THE INSPECTOR TORQUIL MCKINNON SERIES

Books 1-3

Keith Moray

SAPERE
BOOKS

THE INSPECTOR TORQUIL MCKINNON SERIES

Published by Sapere Books.

20 Windermere Drive, Leeds, England, LS17 7UZ,
United Kingdom

saperebooks.com

BOOK ONE: THE GATHERING MURDERS

PROLOGUE

Howard McIvor, the junior partner of McIvor and Son, Funeral Directors, stood in the large dank hallway of the Poplars, wrinkling his nose distastefully at the faintly putrescent odour that seemed to have permeated into the very fabric of the house. He was used to the many smells of death, yet despite himself he always felt ineffably sad when the deceased had died on their own, without anyone present to help or comfort them, or just to watch their passing. Although he himself had never witnessed a death he had a fond belief that there must be something mystical about the moment of transition, when life became extinct and the body turned into the cold lifeless husk that he had to tend.

And this had been a sad case, he reflected. Despite her obvious wealth, the woman had died on her own and the body had started to decay in the Glasgow heatwave. It had been five days before neighbours had been alerted by the rank smell.

He looked down at the blue ceramic urn that he cradled deferentially in his arms, its bottom ever so slightly resting on his developing paunch. Now, of course, there was no smell, no decay, just a few pounds of off-white ashes.

He felt rather awkward about letting himself in, but those had been his instructions. He cast an eye round the hall that he had seen only once before, on the morning that he and Jock Galbraith, the company's on-call assistant mortician, had taken the woman's body away in the body bag. Now, as he waited, he focused on the paintings and photographs on the wall. They seemed to be family pictures of grander days and shooting parties at country houses, portraits of lochs, stags on heather moors and highland gatherings.

He turned at the sound of footsteps descending the stairs and saw a tartan-kilted figure appear.

'I'm sorry, I was expecting ...' he began; trying to suppress the look of surprise that he was aware had flickered across his face.

'You were expecting me, I think,' came the smiling reply. 'I'm her next of kin. We talked on the phone.'

'Of course.' He nodded at the kilt. 'Macbeth tartan, isn't it?'

A nod of assent. 'I'm wearing it as a token of respect.'

'I didn't realize that she was a highland lady.'

This time a slight shake of the head. 'She wasn't. She was a Hebridean, from West Uist. The family had lived there since before the days of Bonnie Prince Charlie.'

Howard McIvor smiled wanly like the professional mourner that he was. Then, in his well-practised funeral director's mode of condolence: 'It was a nice, quiet service as you instructed. Just myself and the minister.'

'She wouldn't have wanted mourning. I'm only sorry that I couldn't get back in time.'

'I understand.' He bobbed his head respectfully, belying the train of thought that was actually running through his mind. *I understand only too well,* he thought. *No mourners, keep the expense down, fumigate the house and sell up as quickly as you can. Forget the old dear ever existed.* No wonder undertakers ended up as cynical as his father. Or as cynical as he himself was becoming.

He reverently handed over the urn and took his leave, his part now done. No need to worry about the fee; that was one good thing about being a funeral director. The first cheque paid out of the deceased's estate, no matter how small that estate, was the undertaker's fee. Regular income, easy money in a way. Dust to dust, ashes to ashes, a life reduced to detritus that would soon be blown by some wind to ephemeral nothingness. Just as the breeze was now blowing away the putrescent odour that had so recently assailed his nostrils. His stomach rumbled and he realized that it was almost lunch time. He smiled at the thought, food being close to his heart. He climbed into his car, all sadness for the old woman left behind with her urn.

He was unaware that he was being watched through the net curtains. A smile spread across thin lips as the black BMW funeral wagon drove away.

'So, just you and me now. Shall we have a cup of tea before we go?'

And a few moments later, with a pot of tea, jug of milk and the best china on a tray, the relative sat and read the letter again. 'I remember you said that you used to like the Gatherings, didn't you? And just look at this letter from the Reverend Lachlan McKinnon. An invitation to the Gathering and the West Uist Literary Festival. He's even put in a list of all the invited guests, all the finest Scottish writers from the west coast and the islands. The bastards will be there!'

The relative finished the cup of tea, and then threw it forcefully into the empty fireplace where it shattered into myriads of jagged pieces. Then, picking up the blue urn and unscrewing the lid: 'Who'd have thought that a thirteen-stone woman like you could fit into a little jar like this.'

Slowly, as if enjoying the deliberateness of the action, the urn was tilted over the hearth. 'All you needed was a little help, wasn't it?'

And the recollection of the simplicity of it all brought the smile back to those cold lips. A large dose of insulin on that last evening, then nature just took its course. The Procurator

Fiscal hadn't even challenged the GP's diagnosis of death through diabetic complications. The inference being that it could have happened at any time.

'You deserved it! You know that, don't you? Just like that rat of a husband of yours deserved it. He never heard me behind him at the top of the stairs. A quick shove, a tumble and a broken neck. Now you've both paid for what you did. And soon it will all be over.'

The first of the ashes began to fall into the hearth. 'Out with the ashes. Remember how you used to make me clean out the hearth!'

But the photograph on top of the mantelpiece halted the action. The sea and sand of West Uist seemed to beckon.

'But that's perfect! You can be really useful after all. I should have thought of it before.' The sound of laughter echoed round the room. The first laughter for many a month.

'We're going to go to West Uist. Home — and then the reckoning!'

PART ONE: THE GATHERING

CHAPTER ONE

Inspector Torquil McKinnon, 'Piper' to most people on West Uist, opened up the throttle on his classic Royal Enfield Bullet 500 and accelerated along the snaking headland road past Loch Hynish with its famous crannog and ancient ruin, then along the edge of the machair, the sand on peat meadow that intervened between the heather-covered Corlin Hills and the seaweed-strewn beach below. As the engine responded and the exhaust gunned noisily, innumerable rabbits scuttled for their sandy burrows and flocks of herring gulls rose from the dunes to fly screeching and squawking protestingly seawards, towards the stacks and skerries that typified the coastland of West Uist.

It was a glorious summer morning and he was anxious to get to St Ninian's Cave for a practice before he turned in for work. With the Gathering just a couple of days away the policing of the event was bound to stretch the West Uist Division of the Hebridean Constabulary to its limits. That is, all three of them were going to have to work like the devil, especially as two of them would be competing as well.

He adjusted his Mark Nine goggles and grinned to himself at the thought of how peeved the Padre would be this morning. He had two pastoral visits booked, then a myriad of tasks related to the Gathering, or rather to the Literary Festival that was his part in the event. All in all it would mean that the old boy would have to forgo his early nine holes of golf. And that meant he'd likely be in an ill humour for the rest of the day.

He changed down gear with a couple of flicks of his right foot, relishing the gun-like exhaust that made the machine's Bullet name seem so apt, then coasted into the lay-by. He switched off the ignition, dismounted and hauled the bike onto its central stand. Then he stripped off his leather jacket, tartan scarf and Cromwell helmet and removed his pipes from the pannier. He was a well-built young man of twenty-eight with raven-black hair and a handsome if slightly hawk-like face. Crunching down the machair sand to the shade of the cliffs and St Ninian's Cave he was grateful for his thick navy blue Arran jumper, the semi-official West Uist Division police uniform.

The Gathering! The whole life of West Uist had become focused on it of late. The population of six hundred could expect to double, if not treble, during the Gathering as visitors, guests and competitors at the various events streamed onto the island. The Padre and his cronies on the Literary Festival Committee were busy arranging lecture venues; the police — that is, PC Ewan McPhee, Sergeant Morag Driscoll and himself, the newly appointed inspector — were embroiled in car parking arrangements and 'security'; and virtually every other family would be involved in one or other of the events, be it field or track sport, music or dance competition or some type of craft show. And, of course, with the kudos of winning an event firing pride and ambition, many an islander could be found practising his or her skill at odd private moments, just as Torquil was about to do with his pipes.

He had timed it just right. The sea had receded down the beach, leaving a fresh crop of multi-hued kelp that sizzled in the early morning sun, filling the air with the fresh tang of brine and iodine. Torquil scrunched across the shingle in his heavy buckled Ashman boots and stood at the entrance to St Ninian's Cave and sighed.

'Latha math! Good Morning!' he called in both Gaelic and English, as he always did when he came to practise in the great basalt-columned St Ninian's Cave, just as so many island pipers had done before him. His uncle, Lachlan McKinnon himself — known locally as the Padre — had practised there in his younger days and had introduced Torquil to its special magic when he was a wee boy. 'Show respect, Torquil. St Ninian's Cave is the best teacher a piper could ever have.'

And as Torquil's echoing voice died away in an instant he smiled. Nature had carved this sea cave beautifully, so that it seemed to hold a sound perfectly for a moment and the piper was able to actually hear the correct pitch of his playing. A natural tape recorder for a musician. He walked into the centre of the great cave, which was as large as a church hall, and hoisted his pipes over his shoulder. He blew up the bag and the inevitable tuneless start-up sounded as uncontrolled air passed through the large bass and two tenor drones before he began to play. His fingers moved over the chanter holes as his left elbow moved bellow-like on the bag to produce a continuous flow of air through the chanter and the three drone pipes.

Torquil ran through his repertoire of warm-up exercises, to get his finger movements right. He played a string of ever more complex movements — *leumluaths*, *taorluaths*, *grace notes* and *birls*. Then he played a strathspey and reel, then a hornpipe and jig, before concentrating on the one that he found the hardest, the *piobaireachd*, the pibroch. At the last three Gatherings Torquil had won cups for the strathspey and the jig, but the pibroch had eluded him. And he needed that if he was to claim the title of Supreme Champion of the Outer Isles, awarded to the winner in all three categories. The trouble was that the pibroch was so difficult to execute well, and Hamish Munro, Pipe Major of the South Uist Pipe Band, had nipped the pibroch prize away from him on those past occasions, thereby depriving him of the chance of gaining the Silver Quaich, that most revered of piping prizes. It had not been won for many years.

Yet one Silver Quaich already rested permanently atop the mantelpiece at the manse, inscribed with the winner's name — Lachlan McKinnon, 1967 Supreme Champion of the Outer Isles.

A sour note from a faulty fingering grated around the cave as Torquil thought with a tinge of envy about his uncle's skill. The old boy had magic in his fingers, even now when he rarely played, since golf had taken over as his number one passion — after motorcycles, literature and his faith, of course. Yet sometimes it helped Torquil to conjure up an image of the Padre standing beside him as he used to do when he gave him piping lessons in the past.

'Play smoothly, laddie. Stroke the holes, don't dab at them. You sound like a constipated crow!' Then he would sing out a series of vocables, the system of oral teaching devised hundreds of years ago by the great MacCrimmons, the hereditary pipers to the clan MacLeod. And putting his *feadan*, his practice chanter, to his lips he would play sublimely, to emphasize the technique and the sound of how the pipes should be played: *'hiodroho, hodroho, haninen, hieachin!'*

'I'm going to win that damned pibroch this year,' Torquil promised himself. And he began to play one of the three pibrochs that he had chosen to put before the judges at the Gathering. Each piece ran to fifteen minutes and had to be played entirely from memory, the judges deciding which of the three they would hear. This morning he was practising *'Cha till MacCruimean'* — 'No more MacCrimmon', a piece composed by Donald Ban MacCrimmon himself, after a vision of his own death, which was to prove true during the 1745 Rebellion.

The three parts of the pibroch built one upon the other, the salute, the lament and then the gathering, each interspersed with the theme, the *urlar*. Torquil played each movement: *siubhal*, *taorluath* and *crunluath*, finishing off with the *urlar* again, all the while looking out to sea, where South Uist could be dimly seen as a low blue shadow on the horizon. And as he looked and played, the words of the chorus ran through his mind:

The breeze of the bens is gently blowing,
The brooks in the glens are softly flowing,
Where boughs their darkest shades are throwing,
Birds mourn for thee who ne'er returnest!

Good, he thought. Not so much like a constipated crow today, Torquil. That was more like it.

And out of the distant haze, coming round far off South Uist and Bara he saw a shimmering speck on the horizon. He let the mouthpiece drop from his lips as the last note of the pibroch reverberated around the cave. 'The ferry,' he mused. He nodded as he walked out of the cave into the sun. 'Time for work then. I best be in the office when the ferry gets in.'

Fiona Cullen stood on the upper viewing platform of the Macbeth ferry, *Laird o' the Isles*. She had stood there smoking a cigarette, watching the hazy blue silhouette of West Uist slowly grow in size as the ferry ploughed through the waves towards it. She was an elegant, slim woman dressed in black motorcycle leathers. Strikingly attractive by any measure, the contrast of her black garb with her short-cut platinum-blonde hair made her stand out.

But to stand out at that moment was the last thing that Fiona wanted. Especially when her writing had thrust her into the limelight of celebrity. Newspaper, magazine and chat-show interviews had done well for her, had boosted her sales into a comfort zone and had opened doors into several areas of society. She had loved it all; revelled in each new experience that came along, the parties, the affairs, the betrayals and the deceits. All good plot material for a writer. Then things just seemed to get too complicated. There seemed to be so many things going on in her life, so many complex threads that had somehow merged together to make the tangled skein that she was now living through. She needed to get away, to sort out her head, to immerse herself in her writing. And that was why the Gathering and Literary Festival had seemed such a godsend. To give a lecture, do a bit of plotting on the already overdue crime novel, and maybe even to see a few old friends — perhaps even one in particular. It had all seemed serendipitous, so right.

Catching the overnight ferry from Oban to Lochboisdale in South Uist had been the first part of her plan. She had powered up the west coast roads on her scarlet Honda Fireblade, boarding the ferry at the very last minute. She had avoided the crowded restaurant and bar to take a solitary supper of cheese sandwiches and coffee in her cabin. Upon arrival at Lochboisdale she had showered, drunk a cup of boiled water, and then found her way up to the viewing platform. It had all gone well until Genevieve Cooper spotted her from the lower deck.

Damn! This is going to be awkward, she thought to herself. *How do I tell my agent it's time to part company?*

Genevieve arrived slightly breathless a few moments later, but not alone. She had a group of eager beavers with her. A coterie of literary groupies that she had undoubtedly ensnared over breakfast. Genevieve was good at that. A big woman in every sense of the word. Rubenesque and overbearing.

'Fiona! Where have you been hiding from your Genevieve?' she cried, advancing along the platform at the head of her troop. She engulfed Fiona in her arms and squashed her against her ample chest. Then before Fiona could get a word out in return, she had turned to the group, hands outstretched like a circus master. Her cheeks bunched up into natural chuckle pouches of gleeful ownership. 'Ladies and Gentlemen, I'm sure you will all have read some of the works of Fiona Cullen — *the Queen of Scottish Crime* — my most celebrated client!'

Then followed a cacophony of banter, adulation for Fiona's books and a scrabbling for concealed paperbacks and autograph books. Fiona went into smiling autopilot: pure literary cocktail chatter and well-practised looped copperplate autograph signatures that she could do in her sleep.

Inevitably, after a flurry of question and answering, the troop dispersed as another writer was spotted and targeted for assault. Fiona waved as they went, all mumbling promises to attend her lecture at the Festival, and to buy drinks, books or to wish her well. A few, as usual, had managed to inveigle her into agreeing to cast an eye over their own amateurish scribblings.

Genevieve lit a Gauloises and held out the packet to Fiona. 'Darling, did you see how well the "Queen of Scottish Crime" thing went down?' she asked in her usual staccato voice. 'They loved it. I have such plans for the new book. What did you say it was called again?'

Fiona suppressed a sigh. "*Dead Writers Tell No Tales*. It's a word play on E. W. Hornung's book, *Dead Men Tell No Tales*. Genevieve I —'

'Hornung! He was Arthur Conan Doyle's brother-in-law, wasn't he? Raffles the gentleman thief and all that. That's good Fiona, that's really good. I like the title, it implies —'

'Genevieve, we need to talk.'

But the agent was smoking furiously, like some sort of engine working up steam. 'I know, I know, Fiona. We need to get together on this one before the Festival gets going. So that we can have a united front. Allegra McCall, your editor from Castlefront, will be about and I need to give her some ideas I'm working on.'

'That's what we need to talk about, Genevieve. About Allegra and about —'

'About Allegra? Oh she's all right. A bit stand-offish, I know, but with a bit of pushing here and there,' she said, with a grin as she jokingly prodded Fiona in the side, 'I think we can get her to go for a bigger print-run this time. I've had a boxload of photographed bookmarks made up for the Festival. You know, the photograph with you at that Japanese Festival in Osaka. It looks —'

'You've what?' Fiona suddenly demanded, clasping Genevieve's wrist and preventing her from raising the Gauloises to her full scarlet lips. 'You've had bookmarks made up with my photograph? Genevieve, how could you. That's so — so tacky!'

Genevieve was momentarily nonplussed. Then she smiled beneficently and shook her head reassuringly. 'No, they're not tacky, darling. They're good, very good, very flattering.' She smiled as she pursed her lips coquettishly and added: 'Smouldering, exotic.'

'You should have asked me first, Genevieve. And that's been half the trouble lately. You just never consult me. That's why I'm leaving.'

Genevieve stared at her uncomprehendingly. 'Leaving? You mean you're cross? Have I upset you, darling? I'm sorry and I'll make it up, I promise.'

But Fiona had picked up her helmet as the ferry's horn blast was followed by the tannoy message advising all passengers to make their way to their vehicles as the ferry would be imminently arriving at Kyleshiffin. She pulled on the helmet and strapped up. 'It's just one thing after another, Genevieve. I think it's time that we parted company. I'm going to look after my own affairs from now on.' And snapping the visor closed she made for the stairs.

The colour drained from Genevieve's face as she stared at Fiona's retreating back. 'But you can't leave now,' she mouthed, her jaw muscles tightening. 'You can't possibly leave me now. I won't let you.'

The crescent-shaped harbour of Kyleshiffin thrummed with activity as a couple of hundred passengers in their cars, minibuses and bicycles rolled off the *Laird o' the Isles* ferry. The main street, a half moon of multi-coloured shop fronts and businesses that had passed down through the generations, resembled an island kasbah. Flags and bunting hung from the lamp posts proclaiming a welcome in both English and Gaelic for the West Uist Gathering and Literary Festival. Locals and holiday makers ambled around market stalls clustered along the harbour wall, inspecting lobsters, crabs, local crafts and second-hand ephemera. Beyond the wall a flotilla of assorted fishing boats, yachts and launches bobbed up and down in the water, attesting to the fact that Kyleshiffin was both a working and a pleasure harbour.

Fiona Cullen's Honda Fireblade roared along the crescent as she made her way to the Bonnie Prince Charlie Tavern, where she had booked a back room without the distraction of a sea view. She planned to do some serious work on her novel.

A slim leather-clad woman on a powerful machine, she attracted many appraising and admiring looks as she rode by. One such observer was Ranald Buchanan, the proprietor of the Kyleshiffin Antique Bookshop, Tobacconist and Fishing Tackle Emporium. As he looked over the shoulder of the customer he was serving he saw the Fireblade zip along the road, the svelte rider conjuring up the pleasing image of a Peter Pan on wheels in his artistic mind. Then he turned his attention back to the important matter in hand. Money — the making of!

'You will be liking this Dragon-fly model, made with these old hands of mine, I am thinking,' he said with a grin, as he handed the package over.

The American in the Chicago Bears baseball hat beamed, his unlit cigar clenched between perfectly capped teeth. 'Looking forward to it. I've fished all over Scotland, but this is my first time in the Hebrides. I hear tell that the fish give you good sport round here.'

Ranald Buchanan ran his fingers through his unkempt pepper-and-salt beard that hung like a curtain to cover his scrawny neck with its prominent Adam's apple. He was a small thin man with shifty grey eyes that had about them a permanent rheumy look. People who had heard of him attributed that look to his poetic vision, as if he were able to 'see things beyond the sense of most'. Those who really knew him, however, put the look down to a surfeit of peatreek, the illicit whisky that he manufactured himself at his croft and stored in his shed on the Machair Skerry to the North of Kyleshiffin, and which he sold illicitly to the cognoscenti throughout the Western Isles.

'*Am fear a thèid a ghnàth a-mach le lìon, gheibh e iasg uraireigin,*' Ranald rattled off in melodic Gaelic. Then, as the American raised his eyes in bewilderment, he translated with a grin: 'If you go fishing a lot, sometimes you'll catch fish. That is to say, you will be finding that most of the creatures of the Isles are singularly intelligent.'

The American departed with a laugh after having left a substantial tip alongside his payment for a 'cut-price' telescopic rod and three over-priced handmade flies, prepared by Ranald Buchanan, the celebrated Gaelic Bard, himself.

Ranald grinned to himself as he surveyed his emporium, half antiquarian bookshop, half angler's-paradise-cum-tobacconist. There were about half a dozen browsers scanning the bookcases and piles of books while the melodic lilt of the Gaelic filled the room. *Bloody brilliant is what I am*, he thought to himself. *A brainwave to tape-record my own poems, first in Gaelic, then in English, and have them on a permanent play-loop to the customers.*

A look of pleasure flashed across a young man's face and he elbowed his companion, a young woman dressed in the modern 'bag-head' style. Ranald grinned at them, as they approached with copies of his latest volume of poems, *Songs of the Selkie*, with both Gaelic and English versions printed alongside each other.

'I can't believe it! Served by Ranald Buchanan, the Gaelic Bard himself,' the young man enthused. 'Would you sign these for us?'

Ranald took the books and scrawled his name in biro on the flyleafs. '*Is ann a tha 'n sgoileam air an sgoilear,*' he said. '"It's the scholar that's the talker", as we say in the Gaelic. You must be reading them aloud to get the real meaning.'

The girl flushed. 'God, that Gaelic is so sexy.'

The fisherman-poet shrugged his shoulders modestly, allowing himself to take a lingering stare at her apple-shaped breasts. He smiled as she flushed in response. Sixty-eight years of age, yet with the loins of a lecher half his age, Ranald Buchanan flirted outrageously whenever the opportunity arose. He loved the advantage that his new-found celebrity had given him.

'Are you here for the Gathering or the Literary Festival?'

'Both,' replied the man. 'We're sort of honeymooning. We graduated this year. We both did Scottish Studies at Dundee, and we're having a fling before we have to find jobs.'

'*Is fheàrr sìor-obair na sàr-obair*,' Ranald mused. 'Better get steady work, rather than hard work. Don't be killing yourselves.'

The couple paid and made their way with their purchases. The girl looked back as they reached the door and Ranald pouted suggestively, bringing another instantaneous flush to her cheeks.

That one would fall like a ripe peach given the opportunity, he thought lasciviously. He sighed at the image of having her in the heather, of cuckolding her new husband. Someone will do it soon, he thought with a malicious grin.

The Kyleshiffin town clock struck ten o'clock and Ranald inwardly cursed, dragged back as he was from his reverie. The letter had said to meet at the Machair Skerry at half past ten. 'It will be to your great profit,' the letter had informed him. 'Destroy this letter and tell no one or you will be unmasked!'

He did not know exactly what to make of it, since his life had been full of so many peccadilloes that it was entirely possible that someone knew something Ranald would rather remained secret. Yet the fact that the writer mentioned profit made him feel more excited than fearful of some sort of blackmail. Profit was always close to his heart.

Fighting back the urge to telephone the only person he ever called for advice, his mentor, he noisily set to and announced the presence of the 'honesty box' in the middle of the room, strategically placed beside a pile of his volumes and a small selection of works by other authors who were scheduled to attend the Festival, then he let himself out.

He crossed the road and climbed down the steps leading to his little boat. He struck a light to a roll-up, started up the little outboard motor and chugged his way out of the harbour. As he did so a red Enstrom Shark helicopter roared overhead, zooming towards distant South Uist. Ranald snorted. That will be the laird himself, off to bring home his guests in style, he thought.

It took him twenty minutes to round the coast and tie up on the iron spike that was the only mooring point on the crude stone jetty of the Machair Skerry, the little sandy islet which he owned and where he came to be alone to write. It was only about a hundred yards or so across the water from his croft, which he had christened *Tigh nam Bard*, the House of the Bard. Behind the cottage were three corrugated outhouses in which he distilled his peatreek and kept a goodly quantity of cases until they were ready to be moved out to the Machair Skerry for final 'distribution'.

The sign at the edge of the skerry proclaimed: PRIVATE PROPERTY — POET AT WORK.

And that seemed to do the job. It kept all and sundry away, even the police, although in their case he knew perfectly well that they knew all about his still and turned a blind eye. Being one of the Padre's oldest friends helped, of that he had no doubt.

But now the inevitable question was on his mind. Who was this mysterious letter writer who wanted to meet him on his own Machair Skerry at half-past ten? There was no one about, and as he approached from the sea, he knew well enough that there was no one approaching from the water.

'*Latha matha,*' he called out. 'A good day to you.'

No reply. He climbed out of the boat and approached the old wooden shed that smelled strongly of the creosote coating that he had given it the week before. He noted that the lock hung untouched from the latch, so no one had forced an entry.

A hoax! Who would go to all that trouble? And the letter had said he'd be unmasked if he didn't go. And what was that about profit? The bastard!

He unlocked the door and carefully peered inside, relieved to see nothing but his lobster creels and the assortment of spare rods and tackle that he kept there whenever he took expensive paying customers out for a day's fishing. And they were all in order, so no one had gotten into his secret press behind, where he kept a subsidiary pot and copper coil, and where every fortnight he ran it for a couple of days to make three quarts of peatreek. Strangely, it actually produced a slightly richer distillate than his big still. This he sold as the *crème de la crème*, a particular favourite of the local fishermen. No one worried about the smoke that rose when the Gaelic Bard was 'in residence', working on a masterpiece they said, and no one noticed the smell for the skerry winds dispersed it continuously.

He suddenly realized that his heart was racing and that his brow was moist. Then it came — the spasm in the chest, followed by the inevitable fear that this would be followed by the big one.

'Bugger this angina!' he cursed, reaching for the glyceryl trinitrate spray that Dr McLelland insisted he carry with him at all times. But as his hand dipped into his pocket and touched his hipflask, he grinned despite the pain and shook his head. *'Uisge-beath' a' bhalaich mhòir, òlamaid gun taing e,'* he whispered, unscrewing the top. 'The water of life, I'll drink it and spit in the devil's eye.'

There was a splash from outside, as if a fish had broken water. He whirled round and saw the black shape emerge from the sea. At first he thought it was a seal. Then head and shoulders rose from the water and he saw a facemask, snorkel and wetsuit.

'Who is there?' He spluttered as the fiery peatreek hit his stomach and he took a step backwards, tripped and felt himself flailing for a moment to land on his back on the dirt floor of the shed.

The figure was out of the water by the time he had sat up. He watched with eyes agog as mouthpiece and facemask were removed to reveal staring eyes that seemed to burn into him.

'Still poisoning yourself with that moonshine?'

Ranald Buchanan blinked at the face in disbelief. 'It cannot be you!' he exclaimed. 'You look just like —'

'That's to be expected, isn't it?'

'Aye, but now you're — different! I was expecting —'

'You were expecting what? A Selkie? Strange isn't it that you should have chosen that subject for your latest volume of doggerel.'

Ranald ignored the heavy sarcasm in the voice. 'It was you who sent the letter?'

'Yes me — your nemesis.'

The Gaelic Bard fumbled for a roll-up and struck a light with his battered old lighter, hungrily drawing on the smoke, like a man trying to suck life into his body. As the nicotine reached his brain, adding to the effect of the peatreek, he felt his nerves calm a little. Enough to ask without his voice quaking, 'Nemesis, eh? Does that mean that you are here to threaten me?'

But despite his bravado he felt the beginning of another spasm in his chest. There was a momentary silence while the Gaelic Bard felt the eyes bore into him, as if discerning that he was in some discomfort, in a state of near panic.

A hollow laugh was followed by words that soothed the poet's nerves. 'Or maybe I'm here to let you profit from your — fame.'

A cunning smile crossed Ranald Buchanan's lips. 'You know about me then? Aye, it's good having friends in high places. They've made me a bit of a celebrity.' He took another swig of his peatreek. 'Ye've nae hard feelings, then? You ken that I only did what I thought was for the best.'

The figure turned and looked out to sea. 'Oh, I have very hard feelings actually.' And then nonchalantly: 'Is that where it "happened"? Or rather, where it didn't...'

Ranald heaved a sigh. 'Aye! The boats were out for two days but they didn't find anything.'

'Except for a scarf.'

Ranald inhaled deeply on his roll-up. 'It was done properly.'

'But you ruined her life. Several lives as it happened. I assume she's in the family plot.'

'Aye, in the cemetery.' He ground his roll-up under his heel and looked up, fear beginning to resurface. 'You've got revenge in your heart, then?'

The eyes bored into him again, and then a hand shot out, grabbing his shirt and pulling him forward to within a few inches of the cruel mouth. The lips softened for a moment as a smile played across them. 'Let's call it — *poetic justice.*'

CHAPTER TWO

The Kyleshiffin police station was a converted bungalow off Lady's Wynd, which ran parallel to Harbour Street. Torquil was at work in his office poring over a map of the island, as he sought to ensure that there would be enough parking facilities. The influx of tourists and visitors from the ferry for the Gathering and Literary Festival had worried him since it had brought an unprecedented number of cars to the island. West Uist's road system simply would not cope. He began to curse his uncle's idea about the Literary Festival.

The commotion from the duty desk was not helping him concentrate. For five minutes he had worked on, hoping that PC Ewan McPhee would calm the situation, but instead, the latter's voice seemed to be getting louder and louder and less controlled. With a sigh he laid down his pen, opened the door and walked into World War III.

It seemed as if a crowd of belligerent faces was haranguing Ewan, Torquil's six-foot-four, red-maned constable. A champion hammer-thrower and Western Isles wrestling runner-up at the last Outer Hebrides Games, he was underneath it all a sensitive and self-effacing twenty-three-year-old. And indeed, although his voice was getting louder it seemed that it was desperation rather than anger that was behind the rise in decibels.

'Ah, Inspector McKinnon!' cried a stout, lank-haired individual in a mustard-coloured anorak. 'Now we'll maybe get some sense, instead of this great lummox's police officiousness.'

'We'll be having less of your lip, Calum Steele,' said PC McPhee. 'I've told you already that parking permits will be required for all vehicles during the Gathering.'

'But the Press need to be exempt, don't they, Torquil? How can I cover all the events if I can't get between them without having to park in your "official" carparks?'

Torquil suppressed a grin. Calum Steele, the editor and chief reporter, meaning the only reporter, of the *West Uist Chronicle*, had been a pain in the backside ever since they had been in Miss Melville's class at the Kyleshiffin School together. He saw himself as an investigative journalist and man of letters, rather than the custodian of the local rag.

'Perhaps we could issue a special permit for Calum's Lambretta, Ewan?' Torquil suggested.

Calum beamed. 'Good lad, Piper. That's just what I've been trying to tell this hammer-throwing hammer-chewer.'

And while Ewan good-naturedly filled out the appropriate docket, Torquil turned and smiled at Annie McConville, a chirpy old lady who had been standing beside the newspaper editor, drumming her fingers on the desk, a large Alsatian dog and a small West Highlander sitting obediently at her feet. She was famed throughout the island for running a dog sanctuary; taking in all waifs and strays from across the Outer Hebrides. 'This by-law is stupidity itself, Piper McKinnon,' she protested with an indignant shake of the head.

'And which by-law is that, Annie?'

'These pooper-scooper bins! You're discriminating against us doggie-owners. I'm going to be up to my armpits in pooper bags.'

'It will be necessary during the Gathering, Annie,' Torquil explained. 'As a responsible dog-owner you'll be aware of the threat of toxoplasmosis.'

Annie pursed her lips tightly together. 'So that's it! The taxman again. It's nothing but tax this and tax that. Well, let me tell you, the taxman will be getting no more out of me.'

'I said *toxoplasmosis*, Annie,' Torquil began. But it was in vain for Annie had turned and begun pushing her way towards the door. People immediately made way for the Alsatian. 'Not a penny!' she cried with contempt.

Together Ewan and Torquil worked their way through the crowd of complainers, enquirers and general busybodies who had nothing better to do than to join a crowd in case they missed something. They were thankful when Sergeant Morag Driscoll came in from her round of the town to lend a hand. She was only a few years older than Torquil, but had seen life. Pretty, despite a slight weight problem, she had been widowed at twenty-six and left to bring up three lusty youngsters on her own. She was efficiency personified, a multitasker who juggled work, home and children with an effortless no-nonsense approach.

'Gosh, Morag,' said Ewan, half an hour later, as the three were sitting sipping mugs of his well-stewed tea. 'Glad I am that the Gathering and this Literary Festival of the Padre's isn't going to be every week.'

Morag beamed. 'Och, you just have to be more organized Ewan. What you need is a lassie and a brood of bairns to make you realize how to keep order.'

Ewan put his mug down and frowned. 'But I'm fed up with half the enquiries we're getting now. Bed and breakfast lists, places to eat. It's an information centre they think we are, rather than a police station. And as for putting up all these signs, isn't that a job for those two lazy special constables to be doing?'

Torquil laughed. 'Now, you know very well that the Drummond twins will still be out with their fishing boat until later this morning. They'll pull their weight right enough once the Gathering gets in full swing.' He winked at Morag. 'What you really mean is that you're not getting enough time to practise the hammer.'

Ewan failed to detect the humour in Torquil's voice. 'Not a bit of it. I'm out at cockcrow every morning, tossing my practice hammer over the roof of the back shed. I...' He hesitated and looked suspiciously at his friends and senior officers, both of whom had burst into laughter. 'You've been spying on me, haven't you, you pair of scunners!'

Torquil leaned over and clapped the big PC on the shoulder. 'Well, Ewan, I see the holes in the shed roof when I go past in the mornings. There seems to be an extra one every day. And I saw your mother scowling at a big one in the shed door before I came in this very morning. She said she was thinking of reporting you for criminal damage.'

Morag almost choked on a mouthful of tea and a slow grin spread across Ewan's face. 'Aye, that's the sort of thing my maw would say.' Then standing up and whirling his arms in a two-handed circular movement, he explained, 'I'm experimenting with the angle of trajectory, you see. If I can just —'

He was interrupted by the door squeaking open. A motorcyclist came in, clad in black leathers and matching black helmet with its black opaque visor down. A fraction of a moment later a tall silver-haired lady of about seventy, dressed in a tweed suit, swathed in a russet-coloured silk shawl entered then deftly bypassed the motorcyclist to reach the desk first.

'Ah, Torquil, thank goodness,' she said. Then her words just tumbled out. 'You're my last hope. I really must find Ranald

Buchanan to organize him properly for his poetry reading. It's too bad that I have to do all these things myself, but some of the other members of the committee just aren't doing what they said they'd be doing. And now Ranald has done a runner. His shop is open, but he has that honesty box thing of his out, so goodness knows where he is.'

Torquil had risen and approached the desk, his heart having sunk at the sight of Miss Bella Melville, one of the Padre's fellow Literary Festival Committee members, and also the Kyleshiffin schoolteacher until her retirement some six years previously. Having taught half of the island's population she was used to being listened to and obeyed. And Torquil's erstwhile teacher's scarce-concealed dig at his uncle did not go unnoticed. 'So — er — what exactly do you want me to do, Miss Melville?'

Over his shoulder he heard Morag begin to deal with the motorcyclist, with a friendly greeting, then: 'Is it a parking permit that you'll be wanting?'

Miss Melville's curt retort brought his attention back to heel. 'You must get your uncle to have words with him. Track him down. He's the only one the old fool listens to.'

'But Miss Melville, I'm rather busy at the moment.'

'Really? You seem quite quiet to me, Torquil. Now come on, we need some action. I'm depending on you, laddie.'

She left as she had entered, in a hurry. Torquil heaved a sigh of relief then turned to see Morag and Ewan grinning at him. 'Look who's here, Torquil,' said Morag, nodding at the motorcyclist who had removed her helmet and was holding it under her arm like a knight's helm.

'Hello Torquil,' said Fiona Cullen. 'Old Miss Melville hasn't changed a jot, has she?' Then when he just stood staring at her, Morag took a hand. 'Maybe the two of you would like a cup of tea,' she said, raising the flap on the desk and pushing Torquil towards his office. 'Ewan, how about a fresh pot of tea — and try not to stew it this time.'

Torquil watched Fiona stroll round his small office inspecting his framed degree, citations and press cuttings. 'So, quite the high-flyer, aren't you — *Inspector McKinnon*,' she said, whirling round and sitting on the corner of his desk with a coquettish smile. 'Last time I was here you were just a wee PC, like big Ewan out there.'

Torquil clicked his tongue. 'And when you left me you were just a reporter on the *West Uist Chronicle*. Calum Steele's side-kick. And look at you now. A famous crime writer.' He pointed at her expensive leathers. 'And you're obviously doing well.'

Fiona folded her arms and gave him a mock interrogatory look. 'So tell me, Inspector McKinnon, how many of my books have you read? All seven of them? Two? One even?'

Then, before he could reply, she wrinkled her nose in that delightful way that used to send shivers up his spine, and stabbed her finger at him with a laugh. 'I'll bet it's none! And why's that, Torquil? Because unless you've changed I bet that *Zen and the Art of Motorcycle Maintenance* still has pride of place by your bedside.'

'You bought that book for me, Fiona.'

'That's true. And I left it by your bedside so that you could think of me. Just like I sent you a copy of each book as it came out.'

'I still have them.'

'Unread! You never even wrote to tell me —' she paused for a moment then went on in a mock piqued tone, 'you never even wrote and pretended that you'd read them.'

Torquil made a point of drinking his tea. '*You* left *me*, Fiona. Don't make out it was the other way round.'

Fiona pushed herself off the desk and slumped down in the chair opposite him. She pouted. 'Oh Torquil, I hoped it wouldn't be like this. Not with us. I want us to be good —'

'What? You want us to be what? Good friends?'

Fiona sighed with exasperation. 'I had to get away from this island. It wasn't that I wanted to leave you. I always meant to come back.'

'After you made your fortune. So are you back here to stay now? Or is it just for the Festival?'

'I think you know that I have to be here for the Festival, Torquil. I'm sure the Padre told you that I have to present the prizes at the short story competition I've helped him to judge.'

Torquil shook his head in disbelief. Damn it, he thought. So the Padre was in on this, the interfering old man! 'I didn't know you were judging anything with the old rogue,' he said. 'In typical fashion he never deigned to tell me. I'll have to have words with him.'

Fiona caught his mood and nodded in agreement. 'And so will I! Why don't we go and berate the old rapscallion together.' She leaned over the desk and smiled. 'But let's go as friends, Torquil. Please!'

He had never been able to resist that smile of hers. He shrugged good-naturedly and handing her the untouched mug of tea, he chinked it with his own. 'As friends, Fiona,' he added with a wink.

And with the ice broken, if not melted and gone, they sat back and chatted about the good times at university, then back on West Uist when they had been a couple. Their idyll was broken by the sound of raised voices from the duty desk outside the office.

'I'm telling you that I saw her come in and I know that's her motorcycle parked outside this police station!' boomed the voice of Calum Steele. 'As the editor of the celebrity page, I demand that you let her know I am here to interview her.'

'God, is he still at the *Chronicle*?' Fiona whispered.

'He *is* the *Chronicle*,' grinned Torquil. 'This seems like a good point to go and see the Padre.'

'But you heard him, my bike is parked outside.'

Torquil reached for his Cromwell helmet and goggles. 'Come on, I've got a *real* bike out the back.'

True to its name, Torquil's Royal Enfield Bullet sped along the west road from Kyleshiffin around the Devil's Elbow.

'Goes like a dream, not bad for a classic old girl, is she?' Torquil shouted over his shoulder, as the dial hovered on the 65 mph mark.

'She's OK if you like wee bikes,' Fiona called back. 'I ride a Fireblade. It's got real oomph!'

'Is that so? Well, it would be no use on West Uist. Can it do this?' And so saying he patted her arms about his waist, a signal for Fiona riding pillion to hang on. And as she tightened her grip about him, he felt a surge of adrenaline that coincided with him raising the front wheel from the road then accelerating to dart off the road through a fringe of bracken onto a sheep track leading across the moors that led up towards the Corlin Hills. As the machine skidded, sped and leapt along over the two-foot-wide track he felt Fiona cling on as she laughed behind her visor. It was as if they had climbed on the Bullet and gone back in time five years.

Five minutes later they rejoined the road for half a mile before sweeping into the gravel court of the manse, where Torquil had lived with his uncle ever since the boating accident

35

that killed his parents more than twenty years before. Dismounting and entering the house it was clear that the Padre was not at home.

'His clubs have gone,' Torquil announced after poking his head round his uncle's study door. 'Looks like he's skiving from school!'

'I see that motorbikes are still high on your mutual agenda,' Fiona said, laying her helmet down on the hall table and pointing to the assortment of carburettor components, oil filters and gears which lay on spread-out oil-stained newspapers along the length of the hall. 'You can tell that this is a bachelor household. Does the Padre still have his Ariel?'

'Aye, the Red Hunter is his pride and joy and he still coaxes it around the parish. But he's also got a Vincent Black Shadow, and we're rebuilding an Excelsior Talisman.' He nodded at the various engine parts. 'The carburettor is proving a bit tricky.'

'You two were always thick as thieves,' said Fiona lightly. 'As well as being a hazard to the environment.'

Torquil smiled. It was true; he had acquired many of the Padre's interests. The pipes and classic motorcycles were twin passions that they shared. He shoved her playfully towards the door and then led her through the garden to the wrought-iron gate, then across the road to the stile that led directly onto the ten-acre plot of undulating dunes and machair that the Padre and several local worthies had converted and transformed into St Ninian's Golf Course. An honesty box hung from the fence for the two pounds green fee per round. Not exactly St Andrews, but it was not far off being a golfing purist's dream. The fairways were tractor-mown once a week, the greens were sheep-grazed to near billiard table smoothness and the bunkers (in the beginning at least) had been excavated by generations of rabbits. Although it had only six holes, players went round three times, each hole having three different tees to introduce different lines of approach and different hazards for errant balls. Carved through steeply undulating dunes covered with patches of thistles and gorse, it was bounded on one side by the Corlins and on the other by the Northern Atlantic Ocean. Because of the forthcoming Gathering, the course seemed deserted.

Torquil looked at his watch. 'I reckon he'll be coming up the eighth by now.'

And cresting the rise they saw him on the 'eighth' green lining up a putt, a tall good-humoured man of sixty-four years with the ruddy cheeks of the outer islander, a pair of thick horn-rimmed spectacles perched on a hawk-like nose and a veritable mane of silver hair that perpetually defied brush and comb. Most incongruous on a golf course these days, however, was his attire, for he was wearing a clerical dog collar and a white summer jacket. He was puffing furiously on a battered old briar pipe as he concentrated. When the putt fell in he punched the air with enthusiasm and Fiona began to clap.

The Padre spun round, immediately recognizing his nephew and the pretty leather-clad girl with him. 'Fiona! The Lord be praised! You're back on hallowed turf,' he called as he covered the ground between them in a short run, sweeping her into his arms and hugging hard. Then immediately releasing her he held her at arm's length, grinning like a schoolboy. 'Did you see that! That was a birdie. If I can par the ninth I'll have played the front nine in two under par.' He playfully prodded Torquil in the stomach with his putter. 'What d'ye think of that laddie?' With a couple of sharp raps he tapped his pipe out on his putter blade and shoved the old briar into the breast pocket of his jacket.

'Great Uncle, but I need ...'

'It's so good to see you again Lachlan McKinnon,' said Fiona, circling the Padre's waist with an arm and walking him back to his bag of clubs. 'I've loved reading all those awful stories you sent me, simply because I was looking forward to seeing you and the old place again,' She sighed. 'I had almost forgotten how beautiful it is.'

Lachlan McKinnon looked over his shoulder at his nephew and grinned. 'Is that so, Fiona? I've been kind of looking forward to seeing you back on the island myself. Now come on, watch me get a par at the ninth for my best round ever.'

And he teed up his ball between the blue tee markers, the middle series for the second circuit of six holes. It was a straight shot played over a slight hill to a green in the hollow between the cemetery on the left and the church of St Ninian's on the right. A bunker in front of the green caught shots played short, while both the cemetery and the church grounds were out of bounds. Like all of the holes on the course it was named, its particular sobriquet being *Creideamh*, meaning 'Faith'.

Lachlan took a couple of easy practice swings, then set up and sent the ball on a perfect parabolic flight over the hill.

'Good shot!' enthused Fiona. 'Can I have a go? I haven't swung a club in anger for a few years.'

The Padre beamed and fished out a ball and a tee from his pocket and handed her his five-iron. 'I remember you had a way with you at sport. Just swing it easy lass, and don't try to knock the cover off the ball.'

Fiona imitated the Padre's moves, swinging twice, then set up for her tee-shot. Being quite petite she swung flat and from inside to out, the result being an inevitable hook. The ball started off on target and then curved viciously towards the left, disappearing over the hill in the direction of the St Ninian's cemetery.

'I think it'll be a dead ball,' said the Padre with a grin. 'If you'll excuse the pun.'

No sooner had he said it than there was a howl from the other side of the hill that could have been either pain or rage.

'Lord hae mercy!' whispered the Padre. 'I did not think to shout "Fore!"' He shouldered his bag and strode off. 'Let's just hope we didn't do any damage to anyone.'

A few moments later they had mounted the crest and could see Lachlan's ball on the green about a yard from the flag. More alarmingly, however, they saw a man on his elbows and knees beside a gravestone in the middle of the cemetery, his hands clasped around his head, as if he was supplicating before an ancient altar. As they approached they could hear a low moaning, and alarmed lest he be badly injured, they all three broke into a run.

Torquil vaulted the fence and reached him first, relieved to find that he was not badly injured, albeit clearly in pain from a bump on his forehead that was swiftly rising. He was a good-looking, well-built man in his late forties, dressed in an open-necked shirt and corduroy trousers.

'Why Professor Ferguson!' exclaimed Torquil, helping him up and gingerly inspecting the bruise. 'Are you all right?'

Professor Neil Ferguson, head of the Department of Marine Archaeology at the University of the Highlands was well known on West Uist, since he had been visiting the Western Isles to study their unique artificial islets or crannogs ever since he had been a PhD student some twenty years previously. He shook his head. 'I'm just shaken, I think. I wasn't expecting it.'

'We should have shouted "Fore",' said the Padre. 'I do apologize.'

'Actually, I suppose it's me that should apologize,' said Fiona, slowly approaching along the gravel path. 'Only I'm not sure that I want to.'

Torquil and the Padre looked at her in surprise for a moment. Then the Padre cut in, well versed as he was in dealing with awkward situations. 'I'm glad you could make it to the Festival, Neil. Your latest book on the crannogs is selling well already, I'm told.'

'Thank you, Lachlan. I'm actually going to be taking some friends diving round the Loch Hynish crannog over the next few days. You'll probably see a lot of us during the Gathering.'

The Padre pointed to the graves about him. 'Can I help you here?'

The professor shook his head, having caught Fiona's persistent look of disdain. 'No thanks Padre, I was just looking for a grave. But it's fine, it'll keep for another time. I — er — must go.'

And once he had gone Fiona nonchalantly hooked her arm through the Padre's. 'Now come on, Lachlan. Let's see you hole that putt for your new record.'

Torquil fell behind them for a few moments until the Padre turned and signalled for him to catch up. Torquil immediately quickened his pace, shrugging off the fleeting impression that someone had been watching them during their strange encounter in the cemetery.

Over a frugal lunch at the manse, where the Padre celebrated his best ever nine with a half bottle of claret, Torquil listened as Fiona and his uncle talked about the short story competition that they were judging together.

'There were three decent ones, I thought,' said Fiona, sipping sparkling water. 'The kidnapping one, followed by the poisoned ice lollies, then by the murderous vicar.'

Lachlan guffawed. 'I agree, although I'd hoped we could maybe ditch the vicar! And I think the order is right as well, so the job's all done. Agreed?'

Torquil coughed. 'Not entirely, Uncle. Miss Melville came into the station this morning and rather suggested that you need to get your finger out and organize Ranald Buchanan. He won't play ball with her about his poetry reading or something. She seems to think you're the only one he'll listen to.'

The Padre quaffed some wine then wiped his mouth with his serviette. 'Och, the woman's havering. The poetry reading is not until the day after tomorrow. Time enough. I'll track him down tomorrow.'

'Your funeral, Uncle.'

'Not yet, laddie! Not yet!' And rising, he dusted crumbs from his jacket. 'Fiona, it's grand to see you. But, as I bet you can imagine, I need to complete the eighteen holes now that I'm breaking records, then I'll sort out my parish visits and nip in to help with the Festival organizing.' And plucking his cold pipe from his breast pocket and a dilapidated old tobacco pouch from a side pocket he took his leave.

'He hasn't changed a bit,' Fiona said with a snigger when they were alone. Then she added, 'Come on, Inspector McKinnon, let's wash up and you can take me back. I have to sneak into my room at the Bonnie Prince Charlie so I can prepare my talk for tomorrow without my agent or my publisher seeing me.' She wrinkled her nose and laughed, 'Or Calum the nose!'

The Bullet hurtled along the road round Loch Hynish in

glorious sunshine. Fiona tapped Torquil's shoulder and called out, 'Can we stop a while at the "wee free ferry"?'

Torquil nodded, and coasted in to the side of the road, then waited while Fiona dismounted, before switching off the engine and hauling the machine up onto its stand. He pulled his goggles up and watched Fiona pull off her helmet and then stroll down the brae to the edge of the loch. Further along, moored to a small jetty, the 'wee free ferry', as the rowing boat was called locally, floated invitingly. Fiona pointed across the water to the crannog, the artificial Iron Age islet in the middle of the loch. In the centre of the crannog, rising from a swathe of bracken and surrounded by dwarf rowan trees, was the ruin of the old tower, once thought to have been a three-storey affair, but now a bare six or seven feet at its highest.

Fiona picked up a pebble and skimmed it in the direction of the crannog.

'It's beautiful, isn't it?' she sighed. Then after a moment with a touch of petulance, 'And that idiot has made a name for himself out of it and all the other crannogs in the Hebrides!'

Torquil had joined her and also selected a skimming stone to send scudding across the surface of the loch. 'You mean Professor Ferguson? He's an expert on them, Fiona. Probably the foremost expert on crannogs in the whole of Scotland. What was all that about on the golf course?'

Skimming another stone and focusing her attention on the ripples, Fiona replied, 'He was responsible for my friend's death and I'm going to expose him.'

'Come again?'

She sighed and sat down on the jetty. 'My friend Esme wrote a book, a New Age book about the crannogs. She was into Celtic tradition, runes, that sort of thing. The book did well and she was invited on a programme for Scottish TV. But they also invited high and mighty Professor Neil Ferguson along at the same time and he rubbished her! Humiliated her on television. She went home that evening and slit her wrists.'

'But you can't hold him responsible for that.'

'Can't I? He's a fraud, Torquil, and I'm going to expose him.'

'How? In a book?'

She shook her head, as if to dismiss any more talk about the professor. She looked him straight in the eyes for a few moments, then reached up and tousled his hair. Snaking her arms about his neck, she drew him towards her, to her waiting lips. Torquil didn't resist, despite his fear of letting this woman get too close to him again. Once more it seemed as if the years had been blotted out and they were together as they were meant to be.

At last, when they parted, she said, 'Do you remember the last time we used the wee free ferry, Torquil? We made love in the ruin.' She nodded towards the boat. 'Can you still row?'

Torquil smiled wanly. 'It's too soon, Fiona. We need time.'

She bit her lip. 'Does that mean you want there to be time for us?'

'I do.'

The noise of a powerful engine approached from the east and they looked up in time to see an Enstrom Shark helicopter zoom over the tops of the Corlins, heading south. On its side it bore the well-known AME entwined logo of Angus MacLeod Enterprises, superimposed on tartan-patterned doors. 'That's the laird flying back in time for the Gathering,' mused Torquil.

Fiona drew his head back and kissed him with her full lips. 'And talking of the great Angus MacLeod, are you going to his ceilidh tomorrow night?'

'The party before the Gathering? Of course. I'm the only practising piper on the island so I've been given the honour of piping in the haggis. All the rich and influential will be there, as well as the paying punters. The Padre, as one of the Festival convenors, will be in his element, poking fun at the establishment as usual.'

'I'm glad you'll be there, Torquil. But I'd like you to be my partner.' She squeezed the back of his neck. 'I'd feel safe having my own police protection with me.'

CHAPTER THREE

The first day of the West Uist Literary Festival, the day before the Gathering itself, was almost in full swing. This was mainly because Miss Bella Melville and her band of faithful helpers, mostly all former pupils, had been whipping round Kyleshiffin organizing venues, workshops, bookstalls and lecture times. The reason it was slightly less than full swing was because the Padre had not quite lived up to his promises.

As Torquil walked along Harbour Street, after being buttonholed by his old teacher, he grinned at the thought of how his uncle was likely to receive an earbashing for failing to pin down Ranald Buchanan. Despite the fact that Torquil had told her the Padre was planning to track the fisherman-poet down today, she was less than impressed.

'He never came back to his shop yesterday and he left it unattended all night.'

'He often does that, Miss Melville,' Torquil protested. 'I think it's the poetic image that he likes to foster. Footloose and fancy-free.'

Miss Melville harrumphed disapprovingly, just as she used to do during her teaching days. 'Poetic *spirit*, more like. I don't know why the police — that's *you*, Inspector McKinnon — allow him to keep producing that illegal peatreek of his. He'll send himself blind one day.'

Torquil grinned. '*Cha choir gòisinn a chur an rathad an doill.* A trap should not be laid in the way of a blind man,' he said, raising his eyebrows quizzically.

Miss Melville suppressed a smile. 'Oh, you always were too clever for your own good, Torquil McKinnon.' She patted his arm. 'You just tell that uncle of yours I'm expecting a result.'

Torquil walked on, passing several posters with pictures of Fiona and the words 'Scotland's Queen of Crime Speaks Out and talks about her latest novel, *Dead Writers Tell No Tales*.'

The carnival atmosphere lifted his spirits, which were already high. Fiona! Had she really walked back into his life? He ambled along between the stalls with his head in the clouds, successfully dodging Miss Melville's helpers who were dishing out flyers about the various literary events.

PC Ewan McPhee was in a similarly light mood when Torquil entered the station. He was still dressed in his waterproof trousers, having just returned in the police Seaspray catamaran from the morning patrol round the Kyleshiffin harbour area. He was whistling as he wrote up his report in the day book.

'I think I've met someone, Torquil,' he confessed. 'A girl as bonnie as a picture.'

Torquil grinned and sat down. 'Give me the facts then. Where, when, how?'

Morag came through with a tea tray and the biscuit tin. 'She's a writer!' she said enthusiastically, indicating that Ewan had already confided in his sergeant.

'I met her last night when I was out for my run. You know, my usual five-miler, down to Loch Hynish, then back through town before going across the school field to home. She was coming out of the Lobster Pot restaurant.'

'So you stopped to chat to her?' Torquil prompted.

'Not exactly. I didn't actually see her. My earphones had come out and I was fixing them. I wasn't really looking where I was going and I — well — I bumped into her and sent her flying into the doorpost.' He blushed and grimaced as Torquil and Morag laughed softly. 'I know, I'm a clumsy bugger, but there you have it.' He sucked air between his lips. 'She was good about it, though. And she's a real good-looker. Long red hair and teabag eyes.'

'He means hazel, I think,' Morag interjected.

'Aye, hazel would be right. And a figure to die for. Anyway, we got talking and I invited her for a drink at the Bonnie Prince Charlie.' He laughed. 'We got on like a house on fire. I even managed to tell her a few things about West Uist.'

Torquil and Morag exchanged expressions of approval.

'She writes travel books,' Ewan volunteered. 'Izzie Frazer's her name. She's here for the Gathering and Literary Festival. She said this was her first visit to West Uist and she was gathering information. She has a wee jotter and she notes everything down. She said that's how she writes. Just absorbs everything about a place and then bashes it into some sort of readable order. Anyway, she was really interested about Ranald Buchanan and his book, and wanted to know all about the Selkie.'

'What did you tell her, Ewan?' Torquil asked, sipping his mug of tea, relishing Morag's brew instead of Ewan's usual stewed version. 'You need to be sure that you didn't give a version that the island folk wouldn't approve of.'

Ewan puffed his cheeks in mock chagrin. 'I'm a police officer, Piper,' he said sarcastically. 'I give the facts and just that. I told her about the Selkie being a seal man, who turns into a handsome lad when he comes out of the water. He usually chooses the best-looking girl and courts her, then leaves her wi' a bairn before disappearing off to sea. Then years later, he comes back and claims his child.'

'And what did your lady friend say to all that?'

'She laughed and said that the old local legends were important in travel books, they were what gave colour to a place.' He smiled as he recounted his tale. 'Then she said she'd better be careful in case I was a Selkie in disguise.' He took a great slurp of tea, sighed with pleasure, then continued, 'And she's coming to watch me practise my hammer tonight.'

'Quite the Don Juan, isn't he?' said Morag, dunking a digestive biscuit in her tea.

Torquil was about to reply when the door opened and a large woman wearing a flowing floral shawl swept in. She had full red lips, bright red fingernails and had a smoking Gauloises cigarette clamped between the first two fingers of her right hand. She waved extravagantly at the desk. 'Ah, the local gendarmerie!' she said airily. 'I have an absolute emergency on my hands. I've lost an author.'

Morag greeted her at the desk with a smile. 'Any particular author, madam? We have a Literary Festival on at the moment and there are quite a few of them around.'

'Oh, not just any author. *My* author, the Queen of Scottish Crime — Fiona Cullen.' With the legerdemain of a conjurer she produced a blue-and-white bookmark with a photograph of Fiona Cullen set against a painted Japanese screen and laid it down on the counter. 'I'm Genevieve Cooper, her agent. I simply have to see her now, because she has a lecture to give at one o'clock and we have so many things to talk about.' She puffed her cigarette and blew out a thin stream of smoke. 'She's just vanished — like smoke.'

Morag coughed and half-turned to see Torquil give the slightest of headshakes. Then she picked up the bookmark. 'Fiona Cullen,' she said, pensively. 'I've read a couple of her books. She's good. If we see her we'll let her know that you're looking for her, shall we?'

Genevieve Cooper nodded. 'I can ask no more. But tell her it's urgent.' She reached for the door handle. 'Oh, you couldn't direct me to the nearest turf accountant, could you?'

'Try Henry Henderson's at the end of the harbour,' Ewan suggested.

'I have to place a bet for a friend,' Genevieve volunteered, before sweeping out.

Once she had gone, Morag turned to Piper. 'I wonder if that could be construed as the police withholding information, Inspector McKinnon? So why the silence?'

'I'd say it was more to do with protecting a friend,' Torquil replied with a grin.

Twenty minutes later Genevieve left Henry Henderson's Bookmakers and looked up guiltily as she heard her name called. A maroon four-by-four was parked by the side of the road next to a Lambretta scooter. A smart thirty-something woman dressed in a grey pin-striped trouser suit was leaning against the door of her car, talking to a scruffy mustard-anorak-clad individual. He was jotting things down in a small wire-bound notepad.

'Allegra! Am I glad to see you,' the agent called, crossing the road and hugging the Castlefront publisher. 'I've just been looking for Fiona.'

Allegra McCall eyed Genevieve suspiciously through round wire-framed glasses that added a touch of severity to her well-groomed image. She was a good-looking woman with high cheekbones, a well-chiselled nose and tightly pulled back hair tied in a ponytail. 'I didn't know that Fiona gambled,' she said, meaningfully. Then added, 'Genevieve, this is Calum Steele, the editor of the *West Uist Chronicle*. He knows Fiona from years back.'

'Aye, you could say I taught her how to write,' Calum said, shaking hands. 'I was her boss on the *Chronicle*. That's before she left the island and you folk made her famous.'

'But now she's disappeared and I need to run over a few things with her,' said Genevieve. 'I saw her on the ferry, but she seemed a bit — stressed.'

Allegra seemed to stiffen a tad. 'And I need to talk to her myself about the next book. I think it's going to make a bit more of a stir than the last one. We need to get a few things straightened out.' She bit her lower lip and stamped her foot. 'Dammit! Why doesn't she use a mobile like everyone else?'

'Ha! That sounds interesting,' crooned Calum. 'Do I detect author-publisher problems?'

Allegra McCall's lips stretched into a smile and she shook her head. 'Of course not, Calum. Castlefront is going to take Fiona Cullen to new heights. I'm in talks with an American publisher.'

'You're what?' demanded Genevieve, her eyes wide with amazement. 'I'm her agent, Allegra! I negotiate any deals with foreign publishers.'

Allegra patted the agent's arm. 'Of course, dear. I wasn't meaning to stand on your toes. I think that you and I ought to have a little chat together, once we've seen Fiona.'

Calum Steele grinned. 'Ladies, you're talking to the Press here. I can sniff something going on.' He cocked his head and his eyelids half-closed, giving him a vaguely reptilian appearance. 'I have connections with a lot of national dailies, who are always on the look-out for a scoop. What gives?'

Allegra and Genevieve exchanged glances. 'If there is any scoop to be had we want you to have it,' Allegra said, dropping her voice to a conspiratorial whisper. 'Just bear with us and we'll keep you informed every step of the way.'

Calum tapped the side of his nose. 'Trust me, ladies. I'm a professional.'

'I just wish Fiona would show up,' said Genevieve.

'Oh, I know exactly where she is,' Calum volunteered. 'She's staying at the Bonnie Prince Charlie Tavern.' He grinned and added: 'Maybe the three of us should go and see her?'

The Bonnie Prince Charlie was almost packed. The influx of tourists, writers, publishers, agents and literary fans had brought a welcome increase in trade to the Kyleshiffin public houses and hotels; and particularly to the well-known Bonnie Prince Charlie, with its own brewery specializing in Heather Ale and its complete stock of all of the Hebridean Islay Malts. The aroma of seafood greeted them as they entered.

Mollie McFadden, the doughty landlady of almost sixty years, was serving behind the bar and came over at Calum's request. She blinked at him from behind thick-lensed spectacles perched on the tip of her nose. 'It's Fiona Cullen you'll be after, isn't it, Calum Steele?'

The jaw of the editor of the *West Uist Chronicle* had fallen open. It clamped shut when Mollie pulled out a piece of paper from her apron and handed it across the bar. 'She told me that you or two ladies would be coming and that I was to show any or all of you this message.' She smiled at Allegra and Genevieve. 'She described you both to a tee, ladies.'

The two women looked over Calum's shoulders as he read the note, written in Fiona Cullen's neat handwriting.

Dear All,

Sorry to miss you, but I've been thinking and preparing for my lecture. See you after it, or at AM's ceilidh in the evening.

Regards, Fiona

'Now would any of you be wanting a drink?' Mollie asked. 'Our Heather Ale is famous, as Calum will tell you.'

But there were no takers.

'Thanks Mollie,' Fiona whispered from the doorway behind the bar, after the trio had gone.

Lachlan McKinnon was thirsty as he rolled up on his 1954 Ariel Red Hunter, a machine famous across the whole island, for it had been beautifully maintained by its owner and used to transport the Padre round his parish for about four decades. Stowing his helmet in the pannier he pulled his pipe out of his breast pocket, applied a light, then strode purposefully into the public bar of the Bonnie Prince Charlie.

A few moments later, after some banter with Mollie, he was just raising his personal tankard of foaming ale to his lips when he felt a prod in the back.

'Lachlan McKinnon! Just where have you been? There have been four lectures this morning and you've missed every one of them. That's so rude! And have you sorted Ranald Buchanan out yet? I've sold so many tickets for the Gaelic Bard's reading session that I've had to turn people away.'

'It's in hand, Bella.'

'And the Fiona Cullen lecture starts in twenty minutes. You're supposed to be introducing her. Have you talked to her? Have you prepared your speech? Have you —?'

'He's done all of those things, Miss Melville,' came Fiona's voice. 'I'm ready whenever you are, Lachlan.'

Miss Melville flashed a cold look at Fiona Cullen, who had appeared, still dressed in her black motorcycle leathers.

'You look and sound just the same, Miss Melville,' said Fiona.

'And so do you, Fiona. I always thought you were —'

'A wee minx,' Fiona cut in, with a mock falsetto voice. 'That's what you used to call me at school.'

Miss Melville straightened up. 'I was going to say that I always thought you were going to be a star.'

The Padre stared regretfully at his full pint of Heather Ale. 'Well then,' he said, detecting a slight frostiness between them. 'Perhaps I'd better escort the star to her admiring audience.' And linking arms with Fiona he wheeled round and escorted her through the crowded bar.

Torquil slipped into the back of the packed Duncan Institute just in time for the start of Fiona's lecture. Fiona was sitting on the stage as the Padre stood at the lectern delivering a few words of introduction. As the audience laughed at some of his little asides and light-hearted jokes, Torquil managed to catch Fiona's eye. He raised his hand and she winked at him. He noted that her reaction had not gone unnoticed by the large woman, Genevieve Cooper, who was sitting with Calum Steele and a smartly dressed woman with a ponytail and round wireframed spectacles a few rows ahead and to the side.

The audience applauded when Fiona took the lectern. And they sat entranced as she began to talk. At first she gave some background to her early life, mentioning in passing her education at the Kyleshiffin School, then her university days at St Andrews before returning to West Uist and her first job at the *West Uist Chronicle*. She spoke of her passion for cinema, fishing and Heather Ale. Then she talked about her move to Edinburgh and her work on various magazines, then about her first novel, *Raw Deal*. It had passed with some acclaim, but little money. Her second, *Nemesis Comes*, had hit the Scottish bestseller lists and was followed by a succession of crime novels, each bringing further success, culminating in her winning a Gold Dagger from the Crime Writers' Association.

Twenty minutes into her talk, Fiona picked up a rolled-up poster and slowly unfurled it.

'But as you can see, my lecture is advertised with the words "Scotland's Queen of Crime speaks out and talks about her latest novel, *Dead Writers Tell No Tales*". Well, now that you know a bit about my background as the so-called "Queen of Scottish Crime", let me give you an inkling of how to do it yourself. And I say that because I know full well that the aspiring authors in the audience want to know exactly what they have to do to get to my stage. Basically, the best advice I can give is to — *tell a story!*'

There was a chorus of mild laughter from around the hall. Fiona smiled as she waited for it to settle, then: 'By "tell a story" I mean you have to base your plot around real life. And that's what I do. I use real life to give me my plots. I aim at what the French call a *roman-à-clef*, literally a "novel with a key".'

She waited, allowing her words to register. 'A lot of you will already know that, of course. You will, I am sure, know exactly who the corrupt health minister was in *Nemesis Comes*. To give you a clue, he resigned from the cabinet three weeks after the book hit the bestseller list. And you may know about the coven of Satan worshippers who ran a village council. There was an exposé in the Sunday newspapers of a group in Glasgow about a month after *Village Coven* came out.'

There was by now a murmuring of realization and of approval running round the hall. From his place at the back, Torquil noticed several people in the audience begin to move about, as if uncomfortable with the direction that Fiona's lecture was taking.

'In a way I suppose I have taken my early journalistic experience and adapted it in my new role as a novelist.'

'That's the way, lassie!' called out Calum Steele, to general merriment from many of the locals. 'Remember your roots — and your first boss!'

'And how could I forget him,' replied Fiona, sardonically. And pointing to Calum Steele: 'Ladies and Gentlemen, be careful of anything you say today because the esteemed editor of the *West Uist Chronicle* is in our midst.'

To his immense delight Calum enjoyed a few moments of good-natured approval and banter, before Fiona went on.

'My last book, *Flesh Trimmers*, caused quite an uproar.'

Torquil saw both Genevieve and the smartly dressed woman shift in their seats.

'I can't say too much about it, because it is *sub judice*. That is, I am being sued by someone who thinks I am talking about them in my book. Guilty conscience perhaps! What I can say is that it relates to certain dubious practices in a branch of the medical profession.

'And that brings me onto my new book, which I am still writing, and which neither my ex-agent nor ex-publisher have seen. It's called *Dead Writers Tell No Tales*. It's about —'

'What did you say, Fiona!' someone cried out. All eyes turned to see a large woman in a floral shawl standing, clutching the top of the chair in front of her. 'What did ... did you just say?'

Fiona looked up and smiled wanly. 'I said I hadn't shown it to either my ex-agent or my ex-publisher.'

A hush fell over the audience then Fiona went on. 'The advert said that I speak out — which is what I'm doing. Things have been happening in my life and I'm speaking out on them, and I'm writing about them. So, to finish my talk, I simply suggest that my readers buy my new book *Dead Writers Tell No Tales*. It's going to be explosive!'

Allegra McCall had been staring at Fiona all this time without saying a word. Now she grabbed Genevieve Cooper's sleeve, nodded to her and walked out down the aisle. Genevieve, ashen-faced, tears in her eyes, followed. A moment later, Calum Steele pulled on his anorak and made after them. Torquil could not help but notice that his old schoolmate had a slight smile on his lips.

By now, the Padre was on his feet, clapping his hands. He took centre stage and held up his hands for calm. 'And now, Ladies and Gentlemen. We thank Fiona for a stimulating and enlightening lecture. Before we break for the next session by Professor Neil Ferguson on his latest book, *The Iron Age Crannogs of the Hebrides*, we have time for a few quick questions.'

Torquil saw Fiona wink at him from the stage. She was a beautiful woman, no mistake. But she still had a brutal side to her.

Torquil signed out the station Ford Escort in order to drive Fiona back to the manse after he finished work. She had changed into a simple black dress that amply emphasized her curves, and wrapped a Japanese silk scarf about her elegant throat. The Padre was just about to set off on his Ariel Red Hunter when they drove into the gravel drive.

'I'm off to get Ranald organized,' he explained. 'I'm betting he's gotten the wind up and is in a peatreek-induced fit of poetic indulgence. The old galoot seems to write his best stuff when he's got a quart of whisky inside him and when he's faced with a deadline. But is that good enough for Miss Bella Melville! Is it thump.'

'Isn't that what poetic spirit really means?' Torquil suggested with a grin.

The Padre smiled at Fiona. 'You look beautiful, my dear.' Then he turned to Torquil, 'You are getting as bad as Miss Melville, laddie!' And pulling down his goggles, he started up the Hunter and rode off. 'Apologize to the laird and the fine folk if I'm late,' he called over his shoulder.

'And now,' said Torquil, 'you've got your lecture out of the way, but tomorrow is my big day. The piping competitions start after the official opening of the Gathering and I'm looking on the ceilidh opening ceremony as a wee bit of final practice.'

Fiona smiled. 'Go on then, get the pipes and put on your glad rags then we'll be off. And I promise not to try peeking up your kilt — not yet anyway!'

Torquil drove into the courtyard of the floodlit Dunshiffin Castle, the thirteenth-century stronghold of the MacLeod family, the hereditary lairds of West Uist. Hired help, the men in kilts and the women in tartan skirts and plaids, all of whom knew Piper Torquil McKinnon, greeted them with trays of champagne and canapés as they entered the main hall. There was a welcoming old-world aroma about the place, enhanced by glass cases of champion-sized salmon and trout, stag heads, antlers, shields, claymores and pikestaffs crisscrossed on the oak-panelled walls. Local dignitaries, celebrities from Edinburgh and the west coast, authors, sportsmen and -women stood about in groups or meandered in and out of the many opened rooms, mingling and moseying among the throng.

Calum Steele, looking uncomfortable in a crumpled and stained tuxedo, was one of the first to break away and join them. 'Well, well, Piper McKinnon and the great Fiona Cullen,' he said, a slight slur indicating how well the editor had already sampled the luxury of Dunshiffin Castle, courtesy of the laird, Angus MacLeod. 'Torquil, you bastard, you have the body and legs for a kilt — even if it is a McKinnon tartan!' He ducked as Torquil playfully raised his pipes to him, then turning to the pretty girl on Torquil's arm: 'Well, any more bombshells, Fiona? Any little nuggets for the *Chronicle*, for old time's sake?'

Fiona graced him with an indulgent smile. 'Only one,' she replied. 'A piece of advice. Buy a dictionary, Calum. I saw a copy of the *Chronicle* today, and you still can't spell.'

The editor of the local newspaper took it in good stead, tossed his head back and roared with laughter.

'And talking about spelling,' came another slightly slurred voice. 'Do you want me to spell out the meaning of your contract — Fiona, *darling*!' said Genevieve Cooper, stopping long enough to glare slightly cross-eyed at Fiona. 'You try and leave me and I'll sue your ass, my girl.'

Allegra McCall was a pace behind her. The trouser suit had been replaced by a sheath-like green designer dress and her hair had been pulled into a topknot. 'Genevieve this isn't the right time or place,' she said, pushing her spectacles higher on her nose. Then to Fiona, 'We shall talk tomorrow, Fiona, civilly and privately. Perhaps a few home truths will be in order.'

Fiona had already quaffed her first glass of champagne and had just accepted a second from a girl in a MacLeod tartan skirt and sash. 'Whatever, Allegra,' she replied. 'Oh, but by the way, you'll be hearing from my solicitor — and my forensic accountant about some *irregularities*.' She raised her glass and drained half of it.

Allegra bustled Genevieve away and Torquil steered Fiona into the main salon, where The Burns Boys, a Scottish traditional band, were playing with fiddle, accordion and tin whistle, while clusters of revellers stood around waiting for food and drink before the dancing began in earnest. At the far end of the room a line of young men in chef uniforms were standing at attention behind tables laden with salvers and bowls of food, also awaiting the beginning of the ceilidh and their part in it.

'I went to one of Angus MacLeod's Edinburgh bashes,' Fiona whispered, accepting a top-up of champagne from a young man in a Campbell kilt. 'I think he's pinched the idea from Jeffrey Archer and is trying to do a Scottish version. Champagne and shepherd's pie suppers have become Champagne, haggis and neeps.' She drained half her glass again and added, 'It's OK, I suppose, if you don't mind offal.'

A trio of men detached themselves from the great fireplace and honed in on them. A tall, distinguished middle-aged man in full highland dress laughed and held out his hand. 'Fiona Cullen, I believe you have perfected the art of whispering so that everyone in a room can hear you,' said Angus MacLeod, the Laird of Dunshiffin and managing director of Angus MacLeod Enterprises, whose business interests included the local malt distillery, hunting, shooting and fishing rights on several of the islands and the well-known chain of cut-price bookshops strung along the west coast of Scotland. 'I did not pinch this idea from anyone. Haggis and turnips were good enough for Robbie Burns, so I don't see why they shouldn't be good enough for the West Uist Gathering.' He nodded to Torquil. 'Glad to see you, Piper. Allow me to introduce you to Roland Baxter, the Scottish Minister for Culture, and my friend Dr Viroj Wattana.' The two men in tuxedos smiled.

Torquil shook hands with the broad, slightly bovine-looking Roland Baxter, well known on Scottish TV for his views about reducing the use of Gaelic in schools. His widely reported belief was that a united Scotland needed a universal language, and that the Gaelic should no longer be a first language, since it promulgated a sense of exclusivity and fostered the idea that the Hebrides were different from the rest of Scotland. The Padre had often been heard saying that such values were typical of the lowland Scot.

'I love the highland dress, Inspector McKinnon,' Roland Baxter enthused.

'*Suas am pìobaires*,' said Torquil raising his glass, 'Up the pipers.'

Baxter laughed. 'I don't speak the Gaelic myself, as you probably know, but I'm a great fan of the bagpipes.'

'And of course, Inspector McKinnon here is the island's best bagpipe player. Apart from the Padre that is,' said Angus MacLeod with a wry smile, before asking: 'Where is the illustrious convenor of the Literary Festival, by the way?'

'He'll be along later,' Torquil replied. 'I believe he's tracking Ranald Buchanan down.'

'That old reprobate Buchanan, eh?' the laird mused, it seemed with a touch of irritation. Then he turned to explain to Dr Wattana, a slight crop-headed man with half-moon spectacles. 'You see, Viroj, we have a...'

But the doctor was paying no attention. He had taken Fiona's arm and was trying to guide her along to chat in her ear. After a few words she threw his hand aside, and with a look of disgust shouted, 'Forget it, Wattana. You're a bungler and I won't let you bugger anyone else up. Just let our lawyers deal with it.'

The laird looked horrified. 'Fiona, please,' he said in an urgent hushed tone. 'Dr Wattana is my guest. I flew in with him yesterday and want him to —'

'To what? Give someone a penis stretch!' Fiona gave a shrill laugh and put a hand on Roland Baxter's arm. 'That could be you, eh, Roland.' She winked provocatively at him, adding: 'Remember.'

The Scottish Minister for Culture shook his head. 'Fiona, you're drunk. And you're insulting everyone. Don't you think you ought to cut back on the booze before you say something dangerous?'

'And what do you mean by that?' Fiona demanded. 'I'll drink as much as I want, say what I want,' she hesitated for a moment, then smiled, feline-like. 'Or write what I want.'

Torquil was indeed beginning to feel embarrassed. Fiona seemed to be knocking champagne back as if it was water, and, as it affected her, she seemed intent on offending everyone around her. He grasped her arm and addressed Angus MacLeod. 'Is it about time to get this ceilidh on the road, Angus? Shall I pipe in the haggis?'

Angus MacLeod, Laird of Dunshiffin, nodded gratefully. He raised his hand above his head and signalled to an elderly manservant who had been hovering silently at the side of the hall. 'Good idea, Piper. Jesmond will take you through to the kitchen. The pipes will bring some order to the place,' he said, smiling uncertainly.

Torquil followed the elderly retainer through the crowd and managed to catch hold of Calum Steele on the way. 'Look after Fiona for a few minutes will you, while I do the piping for the haggis,' he whispered. 'I think she's drinking too quickly.'

The Burns Boys started playing again after Torquil had piped in the haggis and people had begun to form queues to collect plates of food. People patted him on the back and expressed pleasure at his rendition of 'Scotland the Brave'. He was looking round for Fiona when he heard her raised voice again. He saw her berating the laird himself. Calum Steele was standing a few feet away, looking shocked and impotent to interfere. Disappointedly, Torquil noted that her voice sounded even more slurred than before.

'That's right, high and mighty *Mister* Angus MacLeod. I know what you're up to, with your cut-price bookstores, robbing authors so that you can pump money into the Labour Party. Fawning on ministers so that you can buy a knighthood.'

Angus MacLeod caught sight of Torquil as he approached. He hissed through gritted teeth. 'Get her out of here, McKinnon. She's drunk and she's making a spectacle of herself. As usual!'

'I think a little air would help first,' Torquil replied, as he hooked Fiona's arm and drew her away, out onto a balcony. Once there, he asked, 'Fiona, what the hell's got into you? You've insulted everybody you've talked to!'

But Fiona had instantly sobered up. She smiled and slid her arms about his waist. 'I was just having fun. All those prissy people. I needed to stir them up, to get each of them worried about my book.'

'But why?'

'Because it's a game, Torquil. Publishing is just a game. Bestsellers are more than literary effort — the book is just a part of the process — not necessarily even the most important part. Tonight is mainly about getting the publicity machine going.'

'Mainly?'

Fiona laughed and squeezed his waist. 'You're too clever for your own good, Torquil McKinnon. OK, I had a few — points to make with certain folk.'

'And what about me, Fiona? What part does the local inspector play in all this? Am I just part of the game?'

She raised her mouth to his and kissed him gently. 'I'm not playing with you at all, Torquil. I've got serious plans in mind for us.'

As they kissed, Torquil felt himself floating in a sea of bliss. Then his mobile phone went off. Reluctantly, he gently detached himself and fished it out of his sporran to find the Padre's number flashing on the dial. He raised the instrument to his ear.

'Torquil! You better get over here!' came the Padre's agonized voice. There was a rasping sound in the background, followed by a gentle thumping or slapping, then: 'I'm here at Ranald's place on the Machair Skerry with Ewan McPhee.' The strange rasping noise echoed in the background again. 'Ewan can't speak at the moment,' the Padre explained. 'Ranald Buchanan is dead. He's bashed his head and fallen in the water. His feet are all tangled up and his eyes, they, they —'

'They're what, Uncle?'

'They've gone, Torquil. The gulls have pecked them out!'

The rasping sound came again and Torquil vaguely heard his constable's voice cursing in the background. Then he realized that the rasping noise was caused by Ewan McPhee retching his guts out.

CHAPTER FOUR

The post-mortem was held in the Kyleshiffin Cottage Hospital the following morning at seven o'clock, on the authority of the District Procurator Fiscal on Benbecula, whom Torquil had contacted after seeing the body.

It had been a sombre business from the moment of receiving the Padre's telephone call. Torquil had made his apologies to Angus MacLeod, briefly indicating that Ranald Buchanan had been involved in an accident and that he, as the senior officer of the West Uist Division of the Hebridean Constabulary, had been called to the scene. Despite MacLeod's attempts to extract more information Torquil had taken his leave with Fiona, much to the relief of several of the guests at the party.

Dropping Fiona outside the Bonnie Prince Charlie he drove to the police station where he swapped the car for his Royal Enfield Bullet and rode to Binacle Point where PC Ewan McPhee was waiting in the police *Seaspray* catamaran. A few moments later they were scudding over the moonlit waves on their way round the coast to the Machair Skerry. Torquil could see that his constable was badly shaken by the events of the night — the Padre had contacted him as the duty officer to take him over to the Machair Skerry after he had spotted Ranald Buchanan's boat through his binoculars.

'It's awful, Piper,' Ewan informed his superior officer. 'He looks like a dead seal that I saw once, its face all pecked by the gulls.' The thought of it produced another tide of nausea that made him reach for the side of the craft in order to vomit over the side. Torquil took over and steered the boat in towards the small skerry.

Ranald Buchanan's small motorboat was tied up to the iron spike on his primitive jetty. Standing smoking his pipe a few feet back was the Padre.

'He's here, Torquil,' the Padre announced, tapping his pipe out on his heel and depositing the hot pipe in his breast pocket. 'I've given him the last rites, but I havena touched him. Ewan thought I'd better wait for you.'

Torquil hopped onto the stone jetty and, flicking on his powerful flashlight, knelt down to get a closer look at the body. Ranald Buchanan's feet were tangled on the mooring rope and the body was floating in the water a few inches below the surface. His straggly beard waving like seaweed around the already bloated white face gave him a macabre Neptunian appearance. The sight of the empty eye sockets was truly nauseating, the gulls having feasted on the eyes and the sea having washed away the blood. Torquil reached out and caught hold of the dead poet's waistcoat, then with both hands successfully turned the torso over in the water. The gaping wound at the back of the skull was just as nauseating, and despite himself Torquil winced. There was a great depression in the skull exposing a pulpy mass of brain and coagulated blood.

'That seems to have been the culprit,' said the Padre, pointing to a broad blood slick on the iron mooring spike. 'And look at these, a bottle and a copy of his new book of poems.'

Torquil looked at the empty bottle of peatreek and the thin volume of poems, *Songs of the Selkie*, lying open beside it, as if it had fallen as he was reading. He picked up the book and noted a few pencilled underlinings and scorings through words of the penultimate poem, entitled 'The Return of the Selkie'.

'He was too fond of his own peatreek,' mused the Padre. 'And when he was drinking, he was always his own worst critic. It looks as if he was walking back and forth on the jetty, fiddling with his latest work, maybe even working out which poems he was going to use in his reading tomorrow. Then he stumbled on the ropes, fell backwards and bashed his head and —'

'And drowned,' said Torquil. 'Aye, I agree, it looks like it.' He turned to Ewan, who was still looking decidedly ill. 'We'd better get him out of the water and take him back to Kyleshiffin, then I'll report the death to the Procurator Fiscal.'

Dr Ralph McLelland, the local GP and police surgeon, washed his hands after completing the autopsy. 'I'll have to do the histological examinations, of course, but from the morbid anatomical examination and surgical dissection it seems pretty obvious, he died from a blunt injury to the head and probable drowning.'

'Will a diatom test tell you anything?' Torquil asked, as he and the police surgeon stood looking down at the open body of Ranald Buchanan.

Ralph McLelland blew through tight lips. 'Not sure it will tell anything. Some algal diatoms will undoubtedly have crossed the alveolar junction into the bloodstream so I expect we'll find them in some of the histology samples. But whether he died from the head wound or from drowning is pretty academic, isn't it. It's a tragedy any way you look at it.'

'Aye, a tragedy right enough,' agreed Torquil. 'It'll take a few days for the inquest, so it'll be after the Gathering, I am thinking.'

'After the Gathering?' Ralph McLelland repeated. 'Do you think it will be respectful to carry on with it, Piper?'

An emergency meeting of the Gathering and Literary Festival Committee was held an hour later in the dining room of the St Ninian's manse, where Torquil announced the circumstances of Ranald Buchanan's accidental death. 'Of course, this is not official. There will have to be an inquest.'

'Had he any kin?' Angus MacLeod asked.

'None. He had been a widower for thirty years and he lost his only daughter about ten years ago,' the Padre replied. 'She had suffered from schizophrenia for a lot of years. And, you will recall that she had a son that drowned twenty years ago.'

'I suppose the question that I, as the West Uist senior police officer, have to ask is — are you going to go ahead with the Gathering?'

Miss Melville was the first to reply. 'Of course we go ahead, Torquil. It's all very sad, but the life of the island has to keep going. We shall still hold Ranald Buchanan's poetry reading, but someone else will do the recitations. That is only respectful. We shall call it a celebration of his life.'

'I agree, Piper,' said the laird. 'The island is swollen with visitors. And not all of them have come to hear the Gaelic Poet. The majority, I would say, have come for the traditional Gathering. The sport.'

The Padre had struck a light to his briar and was puffing meditatively. 'Glad I am to hear you say this. I am thinking that it is what the old rascal would have wanted.' He looked uncertainly at his nephew. 'And maybe it would be an idea to allow the people who come to hear his poetry have a taste of what Ranald Buchanan was really about?'

'What are you saying, Uncle?' Torquil asked, suspiciously.

'Peatreek!' exclaimed the Padre with glee. 'It was what helped him with his poetic vision. Why not let folk enjoy a sample of his "*spirit*"?'

Torquil suppressed a smile, for he expected Miss Melville's reaction. 'You old fool!' she said. 'It sounds as if his peatreek killed him. Why should we be celebrating it?'

Angus MacLeod put a hand on the retired teacher's shoulder. 'I believe that Lachlan is playing with us, Miss Melville. He well knows that we cannot have anything to do with illicit liquor. But if toasting his memory is what you want, then I am prepared to donate six bottles of Glen Corlin Malt Whisky from my *legal* distillery for those who would wish to celebrate his life and work.'

The Padre clapped his hands. 'There you have it then, Torquil laddie. The show must go on! And if I might make a suggestion to the laird, about the use of his helicopter...'

Calum Steele had also been hard at work throughout the night, which had helped him to work off the hangover that he had anticipated after all the champagne at the ceilidh. Normally the *West Uist Chronicle* appeared twice a week, on Tuesdays and Fridays, but for the duration of the Gathering and the Literary Festival Calum had agreed to produce a special daily news sheet, every morning.

Reading it over a breakfast of boiled eggs, Ranald Buchanan's murderer was pleased to see a mere mention of the Gaelic Poet's demise, presumably from a tragic accident. Then followed a short biography about the fisherman-poet, with a promise of more information in the next issue.

'Poetic justice!' the murderer thought again on scanning the subheadings of the reviews of the Literary Festival lectures:

FIONA CULLEN TELLS ALL AND SACKS AGENT AND PUBLISHER

Our literary editor was well placed in the audience at the celebrated crime novelist's lecture to gather the mood of the meeting. Fiona, who used to work on the West Uist Chronicle, told the audience about the new book she is working on, which is entitled Dead Writers Tell No Tales. Then she surprised everyone by informing the audience that she was sacking her —

PROFESSOR'S BOOK PROVES THE REAL PURPOSE OF THE CRANNOGS OF WEST UIST

Everyone, our editor in chief included, has always accepted the traditional explanation about our beautiful crannogs being artificial Iron Age islets. Yet research over the years by Professor Neil Ferguson, head of the Department of Marine Archaeology at the University of the Highlands, reveals that this is only a part —

GAME, FISH, STOVIES AND WHISKY — WEST UIST CULINARY SECRETS

Mrs Agnes Dunbar, former head cook at Dunshiffin Castle, has just published a small cookbook, which will give us an insight into what is really set before the laird for dinner. In fifty recipes stretching back to —

Anger seethed inside for a moment, threatening to show itself in some way. Then, as it subsided there was a flash of inspiration, followed by an exhilarating sense of anticipation. Gulping down a mouthful of tea and folding the news sheet, lest anyone should notice anything unusual, the murderer smiled with satisfaction and pushed the empty plate aside.

Soon! Retribution was on its way!

Torquil and Morag heaved a sigh of relief after they had given the Drummond twins, the West Uist Division's two special constables, their instructions for crowd patrol. Never slaves to punctuality or to the hierarchy of the police force, the two fishermen had arrived late smelling slightly of herring, Heather Ale and tobacco.

'Och, you should not be worrying. There will be no problems with the crowds,' said Douglas.

'None at all, for we shall be keeping a weather eye out,' added Wallace. The twins were even taller than Ewan, albeit more laid back and with far fewer collective brain cells. Nonetheless, everyone knew them and Torquil was sure that the twins would talk any rowdy revellers out of rowdiness; or bore them out of it.

Not that any problems were anticipated for at least a couple of hours, since it was not the islanders' way to begin drinking before midday. Any problems with rowdy behaviour was expected to come from incomers sampling the island's local Heather Ale at the Bonnie Prince Charlie or one of the other two hostelries in Kyleshiffin.

There had been a couple of well-attended lectures and writing workshops in the morning and now people were beginning to make their way to the village green on the hill above the town, in order to get a good seat or to see what was on offer at the several marquees set up around the roped-off arena.

Torquil called at Fiona's room at the Bonnie Prince Charlie to pick her up at half past eleven. She was still wearing a dressing gown and a cigarette was burning in the ashtray on her dressing table, beside a switched-on laptop and a mound of handwritten notes.

'Poor old Ranald,' she said, shaking her head, as Torquil filled her in on the events surrounding the Gaelic Bard's sad demise. 'Still, he probably went the way he'd have wanted, with a bottle of peatreek and a book of his poems.' Then picking a speck of invisible dust off his tweed jacket and smiling coquettishly up at him: 'You're the most fanciable man on the island, did you know that Torquil McKinnon?'

Torquil lay his bagpipes aside, encircled her waist and drew her close. 'And you are starting to get under my skin again.' He brushed her lips with his own. 'I think we need to have a bit of time on our own later, Fiona. We need to sort out what we're doing here.'

'We're having fun,' she said, kissing him on the nose. 'But first of all, you are going to win that Silver Quaich you've always wanted. Which reminds me, why the tweed jacket and not the full dress job like last night?'

'I'm an individual competitor,' he replied. 'The pipers from the pipe band will all likely be in the full kit, but I'm entitled to be more casual. Just the kilt, tweed jacket, tie and tam-o'-shanter beret.'

'But you're not as casual as me,' she said with a laugh, breaking away from him and pirouetting on her toes. And with a single pull she undid her dressing gown and allowed it to fall open to reveal her lithe naked body underneath.

Torquil closed his eyes and bit his lip. 'Dammit Fiona,' he said in mock agony. 'Like you said, I've got a competition to win. That's not fair.'

'Spoilsport!' she said with a laugh as she skipped into her en suite. 'I'll get dressed then. Like you said, we should talk later.'

A great banner emblazoned with the words '*Ceud Mile Failte* — One Hundred Thousand Welcomes' was strung above the entrance to the green. A light breeze billowed it slightly. At exactly twelve o'clock the South Uist Pipe Band, headed by Pipe Major Hamish Munro, led the procession into the arena. There were six pipers, a bass-drummer, then four side-drummers. As Torquil looked on he felt a tinge of nerves, since at least two of the pipers were above average ability and had their names down for the piping competitions, along with Hamish Munro himself.

Following them came the Chieftain of the Games party. In the centre marched a kilted Angus MacLeod, the current chieftain, his guests and the various specialist judges. Torquil felt Fiona stiffen at his side when she spied Roland Baxter and the surgeon, Dr Viroj Wattana, walking along with him and a coterie of long-legged blonde models in MacLeod tartan skirts with plaids slung over their right shoulders. The pipe band wheeled left and took up a position to the side of the main dais and continued to play, while the VIP party took their seats.

In the middle of the field a youth ceremonially pulled on the lanyard to raise the Games flag. It was timed exactly right, the flag reaching the top of the flagpole just as the band reached the last few bars.

When Hamish Munro whirled his staff to mark the end of their piece, Angus MacLeod stood and tapped the crackling microphone of the PA system. His speech was curt and to the point, welcoming all and sundry, especially Roland Baxter, the Scottish Minister for Culture, and his friend Dr Viroj Wattana from Thailand to the Gathering and Literary Festival; thanking all of the organizers, including Miss Bella Melville and the Padre, Lachlan McKinnon. Then he gave a brief eulogy for

Ranald Buchanan and asked for a minute's silence in his honour, before continuing.

'And now, may the competitors show their strength, speed, skill and dexterity, in whatever event they are competing in. May the spectators be entertained, the stallholders be prosperous and Jack Campbell, the engraver, be ever busy throughout the day, putting names on all the trophies.'

The noise of a powerful engine and rotating blades had gradually increased and from the direction of Dunshiffin Castle a helicopter with the AME tartan logo roared overhead and started on a circuit of the arena, before hovering over a sawdust circle at the far end of the field.

Angus MacLeod pointed at it. 'Our good Padre, the Reverend Lachlan McKinnon, has prevailed upon me,' he said, then paused for effect, 'I suppose you could even say, he has browbeaten me into making the AME helicopter available for the afternoon, to take sightseers on a trip around West Uist. Each spin will cost the munificent sum of two pounds a head, half to go to the Ranald Buchanan Memorial Fund and half towards the West Uist Gathering Appeal for a permanent arena.' He waited for a round of spontaneous applause to subside, then looked heavenwards at the gradually darkening sky and added hopefully, 'And finally, in the hope that the heavens will not open, I declare the Gathering officially open.'

There was another round of applause, accompanied by whistling, catcalls and general high spirits, then the crowd of people started flocking towards the clan tents, displays and various competitions. An almost undecipherable voice crackled on the tannoy to indicate where and when the various events would be taking place.

Torquil spotted the Drummond twins ambling around near the beer tent. For a moment he thought of going over to have a word with them, then he saw the familiar figure of the Padre hailing them, a glass of beer in his hand, and he thought better of it. Instead, he took Fiona's hand and nodded towards the far side of the green where a man with a loudspeaker was just announcing that the field sports were about to begin.

'Let's go and give Ewan a bit of support,' he said.

The big PC was standing outside the hammer-throwing enclosure, wearing a tee-shirt and sporran-less kilt, with his arm around a red-headed, athletic-looking young woman of about his own age. 'Piper! I mean — er — Inspector McKinnon,' Ewan corrected himself. 'You're the very man I want,' he said, still looking a trifle pale after his adventures of the night before, yet with a smile across his boyish face. 'And Fiona. Come and meet Izzie Frazer.'

There was a thud in the arena parallel with them as a twenty-two-pound iron sphere attached to a four-foot wooden shaft plummeted to the earth from the first hammer-thrower.

Izzie smiled and Torquil could immediately see why Ewan had been so smitten by her. She was exactly his type. Redhaired like him, athletic with freckles and large orb-like breasts that amply filled her angora sweater. 'Ah, the famous Fiona Cullen!' enthused Izzie Frazer, her hazel eyes sparkling. 'I caught your lecture yesterday. Most interesting! And I've read every one of your books. I particularly liked *Flesh Trimmers*, your last one.'

The two women shook hands and naturally fell into conversation. While they did so, Ewan signalled his inspector aside and said in a muffled voice, 'Torquil, I'm sorry about this morning. Puking up on duty, I mean. I'm so bloody embarrassed.'

Torquil grinned back. 'Och, I can see that you are cross with yourself, Ewan. Well then, just use that anger usefully. Show

Izzie what you can do with that hammer — assuming that you've got your trajectory right!'

Ewan grinned sheepishly at the dig about his mother's outhouse roof, just as his name was called out by the event referee. The big PC went and took his place behind the trig, the special throwing line. Torquil, Fiona and Izzie watched him swing the hammer round his head, gradually picking up momentum before hurling it over his shoulder to the accompaniment of a bestial roar. The hammer soared into the air and fell a full dozen feet further than the first competitor's marker.

A cheer went up from the watching gallery, testifying to the big local police officer's popularity. Torquil noted with a grin that Morag Driscoll was on the other side of the field, applauding and whistling, eschewing any professional decorum or neutrality that one might have expected from a uniformed police officer.

Izzie Frazer touched Torquil's arm. 'I thought they had to whirl round and round before they threw the hammer?'

'That's the Olympic hammer,' Torquil explained. 'This is the Scottish hammer, and you have probably just seen the winning throw already.'

He noticed Izzie's cheeks flush slightly. 'He's a powerful lad,' she cooed enthusiastically.

'I understand that you are a writer as well?' Torquil asked, keen to change the subject.

'Not as famous as Fiona, but I'm trying. I've got three travel books under my belt so far.'

'Who is your publisher, Izzie?' Fiona asked.

'Wanderlust Press. They're a new publisher, a subsidiary of AME.'

'And where have you been in your travels?' Torquil asked.

'The East so far. I'm doing a series, you see. The titles are not very inspiring, but they seem to be selling.'

Fiona frowned. 'Oh, they'll be selling all right, but if I were you I'd double-check the royalty statement. If Wanderlust have anything to do with Angus MacLeod Enterprises — you need to be careful!'

A female voice from behind them made Fiona spin round. 'And who are you maligning now, Fiona?' Allegra McCall asked. Torquil noted that the publisher had discarded her suit and was dressed in a ski parka and green Wellingtons. Almost inevitably, it seemed, a pace behind her was Genevieve Cooper, slightly out of breath, as if she had been hard put to keep up with the publisher. 'Wanderlust Press is a perfectly good firm.'

'Allegra, eavesdropping is becoming a hobby of yours, I think!' said Fiona.

Genevieve put an arm about Izzie Frazer's shoulder. 'I heard what she was saying though, my dear. Perhaps Fiona is right, you should check your royalty statements. Authors don't always do that, being creative people. That's what a good agent will do for you, make sure you get the best possible deal. Do you have an agent, by the way?' And with the skill of a conjurer she pushed a card into Izzie's hand. 'That's me — Genevieve Cooper, the author's trooper,' she announced. 'Just ask any of my authors.'

There was another thud in the throwing area and they all turned to see a hammer fall ten feet short of Ewan's first throw.

Fiona squeezed Torquil's arm. 'I'm going to have to catch someone for a while, Torquil. You stay and watch Ewan and I'll meet you before your piping.' She stood on her tiptoes and pecked him on the cheek, then turned to see Izzie Frazer chatting with Allegra and Genevieve. As she went by them she touched Izzie's shoulder and half-whispered, 'Remember what I said, Izzie! My best advice to you is to be careful of agents, publishers and cut-price booksellers.' She winked at her, and then smiled thinly at Allegra and Genevieve. 'We'll talk later, ladies.'

She left, oblivious to the looks of contempt bestowed upon her back by the agent and publisher.

Dr Viroj Wattana had been left to his own devices while Angus MacLeod went to give instructions to Captain Tam McKenzie, his helicopter pilot, about the trips round the island. He wandered in and out of the different marquees, feeling slightly bemused by this, his first ever Gathering. It was a feeling that was not lessened when the Padre caught him by the arm and virtually frog-marched him into the beer tent.

Being virtually a teetotaller, Dr Wattana found that the Heather Ale Lachlan McKinnon had introduced him to went straight to his head. As a result, the sound of the music, the dancing and athletic events going on around all seemed to merge into a surrealistic fugue.

'And where did you train, Dr Wattana?' the Padre asked, before quaffing a respectable mouthful of foaming ale.

'Chulalongkom University in Thailand. Then after that I studied plastic and cosmetic surgery at Harvard in the States, then at Oxford in England, and then Edinburgh in —'

'In Scotland,' the Padre finished, with a wink and a quick drink. 'So you know a little of our strange Scottish ways then?'

Dr Wattana sipped his beer. 'Oh yes, I have some good friends in Scotland. I have known Angus MacLeod for some years and I am going diving with him and Neil Ferguson tomorrow.'

'Our celebrated professor of Marine Archaeology? How did you come to know him?'

'As you say, he is a famous archaeologist. He lectured at Chulalongkorn and he — er — he has been a patient of mine.'

'Enough said, doctor,' returned the Padre. 'I understand. Medical ethics and all that. You can't say any more. A bit like us, the clergy.' He eyed the surgeon's glass. 'But come on, doctor, you're hardly drinking. Let me get you a fresh glass then I want to pick your brain about something.'

As the Padre turned to the bar a hand fell sharply on his shoulder. 'Oh no you don't, Lachlan McKinnon!'

The Padre turned, a crestfallen expression on his face. 'Ah! Miss Melville. I was just —'

'I don't care what you were doing, but I'll tell you what you are going to do now. You're coming with me,' Miss Melville announced authoritatively. 'We need you in the Literary Festival marquee, where you are going to put your considerable persuasive talent for salesmanship to good use. You are going to sell at least one copy of every author's work.'

The Padre shrugged helplessly at Dr Wattana. 'Perhaps we can have another drink later, Dr Wattana.'

Dr Wattana nodded dumbly, for he had not been listening properly. He was looking out through the marquee opening beyond the Padre. He blinked hard. He was unsure whether it was the effect of the beer or whether he really had seen someone he had never expected to see again.

Ewan beamed at Izzie Frazer as she ran a French-manicured nail over his bulging biceps.

'You're a strong lad,' she purred. 'A powerful man. I like that.'

Despite himself, Ewan blushed. He raised the gleaming silver cup that he had just been presented with, breathed on it and rubbed it on his hip. 'Och, it was nothing special. I didn't manage my record of last year. I just ken how to give the hammer a good hurl.'

'Mmm, I like a man in a kilt,' she murmured. 'Your inspector, Torquil, he suits a kilt as well — but not as well as you!'

Ewan blushed. 'Will you come and listen to Torquil play his pipes? He's got a rare gift and he's — well, he's a friend as well as my inspector — I'd like to see him win.'

Izzie giggled. 'Actually Ewan, I'd rather not. I can't say that the bagpipes are my favourite instrument. I'll just have a look at that book fair in the Literary Festival marquee then I think I'll try and have a word with that literary agent, Genevieve Cooper. Maybe she can help my career.' And brushing his cheek with her lips she whispered something in his ear that made the big PC blush to the very roots of his carrot-red hair.

No one entering the Literary Festival marquee escaped the eagle eye of the Padre. Using his clerical collar shamelessly he honed in on anyone picking up a book and then successfully prised information from them about their literary tastes, their desires, ambitions and foibles. Within moments a sale was notched up, to the immense pleasure of Miss Bella Melville, who bagged each purchase, took the money then popped a complementary bookmark with Fiona Cullen's smiling face on it into each bag.

'These bookmarks are a popular gimmick,' said Miss Melville. 'That literary agent gave me a great stack of them. I've spread them about all over the place and as a result we've almost sold out of all of Fiona Cullen's books.' She shook her head sadly.

'She's a nice girl, that agent. A pity that Fiona stabbed her in the back yesterday at her lecture.'

But Lachlan was not listening. He had spotted Professor Neil Ferguson chatting with a red-headed girl he thought he had seen cheering on Ewan McPhee at the hammer-throwing.

'Ah, it's Izzie Frazer, isn't it?' the Padre said, stepping up to interrupt their conversation. 'You're the travel writer. *My Sri Lanka* and *My Thai*. Those are your books, aren't they?' And before she could reply he had an arm about her shoulder and Neil Ferguson's and was bustling them towards the travel section. Before five minutes were up he had ensured that the professor had bought a copy of one of Izzie's books and that Izzie had purchased a copy of the professor's *Crannog* book.

'Padre, you have missed your calling,' Neil Ferguson joked. 'I believe that you could make a living selling tickets to hell and back.'

Lachlan tossed his head back and laughed as he stuffed thick-cut tobacco into the bowl of his briar pipe. 'Less of the blasphemy, if you don't mind, professor.' He struck a light to his pipe and beamed at Miss Melville as she handed over their purchases.

But before the professor could reply, the Padre had gone, a trail of tobacco smoke in his wake. He had spied a young hippy-looking couple perusing copies of Ranald Buchanan's latest work, *Songs of the Selkie*.

Good to see that the young were interested in Ranald's poetry, he thought. *Let's see if I can persuade them to make a contribution to the old boy's memory.*

CHAPTER FIVE

Torquil handed the judge his list of selected strathspeys, hornpipes and *piobaireachds* and waited while the panel of three conferred. Then he bowed as the head judge, Major Mackintosh from Mull, handed the list back with ticks against the pieces the panel wanted to hear. He made his way over to the spectator area, just as Pipe Major Hamish Munro began to play his strathspey. Fiona was waiting for him.

'I've got you a programme,' Torquil said. 'There's a note inside that explains everything.'

'The mysteries of the pipes, eh?' Fiona replied with a smile. Then nodding at Hamish Munro, 'He sounds as if he knows what he's doing.'

Torquil frowned. 'Aye, he knows all right. He knows too bloody well, in my opinion.'

Fiona cuffed him playfully on the side of his head, knocking his tam-o'shanter-beret askew. 'Where's the famous McKinnon confidence, Torquil? You're going to win that Silver Quaich today, I just know you will. I spoke to the Padre over in the Literary Festival tent,' she said, holding up a bag containing a couple of books. 'The old devil made me buy a travel book by Ewan's new lady friend and a cookbook by Agnes Dunbar. Anyway, he told me that the only person who can take the quaich away from you is yourself.'

They listened to Hamish Munro for a few moments, Torquil all the while getting more nervous and wishing that he had followed the Padre's oft-quoted advice to take a wee dram before playing in competition. Then, all too soon, it was his turn to take the dais. He kissed Fiona then crossed the grass to the steps. He mounted them swiftly and awaited Major McKenzie's announcement that he was going to play the 'Haughs o'Cromdale', a stirring strathspey. Torquil tuned up and began to play.

It was a piece that he knew backwards and which always brought a tear to his eye, just as he was sure that it did to every piper. Originally, it had been a song written by the Hebridean shepherd poet, James Hogg, telling of a lost Jacobite battle in 1690. But it was the fact that Piper George Findlater had played it with bullets flying around him to encourage his comrades to take a hill at the Battle of Dargai in 1897, despite having been shot in both ankles, that really moved him. For this act of heroism he had been awarded the Victoria Cross. Torquil played as he thought of the words of the song:

As I came in by Auchindoun,
A little wee bit frae the toun,
When to the Highlands I was bound,
To view the haughs of Cromdale...

Playing virtually on auto-pilot, Torquil had fleeting impressions of what was happening in different parts of the field, beyond the judges' table. He saw Fiona standing watching him, looking so damned sexy in her black leathers, tapping a hand on the plastic bag containing her purchases. He saw Professor Neil Ferguson and Dr Wattana, deep in conversation, moving in her direction.

We were in bed, sir, every man,
When the English host upon us came,
A bloody battle then began,
Upon the haughs of Cromdale....

In another part of the field he saw Fiona's agent, Genevieve Cooper, in heated conversation with the publisher Allegra McCall.

But alas. We could no longer stay,
For o'er the hills we came away....

He saw the Padre jogging across the field towards the piping square, arms waving encouragingly at him.

Thus the great Montrose did say,
Can you direct the nearest way?
For I will o'er the hills this day,
And view the haughs of Cromdale.

Up above he saw the AME Enstrom Shark helicopter complete a circuit of the island and head in to land on the temporary helipad at the far side of the field.

The Drummond brothers were still standing near the beer tent, surreptitiously smoking.

Alas my lord, you're not so strong,
You scarcely have two thousand men,
And there's twenty thousand on the plain....

Torquil played on, only dimly aware of the little tableau being played out on the field. Neil Ferguson and Dr Wattana were now close to Fiona, as was Ewan McPhee, coming from the other direction, with his mother — a small round woman with red hair streaked with silver — neither looking where they were going, so focused were they on the silver cup he was carrying. The inevitable happened. All five collided, Fiona stumbled, packages, parcels and purchases flying everywhere. Then they were all picking things up. Dr Wattana, Ewan and his mother looking awkward as Fiona seemed to make some cutting remark to the professor.

Stand rank and file on Cromdale.
Thus the great Montrose did say....

Torquil looked away, wary of becoming distracted from his playing. And his eyes fell on Genevieve Cooper and Allegra McCall. Genevieve seemed to stamp her foot, then the two separated, stomping off in separate directions. Nearby, as if not having wanted to interrupt them, Izzie Frazer walked after the retreating figure of Genevieve Cooper.

Turning back towards Fiona, he saw that the Padre had found her. Fiona was looking distracted for a moment, straightening out her purchases. Then at the Padre's nudge she looked up at Torquil, made a thumbs-up sign and winked.

Torquil closed his eyes, his heart soaring unexpectedly. He played on and on, eventually coming to the last few bars:

... Upon the haughs of Cromdale.
Of twenty thousand Cromwell's men,
Five hundred fled to Aberdeen
The rest of them lie on the plain
Upon the haughs of Cromdale.

He stopped, let his pipes down, bowed to the judges, then made his way down from the dais towards the grinning Padre, Ewan and his mother.

'Torquil you were magnificent,' said Jessie McPhee. 'A credit to the Constabulary.'

'Thanks Jessie,' replied Torquil with a grin. 'I just hope I've done enough there. We'll see what the judges think when they've heard the others.'

'It's in the bag, laddie,' said the Padre, stuffing tobacco into his pipe. 'Unless you've been handing out parking tickets to the judges.'

'Where's Fiona?'

The Padre shook his head. 'She said she had to go somewhere all of a sudden. Said you'd understand. Then she headed off for that thing she calls a motorbike.'

'She said she'll see you with the Silver Quaich, Torquil,' added Ewan.

The Padre had his pipe going to his satisfaction. 'And that's not a bad idea, my lad. You've got a hornpipe to play next, which isn't your strongest discipline. You have no need to be distracted by a bonnie lassie!'

Despite himself, Torquil had to agree, and he forced away the image of Fiona standing in front of him with her dressing gown hanging open.

Later, he thought, suppressing a smile.

The rotary blades of the AME helicopter slowed down and Calum Steele pushed open the door and jumped out. 'Thanks Tam,' he shouted above the noise of the engine. 'I enjoyed every minute of that, so you'll get a good write-up in the *Chronicle*.'

He looked round and saw Fiona Cullen walking briskly in the direction of the carpark.

'Now is as good a time as any, my girl,' he thought. And he rushed after her, turning into the carpark in time to see her familiar form accelerating away on her Honda Fireblade.

'Oh no!' Calum muttered to himself. 'You won't shake the *West Uist Chronicle's* editor off that easily, lassie.' He raced for his Lambretta — only to find that it wasn't there!

He cursed and ran back to the Gathering to find a member of the Hebridean Constabulary. His eye fell on the Drummond twins by the beer tent.

'I've been robbed!' he exclaimed, running across to Douglas Drummond and grabbing him by the elbow. 'My scooter has been stolen.'

Douglas Drummond eyed the newspaperman with good humour, which Calum was pretty sure was fuelled by more than a mug or two of Heather Ale. Or possibly even a spliff or two of marijuana. 'And where did you leave this machine of yours, Calum Steele?'

'In the carpark.'

'And did you leave the key in the ignition of your vehicle?' asked Wallace Drummond, equally good-humouredly, his eyes also looking slightly bloodshot.

'Of course I bloody well did. This is West Uist, no one ever steals anything here.'

The Drummond twins exchanged knowing glances. 'Ah, but there you are, Calum,' Wallace replied. 'You never can tell. You need constant vigilance.'

'Aye, constant vigilance,' Douglas repeated. 'Just about anyone could have taken it. If I were you, I'd report it to the station.'

'But there's no one at the station, you pair of teuchters!' Calum exclaimed in exasperation.

'Of course not,' returned Douglas. 'It's the Gathering today. Everyone is here.'

Calum cursed afresh and, ignoring their protestations about his language, he charged off, having spotted Morag Driscoll popping into the baker's tent with her three youngsters.

Torquil knew that he was up against it an hour later when, after having won the strathspey and the hornpipe and jig, he was sure that Hamish Munro would be out for revenge. He began his pibroch, having just heard a superb version of 'Squinting Peter's Flame of Wrath', by his arch-opponent.

But he was hopeful, as the Padre said he should be, since the judges had chosen to hear him play 'Cha till MacCruimean' — 'No more MacCrimmon', the pibroch that he had worked so hard on over the last few weeks.

He saw the Padre watching him, pipe fuming furiously as he beat out a tattoo on the back of his wrist, as if trying telepathically to send him the *canntaireachd*, the traditional teaching method. He closed his eyes and tried to picture the old boy singing the song, giving him the rhythm, the beat.

But it was emotion that was the key. And it was that emotion that Torquil had been striving so hard to put into his playing for all those practice sessions. It had been that which was missing whenever the Padre had accused him of playing like a constipated crow.

'*Hiodroho, hodroho, haninen, hieachin.*'

He played the final bars, and slowly opened his eyes to see the Padre ecstatically punching the air. He knew that the Silver Quaich was all but his. Fifteen minutes later, the competition over, he shook Hamish Munro's hand and mounted the dais again to receive the Silver Quaich, the traditional cup of welcome given to guests throughout the Highlands and Islands. But it meant much more to Torquil than that.

As he looked down he saw the Padre raise two fingers in salute, meaning that now there were two champion pipers in the family, and that there would be a Silver Quaich for each side of the mantelpiece in the manse.

Through tears in his eyes he saw the Padre wipe a drop or two from his own eyes. It was one of the proudest moments in his life.

The AME Enstrom Shark helicopter landed on the temporary helipad and the door was flung open. A moment later, before the great blades had even stopped, Captain Tam McKenzie, the pilot, was racing across the ground towards the piping square.

'Inspector McKinnon,' he gasped, mounting the steps in two bounds. 'You've got to come,' he cried, grasping Torquil's sleeve and pointing to the helicopter.

Angus MacLeod saw his pilot's agitated manner and ran over to the foot of the steps, to meet them coming down. 'What's the matter, Tam?'

Torquil quietened the laird with a stern gesture. 'Tell me, Tam,' he said quietly. 'What's the emergency?'

'There's a body in the black tower ruins on the crannog in Loch Hynish!' he whispered urgently. 'I saw it as I passed over it. It's a woman's, I think. She's not moving, Torquil!'

A few minutes later the AME Enstrom Shark helicopter zoomed over the waters of Loch Hynish, the blades causing waves to disturb the normally calm surface water.

'The wee free ferry is moored on the crannog,' Torquil said, pointing ahead.

'It was there when I flew by,' Tam replied.

'There isn't room to land on the crannog,' said Morag Driscoll. 'Will you be able to land on the water, Tam?'

'Aye, the Shark has got fixed floats so we can land on sea or loch.'

Torquil was glad that he had been able to get hold of Morag rather than the squeamish Ewan McPhee. The sergeant had always proved to be one of the most level-headed of people.

'Can you just hover above the crannog first though,' said Torquil.

In answer Tam McKenzie manoeuvred the machine closer and hovered above the ruined tower on the crannog. Torquil looked down at the body sprawled inside, and felt a wave of nausea hit him like a battering ram.

The half-naked body of Fiona Cullen was lying on her back in the overgrown interior of the ruined tower, her head turned at an unnatural angle. A ligature of some sort was visible around her throat.

'My God!' Torquil muttered in disbelief. Then he felt himself diving into a pool of dark unconsciousness.

PART TWO: DEAD WRITERS TELL NO TALES

CHAPTER SIX

Torquil came back to consciousness as soon as Tam McKenzie landed the helicopter on the loch surface, within stepping distance of the shore where the wee free ferry rowing boat was moored. His faint had been only momentary and he felt pretty sure that the pilot had not noticed it, although the touch of Morag's hand on his shoulder was enough to tell him that his sergeant had.

'Torquil, do you want me to...?'

'No, I'm fine, Morag,' he replied as he pushed open the door, coughing to try to stave off the wave of nausea that remained. 'Let's take a look.'

His instinct was to rush out and pick Fiona up in his arms, but he had to be professional. He led Morag round the tower wall to the gaping doorway that was invisible from the wee ferry jetty, then pushed his way through the bracken and long grass to where she lay.

It was worse than he had thought. Her face had a blue cyanotic tinge and her mouth was hanging open with the tongue slightly protruding. Her eyes were open and staring into nothingness. Blood caked her blonde hair and blood had pooled from an ugly gaping wound at the back of her head.

'My God!' Torquil exclaimed, as he failed to feel a carotid pulse. He looked up helplessly at Morag. 'Should we try ...?'

Morag was on her knees beside him now, listening for a heartbeat and checking her other pulses. She put a hand on his shoulder and shook her head. 'She's dead, Torquil,' she said gently. 'I'm so sorry, but it is clear that she has been murdered.

Our duty now is to get a doctor here for certification, then seal the crannog off as a Scene of Crime.'

Torquil nodded numbly. 'Someone murdered her,' he repeated. 'They murdered my Fiona!'

Morag slid her arm about her inspector's shoulder. 'Come on, the best thing we can do is to go outside for a while and wait.' She unclipped her police phone. 'I'll send Tam back in the helicopter and I'll phone ahead for the doctor.' She looked worriedly at her friend and senior officer who was clearly still in a state of shock.

Nightmares like this were not supposed to happen on West Uist.

Superintendent Kenneth Lumsden, Torquil's superior officer, was laid up with gout in his son-in-law's house in Benbecula when Torquil rang to report the murder of Fiona Cullen. Not renowned for his temper at the best of times, an attack of gout had rendered him touchy to say the least.

'So get on and investigate it, McKinnon! You are, I gather, an *inspector* now?'

'Yes sir, I gained my promotion six months ago. You were actually —'

'Yes, yes, I know, of course. So, what progress so far?'

Torquil had never liked the big man, a lowlander from Glasgow with an innate dislike for the islanders he now lived amongst. He filled him in on the finding of the body, the sealing-off of the crannog and the setting-up of an incident room in Kyleshiffin police station.

'Post-mortem?'

Torquil swallowed, acid rising in the back of his throat. He coughed. 'It's going to be done almost as soon as I get off the phone to you, sir.'

'Let me have a report straight away. Fax it through. Any suspects?'

Torquil drew in a deep breath. 'Too early to say yet sir, but I think there may be a few.'

'Any motives? Always think of motivation, McKinnon.'

'Yes, sir.'

'Anything else then?'

'I think that in the light of this event we have to reconsider the death of Ranald Buchanan, the man who seemed to have died accidentally last night.'

'That sounds likely. The Procurator Fiscal will want to hold an inquest soon, so start investigating. Any possible link?'

'None that I can think of, superintendent.'

There was a noise from the other end of the phone, as if the superintendent had experienced a sharp pain. 'Right. You'll need to seal the island off. Cancel all ferries to and from the island until further notice. The companies won't like it, but they'll just have to lump it. Well, get on McKinnon, you've got a sergeant and a constable, haven't you? Any specials?'

'Two sir, the Drummond brothers. But do you think that is enough? Shouldn't we get CID assistance?'

'Nonsense! The Hebridean Constabulary has never needed an independent detective service and we shan't start now. That's the Chief Constable's view, so we'll look after this ourselves. But I'll check it out with him, just for your peace of mind. Anything else?'

'There is just one thing, Superintendent,' Torquil said hurriedly. 'What about a press release?'

'I'll leave that to you, McKinnon. Just let the local press know. That will be that Calum Steele fellow won't it? You mark my words; he'll soon see that it reaches the nationals and the television.'

'What about access, sir? Are we going to let outside reporters and TV crews in?'

Superintendent Lumsden's tone was pained, as if he was a teacher having to spend extra time explaining the simplest principle to a dim pupil. 'If the island is sealed off then no one can get in. That will be to your advantage, since you won't have busybodies getting in your way. If you just feed Steele a bit of news then you'll have some control. Nurture him. Keep me in touch.'

The phone went dead and Torquil was left looking at the receiver. 'Thank you for your support, Superintendent Lumsden,' he said, replacing it.

Morag handed him a mug of tea. 'You didn't expect anything else, did you, Torquil?' she asked. 'Drink this,' she ordered, moving into her natural maternal role. 'I've put in extra sugar for energy. You're going to need it.'

While Morag set about phoning round to cancel all ferry movements, Torquil left for the Kyleshiffin Cottage Hospital where Fiona's body had been taken. Dr Ralph McLelland was an experienced police surgeon who had trained with the Forensic Medicine Department at Glasgow University before heading home for the supposedly less stressed life of a Hebridean GP. He had been meticulous in his examination of the body at the crime scene, digitally photographing from every angle, taking pictures of the scene itself, measuring the positions of any loose objects in the area and bagging them for further analysis. He had loaded them onto his computer for Torquil to view.

'I never thought I'd be doing two post-mortems like this in one day, Torquil,' he said, as he continued to make notes of his general external examination of the body, which Torquil was relieved to see was now covered in a green plastic sheet. 'This is a really nasty one. After I do the actual post-mortem examination I should be able to tell you conclusively what caused her death, but at the moment it looks as if whoever did it was taking no chances on leaving her alive.'

'Meaning what, Ralph?'

'She was hit with some sort of bludgeon and she's been strangled. The question is, which came first? Was she knocked out, and then strangled? Or was she garrotted and then bashed on the head to make sure?'

Torquil felt a wave of nausea, mixed with anger. He took a deep breath and willed himself to be calm. 'Was she —?'

'Raped? Not sure yet. Whoever did it had a good go at ripping her leathers off to have a go. I've taken swabs and scrapings from her nails and I'll be looking at them under a microscope after I've done the actual PM. I need to see if she managed to take any chunks out of her killer's skin. I can't tell yet,' he said, holding one of her hands and leaning forward to look at the nails. 'They're broken and there's a lot of dirt under them. She might have struggled.'

Torquil felt his head spin and another wave of nausea threatened to make him topple forward. He reached out for the bench to support himself. The doctor saw his discomfiture and offered a spare stool. 'Are you going to stay for the PM?' he asked.

Torquil nodded. 'Aye Ralph. I'm the investigating officer, so it's my duty.'

'As you wish,' returned Ralph, laying aside his pen and turning to gown up. Once done he wheeled a waiting trolley over, upon which were rows of surgical instruments and saws. 'If you feel queasy at any time, just pop through to the side room.'

He picked up a scalpel and pulled back the sheet to reveal Fiona's naked body.

Torquil squeezed his eyes shut, wishing that he was not there, that he would not have to witness further violation of her body.

To his relief his mobile phone rang. He excused himself and went through to the side room.

'Torquil, I think you'd better come over to the Bonnie Prince Charlie,' came PC Ewan McPhee's excited voice. 'There's something odd going on. Mollie McFadden called me in when she heard about Fiona. The news has gone round the island faster than a summer squall.'

'What did she say, Ewan?' Torquil asked, trying hard to suppress the impatience in his voice.

'She said that she saw Fiona come in and go up to her room, but she never came down again. She's sure it was just before you went off in the helicopter.'

For a fleeting moment Torquil felt a glimmer of hope. As if there could have been some colossal mistake and that Fiona had just been sleeping in her room at the Bonnie Prince Charlie. Then the devastating image of her body lying on Ralph McLelland's mortuary slab made the hope vanish like smoke.

'Has she checked the room?'

'No, and I thought I'd better wait for you.'

'I'll be there in five minutes.'

Steeling himself he pushed open the door to the mortuary room and called through, without daring to put his head round. 'Ralph, I have to go. There may have been a development.'

'That's fine, Torquil. I'll have some news for you later maybe.'

The noise of an electric circular buzz-saw made Torquil beat a hasty retreat.

The Games had finished at about six o'clock and the crowds had all gradually dispersed, in search of food, relaxation, entertainment or drink. But just as Ewan had said, the news had spread about a body having been found on the crannog on Loch Hynish. That it was Fiona Cullen, the famous crime novelist, was also the news on the street and in the cafes, restaurants and bars. Already there was a sense of anxiety and murmurings about what action was being taken to find the killer.

Torquil, now in his police uniform, was inevitably accosted several times as he walked the short distance downhill from the cottage hospital to the Bonnie Prince Charlie Tavern on Harbour Street. To all and sundry who asked him he replied that a body had indeed been found and that the police were making enquiries. He anticipated that the trickle of questions would turn into an avalanche as soon as people realized that the island was being sealed off and that those people who had planned to return to Lochboisdale in South Uist on the late-evening ferry would have to find overnight accommodation.

Or longer, Torquil thought to himself. He had visions of this taking longer than a day to sort out, even though it was just a small island.

He turned into the welcoming tavern and found Ewan standing at the bar, drinking tea with Mollie McFadden. The bar was busy, her staff dispensing Heather Ale and taking orders for food.

'Torquil, it is sorry I am to hear about Fiona. But I canna understand it. I saw her go upstairs to her room and she hasn't been down.'

'Let's get out of the bar, Mollie,' Torquil said. Then, once in the hall, 'When did you see her?'

Mollie blinked and pushed her spectacles farther back on her nose. 'About half past four, I think. There was no one here, of course, since the Games was still in full swing. I was just bottling up in the cellar and I heard that big bike of hers draw up into the back carpark. I heard the door open and I went up to ask how the Games had gone. I saw her dashing up the stairs and I called out to ask, but she didn't seem to hear me. I heard her door close and thought no more about it.'

'You're sure it was Fiona?'

Mollie McFadden's eyes grew huge behind her thick spectacle lenses. 'She was wearing her black leathers and her helmet!' She grabbed his arm. 'Mother of God! Torquil, could that have been —?'

'Ewan and I will see, Mollie. Have you a master key?'

Mollie scuttled into her small reception area and came back with a heavy key. 'Take care, the pair of you.'

Somewhat apprehensively Torquil led the way up to the Flora McDonald Room, where he had last seen Fiona alive that very morning. As he expected, the door was locked from within, and peering into the keyhole he saw that the key was still in the door.

'This key is useless,' he told his constable. 'We don't have enough time to wait, Ewan. Will you do the needful?'

The big hammer-throwing champion nodded and with two shoulder charges the door burst open, to reveal a scene of devastation. The room was not just untidy; it had been destroyed, as if someone had trashed it in a frenzy of fury and passion. Fiona's helmet lay in a corner of the room as if it had been discarded and had rolled there. The bedclothes were scattered over the floor, her soft motorcycle panniers had been emptied and the contents thrown hither and thither. Torquil felt his anger rise as he spotted a pile of underclothes which had been slashed with some sort of sharp blade, just as had several loose blouses and the dressing gown that he had seen her wearing that morning. Several personal effects lay scattered about the floor.

'We've got a sicko bastard on our hands, Torquil!' Ewan growled, working his hands open and closed. 'If I could get my hands on him —'

But Torquil silenced him with a raised hand. 'We have to be professional, Ewan.' He pointed to the open window. 'The room looks out over the back carpark. So that's how the killer, assuming it was the killer that Mollie saw, made off.' He crossed to the window and looked out. 'Her bike is there all right.'

'He must be a cool bastard, riding her bike back here,' Ewan gasped.

Torquil shook his head. 'We can't assume it was a man, Ewan.' He bit his lip, then mused. 'But why did whoever it was risk coming here? What did they want?'

Ewan pointed to the shredded frilly underwear. 'I told you, Torquil. A sicko!'

'Don't touch anything Ewan. We just need to get the room photographed and dusted for prints. Morag can sort that out. She's done her CID training and can bring her kit.'

He looked around the room; his eyes searching amid the mess for something that he knew should be there. He tapped his teeth with his fingernail as he contemplated. Then he snapped his fingers as realization dawned.

'Her notes and her laptop! They're not here. That's what the murderer came for, Ewan.'

'Sick bastard!' Ewan cursed, shaking his head in disgust.

Angus MacLeod was not himself. He was either angry, anxious or a combination of the two. The Padre could not quite work out which, as he sat with the laird, Miss Melville and the rest of the Gathering Committee in the Duncan Institute that evening. All of them were feeling shocked, of course, but needs must and they had to decide what to do now, since the news had percolated around that all ferries had been cancelled, pending police investigations. The Padre had tried to contact Torquil to find out what was happening, and to try to console the lad, but as he expected Torquil was run off his feet and unable to talk.

Poor Fiona! Dead! Murdered! How could it happen to her? He had talked to her just a few hours ago, watched her head off on her motorbike, seemingly full of spirit and *joie de vivre*. And he was sure that a lot of that *joie de vivre* had been due to Torquil. It's a cruel world, he thought.

'I know that we're all more upset about Fiona Cullen than we could ever adequately express,' said Miss Melville, interrupting his reverie, 'but we do have to sort these problems out this evening. Sergeant Morag Driscoll has given me a list of all the pubs, bed and breakfasts, hotels and hostels that might be able to put people up for the night, but I think it might come to providing sleeping bags and blankets and finding whoever has got room for strangers to bed down in their living rooms.'

'You can put me down for twenty or so, Miss Melville,' Angus MacLeod volunteered. 'Dunshiffin Castle is at your disposal.'

'And we can use the Duncan Institute,' piped up Rabbie Roberts, the caretaker. 'But I canna say that I can do anything about breakfasts,' he added, hastily.

'St Ninian's Hall is free, of course,' said Lachlan McKinnon. 'And all of the marquees are still up. It might be a wee bit windy if there is a squall, but on the whole I think we should be able to manage.'

Angus MacLeod stood up, examining his wristwatch for the umpteenth time. 'Right then, if I can leave these things in your capable hands, I must be off. I have to look after Roland Baxter, our esteemed Minister for Culture.' He shook his head. 'This couldn't have happened at a worse time,' he mused, making for the door. 'Just send however many people you want and I'll get the staff to make them comfortable.'

Lachlan also stood. 'And I'm afraid that I'm going to have to go as well, ladies and gentlemen.' He nodded and smiled at the other council members, in that reassuring way that the clergy manage during times of tragedy and suffering. 'I need to go and see Fiona Cullen's — body. It's time that I give her the Lord's blessing.'

'*A Thighearna bheannaichte!*' said Bella Melville, her eyes immediately welling up with tears as she verbalized the thoughts of everyone in the room. 'Let the lassie rest in peace.'

The recreation room at the back of the Kyleshiffin police station had been converted into an incident room. The net of the table tennis table had been taken down and stowed away to provide room for all the documentation that was bound to accrue. Four large pinboards had been put up on the wall for all sorts of snips and snaps of information that may or may not be relevant. The whiteboard that was usually used to record table tennis scores and supply lists had been cleaned down in readiness and extra supplies of milk had been obtained for the innumerable brewings of tea that were anticipated.

Torquil, Morag and Douglas Drummond were sitting waiting for Ewan to come through from the front office so that the meeting could begin. But the heated voice of Calum Steele made Torquil shudder.

'Ewan will deal with the wee nyaff, Torquil,' Morag said, sensing her boss's irritation.

'No, I'd better have a word with him,' replied Torquil. 'Best to get the press conference over and done with.'

'Ah, Torquil. At last! The organ grinder, not the monkey.'

Ewan smouldered. 'You just be having a care with your words, Calum Steele or I'll —'

'Ewan, why don't you go and brew up some tea while I talk to the editor of the *Chronicle*.'

'The editor has a complaint, Torquil,' Ewan returned, as he left the office. 'About his stolen Lambretta.'

Torquil leaned on the counter and rubbed his eyes. 'Calum, this is a bloody awful business. I'm going to nail the bastard that did this.'

'You will be having the full backing of the *Chronicle*. But I ought to warn you that the big boys, the nationals and the TV, will be hard to handle. They have ways of inveigling information; they winkle it out of you.' He nodded meaningfully at the now closed office door. 'Some of your people may not be as adept as they need to be at keeping their mouths closed.'

'The only media involved will be the *Chronicle*,' Torquil replied. 'My superintendent has imposed a press embargo.'

The ghost of a smile flickered across Calum's lips. 'But you can't totally blank this from the news, man. Fiona Cullen is famous; it will need to be on the television news.'

'You can be the link, Calum. But the island is being sealed off, no ferries, boats or helicopters. Anyone landing will be arrested and held for questioning.'

Calum whistled. 'You're going to have to sort this out quickly.' He winked as he drew out his ubiquitous notepad. He licked the end of a stubby pencil, then continued, 'Can you officially confirm that Fiona Cullen is dead?'

'She is. She has been formally identified by me and by her agent, Genevieve Cooper. We are treating this as suspicious.'

'Suspicious, I'll say,' agreed the little reporter. 'Half-naked on a crannog in the middle of Loch Hynish. How did she get there?'

'We're making enquiries.'

'Any leads as to who did it?'

'We're following up several leads, but it is too early to report.'

'What about manpower? Have you enough folk on the job?'

'The West Uist Division of the Hebridean Constabulary is ... *stretched.*'

Calum shook his head. 'Oh, come on Torquil, give me something! I could have replied to each of those questions myself.'

They were interrupted by Torquil's mobile phone. Wallace Drummond's name flashed on the little view-panel. He excused himself and answered it, nodding as his special constable talked to him. 'OK, Wallace, get it covered and don't disturb it. We'll have to have it dusted for prints. Come back now, then you and Morag can check it after our meeting.'

Once he had finished, Calum asked eagerly, 'Have you got something there? A lead?'

'Perhaps, Calum,' Torquil replied. 'We don't know how Fiona Cullen got to the crannog, but we do have an idea as to how her murderer got out to Loch Hynish.'

'Well?'

'I had a suspicion that we would find something near the lochside. Wallace Drummond has just pulled a Lambretta out of the bracken.'

'Well, I'll be buggered!' exclaimed Calum. Then, horrified, 'The cheeky bastard!'

Ralph McLelland arrived in time for the start of the meeting. He sat in the corner, his hands clasped over his slight beer-belly while Torquil stood by the whiteboard with a marker pen in his hand.

'OK, so we are here to hold the first formal meeting of the investigation into the death of Fiona Cullen.' Torquil talked slowly, enunciating every word, as if he still could not accept the fact that she was dead. 'This afternoon Dr Ralph McLelland conducted a post-mortem examination and he is now going to give us his findings.'

Ralph McLelland stood and took over from Torquil. He opened the file on the desk in front of him and began reading out his general findings at the murder site and then his observations of her body at the mortuary. As he did so, Torquil pinned the photographs of the murder scene to the first pinboard.

Morag and Ewan busily took down notes.

'It is not possible at this time to be certain about the cause of death. There was a major blow to the back of the head with a blunt instrument. That could have been fatal. But there was also a ligature around her neck with which she was strangled. Whether she was already dead or not, I cannot determine as yet.'

'Will further forensic testing tell you, Ralph?' Torquil asked.

'I'm not sure. The gross morbid anatomical examination can't tell me. Certainly there were punctate haemorrhages over the face, and in sections of the brain. That would occur with both a blow to the back of the head and strangulation, if either was a single event.' He bit his lip and frowned. 'There were no such haemorrhages in the lungs or upper airways, which is unusual in a case of strangulation.'

'Meaning what?' Torquil queried.

'That on balance, although I cannot be certain, my opinion is that she was already dead before the strangulation.'

Despite himself, Torquil heaved a sigh of relief. He had hated the thought of her being strangled. 'But what about the broken fingernails and the dirt under them?'

'It could have been reflex action after death,' the doctor replied without conviction. 'But again, my opinion is that her hands were raked along the ground after death. I didn't find anything except dirt on microscopy.'

'So it could have been done to make it look as if she'd struggled,' Torquil said with a shudder. 'What about the state of her clothes? She was half-naked. Her leathers had been pulled off her top and halfway down her thighs. Had she —?'

Ralph McLelland anticipated Torquil. 'No, I can say categorically that she wasn't raped. There were no signs of penetration, no bruising, no evidence of semen anywhere. The murderer might have been interrupted or panicked and left.'

'Or it could have been done to make it look as though it was a sexual crime.'

'That's possible,' the police surgeon replied, picking up his mug of tea and draining it. He looked at his watch. 'Well, I think that's about all I have to tell you for now, Torquil. Do you mind if I get off? I have a couple of house calls to make.'

While Ewan showed him out, Torquil went to the whiteboard and wrote in the top-left corner three words: MURDER, INVESTIGATION, ARREST.

'OK, everyone,' he said, a few moments later as Wallace Drummond came in. 'We have a murder case on our hands.' In the centre of the board he wrote FIONA CULLEN, and underneath added arrows to subheadings of: writer, local girl, motorbike, the Gathering, Bonnie Prince Charlie. He tapped the board and spread out his hand to the other pinboards. 'This is the control centre and we're going to get this bastard, whoever it is. We're going to spend an hour putting all that we know up on this board and on these pinboards. We're going to build up a web of all the possible motives, all the possible suspects, anyone who had any dealings with Fiona while she was on the island, and any dealings before she came here for the Gathering.'

'Is it a sort of brainstorming that you are after having?' asked Douglas Drummond.

'Exactly,' Torquil replied. 'Absolutely anything goes up there, then we'll work backwards and establish links.'

'So we'll catch this bastard in the web!' exclaimed Wallace Drummond. 'Better put up Calum Steele and his Lambretta scooter then, boss.'

'Genevieve Cooper, her agent,' volunteered Morag. 'Allegra McCall, her publisher.'

Torquil put each name in a circle on its own, with little explanatory notes attached to each, and arrows linking them to Fiona's name at the centre of the board. He added the names of Professor Neil Ferguson, Roland Baxter, Angus MacLeod, Izzie Frazer, Miss Bella Melville, the Padre — Lachlan McKinnon.

'And I declare my own name.' he said, adding his name and circling it, annotating it with 'friend'.

'Torquil you were at the Gathering when this happened,' Morag protested. 'I saw you myself.'

106

'I was,' he admitted. 'But we shall conduct this investigation with rigour and diligence. You shall interview me in due course, Morag.'

And so they worked for a good hour, dragging possible times, connections and hunches together and adding them to the board.

'Now, let's just take a sideways step.' The others looked curiously at him as he went to the other side of the whiteboard and wrote the name RANALD BUCHANAN in large letters, just as he had done Fiona's. 'Fiona's murder forces us to reconsider the death of Ranald Buchanan.'

Ewan spluttered. 'It was horrible, Torquil. Shall I go and make some tea, I feel kind of sick just thinking about it?'

Torquil nodded, and as the big constable retreated to the kitchen, he drew a dotted line between Ranald's name and Fiona's. 'Is there a link of any sort between them? I don't know.'

'They were both writers,' suggested Morag.

Torquil nodded and jotted notes. 'And Fiona's laptop and all her notebooks were missing.'

'Perhaps Calum Steele may have an idea,' Morag suggested. 'She used to work on the *Chronicle*, didn't she?'

'We will be speaking to Calum about his scooter and other things,' Torquil agreed.

Ewan came in a few moments later with a tray full of fresh mugs of tea. 'I heard what you were saying, Torquil, and it worries me. About Ranald and Fiona both being writers.'

'Go on, Ewan.'

'Well, all these people on the island are here for the Gathering *and* the Literary Festival. It might be a stupid suggestion, I know, but if there is a link and they were both killed, murdered I mean. Well, couldn't —?'

'I see what he means!' Wallace Drummond exclaimed.

'A serial killer on the loose! On West Uist,' added Douglas Drummond.

Morag shook her head. 'Oh, come on now, that's a quantum leap isn't it?'

Torquil shook his head. 'Maybe not, Morag,' he said, tapping the pen against the whiteboard. 'Do you remember the title of Fiona's next book?'

The sergeant's eyes rolled up in alarm.

'That's right,' said Torquil, as he began to write the title in capital letters: DEAD WRITERS TELL NO TALES.

'We need to find that manuscript,' he said. 'Or, at least, we need to know what it was going to be about.'

CHAPTER SEVEN

The alarm went off at 7 a.m. and woke Torquil from a wretched nightmare. He shot up in bed, bathed in cold perspiration.

In his dream he had seen Fiona row out to the crannog on Loch Hynish, a peal of laughter following her as she left him on the shore. Unable to get across to the island he kept calling out her name, only to be greeted by more laughter. And then he heard a noise, a scream he thought, followed by someone else's laughter. But still he could not get out to her and he called more frantically. Then he heard the whirring blades of a helicopter, getting louder and louder until their noise reached a crescendo, and he found himself sitting up in bed, his hand stretching out to switch off the alarm.

The stark realization that Fiona was dead was like a knife through his heart.

Yet the content of the dream would not leave him as he rose, shaved and showered. There was something in the dream — something important that he could not quite put his finger on.

He descended the stairs to the smell of porridge, but found the big kitchen was empty. A simple note on the large kitchen table read:

Torquil,

There is porridge in the bottom of the Aga. I'm on the golf course if you need me.

Lachlan

Torquil read the note in disbelief, then screwed it up in his hand and contemptuously threw it in the pedal-bin.

'Oh man!' he exclaimed as he served himself porridge and sprinkled salt over it. 'How the hell can anyone play golf at a time like this!' He poured milk and forced himself to eat, despite having no desire whatsoever for food. When he had managed half of the portion he shoved the bowl aside and rose to make tea. But that too had no taste and picking up his mobile phone and wrapping his tartan scarf about his neck he left the house, strode down the path and out the iron gate, over the road and onto St Ninian's Golf Course.

The Padre was nowhere to be seen.

But then Torquil heard him. Or rather, he heard the repeated click of an iron club hitting balls and he realized where his uncle was. Jogging across the dunes he crested a rise and saw him standing on the ninth tee, hitting ball after ball over the small hill towards the out-of-sight green.

'Ah, Torquil laddie,' Lachlan called, seeing his nephew strutting towards him. 'I needed to come out and hit a few balls at *Creideamh*.'

'I wondered what you were doing out this early — playing golf, today of all days!' Torquil replied stiffly. 'Fiona is dead you know!'

The Padre nodded his head. 'I know that Torquil. And I cannot believe it any more than you. Do you know why I called this hole *Creideamh* when I designed it?'

'Of course. It means Faith. It's beside the kirk and the cemetery and it takes an act of faith to knock it between them.'

The Padre hung his head and swished the club along the grass. 'It was partly that, Torquil. But it was to remind me that life goes on.'

'Not for Fiona,' Torquil snapped. 'She was murdered yesterday. And I'm going to find her murderer.'

'And do what, Torquil? Have your revenge?'

'I'm going to bring whoever did it to justice. I'm going to get justice for Fiona.'

'I hope you do, laddie, I hope you do. Just make sure it is justice and not revenge.' He pulled his pipe out from his top pocket and began filling it from his dilapidated pouch. 'But you know as well as I do that your parents are both buried in that graveyard. You never want to talk about it, but the fact is that they are there. I designed this golf course so that I could test my faith to keep going whenever I came this way.'

'Like you are testing it now? By hitting golf balls?'

The Padre tamped the tobacco down in the bowl of his pipe. 'That's right. Your parents died tragically, Torquil. Drowned in the Minch, and I became your guardian.'

'And I'm grateful, Uncle.'

The Padre shook his head. 'I don't want your gratitude. You are my brother's son and I was happy to look after you. Just as I have been proud of all the things you have achieved, like the Silver Quaich that you won yesterday.'

Torquil waved his hand dismissively.

'No, Torquil, I am proud. But this hole, Faith, has meant a lot to me. It hasn't always been easy bringing a lad up all on my own. And I don't think that I made a half bad job of it. But I've always been able to test my faith here on this little golf course.'

'I don't like to think about my parents being here,' Torquil admitted, hanging his head.

'I know that. And I know that you think I'm showing disrespect by hitting golf balls the day after Fiona — passed over. But I'm testing my faith again. I'm hurting inside. I'm sad and I'm as angry as hell. And these golf balls are feeling every little bit of my anger.' He gave his nephew a wan smile. 'And when I'm angry I mishit the ball, just as Fiona did the other day. Like when she hit Professor Ferguson.'

'What are you getting at Padre?'

'Let your emotion out, laddie! Your task is to find whoever did this dreadful thing, but you can't do it when you're full of anger and hate. Hit some balls, or go to St Ninian's Cave and play a few tunes, just do something to let it out. Then you'll be able to get things in perspective, be able to ask the right questions.'

'You mean about things like Fiona's reaction when she hit Professor Ferguson?'

The Padre struck a light and applied it to his pipe. 'Aye, Torquil. Questions just like that.'

Torquil rode the Bullet fast along the snaking Loch Hynish road towards Kyleshiffin. And as he did so, putting the machine through its paces, he realized that the old boy was right, as he so often had been. Riding aggressively, losing some of his frustration was therapeutic.

There were so many issues going through his mind; so many things that had given him cause for anger, yet he had pretty well suppressed them. He was good at that. His parents had died in a freak accident in the Minch when he was a youngster of five. He barely remembered them, having bonded with the Padre and been brought up by him. And in that he realized that so many of the Padre's interests were now his, like motorbikes and the bagpipes.

But not the faith! Early on, Torquil had expressed disquiet about religion and the Church. He had assumed it was because he didn't like to think that his parents were lying dead in the cemetery. Yet now he knew that it was more than that. It was to do with a feeling of anger that he had about God.

He opened up the throttle and accelerated out of a corner. And it was anger at his parents for getting themselves killed.

A shiver ran up his spine and the involuntary movement made the bike wobble dangerously. Fiona! Was he angry with her for getting killed? He applied the brakes and skidded to a halt. 'You bloody idiot, Torquil McKinnon!' he screamed at the top of his voice. And as if suddenly startled by his cry, a flock of gulls rose from the sandy machair and squawked noisily across the loch. *I loved her! I always loved her and I should have been there to protect her!*

Anger coursed through him like hot lead. And again the Padre's words struck a chord. *'Just make sure it is justice and not revenge.'* He wasn't sure which he really wanted. First of all he just needed to find the bastard. And in that respect the Padre was right. He needed to be dispassionate and clinical. A thinking machine.

He started up the Bullet again and headed for Kyleshiffin.

First, find the bastard! he thought. *Then I'll see what I want.*

Morag was hard at work by the time Torquil arrived at the station. Despite having had less than four hours' sleep, for she had gone with Wallace Drummond to photograph and fingerprint Calum Steele's Lambretta immediately after the meeting the night before, she looked as fresh as a daisy. No mean task since prior to setting off she had to organize her three children. Torquil admired his sergeant's ability to multitask, which she was forever telling him and Ewan, was a quality of the female sex.

'Tea, boss?' she asked, handing him a copy of the morning's special festival edition of the *Chronicle*. 'Calum wasted no time there. Look at the headline.'

The words stood out boldly:

THE GATHERING MURDER!
FAMOUS WRITER'S BODY FOUND

Torquil winced as he read the report of the finding of a body on the crannog on Loch Hynish as the Gathering drew to a close. In his most sensational journalese Calum Steele recounted how the famous crime writer Fiona Cullen had mingled with the crowd at the Gathering, then disappeared for a while, only to be found after her body had been sighted by the AME helicopter, which had been giving visitors aerial trips around the island all afternoon.

Somewhat indignantly he had added the theft of his Lambretta, hinting strongly that 'the police suspect the killer may have used the editor-in-chief's vehicle to get to Loch Hynish'.

Torquil looked up from the paper and asked, 'Did you find anything on the scooter?'

Morag put a mug of strong tea by Torquil's elbow. 'Nothing at all. The handlebars had been wiped clean. It's probably never been so clean, actually. You know how scruffy Calum is.' She wrinkled her nose at the thought of the local journalist. 'And I think he must have been on the phone to the mainland newspapers and TV channels straight away. Did you see the news on Scottish TV this morning?'

'No. I had other things on my mind than television,' he replied, feeling a tad guilty over his contretemps with the Padre.

'The TV is always on at my breakfast table,' Morag said. 'It keeps the kids occupied while I do their eggs or kippers. Anyway, they basically gave a resumé of Calum's article.'

'Well, let's hope we can get a swift result before the media circus is forced upon us. Where's Ewan?'

Morag had picked up a pile of reports and had begun arranging them into alphabetical order. 'I sent him out in the *Seaspray* to do a reconnoitre to make sure we don't get any investigative reporters from the big papers trying to break the embargo.'

'It won't be easy to stop them, Morag. You had better get Fergus McAllister, the harbour master, to keep a watch as well and let us know if any boats try to land.'

'I've done that, boss.'

Torquil grinned. 'You're a wonder, Morag. What would I do without you?'

She saw his face suddenly pale and she patted his shoulder. 'You're going to be all right, Torquil,' she said soothingly, in her big-sister manner. 'We'll nail this bastard.'

'Bloody right,' he replied, picking up his mug and swallowing tea. Then, slapping the desk with the flat of his hand, he added, 'OK then, time to get started on the interviews. We'll have to split them between us.'

'Who do you want to see first?'

Torquil's lips tightened. 'Professor Neil Ferguson. I want to know why he was ferreting around the St Ninian's cemetery the other day.'

Professor Neil Ferguson had breakfasted on orange juice and half a slice of toast, his usual morning fare, at about six o'clock before heading out to sea in his 28-foot cabin cruiser. He anchored about a quarter of a mile from the west coast, donned his wetsuit and dived into the sea.

Ewan spotted the boat as he came round the Machair Skerry on the north of the island and headed towards it. He sounded the claxon, then cut the engine and coasted alongside just as the professor was hauling himself back on board.

'Good morning!' he called out. 'It is glad I am to be finding you, Professor. There are two good reasons,' he explained. 'First, it is not permitted for anyone to leave the island at the moment.'

'Ah, I'm sorry,' Neil Ferguson replied, sitting down and removing his face mask and snorkel. 'I wasn't thinking. And what is the second reason, Constable?'

'My inspector wants to interview you. He just called from your hotel.'

The professor nodded, showing no surprise. 'Of course. I rather thought he would want a chat.'

Ewan eyed him suspiciously. *Why isn't he surprised? I had better tell Torquil about that*, he thought.

Dr Viroj Wattana had been unable to sleep. There were so many questions buzzing through his mind, so many anxieties.

The bitch was dead!

Yet the implications were immense. The whole afternoon at the Gathering had been a blur, partly due to that idiot priest and the alcohol he forced down him. But he had been sure that he had seen —! Yet it couldn't have been, surely not?

Unable to toss and turn any longer he rose, dressed and silently made his way through the corridors of Dunshiffin Castle, passing several rooms from whence a cacophony of snoring was being emitted by the multitude of largely unwanted guests that had been billeted at the castle the night before.

Fresh air. He needed to get outside so that he could think what to do next.

A muscle flinched in Torquil's jaw as Ewan reported to him about how he had found the professor of Marine Archaeology snorkelling off the side of his cabin cruiser.

'Is he in the interview room?'

'Aye. With a cup of coffee.'

'And you followed him back to the Kyleshiffin harbour?'

'I did. I waited for him to set off. I thought that would be best.'

'And you left a marker buoy over the spot where he was swimming?'

The big constable's face went puce and he fidgeted from foot to foot. 'I — er — no, Torquil. I didn't think about that.'

Morag was watching from her desk, all too aware that Torquil's temper was beginning to rise. She half expected an eruption any moment; as did Ewan. But it didn't come. Torquil merely nodded. 'That's a pity, Constable McPhee,' he said coldly. 'It may be of no importance whatever — or it could be vital information that we have now lost.'

'I'm sorry — er — Inspector,' Ewan blustered. 'But why would it be important?'

Torquil turned to Morag. 'Explain, will you, Sergeant,' he said, heading for the interview room. 'I'm going to have a chat with the professor.'

When he had gone, Ewan turned desperately to his superior. 'Morag, what have I done? I've never known Torquil pull rank like that before.'

'Oh sweet Lord!' Morag exclaimed with a gentle shake of the head. 'Just think, Ewan. A murder has been committed with some sort of bludgeon. Where do you think would be a good place to lose it if you were a murderer?'

Ewan gasped as realization dawned. Then he quickly shook his head. 'But you can't be serious. No one could think that Professor Ferguson could have done it.'

Morag clicked her tongue. 'Ewan, my love, right now everyone on West Uist is a suspect!'

Professor Neil Ferguson was used to public speaking. He had taught in lecture halls full of two hundred students, given papers at world scientific conferences of several hundred, and presented a popular television series, *The Treasures of the Deep*. Despite this, he was more nervous about his interview with a Hebridean police inspector than he had ever been before.

'Had you known Fiona Cullen for long?' Torquil asked, after briefly informing the professor of the purpose of his interview, namely that it was part of his investigation into the murder of the famous crime writer.

'A few years. I first met her when she was a reporter with your local newspaper here.'

'That would be five years then,' Torquil volunteered. 'Before she left to become a full-time writer. Have you read any of her books?'

The professor shook his head. 'No, crime fiction isn't my thing.'

'Were you on friendly terms with her, Professor?'

The academic raised his eyebrows slightly at the use of his title. A frequent visitor to West Uist for the better part of twenty or so years, he had always been on first-name terms with Torquil McKinnon.

'We used to be.'

'What changed that?'

Neil Ferguson looked down at the table in front of him and wiped an imaginary speck of dust away. 'I'm afraid that she blamed me for the death of a friend of hers.'

Torquil was making notes as they spoke, rather than using the more formal tape recorder. He gestured for the professor to explain.

'As you know I have a certain reputation as an expert on crannogs, the artificial islands to be found on the lochs and lakes of the northern parts of the British Isles. The majority date from the Iron Age. Originally they seem to have been constructed as defensive islets, but later on they became a sign of power, of wealth. Sort of archaic follies.'

Torquil could see that the professor was warming to his subject and beginning to relax.

'I have studied the crannogs of the Hebrides extensively over the last twenty years or so. I did my doctoral dissertation on the crannogs of the Uists.' He sucked air in between his teeth. 'What I'm trying to say, Inspector, is that I have a detailed knowledge of the way the crannogs were constructed. I can outline the different styles, just as an expert drystone waller can look at a dyke and tell you all sorts of things about the way it was built, and why a particular technique was used.'

'Your point being?'

Neil Ferguson sighed. 'Egyptology is the sexy side of archaeology, Inspector. Everyone and his dog knows about the pyramids of Egypt. They were built with massive manpower over decades with ropes and pulleys. We all know that.'

Torquil was beginning to feel his irritation rise, just as the professor's nerves seemed to be calming. 'Has this a bearing on my investigation, Professor Ferguson?'

'Absolutely! Despite the fact that we know scientifically how the pyramids were built, there are still people — New Age folk

— who are convinced that the pyramids were built by some extra-terrestrial beings or by survivors from the lost civilization of Atlantis. They are called "Pyramidiots" by bona fide Egyptologists. Well,' he took a breath, his face a picture of exasperation, 'we have the same problem in Marine Archaeology. There is a thriving market in Atlantean and extra-terrestrial theories about crannogs. We have oddballs insisting that the crannogs were built as landing platforms for UFOs, or as islands on which to build mini-Atlantean-style temples to encircle the globe.'

'And you think that is nonsense?'

Neil Ferguson shoved his fingers through his thick brown hair. Although now in his forties he still had the look of a man ten years younger. 'Of course it's rubbish. And that is what I said — perhaps a trifle forcefully — on a TV chat show one afternoon. You may have seen the sort of show. A husband-and-wife team sitting on a sofa, sipping tea and giving all kinds of eccentrics an easy ride. Anyway, this woman, Esme Portland, was expounding about her book, *Mini Temples of Atlantis* I think it was called. I was there as a supposed tame archaeologist. Only I didn't feel tame about the rubbish she was spouting. It demeans my profession.'

'And the result of the interview was what?'

'I showed her up as a simpleton on TV.'

'And?'

The professor bit his lip. 'I'm not sure there was an "and",' he replied. 'I mean, I don't know whether one can make a connection between the television programme and the — er —'

'The what?' Torquil asked blandly, making it seem as if he was unaware of any of this.

'Esme Portland cut her wrists the evening of the show. Fiona Cullen was a friend of hers. She phoned me up and told me that I was responsible for her friend's death.'

'Did you have any other contact with her?'

'She harassed me for a few months. Phone calls, letters, that sort of thing. I ignored them actually.'

'And when was all this?'

'About eighteen months ago.'

'And there was no further contact between you.'

Neil Ferguson shook his head. 'Not until I came to West Uist, when I saw her with you and the Padre.'

'Ah yes,' Torquil admitted. 'On the golf course — or rather, in the St Ninian's cemetery.'

Almost unconsciously the professor touched his forehead where a slight bruise was visible. 'What was she doing there?' he asked.

This was potentially tricky ground, Torquil knew. It would be so easy to lose the initiative if he allowed himself to have the interview turned on him by a clever interviewee. And there was no doubt that the professor was a clever man.

'She wanted to have a chat with the Padre as one of the Literary Festival judges,' Torquil replied, then added, 'but more to the point, what exactly were *you* doing in the cemetery, Professor?'

The archaeologist seemed to ponder this for a moment before replying. 'Research. I was following up on a story I came across recently about the 1745 uprising and the hunt for Bonnie Prince Charlie after Culloden.'

'Indeed? Tell me more.'

The professor shrugged. 'I'm not sure about the veracity of the tale. I was told that in 1746, when Bonnie Prince Charlie was on the run throughout the Hebrides, there were eight days that have never been properly accounted for. As you probably know, it is believed that he spent five of those eight days on West Uist and three days sailing between here and the other Western Isles trying to liaise with the French vessel sent to pick him up.'

'You mean the *Hirondelle*?'

'No, that was the vessel that finally did pick him up from Skye. No one knows much about this other French vessel, except that it is thought to have sunk somewhere off West Uist in deep water after holing its hull on rocks.'

'Aye, we all know the tale,' Torquil said. 'But it's always been linked up with the Selkie legend. The seal-folk took the souls of the sailors.'

Neil Ferguson nodded. 'Yes, I was told that the whole crew drowned, except for the ship's pet marmoset monkey. It floated onto the beach on driftwood and was promptly hanged as a French spy by English Dragoons stationed on the island.' He took a deep breath. 'I was looking for the grave of the monkey in the cemetery.'

Torquil forced a laugh. 'That's a new one on me, professor. But I'll check it with the Padre. He'll know.' He made a few more notes then laid his pen down on the table. 'I seem to recall that you said you'd be going diving with friends over the next few days.'

'With Angus MacLeod and Dr Viroj Wattana around the crannog, and maybe a bit of deep-water diving.'

'You realise that will not be possible now?'

'Of course, Inspector. You don't want us muddying the waters around the murder site.'

Torquil nodded. 'I'm glad you understand, Professor Ferguson. Now, let me ask you candidly, did you like Fiona Cullen?'

The marine archaeologist looked as if he wished he was somewhere else. Perhaps underwater wearing a mask to protect himself from involuntary facial expressions. 'Are you suggesting that I need a lawyer with me now, Inspector? Are you suggesting that I know something about this unfortunate death?'

Torquil was unflustered by the professor's sudden irritability. He shrugged. 'I will be asking all interviewees similar questions, Neil. It is just routine.'

The professor seemed to relax at the use of his Christian name. 'In that case I can say that I honestly had no strong feelings about her at all. I think she felt an antipathy towards me because she thought I was in some way responsible for her friend suddenly snapping and committing suicide.'

Torquil jotted down a few more notes. 'And what exactly were you doing this morning when PC McPhee found you swimming from your boat?'

'I often go for an early morning swim when I'm here. The water is so clear at this time of the year. Apart from that I wanted to check out a new wetsuit and some equipment before I met up with my friends.'

'You weren't disposing of anything?' Torquil asked bluntly.

Neil Ferguson shot to his feet. 'Absolutely not! What the hell do you mean?'

'Just routine questioning,' Torquil replied with a soft smile. 'So where were you yesterday afternoon at the end of the Gathering?'

'I was watching you, actually. I had a chat with Viroj Wattana and then, when he went off, he had a headache from drinking Heather Ale with the Padre, I had a look at some of the clan tents.'

Torquil nodded. 'Oh, just one more question — why did you decide to come to the Gathering this year?'

The ghost of a triumphant smile hovered over the professor's lips. 'Your uncle, Lachlan McKinnon, asked me to come.'

Torquil nodded and closed his notebook. 'Thank you, Professor. That will be all for now.'

Dr Viroj Wattana was in an ill humour. And the cause of that ill humour was the man standing opposite him, lecturing him about being discrete.

The little Thai surgeon was smarting, but he merely bowed. Soon, there would be a levelling of scores, he thought.

CHAPTER EIGHT

Miss Bella Melville was giving Morag Driscoll a hard time. Having taught every member of the West Uist Division of the Hebridean Constabulary, she maintained, in her own mind at least, the right to talk to them as if they were still her pupils.

'And I don't care what your superior officers are telling you, Morag Driscoll, I am telling you that you will not be able to keep the island sealed off. It is unfair to the local people and it is grossly unfair to the tourists who want to leave.'

Morag smiled as sweetly as she could. 'We *are* investigating a murder, Miss Melville.'

'And don't try that tactic with me, young lady,' returned Miss Melville. 'I am as deeply upset about Fiona Cullen as anyone else. I taught her as a wee girl, you know.' Her cheeks reddened slightly beneath her carefully applied Elizabeth Arden make-up. 'The media will have a field day with you all unless you play ball with them. You do yourself and Torquil McKinnon a favour and get him to telephone his superior officer now and get this silly rule overturned.'

Morag nodded conspiratorially. 'I'll have a word with him, Miss Melville.'

'Be sure that you do. I know he's under pressure at the moment, but just give him one other message from me.'

'Yes, Miss Melville? What?'

'Tell him that Miss Melville said TDG!'

'TDG?' Morag repeated.

Miss Melville came close to smiling. 'That's right, Morag Driscoll. He'll understand.'

And indeed, ten minutes later when Torquil emerged for a cup of tea, having let Professor Ferguson out of the station by the back door, he knew only too well what his old teacher meant.

'She used to tell me to "Take a Dose of Gumption",' he explained as he and his sergeant sipped hot strong tea in the office. 'She used to think that I was sometimes too timid. That I needed to be more like the Padre and show more gumption, more oomph!'

'Och, you've done just fine, Torquil,' Morag said defensively. 'Look at you. You must be about the youngest inspector in the whole of the west of Scotland.'

'But she's right, Morag. We can't just seal off the island like this. I need to talk to the superintendent again. That's what she meant — I should do it straight away and not procrastinate.'

Morag looked doubtful as Torquil reached for the phone.

As usual it seemed to be a pretty one-sided exchange.

'I think he'd had second thoughts himself,' Torquil told her as he put the receiver down after his call. 'He's apparently talked it over with the Chief Constable and they agree, we have twenty-four hours to investigate, then the ferry service must resume as normal.'

'And what about media coverage?'

'We've still to use Calum Steele as a go-between.'

'So we have twenty-four hours to catch this maniac?'

'There's worse, Morag.'

'Out with it, boss.'

'Twenty-four hours and then he may come across himself.'

Morag groaned.

After he had hit enough balls to raise blisters on the insides of both thumbs, the Padre went into his study and tried to write a sermon. But it was a thankless task. His mind would not settle. He kept thinking of Fiona and Ranald Buchanan. Finally, he went out, got on the Red Hunter and chugged around the island to Ranald Buchanan's cottage, *Tigh nam Bàrd* — the House of the Bard. He had no particular purpose in mind; he just felt that he needed to think. And he suspected that if he just stayed and pottered about the manse, he would be bound to receive a call from Bella Melville.

Also, there was something worrying about Ranald's death. They had all been too quick to assume that he'd slipped on that jetty while he was drunk and bashed his head on that spike. The fact was that Ranald Buchanan had always managed to function even when he'd drunk enough peatreek to sink a battleship.

The House of the Bard was a fairly basic croft, literally built within a stone's throw of the sea. There was a jetty where he moored his boat, and just a hundred yards distant the Machair Skerry jutted out of the sea. The Padre stood looking at it for a few moments, seeing the water lapping at the jetty on the skerry, where they had found Ranald's body floating just under the surface. And behind it was the shack where he kept his fishing tackle and a good quantity of his best peatreek.

The Padre turned to look at the cottage, a three-roomed affair, surrounded by a low wall containing a garden overgrown with nettles and thistles. Behind it there were several large corrugated-iron outhouses where, everyone knew, the Gaelic Bard made his fishing flies, repaired fishing tackle and distilled his peatreek — a cottage industry in every sense of the word.

The Padre walked round the outside of the cottage, looking in through the windows and marvelling at the primitive furnishings and the lack of proper amenities. He pulled out his pipe and stuffed the bowl with the dark thick-cut tobacco that he favoured. *Aye, basic was the way you liked it, wasn't it Ranald?*, he mused as he strolled on, leaving a trail of smoke in his wake.

But it wouldn't have been much of a life here for her or the boy, he thought. And he felt sad to think of how tragic Ranald Buchanan's life had been. His daughter going mad after the birth of her son, and then her son drowning beyond the Machair Skerry. *I guess that's where the creativity came from, Ranald*, the Padre thought.

He walked over to the outhouses where he had found Ranald distilling his peatreek on so many occasions. He smiled as he thought of the old chap's defence — 'Mind that dog collar o' yours, Lachlan. You cannot tell anyone! It would be unethical for a man of the cloth to grass on his supplier of peatreek.' Then he would lock the padlock and take him round to sample one of his best flasks of peatreek in his front parlour.

The Padre was still grinning when he realized that the padlock he had been thinking of was not securing the door, but was lying open in the dust.

He was about to try one of the doors when he thought better of it. He was on his own at a deserted croft, and there was an unknown murderer somewhere on the island. What on earth was he thinking of? He made his way back on tiptoe to the Red Hunter, slipped on his goggles and kick-started the bike into action.

When he had ridden a quarter of a mile along the road he stopped, pulled out his mobile phone and called Torquil.

'Where's Ewan?' Torquil snapped after speaking to his uncle on the phone.

'He'll be back in a moment,' replied Morag. 'I sent him out to get some milk. He's upset that you're cross with him, Torquil. About not leaving a buoy. He's kicking himself.'

Torquil frowned. 'We're all going to have to be on our toes, Morag. So far we've no idea who did this thing. Ewan occasionally needs a prod.' He stood and made for the door. 'That was the Padre. He's just been to Ranald Buchanan's croft — Lord knows why — and it looks as if someone's tampered with his sheds. I'd better go and have a look.' He scowled. 'I was going to interview Genevieve Cooper, but I think you'd better do that while I'm out at Ranald's place.'

'Any particular line you want me to take, boss?'

'The quickest one to the truth. We know that Fiona was going to fire her, but we don't know why.'

'I'll go as soon as Ewan comes back.'

Ten minutes later Torquil coasted to a halt beside the Padre, then together they set off back to the House of the Bard. Over the years they had enjoyed many a ride together on their classic bikes, had many a breakdown and repair session, and occasionally one or other would have a spill. More often than not their trips had been full of good spirits, yet now there was no sense of enjoyment, just urgency and desperation to get to the bottom of this tragedy as swiftly as possible. And it was just possible that a break-in at Ranald Buchanan's could be relevant.

'What were you doing out here, Lachlan?' Torquil asked as they dismounted by the moss-covered garden wall in front of the cottage.

'Seeking inspiration. My sermon wasn't going very well,' the Padre explained. 'Come on,' he said, leading the way round the back to the corrugated outhouses. 'You know what he kept in these sheds, don't you?'

Torquil gave a thin smile. 'Peatreek, of course. But I didn't think it was doing any harm, so I never made an issue of it.' He bent down and, without touching it, he examined the padlock that lay on the ground. From his pocket he pulled out a handkerchief and laid it over the padlock, using a few pebbles to stop the handkerchief from blowing away. 'Morag will come and do the forensics on it later.' And so saying he inserted a pen into the door crack and pulled the door open.

The smell of alcohol that was released was almost overpowering. Dozens of bottles lay smashed on the ground, their contents having seeped into the earth floor.

'Looks like someone went berserk in here,' Torquil said, pointing to the evidence of bottles having been indiscriminately smashed on the corrugated walls. 'And it was done a while ago.'

'Not long after he died, I expect,' the Padre agreed.

'We'd better have a look in the house, Lachlan.'

'The door won't be locked, of course,' the Padre said. 'Ranald had nothing he considered of any value in his house.' He cast a sad look at the detritus in the shed. 'This was what he thought he was really good at. Making peatreek.'

'How much did he make? How many folk did he supply?'

'Around the islands? To his fishing cronies and customers?' the Padre pouted reflectively. 'Enough for his meagre needs and much more, I guess.'

As the Padre had predicted, the door was unlocked. Inside, the house looked as if Ranald Buchanan had just left it and intended to return shortly. There was the odour of stale cigarettes and marijuana smoke. Thick dust covered the furniture, a few used coffee mugs and fishing paraphernalia littered the table, while in the grate and over the hearth there was a heap of black ash. To the side of the fire was a broken bottle with some amber-coloured liquid still in the bottom.

'Looks like either Ranald or someone else has been burning papers,' Torquil said, bending and inspecting an unburned fragment of paper. 'It's part of a poem, I think,' he said. He nodded at the broken bottle. 'It looks as if someone, probably the breaker of all his bottles, kept one bottle to burn a stack of paper.'

'His poems! His work!' exclaimed the Padre, in exasperation. He shook his head. 'That wouldn't have been Ranald. He was too conceited ever to do anything like that.'

Torquil stood up to face his uncle. 'I agree with you there, Lachlan. It looks like someone wanted to destroy all that Ranald Buchanan held dear. His peatreek and his poetry.'

'He was murdered, wasn't he?'

'I believe so. I'm sorry. I know that you were close to him.'

The Padre shrugged. 'He was an eccentric, laddie. We need folk like that.' He puffed up his cheeks. 'Oh, he could be a cantankerous old fool. And in his younger days he'd been a bit of a — er — well, a bit of a lecher, but he wasn't a total bad lot.'

Torquil nodded. 'And a poet. One of the last great Gaelic poets. West Uist has lost a lot with his death.'

The Padre inexplicably tossed his head back and guffawed. After a moment, he took a deep breath, then said, 'Well, I agree that he was a Gaelic speaker, Torquil — but a great poet? Never! He wrote doggerel. As a poet he was a non-starter.'

'Are you serious, Lachlan?' Torquil asked incredulously.

'Afraid so, laddie. Ranald Buchanan was a rogue in many ways. A likeable rogue, I thought, but a rogue nonetheless. He was a versifier, a doggerel-peddler. If he wrote in the straight dialect, like William McGonagal, he would have been denounced straightaway, but because he wrote in the Gaelic, and since most people no longer speak the native tongue, he is forgiven for his mistranslations into English. Patronage! That is what made Ranald Buchanan's reputation. It does no harm having a large chain of bookshops pushing your work.'

'You mean AME Books?'

'Exactly.' The Padre looked over Torquil's shoulder. 'What does the fragment say?'

'It's just a few handwritten words. Presumably lines from a poem: "by the providence" and "Selkie returns"!' Then he added, 'And they're in English, not the Gaelic,' he added.

'Hmm. I expect that was a translation of a poem. As far as I know, he composed in Gaelic, then translated.'

Torquil took out his pocketbook and inserted the fragment inside the cover. He then turned to his uncle. 'Do you have a list of all the writers who attended the Festival?'

'Of course. Back in my study. Why?'

'Because it's possible that some of them could also be at risk.'

The Padre eyed his nephew quizzically and Torquil explained about Fiona's missing laptop and notebooks. 'Her latest novel was to have been called "Dead Writers Tell No Tales",' he said. 'It looks as if we've had the murder of two writers. We don't want a third.'

It did not take Morag long to track Genevieve Cooper down. She had left her room at her bed and breakfast after a frugal repast, consisting of a glass of orange juice, an Aberdeen buttery and two back-to-back Gauloises cigarettes, then gone for an amble along the bookstalls and stands that were still up and running. Her distinctive appearance in the small harbour town made her easy to stalk. Morag followed the sightings to Henry Henderson's Bookmakers, where she had placed a few bets, then into the Bonnie Prince Charlie, where she found her in a corner seat nursing a large vodka and tonic and smoking one of her trademark French cigarettes.

'Genevieve Cooper?' Morag asked, holding out her warrant card. 'I'm Sergeant Driscoll of the Hebridean Constabulary. May I have a few minutes of your time?'

'Ugh! The dreaded interview,' Genevieve returned, downing her drink in one go. 'I think I'd better have another of these before we start.'

Morag waited for the literary agent to return from the bar with a fresh drink, and then produced a silver pen and notebook. 'I'm afraid that I need to ask you a few questions about Fiona Cullen.'

In answer, Genevieve dissolved into tears, which immediately merged into an attack of hiccups. Another few moments passed while they gradually subsided. Then, with a freshly-lit cigarette, Genevieve sat back and smiled. 'Ask away then Sergeant, dear, Genevieve Cooper, the author's trooper, is at your service.'

'How long had you been Fiona Cullen's agent?' Morag asked, poised with her pen.

'Five glorious years. I guided her from rags to riches. And never a cross word spoken between us.'

'Yet, I understand that she recently announced that she was firing you?'

Genevieve blinked several times as if her brain was having difficulty registering the question and computing an answer. Then she replied, 'Not firing me, just parting company, dear.'

'Is there a difference?'

'You get fired when you've done something wrong. I hadn't.' She puffed her cigarette then waved her hand extravagantly. 'These things happen between authors and agents.'

'Has it happened to you before, Genevieve? Have other authors parted company with you?'

Genevieve blushed and reached for her vodka and tonic. 'I may have had a lean patch recently.'

'Any reason for that?'

'It's a mystery.'

'It couldn't be anything to do with gambling, could it?'

The literary agent suddenly stiffened. 'Why do you ask that?'

Morag made a play as if she was doodling. 'Oh, just because you've been seen in Henry Henderson's Bookmakers several times so far. And you placed a couple of bets already today — the day after Fiona Cullen was murdered. Some people might think that was unusual. They might even suggest that you had a problem, an addiction.'

Genevieve stubbed out her cigarette in the ashtray and immediately lit another. She looked at the cigarette and shrugged. 'OK, so I admit that I have an addictive personality. But my drinking and gambling have nothing to do with our parting company.' She coughed. 'Not directly, anyway.'

'So it had an indirect effect?'

Genevieve bit her lip. 'Look, Sergeant, I may not be the best literary agent in the world, but I'm not bad. I have a knack for certain things and not others. I'm good at getting authors published, getting them linked up with the right publisher and ironing out any flaws in that vital first contract. And I'm good at getting people to keep an interest in an author. Sometimes I may go too populist, that's all.'

Morag looked puzzled. 'But surely every author wants to be popular?'

Genevieve smiled. 'They want to be popular, not populist! I may be too brash for some people.' She inhaled deeply on her cigarette then tapped the lengthening ash off. 'Fiona said I didn't consult her often enough, and that my taste in advertising could be a bit tacky. She thought I sometimes went too far down-market — like getting her to do a sexy pose in Japan. She said that I dumbed down her writing and created the image of her as a kind of literary slapper.' She shook her head emphatically. 'As if I'd do that to one of my authors!'

Morag felt herself warming to Genevieve. 'Can you give me an example of what she meant?'

'She criticized me about some of the publicity pieces I managed to get into magazines. She wanted to be in the literary reviews not the girlie mags. In a way she was a snob, I think. She saw herself as a real writer, a potential Booker prize-winner, rather than a crime writer.'

'Was her writing good enough for that?'

Genevieve took a meditative puff on her cigarette. 'No,' she said decisively. 'She was a born story-teller, but her writing was a little crude. The truth is, my lovely, that although we all want to live in a class above our own, only the extraordinarily talented make it work. I don't think I could have gotten a literary publisher to look at her stuff.'

Morag grimaced. 'That sounds harsh.'

'But realistic, Sergeant, dear. Fiona, on the other hand, was not realistic. I think she had a thing about tackiness. What she didn't realize was that tackiness was her bread and butter. It wasn't a literary audience that was buying her books; it was tacky old Joe Bloggs and his sister Sharon who liked her work.' She took a final drag on her cigarette then stubbed it out. 'I think that's why she took such an aversion to the bookmarks I had made up.'

'The bookmarks that were given away at the Literary Festival?'

Genevieve nodded. 'I think they were a tour de force. Everyone would see her in Osaka — and it is a sexy pose, but it's also sophisticated, whatever she said — and want to buy a copy of one of her books.'

'But she didn't like it?'

The agent vigorously shook her head. 'She hated it! I still don't know why. And that's when she said we should part company.'

'When exactly did she say this?'

'On the ferry over here.'

'Oh!' Morag exclaimed in surprise. 'So you had plenty of time to mull it over!'

Calum Steele had a strong Walter Mitty streak, which he was blissfully unaware of himself. He saw himself as a man of letters, an editor of literary excellence and an investigative journalist at heart. He loved the celebrity status that being editor of the *West Uist Chronicle* gave him, even though the population of the island was small enough for most people to know the majority of their neighbours anyway. The flipside of the coin, to his chagrin, was that because so many people knew about other people's business, there was little scope for actual investigative journalism. Until now! The sudden swell in the island's population, and the murder of the celebrated Fiona Cullen, meant that not only was he the main link to the outside world, but he was also in a position to do some real investigating and maybe even find the murderer before Torquil McKinnon did.

And to best Torquil at anything would give him great pleasure. All his life he had played at least second fiddle to

Piper, and although he was probably one of his best friends, it pissed him off! To outstage him — to have a national scoop — would, he felt, salve the wound he had received on that day in Miss Melville's class when Torquil had won the Robert Burns Poetry Recitation Prize for his rendition of 'To A Mouse', after Calum had stuttered and stumbled over his potted version of 'Tam o'Shanter'. It hadn't so much been the fact that Torquil had won that bothered him; it was more the fact that Fiona Cullen, an eight-year-old blonde angel, had been inspired to give the winner a kiss. And then, twenty years later, after she had worked for Calum then gone on to far bigger and better things, she had come back to West Uist and had Torquil in her sights.

When she was working for him as his reporter, she had slept with Torquil! It still hurt, even though he was sad that she was dead.

He rankled inside. Perhaps he could scupper Torquil in the media. He had the power. Or perhaps he could do it more effectively some other way. It was nice, he reflected, to have some choice in the matter.

Arming himself with this knowledge, he stepped up to the unusually quiet public bar of the Bonnie Prince Charlie and winked at Mollie McFadden, who peered myopically at him, her expression that of mild suspicion.

'And what can I do for you, Calum Steele?'

'I'll take a pint of your best Heather Ale to begin with, Mollie.'

He watched her pull the pint, her right forearm noticeably more developed than her left after having pumped a seaful of beer over the years. Calum took a hefty swig then wiped foam off his upper lip as he replaced the glass on the counter.

'A sad business,' he remarked casually. 'A bad ending to the Gathering.'

Mollie leaned on the bar. 'Terrible. And it makes me feel awful, her having stayed here in my tavern.'

'Fiona used to work for me, you know,' Calum said. 'We were at school together. Same class as Torquil.'

'Aye, I recall. That was before she became famous.'

Calum's cheeks burned and he took another swig of beer. He hadn't realized it before, but he was jealous of his former employee. They had both gone off to university, as had Torquil, and they had all come back to West Uist. Both he and she wrote words for a living, but she had achieved something really big, while he was still reporting on Gatherings, the price of fish and who was selling what at the church jumble sales. He forced the emotion from his mind, for now he was chasing the biggest story of his life, ironically thanks to Fiona!

'Was she working while she was here?'

Mollie smiled at the *Chronicle* editor's efforts to winkle information from her. 'Aye, she was working on her new book, just as she said at her talk the other day.'

'Have the police taken her things away? Her writing, her notes and everything?'

Mollie shook her head. 'You will have to be asking Inspector McKinnon that question, Calum Steele. And while you're at it, you'd better ask him about the ghost!'

Calum raised his eyebrows quizzically, his journalistic antennae quivering. 'Did you say *ghost*?'

'Aye, a ghost. I saw Fiona Cullen go up those stairs to her room yesterday at about five o'clock, when they say that her body had already been found.'

Calum leaned closer and dropped his voice. 'Mollie, do you realize what this could mean to you?'

'Aye, I do. I'm sorry about poor Fiona, but I'm a working lassie with a living to make.'

'You know that I'm handling all the media coverage at the moment?'

Mollie McFadden's eyes gleamed behind her spectacles. 'That's what I heard. Would you care for a dram of malt to follow that pint?'

Calum nodded with a sly smile as she poured a good measure of Glen Corlin from one of the special bottles that she kept under the bar. 'The public has a morbid streak of curiosity, Mollie. If the publicity about Fiona Cullen's ghost is handled right it could prove very profitable in the long term for the landlady of the Bonnie Prince Charlie Tavern in Kyleshiffin.'

As he sipped his malt and imagined the headlines in *Scottish Life* magazine, Mollie greeted another customer. 'I'll just serve this gentleman,' she whispered, 'then we can have a wee chat over in the corner.'

'*Slàinte mhath*,' said Calum, as he downed the rest of the glass. He smiled as the fiery water of life hit the spot.

At the same moment, Genevieve Cooper put her glass down on the table and snapped her Zippo lighter to puff a further cigarette into life. Morag, a passionate non-smoker, suppressed a wince and sat stoically enduring the smoke. 'Did you arrange many trips for her?'

'Loads. France, Germany, Japan and Thailand. I got her published in eight languages and arranged tours in each country.'

'Are there any of her foreign publishers here?'

'No, this is just an experiment. It's hardly the Edinburgh Festival, is it? As far as I've seen, the only person from foreign parts is that funny little Dr Wattana.'

'Did Fiona have a literary connection with him?'

Genevieve laughed. 'Good Lord, no! Fiona often combined business with pleasure when she was away.'

'She had a relationship with him?'

This time the agent sniggered. She dropped her voice. 'She had a boob job in Thailand.'

'He operated on her?'

'Yes, but not to her satisfaction. She ranted about him botching the job. Didn't use big enough implants. There's a court case between them.'

'Do you know what he's doing on West Uist?'

'No idea, my lovely. But I think they had words at the Gathering yesterday.'

Morag made another entry in her notebook, then continued, 'She was an attractive woman. Any men in her life?'

A twinkle formed in Genevieve's eyes. 'I rather had the impression that there was a current man in her life, a certain inspector of the local police.'

Morag glossed over the remark. 'I meant before she came to West Uist for the Gathering.'

'Fiona was socially gregarious. She had quite a few men friends. She liked to party. She was close to Angus MacLeod for a while, and I think — only think, mind you — that she may have had a fling with Roland Baxter.'

'The Scottish Minister for Culture?' Morag asked in surprise.

Genevieve stubbed her cigarette out. 'I don't know details, but Fiona hinted that the minister was — er —' She hesitated a moment, '— less potent than people might imagine.'

Morag jotted a few lines. 'One more question. Would losing Fiona Cullen's custom cause you cash flow problems?'

Genevieve Cooper stiffened. 'Why do you ask that?'

'This is a murder investigation. It's my job to ask questions, no matter how unpalatable or unpleasant. Henry Henderson tells me that in the short time you've been in Kyleshiffin you've laid several bets and lost over seven hundred pounds.'

A muscle twitched near the corner of the literary agent's mouth. 'I like a flutter. I've told you that already.' She hesitated, then nodded, as if having made up her mind about something. 'OK, so maybe I like it a bit too much, but I've always been strictly honest and fair with my authors. That's maybe more than some pub—' She bit her lip and leaned forward. 'Look, Sergeant, I don't want to say anything out of turn or get anyone in trouble.'

Morag eyed her sternly. 'I repeat, Genevieve, this is a murder investigation. Withholding information could get *you* in trouble. So, come on, what do you mean?'

'Christ! Look, Fiona Cullen was a very sexual woman. What you may not know is that she swung both ways.'

'Go on.'

'She had an on-off affair with Allegra McCall for a couple of years. I think that Fiona ended it because she thought...' Once again she hesitated and looked doubtful, but a look from Morag urged her on. 'She thought that Allegra may have been holding money back. Rooking her! Not paying her for various print-runs, that sort of thing.'

'Any truth in that, do you think?'

Genevieve shook her head. 'I think Allegra McCall is one of the most honest publishers I deal with. I think it was another of the bees that Fiona got in her bonnet.'

Morag shook her head sadly. 'But now she is no more. Tell me though; what were you doing at the close of the Gathering?'

Genevieve Cooper gave a small guilty-looking smile. 'I was avoiding people. I had a bit of a tiff with Allegra actually. Nothing serious, I think we were both just pissed off with Fiona. I went to see if the bookies was open — but of course it was closed for the Gathering.'

Morag glanced at her watch and put her pen away. 'Thank you, Genevieve. You've been most helpful.' She rose to go.

'Could you do me one favour, Sergeant?' Genevieve asked. 'Please don't tell Allegra I said anything.'

Morag maintained her professional poker face. 'All I can say is that we never divulge our sources.'

PC Ewan McPhee was feeling miserable. Manning the station desk had been really tough since he had had to deal with a constant stream of queries, complaints and all manner of sightings and suggested theories from locals and tourists. Dutifully he had recorded them all, dealing with them as best as he could. The problem was that he was feeling bad about letting Torquil down, especially when he must be going through his own personal hell. It had been clear to everyone that he and Fiona had been picking up on their old relationship.

He was only half listening to Annie McConville as she gave him the benefit of her advice, while Zimba, her large Alsatian, sat patiently beside her.

'So if you want to scour the entire crime scene for clues, just get back to me. Zimba has a better sense of smell than any bloodhound; you just take it from me.'

Ewan nodded and forced a smile as the old lady turned to go. 'I'll tell my inspector, Annie.'

His forced smile turned into a real one a moment later when Izzie Frazer came in. She was wearing jeans and a green poncho, her shoulder bag slung diagonally across her breasts like a bandolier.

'Am I glad to see you, Izzie,' Ewan said with relief. 'I need something to cheer me up. It's been a bloody awful time. I —'

She reached across the desk, grabbed both of his ears and pulled him forwards to plant a kiss on his lips.

'Is that better?'

He grinned like a Cheshire cat. 'Aye, it's just got a lot better.'

Izzie shivered. 'I can't believe it. I talked to her at the Gathering yesterday and now she's gone. How could something like this happen?'

Ewan bit his lip. 'I don't know, Izzie. I feel so sorry for Torquil, and he's got the job of finding the bastard. At a time like this when he must be going through hell himself.'

'I missed you after the Gathering.'

'Aye, I know, it was just pandemonium. But did you manage to get hold of that agent woman?'

Izzie shook her head. 'No. It was odd. I saw her leave the grounds and I ran after her, but she just seemed to disappear. She's faster than she looks.'

'What are you doing now?'

'Visiting you, silly. I thought we could have lunch or something.'

The big constable shook his head. 'I'm afraid I've got to man the fort. But maybe we could meet this evening — whenever I get away. But it could be late, awful late.'

Izzie reached out and tousled his hair. 'It doesn't matter how late. I think with everything that's going on I could do with a cuddle from a big strong constable.'

Ewan flushed to his roots again.

CHAPTER NINE

Ewan grimaced when Morag came in. He nodded in the direction of Torquil's closed office door. 'The boss has been buttonholed by Calum Steele. The sly dog was in here thirty seconds after Torquil and almost demanded to have a word with him. I think he sees all this as a chance to get famous.'

'How long have they been in there?'

'About twenty minutes — and without any request for tea or coffee.'

'The boss is obviously not wanting to encourage him then,' Morag murmured. Then she smiled. 'But I could do with a cup, my wee sweetheart.'

Ewan grinned. 'Coming right up, Sergeant.'

And while he was in the kitchenette rattling cups and making tea, Morag went through to the incident room, sat down and wrote up her report from her notes. Ewan joined her a few minutes later with a tea-tray and the biscuit barrel.

'Any progress?' he asked, dunking a ginger biscuit in his mug of tea.

'A lot of interesting facts that may or may not be relevant,' Morag replied, sipping her tea and reluctantly ignoring the biscuits since she was in one of her diet phases. Although only a few pounds overweight she felt a duty to stay as fit and slim as she could in order to prevent a heart attack, like the cruel early one that had taken her husband away in his thirty-third year and left her a widow with three children to look after.

Torquil's outer office door opened and they heard the inspector walking Calum Steele to the door.

'I'll have to let this one out, you know that, don't you, Torquil.'

'Just the facts, Calum. No embellishments and no theorizing.'

Calum Steele's voice was indignant. 'I'm a responsible journalist! You know I always shy away from sensationalism.'

The rest of the conversation was inaudible to them. They heard the outer door close and a few moments later Torquil came in. He spotted the tea then shook his head as he poured himself a cup. 'He may prove a liability to this investigation!' he volunteered. 'Somehow or other he found out that someone went into Fiona's room after she was murdered. He was trying to find out about what she was writing. The sly dog.'

Morag pushed the biscuit barrel across the desk, then enquired, 'What about the Padre's call, boss? Was everything OK?'

Torquil munched a ginger biscuit. 'Are these your mum's biscuits, Ewan?' The big constable flushed and began to nod. 'They're delicious! Thank her for me, will you.' He flashed a smile at the constable. 'Sorry I snapped this morning, I was —'

'Upset,' Ewan interjected, eagerly. 'Of course you were, boss. Losing Fiona like that.' His face went crimson and his voice trembled. 'And what with me acting the gowk! I'll think next time, you just wait and see!' And picking up his mug he stood. 'Maybe I'd better man the desk — unless I can do anything now?'

Torquil smiled. 'You're a good lad, Ewan. I'll brief you later.'

When they were alone Torquil picked up a marker pen, stood up and tapped its end on the whiteboard, beside Ranald Buchanan's name. 'There's no doubt, it was murder, Morag.' And he told her about his investigation with the Padre. 'We'll need to forensic the place, of course. I'm thinking that you may need some help from South Uist, so if you do —'

'I'll manage, boss. We want to sort this ourselves, don't we?'

Torquil gave her a half-smile and then drew a box around Ranald's name. 'And what about your interview with Genevieve Cooper?'

'Here's my report, boss. Hot off the press and illuminating.' But as he reached out for it she held the papers firmly for a moment. 'But I think you should just steel yourself, Torquil,' she said concernedly. 'You may find out a few things about Fiona that you didn't know.'

Kyleshiffin was thrumming with activity. The market stalls on Harbour Street were doing a roaring trade and so were all the shops as people resigned themselves to their enforced stay on West Uist.

Torquil was pleased to leave the hustle and bustle for a while and headed off on his Royal Enfield Bullet for Dunshiffin Castle. After reading Morag's report he decided to put off his interview with Allegra McCall, at least until he got his head cleared. News that Fiona had had an affair with another woman had thrown him and he felt the need to disconnect for a while.

But as he rode into the Dunshiffin Castle forecourt he found himself transported back to the ceilidh of the other night. There were people all over the place, just as there had been then.

Of course, he told himself. They've been staying here. Billeted by the Padre and Miss Melville!

People were getting into cars and mini-buses, presumably to be transported back to Kyleshiffin in search of food and refreshments.

He stripped off his gauntlets, goggles and Cromwell helmet.

'Ah, Piper McKinnon! Up here!'

He looked up at the sound of his name and saw the elegant torso of Angus MacLeod, the laird of the Dunshiffin estate, beckoning him from an open first-floor window.

Jesmond, the laird's butler-cum-general-factotum, met him at the door and directed him up the great stairway to Angus MacLeod's sumptuous oak-panelled study, where the man himself was sitting on the corner of his desk, puffing on a large Havana cigar.

'Ah, Piper, come in. Have a seat. A cigar?' He held out his hand.

Torquil shook hands, but refused the cigar humidor and sat down. 'Angus, I need some information.'

Angus MacLeod nodded as he blew a stream of smoke ceilingwards. 'About Fiona Cullen's murder, of course.' He shook his head. 'I'm afraid that I probably know nothing of any use to you. I was at the Gathering all afternoon.'

Torquil raised a finger. 'We'll talk about Fiona in a minute. In fact, I'm here to investigate two murders. It's the first that I want information about.'

Angus MacLeod stared at him in amazement. 'Two murders?'

'Aye. I'm investigating the murders of Fiona Cullen and Ranald Buchanan.'

The Laird of Dunshiffin visibly paled. 'Are you serious? You think that Ranald Buchanan was murdered too?'

Torquil nodded. 'That I do. And I believe that you have important information for me.'

Angus MacLeod stared at the glowing tip of his cigar. 'And why would you think that?'

'Because, for one thing, you were his sponsor. You've been pushing his books in your chain of bookstores all over the west of Scotland. You brought him to prominence, made him famous.'

'He deserved his success. I just gave him a hand on the way.'

'Am I right in thinking that it was you who first called him "the Gaelic Bard"?'

The laird puffed his cigar and blew a ribbon of smoke from the corner of his mouth. 'Who told you that?'

'The Padre.'

Angus MacLeod smiled. 'The Padre doesn't miss much does he? But that still doesn't detract from the fact that Ranald deserved his success. He was a great poet and his book sales back that up. He is one of the few Scottish poets to ever make the bestseller lists.'

Torquil gave a slow whistle. 'Now that's no small feat for any poet is it? I thought it was a miniscule market. They can get great kudos, but it's basically pocket money stuff. The Padre tells me that not even the poet laureate makes a living from his poetry.'

'Perhaps the Padre knows less about the book industry than he thinks.'

Torquil smiled and leaned forward. 'Do you know, I think I will take you up on that offer of a cigar. Ordinarily I only ever smoke when I'm amongst the midges, but that aroma is tempting. Havana, isn't it?'

'The finest. Montecristos. Help yourself.'

Torquil opened the humidor and selected a cigar. He snipped its end with the gold cigar clipper that lay inside and picked up the box of Swan Vestas. The laird watched him through narrowed eyes as he methodically lit it.

'Hmm. That's good,' said Torquil. 'Did Ranald like cigars?'

'Why do you think I should know that?'

'Because he was often here, wasn't he?'

'He was. And now that you mention it, I don't think he ever did smoke cigars. He was addicted to those foul little roll-ups of his.'

Torquil savoured his cigar. 'Did he smoke tobacco here, or weed? Marijuana, that is.'

'Tobacco, of course!' snapped the Laird. 'Look, Piper, what are you getting at?'

'Ranald Buchanan smoked cannabis regularly. You know it and I know it. I admit that I never pulled him in for it, since he was not exactly causing a problem on the island.'

'Magnanimous of you.'

Torquil shrugged. 'That's the way things work in life, though, isn't it, Angus? People do each other favours.'

'I don't follow.'

'Well, I've always wondered why you, as the owner of Glen Corlin distillery, the only West Uist distillery, didn't try to stop Ranald Buchanan from supplying half the islands with his peatreek.'

Angus MacLeod shot to his feet. 'Illicit alcohol! Are you suggesting that Ranald Buchanan ran an illicit still?'

Torquil looked at the accumulating ash on his cigar. 'That's exactly what I'm saying. And I believe that you knew that very well — as just about the whole island did.'

The laird smiled triumphantly. 'So you admit that you, an officer of the law, knew about this?'

'I suspected, but never investigated. It was hardly in the public's interest. Besides, the distilling of peatreek is a traditional craft of the outer isles.'

'But it's illegal. Immoral even.'

Torquil smiled benignly. 'I don't think it is all that immoral.'

'It's dishonest then. It deprives the government of revenue.'

'Ah, dishonest. You mean less than honest?' Torquil stood up and took an extra puff on his Havana. He walked across to the bay window, leaving a trail of smoke in his wake. 'Tell me, do you think that touting a meagre talent and pretending that it was a major one was strictly honest?'

'What do you mean, McKinnon?'

Torquil turned and grinned at the laird's obvious discomfiture. 'Come on, Angus. We both know that Ranald Buchanan smoked cannabis, that he was an illicit distiller — and that he didn't rate as a poet! Yet somehow you ignored his peatreek making, which was directly against your personal financial interests, and for some reason you pushed his books in your bookstores.'

The laird seemed to have gone slightly pale. Torquil noticed him unconsciously looking towards the tray of assorted decanters on the side table, as if he suddenly felt in need of a drink. But the laird quickly regained his composure. He picked up the box of matches and slowly relit his cigar. 'OK! I admit that I helped him by pushing his books in my shops. What's the problem there? He was a fellow islander and I wanted to see him become a success.'

'But how do you account for the number of books you sold, Angus? That many people just don't like poetry.'

'What are you suggesting?'

'That perhaps for some reason someone bought his books in large quantities.' He smiled sarcastically. 'Perhaps the books were literally cooked.'

Angus MacLeod sat down in the plush leather chair behind his desk. 'I think you should be careful what you say, Inspector McKinnon.'

'Oh, I will, Angus. Which brings me to the second murder.'

'You still haven't told me why you think Ranald Buchanan was murdered,' the laird interrupted.

'That's police business at the moment, and I can't discuss it.' Torquil laid his cigar in the ashtray and brushed the palms of his hands against each other. 'Fiona Cullen had a grudge against you, didn't she?'

Angus MacLeod shrugged his shoulders. 'She didn't approve of my bookstore policy. Many authors don't. They want sales, big sales, but they don't like cut-price books, or anything that could affect their royalties.'

'And you sell cut-price books?'

'I'm a businessman. I make money for the publishers, the authors and myself.'

'Do you deal directly with the publishers?'

'Quite often, yes.'

'And could some of the deals affect an author's income?'

The laird considered for a moment, then nodded. 'In a way, yes, that's possible.'

'Did you do a deal with Fiona Cullen's publisher?'

Angus MacLeod folded his arms. 'I'm not prepared to say.'

Torquil nodded and decided not to pursue the matter. Instead, he asked, 'Did you ever have a relationship with Fiona Cullen?'

The laird's face reddened and he too laid his cigar in the ashtray. 'I may have done — for a while.'

Torquil felt the hairs at the back of his neck begin to rise. But he dared not allow any personal emotions to show through. 'A sexual affair?'

'Of course!' the laird replied curtly. 'But not for long. Only a month or so. It started at one of my parties.'

'And it ended when?'

'When I caught her cheating on me.' He frowned, got up and crossed to the tray of decanters. He poured himself a couple of fingers of Glen Corlin, which he downed in one go. Then, through gritted teeth, he added, 'With Allegra McCall, her publisher at Castlefront, as it happened. I was furious, I stopped stocking her bloody books altogether. And any others by Castlefront.' He pulled a handkerchief from his breast pocket and dabbed his forehead. 'There! Are you satisfied now, McKinnon?'

Torquil felt anything but satisfied and was about to reply when the noise of an engine starting up was followed by the gradual build-up of whirring rotor-blades.

'What the hell is that?' Torquil blurted out.

'It's my helicopter,' Angus MacLeod replied nonchalantly. 'Roland Baxter has to get back to the mainland. I said he could get Tam McKenzie to fly him back today.'

'Like hell he can!' Torquil snapped. 'I'm investigating what could be a serial murder case and no one leaves West Uist until I say so.'

The laird raised his eyebrows. 'I think you may be too late, Inspector.'

Torquil stepped very close to the laird. 'And I'm asking you to get straight on your radio to Tam McKenzie and tell him that he must under no circumstance leave West Uist. I want to talk to Roland Baxter — right now!'

The Padre had gone on from Ranald Buchanan's to do a couple of pastoral visits before riding into Kyleshiffin for a meeting with the Literary Festival Committee about the situation. He had parked the Red Hunter beside the harbour wall and was just stripping off his goggles and helmet when he spotted Dr Wattana a little further along the harbour, trying to peep through the cabin window of a cabin cruiser, which was gently bobbing up and down next to the police *Seaspray* catamaran.

'Dr Wattana,' the Padre called out in greeting. 'Do you fancy a boat like that?'

The doctor turned and blinked at him. 'Ah, yes, you're the drinking priest!' He exclaimed. 'I was just looking for a friend of mine.'

The Padre had mechanically struck a light to his briar pipe and tossed the match carelessly into the gutter. He looked right and left to make sure that no one was in earshot. 'Actually, I'd rather you didn't use that particular description, Doctor,' he said with a twinkle in his eye. 'It doesn't do for a man in my profession to have that sort of reputation.'

Dr Wattana blushed and executed a nervous little halfbow. 'I didn't mean offence — that is, I only meant that you introduced me to your beer.' He shook his head as if recalling an unpleasant memory. 'It made my head spin.'

The Padre gave a short laugh. 'Good old Heather Ale!' He pointed to the sign above the door of the Bonnie Prince Charlie Tavern. 'Would you care for a half pint?'

Dr Wattana held his hand up and looked horrified. 'No! I mean, I need to find my friend and talk to him. I hoped that he would be here.'

The Padre glanced at the cabin cruiser, with the name 'Unicorn' emblazoned across its prow. 'So you're looking for Neil Ferguson? This is his cruiser.' He snapped his fingers. 'Yes, of course, I remember you telling me you were supposed to be going diving with him and Angus MacLeod today.'

Dr Wattana bobbed his head. 'But everything has changed now. This regrettable murder!'

'Aye, awful, isn't it. Nothing like it has happened on West Uist before.'

'She was so — *talented*,' mused the little surgeon, as if carefully selecting his words.

'How about a cup of tea if you don't want beer?' the Padre suggested, tapping his pipe on the harbour wall and immediately shoving it into his breast pocket.

'Thank you, but no. I have just seen someone I'd rather not speak to right now. I must go. And I need to speak with that police inspector most urgently.'

The Padre looked at him in surprise. 'You mean Torquil? Well, if you like I could —' But Dr Wattana had already gone and had scurried towards the crowds still milling around the market stalls.

A hand dropped on his shoulder and he turned to see the grinning face of Calum Steele. 'Wasn't that the wee Thai surgeon?' Calum asked.

The Padre nodded. *I wonder how he knew to avoid Calum*, he thought with a grin.

Roland Baxter was in a furious mood when he stormed into Angus MacLeod's study.

'Just who the hell do you think you are, McKinnon?' he barked at Torquil. 'I'm a minister in the Scottish parliament and I have important business to attend to.'

'Since when?' Torquil asked with an innocent smile.

'Don't push your luck, Inspector.'

Angus MacLeod had stood up to try to placate the irate minister. 'Easy now, Roland. Inspector McKinnon is investigating a murder after all.' He glanced at Torquil, then added: 'Two murders actually.'

Roland Baxter looked amazed, but before he could get a word out, Torquil interrupted. 'Angus, I'd be grateful if we could have the use of your study for a while.'

In answer, the laird nodded. 'Of course.' And, addressing the minister, 'Take it easy Roland.'

Torquil gestured the minister to the plush armchair. 'So minister, could you answer my question? Since when did you have important business to attend to? As I understood it, you were planning to stay a few days on West Uist with your friends.'

The minister seemed to have regained his composure, the only sign of any antipathy or stress being a slight flaring of his nostrils. 'That was the plan, yes. I was going to enjoy a break and go fishing with Angus.'

'Not diving?'

'No, I don't dive myself. But Neil Ferguson was going to take Angus and Dr Wattana out for a dive around the crannog, and probably also do a bit of deep-water diving too.' He crossed his legs and flicked an imaginary speck of dust off his immaculately pressed trousers. 'What did Angus mean, you're investigating two murders?'

'We have reason to believe that Ranald Buchanan was also murdered.'

'By the same person?' Roland Baxter asked in disbelief.

Torquil shrugged. 'I am not yet in a position to answer that, but it is suspicious. Let's talk about Ranald Buchanan first. What was your relationship with him?'

Baxter looked bemused. 'I had no relationship with him. None, that is, except for my position as Scottish Minister for Culture and his status as a major Gaelic poet. As such he had to be regarded as a national asset.'

'Yet, you are not a fan of the Gaelic?'

Roland Baxter gave a dry smile, the practised smile of a politician. 'I am not personally in favour of extending the use of the Gaelic, because I see it as potentially divisive. But I am in favour of promoting anything to do with Scottish culture. I see Ranald Buchanan's significance as a poet, Gaelic-speaking or not.'

'And Fiona Cullen? How significant did you see her?' Torquil asked in an attempt to catch the minister on the hop.

'She was an able crime writer.'

'What was your relationship with her? Were you involved with her?'

Roland Baxter eyed Torquil with a hint of hostility. Then again the politician took over. 'We had been involved, but not for long.'

'Tell me about it.' And once again he felt an inner heat, as if his temper was rising, but he suppressed it as best he could.

For a moment it looked as if the minister was not prepared to cooperate. Then he shrugged. 'We had a fling for less than a week. It was after a party at Milngavie in Glasgow. A friend of hers had just written a book and she was expecting great things. I was —'

'Who was the publisher?'

'Castlefront. They publish a wide range of books. A strong fiction list, but also strong on equestrian, crafts and New Age stuff.'

'And Fiona Cullen was a Castlefront author?'

The minister nodded. 'My presence at the party lent it a certain — respectability and solidity. Fiona was pleased for her friend, because she thought it would help the book. It —'

'Did the book do well?'

The minister looked put out by Torquil's repeated interruptions to his narrative. 'No! I'm afraid it had a bad TV review.'

'Was that TV review after your affair with Fiona Cullen?'

Roland Baxter stared open-eyed at Torquil as if his question had suddenly answered a question of his own that had been posed over and over in his mind. Then slowly, he replied. 'Yes, as a matter of fact it was. It seemed that for some reason Fiona decided we weren't going anywhere.' A muscle in his jaw twitched, then he stiffened and sat upright. 'Fiona Cullen was one complex woman.'

Torquil found himself nodding his head. A complex woman indeed.

'Finally, where exactly were you between four and five o'clock yesterday?'

'I was at the Gathering all afternoon. I'm the Scottish Minister for Culture, damn it! Everyone knows me and would have seen me there.'

Or they would think they had, you pompous git! Torquil thought.

Superintendent Kenneth Lumsden had been feeling reasonably well until he switched on the news. Kirstie Macroon, the bonnie red-headed newsreader for Scottish Television, was a particular favourite of his. Yet when she reported on the murder inquiry on West Uist he jumped to his feet and experienced a sudden lancing pain that shot from his big toe straight up his spine. His leg buckled and he fell down with a yell.

Thirty seconds later he was dialling the Kyleshiffin police station. It took a further thirty-five minutes before he was connected to Inspector Torquil McKinnon at Dunshiffin Castle. The superintendent was not a happy man.

'What the hell is happening?' he thundered down the phone. 'Why haven't you got an arrest? Why haven't you reported back to me with a progress report? And why on earth is Scottish Television giving a report about ghosts?'

Torquil had not seen any of the reports, so asked the superintendent to explain what he had heard. After he listened to his superior's histrionic rendition of the news he replied: 'I wasn't aware that the newspapers had given the television that information, Sir.'

Superintendent Lumsden was not impressed. 'Well, you bloody well should know, McKinnon. You give that Calum Steele his information, don't you?'

'That must be information he's given out himself, Sir. It didn't come from us. It's just a bit of sensationalism. But what harm can that do?'

'What harm! The harm lies in the fact that we have no arrest. What are you playing at, McKinnon? It's a tiny bloody island.'

Torquil took a deep breath. 'We are investigating two murders, Sir.'

'Exactly! So why no arrest yet?'

There was silence for a moment then Torquil asked, 'What do you suggest I do, Superintendent Lumsden?'

'Get out and arrest a suspect! You have until tomorrow, then I'm coming over.'

There was a click then Torquil found himself staring at his phone.

'And thank you for your support, Superintendent Lumsden,' he said softly.

Torquil left Dunshiffin Castle and took the long snaking coastal route back towards Kyleshiffin. As he sped along the chicane of turns and bends leading to the lay-by overlooking St

Ninian's Cave, he momentarily wished he had his pipes in the pannier. His mind was swimming and his heart ached as if the blood flowing through it carried a mix of negative emotions. Anger, guilt, jealousy and an almost unbearable sorrow each seemed to rise in peaks, then plummet downwards to be replaced by a different emotion.

He gunned the Bullet as he changed gear to take the final bend, and as he did so he saw the large four-wheel drive parked in the lay-by. He braked and stopped beyond it. The vehicle was empty.

Then suddenly the air was broken by a woman's scream.

CHAPTER TEN

Torquil jumped down to the beach and sprinted across the shingle towards St Ninian's Cave, from whence the screaming continued to ring out.

Allegra McCall was on her knees inside the cave, her head in her hands as she stared upwards screaming like a banshee.

Torquil spotted the half empty bottle of clear spirits beside her.

Thank Christ! he thought with relief. For a moment he had thought someone was being —!

He pushed the thought from his mind and went over to the woman, his emotions turning from relief to a mixture of anger and jealousy. Anger that the woman was intruding in his cave, tainting its echo with her screeching. And jealous that she might have slept with Fiona.

He shook her gently and called her name. 'Miss McCall! Allegra!'

But she didn't even seem to register his presence. Her eyes seemed to be looking upwards, staring straight through the rock of St Ninian's Cave.

She's drunk and hysterical, he thought. His hand itched to strike her, to slap her across the face and jolt her back to reality, just as they did in the old movies. But his logical side told him that was the worst thing you could do to someone in such a state. Apart from that, the islanders' innate respect for womankind was like a solid barrier to such an act.

Damn you! Stop it! he yelled internally.

He picked up the bottle and sloshed it across her face. The effect was instantaneous. Shocked out of her screaming frenzy by the cold liquid she stared up at him for a moment before falling forward and dissolving into tears. Torquil let her lie there for a few moments then gently eased her up onto her knees.

'I … I'm sorry,' she eventually gasped, her eyes focusing hazily on him. 'You're him, aren't you? Fiona's latest conquest.'

Torquil scowled. 'Actually, I was an old conquest,' he replied bitterly. 'Or maybe a rediscovered one.'

'The bitch!' Allegra McCall cursed, before once more dissolving into uncontrollable sobbing and screaming.

Once again Torquil came close to slapping her. And once again his scruples kept him in check.

The Padre and Miss Melville had spent a couple of hours trying to placate disgruntled visitors who wanted nothing more than to leave the island. Explaining that the enforced quarantine was none of their doing didn't seem to help overmuch. Accordingly, they opted for the strategy of trying to provide further entertainment and diversion with lectures and workshops. Fortunately, several of their authors were more than willing to help, yet they knew that there would only be so many talks and lectures that people would be willing to listen to.

It had clouded over and started to drizzle as Lachlan headed for his Red Hunter. On his way he saw Professor Neil Ferguson striding along the harbour towards his cabin cruiser.

'Ahoy there, Professor!' he yelled, trotting along the quay with the intention of persuading the marine archaeologist to give another talk.

'Ah, Padre,' said the professor, turning quickly with a pile of magazines and assorted paperwork cradled in his arms. The inevitable happened and several magazines slipped from his grasp into a puddle. 'Damn! I was just going to put some of this stuff into the hold.'

Lachlan helped him gather up an assortment of soggy archaeological journals, magazines and programmes from the Gathering. The professor took them from him and swiftly climbed on board. 'Back in a moment,' he said, sliding open the cabin door and disappearing inside with the pile.

'I want to be ready to go as soon as I can,' he said a few moments later when he emerged again. 'I've had enough of West Uist for a while — and of police interviews!'

'Interviews?'

'Torquil had a lengthy chat with me this morning,' he explained. 'I'm afraid I'd been a bad boy and broken his embargo in my boat. I went out for an early morning swim. I didn't think it would matter.'

'He gave you a rough time, did he?'

'A bit.'

The Padre had mechanically filled his pipe from the yellow oilskin pouch that he seemed to keep several ounces of tobacco in at any time, and struck a light to the cracked briar bowl. 'Torquil is upset himself, Neil. Don't worry if he seemed a bit abrupt.'

Neil Ferguson sighed. 'Of course, I feel guilty about her.'

Lachlan blew out a thin stream of blue smoke. 'Guilty? Why ever should you feel guilty?'

'Because I don't think ...' He sighed again and bit his lip. 'I've explained it all to Torquil this morning,' he replied, after seeming to consider his words. 'I expect he'll tell you himself.'

The Padre shook his head. 'I doubt it. Torquil is the senior officer in a murder investigation. I'm not sure that he'll feel able to confide in his old Uncle Lachlan.' He shook his head then repeated, 'He's a bit fraught himself.'

Neil Ferguson nodded his head. 'It will be a relief when they catch the bastard. Then we can all go home.' He touched Lachlan's arm. 'Tell Torquil I'll...' He hesitated, then added, 'Tell him I'll catch up with him later.'

The Padre nodded and clenched his pipe between his teeth as he watched Neil Ferguson walk off in the direction of the Bonnie Prince Charlie. The professor was out of sight before he realized that he had not asked him about giving another lecture.

Sitting in Allegra McCall's Mitsubishi Shogun four-by-four after having phoned to Morag to send the Drummond twins over to bring her and her vehicle back to Kyleshiffin, Torquil hefted the empty bottle of vodka in his hand. Outside, the rain was lashing the windows.

'Why Allegra? Why the vodka?'

The publisher looked back at him with red-rimmed, bloodshot eyes. 'I haven't drunk all that. It was only half full.'

'But you've drunk too much to drive back to town. We may only be a wee island but we have the same laws as the mainland.'

'So breathalyse me!' she said indifferently.

'I should do, Allegra. But I want information from you and I want you to give it to me.'

She bent her head and trembled. Her hair was astray and she did not look remotely like the straight efficient bastion of respectability he had seen at Angus MacLeod's ceilidh and at the Gathering. She pulled back a sleeve to glance at an ornate expensive-looking Rolex watch that Torquil reckoned would be worth half a year's salary to him, then she took a deep breath and eyed him unsteadily. 'How do you know that I was planning to come back to Kyleshiffin at all?'

Torquil raised his eyebrows. That surprised him. 'What do you mean, Allegra?'

'That I was toying with the idea of killing myself.'

'Now why would you want to be doing that?'

For a moment her cheeks suffused with colour and he feared that she might be about to drift back into hysteria. But then the colour disappeared just as suddenly and her shoulders dropped. 'Because I don't know if I want to live any more. The person I loved is dead. Killed by some ...' she hesitated as she sought for a word, 'some monster's hand.'

'And how did you plan to do it?'

Allegra McCall shrugged matter-of-factly. 'I was going to drink enough not to care, then I was going to load my pockets with stones just like Virginia Woolf.'

Torquil eyed her dispassionately. 'Why kill yourself though? Do you feel guilty about Fiona's death?'

'Of course I bloody do.'

'Did you kill her, Allegra?'

Fires blazed in her eyes, then just as suddenly extinguished themselves. 'That's a stupid question! I loved her.'

Torquil maintained his dispassionate poker face. 'You were her publisher, so you mean that you loved her as an author?'

Answer that, he thought, but then he realized that he was pushing her, not because he wanted her to give him information, but because he wanted her to give him a reason to validate the emotion of hate that was rising within him just then. He had a demon on one shoulder and an angel on the other, each prompting him one way or the other. The demon wanted to bully her, to make her say things that stoked up his internal fires. The angel tried to calm him down, telling him to be calm, clinical and dispassionate. So far the demon had been winning, but now the angel was gaining the upperhand. Yet in that he felt his heart aching, for he had to negate his own feelings.

You have to be detached, the angel's voice said in his head. *For just now you have to think that Fiona meant nothing to you — that she was someone unfortunate enough to get herself killed — and you have to find out who killed her.*

Allegra McCall sniffed. 'I was her publisher, Inspector. I was the person who first lifted the stone and let her crawl out. I nurtured her, groomed her, I turned her writing into something the world wanted.' She took a deep breath. 'Yes, I loved her as a writer, but I ... I ... just loved her.'

Torquil refused to let her off the hook so easily. But now he was pursuing his questioning with a more professional motive. The effect was just as brutal. 'You mean in a sisterly manner?'

Allegra McCall looked sober for the first time. She shook her head. 'I loved her, Inspector. And she told me that she loved me too.' She smiled and her eyes went misty, as if she was looking into the past and seeing a happy memory rekindle itself. 'We were lovers for two years.'

Despite himself, Torquil was aware that the angel had suddenly dropped off his shoulder.

Roland Baxter and Angus MacLeod were drinking malt whisky in the laird's oak-panelled library-cum-billiard room. They had both felt unsettled ever since Inspector McKinnon had left, and their tempers were fraught. None of this helped their ball-potting and neither of them had much interest in the game of snooker they were playing.

'You were a fool to ever get involved with him!' said Roland Baxter. 'He could drop you right in it.'

Angus MacLeod picked up his smouldering cigar and puffed thoughtfully on it for a moment. 'Yes, it has all suddenly gotten out of hand. I thought having him here would have sorted everything out.'

'Well it hasn't, has it!' the minister snapped.

Angus MacLeod's voice was as silky as ever. 'But you know what they say, Roland — mud sticks.' He blew out a ribbon of Havana smoke. 'And of course, mud also splashes and gets on other people.'

'Are you threatening me, Angus?'

'Just warning you, old chap.'

Roland Baxter leaned over the table and lined up the black ball, then deftly potted it in the corner pocket. 'In that case we'd all better be careful hadn't we?'

Although Morag's report on her interview with Genevieve Cooper had already prepared Torquil, Allegra McCall's answer struck home like a dart dipped in the poisonous cup of jealousy.

But she has valuable information that might lead to the murderer, he chided himself. I have to get her to tell me. 'Was she faithful to you during that time?' he forced himself to ask.

'She was never faithful. She liked sex. Lots of it.'

Torquil swallowed a hard lump that suddenly appeared in his throat. 'And were you faithful to her?'

'She was all I ever wanted.'

'And so what happened?'

The publisher shook her head. 'I don't really know. She just suddenly became suspicious of me. She started to think that I was holding money back on her.'

'Were you?'

'Don't be ridiculous. I loved her and would have done anything for her. In fact, I was doing everything possible to help. Genevieve Cooper and I transformed her from a small island journalist into what she is —' She stopped, her face mirroring the pain that she felt. 'We turned her into the Queen of Scottish Crime. She was rich, well on her way to millionaire status.'

'Tell me about Angus MacLeod.'

Allegra stared blankly back at him. 'Tell you what?'

'Where did he fit in? Why did she dislike him so much?'

She darted her eyes heavenwards and whistled. 'Again, she had a crazy idea that he was making money out of her and not letting her reap her just rewards. You know that he runs a string of cut-price bookshops along the west of Scotland?'

'AME Books.'

'That's right. The thing is that he sells vast numbers of books. She was still getting her royalties, but she hated the idea of her books being sold for less than the recommended retail price.'

'That was all?'

'As far as I know.'

'Could she have been having an affair with him?'

'No way!'

'What about our esteemed minister for culture, Roland Baxter?'

Allegra hung her head. 'Yes,' she replied, almost in a whisper. 'She used him, I think. Used his power, used him for sex, and then bad-mouthed him.'

'How so?'

'She put it round that he was impotent. And she hinted that she was going to do an exposé of him in her next book. Just like she did in her last one, *Flesh Trimmers*.'

'Explain that to me.'

The publisher waved her hand in front of her eyes as a mini swarm of midges opportunistically flew through the slightly open window and began biting. She flicked the automatic window button and the glass slid up. 'Mind if I smoke?' she asked, reaching into the glove compartment and taking out a pack of low-tar cigarettes. Torquil declined one and waited as she lit up; feeling grateful for the smoke that so rapidly discouraged the midges.

'You do realize that Fiona more or less wrote to a formula. She used a *roman-à-clef* in each of her books.'

'My schoolboy French tells me that means a novel with a key? I don't understand,' he lied. He recalled Fiona's very own words at her lecture. 'What does that mean?'

'It means that some of the characters were thinly disguised allusions to real people. Effectively, she wrote a crime novel round real-life celebrities, generally doing a real hatchet job on them, showing all of their inadequacies or peccadilloes so that the reader would cheer when they were bumped off, as they invariably were. Take her last book, *Flesh Trimmers*, for example. The person she based it on, Dr Viroj Wattana, is suing her for defamation of character.'

Piper stroked his chin and nodded. 'Does he have a case?'

'He has a gripe. I guess he could legitimately claim to be upset, but for him to win his case he would have to prove that he was her subject for the cosmetic surgeon in the book. And he may have a job doing that.'

'What's so bad about being in the book?'

'She implies that he doesn't do straight cosmetic surgery, and that he is a butcher and a botcher.'

'Was he definitely the subject of the book?'

'Yes. And she used him because she wasn't happy with the boob job he did on her. She felt that he left one breast higher than the other.' She took a long puff on her cigarette and let out a plume of smoke. 'And she was right, there was a slight difference, but nothing to speak of. I thought her breasts were beautiful.'

'Could he have had a motive to kill her, do you think?'

She eyed him quizzically. 'Is that an ethical question, Inspector?'

'Murder is an unethical business, Allegra. I'll do whatever it takes to find Fiona Cullen's murderer.'

She nodded. 'He had no warm feelings for her and a court case would have been costly. It could have crippled his reputation if he lost.'

'And what about her new book?' he asked.

'I don't know much about it, except that it was to be called *Dead Writers Tell No Tales*.' She shivered involuntarily. 'God! That's eerily prophetic.'

'Was it going to have a *roman-à-clef*, too?'

'I expect so.'

'And if that is the case then whoever was going to be the main character could have been in for a hatchet job?'

Allegra nodded. 'The full Fiona Cullen treatment! Poor sod!'

And Torquil realized that there were indeed several people who could have found themselves inside the covers of her new book — a number of people with a possible motive for wanting her dead.

That made it ever more important to find that missing laptop.

Morag had been busy. After Torquil had left Kyleshiffin for Dunshiffin Castle she had been working at the duty desk dealing with the constant stream of tourists, idlers and busy-bodies. Then a young couple had come in. A young man with long lank hair and a girl with corn-blonde hair with ringlet extensions. They were both dressed in baggy jeans and tee-shirts; each had a rucksack on their back. Morag noticed the gleaming new wedding ring on her hand.

'*Latha math*,' Morag greeted. 'Good morning to you.'

The young woman smiled. 'I just love that Hebridean accent. Is the Gaelic easy to learn?'

Morag smiled. 'I cannot be saying very easily, I have been speaking it all my life. Now what can I be doing for you?'

The young man slid his rucksack off his back. 'We found something and wonder if it could be important.'

'Important in what way?' Morag queried.

'In your murder investigation,' the young woman replied. 'Show her, Simon.'

Morag watched as Simon opened his rucksack and pulled out a plastic bag. He laid it on the counter and unrolled the plastic. 'I didn't touch it,' he said with a half-smile. 'I know that you'll probably want to send it for forensic analysis.'

Morag leaned closer and saw a battered black plastic case. It was unmistakably a laptop computer that someone had tried very hard to smash to bits.

'Look,' said Simon triumphantly. 'You can see her nametag on it. Fiona Cullen.'

Morag nodded noncommittally. 'It could be useful,' she said, wrapping the bag round the laptop again. She raised the flap on the counter. 'Perhaps we'd better have a word through here.'

Genevieve Cooper was smoking even more heavily than usual. Ever since she had received the call on her mobile from *him*. Damn him! Why was *he* pushing her now of all times? Everything was going wrong. Desperate measures might be called for.

Ever methodical, Morag made notes as she interviewed the couple:

Mr and Mrs Simon Sturgess, newly married, enjoying honeymoon on West Uist. Came for the Gathering and Literary Festival. Both recently MA graduates in Scottish Studies from Dundee University. Met Ranald Buchanan in his shop two days ago, and purchased a copy of his book, Songs of the Selkie.

'And how have you spent your time on West Uist?'

'At the Gathering and just ambling around the island. We've bought loads of books, talked to lots of authors,' Simon volunteered. 'Carol wants to be a writer.'

Carol flushed. Morag noticed that she seemed to blush easily. 'One day, maybe,' Carol said. 'I'd like to be a crime writer, like Fiona Cullen. Or a poet, like Ranald Buchanan.'

Who are both dead, thought Morag. She jotted notes, smiled at Carol, then said to Simon: 'And where did you find this laptop?'

'In a bin in a carpark.'

'Which carpark?'

'The one behind the Bonnie Prince Charlie.'

Morag involuntarily took a deep breath.

'I'm surprised that the police hadn't found it. What with her having stayed there.'

Despite herself, Morag felt she was beginning to take a dislike to Simon Sturgess as he sat back looking smugly at her. 'And why were you looking in a bin in that carpark?' she asked.

He grinned. 'Carol wants to be a crime writer. Me, I want to be a detective. I thought it would be fun to investigate a real-life murder.'

'Interesting,' Morag mused as she continued to make notes.

171

Wallace Drummond drove Allegra's Shogun back to her hotel in Kyleshiffin while Douglas went on, under Torquil's instructions, to check that nothing had been touched at the crannog on Loch Hynish, and in particular that there were no ghoulish tourists.

Torquil rode back to the station on his Bullet, stopping at Miss Melville's main Festival book stall to buy a copy of Fiona Cullen's last book, *Flesh Trimmers*.

Morag had gone out some ten minutes previously, Ewan informed him when he arrived back at the station.

'She tried phoning you, but she said your phone wasn't picking up. She's pretty excited about something and said she'd explain when she came back.'

'Did she say where she was going?'

'To find the Padre, actually. Would you like a cup of tea?'

Torquil nodded and retreated to his office, while Ewan went to get him some stewed tea. Slumping into a chair he thumbed through the book, trying to get the gist of Fiona's *roman-à-clef*. He quickly found the first description of the main character and realized that it did not take too much imagination to identify the maverick surgeon in the novel as Dr Viroj Wattana. Scanning the first chapter, he gained some idea of the fictional surgeon's activities.

'*Mac an diabhoil* — son of the devil!' said Ewan coming in with a tray of tea and biscuits. 'An evil bugger that doctor is.'

Torquil glanced at the gory book cover, illustrating a masked, bespectacled surgeon with a blood-stained scalpel in his gloved hand. 'Have you read this book, Ewan?' he asked in surprise.

'Och, I've read all of Fiona's books,' Ewan returned, his eyes narrowing. 'Haven't you?'

Torquil shook his head. 'None of them. I'm not a fiction fan really.' And as he said it he felt a deep regret, almost mounting to guilt.

Ewan pouted, then shrugged his big shoulders. 'She's really good, Torquil. She can —' Then he knocked the side of his head with his knuckles. 'There I go again. Talking without thinking. I meant that she told a good story, kept you guessing.'

'Well, go on Ewan, tell me about this book. Why don't you like this surgeon?'

Ewan looked doubtful. 'But I don't want to spoil the story for you!'

Torquil picked up his mug. 'I need to know, Ewan. This could be important for the investigation. You will save me time by giving me the low-down.'

Ewan sat down and picked up his own mug of tea, dunking a ginger biscuit in it. 'It's all set in Thailand, you see. This surgeon is supposed to be a posh cosmetic surgeon, but he makes most of his money by doing cheap organ transplants and sex change operations for rich foreigners. Oh yes, and he also has a side-line in doing operations for the gangs. Instead of the gangsters shooting people's knee-caps off like they do in London and places, the gangsters arrange castrations. He does it for them at a special clinic.'

'I can see why you don't like the guy,' Torquil remarked.

Ewan grinned. 'But don't worry. Fiona made sure that he got his just deserts.'

Torquil nodded and sipped his tea. *And maybe that's why the real Dr Wattana had a grudge against Fiona.*

Putting down his mug he rose and went through to the incident room where he began adding notes to the whiteboard.

The Padre was enjoying a ploughman's lunch at the bar of the Bonnie Prince Charlie when Morag caught up with him. He beamed at her over the rim of a glass of Heather Ale. '*A Mhorag, slàinte mhór*,' he called across the crowded bar.

'And good health to you, too, Lachlan,' she returned, refusing his offer of a drink. 'I need a bit of information.' And she described the young couple she had just interviewed.

'Aye, I remember them clearly. Bookish types. They were at all of the lectures. She was quiet, but he seemed keen to ask questions of all of the lecturers. As my auld father would say, he'd speir a snail out of its shell.' He sipped some beer then wiped foam off his upper lip. 'Why the interest in them, Morag? They seemed an innocent enough couple.'

'You're probably right, Lachlan. But they found Fiona Cullen's laptop.'

The Padre raised his eyebrows. 'Does Torquil know?'

'Not yet. He hasn't picked up his phone for a while.'

'And why are you suspicious of them?'

Morag shook her head. 'I don't know if I am or not. It's just that she says she'd like to be a crime writer like Fiona or a poet like Ranald.'

'It is a commendable ambition to be a scribe.'

'And he says he wants to be a detective. To tell you the truth, there's something morbid about him that I don't like.'

The Padre popped a piece of oatcake with Orkney cheese into his mouth. 'And why did you come to me, Morag Driscoll, and not Bella Melville?'

Morag grinned at him. 'I'm still frightened of her.'

Lachlan began to chuckle, then elbowed her and dropped his voice. 'I don't blame you, lassie. She still scares me!'

Morag's mobile beeped and she accessed a text message, with a puzzling smile. 'Torquil's back,' she announced. 'And he said I have to find you and bring you with me!'

In the incident room they looked down at the smashed laptop. 'Will we be able to find out anything that was on it?' Torquil asked.

Morag shrugged. 'Who knows. The Forensic Department at Dundee University may be able to, but it just depends whether the hard drive has been destroyed or no. My cousin is a dab hand with computers. I can get him to look at it if you like.'

'Please do. It'll be quicker than getting it over to Dundee. Were there any CDs or floppies?'

'This was all they found. He seemed smug that he had found it and that we hadn't.'

Torquil leaned back in his chair with his hands linked behind his head. 'Uncle, I have a couple of things I need to ask you.'

Despite the no smoking signs the Padre had already filled and struck a light to his pipe. No one except Bella Melville ever had the nerve to ask him to desist from his pipesmoking. 'Ask away, laddie.'

'What do you know about a monkey's grave in the St Ninian's cemetery?'

The Padre puffed furiously for a few moments, as he often did when deep in thought. Then he tapped his teeth with the stem of his pipe and shook his head. 'There is no monkey buried in St Ninian's. Maybe you are thinking of the legend about the Boddam monkey. It's a fishing village near Peterhead, where it is said the villagers found a wrecked ship after a storm. There was no one on board except a monkey. Knowing that according to the law of salvage they had no right to it, because there was a living creature aboard, they hanged the monkey.' He tamped the tobacco down in his pipe with his thumb. 'That is the source of the monkey story, I think.'

'That's interesting,' Torquil said after a moment, 'because Professor Ferguson tried to tell me that he was researching a tale he'd been told about a wreck associated with Bonnie Prince Charlie. He said someone had told him about the ship's marmoset having made it to shore and then been hanged by English dragoons.'

'I think someone was pulling his leg.'

'Or he was pulling mine,' Torquil replied. 'I was asking him what he was doing in the cemetery the day Fiona and I met you on the golf course.'

'The day she hooked her ball and hit him? I tell you what, laddie — I'll go and have a look at all those graves and report back to you.'

'Before you go, Uncle,' Torquil said, picking up the copy of Fiona's book *Flesh Trimmers*, 'you had a chat with Dr Wattana at the Gathering, didn't you? Did you realize that Fiona may have used him in this book?'

The Padre nodded his head. 'Aye, I had a drink with him at the Gathering. But I didn't know about the book. Is that significant?'

'He may have had reason to be happy about Fiona's death.'

The Padre whistled softly. 'He's a nervous little fellow. I saw him earlier today, hovering about Neil Ferguson's boat. He seemed a bit preoccupied, a bit distressed in fact. Said he wanted to talk to you.' The clergyman looked pensive for a moment. 'As did Neil Ferguson. I saw him afterwards.'

Torquil looked over at Morag, who had remained silent as she took notes. 'I think it's time we brought Dr Wattana in for questioning. Send Ewan on this one, will you Morag?'

Ewan had telephoned Dunshiffin Castle to see whether Dr Wattana had returned, but had been greeted with a stiff negative from Jesmond, the Dunshiffin butler. Other enquiries at hotels, pubs and restaurants also drew blanks. So Ewan met up with the Drummond twins and together they set off to see whether the doctor could be found anywhere in Kyleshiffin.

The rain meanwhile had turned into that extra fine variety called Scotch mist, which typified the Western Isles. Halfway between drizzle and mist, it was wet enough to drench you slowly and thick enough to get lost in.

Parked up a side alley behind the lifeboat house, they found the AME car the Thai doctor had been seen driving about in that day.

Suddenly, the noise of a powerful boat revving up broke the silence that had hung over the harbour ever since the embargo had been passed on using boats. All three rushed down the alley in time to see a boat accelerating out of the harbour and disappearing in the mist in the direction of far-off South Uist.

'That's Professor Ferguson's boat, the *Unicorn*!' cried Ewan. 'Come on you two, let's get the *Seaspray*. I don't know what he thinks he's up to.'

'He's going to have a good start, Ewan. We'll be pushed to catch him,' said Wallace as the trio broke into a nm.

'I'll catch the bugger!' returned Ewan. *And this time I won't be letting Piper down*, he thought to himself.

PART THREE: THE SELKIE RETURNS

CHAPTER ELEVEN

The catamaran scudded across the waves, in and out of patches of sea spray and mist, gradually gaining on Professor Ferguson's *Unicorn*. They could hear the drone of its powerful engine as it raced on towards the slow-rising silhouette of South Uist. As they came within hailing distance Ewan picked up the microphone and flicked on the loudhailer.

'This is the Police. You are ordered to stop. Cut your engine immediately!'

But the boat raced on regardless.

'What are you thinking we should be doing, Ewan?' asked Wallace Drummond.

'Aye, how will we be stopping him if he doesn't want to be stopped?' Douglas queried.

Ewan rubbed his lantern jaw. A thorny problem it was proving, right enough. They could hardly ram the boat. Far less could they draw alongside at this speed on a choppy sea and try to board.

'We'll keep on his tail and take him when he stops,' Ewan said, decisively. 'At this rate, it will be in Lochboisdale. Then we'll arrest the bugger.'

Wallace wiped sea spray from his eyes. 'Why would the professor be making a run for it? He's nothing to hide, has he?'

Ewan bit his lip at the recollection of his encounter with the marine archaeology professor earlier in the day. 'Maybe he has, maybe he hasn't,' he mused, deciding that the twins did not need to know about his slip-up with the buoy. 'But running away from the island when all boats are banned from leaving is suspicious in my book. As is ignoring police orders to stop!'

The professor's boat started to veer towards starboard, describing a slow turn.

'He's making for Barra, I think,' Wallace suggested.

Then the boat started to chug, its engine spluttering.

'He's running out of fuel!' Ewan cried triumphantly. 'Now we'll have him, lads.'

And sure enough a few moments later the boat's engine gave a final splutter then went dead; with its speed cut, the boat began to flounder.

Ewan again flicked on the loudhailer. 'This is the police, Professor Ferguson. You are under arrest for leaving West Uist without permission. Please anchor and submit yourself.'

Wallace took the helm and manoeuvred the *Seaspray* close to the *Unicorn*. There was no sign of movement aboard.

'I am not liking this!' said Douglas Drummond. 'It's like the bloody *Marie Celeste*!'

And as the mist started to curl in around them, all three police officers felt shivers run up their spines.

'I don't like it either,' agreed Wallace.

Calum Steele was drinking a whisky and water at the bar of the Bonnie Prince Charlie and going over details with Mollie McFadden for his next news bulletin to Scottish TV.

'It's going to be the making of this pub, Mollie,' he said with a wink.

Mollie tapped him on the back of his hand. 'Like my auld mother said, Calum. You scratch my back and I'll scratch yours.' With this she ambled off to the other end of the bar to serve another customer.

Calum swallowed the last of his whisky and stood contemplating the bottom of his glass when someone coughed next to him. It was the cough of someone wanting to attract his attention. He turned to find a young couple standing smiling at him. He recognized them from somewhere, possibly from one of the lectures at the Festival, he thought.

'Can we buy you a drink, Mr Steele?' Carol Sturgess asked.

'We love your paper and the articles you've been writing about the Gathering,' enthused Simon. 'This murder is going to make you famous.'

Calum felt slightly nonplussed, an unusual feeling for him. 'Sure, it's a sad way to gain recognition,' he said at the same time nodding at the offer of a drink and tapping the bar to attract, Mollie's bar-helper's attention. 'What can I do for you both?' He had spotted their wedding rings: 'Mr and Mrs...?'

'Sturgess — Simon and Carol. We've been here for the Festival,' Carol volunteered, while her husband ordered a round. 'I want to get into the media like you, too.'

Calum accepted his whisky and topped it with an equal measure of water from the small Bonnie Prince Charlie jug on the bar. 'Well, journalism is a hard life. Rewarding though.' He raised his glass. '*Slàinte mhór!*'

'Could we have a word with you, Mr Steele?' Simon asked, pointing to a corner table under the portrait of the Young Pretender, Charles Edward Stuart. 'In private.'

'We have some information that you might want to use. We found something, but the police didn't seem too interested ...'

Calum eyed them with renewed interest. 'Come away with me, my friends. You'll not find Calum Steele uninterested.' He put a hand on Simon's arm and dropped his voice. 'But I'm afraid that the *West Uist Chronicle* doesn't have a very big cheque book.'

Carol squeezed his arm. 'Don't worry, Mr Steele. You won't need a cheque book.'

Having secured the becalmed *Unicorn* with grappling hooks, Ewan jumped on board. There was no one at the wheel, which had been locked off. He slid back the cabin door. The twins watched him disappear below, prepared to leap to his assistance should the occasion merit it. But after a few moments the big constable reappeared, his face pale and confused-looking.

'What the hell!' he exclaimed. 'There's no one here. There's a dreadful mess though. Bottles and pills and papers everywhere. I think the professor has flipped and done away with himself!'

'He must have jumped into the sea before now and we missed him in the mist,' Wallace deduced. 'We'd better get on the blower and get the coastguard helicopter out.'

'And we'd better get on back and see if he's still alive,' said Douglas. He thumped his head with his fist. 'Gah! We're a right trio of fools!'

'Oh boy!' Ewan exclaimed. 'I'd better phone Torquil first and see what he wants us to do.'

Torquil was not in a good humour when Ewan called him. 'Right, you'd better bring the boat in. Have you got enough fuel?'

'Aye, there's spare in the boat and we've got reserves in the catamaran in any case.'

'Good, you'd better get going then in case he's managing to stay afloat. But don't touch the cabin, Ewan, whatever you do. Use gloves and make minimum contact with the controls.'

'That's what I was planning, Inspector.'

'Do a good sweep and get the Drummonds to do the same. It'll not be easy but try and chart a course on the way back, as close as you can to the route you took there. And leave —'

'Leave a buoy! I know, sir. I've dropped one already.'

'On you go, Ewan.'

Damn it! Torquil thought a moment later as he put the phone down. If Neil Ferguson was a killer the last thing he wanted was for him to commit suicide. He had wanted to look Fiona's killer in the eye. Or even better, catch him alone somewhere!

The commotion from the outer office was an irritation he felt he could have done without. He tried to ignore it, sure that Morag would deal with it quickly. But in this he was not quite correct. A few moments later she tapped on his office door then popped her head round. 'Torquil,' she whispered. 'I think you'd better come through. Professor Ferguson is here and he's hopping mad because someone's stolen his boat.'

Torquil stared at her incredulously for a moment. Neil Ferguson was alive! So who the hell was on the boat? *Things are getting crazy,* he decided with a silent shake of the head.

And in fact, hopping mad was an understatement to describe the professor's state of agitation. He was furious. Almost irrational, Torquil thought. When questioned as to why he was so angry the marine archaeologist replied: 'My research papers, my work over the last year is on that boat.' He crossed his arms as if expecting this answer to explain everything. 'There's at least a quarter of a million words in that cabin.'

'Well, we'll see if it's all still there, Neil,' Torquil replied. 'Ewan is bringing your boat back now.'

Calum Steele woke up in the camp bed that he kept in his office for emergencies when he was either working late or when he felt too drunk to ride his Lambretta home. His tongue stuck to the roof of his mouth and a pounding headache made him groan as he fought to recall just how he had gotten there. The fact that it was still daylight confused him. Then he remembered getting into a drinking session with that young

183

hippy couple, Simon and Carol Sturgess. Not that they seemed to have drunk as much as him. Three pints of Heather Ale and about four whiskies; a mere bagatelle for him under ordinary circumstances. He hadn't really wanted to drink all that much, but he felt flattered by their attention. Especially by hers, sticking her tits at him that way. And then they had left the Bonnie Prince Charlie — he remembered waving to Mollie who had eyed him in that withering, disapproving way of hers — then they had come back to the *Chronicle* office. And then what?

The whirring of distant helicopter blades impinged upon his thoughts for a moment, which seemed strange, what with the ban that Torquil had placed on all travelling from the island. But then a sudden gut-wrenching spasm of utter nausea and dizziness overcame him and he leaned out of the camp bed and vomited on the floor. He felt himself slipping into a pool of unconsciousness.

The coastguard helicopter was joined by a helicopter from RAF Macrahanish which had been quickly scrambled after Morag had sent off the details of a person lost overboard. While they continued to sweep the area, the Drummond twins came in with the *Seaspray*, followed by Ewan in Professor Ferguson's *Unicorn*.

Torquil was waiting for them at the harbour.

'No sign of anyone?' he called out as he caught the rope to secure the *Seaspray*.

'Not a —' began Wallace Drummond, suddenly seeing Professor Neil Ferguson approach along the harbour. 'The professor is alive!' he gasped, as if he had just seen a ghost.

'Of course I'm alive,' Neil Ferguson snapped. 'Who stole my boat? Who have you got there?'

Ewan had cut the engine of the *Unicorn* and hopped ashore to tie up. 'We've no idea, Professor Ferguson,' he said with a half-smile. 'But we are glad to see you.' He shook his head and looked at Torquil. 'It's a mess in the cabin, though, Inspector.'

Torquil boarded. 'You haven't touched anything have you, Ewan?'

The big constable shook his head.

'I'll tell you if anything is missing,' said Neil Ferguson, climbing aboard after Torquil.

But Torquil stopped him with a hand on his arm. 'I'll go first, Neil. You can come, but I must insist that you don't touch anything. This is still an official investigation you know.' He looked back at Ewan, then continued, 'Give Morag a bell. I want her down here pronto with her camera and fingerprint kit.'

Slipping on a pair of rubber gloves from his pocket he slid the cabin door open and went down the steps with Neil Ferguson close behind.

'Bloody hell!' exclaimed the professor. 'All my papers have been scattered. And some bastard has drunk a bottle of my best whisky.'

'Was it a full bottle, Neil?'

The professor nodded.

'And what about this empty bottle of paracetamol?'

'That wasn't mine.'

Torquil knelt down to look at another empty bottle that was lying on its side on the floor. 'And this wasn't yours either,' he said. 'This bottle was made out to Dr Viroj Wattana. Nitrazepam — sleeping tablets.'

'Viroj!' the marine archaeologist exclaimed. 'You think Dr Wattana was here?'

Torquil straightened up and shrugged. 'I'm not saying anything, Neil. But an empty bottle of tablets made out to Dr Wattana is lying on the floor of your boat. I'd say it looks suspicious, wouldn't you?'

'Do you — do you mean he's killed himself?'

'That is a possibility,' Torquil replied, looking round. Then, having sighted a loose paper on the floor underneath the cabin table, he exclaimed, 'Hello, what have we here?' He bent and picked up the single sheaf of paper by its corner and laid it flat in the middle of the table. In a shaky hand was written the name 'Fiona' followed by a pattern.

Neil Ferguson looked over his shoulder and whistled softly.

'Do you know what that means?' Torquil asked.

'It's Thai. It says "Fiona", then "I am sorry".' He looked at Piper. 'Does that mean ...'

A muscle twitched in Torquil's jaw. 'Does it mean that we've found Fiona Cullen's murderer?' He bit his lip, then nodded. 'It could be a confession before he killed himself. I'm afraid it looks like it.'

'I can't believe that. Not Viroj —'

But he did not finish. He flinched as Torquil McKinnon suddenly leaned forward and pounded the table with his fist.

'*Mac an diobhoil!*' Torquil cursed. 'I wanted to take him alive!'

By 7 p.m. Morag had photographed the cabin of the *Unicorn* and dusted it for fingerprints. In a corner of the cabin, underneath a pile of scattered journals and papers, she found a pair of wire-rimmed spectacles.

'Those are almost certainly Dr Wattana's,' said Torquil as he, Morag, Ewan and the Drummond twins sat round the table in the incident room after tea that evening. Outside, mist swirled against the window panes.

The helicopter teams had been in contact, informing Morag that they were going to do one further sweep before returning to their respective bases. They had found nothing whatsoever and the sea squall and mist were making the search hazardous.

While Morag had talked to the helicopter crews Torquil had been on the telephone to report on the finding of the boat to Superintendent Kenneth Lumsden, who was still staying at his son-in-law's house in Benbecula.

'Well, I think it sounds clear that the chap has done himself in,' the superintendent had barked down the phone. 'Do you feel confident about it?'

'I'd like to go over things with my team, sir.'

'Do so, then ring me, then we can let folk off the island and back to civilization.'

As usual Torquil had been left staring at the receiver as the superintendent disconnected without courtesy or warning.

Well, let's deliberate, he thought as he looked at the wireframed spectacles, one lens of which was cracked, presumably after the doctor had thrown them down in a semi-drunken, drug-fuelled haze, or when they had been skittering around the floor during the boat chase.

'Did you go over the ship's inventory with the professor?' he asked.

Morag nodded. 'There was a spare anchor. That's gone.'

'I'm betting that he used that to weight himself down,' Douglas Drummond volunteered.

His brother nodded sombrely. 'Aye, to take him down to Davy Jones's Locker.' He made a sign of the cross over his heart. 'Poor man!'

'If he was a murderer then he was not a poor man,' Torquil rebuked sharply, standing up and going over to the whiteboard.

He picked up the marker and wrote the name 'Viroj Wattana'. Under it he made several notes:

Doctor/Thailand/cosmetic surgeon

Book character/ Legal action

Spectacles

'Fiona, I am sorry' (written in Thai)

Boat/missing spare anchor

Whisky/paracetamol/Nitrazepam (sleeping tablets)

Then he drew lines between Wattana's name and that of Professor Neil Ferguson and Fiona Cullen. He tapped the board with the end of the marker. 'What do we make of it then? Anybody?'

'He did it!' blurted out Douglas Drummond. 'It is as plain as day.'

'I agree with my brother,' said Wallace. 'He was cross about Fiona writing her book about him.'

Ewan nodded. 'That's right, Piper. I told you about it, remember?'

'Well,' Wallace went on. 'While we were all at the Gathering he persuaded her to meet him at the crannog on Loch Hynish, then he — did her in!' He saw his inspector's sudden pained expression and frowned. 'Sorry Torquil, I mean that he murdered her.'

His brother took over, as if they were thinking along the same train of thought. 'But with all this police investigation he panicked. Decided to do away with himself and so he stole Neil Ferguson's boat and headed out to sea.'

Ewan nodded again. 'I think that makes sense. And while he was out there he drank a bottle of whisky for courage and swigged a couple of bottles of pills, then threw himself overboard.'

'And what about the note?' Torquil prompted.

'That confirms it,' Douglas said eagerly. 'It stands to reason he'd say it in his own language.'

Torquil looked at his sergeant, Morag Driscoll, who had remained silent with her lips pursed pensively. 'What do you think, Morag?'

Morag clicked her tongue. 'It seems logical. But there are still a lot of loose ends. That and —'

'Go on.'

'Well, he had a motive, perhaps. Means — who knows? Anyone could have stolen Calum's Lambretta. As for opportunity — yes he had that, too — but so did a lot of people. His note says sorry, but it doesn't say what for.'

'And we don't have his body either, do we?' Torquil added. 'There weren't any oxygen cylinders missing were there?'

Morag shook her head. 'No, I specifically went over the diving equipment. Everything is just where it should be.'

Again Torquil tapped the whiteboard. 'Like you, I'm not entirely happy. And it's not just the loose ends, either. It's the connections as well. We've got a board here that's beginning to look like a spider's web. Two webs even. Too many connections.'

'I still think he did it, Torquil,' said Douglas.

Torquil sighed. 'Certainly, at the moment Dr Wattana is our chief suspect. And the very fact that we can't find him makes the theory that he may have taken his own life seem very likely. And if that is so, it strengthens the case against him.'

Despite her great sorrow, Bella Melville had enjoyed her day, what with organizing talks, and dashing here and there between showers in her best schoolmarm manner trying to keep tempers calm. It had been tough, challenging and draining all at once. Quite like the old days, she reflected, when she had striven to keep the Kyleshiffin School running with the minimum of support from the Highland and Island Education Department.

The news on the street about the professor's boat and the fact that the helicopters had been dashing back and forth in the lashing rain and the mist had led to a mass of rumours.

He's struck again!

The murderer has been caught!

The bastard committed suicide.

Like the sensible Hebridean woman that she was, Bella Melville had squashed each rumour that she came across with the irrefutable logic that you could not come to a proper conclusion without knowing the facts. When Sergeant Morag Driscoll telephoned her with the news that the embargo on travel had been lifted and that a special Macbeth ferry was on its way from Lochboisdale, she was delighted. And curious!

'And tell me why it has been lifted? Who has been found?'

Morag was silent for a moment. 'No one has been found, Miss Melville.'

'Now remember what I used to tell you about being obtuse, Morag. Now just tell me —'

'I suggest that you listen to the news,' Morag blurted out. 'I'm not at liberty to divulge anything else.' And with a hasty goodbye, she had rung off.

Torquil nodded at Morag as she replaced the phone. 'I think we can leave it to Bella Melville to alert the whole of West Uist,' he said with a half-grin. 'I bet she's loving being in charge again.'

'Does the superintendent feel comfortable about letting everyone go now?' Morag asked.

Torquil nodded. 'He just wanted a quick answer so that we can get the island back to normal. He thinks it is an open and shut case.'

'But you don't, do you?'

'I'm uneasy, Morag,' he admitted. Then with a sigh he added, 'Still, I guess it's time that we got Calum over here to give him the news.'

Torquil himself called at the *Chronicle* office after being unable to get hold of the newspaperman by telephone, either landline or mobile. Letting himself in by the back door (knowing from experience the loose brick behind which Calum kept his spare key) he ascended the stairs to find the journalist in his underpants, huddled over his toilet.

'A bit early for you, isn't it, Calum,' he said, upon smelling the alcohol-vomit odour that emanated from the bowl.

'That bloody hippy couple spiked my drinks!' Calum moaned between retches. 'And they've robbed me!'

Torquil patted Calum on the back and poured him a glass of water from the tap. 'Here, drink this, brush your teeth, then tell me what happened. If you've been robbed, we'll get the culprits. And maybe you'll want to know the news!'

Upon hearing the last words Calum took a deep breath then steeled himself manfully. 'What news?' he asked, pushing himself to his feet and reaching for the water.

'Teeth first!' Torquil insisted. 'I'll make tea while you get ready.'

And with a greasy-looking patched dressing gown about his shoulders and a mug of sweet tea clutched in his hands, his teeth chattering and his face alabaster pale, Calum Steele reported his theft as Torquil insisted.

'They've taken all my notebooks. And my camera and photographs. Everything to do with the case.'

'That's bizarre.'

Calum curled his lip contemptuously. 'They're a bizarre couple right enough.' He cringed. 'They could have done anything while I was out cold. They could have killed me!'

'We'll bring them in for questioning, Calum,' Torquil soothed. 'And if they have any of your things we'll charge them.' He took a sip of tea, then gave the local newsman an update on the boat chase and the disappearance of Dr Wattana.

'He was a weird wee man,' said Calum, jotting it all down on a scrap of paper, his hands visibly shaking. 'He was talking to the Padre earlier today, by Neil Ferguson's boat as it happened, but he skedaddled as soon as he saw me coming to chat with him.'

'Did he indeed?' mused Torquil.

The late Scottish TV newscast that evening was given by a glamorous red-headed reporter standing on the quay at Oban in front of a newly arrived Macbeth ferry. It was a synopsis of the report that Calum had rang through.

'The murder enquiry on the Island of West Uist, into the death of the celebrated crime writer Fiona Cullen, has taken a huge leap forward. The West Uist Constabulary, headed by Inspector Torquil McKinnon, had been anxious to interview a Doctor Viroj Wattana, a cosmetic surgeon from Thailand, who is believed to have stolen a motor launch and headed off in the direction of Bara. When the boat was finally boarded by police officers, it appears that Doctor Wattana had vanished overboard.

'A coastguard helicopter was joined by a rescue helicopter from RAF Macrahanish, but no body was found. The search was discontinued due to adverse weather conditions, but will continue tomorrow morning.

'Happily, movement to and from the Island of West Uist is now returning to normal service.'

The camera shot then zoomed in on the ferry, just as a great hoot resounded from the boat.

Allegra McCall sat on the edge of her bed in her hotel bedroom and flicked the remote control to change channel. On the table in front of her was a half empty bottle of vodka, which she had purchased from the hotel bar upon her return to Kyleshiffin. She raised the glass.

'Fiona! Why? Why?'

Her head slumped forward and she dissolved into tears, unaware of the soft footsteps behind her.

There was a dull thud and a moment later she slithered to the floor, a patch of blood flowing from a wound at the back of her head.

CHAPTER TWELVE

The Padre had bathed and was comfortably settled in his study, dressed in an ancient maroon dressing gown, his pipe billowing plumes of smoke as he worked on the eulogies for Ranald Buchanan and Fiona Cullen, when Torquil arrived home.

'Are you OK, laddie?'

Torquil nodded, although he was unsure how he actually felt. 'Did you hear about Dr Wattana on the news?'

'Aye. Do you think he did murder Fiona?'

Torquil sighed. 'It certainly looks like it. Then his nerves or his conscience got the better of him and he ended it all.'

The Padre blew smoke ceilingwards and laid his pipe down in a large brass ashtray. 'He seemed a nervous, vulnerable little chap to me.'

'Calum Steele said something similar earlier. He also mentioned that he saw him talking to you on the harbour, but that he scuttled away when Calum approached.'

The Padre had crossed to a side table and picked up a decanter of malt. 'That's right. It was near Neil Ferguson's boat, I told you, remember?'

He poured two good drams, topped them up with water and handed one to his nephew, then perched on the corner of his desk. 'He was trying to look into the boat. He said he was looking for Neil Ferguson.' He gave a rueful smile. 'He made a wee jibe about me being the "drinking priest". I asked if he was supposed to be going diving with Neil and Angus MacLeod, and he went all sad and said everything was different after Fiona's "regrettable" murder. It seemed a strange word to use about a murder, but I don't suppose there can be an appropriate one. And he did dash off. I just assumed it was because he didn't want to get pinned down by our local newshound.'

Torquil sank into the big armchair and sipped his whisky. 'Maybe so. But talking of Neil Ferguson, did you check out those graves?'

Lachlan put down his drink and picked up his pipe. 'As a matter of fact, I did,' he said, tapping the pipe out and reaching for his oilskin tobacco pouch. 'There was no monkey grave, of course. But there was a grave there that I had just about forgotten all about. It was Flora Buchanan's. Strange that I didn't remember it being there.'

'Wasn't she Ranald Buchanan's daughter?'

'Aye. She was a chronic schizophrenic, ever since her son was born. You may recall that he was drowned out beyond the Machair Skerry. Dr Crompton McLelland, Ralph's father, thought that some trauma had unhinged her mind. She had to be committed to a mental hospital on the mainland, and there she lived and died. She was buried here ten years ago.' He struck a light to his pipe. 'I remember that Ranald himself had engraved her headstone, but I had never noticed until now the inscription he had written underneath her name.'

'What did it say?'

'He wrote "*Finally safe from the Selkie*".'

'And why is that significant?'

The Padre puffed on his pipe. 'Don't you see, Ranald had a thing about the Selkie. It was a common theme in a lot of his poetry. A cynic might say that he capitalized on it.'

Torquil nodded slowly. It was becoming clear. Part of Ranald Buchanan's success seemed to depend upon the fact that his grandson had drowned, and that the island folk had been willing to accept the rumour that a Selkie, a seal man, had impregnated Ranald's daughter and then had come back years later to claim the boy as his own and carry him off to his home beneath the sea. The superstition about drowning was somehow embedded in the islander psyche.

'Who was the father?'

The Padre shrugged. 'I honestly have no idea, Torquil. Ranald would never talk about it, except to affirm his belief that it had been a Selkie.'

'What was the child's name? And how old was he when he drowned?'

Lachlan screwed his eyes up as he delved into his memory. 'Archie. Young Archie and he was four. Ranald had brought him up himself after Flora was committed.'

'Four years old?' Torquil gasped. 'How the hell could a four-year-old go out in a boat all on his own? That's impossible, Lachlan.'

The Padre nodded. 'Nowadays it would be considered so. But it was just assumed that the youngster had somehow gotten into the rowing boat at Ranald's jetty and managed to untie the mooring.' He shrugged. 'When Ranald discovered the boat had gone, a search was started. The lifeboat went out and found the boat about a mile out from the Machair Skerry. It would have drifted that far. Young Archie's scarf was hanging over the side, but the lad had gone.'

'But that's negligence. Why was there no action against Ranald?'

'Things were different then. Ranald seemed to be broken. I suspect it was felt that he'd been through enough. It was just considered an unfortunate accident. West Uist folk have always lived with the sea, as you know yourself.'

Torquil sipped his whisky. Selkie legend or not, he thought, it was strange that Neil Ferguson should be looking in St

Ninian's cemetery for a grave. Clearly it wasn't for the grave of a monkey as he had told him. But why would he have been looking for Flora Buchanan's grave? And did this somehow indicate a link between the deaths of Ranald Buchanan and Fiona?

Roland Baxter and Angus MacLeod had dined and were sitting in the library of Dunshiffin Castle drinking brandy and smoking cigars.

'I never drought Viroj would do anything stupid like that,' said the Scottish Minister for Culture.

'Suicide, you mean?'

'Actually, I meant murder. He was a cold-blooded fish as we both know, and I think he would have been perfectly capable of taking a life, but careful planning and clinical execution would have been Wattana's way. A crime of passion doesn't seem his style.'

Angus MacLeod idly swirled his brandy. 'But he hated her all right,' he said reflectively. Then continued, 'Do you think he's done us a favour?'

Roland Baxter's eyes shot up. 'Only if he hasn't left any records.'

The laird shivered involuntarily. 'If he has, we're buggered!'

'You mean you are, Angus.'

A cold, humourless smile flickered across Angus MacLeod's face. 'No Roland, I meant what I said. *We* would be buggered.'

Ever the practised politician, Roland Baxter smiled genially as he savoured his brandy. 'In that case we'd better see that there are no silly pieces of paper left lying around. I assume that you can check on that?'

'I suppose I'll have to,' the laird snapped. 'But what about Ferguson?'

'What about him?'

'Could he ...?'

The Scottish Minister for Culture pursed his lips and blew out a perfect smoke ring. 'I think that I can put the right type of pressure on him.'

Its head rose majestically out of the water and stared at him with large brown eyes. He stood transfixed, hypnotized even, as it swam towards the shore. Then once it reached the shallows it shuffled its great body onto the shingle beach, never once taking its eyes off him.

And then it transformed itself, its lower half tapering, its back flippers elongating, changing into legs. It rose, and began walking towards him.

The Selkie! He wanted to scream, to run away, yet he could not move. In desperation he held out the Silver Quaich.

But it ignored him. It walked past him, towards the waiting motorbike. It mounted it, kicked the engine into action and accelerated away.

He must stop it! His legs seemed unwilling to move, as if they were anchored in mud. But gradually they obeyed his will until he was running, chasing after it with all his might. He hated it. He would kill it. He ran faster and faster until he lost his balance and began to fall, down the edge of the cliff.

Torquil landed with a thud in a tangle of bedclothes, his mind swirling, his skin damp with perspiration and his heart pounding. It was pitch-dark, the luminous hands on his bedside clock showing that it was almost five o'clock.

So the Selkie returned after all, he mused. He lay pondering the events of the last few days for another half hour then flung himself out of bed and showered.

By the time the Padre shuffled downstairs at six o'clock, his usual time to rise, there was a delicious aroma of fried herrings emanating from the kitchen.

'Come in Uncle,' Torquil greeted him with a grin as he dished a pair of oatmeal-coated herrings from a skillet onto a couple of warming plates. 'I have to be off in a few minutes.'

'You seem in brighter spirits than I've seen you for ages, laddie.'

Torquil had already started to work on his herring. 'I had a dream last night.'

'I heard a bump. I thought you'd had a nightmare.'

'A revelation, actually. I dreamed that a Selkie came out of the water for me.'

The Padre stopped with a forkful of fish halfway to his mouth. 'It must have been our chat last night about Ranald Buchanan.'

Torquil took a sip of tea. 'Maybe. But in any case it showed me something that's been puzzling me since the murder. How did the murderer get from Loch Hynish to the Bonnie Prince Charlie Tavern on Fiona's motorbike without anyone spotting him?'

'I thought Mollie McFadden saw him — or her? She thought it was Fiona, didn't she?'

'Exactly. And so whoever it was must have been in leathers — right?'

'Aye. You have Mollie's testimony there.'

Torquil shook his head. 'But I don't think they were wearing leathers. They certainly weren't Fiona's. She was wearing hers.' He shuddered, then shook his head as if to clear it of the image of Fiona Cullen's body with her leathers half pulled off. 'Lachlan, I think the murderer was wearing a wetsuit.'

The Padre thumped his fist on the table. 'And so —'

Torquil nodded. 'And so it would explain how he was on the crannog waiting for her. He'd swum out. And it explains why the wee ferry was still tied up at the crannog. Fiona had used it to row out to the crannog, but he swam back. Then he simply pulled on her crash helmet and rode back to the Bonnie Prince Charlie on her Fireblade.'

Lachlan poured himself a cup of tea. 'It could have been Wattana, right enough. He was a slight chappie, and in a wetsuit from behind he could easily have fooled Mollie.'

Torquil polished off the rest of his herring and took a mouthful of tea. 'Now I need to head off to the station. I've got to sort a few things out. Will you be staying here?'

The Padre nodded. 'I'll be chained to my desk all morning. I have the funeral service and a suitable sermon to prepare, then I have a pile of unanswered correspondence to attend to, thanks to the Gathering and Festival. Why, do you need me to do anything?'

'Just let me know if a fax comes through from Thailand. I've broadened the net a little and I'm waiting for some information to come back.'

Once Torquil had gone the Padre finished his herring, drank another cup of tea and then went across the road to his Kirk. And there he knelt before the altar and muttered prayers for the departed spirits of Ranald and Fiona, and for his dearest nephew and ward, Torquil.

The whiteboard in the incident room now looked like a complex spider's web, for Torquil had added several other connecting lines linking the two webs together. The pinboards were covered with a mass of papers and photographs, and the desk was laden with piles of notes and the contents of Neil Ferguson's cruiser cabin. It was this heap that Torquil was now meticulously working through. There was something there, he knew. The problem was that he was not entirely sure how to find it.

By his side was a blown-up photograph of the note that Wattana had left.

He leafed through a couple of scientific papers that the professor of marine archaeology had obviously been working on. Then he looked at a sheaf of letters from various institutions. They all seemed to be from his opposite numbers at the universities of Oxford, Massachusetts and Chulalongkom.

'What's this?' he said, sitting upright to read a handwritten letter on letter-headed notepaper from Chulalongkorn University in Bangkok. Only he could not read a word, for it was written in Thai.

So you really are fluent in Thai, aren't you Professor Ferguson? he mentally asked, glancing again at the photograph by his side.

While he did so he reached across the desk for his cup of coffee and inadvertently knocked over another pile of papers which went crashing to the floor. With a shrug he bent to pick them up, his eye being drawn to a programme for the Gathering. A bookmark with Fiona's smiling face had fallen out and startled him. Then he saw that the programme was open at the listing of the main events, and there were a few notes written in the margin in ballpoint pen.

Dhuine, Dhuine! he breathed in amazement. *This is my writing! And this is the programme that I gave Fiona myself! What the hell is it doing in Neil Ferguson's papers?*

Sergeant Morag Driscoll had been up half the night nursing a semi-delirious eight-year-old daughter with tonsillitis. She had been on the verge of calling Dr McLelland out when the temperature finally broke at six o'clock and she had stumbled back to bed, to doze fitfully until her official waking-up time at seven. The bedside telephone rudely intruded upon her slumbers five minutes before then and she struggled up onto one elbow to answer it.

'Morag, I've found something!' Torquil's voice rapped out. 'Neil Ferguson had Fiona's programme among his things.'

Morag swung her legs out of bed. 'I'm sorry Torquil, but what programme?' She tried to force her mind to focus.

'He had her programme of the Gathering events,' Torquil explained. 'And that means that it looks as if he swapped programmes with her at the Gathering. I had made some notes in a programme explaining about the times I was going to play in the piping competition. I'm thinking that he must have swapped programmes and maybe inside his was a message to meet him at the crannog on Loch Hynish.'

'I see!' gasped Morag. 'So what do we do now, boss?'

There was a pause for a moment, then Torquil spoke. 'It's still all a bit flimsy, but there are a few things that Neil Ferguson needs to explain. I'm going to go and see him now.'

'Are you arresting him?'

'There's nothing concrete yet, so I'll have to play it by ear. I'll have gone by the time you get in.'

'Be careful, Torquil. Are you sure you don't want Ewan to come with you?'

'You look after Ewan, Morag,' he replied sardonically, then hung up, leaving Morag looking at the buzzing receiver in her hand.

Calum Steele had managed to control his thundering headache and successive waves of nausea for long enough to produce another 'special edition' of the *Chronicle*. Having then sent off the handful of teenagers who delivered it to the outlets across the island he settled down to watch the early morning Scottish TV news with a mug of sweet tea and a couple of rounds of jam and bread.

He smiled at the sight of Kirstie Macroon, the pretty redheaded newsreader with pert breasts that he lusted after and fantasized about. She was sitting in front of a backdrop of Kyleshiffin harbour as she read the latest bulletin:

The search for the body of Dr Viroj Wattana continued at first light this morning, but without success. The surgeon from Thailand is wanted for questioning by the island police who have been investigating the murder of Fiona Cullen, the famous crime writer, whose body was discovered on a crannog on Loch Hynish.

The picture behind her changed to one of the crannog, with an inset photograph of a smiling Fiona Cullen in some exotic Oriental setting.

Mr Simon Sturgess and his wife have been on honeymoon on West Uist these last few days and have been keeping a close watch on the investigations.

A picture of the young couple who had befriended Calum and who were responsible for his hangover flashed onto the screen.

Mr Sturgess actually found a smashed laptop computer believed to belong to Fiona Cullen. His literary contacts on the island, including Calum Steele, the local newspaper editor who has until now been supplying us with news bulletins, have confirmed his belief that the laptop could well contain information that could lead to the murderer.

Calum stared at the screen. 'You wee bastard! What drivel is this? Me! One of your literary contacts!'

Mr Sturgess was also able to inform us that his friend, Calum Steele, had told him that Torquil McKinnon, the inspector in charge of the case, known locally as Piper McKinnon, had a close personal relationship with the deceased, Fiona Cullen.

Calum smacked the side of his head. 'You bloody idiot! What did you tell them?'

Mr Sturgess, who has recently begun work as a private investigator, and his wife Carol, a writer, tell us that this information was well known on the island, and that despite his conflict of interests, Inspector McKinnon has continued to lead the inquiry.

Calum reached for his mobile telephone. *The snakes! What would Torquil say about all this?*

But Kirstie Macroon had not finished her report.

Mr Sturgess is considering reporting this to HM Inspectorate of Constabulary in Scotland, since he feels that the police inquiry on the island has been heavy-handed, citing the fact that several hundred people were effectively detained on the island against their will by Inspector McKinnon. He also believes it was —

But Calum had heard enough. He pressed the hold button on the control and typed in the Kyleshiffin police station number on his mobile phone. *Torquil, I am sorry*, he thought. *I am so sorry! I'm just a jealous wee idiot!*

Superintendent Kenneth Lumsden's gout had kept him awake half the night and the early morning news had not helped him one iota. He had listened in amazement and horror. Finally, banging his cup down and breaking the saucer, much to his wife's consternation, his daughter's embarrassment and his son-in-law's increasing irritation, he rose from the breakfast table and reached for the telephone.

'What the hell is McKinnon playing at? Why didn't he tell me that about being in a relationship with the Cullen woman? By the time I finish with him he'll be pounding a beat in Ullapool!'

Neil Ferguson hated the immediacy of the mobile telephone with its texting facility. It just leant itself as an instrument of blackmail. And that was something he was beginning to feel, for he was conscious that he was being manipulated. So far there had been no mention of money, merely threats of exposure and scandal. A man in his position could not afford either.

Who the fuck was it? And what did the evil fuck actually want of him? Hadn't enough happened? And just what did the last text message mean? Should he ignore it? Go to the police, maybe?

He poured milk into his coffee and added a large measure of whisky. He felt he needed the alcohol, yet by mixing it with coffee he didn't feel that he was really drinking. Psychologically he still felt in control.

'Baxter can screw himself!' he muttered to himself. Just where did he think he was coming from, warning him about the funding for his chair. Bloody politicians! Always careful to hide their dirty secrets, never talking in plain English but using hyperbole and veiled threats.

He swigged his Gaelic coffee and started to feel better as it hit his stomach. He stood and looked out of the window of his room in the Commercial Hotel. It was a gloomy morning with poor visibility due to the fine drizzle or Scotch mist that had enshrouded the island overnight.

What does he want now? he thought as the mist swirled and he saw P McKinnon park his Royal Enfield Bullet opposite the hotel, then stride purposively towards the front door.

He looked again at the last text message, then pocketed the phone. There was time. The bastard said he'd text the hour and the place.

Annie Campbell, the Masonic Arms' early morning room-maid knocked on the door of room seven, fully expecting the occupant to be up and about as usual. Every morning for the past few days she had enjoyed a chat with Allegra McCall when she called to change the towels and make up the room.

A nice lady, Annie thought. A bit like herself, disciplined. An early starter.

The sound of the television meant that she was in there, of course. But why wasn't she answering? She couldn't still be in the shower, could she? She was usually up and working away on something by now.

Annie was a naturally curious girl. She reckoned that she would make a pretty good spy or one of those investigative journalists — if only she could write, she chided herself. She knelt down and squinted through the keyhole.

'Oh my God!' she gasped. *She's lying on the floor!*

She stood up and tapped again on the door.

No answer. She tapped again — louder this time.

But still no answer.

Maybe the poor thing was ill? She pulled out her master key and opened the door.

Her scream woke several of the guests and brought George MacFarlane, the manager, springing up the stairs. He found Annie rooted at the entrance, her shaking hand pointing to the body lying face down on the floor, a pool of blood surrounding her head.

Neil Ferguson opened the door in answer to Torquil's knock.

'Morning Neil,' Torquil said. 'I need to have a chat.'

'An official one? I thought you had this mess sorted out after Wattana's suicide.' He stood back and let Torquil enter.

'We don't know that he did commit suicide, Neil. We have no body.'

'But he took my boat out to sea! The whisky, the pills and the note.'

'Indicative, but not conclusive. But I want to ask you some questions on another matter. For starters, why did you tell me that cock and bull story about a monkey's grave?'

The professor shrugged. 'I wasn't aware that it wasn't true. I was following up on a curious tale, that's all.'

'Are you sure that you weren't looking for an actual grave? The grave of Flora Buchanan, for example.'

Two small pink patches appeared on Neil Ferguson's cheeks.
That's hit home all right, Torquil thought.

'Flora Buchanan is buried there? Ranald's daughter?'

'Did you know her?'

'We were — close, once upon a time. A long time ago, when I first came to West Uist to do research on the crannogs for my doctoral thesis. I understand that she died?'

Torquil nodded. 'She was schizophrenic, Neil. She died in a mental hospital.'

'I'm sorry to hear that, but in answer to your question — no, I wasn't looking for her grave.'

'Well would you have any idea why Ranald had the words "*Finally safe from the Selkie*" carved on her headstone?'

Torquil fancied that the professor's brow had suddenly developed a patina of perspiration.

'As far as I know the Selkie is just an old myth. I'm a scientist, not a mythologist.'

'But for some reason Ranald Buchanan was obsessed with the whole Selkie story,' Torquil went on. 'He wrote reams of poems about it. A seal man who seduces young women and impregnates them before returning to the sea. And then he comes back years later to reclaim his child and carry it off beneath the water.'

'What are you getting at, Inspector?'

Torquil was about to reply when his mobile went off. He answered it, his face hardening as he listened. 'I'll be there in five minutes, Morag. Keep everyone away.'

'Trouble?' Professor Ferguson asked.

'Another murder!' Torquil replied. He made for the door. 'Look Neil, don't leave the island yet. We need to finish this talk later.'

'Who has been murdered?'

'I can't say yet. But we'll talk later, OK.'

When Torquil had gone Neil Ferguson opened a drawer and poured more whisky into his coffee cup. 'Maybe we'll talk, Piper. And maybe we won't.'

CHAPTER THIRTEEN

Dr Ralph McLelland was kneeling beside the body by the time Torquil arrived at room seven of the Masonic Arms Hotel. Morag was standing by the window, ready and waiting with her camera and fingerprint kit.

'She's dead all right,' Ralph McLelland said, rising to his feet as Torquil came in. 'The blow to the back of the head with some sort of bludgeon looks to have been instantly fatal. Rigor mortis has set in.' He pouted thoughtfully. 'The room is warm; the television set is still on. I'd say she's been dead for at least eight hours. Maybe a couple of hours longer.'

'Any idea about the murder weapon?'

'It's in the shower, Piper,' Morag volunteered. 'It's a brass candlestick.'

'You are joking!'

'It's in there and it has been washed clean.'

Torquil bashed one fist against his other palm. 'Dammit! Any idea where this candlestick was from, Morag?'

His sergeant pointed to the side table just inside the door. At one side there was a large brass candlestick beside a doily. 'It was one of a pair. Whoever did it had a weapon ready at hand.'

'Have we a motive here?' Torquil asked. 'Anything stolen? Bags searched?'

Ralph McLelland nodded. 'She's had something pulled off her wrist, a bracelet or a watch, I think. You can see where she's been scratched as it was pulled off. A couple of rings also look to have been taken. You can see her hands are fairly tanned, and she's got ring marks.'

Torquil closed his eyes for a moment, picturing the watch she had been wearing when he 'interviewed her' in her four-by-four Mitsubishi Shogun the day before. 'It was a gold Rolex,' he volunteered. 'I bet it had to be worth at least fifteen grand, maybe more. So, we have a possible motive. Has anyone seen anything suspicious? Did she have any callers?'

'No one noticed anything. Except that she bought a new bottle of vodka and took it upstairs with her last night. She bought it from George Macfarlane at the bar.'

'Who found the body?'

'Annie Campbell, the room-maid. She's upstairs in a spare guest room,' Ralph volunteered. 'She was well nigh hysterical so I gave her a sedative.'

Torquil shook his head. 'And so it goes on. But why, for God's sake?'

Morag bit her lip. 'I think it's about to get even worse, boss. The superintendent phoned just before I called you. I'm sorry, in the heat of the moment I forgot to tell you when I rang. He's on the warpath and wants you to ring him back straight away.'

Torquil shrugged. 'He's going to really love this then.'

Back at the station an hour later Morag tapped on Torquil's office door and popped her head round. 'Well? What did he say?'

'That I'm an incompetent oaf and that I should have told him about Fiona and me. He was livid that it had been splashed across the television.' He sighed. 'And now with Allegra McCall's murder he's beside himself. He's already on his way across to take charge and could be here literally any minute. He's coming care of a Scottish TV helicopter.'

'Rushing in like the seventh cavalry, complete with the media to record the event,' Morag said sneeringly. 'I'm sorry, Torquil. Can I do anything?'

Torquil shook his head. 'We'd best get all the information together. Anything useful to report about the laptop?'

Morag's face brightened. 'Actually, yes. My cousin Hughie had a good look and was able to find a few files. They're separate book chapters, but none of them are new. Hughie is a Fiona Cullen fan himself and he's pretty sure that they are all to do with her last book — *Flesh Trimmers*.'

'Dammit! So there is no clue there after all. Come on then, let's get on with it. Is everyone here?'

Ewan had put up a new pinboard and was waiting with the Drummond twins and Ralph McLelland for an initial meeting.

'I'll be doing the post-mortem as soon as you can give me the go-ahead from the Procurator Fiscal,' said the GP-cum-police surgeon. 'But as you know already, an initial external examination makes it look as if death was instantaneous from a blow to the back of the head with a blunt instrument, almost certainly the brass candlestick found in the shower.'

Torquil nodded at Morag who stood up to give her report. 'There were no fingerprints. It looks as if whoever did it only touched the candlestick and washed that immediately. I haven't even tried to do anything with it. It would probably be a job for the Forensic Department at Dundee.'

Torquil stood and crossed to the whiteboard, adding Allegra McCall's name and drawing lines between some of the names, to complicate the web even further. 'It's a tangled skein and no mistake. And all to do with writers and books.'

'Do you think she knew who killed Fiona?' Morag asked.

Torquil shrugged. 'Maybe. But if so, why was she robbed?'

Wallace Drummond clicked his teeth. 'She was an attractive lassie. Classy too I thought when I drove her back yesterday. Had she been ...?'

'Molested?' Ralph McLelland said, then shook his head. 'No, I'm pretty sure she wasn't. She seemed to have been bashed on the head as she sat on her bed, then fallen straight over.'

Ewan shuffled in his chair. 'Piper, can I just say —'

But precisely then there was a banging noise from the outer office, as if someone had just thumped the counter several times. It was followed by the noise of creaking metal, a heavy slapping sound and several other footfalls.

'I'll go and see,' Ewan began, crossing to the door which at that moment was hurled back and a large uniformed man on crutches appeared. He was red-faced with a crisp, unfashionable black moustache and an aggressive square chin. Behind him was a television crew consisting of a producer, a female reporter and a cameraman, who was already taking pictures.

'Why isn't there an officer on the desk?' the big man barked.

'Superintendent Lumsden,' said Torquil, advancing with his hand outstretched. 'Welcome to Kyleshiffin. We are just in the process— '

'Aren't you forgetting something, Inspector McKinnon? How do you greet a senior officer?'

Torquil eyed the superintendent dispassionately, his hackles rising. 'If you will step in, Superintendent Lumsden, out of sight of the cameras, which are not authorized in my station, then I will brief you.'

And stepping past him he put his palm over the video camera and gently, but forcefully, marched the crew backwards. 'This is a police station and the media are not permitted into the offices. One of my officers will be with you

212

in a moment to answer your questions.' He turned and ignored the protestations of the trio.

'Ewan, can you look after the Press?' Torquil asked a moment later.

'But Piper, I wanted to tell you —'

'Later, Ewan,' Torquil said, a hand on the big constable's back urging him forward. 'And now, Superintendent Lumsden, let me fill you in.'

Lumsden was clearly seething, his moustache almost literally bristling. 'That was bloody stupid, McKinnon. Antagonizing the media like that. Don't you see that we need them right now, after this pig's ear that you've made of the investigation.'

Everyone in the room squirmed and felt for Torquil. Only Ralph McLelland felt able to say anything, since his position as police surgeon was not directly under the jurisdiction of the superintendent. 'I take exception to that, Superintendent Lumsden. This investigation has been dealt with efficiently and —'

'Efficiently!' Lumsden exclaimed. 'How many people are going to die before this investigation is over? I make it four deaths so far. That's more than bloody Glasgow gets, let alone a twopenny Western Isle.'

'Steady now!' said Douglas Drummond, coming swiftly to his feet. 'This is our island. Our home.'

Throughout these exchanges Torquil had stared resolutely at his superior officer, his temper rising exponentially. Yet somehow he managed to keep the lid on it. He had developed a facility for keeping his emotions in check ever since Fiona's death. 'Do you want to know what's been happening, Superintendent?' he asked calmly. 'Or do you just want to scream and behave like a prat.'

Superintendent Lumsden stared in disbelief, then his face went even more puce. 'The sergeant will brief me,' he said slowly. 'Then I'm going to take over and get a result. As for you, McKinnon, you are officially suspended forthwith. Now please leave the station.'

Once again Ralph McLelland began to protest, but Torquil placed a hand on his arm. 'It's OK Ralph, I'll go. Perhaps the superintendent is right. I haven't got the result we need.' He picked up his scarf and wound it round his neck. 'I'll see you all later,' he said, walking past the superintendent and letting himself out.

Ewan was busy with the reporter, a pushy young woman who would undoubtedly prove too much of a match for the big constable. Torquil let himself out and passed Izzie Frazer as he made for his Bullet.

'Inspector McKinnon,' she said, catching his arm. 'Ewan told me about that poor woman. Did he tell you about —?'

But Torquil was in no mood to stop. He shook his head. 'I have no official position here anymore, Izzie. There is a superintendent on the case now.' And he went over to his bike, pulled out his Cromwell helmet from the pannier and started the bike up.

'But it could be important,' Izzie muttered as she watched the tail light of the Bullet disappear into the mist as he headed up the hill road out of Kyleshiffin.

After a hard morning the Padre had taken half an hour off to play the first, the third and the sixth holes, then returned to his study where he set about cleaning his irons and polishing his woods. He was surprised to hear his nephew come back so soon.

'You obviously haven't heard the news,' Torquil said when the Padre beamed a greeting at him. 'Allegra McCall has been murdered.'

Truaghan! Poor creature!' he exclaimed. 'Have you any idea who did it?'

'And I'm off the case. I've been suspended by Superintendent Lumsden. He thinks I've been incompetent.' He gave a wan smile. 'And I suppose calling him a prat didn't help.'

The Padre shook his head. 'I don't know what to say, laddie.'

Torquil shrugged, then threw himself down in the chair and rubbed his temples. 'At least I didn't deck the bugger!' He sighed, then went on. 'Nothing much seems to matter anymore. I think I've been wandering around in shock since Fiona's death.'

'Are the deaths linked? It seems odd, her being Fiona's publisher.'

'Oh, it's linked somehow, I'm sure. The odd thing is that she was bludgeoned to death and then robbed.'

The Padre patted his nephew on the shoulder, and then snapped his fingers. 'I almost forgot. That fax you wanted, it came through.' He handed Torquil the sheet and waited while he read it.

'So! Wattana's clinic does all sorts,' mused Torquil. 'Cosmetic surgery, gender reassignment, transplantations. And it has been under investigation by the Medical Association of Thailand and by the Bangkok Police Department. It is entirely private, with a lot of foreign money pumped into it.'

'That's no surprise.'

'You obviously didn't look at the list of sponsors, Lachlan. Top of the list is AME — Angus MacLeod Enterprises. And the concern about the clinic is that it might be acting unethically, doing operations without too many questions being asked. You know, buying kidneys from the local poor people and selling them on to rich ill folk who have no inclination to wait for a legitimate tissue typing.'

'Wow! So that could be why Wattana was here as Angus MacLeod's guest!' The Padre struck a light to his ever-ready pipe. 'And I have another interesting piece of news. It was in that heap of correspondence that I have neglected.' He reached across his desk and picked up a letter. 'It's from a solicitor in Glasgow acting on behalf of the estate of a Mrs Rosamund Armstrong of Milngavie, née *Rosamund MacLeod* of Dunshiffin Castle, West Uist. That's Angus MacLeod's sister! She died a few weeks ago and wanted her ashes to be placed in the family vault in the St Ninian's crypt.'

Torquil had sat upright on hearing this news. 'Now why on earth hasn't Angus MacLeod mentioned this? His own sister.'

'It doesn't make sense, does it?' the Padre agreed. He scanned the letter again. 'It mentions that her son may well be in contact himself.'

'Her son? Angus MacLeod's nephew. That means he would be —'

'Angus MacLeod's heir to the Dunshiffin estate, and that presumably would include AME.' Lachlan puffed on his pipe, sending billows of blue smoke ceilingwards. 'The plot thickens, laddie.'

'And gets very muddy indeed!' said Torquil. He reached for the telephone. 'I think a call to the Milngavie Registrar of Births, Deaths and Marriages is called for.'

Despite what many people thought, Superintendent Kenneth Lumsden had a very fine police brain. He had the ability to absorb facts fast, see links and act quickly. And in this case, this was precisely his aim.

'A swift arrest should now be on the cards,' he said into the camera, as it trained on himself and Donna Spruce, the Scottish TV reporter, as they stood in front of the whiteboard with its network of leads and connections. I have personally taken over the case.'

Outside, in the main office, Izzie Frazer stood leaning on the counter as Ewan talked to Morag.

'I kept trying to talk to Piper, but yon muckle superintendent arrived and I couldn't get a word in,' Ewan told his sergeant.

'Well, tell Morag now,' Izzie urged.

Ewan smiled at her, then turned to Morag. 'Izzie saw Genevieve Cooper go into the Masonic Arms Hotel last night, before she came over to my place.' He blushed. 'We didn't think anything about it until I got to work this morning and we heard.'

The sound of laughter, the bluff snort of the superintendent and a trill flirtatious peel from Donna Spruce preceded the door to the incident room opening. 'We'll be over at the Masonic Arms filming a piece while we wait for your call with any developments then, Kenneth.'

When the film crew had gone Morag addressed the superintendent. 'PC McPhee has some information you should know about, sir. It's a possible lead. A possible suspect.'

Lumsden rubbed his hands together. 'Into the office then, lad. All leads are worth looking at.'

'What a smug git!' said Izzie as the incident room door swung closed behind them.

'That's official,' agreed Morag.

Genevieve had just popped into the Bonnie Prince Charlie for a swift drink before making her way along Harbour Street to catch the Macbeth ferry *Laird o' the Isles* back to the mainland, via Lochboisdale. And it couldn't be too soon now.

The bastard, calling in her debt like that. Making her do that thing. She shivered involuntarily and reached for the packet of Gauloises cigarettes on the table in front of her. *Just one more cigarette and one more drink then I'll be off.* She flicked her Zippo and inhaled greedily as the strong smoke seemed to calm her. Then she rose and went over to the crowded bar and signalled to Mollie McFadden for replenishment.

'Genevieve Cooper?' someone asked behind her.

She spun round, her Jack Daniels-induced smile ready to greet whoever it was. She didn't recognize the big man on crutches, but she did recognize the nice sergeant and the tall hammer-throwing constable who flanked him.

'My name is Superintendent Lumsden. We'd like to ask you a few questions about the recent death of Allegra McCall.'

Genevieve's lips quivered, then her eyes rolled upwards and she dropped to the ground in a dead faint.

Roland Baxter watched the colour drain from Angus MacLeod's face as the latter read the new text message on his mobile. He muttered and turned away to face his desk.

'Bugger! It's all going pear-shaped!'

He tossed the phone down on the desk and drew out a key to unlock a drawer. The Scottish Minister for Culture's eyes opened wide when he saw his friend reach in and draw out a Beretta Vertec handgun.

'Some personal stuff I need to sort out,' he explained tersely.

'Angus, I want no part in any shooting.'

'Then bugger off.'

'Can I use your helicopter?'

The laird just grunted and made for the door. 'Do whatever you want.'

Genevieve Cooper's confession tumbled out of her upon questioning at the station. Gambling debts, huge ones thanks to an addiction, poor judgement and foolishness beyond measure had put her into the hands of one Albert Conollan, Glaswegian money-lender and agent for one of Glasgow's oldest mobs. Her debt had been called in suddenly a few days ago, along with threats of personal violence and worse, as far as she was concerned: a promise to exterminate her dog unless a payment of ten thousand pounds was made by the following day.

Genevieve had drunk herself into a state. She had gone to Allegra McCall's room at the Masonic Arms Hotel with the intention of asking the publisher for a loan. The door was open, Allegra was sitting on the end of the bed drinking neat vodka and sobbing her eyes out, mumbling about Fiona. Then Genevieve saw the Rolex, a timepiece that would easily take care of the ten grand and save her kneecaps and her dog. It was an impulse. She had picked up the candlestick, intending only to stun the publisher, knock her out. But she had hit her too hard — and panicked.

'I never meant to do it,' she sobbed, looking up at the officious Superintendent Lumsden while Sergeant Driscoll made notes and from time to time checked the tape recorder at her side. 'You won't let them hurt Ozzie, my Labrador, will you?' she asked pleadingly.

Superintendent Lumsden eyed her dispassionately. 'I make no promises, Miss Cooper. It's the unlawful killing of Allegra McCall by your hand that concerns me.'

Half an hour later, inside the public bar of the Bonnie Prince Charlie, the afternoon film on the big, broad television screen was interrupted by a newsflash. Kirsty Macroon's familiar features appeared as she announced the news just received from West Uist. The picture changed to a live picture of Donna Spruce standing outside the Kyleshiffin police station.

Further tragedy hit the island of West Uist as another body was discovered this morning. Allegra McCall, the publisher of Fiona Cullen's crime novels, was discovered bludgeoned to death.

Inspector Torquil McKinnon who has been leading the investigation into the novelist's murder has apparently been suspended from duty in circumstances yet to be explained. His superior officer, Superintendent Kenneth Lumsden, flew in this morning to take over the case and — we have it on good authority — it appears that an arrest has been made, a confession received and charges are about to be made.

We believe that a serial killer may have been apprehended.

This is Donna Spruce reporting for Scottish TV from Kyleshiffin, West Uist.

Wallace and Douglas Drummond, who had popped in for a swift half pint of Heather Ale, grimaced at one another as the film continued.

'They're making a scapegoat of Piper,' said Wallace.

His brother nodded, then drained his glass. 'Aye, we'd better get back and see —'

A hand clapped him on the shoulder and made him jump. It was followed instantly by Calum Steele's indignant voice. 'Did I hear right? Have you got someone? How do the television people know and me not?'

Douglas turned to the local newshound. 'We have someone. But as you know we are just a couple of lowly minions and are not at liberty to divulge —'

Calum held up his hand. 'Spare me the usual excuses. I'm used to being sold down the river, just like poor Torquil. Anyway,' he went on, changing the subject, 'I looked through the window and saw you two drinking on duty as usual. I won't bother reporting you because I need to report a crime!'

'Not another one, Calum?'

'Aye, another crime has been committed. And it is seriously pissing me off almost as much as all those fancy TV news-usurpers. My Lambretta has been stolen again.'

Torquil roared into the courtyard of Dunshiffin Castle and braked hard, the Bullet's wheels spraying gravel as he abruptly halted by the grand steps leading up to the main door.

Jesmond, the laird's retainer opened the door so swiftly that Torquil wondered if he had been waiting for his arrival. 'The laird has gone out,' Jesmond announced in his usual haughty tone.

'Is Baxter still here?' Torquil snapped.

'I'm still here,' came the Minister for Culture's smooth voice from an open door to the left of the hall. 'But only just. Tam McKenzie has gone to start the helicopter up. I'm heading back to civilization in a couple of minutes.'

Torquil brushed past the butler and entered the drawing room to find Baxter dressed in a sheepskin jacket, a brandy in one hand and a Montecristo cigar in the other.

'Where's MacLeod?' Torquil demanded.

Roland Baxter shrugged his shoulders and languidly drew on his cigar. 'Business to attend to, he said. He's graciously given me the use of his helicopter.'

Torquil stepped close to the minister. Too close for Baxter's comfort. 'Business connected with Dr Wattana's clinic in Thailand, by any chance?'

Roland Baxter coughed, and then spluttered.

That caught him off guard, Torquil noted.

'Dr Wattana's clinic? No idea, old fellow.' He took a sip of brandy, then asked, 'Cosmetic surgeon, wasn't he?'

'You know very well he was,' Torquil replied. 'As well as all sorts of other surgery. Some of the operations he was carrying out were ethically questionable, so I understand. The clinic is currently under investigation by the Medical Association of Thailand and by the Bangkok Police. Apparently a lot of British businessmen are involved in financing the clinic — including Angus MacLeod.'

Roland Baxter drained his brandy. "Really?' he looked at his watch. 'I'm afraid I'll have to go, Inspector.'

'I'll find out, you know. I'll find out about every connection that Angus MacLeod has with Wattana's clinic. And I'll discover all the people who he's fronting for.'

Torquil noted the beads of perspiration forming on Baxter's brow. He stared him straight in the eye, sensing the politician's nerve beginning to buckle.

'He had a text message a short while ago and he said it was something to do with someone called Selkirk.'

'Selkirk?' Torquil repeated. 'You're sure he said Selkirk?'

Roland Baxter shrugged his shoulders helplessly, his whole demeanour becoming like a frightened rabbit. Then his eye fell on the mobile phone on the desk. 'Look, he left his phone,' he said pointing it out. 'He had to get something from that drawer and he must have forgotten to pick it up again.' He neglected to say that the something was a gun.

Torquil picked up the phone and accessed the message file. He pressed the button and the last message showed up on the screen:

THE SELKIE RETURNS.

I KNOW ABOUT THE POET.
MEET ME AT 3 OR BE EXPOSED.

Torquil looked up at the Minister for Culture. 'Baxter, you're a fool,' he said as he made quickly for the door.

The politician felt himself begin to tremble and he stood for a moment, unsure of his next course of action. He started for the door. 'But what about Wattana? You won't say anything about me will you?'

The screech of tyres on gravel indicated that either Torquil had not heard or that he was not interested.

The Padre had felt a growing indignation ever since he watched Torquil ride off on his Bullet. Grabbing his six-iron and a bag of old balls he had gone outside with the good intention of hitting their covers off to relieve his frustration. But he had thought better of it and instead stuck the golf club and bag of balls in the pannier of the Red Hunter and headed off to Kyleshiffin. As he rode through the patchy mist, his machine splashing through puddles, he went over the tonguelashing that he intended to give Superintendent Lumsden.

Then riding along Harbour Street he saw Professor Neil Ferguson striding along in the direction of the *Unicorn*. The Padre honked his claxon and coasted to a halt alongside the professor.

'Heading off now, Neil?'

Neil Ferguson looked distracted. He nodded assent. 'Yes Padre, but I've got some unfinished business to attend to first. Can't stop I'm afraid.' He strode on, adding over his shoulder, 'See you — sometime.'

Lachlan gunned the Red Hunter and set off again, up the hill to the station. He had business of his own to finish.

Ewan McPhee was chatting to the Drummond twins behind the counter when he entered.

'Is that superintendent of yours in?' he asked.

'He is, Padre,' Ewan replied. 'But I'm afraid he's busy just now.'

'Well you can tell him I want —'

Sergeant Morag Driscoll appeared from the incident room at the sound of his voice. 'Tell the superintendent what?' she asked.

The Padre was about to go into his carefully rehearsed diatribe, but thought better of it. Instead he shook his head and said, 'I'm just worried about Torquil, Morag.'

Morag lifted the counter-flap and came through. 'Come outside for a minute, Lachlan,' she said, hooking his arm and guiding him towards the door. Then, with a nod to Ewan and the Drummonds, 'Look after the shop for a bit, OK.'

Outside the station she led him down the road. 'We're all concerned, you know. Torquil has been through hell these last couple of days.'

'It's not fair, Morag. The lad has done all that he reasonably could.'

'I know. But maybe he can have a rest now that Superintendent Lumsden has got Genevieve Cooper to confess.'

'Has she confessed to killing Fiona and Ranald?'

'No, but he's convinced that she did. She has huge debts you know.'

Morag's mobile beeped to indicate that she had received a text message. She accessed it, then muttered a curse. She showed it to the Padre.

I'M GOING FOR THE SELKIE
I'LL FINISH THIS CASE.

TORQUIL.

'What does he mean?' Morag mused. And before Lachlan could reply she tried calling her erstwhile inspector.

'Blast! He's turned off his mobile now. What does he mean "finish this case"?'

'I'm not sure, lassie,' replied the Padre. 'But I just saw Neil Ferguson and he was talking about finishing some business as well.'

Torquil cut the Bullet's engine and coasted to a halt about a hundred yards from *Tigh nam Bàrd*, Ranald Buchanan's House of the Bard, which stood shrouded in mist. He advanced stealthily on foot.

To his right, through the mist, he saw the outline of a boat, undoubtedly the *Unicorn*, tied up to the jetty.

'So, you are here already, aren't you, Neil Ferguson,' he muttered to himself. As he edged forward, carefully lifting and placing his feet to avoid kicking any loose pebbles, he was grateful for the cover of the mist.

He climbed the outer wall then flattened himself against the wall of the cottage and carefully peeped through the window into the front room.

Dr Viroj Wattana was sitting on the settee, a gun in his hand. Beyond him, in shadows, another figure was sitting upright in a chair, the posture distorted as if tied to the chair with the hands tied behind the back.

His eyes widened further as he saw a dim shape on the floor between them, almost certainly another body.

Inwardly cursing himself for not having his truncheon, Torquil looked for something to use as a weapon. A loose stone from the wall would have to suffice, he decided, as he edged round the side of the cottage. Somehow he would have to sneak up on the gunman.

The back door was unlocked and thankfully opened without a creak. Torquil crept across the kitchen and peered through the crack of the open door where he could clearly see Dr Wattana with the gun in his hand.

Suddenly, there was a crack and he felt a searing pain in the side of his head. For a brief moment he felt himself pitching sideways, diving into a pool of blackness. And yet dimly he thought he heard Angus MacLeod's voice, followed by a laugh — a peal of hysterical laughter that accompanied him to the depths of unconsciousness.

CHAPTER FOURTEEN

Torquil was vaguely aware of motion, of being dragged along the floor by his wrists, then of being rolled over onto his belly and having his hands bound behind him and then being hauled into a sitting position and propped against a wall. He struggled against nausea and almost unbearable pain in the head as he felt himself returning to consciousness.

Angus MacLeod was still laughing. 'Welcome back to the land of the living, Piper,' he said, 'for the time being!' His laugh turned into a strange giggle that sent a shiver up Torquil's spine.

He shook his head and blinked, his eyes perceiving the body of Neil Ferguson lying face down in front of him.

'Don't worry, he isn't dead,' came MacLeod's voice. 'He just can't move. As you can see, he's effectively hog-tied — and gagged.'

Torquil saw the rise and fall of the professor's chest. He shook his head again and looked towards the settee where Dr Wattana was sitting with the gun held unwaveringly in his hand.

'But I'm afraid poor Viroj was not so lucky!'

And as Torquil's eyes began to focus in the half-light of the room with the mist swirling against the windowpanes, he saw that the surgeon's eyes were staring sightlessly ahead, like a doll's, and that his skin was mottled and his lips were almost purple. Just above the collar of his shirt a garrotte was visible, so tight as to have almost cut into the flesh. Torquil felt a threatening wave of nausea begin to rise.

Angus MacLeod laughed again, the same hysterical peal of laughter. 'And soon we'll all be dead!'

Torquil looked round at the speaker for the first time, and was surprised to see that he was sitting in the shadows, ropes binding his torso to the chair, his hands behind his back. Blood had oozed down the side of his face from a gash on his temple and soaked into the collar of his Harris tweed jacket.

The light suddenly went on and Torquil turned to see Izzie Frazer standing by the door with her hand on the switch. She was dressed in a black wetsuit, her hair tied back in a pony tail.

'Izzie?' Torquil breathed.

'That's me,' she replied with a broad feline smile. 'Welcome to my parlour.'

Torquil gave a short humourless laugh. 'But of course! It used to be your parlour didn't it — *Izzie.*'

Izzie Frazer smiled and crossed the room to remove the gun from the hand of Dr Wattana. She bent in front of his immobile face. 'Thanks for looking after Angus's gun for me,' she said, wrinkling her nose at him, then with a shove she pushed his body sideways and he slumped to land in a grotesque heap on the floor. Izzie straightened and slipped the gun behind a belt, from which also dangled the two ends of a doubled-over bag, rather like a wheatbag.

'You're cleverer than I gave you credit for, Piper McKinnon. You surprised me by showing up here.' She waggled a finger at him. 'You almost cramped my style, you naughty boy!'

'You mean I cramped your style the same way that Dr Wattana did?'

She bent down and caught Neil Ferguson by the belt of his trousers and dragged him with surprisingly little effort towards the same wall that Torquil was propped up against. 'My word, you are astute,' she said, reaching up and pulling masking tape roughly from the professor's mouth. She grinned at his gasp of pain, then went on, 'Yes, his death was unfortunate — but necessary! And my little ruse with the note seemed to work.'

'That was clumsy,' Torquil said. 'It was too pat.'

Izzie shrugged her shoulders dismissively. 'It served its purpose.'

Neil Ferguson's voice quavered. 'Wh … what the hell is this all about?'

Izzie reached out and gently stroked his cheek. 'Oh, don't be nervous, Professor Ferguson,' she said soothingly. 'Not here when you're with friends. No need to be nervous — yet!'

Angus MacLeod began to giggle again, but went quiet when Izzie turned her head to stare him down. 'That's better Angus,' she purred. 'Let's keep some sense of dignity, shall we?'

Again she turned to Neil Ferguson. 'But do you really not know what this is about? After all my little messages.'

'Your messages?' he gasped. 'It's been you? My God! Why? I don't even know you.'

'I think you'll find it's to do with the Selkie, Neil,' Torquil ventured. 'That's right, isn't it Izzie?'

Angus MacLeod took a sharp intake of breath and made a guttural sobbing noise.

Immediately, the smile vanished from Izzie's face to be replaced by a thin-lipped piercing glare. 'I think that you seem to know too much for your own good, Inspector McKinnon. Enough to sign your own death warrant, in fact.'

'In that case I think that I deserve to know why I'm going to die,' Torquil replied. 'And I think that we all need to know why you're planning to murder us. Just like you murdered Ranald Buchanan and Fiona Cullen.'

'Do you really think that I wasn't going to tell them?' Izzie returned. 'They need to know exactly why they're going to die, just like Ranald Buchanan did. The Selkie returned for him!'

'And by the wetsuit I see that you are the Selkie,' Torquil said.

'No I'm not,' Izzie returned with an emphatic shake of the head. 'But the wetsuit is symbolic of the Selkie coming back from the water to collect his own. I'm symbolic of the Selkie coming back to deliver retribution.'

'Y ... you are mad!' Neil Ferguson exclaimed, tremulously.

Izzie's eyes blazed. 'Don't call me that! I'm the sanest person here.'

'There's no shame in mental illness, Izzie,' Torquil said. 'Take your mother for instance.' He watched her closely to see if there was any stirring of emotion. 'Flora Buchanan *was* your mother, wasn't she?'

'Very good, Inspector! Go on!' she urged, the feline smile returning.

'Ranald Buchanan was your grandfather. And he arranged for you to disappear. Seemingly, to drown. And he fostered the rumour that the Selkie had returned to claim you.'

Angus MacLeod stifled a gasp.

'And then your mother had her breakdown. But you never knew her properly, did you? She was committed to a mental hospital with schizophrenia and never recovered. Ranald never visited her, the only thing he ever did for her was to bury her and carve an obscure note on her headstone.'

Tears seemed to form in the corners of Izzie's eyes. She turned abruptly and pointed an accusing finger at Angus MacLeod. 'And he bought me from the bastard Buchanan and gave me to his sister!'

'Who died recently in Milngavie,' Torquil announced.

The Laird of Kyleshiffin began to sob.

Izzie Frazer sneered. 'But not before I got the whole story out of her. And out of her bastard husband, before I pushed him down the stairs. Then I gave her an overdose of insulin.' She smiled as she patted the bag hanging over her belt. 'And you're here with me, aren't you, Rosamund? You've been the instrument of retribution — several times!'

'Her ashes are in that sandbag, I assume,' Torquil queried. 'So you used her ashes to batter Ranald Buchanan?' He swallowed hard, forcing the lump out of his throat. 'And you used it to bludgeon Fiona Cullen before you strangled her and tried to make it look like a sexual crime.'

'Don't mention sex to me!' Izzie hissed. 'I hate it! I hate all you bastard men. That bastard Buchanan buggered me senseless before he sold me to that sod. I ... I remember —'

'And that's why you wanted to become a woman, wasn't it?' Torquil continued. 'You had been abused.' He tried to make his tone sound sympathetic. 'And that's why Dr Wattana had to go, wasn't it, Izzie? He recognized you. He had performed the sex change operation in Bangkok. And modified your features a fair bit as well, I guess.'

'That's right. And then the bastard showed up on West Uist, as a guest of that creature,' she almost spat, pointing at the laird. 'He saw me at the Gathering and he had to go as well.'

'And so you took the professor's boat and headed off to sea, then dived in and swam ashore.'

'That's right. Wattana was already dead,' she replied, with a hint of pride. 'He's been sitting here all this time.'

'But I still don't understand,' Neil Ferguson said. 'Why have you been sending me those messages? I thought you were just someone trying to blackmail me.'

Her eyes turned to the professor of marine archaeology, hatred emanating from them. 'Just blackmailing you? You bastard. Don't you realize what you are? *You* are the fucking Selkie!'

'I ... I ... don't understand!'

She hit him ferociously with the back of her hand, sending his head crashing against the wall. 'You're my father! You abandoned me. You caused all this!'

Neil Ferguson looked aghast. 'You, you are my daughter? It isn't possible.'

'I was your son! But you never came back, did you. I had to bring you back. But you had the luck of the devil. Like that day in the St Ninian's cemetery, when I sent you to find that grave. *Her* grave!'

'You did that? But I never found it. I ... I was hit on the head.'

'By a golf ball!' Izzie wailed, then touched the sandbag hanging from her belt. 'Not with this little beauty, like you should have been. I was waiting in the porch of the church.' Her eyes blazed. 'But now I'm going to send you to hell.'

Torquil's mind went back to that day, to that moment when he, the Padre and Fiona had rushed over the crest of the fairway to see Neil Ferguson curled up by a gravestone, his hands about his head. He was speechless at the realization that it had been Fiona's miss-hit tee shot that had ironically saved him; and that Izzie had been hiding a few feet away, ready to commit cold-blooded murder — a murder that, if she had committed it, would have meant Fiona would probably still be alive today. His blood boiled.

Izzie reached behind the settee and pulled out a crate of bottles. 'The bastard Buchanan's peatreek,' she explained, pulling the cork on one bottle and casually pouring its contents over the prone body of Dr Wattana.

'It's all been about Professor Ferguson, hasn't it, Izzie?' Torquil said. 'You just botched it up.'

'I botched nothing up!' she hissed. She uncorked another bottle and poured the contents over the floor, and over Neil Ferguson's legs.

'But you did botch it up. You had left a message to him in the programme at the Gathering and didn't expect it to get switched. It was an accident, actually. Ewan McPhee bumped into the professor and Fiona, and their programmes got mixed up. Fiona found the message and thought —' Again he forced back the rising lump in his throat — 'and thought that the message was from me. It said to meet at the crannog, didn't it?'

Izzie nodded. 'I took that newspaper idiot's scooter and rode out to the loch, then dumped it in the bracken. I swam out and was waiting inside the ruins. Then she came over in the boat. The stupid bitch! I had no choice.'

Torquil's blood was boiling. He wanted to get his hands around her neck, to choke the life from her. But it was not possible.

'Then you swam back, put on her helmet and got on her bike. And then you got clever with the laptop.'

'I had been at her lecture and I'd read her books. I knew that she wrote thinly disguised hatchet jobs. It gave me time to think again; to plan how to get the two people I hate most in the world to come here together. I was going to kill them — and you, you interfering pig, at one stroke.' She pulled another cork and let the liquid flow all over Torquil.

'And then you were going to sail away in the professor's boat?'

Neil Ferguson shook his head. 'I had no idea,' he said in astonishment. 'If I had I would have —'

'What? What would you have done? Claimed me as your own?'

'If you hate me so much, then kill me,' Neil said. 'But don't add to your crimes. Let them go.'

Izzie sneered as she uncorked yet another bottle and went over to Angus MacLeod, who was now simpering like a baby. She poured the contents over his head and shoulders. 'What's this? Self-sacrifice? It's a bit late for all that now — *daddy*!'

She reached for a lighter on the mantelshelf and backed towards the door. 'You're all going to burn in hell. Where all men deserve to go!'

She flicked the lighter into flame. 'Goodbye!'

But suddenly through the door rushed Morag, crashing into Izzie's midriff and propelling her to the floor in a near perfect rugby tackle. The lighter arced through the air, to fall on Dr Wattana's prone body, where it ignited the alcohol with a whump.

'No you don't, you sick bastard!' Morag cried, attempting to pin Izzie down. But in a trice Izzie head-butted the sergeant who recoiled for a moment, blood streaming from her nose. And in that instant Izzie Frazer reversed their positions. She manoeuvred herself astride Morag and began pounding her head with her fists.

Torquil seized the opportunity to struggle onto his knees. Somehow he had to do something to help Morag.

The flames were engulfing the dead Dr Wattana and threatening to leap across the floor to absorb Neil Ferguson and Torquil in a fireball.

Angus was screaming and Morag was grunting in pain as she continued to take a pounding from the maniacal Izzie Frazer.

Then the Padre entered, a six-iron in his hands. With a single well-aimed swipe he connected with the side of Izzie's head and she collapsed on top of Morag. 'God forgive me!' he muttered, staring momentarily heavenwards. Then in a trice he had pulled a blanket from the settee and began trying to beat the flames.

'It's no use, Lachlan,' Torquil cried, 'we need to get everyone out.' He had made it to his feet and turned his back to his uncle. 'Get a knife and cut me free and I'll help.'

The Padre went into the kitchen and returned instantly with a bread knife. He sliced through Torquil's bonds and together they pushed Izzie aside and pulled Morag free. Lachlan carried the stunned Morag out while Torquil tried to help Neil Ferguson up.

The flames jumped from Wattana's body igniting the peatreek and spreading instantly across the room. They engulfed Neil Ferguson's legs and Torquil's clothes.

'Come on!' Torquil screamed, dragging the professor out the door and out through the kitchen. He threw him to the ground and followed by throwing himself down. 'Keep rolling over! Try and smother ...'

The Padre and Morag immediately sprang to help, pulling off coats and sweaters and trying to stifle the flames. It seemed to take forever, but finally the flames were out, leaving clothes and flesh badly burnt.

Looking back, the cottage was already blazing furiously, the doorway now an impassable wall of flames.

Angus MacLeod was screaming his head off, in fear and in pain.

'We must be able to reach him — them!' gasped Torquil.

And then suddenly there was the noise of breaking glass and a nerve-jangling screaming. They ran round the side of the house in time to see a fireball running from a window and racing towards the *Unicorn*.

'There she goes! I'll get her!' cried Torquil, setting off at a sprint. The smell of burning rubber and flesh was awful. Yet screaming in agony, Izzie Fraser made it to the boat.

'Get in the water! It's your only chance!' Torquil screamed.

But the fireball that was Izzie Frazer ignored him. Probably past all sentient thought, it stood teetering on the boat, the rubber wetsuit burning brightly and bubbling, sending out billowing black clouds.

The explosion as the flames ignited a petrol drum was deafening. Torquil was thrown to the ground where he lay with his hands over his head as the debris from the boat cascaded around the area.

A few moments later, once the detritus settled, he rolled over onto his knees. Just in time to see the roof of the House of the Bard collapse. Angus MacLeod had stopped screaming.

Superintendent Lumsden had been furious upon hearing that Sergeant Morag Driscoll had gone without leaving any message. But when he received the telephone call and the brief report about the events at Ranald Buchanan's house he mobilized the necessary help. He was enough of a policeman to realize that a result was a result. Apart from which, he had quickly understood that Genevieve Cooper was no serial killer.

The sight of the burning ruin of *Tigh nam Bàrd* sickened everyone. The fact that it had been impossible to save Angus MacLeod left everyone with a heavy heart. PC Ewan McPhee felt particularly unwell when he heard of how he had been duped by the killer.

'She — she used me, Piper. I am so sorry.'

Torquil had patted his friend and constable on the arm.

'We'll talk about it all later, Ewan. Right now I think that the professor and I need a bit of medical attention.'

'And don't forget your sergeant,' Lachlan added.

Torquil put an arm round Morag's shoulder. 'How could I ever forget the woman who saved my life?'

'It was the Padre,' Morag said as Ewan phoned for Dr McLelland. 'He brought me on that evil old Red Hunter of his. He almost did for us both on some of those bends.'

A whirling noise sounded from a distance away and a few moments later a Bell 429 helicopter, emblazoned with the Scottish TV logo, broke through the mist, hovered overhead, then landed in the pathway behind the West Uist police Ford Escort. The doors opened and Donna Spruce and her camera crew climbed out and advanced towards them, bending low under the gyrating helicopter blades.

Superintendent Lumsden broke away and hobbled over on his crutches to meet them. He talked with her for a few moments then turned and came over to Torquil, Morag and the Padre.

'A word with you, Inspector McKinnon,' he said, a half smile playing across his lips. And drawing Torquil aside he went on in hushed tones. 'I have explained that we have solved the whole affair, but I have not told them all the details. I said that we need to complete our investigations first.'

'Our investigations, Superintendent Lumsden?' Torquil queried. 'I understood that I was suspended.'

Lumsden snorted dismissively. 'You have been reinstated, Inspector, with a clean copy-book. Clearly you've got information that I don't know about yet, so I look forward to reading your report ASAP. But for now I want you to come and give an impromptu interview with me. I'll lead, but you back me up. The Division can come out of this pretty well, I think, all things considered.'

'Apart from the fatalities.'

Lumsden bit his lip. 'McKinnon, you're a maverick, but I think you might have the makings of a good officer inside you. Play ball with me and I'll play ball with you. Now come on, let's do this TV thing.'

'Was that an apology, sir?'

'I suppose so. But just one other thing. Never call me a prat again!'

Torquil shrugged. 'As long as you don't behave like one.'

Purple patches formed on the superintendent's cheeks and he seemed to consider his words for a moment. He nodded his head slowly, then whispered, 'I think we understand each other, McKinnon.'

'I think we do, Superintendent.'

Later that evening, after a simple meal of cold roast pheasant and a bottle of good claret, the Padre and Torquil sat on either side of the fireplace in the sitting room of the manse.

'It's been a hell of a day, laddie,' the Padre remarked as he stuffed tobacco into his briar. 'But at least we know the truth now.' He shook his head in disbelief. 'I always thought of Ranald Buchanan as a bit of a rogue, but I would never have thought him capable of what he did.'

'Which do you mean, Lachlan? Of child abuse or of selling his own daughter's child, his grandson?'

'All of it. He screwed up their lives, didn't he?'

Torquil sipped his wine. 'I think that young Archie Buchanan must have had a hell of a life. My guess is that he was so traumatized by his abuse as a child that he had developed a disgust of being a male himself. And that was why he had gone off to Thailand and had a sex change and cosmetic surgery by Dr Wattana. It was ironic that Angus MacLeod had been pumping money into Wattana's clinic.

'And later, when he wheedled the truth out of his stepmother, he must have snapped. And worked out a plan to kill all the people he felt were responsible for his real mother's fate.'

The Padre had puffed his pipe into life. 'Those people being Ranald Buchanan, Angus MacLeod and his father — Neil Ferguson.'

'And all because of a mix-up with the programmes at the Gathering, Fiona ended up in the wrong place at the wrong time. Neil Ferguson was supposed to meet Izzie on the crannog. And after she had disposed of him I expect that Angus MacLeod would have been next.'

'And Wattana also happened to be in the wrong place — on West Uist that is.'

Torquil nodded. 'The fall-out from all this will be considerable. There's bound to be an exposé of Wattana's clinic and an investigation of all the investors and the clients that were treated. The blackmarket in organ transplantation needs to be brought out into the open.'

'And you think Roland Baxter and Angus MacLeod knew about it?'

'I have little doubt, Uncle.'

The Padre nodded. 'I am sorry that Angus MacLeod lost his life, but I have little sympathy with Roland Baxter. A politician needs to be squeaky clean.' He puffed on his pipe for a moment, then asked, 'But what about Genevieve Cooper? There is no doubt, I suppose, she killed Allegra McCall?'

Torquil bit his lip. 'I'm afraid not. She was a desperate woman and she'd drunk too much. Apparently she'd gone to ask Allegra for help, but saw the watch and on the spur of the moment had the idea of stunning and robbing her. It seems completely out of character. She didn't mean to kill her. I'm guessing she'll go down for manslaughter.'

'And Izzie — or Archie Buchanan has gone, too. A dreadful way to go. Burning to death and then being blown to bits.'

Torquil unconsciously laid a hand on his own heavily bandaged leg, which Dr Ralph McLelland had treated that afternoon. 'I don't know how it will affect Neil Ferguson. Apparently he'd been receiving letters from Izzie for some time. He'd thought they were the work of a crank, yet there was enough in them to have him both intrigued and a bit wary.'

'So he knew nothing about Izzie?' Lachlan queried.

'Nothing until she told him that he was her — or his — father. And that she was going to kill him. I think he's going to need pretty intensive counselling.'

The Padre looked concernedly at his nephew. 'And how about you, laddie? How can I help you?'

Torquil pushed himself to his feet and pointed to the two Silver Quaichs at either end of the mantelpiece. 'By having a drink with me. Shall we put them to their true purpose, Lachlan? A dram for Fiona.'

And a few moments later, with their quaichs charged, they saluted each other and drank to the memory of Fiona Cullen and what might have been.

BOOK TWO: DEATHLY WIND

PROLOGUE

The assassin edged closer, sliding forward on his belly through the sand of the machair, gradually steering a course between the thick tufts of coarse grass and clumps of yellow-blossomed gorse. It was slow going, but he was prepared to take as long as it needed to get in position in order to carry out the execution crisply and cleanly.

It was an unexpectedly hot day with hardly a cloud in the cobalt blue sky. A day to soak up the sun, or so his targets might have imagined when they found the isolated strip of beach. The parents were snoozing while the two youngsters frolicked in the shallows.

Quite the little family group, he thought, with a sneer of contempt. He adjusted the silencer on the barrel of his Steyr-Mannlicher rifle and slid it through a clump of tall coarse grass, resting it on the bipod and squinting through the Leupold 'scope to take a bead on the father.

The youngsters were making a lot of contented noise, yet despite that, perhaps due to some sixth sense their mother suddenly shot up, her beautiful eyes wide with alarm.

She opened her mouth as if to cry out, but the assassin shifted his aim with unerring speed and squeezed the trigger. There was a dull popping noise, at variance with the effect of the bullet as it smashed into her throat, hurling her back against the sand to thrash wildly as her life began to ebb swiftly away.

The youngsters looked up, suddenly fearful and panicking. The father, awakened by the spray of blood across his face shot upright, his eyes sweeping round to fix the assassin. For one so big he moved surprisingly fast, instinctively trying to protect his family. But he was not fast enough. The assassin coolly aimed and fired, another popping noise belying the power of the bullet that bored its way between the eyes, exiting almost instantly from the occiput in a spray of blood and brain pulp.

Then the assassin was on his feet, the blood lust taking over. The youngsters were cowering, edging backwards from the bodies of their parents and the expanding pools of blood soaking into the sand. He had no compassion, no pity. He dispatched them both with a shot to the head.

He smiled contentedly as he looked up at the bright blue sky. It was the sort of day that made one feel good to be alive, he reflected. Especially when a commission like this one had been so easy and so pleasurable.

Five minutes later, he had dragged the parents' bodies up onto the machair and was just returning for the youngsters when he heard the motor of a boat approaching from the other side of one of the small islands. He hesitated for a moment then ducked down and made his way back to his sniper's position in the tall grass of the machair.

PC Ewan McPhee had set off on his round of the West Uist waters early that day and he was hungry. He came round the small island in the West Uist Police *Seaspray* catamaran and slowed down to coast towards the beach. He intended to snatch a break and have a cup of tea from his flask.

But then he saw the bodies and the blood soaking into the sand.

He cruised into the shallows, cut the engine and jumped over the side, running towards them. And, as he squatted beside them, he felt an overwhelming wave of nausea come over him.

He doubled up and began retching.

He never heard the soft footfalls coming towards him from the machair, and he never felt the blow that sent him flying face down beside the dead bodies.

CHAPTER ONE

The Reverend Lachlan McKinnon, known throughout West Uist as the Padre, was in a subdued mood, just as he had been for the last three days. For twenty-four hours following the discovery of the West Uist Police *Seaspray* catamaran, drifting empty like a latter-day *Mary Celeste*, he had hoped that they would find Ewan McPhee alive. On the second day, as hope started to peter out he had prayed fervently that the big police constable, the hammer-throwing champion of the Western Isles, would have somehow kept himself afloat on the sea until he was rescued. First thing that morning he had simply prayed that they would find the constable's body before too long, so that Jessie McPhee, his elderly mother, would be able to get on with her grief.

And then there was poor old Gordon MacDonald. His had been a sad and lonely way to die, but at least he could be put to rest. He ran over the notes that he had made in readiness for the funeral then tossed them on the desk and sat drumming his fingers on the surface for a moment. Finally, with a sigh, he got up and put on his West Uist Tweed jacket that was hanging on the back of his study door. He glanced in the mirror, adjusted his clerical collar a mite and ran his hand through the mane of white hair that permanently defied both brush and comb. He pushed his horn-rimmed spectacles higher up on his nose and reached for his golf bag that leaned in readiness beside the bookcase.

Life had to go on, as he told everyone. And golf was one of his ways of coping; apart from giving his bagpipes a good airing. Yet with his nephew, the local police inspector, Torquil

McKinnon, still away on a protracted leave of absence after his own recent personal tragedy, the pipes held little attraction for him.

A few moments later, with his golf bag slung over his shoulder and his first pipe of the morning newly lit and clenched between his teeth, he let himself out of the front door of the house and scrunched his way down the gravel path to the wrought-iron gate, then crossed the road and mounted the stile that led directly onto the ten-acre plot of undulating dunes and machair that he and several local worthies had converted and transformed into the St Ninian's Golf Course.

There was a fine early morning mist, and under its cover a few terns were dive-bombing some of the sheep that grazed freely over the coarse grass fairways of the links. He stopped on top of the stile and removed the spectacles that had already misted up. When he replaced them and dismounted he saw that three men were standing by the first tee.

'*Latha math*! Good morning!' Lachlan greeted them. 'If you are already playing don't let me hold you up.' He glanced at his watch. 'Not many start this early at St Ninian's.'

'It is the Reverend McKinnon, isn't it?' replied the eldest of the trio, in an unmistakable Glaswegian accent. 'See, I heard that you usually have an early round and I wanted to try out this famous golf links of yours. Maybe we could have a game?'

He was an olive-skinned, well-built man in his mid-forties, of medium height, with cropped black hair and a small, slightly upturned nose. Neat though it was, however, it seemed a tad smaller than one would have expected from his overall bone structure. That and a certain tautness of the skin on his face suggested to the Padre that at some time he had submitted himself to the skill of the cosmetic surgeon.

A bit of a peacock; a preening peacock, the Padre silently

concluded.

'I'm Jock McArdle,' the man went on, assuming that the Padre had accepted his invitation. He extended a muscular hand bedecked with expensive thick gold rings. 'I've just moved into —'

'You've just moved into Dunshiffin Castle,' Lachlan interjected with the affable welcoming smile of the clergyman. 'Which makes you the new laird of Dunshiffin. I heard that you bought the estate a fortnight ago, Mr McArdle, and intended paying you a visit as soon as you took up residence, but I am afraid that we have had a few upsets on West Uist lately.' He shook hands and suppressed a wince at the power of the other's grip. He assumed that it was the habitual grasp of a hard-bitten entrepreneur, designed to indicate dominance. He duly ignored it, having long since refused to feel intimidated by anyone.

'No worries, Reverend, I only arrived four days ago. I've had to tie up a lot of business before I could move in. But I'll be living at the castle most of the time. I have big plans for the place.'

The Padre smiled unenthusiastically. 'Are you all three playing this morning?' he asked, his eye hovering over the single professional-spec leather bag and the two men standing a pace behind Jock McArdle.

'Naw, Reverend, it's just me,' Jock McArdle returned with a grin. 'These are two of my employees that I've brought from Glasgow. I thought that a bit of good clean sea air would be good for their health. Isn't that right, boys?'

'It's a bit deathly if ye ask me,' returned the one holding the golf bag. 'There's no night life. Just a handful of pubs.'

Jock McArdle guffawed. 'This is Liam Sartori, Reverend. As ye can see, he's a wee bit lippy, but he's a good lad.'

The Padre shook hands, his practised pastoral smile belying the shrewd appraisal that he had made of the two young men. Liam Sartori was a tall, well-built and excessively tanned fellow, probably the result of a sunbed rather than the sun's rays, the Padre reflected. Possibly a third or fourth generation Glasgow Italian. His clothes were casual and brashly expensive. A gold medallion hung from a heavy gold chain on the front of a red, white and blue sports shirt. He was unsure whether Jock McArdle's criterion of goodness matched his own.

'And this is Danny Reid,' Jock McArdle said, introducing the other young man who was in the process of opening a cigarette packet and offering it to Liam Sartori. 'See, he's the quiet one.'

'I'm the thinking one, Reverend,' said Danny Reid, clipping the cigarette in his lips and shaking Lachlan's hand.

He was a shade shorter than his associate, possibly a touch under six foot, well-muscled, with a tattoo of a claymore on his right forearm and at least six body piercings that the Padre could count on lips, ears, eyebrows and nose. Like his associate he had a medallion on a thick gold chain. His blond hair was spiky and most probably the result of peroxide. Lachlan watched as he lit their cigarettes with a gaudy Zippo lighter.

'I can only manage nine holes, I'm afraid,' Lachlan said. 'I have a funeral to conduct in a couple of hours.'

'Nine holes would be excellent,' returned Jock McArdle, enthusiastically. 'But see, would I be insulting your cloth if I suggested a wager?'

The Padre struck a light to his pipe, then replaced his box of Swan Vestas in his jacket pocket. 'A small wager always adds a frisson to a game, so I don't see why not. Match play or Stableford?'

'I prefer simple match play, Reverend. Winner takes all.'

The Padre blew a thin stream of smoke from the side of his

mouth and nodded. It fitted with his assessment of the Glaswegian. The new laird was clearly a man confident in his own abilities. 'Shall we say five pounds for the winner? What's your handicap, Mr McArdle?'

'Fourteen.'

'And mine's a rather shaky eight. Exactly one eighth of my age. So, that means I give you three shots over the nine holes. That will be at the second, the fifth and the ninth.'

Jock McArdle nodded to Liam Sartori who unzipped a side pocket of the golf bag and extracted a box of Dunlop 65 balls, and a tee, then pulled out a Callaway driver. 'You'll be needing the big one, boss,' he said with a confident grin.

The Padre puffed thoughtfully on his pipe and pulled out his two iron, the club he favoured for the tricky first drive, especially when the wind was gusting as it tended to do on the first three holes.

'I'm thinking that you will enjoy the course, Mr McArdle. It isn't exactly the Old Course at St Andrews, but it's a good test of golf. Nature designed it with the Corlins on one side and the North Atlantic Ocean on the other, and we just added a few refinements. It has six holes dotted about the sand dunes of the machair, with three tees for each one, so you can either play a straight eighteen, or, when it is quiet, string any number of combinations together. The fairways are mowed once a week, the sheep nibble the green to billiard-table smoothness and the bunkers have been excavated by generations of rabbits. Watch out for the gorse and the thistles; think your way round and you'll be all right.'

He puffed his pipe again and nodded at the honesty box hanging from the fence. 'And, of course, the green fee is pretty reasonable.'

Jock McArdle grinned and nodded to Danny Reid, who drew

out a roll of money and peeled off a five pound note. 'Is this safe here, Minister?' Danny Reid asked incredulously as he deposited it in the box.

The Padre pointed to the nearby roof of the church. 'This is West Uist, Mr Reid. St Ninian's Golf Course is beside church land. Who would steal from the church?'

Liam Sartori sneered, 'I'm willing to bet that you've never been to my part of Glasgow, Minister.'

Jock McArdle eyed the yardage marker by the side of the first tee, then the two iron in the Padre's hand. He handed his driver back to Liam Sartori and pulled out his own two iron. 'Aye, golf is a thinking game, Reverend. A careful game.' He grinned, a curious half smile with no humour in it. 'You'll find that I am always careful. It's a good policy in my book.'

Jock McArdle was a bandit off a handicap of fourteen, Lachlan decided, after they had played three holes and he found himself three holes down. Or rather, he was a 'bandit chief', on account of the fact that his two boys seemed to take it in turns to caddy and to find their boss's ball, a task that they seemed to achieve with miraculous skill. Indeed, knowing the extent of the gorse and thistle patches on the undulating dunes as well as he did, the Padre was almost certain that twice the ball had been discovered at least twenty yards further on than it should have and, on both occasions, had seemed to fortuitously find a nice flat piece of fairway.

'You play well for a fourteen handicapper, Mr McArdle,' the Padre said, as they walked onto the fifth tee. 'And your two *finders* have done sterling work this morning.'

'I like to win at everything I do, Reverend. That's why I've been successful in business. That's how I came to buy the Dunshiffin estate.'

The Padre pulled a dilapidated pouch out of a side pocket of his jacket and began stuffing tobacco into his battered old briar pipe. 'Am I right in sensing that you have something more than golf on your mind this morning, Mr McArdle?'

'You're a shrewd man, Lachlan,' returned Jock McArdle with an ingratiating grin. 'Do you mind if I call you, Lachlan?'

The priest shrugged. 'Most people on West Uist just call me Padre.'

'OK then. Padre. I'm not the sort of guy who beats about the bush.' He nodded to his two boys and raised his voice: 'You two go and have a smoke over by that pot bunker. But keep your eyes open. I'll be driving over your heads in a minute, so mind and duck.' When they were out of earshot he went on, 'Do you know how I came to buy the Dunshiffin estate, Padre?'

Lachlan had won the last hole and gained back the honour to drive first. He shoved a tee into the ground and perched his ball on top. 'I was aware of the liquidation of Angus MacLeod Enterprises after the death of the last laird of Dunshiffin, Angus MacLeod.'

'I picked the estate up for a song. Two and a half million, if you want to know.' His mouth twisted in a curiously self-satisfied way. 'That's not bad for a lad who started selling cones and wafers from a fourth-hand ice-cream van. I built up the biggest confectionary business in Midlothian over the last twenty years. And I have plans. Padre. Big plans.' He bent and picked up a few blades of grass and threw them into the air where they were caught in the breeze and wafted sideways. 'The wind is not too bad here, is it?'

'No, the Corlins give us a bit of shelter.'

'But it is really windy on the west of the island, isn't it? Especially over by the Wee Kingdom.' He seemed to puff up his chest. 'You know that as the owner of the Dunshiffin estate,' he beamed and corrected himself, '— or as you rightly said, as the new *laird*, I own all the land on the Wee Kingdom.'

The Padre stiffened a tad. 'Aye, you own it all right, but there are crofters there. They lease the land from the estate.'

'Exactly. See Padre, I'm their new landlord.'

'And you are thinking of erecting windmills on some of your land?'

Jock McArdle tossed his head back and laughed. 'So you know all about the wind farm idea?'

'Mr McArdle, I've been the minister on West Uist for thirty-five years. People have been talking about introducing wind farms in the Hebrides for a decade. They are almost a reality on Lewis already. It's only our remoteness on West Uist that has prevented talk of them coming here. That and the cost.'

'I am an entrepreneur, Padre. I have no ties to the energy department, or the electricity boards. I see an opportunity to generate a lot of electricity on this windy island, enough to supply every family and every business at a fraction of the cost. And where better than to start up a wee wind farm than on the Wee Kingdom? The most westerly point of the most westerly island. The wind is roaring in from the sea; it's a power source just waiting to be tapped.'

'I doubt if you'll have much support. They're unsightly things and we are proud of our wildlife on the island.'

Jock McArdle shrugged. 'There is little evidence about it affecting wildlife, Padre,' he said dismissively. 'In any case, I'm used to resistance. It doesn't worry me.'

The Padre glanced at his watch. 'I have to give you a shot at this hole, so I'd best nail this drive down the middle.' And taking his trusty three-wood from the bag, he did just that.

For the next four holes, the Padre watched his opponent's ball like a hawk and himself played with grim determination.

Despite the strokes he had to give away, by the time they had reached the ninth green they were all square on aggregate.

'How many of these windmills are you thinking of having?'

'I'd be starting small. Just two or three to see how it goes, then who knows? My boffins tell me that twenty-five would produce a sizeable amount of power. That would be my target in the first year.'

The Padre stared aghast at him. 'You cannot be serious! There is no room. And you would need to be building pylons to carry the electricity.'

The Glaswegian nodded. 'I know all that, Padre. I have had it all researched. I have the means to invest and I have the permission to go ahead. I've had my lawyers check with everyone that matters — the Land Court, the Crofters Commission — you name it, I have had it checked and double-checked.'

'But you don't have the crofters' permission. They'll never agree to this.'

Jock McArdle smiled. It was a strange crooked smile that seemed to be formed by two very different halves of his face. One side was all innocence while the other was cunning personified. 'Technically, I don't need their permission, Padre. The original deeds that go with the Dunshiffin estate are quite clear: it is my land to do with as I please.' He looked at their two balls, comparing the distance of each from the hole. 'I'm on in three and you're there for two. With my stroke that makes us all square. And it looks like it's me to putt first.' He lined up his putt and struck the ball, cursing as it slipped a yard past the hole. 'I'm going to begin with the MacDonald croft. I have a couple of boys on their way to West Uist now with the components for a couple of wind-testing towers.'

The Padre eyed his opponent askance. 'This funeral that I

have to take, did you know that it was Gordon MacDonald's?'

Jock McArdle nodded as he lined up his return putt. 'Aye, I knew that, Padre. I never knew the man myself so I won't be going to his funeral.' He tapped the putt and grinned with satisfaction as it rattled into the cup. 'A five, net four. You have a putt for the match.' His two boys smirked and lit fresh cigarettes.

As the Padre lined up his five-foot putt, McArdle remarked casually, 'Of course, as the new laird, I thought it my duty to attend the wake after the funeral.'

If the remark had been intended to make the Padre miss the putt, it did not succeed. Lachlan struck the ball smoothly and it disappeared into the cup with a satisfying rattle. The Padre retrieved it and held out his hand. 'My game, I think.' After shaking hands he pulled out his pipe from his top pocket and struck a match to it. 'I am thinking that is your right, Mr McArdle, but perhaps you should go easy on the wind-farm information.'

Jock McArdle again gave his curious half smile. 'I was hoping that maybe you could smooth the way a little. See, Padre, I am a good man to have on your side. I am always grateful for help shown to me.'

Liam Sartori smirked and was rewarded with an elbow in the side from Danny Reid.

'I'm thinking that you will find that the folk of West Uist make up their own minds, Mr McArdle.'

The Glaswegian gave a wry smile and gestured meaningfully at Danny Reid. 'Well, it was good to play and talk with you anyway, Padre. And so I owe you five pounds. That's one thing that you should know about me: I always pay my debts — in full.'

The Padre smiled as he accepted a five pound note from the

roll of notes that the be-pierced Danny Reid peeled from the roll that he produced with the dexterity of a conjurer.

'Well, let's just hope that you don't run up too many debts on West Uist, Mr McArdle. West Uist folk are pretty keen at calling in debts themselves.'

CHAPTER TWO

The Wee Kingdom was almost another island of the archipelago that formed West Uist. It was a roughly star-shaped peninsula with steep sea cliffs, home to thousands of fulmars and gannets, facing the Atlantic Ocean on its north-west coastline. Gradually the terrain descended to sea level at its most westerly point, where three successive basalt stacks jutted out of the sea. On the top of the last one was the ruins of the old West Uist lighthouse and the derelict shell of the keeper's cottage. Moving inland, the machair gave way to lush undulating hills and gullies surrounding the small central freshwater Loch Linne. To its inhabitants, this oft-times wind- and sandstorm-swept islet was heaven on earth.

The name, the Wee Kingdom, had been coined back in 1746 by the families that farmed the islet after the Jacobite laird, Donal MacLeod had granted the land in perpetuity to them and their descendants and heirs in gratitude for the sanctuary they had given the fugitive Bonnie Prince Charlie during the five days that he had stayed on the island while waiting for a French vessel to take him to safety. It had been the sighting of a heavily armed English frigate by Cameron MacNeil, the lighthouse-keeper, that resulted in the change of plan to move the prince back to South Uist from whence Flora MacDonald helped to take him over the sea to Skye and thence to freedom.

An automatic beacon on the cliff tops above had rendered the old venerated lighthouse obsolete in the mid-1950s, and it remained a ruin, accumulating a veneer of guano from generations of seabirds.

There were six smallholdings on the Wee Kingdom, each

lived in and worked by a person or family, who had inherited it from a forebear or patron in keeping with the original dictates of Donal MacLeod's grant. Essentially, only six holdings were ever to be worked on the Wee Kingdom, the lease for each depending upon a peppercorn rent paid to the current laird in goods manufactured on the Wee Kingdom by the holders themselves. Effectively, the holdings pre-dated the crofting system by a full fifty years.

All six crofts were granted the right to use the natural resources of the islet of the Wee Kingdom and the surrounding waters up to a good stone's throw off the coast, including the same area around the three stacks and the lighthouse. And well stocked it all was. In days gone by the crofters had taken the eggs and birds from the cliff-faces, just as their distant neighbours, the St Kildans, had done for centuries. Like them, they cut and burned peat, farmed Soay sheep and kept a few cattle, goats, ducks and geese. They grew crops of potatoes, cabbages, turnips and beetroots on the traditional *feannagan*, or 'lazy beds' that had been artificially built up in long swathes and fertilized with innumerable barrowloads of seaweed over two and a half centuries. They each operated a treadle loom, using their own wool and traditional methods to produce the famous West Uist Tweed that was bought and sold down the west coast of Scotland. And in the shallow southern waters between the causeway and the edge of an underwater shelf they collected edible seaweeds for cattle fodder and fertilizer, and farmed the rich oyster bed, using their own boats and ten-foot long oyster tongs to rake up the valuable delicacies that were in much demand on West Uist and the other Western Isles. All in all the Wee Kingdom Community was a throw-back to the old days. Although each croft was worked as a separate enterprise, they still cooperated, shared and bartered; and they produced West Uist Tweed, pâté and oysters which were marketed under the label of the Wee Kingdom Community. All profits were poured back into the community and used or shared in equal measures. It was a system that had worked successfully for two and a half centuries.

An unmetalled road that was in a continual state of disrepair had been constructed across the causeway, wide enough for a single vehicle. It was just after noon when the Padre zipped across on his Ariel Red Hunter, the classic motorcycle that was his trademark, as he followed the wake party led by Rhona McIvor's erratically swerving minibus and a motley assortment of cars, vans and wagons. The state of Rhona's battered minibus was testimony to her propensity to bump car fenders, roadside rocks, gates and harbour walls. Her corner-taking was renowned and most people were aware that her vision had been progressively deteriorating to the point where she should not be driving, yet no one had so far had the temerity to suggest it to her.

The cortege followed the minibus up the rough pockmarked road to Wind's Eye, the late Gordon MacDonald's croft, then parked up amid the pens and outhouses and disembarked. Inside the austere thatched cottage with its mixed smells of seaweed, brewing yeast, turnips and stale tobacco, Rhona had already set out a spread of sandwiches, beer and whisky.

There were about a dozen mourners standing awkwardly in the low-ceilinged main room that had served the old crofter as a sitting-room, kitchen and workroom. The old thatched cottage, which had been built on the site of one of the old medieval 'black houses' reflected the late crofter's personality and had never been renovated or added to, as had most of the other Wee Kingdom dwellings. Fishing nets and rods were stacked in a corner; a large brewing bin took up space beside the plain porcelain sink and on a shelf lay a well-thumbed King James Bible, the only book in the cottage.

'He was a religious man in his own way, Padre,' Rhona said, as she lifted a tray of glasses, a whisky bottle, a jug of beer and a jug of water. As she did so, Lachlan noticed how pale she suddenly looked. He also noticed the slight intake of breath, as if she had experienced a spasm of pain.

'I'll take that, Rhona,' he said, reaching for the tray, his manner brooking no argument. 'Is it the angina again?'

A thin smile came to Rhona McIvor's face. She nodded and pushed her thick-lensed wire-framed spectacles back on the bridge of her nose. She was a slim woman of about his own age he guessed, since it was not a statistic the remarkable Rhona ever cared to divulge. Lachlan remembered when she had taken her croft some twenty odd years before. Back then she had been a glamorous redheaded woman of the world. A freelance investigative journalist and a prize-winning cookery-book writer, she had come to the Wee Kingdom upon inheriting her holding, having made the decision to retire from the rat race forever. And that she had done, immersing herself in the crofting traditions and lifestyle of her forebears. 'It's a paradise, Padre,' she had told him one Saturday morning many years ago when he called in on one of his pastoral visits to the residents of the Wee Kingdom. 'No telephones, no deadlines, no editors breathing down your neck. You just have to put bread on the table and wool on the backs of the rich folk of Inverness.' He remembered her peal of laughter, as she then set about shearing a sheep, a cigarette in an ebony holder clasped between her small pearly teeth. In her dungarees and Wellingtons she made an impressive, if incongruous, sight.

The Padre had looked at her concernedly, but was relieved to see the pained expression quickly disappear. She was dressed in a smart trouser suit, her once tumbling Titian locks now iron grey, pulled back in a pony-tail that exposed her intellectual brow and the long neck that had attracted so many would-be suitors over the years. It was widely believed that she had had several lovers since she came to live on West Uist, yet neither she nor they ever broadcast the fact. Discretion seemed to be a guiding principle in Rhona's life.

'Aye, this angina is a bugger, Padre,' she said with a twinkle in her eye as she produced her trade-mark ebony cigarette holder from her shoulder bag and slipped a fresh cigarette into it. Lighting it with a small silver petrol lighter she blew out a stream of blue smoke. 'These things will be the death of me, I suppose.' Then she sighed. 'But we all have to go some day. Gordon was only a couple of years older than me, you know?'

'You'll go on forever, Rhona,' said the Padre.

'God, I hope not,' she returned, picking up a couple of plates of sandwiches. 'Look, you do the drinks and I'll feed the hoards.' Saying which she was off, a trail of smoke following in her wake.

Lachlan turned and went over to the two McKinleys standing by the merrily burning peat fire. Father and son, they worked Sea's Edge, the most westerly croft on the Wee Kingdom. As he held the tray and muttered a few words about the funeral he let them help themselves. Unconsciously, he found himself appraising them.

Alistair McKinley was a smallish wiry man in his mid-fifties with the gnarled and wrinkled skin of a man used to the elements. He was bearded with short cropped hair and an almost perpetual scowl on his face. He helped himself to a whisky from the tray while his son, Kenneth, took a glass of beer. In contrast to his father he was tall and broad-shouldered, his eyes blue like his dead mother's. His expression was not as severe as his father's scowl, yet there was about him a suggestion of unease, as if he was anxious to be off somewhere. Lachlan had seen that look so often among the young islanders as they began to hanker after some of the comforts, luxuries and attractions of civilized life. He wondered if the younger McKinley would soon announce to his father that he was going to cut loose.

'Is the croft going well?' the Padre asked Alistair.

'Passable, Padre. Passable.' The older crofter flashed a look at his son. 'It would be better if we were more focused.'

Kenneth McKinley shook his head slightly. He was twenty-two, but looked five years older. 'Och, we're doing fine. Father. We just need to ask —'

'We need to be patient, Kenneth,' Alistair said curtly. He sipped his whisky, and then turned back to Lachlan. 'You best see to the others, Padre.'

Lachlan nodded, quite unperturbed by the other's curtness, since he was renowned for it throughout West Uist, just as his father and grandfather before him had been. He went over to a trio, two young women and a man, standing by the door. Katrina Tulloch, the local vet was chatting with the two newest crofters, Megan Munro and Nial Urquart.

'Anyone for a dram?' he ventured. 'To see old Gordon off.'

A pretty girl in her mid-twenties with finely chiselled features and spiky blonde hair smiled and took a glass of water. 'I'd love to have a beer, Padre, but I'm afraid I am still on duty. A vet is always on the go in the Hebrides, you know.'

'Like a minister, eh Katrina?' said Lachlan, giving her a wink. 'I doubt if the sheep will notice the smell of beer. They never seemed to mind your uncle when he had the practice.'

'I'll have a glass of water as well, thank you, Padre,' said

Megan Munro who was about the same age as Katrina. Unlike the other mourners, Megan had come in her work clothes, a beanie hat pulled down over her auburn hair, and almost over her earlobes from which dangled large hooped ear-rings. Despite her lack of make-up and grooming she still had the looks and curves that would make many men turn their heads. Her features were only slightly marred by a certain sternness of expression that seemed fastened around her mouth. 'I don't approve of alcohol,' she said firmly. 'I don't know why everyone thinks they should drink at funerals. I think it's a sad occasion.'

The Padre was about to say something when Nial Urquart, her partner, chipped in. 'That's a bit harsh, Megan. Gordon was a neighbour and we're all sad to see him go, especially the way he did, but it is natural to have a little party. Give him a send-off so to speak.' He nodded at Lachlan. 'That was a beautiful funeral service, Padre.'

Lachlan smiled, noticing that two pink patches had formed on Megan Munro's cheeks; a mix of ire and embarrassment, he thought. Although the couple had only lived on their croft for six months, he had already had enough contact with her to form an opinion on her character. She was strong-willed, passionate about animals and the environment, and moderately outspoken.

'This is a community, Nial,' she said, arms hanging rigidly at her sides. 'Poor old Gordon died in this cottage and no one noticed for two days — and that's us included.' She looked about the room melodramatically, then asked, 'And just where are the rest of the Wee Kingdom residents? Where is Vincent Gilfillan? Where are the Morrisons? They should be here now.'

'Vincent was at the funeral, Megan,' said Lachlan, turning to dispense drinks to a party of mourners, consisting of various tradesmen and shopkeepers from Kyleshiffin, who had known the deceased crofter for decades.

'But why isn't he here now?' he heard Megan persist. 'This is a time when a community should pull together.'

The Padre smiled to himself as he heard Nial remonstrate with her. Lachlan quite liked the young Scottish Bird Protection officer, and thought that he had taken on a challenge when he moved into Megan Munro's holding with her. The word was, of course, that she had seduced him after one of the public protest meetings she had organized after the announcement that there was to be a cull of the hedgehogs on the island. Nial Urquart was there to lend strength to the argument that the hedgehogs were devastating the seabird population by stealing eggs. However she did it, whether by art, craft or sexuality Lachlan did not know, but he had moved in with her and now he helped her to run her croft.

'Would you listen to her, the wee madam,' Rhona whispered in his ear, as she met him back at the big table where she was picking up another salver of sandwiches. 'She's only been a crofter for six months and she's telling everyone where they should be. She's really put old Alistair's back up with her hedgehog sanctuary and all her vegetarian propaganda.'

'Alistair has been appointed in charge of the hedgehog culling, hasn't he?' Lachlan asked in a half whisper.

'That's right, and a fine to-do they had over it. And there's another war brewing over the way he slaughters the livestock. And she's already made it clear to me that she doesn't think we should be making pâté from the duck livers.'

Lachlan frowned. 'But he's been doing it for years. He's a trained butcher, isn't he? And the Wee Kingdom pâté sells all over the islands.'

Rhona shook her head as she screwed another cigarette into

her ebony holder and lit it. 'But that doesn't cut any ice with Megan. She thinks we should all turn vegetarian.' She sipped a whisky. 'I doubt that she will last long as a crofter. We never had any trouble with her great uncle, Hector Munro. He'd be turning in his grave at the way she carries on. And that poor Nial.' She shook her head sympathetically.

'Where is Vincent, by the way?' Lachlan asked.

'On his way to Benbecula. Oh it's quite legitimate. He talked to me after the funeral. He has to be there to meet the tweed buyer. It's normally Geordie Morrison's job, but he's gone off somewhere and taken the whole family with him.'

The smell of tobacco had given the Padre a craving and he pulled out his cracked old briar from his breast pocket and filled it. 'But it's still school time. He surely can't have taken wee Gregor and Flora away with him?'

'Och, Geordie is a law unto himself. Sallie Morrison has just about given up. He gets a bee in his bonnet about going off looking for whales or something, and just tells her that it'll be educational for the children. And off they go. They'll be back in due course.'

'So they don't know about Gordon's death?'

'No, they'll be devastated when they find out, but we have no idea where they are just now.'

Lachlan struck a light to his pipe and picked up a glass of beer. He was about to take a sip when Megan Munro's raised voice carried across the room and caused all heads to turn.

'But you're a vet, Katrina! You can't condone the killing of innocent hedgehogs.'

'Megan, we've been through all this before,' Katrina returned, patiently. 'The hedgehog population is getting out of control.'

'It's no good, Katrina,' came Nial Urquart's voice. 'Megan

just won't accept that point. She doesn't like birds; she's just into cute little hedgehogs, hence her Mistress Prickle-back Sanctuary.'

'I might have known you'd bring it round to your precious birds,' said Megan, heatedly.

'It's not that simple, Megan,' Nial returned. 'The golden eagles up in the Corlins may take a lot of eggs and young seabirds, but not as many eggs as the hedgehogs. In any case they are a protected species, unlike the hedgehogs. Here the hedgehogs are regarded as vermin.'

Megan was about to reply, when the McKinleys joined the discussion. 'They're vermin right enough,' said Alistair, his beard bristling. 'But so are those eagles in my opinion.'

Katrina Tulloch looked aghast. 'You can't be serious, Alistair? The golden eagles are a national asset. We're lucky that they are nesting on West Uist again.'

'Not when they take our young lambs,' cut in Kenneth McKinley.

Katrina shook her head and smiled at him. 'I think you'll find that's a superstition, Kenneth. Eagles don't take lambs.'

Kenneth stood up straight. 'Don't patronize me. You may be a vet, but I've lived on Sea Edge all my life and I've seen them.' And suddenly his eyes widened and he pointed out of the window at the majestic sight of a golden eagle in the distance flapping its way towards the Corlins. 'If I only had a rifle now, I'd get that one.'

'And you'd end up in jail,' Nial Urquart returned. 'They're beautiful birds and as Katrina says, they are protected.'

Megan Munro had been seething for a few moments. 'That's everyone's answer to everything here, isn't it? Kill it! Shoot it! Well, you won't touch any of the animals in my sanctuary. If you do I'll have the police on to you straight away.'

'The police!' Kenneth exclaimed with a sarcastic tone. 'If you can find a police officer on the island, you'll be lucky. They all seem to be disappearing faster than smoke around here.'

Katrina Tulloch spun to face him, her eyes registering disbelief mixed with ire. 'Kenneth McKinley! You — you insensitive oaf!' She snapped her glass down on a window ledge, swung her bag onto her shoulder and with an involuntary sob, ran for the door.

Lachlan was about to go after her, but Rhona stopped him with a hand on his arm. 'Let her be, Lachlan,' she said, as the silence that had momentarily followed Katrina's exit was immediately broken by a cacophony of raised voices.

'Maybe we ought to break it up,' the Padre whispered to Rhona. 'It looks as if there's going to be a civil war in the Wee Kingdom.'

But before they had time to move, there was a loud rap on the door which was shoved open to reveal Jock McArdle and his two boys. Lachlan noticed that they were all dressed as they had been that morning, except that Jock McArdle was now wearing a pair of wire-framed spectacles and a black blazer on top of his golf clothes.

'Correction, Padre,' said Rhona, suddenly stiffening. 'It might be the start of World War Three. Unless I am mistaken, this is the new laird.'

Jock McArdle stood nodding his head at the assembled mourners and took off his wire-framed spectacles. 'It's a sad day. A lassie just ran past us as we came in. Greeting her eyes out she was.' He pulled out a handkerchief and swiftly and noisily blew his nose, then, 'For those of you who don't know me, and I think that is probably you all except for the Padre there, I am Jock McArdle.' He paused for a moment, then added emphatically, 'I am the new laird of Dunshiffin.'

Rhona was the first to say anything. 'You will have come to pay your respects to Gordon MacDonald. That's good of you, Laird. Would you and your sons like a drink?'

Jock McArdle stared at her in bemusement for a moment as his two minders smirked. He shook his head. 'Oh no, these are my boys, but not my sons,' he replied cryptically. 'But a drink would be good, thank you. And I thought that this would be a good time to meet my tenants. A good opportunity to let you know a few of my ideas.'

The Padre, being used to organizing groups, introduced everyone while Rhona poured drinks.

'We are not all here, though,' Rhona said, as she lit another cigarette. 'Vincent Gilfillan is doing business on behalf of the Wee Kingdom Community in Benbecula and the Morrison family have gone — off somewhere. You will be meeting them in due course, I am thinking.'

'What about Gordon MacDonald's croft, Laird?' Kenneth McKinley asked.

Alistair McKinley gave his son a poke in the ribs. 'My son has pre-empted me, Mr McArdle. I was going to make an appointment to see you. We have some business I need to ask you about.'

Jock McArdle shoved his hands into his golf trousers and stood facing the old crofter. 'Ask away. I am here now.'

Alistair McKinley cleared his throat. 'Could my son here take on the lease for the Wind's Eye croft? Gordon MacDonald died without issue and it is traditional that the holding —'

'No!' the new laird replied emphatically. 'He cannot take it on.'

'And why not?' Kenneth McKinley demanded, heatedly.

'The holding will not be re-leased.'

Rhona McIvor removed her cigarette holder from her

mouth. 'You are not serious! The Wee Kingdom Community has always had the right to pass on the holdings to family or appointed heirs.'

'I am rescinding that right,' the laird replied, removing a hand from his pocket and languidly taking his glass of whisky from Liam Sartori. 'It will not be the case in the future.'

'Are you sure that is legal, Mr McArdle?' the Padre put in.

'Oh, it is absolutely legal, I assure you, Padre,' McArdle returned, his eyes glinting behind his spectacles. 'I have had my lawyers check over the original agreement. If any of the holders had ever taken the trouble to research it they would have seen that it was written up in such a way as to give the laird the right to do whatever he wanted with the land, subject to certain minor restrictions.'

'Lairds! I knew this would happen!' barked Kenneth McKinley. He made for the door, but found his way barred by Liam Sartori and Danny Reid. He squared up to them. 'Out of my way! Now!'

Neither seemed inclined to move, the same challenging grin having appeared on each of the two minders' faces.

'Let him pass,' McArdle barked. Then once the younger McKinley had stomped out, he turned back to the assembly. 'I will be putting up several wind installations on this croft in the next few days.' He grinned patronizingly. 'It will be good for the whole island, you'll see it will.'

Rhona had been standing beside the Padre, her face getting whiter and whiter as anger seethed inside her. 'We'll not permit this. We will fight you.'

'That is not recommended, Rhona,' he replied smugly.

'You'll not break up the Wee Kingdom Community. If you do, it will be over my dead body.'

Liam Sartori sniggered.

Rhona saw him and made to cross the room towards him. 'You young whelp! I'll teach you —' She had taken two steps then suddenly halted, clutching at her chest before collapsing on the floor.

Lachlan was by her side instantly, feeling for a pulse. His face was like thunder as he turned and rattled out the order, 'Somebody call Dr McLelland. Now!'

CHAPTER THREE

The Macbeth ferry *The Laird o' the Isles* slowly loomed out of the morning mist and manoeuvred into the crescent-shaped harbour of Kyleshiffin. As the great landing doors slowly and noisily descended to allow the walking passengers to disembark before the inevitable cavalcade of traffic, Sergeant Morag Driscoll blew into her hands and stamped her feet. She felt cold and shivery, and not just because of the outside temperature. She was waiting for her boss, Inspector Torquil McKinnon, to return to the island after his extended leave. And she did not relish the news that she had to give him.

'Morag! I thought I would find you here,' came the Padre's booming voice. She turned to see Torquil's uncle hurrying along the harbour to join her, his mane of white hair blown awry.

'Lachlan, have you been on that motorbike of yours without a helmet again?' she chided him with a smile. 'You know full well it's against the law.'

'Och Morag Driscoll, I was in a hurry to meet Torquil. He's been away a good long while, you know.'

'I know, Padre, and I was just teasing.' Her face became serious again. 'How is Rhona?'

Lachlan clicked his tongue. 'As well as can be expected. Doctor McLelland has her trussed up with wires all over the place and a monitor that bleeps every second. There's a no-smoking policy in the cottage hospital and she's threatening to discharge herself because of that alone. She hasn't had a cigarette since the wake yesterday. That's an age and a half for Rhona.'

'Was it a heart attack, then?'

He nodded. 'Her third. She's going to have to take it steady from now on.'

'Not easy when you work a croft in the Wee Kingdom.'

'Not easy when your name is Rhona McIvor, you mean.'

'It sounds as if the new laird of Dunshiffin Castle is causing quite a stir in the Wee Kingdom. There are a lot of rumours going around.'

They moved aside as a stream of walking passengers disembarked from the ferry, fully expecting that Torquil would be among the motorcyclists that were usually permitted off ahead of the heavier vehicles. After the foot passengers, half-a-dozen motorcyclists rode down the gangway with much gunning of engines, but there was no Torquil. Instead, a large container lorry edged off.

'I wonder if he isn't coming after all,' mused the Padre.

Morag bit her lip. 'I hope he comes soon, or I'm in a fix. There's only me and the Drummond twins to run the show, and they're only special constables.'

'Aye, and they have their fishing business to run,' the Padre agreed.

The container lorry stopped and the driver wound his window down. 'Excuse me, darling,' he called to Morag. 'Are you with the police?'

Morag smiled up at the man, a large fairly good-looking man with a pony-tail and tattoos on hefty forearms. She understood his question since the West Uist division of the Hebridean constabulary had a fairly liberal attitude towards uniform. She was dressed in jeans and trainers, the only indication that she was in the force being the blue Arran pullover with three small white stripes on the right sleeve. 'Right this minute, I am the police. What can I do for you?'

The man nodded at a swarthy, surly-looking youth wearing a red baseball cap sitting in the cab beside him. 'Me and the young 'un here need to find a place called the Wee Kingdom. We've got a consignment for the Laird of Dunshiffin.' He grinned and winked at her, adding, 'It's the first of many. I'll be coming here fairly regularly, you ken.'

Morag was a pretty, thirty-something, single mother of three. She recognized the man's unsubtle meaning and treated it with the contempt she thought it deserved. 'Follow the road past Loch Hynish, then turn left at the big T junction. The Wee Kingdom is signposted from there. Watch out for the sheep by the roadsides and don't exceed the speed limit at any time. My colleagues are out with the mobile speed cameras today and we always prosecute.'

His charm, having failed to impress her, evaporated, the smile vanished from his face. He muttered a remark to the silent youth beside him then looked back at Morag, tapped his forehead and started off again.

'That was a wee bit harsh, was it not, Sergeant Driscoll?' said Lachlan with mock severity. Then before she could reply he pointed to the side of the lorry as it passed. It bore a large picture depicting a row of windmills linked by lightning bolts. Underneath in red lettering were the words: NATURE'S OWN ENERGY.

'So it's really going to happen, is it?' Morag asked. 'The new laird is going to build a wind farm.'

A stream of cars followed the lorry off, drowning out the Padre's reply. Then came a familiar noise as Torquil's Royal Enfield Bullet gunned its way down the ramp towards them. He was wearing his usual goggles and Cromwell helmet and looked tanned and healthy, despite several days' growth of stubble. He swung the classic motorbike up onto the harbour road and dismounted. He swept Morag off her feet in a warm hug and then pumped his uncle's hand.

'I'm so glad that you two are here to meet me.'

'Torquil, we need to —' began Morag.

'I've been with the Tartan Army in Belgium,' Torquil went on. 'There were about a dozen of us with our pipes,' he said, pointing to the pannier on the Bullet, from whence his travel sticker-covered bagpipe case was protruding. 'The football wasn't up to much, but that Roi Baudouin stadium in Brussels is something else. And the Belgians just love the kilts and the pipes. It was just the break that I needed.'

'Torquil, Morag has —'

'And then I caught the ferry from Zeebrugge back to Rosyth and just tootled up the East coast. I even managed to take in a couple of Highland Games Days.'

He clapped his uncle on the shoulder. 'I won a pibroch cup at Strathpeffer and a Strathspey at Dornoch.'

He looked at them. 'I've had lots of time to think things over and I've made a decision: I'm leaving the force.'

Morag and the Padre stared at each other in astonishment.

'But you can't leave, Torquil!' Morag exclaimed.

Her inspector put an arm about her shoulder. 'I know, we've been through a lot together, Morag. But it will all be for the best. After Fiona's death I need to move on. I want you to be happy for me. And I —'

The Padre grabbed his nephew's wrist and held it firm. 'Torquil, hold your breath for a minute and listen to Morag.'

Torquil turned to his sergeant and raised an eyebrow quizzically. Then he realized how pained she looked. He felt a shiver of dread run up and down his spine.

'Torquil you can't leave,' said Morag, her voice quaking. 'Ewan is missing! He's gone!'

Torquil stared from one to the other, his dark, handsome features registering bewilderment. 'Gone? Gone where?'

The Padre put a hand on his shoulder. 'This is the fourth day since he disappeared.' He took a deep breath; then, 'We think he's drowned.'

Ten minutes later in his office in the Kyleshiffin Police Station off Kirk Wynd, with a mug of hot, sweet tea in front of him, Torquil listened in shocked amazement as Morag recounted all that they knew about Ewan's disappearance.

'He was on the morning round of the islands and due back at ten o'clock, but he never showed up. The Drummond twins were out fishing and found the *Seaspray* drifting beyond the Cruadalach isles at about two in the afternoon.'

'And Ewan?'

Morag shook her head. 'There was no sign of him. The boat was just drifting and had run out of fuel.' Her normally unflappable visage was showing signs of strain. Tears were forming in the corners of her eyes. 'We think that he must have tumbled overboard.'

Torquil rubbed his eyes and sighed. 'It's not possible, Morag. Ewan McPhee, the Western Isles hammer-throwing champion, who's been a strong swimmer since he was a lad — there's no way that he could have just fallen overboard. And even if he had, he would have pulled himself back on board, no bother.'

'We've agonized over all that ourselves, Torquil,' the Padre pointed out. 'But if the boat had been moving fast —'

'And he may not have been well, Torquil,' said Morag. 'There was blood on the side of the catamaran.'

Torquil eyed her quizzically. 'You think he may have banged his head and fallen overboard?'

'No. I think he may have had one of his nose-bleeds. You

know how prone he is to them when he's stressed.'

'And how squeamish he is,' the Padre added.

Morag went on, 'The Drummonds notified me immediately and they tried to retrace the route of the *Seaspray,* but they could only guess at the direction he had taken. I called out the coast-guard helicopter from Benbecula and the RAF at Macrahanish despatched two Sea Kings — they spent two days looking for his body. They combed the whole area but found no trace of him. And you know full well that's what usually happens. We are waiting day by day to hear about the body washing up somewhere along the coast or on one of the islands.'

Torquil picked up his mug of tea and began pacing the room. He sipped it, thinking of the many gallons of stewed tea that Ewan had made him over the years. 'I just can't believe it. He was my friend.'

'He was a good friend to all of us, Torquil,' Morag said. 'The Drummonds are both cut up about it and even Calum Steele has been writing sentimental pieces in the *Chronicle* about him.' She stood up and put a hand on his shoulder. 'Now do you see why you can't go resigning? I need you, Torquil.'

He turned and smiled down at her. Like Ewan McPhee, Morag was a good friend, as well as being his sergeant. He noticed how tired and drained she looked. And how much weight she had lost, although now he realized that it must have been from worry. He gave her a big hug. 'Och, of course I won't leave, Morag — for now anyway.' He released her, then asked, 'How is Jessie?'

The Padre struck a light to his pipe despite the prominent No Smoking notices scattered all over the station. 'She's struggling, Torquil. But she's a tough old lady. She lost her husband in a fishing-boat accident when Ewan was only five, so it's bound to be stirring up old wounds.' He sighed. 'But until the Fatal Accident Enquiry, whenever that is, we can do nothing.'

'Poor Ewan, he'd been through the mill, hadn't he?' Torquil said. 'What with that last relationship and everything.'

'A relationship may have had something to do with this, Piper,' said Morag, using the name that Torquil was often known by throughout the island. 'You know how involved Ewan can get? Well, I think he had fallen head over heels. His mind hasn't been on the job for days. The trouble was, I don't think the lassie knew exactly how much he felt for her.'

'Who is she?' Torquil queried.

'Katrina Tulloch — the new vet.'

Torquil nodded his head as he put the face to the name. 'Old Tam Tulloch's niece. I met her a couple of times before I left. She's a bonnie lassie, right enough.'

The Padre blew smoke ceiling-wards. 'Actually, I think she did know he liked her, Morag. She was upset yesterday at Gordon MacDonald's wake. She left in a hurry after Kenneth McKinley said something to her about there not being many police officers left on West Uist.'

'Gordon MacDonald is dead?' Torquil repeated.

'Aye, from a stroke. That was Ralph McLelland's opinion, and he'd been Gordon's GP for years. He'd been dead for a couple of days before he was found. Rhona McIvor discovered him when he didn't show up to help her with the geese.' He shook his head. 'And now poor Rhona is in the cottage hospital herself after having another heart attack.' He told Torquil about the events at the wake.

'So the new laird, this Jock McArdle, is really going to set up a wind farm?' Torquil asked in disbelief. 'Here on West Uist? There will be an outcry.'

'Morag and I just saw the first one,' said the Padre. 'That lorry that just came off before you looked as if it was carrying the components for a windmill.'

'I can't believe that all this has happened since I went away,' said Torquil with a sad shake of the head. 'Especially Ewan ...'

'We're all trying to get our heads round it, laddie,' agreed the Padre.

At that very moment Katrina Tulloch, the veterinary surgeon in question, was not feeling at all caring towards one of her patients. She had been feeling tense and on edge ever since Ewan had disappeared. She knew perfectly well that the big constable had fallen for her, but over the last couple of weeks he had seemed to be preoccupied with something and his attitude towards her had been slightly strained, as if he was suspicious of her.

God! How do I get myself in such emotional messes? she mentally chided herself. Without any active encouragement she seemed to have had at least three men fawning over her since she had taken over her uncle's practice. And she had felt torn and confused to say the least. Which of them did she really want? Dammit, it was all so bloody —

Her wandering attention was brought back to bear on the large dog that had begun to snarl at her again.

'Zimba has always been a wee bit protective of his bottom,' explained the dog's owner, Annie McConville, one of Kyleshiffin's renowned eccentrics. She ran a dog sanctuary that covered the whole of the Western Isles, and she was an almost daily visitor at both the local police station, where she would lodge complaints about local ordinances, and the local veterinary practice with at least one of her many canine charges. Zimba was a large Alsatian who had developed a limp over the preceding week which had done nothing for his somewhat mercurial disposition.

'I think I'll have to take him in for a general anaesthetic, Miss McConville,' Katrina said, edging backwards, peeling off her latex rubber gloves as she did so. 'Zimba isn't going to let me near enough to examine that abscess.'

'Oh, so it is an abscess that he has? And there was me thinking it was just a bad case of worms again. He sits down and pulls himself along to scratch his bottom a lot.'

Katrina smiled uncertainly, scarcely believing that Annie McConville hadn't seen the abscess as large as a duck's egg to the left of the Alsatian's anus. Attempting to examine the brute had almost cost her a couple of fingers.

'I'll make an appointment then shall I, Miss Tulloch?' Annie asked, alternately stroking the Alsatian and tugging on the chain leash to encourage him off the examination table.

'Just see Jennie at the reception and we'll get him in tonight. He'll need an operation tomorrow.'

The Alsatian jumped down and yowled with pain.

'See, he's not liking that proposition,' said Annie.

And while Katrina sprayed the table with disinfectant and then washed her hands in preparation for her next client, she mused that in many ways human medicine seemed preferable to veterinary work.

'Hi, Katrina,' came a familiar male voice.

She spun round at once, her face registering surprised joy, which was quickly suppressed by professional bedside manner. 'Oh, Nial,' she said, on recognizing the Scottish Bird Protection officer-cum-smallholder. He was holding a cage containing a young fulmar. 'You sounded just like someone else.'

Nial Urquart pressed his lips together. 'I'm, sorry, Katrina.

You mean Ewan McPhee, don't you?'

Katrina shook her head and smiled dismissively. 'Forget it. What can I do for you? A wounded fulmar is it?'

The bird protection officer nodded and laid the cage on the table. He undid the front grille and, reaching in gingerly, removed the bird.

'Just hold her on the table while I give her the once over,' Katrina said. She swiftly and skilfully assessed her patient. 'She's been lucky,' she announced. 'She's got a pretty bloodstained wing, but the wound is superficial. No bone damage that I can find.' She looked up at him, instantly aware that his eyes had been roving appreciatively over her upper torso. She pretended not to notice, instead asking, 'What was it, an eagle?'

'It was one of the golden eagles from up in the Corlins. I saw it swoop on her in mid-flight, and just failed to keep hold. I saw her fall and the eagle just flew on and took the next fulmar it spotted. The last I saw it was heading back towards its eyrie in the Corlins.'

'You really love those eagles, don't you?'

He nodded enthusiastically. 'They are majestic creatures, Katrina.' He put the fulmar back in its cage, then turned to her with a smile. 'I love all beautiful creatures.'

Katrina chose to ignore the flattery, if flattery was intended. Instead, she continued conversationally, 'I'm heading up to the Wee Kingdom after I finish surgery here. I've got to go and see Alistair McKinley's sheep. He's worried that a couple might have a touch of foot rot.' There was silence for a moment, then she asked, 'Any news of Rhona?'

'I've just been to the cottage hospital. She was really out of it, with morphine I guess. She just came round enough to ask me to get her some cigarettes, then she fell asleep again. I don't

279

know if she actually realized that it was me. That set-to with the new laird didn't help one iota.' He gritted his teeth. 'The bastard! Him and his two Glaswegian lackies.'

'Yes,' Katrina agreed. 'He's got a lot to answer for if he caused Rhona to have a heart attack.'

Nial picked up the bird cage and prepared to leave. Then, almost as an afterthought, he plucked a couple of leaflets from a side pocket of his waterproof jacket. 'Could I leave a few of these in your waiting-room? They're for a protest meeting against the wind farm.'

Katrina looked at him with concern. 'Be careful, Nial. The new laird doesn't sound as if he's the sort that it is wise to cross.'

The bird protection officer grinned. 'I didn't know you cared.'

'It's Morag I'm worried about,' she lied.

It was after lunch before Katrina could get out to the Wee Kingdom to see Alistair McKinley's sheep. It was misty for one thing. For another the causeway across to the little islet was blocked by a large container lorry that could only just get across, by literally edging its way inch by inch, each move directed by a swarthy well-built youth in a red baseball hat. After waiting behind it for quarter of an hour, she zipped past in her battered old Mini-van, ignoring the wolf whistles from the driver and his mate as they pulled into the side of the road prior to negotiating the pock-marked drive up to Wind's Eye croft.

As Katrina expected, she found the old crofter working away at his hand loom in one of the outhouses, outside which Shep, his nervous but friendly old collie stood guard. After a cursory bark, the collie advanced with tail wagging at half-mast. Katrina patted him, stroked his head then entered the outhouse. 'You never stop, do you, Alistair?' she said admiringly.

'Time is money, Vet,' he returned, barely looking up to acknowledge her entry. 'Just let me finish off this bit of weaving, and then I'll be with you.'

Katrina watched admiringly for a few minutes as he operated the foot treadles which raised the heddles to open a shed for the shuttle, which was thrown across when he pulled a string with his right hand. That done, he swung the sley back and forth, gradually transforming a seemingly impossibly complicated arrangement of threads of yarn into the famous patterned West Uist cloth. There was something almost hypnotic about the pleasing rattle-tattle noise of the most basic technology.

'It really is a cottage industry in every sense, isn't it?' she commented. 'West Uist Tweed is sold all over the west of Scotland, yet I guess few buyers in the fancy shops realize that it is all made by hand in the crofts of the Wee Kingdom.'

'Aye, that's right. We don't have the market of the Harris Tweed, of course, but we have our own style. All of the crofters contribute and we all aim to make our quota each month. It's the way it has always been.'

'And will it always be done like this?'

Alistair finished and tapped the shuttle, 'I have my doubts. Especially if that new laird has anything to do with it.' He looked as if he was about to spit, but thought better of it. 'Windmills!' he exclaimed in exasperation. 'He's just sent poor Rhona into hospital and as for my Kenneth —'

'He's sent Kenneth where?'

The old crofter turned sharp penetrating eyes on her. 'Are you interested in Kenneth, Katrina? I saw he got your blood up yesterday at the wake.'

Despite herself, Katrina flushed. 'I interrupted you. What do you mean, am I interested in Kenneth?'

'Are you just being polite when you ask where he is, or are you interested in my son?'

Katrina smiled and gently shook her head. 'I think we are talking at cross purposes here, Alistair. I had heard that Rhona had been sent to hospital and I somehow thought you meant that Kenneth had gone too. And to answer your question — your very direct question — I am not interested in Kenneth as a boyfriend. He's a good-looking lad, but he's ... a lot younger than me.'

'Not all that much, lassie. He's twenty-two now.' Still the penetrating eyes fixed on her. 'And he likes you, you ken.'

Katrina pursed her lips and folded her arms across her chest. 'OK, how can I say this,' she said pensively. 'I am interested in —' She hesitated and bit her lip. 'I was interested in someone else.'

'Young McPhee, the policeman?'

Katrina stared at him for a moment, saying nothing. Then she glanced at her watch. 'Maybe I could see those sheep you're worried about.'

Alistair shrugged and stood up. 'This way then,' he said. At the door he stopped and looked at her pointedly. 'But look, lassie, I think you need to be realistic. It's been days since the accident. I doubt that we'll ever see Ewan McPhee again.'

The mists had rolled down from the tops of the Corlins making the ascent perilous. Yet the assassin was as sure-footed as a mountain goat. Or rather, he usually was. Having slept rough overnight, he had only eaten snails, a few worms and taken a goodly few drams of whisky from his flask. The combination had slightly numbed his senses and he was aware that he had taken one or two chances that he would not normally have taken. Even so, he shinned up the almost sheer slope of the crag that levelled to a small shelf in a little less than half an hour. He pulled himself over the jutting overhang and, after resting for a moment or two to get his breath, he stood up and adjusted his rucksack. The mist swirled around him making it hard to see more than an outline of the upward crag, atop of which he knew rested the eyrie.

'It's illegal to steal golden eagle eggs, you know,' said the voice from out of the mist.

He started despite himself, his hand reaching over his shoulder for the rifle in its shoulder bag. Then he regained his composure, and he laughed. 'It is also illegal to kill eagles, but I am going to.'

The figure came out of the mist. 'No, you will not! You will restrict yourself to the tasks I give you. And there will be no more killing.'

He scowled angrily. 'I take orders from no one.'

'What did you do with the bodies anyway?'

'I ... disposed of them.'

He swung his rucksack off and delved inside, pulling out a small thermos flask. He tossed it over and watched with amusement as the other raised it and gently shook it. Their eyes locked, then, 'Are they iced?'

'Just as you said.'

He watched as the lid was unscrewed and some crushed ice was allowed to escape before a polythene bag fell out into the waiting hand. He half-expected a reaction upon seeing the gory contents, but there was none. Instead: 'And what about the policeman?'

He sneered, 'I already told you.'

'You were lying.'

His eyes narrowed, then he bit his lip. 'He got in the way.'

'You fool!'

'Never call me that!' he snapped, swinging the rifle bag off his shoulder and undoing the press studs to withdraw the weapon. 'I did what I had to do and that's that. And maybe now I should be the one to give orders.'

They both heard the sound of flapping wings followed by the characteristic chirping noise as the eagle returned to its nest. The assassin screwed on the silencer on the barrel of his Steyr-Mannlicher rifle.

'What did you do with —?'

'With him?' He laughed. 'That's my wee secret. Now get out of my way. I've got another job to do.'

'I won't let you this time.'

'Don't try to stop me.' He put the rifle to his shoulder and squinted through the mist in the direction of the last screech. 'Come to me, birdie!' he said, his voice dropping almost to a whisper.

'I said — no!'

'Shut up!' he hissed.

The mists swirled and he thought he saw a shape flit across the Leupold 'scope. He swung the weapon, squeezed the trigger and there was a popping as the report was muffled by the silencer. Looking up he scowled and took a step backwards towards the ledge to get a better view upwards.

He had no time to deflect the blow. He felt a thump on the side of his head, a searing pain in his face — and then he was falling backwards, the rifle slipping from his hands as he clawed futilely at space. His scream rang out and died upon the moment of impact on the rocks below.

The other stared down, only dimly conscious of the flap of retreating wings.

CHAPTER FOUR

Megan Munro's libido was always at its best in the early morning. As a self-styled neo-pagan, she believed that it was because she felt closest to the earth when her mother-earth force awakened and demanded satiation. Regardless of morning breath, overnight perspiration or flattened hair, the need was there, like a powerful itch. And the means of assuaging it was also there in the form of Nial, always eager to please, and to be pleasured by her.

Afterwards they lay side by side, heart rates gradually recovering, thoughts turning from the carnal to the more mundane business of the day ahead. And as usual it was Megan who threw back the duvet and ran naked to the bathroom to brush teeth and perform ablutions before hitting the kitchen to make that first post-coital cup of tea.

Nial took a few sips then lay back dozing contentedly. Morning sex with Megan had been a revelation. It lifted him to heights of delirium then plummeted him into pleasant somnolence. She was like an enchantress, he mused, as he rolled over and burrowed further under the duvet. In many ways she liked to project a simple persona. She eschewed make-up, avoided alcohol, tobacco and drugs. She dressed simply and made no secret of her beliefs and opinions. She was vegetarian — on moral grounds — a former animal rights campaigner — as was he — and a paid up member of the Green Party. Yet in the bedroom, or any other room where the fancy took her for that matter, she was primal passion itself. Yes, that was it, he thought, passion was the key to her personality. She was passionate in everything that she thought or did.

Animals seemed to come first with her, even more so than they did with himself. But especially those blasted hedgehogs of hers. He grinned through his semi-conscious haze as he pictured her now, buff naked, running through the dew, to check the runs of her 'Mistress Prickleback Sanctuary'. The islanders all thought that she was a nutter of course, with her New Age ideas, her views on animal rights and her obsession with the West Uist hedgehog population. To him she was more than that. She was a wonderful, eccentric nymphomaniac that he was happy to live with — for now. As to whether he would want to spend the rest of his life with her, however, was another matter. But, as he inhaled the scent of her body on the bedding, he felt the stirring of a fresh erection. And because she was not physically there, his mind spiralled off in another direction, conjuring up an image of that other woman whom he found so attractive. He grinned as he thought how wonderful it would be ...

Megan's scream broke through his reverie and he shot out of bed, stopping only long enough to pull on a pair of underpants. The kitchen door was open and through it he saw her slowly walking up the path, as naked as she was born, her face contorted in horror as she stared at her outstretched, bloodstained hands.

Her eyes slowly rose to meet his and she screamed again.

The Padre was busily stirring a porridge pot on the Aga while a couple of herrings in oatmeal sizzled in a pan when Torquil slinked into the kitchen in a towelling dressing-gown and bare feet.

He was a tall, dark-haired young man of twenty-eight, handsome in the opinion of many an island lass, albeit with a slightly hawk-like profile that he himself disliked. Despite his exhaustion after all his recent travel, he had slept poorly, because his mind refused to stop thinking about Ewan, his friend as well as his constable. He had showered and shaved off his accumulated stubble, much to his uncle's approval.

'That's better, laddie,' he said, lifting the porridge pot and taking it over to the table. 'You look more like an inspector now and less like a tramp.'

Torquil grinned and ran the back of his hand over his freshly shaved chin. 'And there was me toying with the idea of letting the beard grow.' He took his seat and sniffed the air appreciatively. 'I must say, I had dreams about having a good West Uist herring while I was away.'

'Porridge first though, eh,' said Lachlan, ladling out two bowls. He smiled at his nephew, then, 'It's good to be having you home, laddie. I just wish it could be under happier circumstances.'

'Like it was before we lost Ewan?'

The Padre nodded. 'And before we lost Fiona.'

Torquil sighed. 'It was losing Fiona that made me take time off. I thought I had it all sussed. That's why I'm thinking of leaving the force.' He sprinkled a little salt on his porridge. 'But I'll have to put my plans on hold for a while. The Procurator Fiscal will need to be consulted, and a Fatal Accident Enquiry is likely.'

'I keep hoping that we'll find the lad's body. There's nothing worse than knowing somebody's drowned, but not being able to pay your respects properly. I've been praying every day that we'll find him washed up on some shore.'

Torquil shivered despite himself and reached for the previous day's copy of the *West Uist Chronicle* that his uncle had been reading as he prepared the breakfast.

287

'Calum Steele has written a fine piece about Ewan,' Lachlan said. 'He's written a review of all of Ewan's sporting achievements since he was a boy at the school. I doubt if his hammer record will ever be beaten.'

Torquil scanned the two-page article, then jabbed at a photograph of a row of windmills. 'Calum is taking up cudgels about windmills, I see. A regular Don Quixote, eh?'

The Padre raised his eyes heavenwards. 'Windmills indeed! Here on West Uist.'

'But there has been talk of wind power in the Hebrides for years. Why are you against it, Lachlan?'

'I'm not, in principle. I don't much like the new laird of Dunshiffin though.'

'That's not like you. You usually give everyone the benefit of the doubt. What have you got against the man?'

The Padre shook his head disdainfully. 'He cheats at golf for one thing. You can tell a lot about someone's character by the way they play golf.'

'Ah, the hallowed game,' Torquil said with a grin.

'Aye, laddie, you may laugh, but it takes a lot —' Then seeing his nephew's grin growing wider he shook his head. 'Suffice it to say that despite his cheating I took a fiver off him and put it straight into the *Say No to Windfarms'* kitty.'

Torquil finished his porridge and sat back. 'So what exactly is the laird proposing?'

'We don't know precisely yet, beyond the fact that he's already ordered the first one and is having it set up on Wind's Eye, Gordon MacDonald's croft on the Wee Kingdom. From what he said the other day I don't think he's planning to let anyone work the croft in the future.'

'But I thought the crofters had a right to transfer their crofts to family or close friends if they had no offspring.'

'That's what everyone thought, but it doesn't look to be the case. The laird has looked into it.' Lachlan finished his own porridge then stood up and went over to the Aga where he had left the herrings at the side of the simmering plate. Transferring them to plates he returned to the table. 'Och! And I don't like the way he's taken on the title of 'laird.' He's a puffed up Glaswegian —'

'A Glaswegian what?'

'I don't know exactly, Torquil. But I suspect that he's a bully as well as a cheat. And I cannot abide a cheat.' He sighed as he poured tea for them both. 'The trouble is that I have seen his like before and I fear what may happen in the future. I am concerned about Rhona McIvor and the other crofters. I don't like to take issue with the Good Book, but the fact is that the meek do not seem to inherit the earth. It is the bully-boys who do, and they are the ones who seem to know how to hang on to things.' He started on his herring with gusto.

'What is his background?'

'Bakery, I think. He calls himself an ice-cream and confectionary millionaire, but that's a bit suspicious if you ask me. You know about the ice-cream wars in Glasgow back in the eighties? Well, he's got a couple of heavies that he refers to as his boys with him.'

'Sounds like I should check out his background.'

The Padre buttered an oatcake. 'It would do no harm to let him know that we have law here on West Uist.'

Torquil nodded. 'Maybe I'll take Ewan —' He stopped, realizing that he had momentarily forgotten that he would never be able to take Ewan on official business again. He hit the side of his head with his fist and scowled. 'Maybe I'll take the Drummond lads with me.'

The Padre smiled sympathetically and nodded. 'Aye, they are

good lads and will not be intimidated by any number of Glasgow heavies.' He sipped his tea then nodded reflectively. 'So tell me, what were you planning to do if you left the force?'

Torquil leaned back and stretched his legs under the table. He nodded towards the open kitchen door where a half-stripped carburettor from one of their classic motorcycles could be seen leaking oil onto an old newspaper. The whole hallway was similarly littered with bike parts and repair equipment. 'Mend motorcycles maybe,' he said with a grin. 'Or perhaps something to do with music and the pipes. Teaching maybe, or even set up a business.'

'A piping business here on West Uist? You would starve, laddie! There's only really you and I who play the pipes on the island.'

Torquil grinned. 'The internet, uncle. Technology has changed the world. If you set up a decent website and do your homework you can soon have customers all over the world. And you'd be surprised how many people are interested in piping now. The Tartan Army showed me that. People love the Scottish football fans and their pipers.'

'But you've put the idea on the back burner? You're not going to leave the force? Morag really needs you right now.'

Torquil stood up and stretched. 'Aye, I'm staying put for now. But later on, who knows.'

Nial Urquart stared transfixed at the blood on Megan's hands and at the way her jaw trembled as she shifted her attention from them to him. But no words came, instead she screamed again, startling him into motion. He ran to her and gingerly put an arm about her shoulders, but she shrugged him off, her eyes wide with horror.

'It's awful!' she exclaimed. 'The body! It's been —'

She did not finish, but suddenly bent double and vomited.

Nial patted her back, feeling uncertain how he could best comfort her. Then, as she continued to retch, he decided that action was the best course. 'I'll take a look, Megan,' he said. He ran down the path and passed the outhouses, beyond which were the hedgehog runs and the tiny sheds filled with straw that were used to house Megan's prickly waifs and strays.

The body was lying in between two of the runs, covered in blood and with deep lacerations from which the vital fluid had oozed. It looked as if it had literally dropped from the sky. And indeed, looking at its position between the runs, he assumed that must have been exactly what had happened.

He steeled himself and bent over the body of the dead hedgehog and pictured what had happened. He was sure that he had witnessed something similar the day before. The golden eagle swooping on the flock of fulmars, catching one, then dropping it and nonchalantly taking the next with barely a break in its flight. And now, in his mind's eye, he saw the great bird swooping down from above, having spotted the hedgehog run. Grabbing one in its two-inch talons, rising, then dropping it and returning for the next unfortunate hedgehog that had not scurried to the safety of the small sheds, and flying off with it to the eyrie up in the Corlins. A natural killer, it wouldn't have given a second's thought to the exsanguinated hedgehog that it had left behind.

'You're a bit of a butterfingers, aren't you!' he mused with a grin.

He heard Megan behind him and instantly the grin on his face disappeared.

'I ... I thought it was still alive,' she sobbed. 'I picked it up — ' She looked down at her bloodstained hands, still held well away from her naked body. 'They're evil, Nial. They're murderers. They enjoy killing.'

He was worried by the glazed stare in her eye. She was bordering on the hysterical. He stood to put himself between her and the sight of the dead hedgehog. 'Come on, let's get you into a bath then I'll make you a good strong cup of chamomile tea.'

'You'll bury it, won't you?'

He put an arm about her shoulder and shepherded her back to the cottage. 'I'll do it while you are having a bath,' he assured her.

'We have to get them, Nial. Kenneth McKinley was right. They're vermin! Vermin!'

Vincent Gilfillan stood at the end of Rhona McIvor's bed in the four-bedded unit of the Kyleshiffin cottage hospital. The fact that she was the only patient seemed oddly poignant, as if her health was particularly precarious. Tears threatened to form in the corners of his eyes as he looked down at the middle-aged woman who meant more to him than his own mother. This is all wrong, he thought. It shouldn't be happening this way. Not to Rhona. Although she was twenty years older than him, he loved her dearly.

He shuddered as he looked at the wavy green trace on the oscilloscope of the heart monitor, at the wires attached to her chest and the intravenous line that ran into the back of her heavily bandaged left wrist. There seemed to be flowers, fruit and Get-Well cards everywhere. He looked at his own modest collection of freesias and let out a disdainful puff of air through tight lips. It was enough to wake the dozing Rhona. She turned her head and saw him, her eyes momentarily opening wide in alarm. It was not the sort of reaction that he was used to from Rhona. She reached for her spectacles on the cabinet and put them on. Then, recognizing him, 'Vincent,' she said dreamily, almost with relief as if she had woken from a troubled sleep. She held out a hand to him. 'You startled me.'

He took her hand and pressed it to his lips. 'Rhona, I'm sorry,' he mumbled apologetically. 'I heard as soon as I came off the ferry. I should have been here.'

'For what?' she said with a smile. She reached up and stroked his wiry black beard that had recently begun to display a peppering of silver hairs. 'Would you have stopped this old ticker of mine from having a heart attack?'

He shrugged awkwardly, indicating a particularly large bouquet of red roses that dominated the display. 'It looks like someone has sent the contents of Betty Hanson's florist shop.'

Rhona pushed herself up against the bank of pillows and harrumphed. 'They're from the new laird, Mr Fine And Dandy Jock McArdle. A peace offering, I think. Did you hear what happened?'

Vincent sat down on the side of the bed and handed her his Get Well card. 'I saw Morag Driscoll on Harbour Street. She told me about his plan to put up windmills on Gordon MacDonald's croft.'

'And I told him it would be over my dead body,' Rhona said, with a shake of her head as she opened the card and smiled at the picture of an old goat in bed. She perched it on the bedside cabinet alongside the others. 'And then one of his toadies sniggered and I saw red. I was about to give him a good skelp on the side of his head — and then I ended up in here.'

Vincent's jaw muscles tightened. 'I think I'll be having a word with this lad then. He sounds as if he needs teaching a lesson.'

Rhona noticed the way his fist opened and closed. 'You'll do no such thing. I can fight my own battles and I'll not have you getting into trouble with the likes of him. It's not your battle.'

'It sounds as if it is a battle for all of us on the Wee Kingdom. What have the others said about it?'

Rhona pouted. 'Nial Urquart was round yesterday and he said that Megan was upset, of course. And they've had a bee in their bonnet about the wind farm threat anyway for a while. This has just sort of focused everything a bit.' She bit her lip. 'God, I could murder a cigarette!' She looked at him pleadingly. 'You couldn't sneak in a pack for me, could you?'

'More than my life is worth. And it's time you were stopping anyway.'

'Ach! It's too late for me now.' She made to fold her arms, but being unable to do so because of the heavily bound wrist with its drip-line she swore volubly.

'I see that you can't be too ill then,' came Alastair McKinley's voice from the end of the unit. He came forward, nodded to Vincent and bent to kiss Rhona on the cheek. 'That was some fleg you gave us yesterday, Rhona. You'll not be planning another, I'm hoping.'

Rhona scowled, then looked worried. 'Will you manage my goats?'

'Everything is taken care of,' said Alistair. 'All the animals are fed, the crops are doing well and the weaving will get done as and when we've time.'

Rhona gave a smile of resignation. 'Of course, like always, the Wee Kingdom folk will pull together.'

Vincent put a hand on Alistair's shoulder. 'Will you point out the young fool that caused all this to me?'

'Vincent!' Rhona exclaimed. 'I've told you already.'

'Of course I will,' Alistair said, ignoring Rhona's look of exasperation for a moment. 'But I'm thinking that you might need to stand in line if you're contemplating violence. Kenneth went off in one of his huffs and you know what a temper he has. He didn't come home last night. He does that when he's working himself up about something. And he's been doing that a lot lately.' He shoved his hands deep into his pockets and stared at the floor for a few moments, as if deep in his own thoughts. Then he added, 'And as for that mad woman —'

'Alistair! I've told you before about calling Megan Munro names! We have to be united in the Wee Kingdom.'

'Ach, well, she is mad,' replied Alistair. 'Her and her hedgehogs. I don't know what she gets up to sometimes, but I heard her screaming away this morning. Her man dropped another of those flyers of his on my doormat, but didn't stop long enough to talk to me. No manners!'

'What flyer was this?' Vincent asked.

'This meeting he's been on about for a while. The anti-windmill thing this afternoon. I suppose under the circumstances we should be there, don't you?'

Rhona sat forward. 'Of course, the pair of you should go and represent our interests. But don't do anything silly. No violence, or any of that nonsense.'

Vincent smiled and clicked his tongue. 'This coming from the woman who was going to give that lad a "good skelp" herself!'

CHAPTER FIVE

No one on the island of West Uist had ever known Jesmond's first name. He was not a local man, but had come to the island to serve Fergus MacLeod as a footman in the 1950s when he was about sixteen. The household at Dunshiffin Castle had been trimmed right back with the last laird, Angus MacLeod, but Jesmond had worked loyally for his master and had come to be associated with the very fabric of the building. Indeed, when Jock McArdle had purchased the estate, he found to his delight that he had also retained the services of a butler.

The elderly retainer seemed to have all the qualities one could have wished for in a butler. He was old, lean as a rake and so straight that he could well have had such an instrument thrust up the back of his ever present white jacket. He had a slightly bulbous nose speckled at the sides with tiny red veins, suggestive of a partiality for the castle brandy, and a comb-over that perpetually threatened to fall back whenever he bowed. And the deferential bow was something that he had down to a fine art. All in all, Jock McArdle couldn't have been happier with him.

But the feeling was not reciprocated by Jesmond. He had been a loyal butler to the MacLeods for fifty years. And in his book, being loyal to the laird meant being loyal to the estate and all that the estate represented. He did not like the new laird's two heavies from Glasgow. He did not particularly like the new laird himself, whom he thought to be boorish and bullying. He did not approve of the laird's plans for the development of the estate, such as he had overheard while serving dinner or port to him and the two heavies whom he seemed to dote on as if they were his own sons. But more than any of that, he did not approve of Jock McArdle's two pet Rottweilers. Nasty-tempered buggers, he thought them, leaving hairs all over the place, skidding on the polished floors and barking whenever a fly landed. His nerves were shot to pieces, but he judged that it was too soon in the relationship with the new laird to protest about them.

He came into the billiard-room where the laird was playing snooker with Liam and Danny. The air was thick with tobacco smoke and he eyed with disdain Liam's habit of leaving a cigarette-end balanced on the edge of the billiard table while he took a shot.

Dallas and Tulsa, the two Rottweilers, lay sprawled on the mat in the window bay, both growling menacingly at his entry.

'This note was dropped through the letterbox, Mr McArdle,' he said, executing his bow and proffering the envelope on his little silver salver.

Jock picked it up and tore the envelope open. As he read it his eyes widened and anger lines appeared between his eyebrows. 'Did you see who left this?' he demanded.

Jesmond had moved a crystal ashtray from the side table onto the edge of the billiard table, beside Liam's cigarette-end. 'No, sir, it was lying on the mat. But as you can see, it was hand-delivered rather than mail-delivered.'

'What's it say, boss?' Liam asked.

In response, Jock tossed the single sheet of paper down on the table for them to see. Upon it, with words cut out of a newspaper, was the message:

THERE IS A WIND OF DISCONTENT
NO WINDMILLS
WE'RE WATCHING YOU

Liam laughed his strange laugh. 'Is that someone trying to frighten you, boss? That's a good one that is. That's original.'

'Shut it, Liam!' snapped Danny, indicating Jesmond with a slight motion of his eyes.

'Should I call the police, Mr McArdle?' Jesmond asked.

'Naw, pal,' replied the laird. 'I don't think we need bother anyone about this. See, it'll just be kids playing a joke. Don't worry about it.' He patted Jesmond's arm and picked up a Moroccan leather cigar ease and tapped out a Montecristo Corona. He clipped the end and winked at the butler. 'We'll be OK, pal. Thanks.'

When Jesmond left, Danny asked, 'What do you really think, boss? Is somebody playing silly buggers?'

Jock struck a light and puffed the cigar into life, 'They'd better bloody not be, lad. These island yokels don't know what trouble really is.' He glanced at his Rolex watch. 'See, it's almost time for that windmill meeting. You two had better get there in order to ... represent my interests.'

Liam laid down his cue and picked up his cigarette. He took a deep inhalation on it and smiled at his employer. 'We'll do you proud, boss.'

'You do that. As for me, I'm going to take the girls for a walk.'

The Duncan Institute was packed and the meeting was in full swing when Torquil arrived. The Padre had suggested that it would be a good idea for him to be there to get a flavour of the strength of local opinion about the wind farm issue.

Nial Urquart and Megan Munro were sitting behind a long table on the dais, together with Miss Bella Melville, the local retired schoolmistress who had educated most of the local people on West Uist between the ages of twenty and fifty. She was a sprightly looking seventy-something woman dressed in tweeds and a rust-coloured shawl. A tubby fellow of Torquil's age with a double chin and lank hair, wearing a yellow anorak was standing in the front row of the audience addressing a question to the committee. In his hands he held an A5 spiral notebook with a pencil poised above it.

'As you are all aware,' he said, 'the *West Uist Chronicle* has been running a series of articles on the pros and cons of wind energy for the last month. The SNWF committee say that windmills are injurious to wildlife, but could you give us any evidence that this will be a problem on West Uist?'

Torquil grinned. Calum Steele, the editor-in-chief, and in fact the only reporter on the *Chronicle* was one of his oldest friends. They had been classmates together and both shared a healthy respect for Miss Bella Melville. As Torquil anticipated, their old teacher came out on the attack.

'Calum Steele, you are fishing for a quote. You were always a nosy boy at school. That's why I told you to become a journalist —' Calum swallowed hard and two red patches began to form on his cheeks as general laughter went round the hall. '— and you already know about the damage that windmills do to bird populations. I sent you a paper about the European experience, which you quoted in an article last week.' She glowered at him, daring him to refute her statement. 'You know and I know that it will be just the same here on West Uist if these things are allowed to be erected.'

Calum raised his hand again. 'Yes, but — er — how do you know it will be the same?'

Miss Melville sighed and shook her head in exasperation. 'Nial, will you illuminate the *Chronicle* editor?'

Nial stood up and grinned. 'Absolutely, Miss Melville. The

problem relates to location. If wind farms are based near the coast then there is a significant danger to seabirds. And, of course, on West Uist, we have an incredibly diverse seabird population. As the local Scottish Bird Protection Officer, I have been surveying the coastal birds for the better part of a year. We have fulmars, puffins, shags, oyster- catchers —'

Calum raised a hand. 'Excuse me for interrupting, but these are all common birds, are they not? What about our other birds, the protected species? The golden eagles, for example?'

Nial suddenly looked uncomfortable. 'They would be at risk too. They are master predators and will take any food they can. If they were hunting near windmills, they might be in danger of flying into the arms.'

'A good riddance, too!' exclaimed Alistair McKinley. 'They take young sheep.'

Nial smiled humorously. 'That is a myth, Alistair.'

'They kill hedgehogs!' Megan Munro piped up. 'And you know that, Nial. They are vermin! Vermin!'

'Ach! Not the hedgehog thing again!' exclaimed Alistair McKinley. 'Now they are real vermin and we'll soon be taking care of them.'

Megan Munro shot to her feet. 'They are not vermin. They are God's own creatures and you will not touch one of my hedgehogs.'

Nial held a hand out to appeal to Megan for calm, but she shrugged him off angrily.

'I'll not touch your wee hedgehog farm, don't worry, lassie,' returned Alistair, 'but I make no promises for all the other hedgehogs I find on the island.'

'It is not a farm, it's a sanctuary,' Megan snapped, and slumped petulantly back into her seat.

A background murmur of merriment ran round the hall and

Calum gleefully made notes. It was just the sort of heated exchange that he had been looking for. Indeed, despite his fear of Miss Melville, he had been machinating for such a reaction. Bella Melville eyed him with displeasure, but he just kept his head down and continued jotting.

Vincent Gilfillan stood up. 'Are we not getting a bit off the track here? Let's be honest. The issue is about a wind farm being set up on the Wee Kingdom, is it not?'

Torquil noticed the two men who had been sitting on the back row, from time to time guffawing and mumbling to each other. Their faces had become serious as Vincent started to talk.

'What does this new laird plan? Do we know if he's got a significant wind farm plan in mind?'

Liam Sartori swiftly stamped to his feet. 'Mr McArdle, the new laird, is not prepared to comment on that.'

'And would you mind introducing yourself?' Miss Melville asked. 'Do you represent the laird?'

Liam grinned. 'I am in his employ. Sartori is the name. And yes, I represent his interests at this meeting, as does my colleague here, Mr Daniel Reid.'

'And can you enlighten us?'

Liam grinned and shook his head. 'No comment, that's all we are permitted to say.'

'Except,' added Danny, 'that Mr McArdle is a staunch believer in renewable energy. Surely that's a good thing in this day and age.'

The comment evoked a mixed reaction from the audience. Indeed it became obvious after a few moments that there was about a fifty-fifty balance, many people being in favour of anything that might increase the number of jobs and pump money into the island.

'We want to be the first!' yelled a young man in the middle of the hall.

'That's right; we need to get in before they build one on Lewis.'

Torquil looked over the audience and saw Alistair mumble something to Vincent, and gesture with a nod of his head towards Liam Sartori. Then he saw Calum raise a hand and take to his feet again.

'It seems that there are a lot of islanders who would welcome wind energy.'

The number of nodding heads and a chorus of assent left no doubt but that the audience was not as anti-wind farm as the SNWF committee had anticipated. It was immediately followed by a chorus of anti-windmill comments, then by a general murmur of disagreement, which prompted Miss Melville to take to her feet and try to subdue it. As she did so, Torquil stood aside as Liam Sartori and Danny Reid edged their way out of the hall with amused expressions on their faces. He looked over at Calum, who was scribbling away as if there was no tomorrow, clearly enjoying the melée.

He was unsure himself exactly how he felt.

From the meeting Torquil went to pay a visit to Jessie McPhee. A typical West Uist mist had descended suddenly from the Corlins, and its presence was enough to dampen his spirits. He smiled wistfully as he rode up to the shed at the back of the McPhee cottage. There were at least five holes in the shed roof, a result of Ewan's hammer-throwing practice. Torquil pictured the big red-haired constable winding himself up and hurling the Scottish hammer over the roof as he worked on getting the trajectory just right to get maximum distance. Getting around to repairing his 'low shots' had been a frequent bone of contention between Ewan and his mother.

'He was a strapping lad,' Jessie said, with tears in her eyes and a cup and saucer in her hand, as she and Torquil sat before a peat fire in the front parlour.

'We must not give up hope, Jessie.'

Torquil had known and respected Jessie McPhee all of his life. She had been widowed when Ewan was a child. Her husband, Balloch, had been a fisherman, like so many of the islanders of his generation. And in his spare time he had been a special constable, one of the stalwarts of the Hebridean Constabulary.

'You were always a good friend to Ewan,' Jessie replied, finishing her tea and laying the cup and saucer down on the basketwork tray on the coffee table. She sighed. 'But who are we trying to kid? First it was Balloch and now it's Ewan. Both drowned. It is something we islanders have to live with. You yourself lost your parents to the sea, and I am not the first West Uist woman to lose her menfolk, and I doubt if I will be the last. I just hope that his body will wash up on the shore someplace and then we can lay him to rest properly.'

Half an hour later as he rode his Royal Enfield Bullet along the snaking headland road, scattering countless gulls from the dunes, he had to agree with Jessie McPhee's pronouncement. He slowed up as the mist suddenly became thicker and he flicked on his full headbeam.

He just could not get his head round the loss of Ewan. He was so big, so strong and robust. He was not looking forward to the inevitable Fatal Accident Enquiry on his friend and colleague.

'Damn it!' he exclaimed, as he slowed and swung the Bullet off the road and through thick bracken onto a thin track through the heather towards the Corlins. It was a shortcut that he often took on his way back to the manse.

He heard a cacophony of dog barking ahead of him and a moment later the Bullet's headlamp beam caught the eyes of first one then two dogs advancing towards him through the mist. He slowed down as he saw a figure appear behind the dogs, frantically waving to him.

'Heel, Willie! Heel, Angus!'

Torquil immediately recognized the two West Highland terriers and their elderly owner, Annie McConville. The old woman's eyes were wide with alarm and she looked shocked.

'Annie, what are you doing out here?' he asked, as he cut the engine and dismounted. He pulled the machine onto its central pedestal and pulled off his gauntlets. Annie was well known throughout West Uist for her dog sanctuary in Kyleshiffin. She was breathless and, for a moment, unable to speak. She grabbed the sleeve of his leather jacket with shaking hands.

'We've found a body! Over there!'

Torquil looked to where she was pointing and, on the rocks at the foot of an almost sheer cliff-face, lay the broken body of Kenneth McKinley.

CHAPTER SIX

Annie McConville was a formidable lady. Some people thought of her as an old dog-loving woman who was losing her wits, while others were more generous and averred that she was simply a glorious eccentric. The longer Torquil had known her, the more he had become aware of the strong personality that lurked behind the façade of eccentricity. He was sure that she fostered the image, just as Miss Melville played up to her image as the retired local schoolmistress.

Yet there was one quality possessed by Annie that was now abundantly clear to Torquil. The old lady had a level head. She had discovered a body under tragic circumstances and had neither panicked nor gone hysterical. What she had done before Torquil arrived was to examine the body for any signs of life.

'The poor soul has been dead since yesterday, I would be betting,' she said, looking over his shoulder as Torquil squatted beside the body of the crofter as soon as he had telephoned to Kyleshiffin for assistance.

'He's had a fall, that's for sure. Dashed his brains out,' she said conversationally, as she clipped leads on the two West Highland terriers who were both cowering unhappily at her ankles, clearly anxious to get away from the disquieting dead body.

Annie sucked air between her teeth. 'Aye, it looks like an eagle killed him.'

Torquil had noticed the three long gashes on Kenneth's face, extending from above the left eye and running diagonally down across his cheek to the corner of his mouth. It was an obvious wound that stood out from the gashes and contusions that he seemed to have sustained in his fall.

Gingerly, and futilely he knew, he felt the neck for a carotid pulse. The cold skin was a shade somewhere between blue and purple and felt rock hard as rigor mortis had long set in.

'He'll have been after the eagle eggs up there, I'm thinking,' Annie went on.

'You may be right,' Torquil said, pursing his lips pensively. 'But perhaps he was after the eagles themselves?'

'Now why would you be saying that, Inspector McKinnon?' Annie asked in a voice that almost seemed indignant, as if she was irritated that he had come up with an alternative theory to her own.

Despite himself, Torquil answered automatically, for he was mentally trying to piece things together. 'Because you don't necessarily need a rifle to rob a nest of eggs.' He pointed mechanically to the bullet that lay beside the body, as if it had been thrown out of Kenneth's camouflage jacket pocket upon impact with the rocky ground. 'It looks like a .308 rifle bullet.' He straightened up and peered round in search of the rifle. When he saw no sign of it he looked up at the sheer rock face and the ledge high above. Perhaps it is still up there, he mused to himself.

Annie tugged the Westies' leads and the two dogs stood upright eagerly ready to retreat.

'I didn't see that,' she said coldly. 'We'll be away then, Inspector. You know where I am if you are requiring a statement.'

Torquil noted the angry tone that had suddenly entered her voice. 'Are you all right, Annie?' he asked concernedly.

'I am perfectly well, thank you. I just do not want to say something now that I might regret later on.'

Torquil eyed her quizzically. 'What do you mean? Why would you say something that you regret?'

In response, Annie zipped up her anorak to its limit and sniffed coldly. 'Oh don't worry, Inspector McKinnon, I didn't mean that I have anything to hide! I meant that I don't want to say or think anything ill of the dead. Especially not when someone has lost their life so young. It is just that I don't have a lot of sympathy for anyone who harms one of the Lord's creatures — be that animal, bird or man.'

Torquil watched her walk off with the two Westies tugging at their leads.

Her parting words had given him a strange feeling. 'Animal, bird or man.' He looked down at the bullet lying beside the body. He had left it there deliberately, since it would need to be photographed beside his body. It was certainly a calibre that would be enough to kill a man.

Doctor Ralph McLelland arrived in the Kyleshiffin Cottage Hospital ambulance about quarter of an hour later. It was not a purpose-built ambulance, but was in fact a fairly ancient camper van that had been donated to the cottage hospital by the late Angus Macleod. Sergeant Morag Driscoll arrived moments after him in the official police Ford Escort.

Torquil led them to the body and explained his findings before the GP-cum-police surgeon went to work, assisted by Morag, who was forensically trained.

Ralph McLelland was one of Torquil's oldest friends. He was the third generation of his family to minister to the local people of West Uist. He had trained at Glasgow University then embarked on a career in forensic medicine, having gained his diploma in medical jurisprudence as well as the first part of his membership of the Royal College of Pathologists. But then his father had fallen ill and he had felt the old strings of loyalty tug at him, so that he returned to the island to take over his father's practice and look after him in the last six months of his life. He had been in single-handed practice for six years.

As for Morag Driscoll, she was a thirty-something single parent of three children. She too had for a time striven to break loose from her island background and had undergone CID training in Dundee before returning to West Uist, marriage and parenthood. Her husband's early demise from a heart attack had given her a personal drive to keep healthy — which she managed in the main, except for a slight problem with her weight — so that she could provide for her 'three bairns,' as she called them.

Together, Morag and Ralph were a formidable team, forming as they did the unofficial forensic unit of the West Uist division of the Hebridean Constabulary. They knew unerringly what the other needed in terms of the examination of the body and the scene.

'Is it a straightforward accident, do you think?' Torquil asked, after the pair had spent about half an hour examining and photographing the body, the surrounding area, collecting bits and pieces and bagging them up in small polythene envelopes.

Ralph and Morag looked at each other. Ralph raised his eyebrows and Morag shook her head.

'Well, it looks like it could have been an accident,' said Ralph. 'But I don't like the look of that bullet you found.'

'That's my view as well,' agreed Morag. 'And where is the rifle?'

'That's what I thought,' replied Torquil. 'I took a walk up to that ledge and saw where he must have tumbled over. But there is no sign of a gun there. So either he didn't have one with him.' He paused and stroked his chin worriedly. 'Or he had one — and someone for some reason has removed it from the scene.'

Death has a galvanizing effect upon people. An hour and a half later Torquil stood beside Alistair McKinley in the mortuary of the Kyleshiffin Cottage Hospital. He could empathize with the old crofter as he pulled back the sheet to expose the corpse of Kenneth, for he himself had personal experience of having to identify the dead body of a loved one. He remembered that it was like being hit with a sledge hammer, then having your insides twisted like an elastic band. He recalled the scream that threatened to erupt from the depths of his being, the instantaneous dryness of mouth and the overwhelming sense of disbelief.

Alistair's normally ruddy complexion suddenly went pale, as if he had instantly haemorrhaged three pints of blood. And he teetered for a moment as if on the point of fainting. But he didn't. He immediately straightened up and swallowed hard, fighting down rising bile in his throat.

Then, 'That is my son, Kenneth McKinley,' the old man volunteered. 'As you know well enough, Inspector McKinnon.'

'I am truly sorry, Alistair. I am also afraid that —'

'That bastard McArdle is going to pay for this!'

'I'm sorry,' Torquil said quietly, with the intention of keeping Alistair calm. 'What connection is there between them?'

'This is his fault. The lad was as mad as a hatter after Gordon MacDonald's funeral. He was disappointed that the — *laird* — told him he couldn't have Gordon's croft. He went off in a foul mood. When he was in one of those dark moods you couldn't —' His face creased into a woeful expression of pain, '— you couldn't argue with him. He was capable of doing anything.' He shook his head. 'Only this time he went and got

309

himself killed.'

'What did you mean about Mr McArdle, Alistair? About him paying?'

Alistair held Torquil's gaze for a moment, before shaking his head. 'I meant ... nothing, Inspector. It is not for me to say what will happen. But the good Lord may have designs on those with blood on their hands. That's all I have to say.'

Suddenly, his weather-beaten face creased and tears appeared in his eyes as a sobbing noise forced itself from his throat. He wiped his eyes with a pincer-like movement of his right finger and thumb. 'I should have stopped him. It's my fault.'

'How so?'

'I was cross with him. We had an argument as well. I told him he needed more backbone. I said I was fed up with his fantasies. When he went off with his rifle, I should have stopped him. I should have locked him in his room, the way I used to.'

'He had a rifle with him when he left, did he? You are sure about that?'

'Absolutely sure.'

Torquil did not think it an appropriate time to mention that the gun was missing.

The Padre was pulling into the Cottage Hospital carpark on his 1954 Ariel Red Hunter motor cycle on his way to visit Rhona when he saw his nephew come out of the back door of the little hospital with Alistair McKinley. The old crofter's demeanour and posture told him that some tragedy had occurred. The fact that they were coming out of that particular door immediately rang alarm bells since the door only opened from the inside, and he knew full well that it meant they had come from the mortuary.

He crossed the car-park to meet them. After seeking Alistair's permission, Torquil explained about the finding of Kenneth's body at the foot of the cliff.

'Do you need some company, Alistair?' asked the Padre.

The crofter scowled. 'If you are going to the Bonnie Prince Charlie, the answer is yes, but if you mean do I want God's company, the answer is definitely no!'

Lachlan glanced at his watch as Torquil retreated, but not before he had given him a look that meant 'look after him'.

The Padre sighed inwardly. He felt profoundly sad at the loss of a young islander. He put a comforting hand on Alistair's shoulder. 'No, it will just be me. The Lord never pushes Himself on folk, but He's there if you need Him later.' He squeezed the shoulder. 'Come on then, we'll drink to your lad's memory. Just the one drink, though. The whisky bottle can be a false comfort at a time like this.'

Alistair McKinley said nothing but allowed himself to be steered down Harbour Street to the Bonnie Prince Charlie Tavern. The aroma of freshly cooked seafood assailed their nostrils as they entered the bar, behind which the doughty landlady Mollie McFadden and her bar staff were busy pulling pints of Heather Ale and engaging in healthy banter with the clientele.

'And what can I be doing for you gentlemen?' Mollie asked, as she finished serving another customer and greeted them with a smile. She blinked myopically behind a pair of large bifocal spectacles perched on the end of her nose. She was a woman of almost sixty years with a well-developed right arm that had pumped a veritable sea of beer over the years.

'A drink in memory of my boy,' Alistair McKinley said; then raising his voice above the background of chatter, 'And a drink for anyone who will drink with me.'

Mollie's face registered a succession of emotions from shock to profound sadness. 'Oh Alistair, I am so sorry to hear that. An accident, was it?' she asked, as she signalled to her bar staff to begin dispensing whiskies from the row of optics above the bar to the assembled customers willing to join the crofter in a drink.

'A tragedy,' Alistair returned. 'He fell from a cliff at the base of the Corlins.'

Mollie paused momentarily from pouring a couple of large malt whiskies for Alistair and the Padre. 'Was he climbing in the Corlins?'

The crofter shook his head. 'He was after shooting the eagles, I'm thinking.' He picked up one of the ornamental Bonnie Prince Charlie jugs of water that lined the bar and added a dash to his whisky.

Mollie nodded sympathetically. Being well used to orchestrating toasts and all sorts of drinking ceremonies, both joyous and tragic, she clanged the bell above her head. As the bar went silent she drew attention to the crofter standing in front of her.

'To my lad, Kenneth McKinley,' called out Alistair, raising his glass.

A chorus followed, then about twenty glasses were raised, drained and then snapped down on the bar. Half a minute or so of silence ensued, then the customers dutifully and respectfully came up and offered their condolences to the bereaved father.

When the throng had passed Alistair McKinley fixed Lachlan with a steely gaze. 'You said just the one, but I have a mind to drink this place dry. Will you be staying with me?'

The Padre had charged his old briar pipe and was in the process of applying a match to the bowl. He blew smoke ceilingwards.

'My words were merely cautionary, Alistair,' he said. 'I will happily have one more drink with you, but then I will take you home myself. If it is your wish to drink more then I suggest that we get you a small bottle to take home. You need to keep the lid on it.'

'Padre, you mean well, I know. But at this moment I don't give a monkey's curse for anyone. I've lost my boy today and that means I've lost my whole damned reason for life.' He tapped his glass on the bar and nodded meaningfully at Mollie, for her to replenish their glasses.

Lachlan laid his pipe in an ashtray and put a hand on the crofter's arm. 'Alistair, I know you are hurting right now, which is only natural. But it would be best to deal with it naturally. Drinking will only make the hurt worse.'

Alistair did not bother with water this time. He drained his glass and immediately signalled for another. 'I'll find my own way home, Padre. And right now, the only person that needs to worry about me drinking isn't you — it's that bloody laird!'

One of the things that Torquil had not missed while he had been away was the twice weekly telephone call he was obliged to make to his superior officer, Superintendent Kenneth Lumsden.

'Time to phone the headmaster,' he said to Morag when he arrived back at the converted bungalow on Kirk Wynd, which served as the Kyleshiffin police station.

Morag had been engrossed with paperwork at the front desk. 'Rather you than me, boss,' she replied, laying her pen down and jumping down from her high stool to lift the counter flap. 'Would you like a wee fortifying cup of tea to set you up?'

Torquil sighed and shook his head. 'I've gone off tea for

now,' he shrugged his shoulders dejectedly. 'I'm sorry, Morag.'

Morag nodded, her own face dropping. They were both thinking of Ewan and his ever-willingness to make tea. 'That's OK, boss. I guess it wouldn't taste the same without being stewed!'

Despite themselves, they both grinned at the reference to Ewan's ineptitude at brewing tea.

'Do you think there's a still a chance, Torquil?'

He bit his thumb. 'Of finding him alive?' He gave a slight shake of the head. 'I can't see it. But I hope to God we can find his body, for Jessie's sake. I'm going to go out in the *Seaspray* first thing in the morning. Are the Drummond twins going to be about?'

'Aye. They said they'd be in to see you at nine-thirty. They've been a couple of stars while you've been away, but they still have to make their living.'

'Thank heaven for our special constables,' agreed Torquil, walking into his office. He dialled Superintendent Lumsden.

To say that there was a personality clash between Torquil and his superior officer would be an understatement, for they had clashed horns on several occasions, and on one it had even resulted in Torquil being suspended from duty for a short spell. The superintendent hailed from the lowlands of Scotland and seemed to loathe and despise the Hebridean way of life. He was a big man with a ruddy face, a walrus moustache and a chin that could have been carved out of wood. He was a widower and had applied for the post with the Hebridean Constabulary because his only daughter had married a teacher on Benbecula and he wanted to be close to her. A police officer of the rules-and-regulations variety, he had never found it easy to deal with the more laidback approach to life of the islanders. Although he lived on Benbecula and worked between offices on North and South Uist, his jurisdiction ran throughout the whole of the Outer Hebrides. The running of the West Uist division of the Hebridean Constabulary particularly incensed him. Although it only consisted of an inspector, a sergeant, a constable and two special constables, he considered it shambolic to the point of chaos. He disliked the disregard for uniform, schedules and rank. For this he held Torquil McKinnon personally responsible. He felt that twenty-eight was too young to achieve the rank of inspector, he himself having to wait until he was in his mid-thirties.

'I had been expecting your call yesterday, McKinnon,' his voice boomed down the phone as soon as Torquil was put through to him.

'I have been catching up, Superintendent Lumsden. Would you —'

'What's the latest on McPhee?'

Torquil bristled. Somehow to have his friend referred to by his surname, as if they were discussing a local crook rankled. Part of him felt he should remonstrate, but he choked back the feeling and replied calmly.

'He is still missing, sir. I am going out to look around the island myself first thing in the morning.'

There was a moment's silence, then a soft creaking noise from the other end of the phone. Torquil imagined the beefy superintendent shaking his head disdainfully, his stiff collar producing the creaking.

'Do what you have to do, McKinnon. But bear in mind it is five days now since he went missing. He is bound to be dead.'

'I know that, sir. I just want to find his body. He is — was, my friend. I'll be going out with the Drummonds.'

At the mention of the Drummond name Torquil imagined that he heard the same neck-creaking noise. Then, 'If there is no news by tomorrow, I feel that a first report to the Procurator Fiscal should be made. It looks as though there will have to be a Fatal Accident Enquiry.' There was a sigh. 'It would be better if we had a body, though.'

Torquil's hackles rose again, but he suppressed his ire. 'Speaking of a Fatal Accident Enquiry, Superintendent, I have to report that there has been another death. A climbing accident, I think. We found a body at the foot of a cliff at the base of the Corlins.' He declined to mention that Ralph McLelland, Morag and himself all had reservations about the death.

'Damn it, McKinnon. Are you some sort of jinx? You go away for a holiday then all hell breaks loose, people fall in the sea and go missing, or fall off cliffs.'

Torquil was about to reply, when his superior snapped, 'Fax me a full report by the end of the day.'

The line went dead and Torquil found himself staring at the receiver held in his white-knuckled fist. 'Thank you for your usual support, Superintendent Lumsden,' he said.

CHAPTER SEVEN

Wallace and Douglas Drummond, the two West Uist Police special constables, were only fifteen minutes late, which was actually pretty reasonable for them. They had been out fishing from the early hours and were still dressed in their yellow oilskins and smelled strongly of fish with just a hint of tobacco. They were drinking tea from thick mugs and chatting with Morag when Torquil came out of his office. They both shuffled awkwardly and shook hands with their inspector, whom they had known since their childhood.

'It is a sad business, Piper,' said Douglas.

'And it will never be the same without Ewan,' agreed Wallace. There was a tear in his eye and a rueful smile on his lips as he held up his mug. 'He liked a strong cup of tea.'

Torquil nodded. Although six foot tall himself, he had always felt small in comparison with Ewan and the two Drummond twins, who towered over him.

They were like peas in a pod, both about six foot five inches in height and with lithe, strong bodies that had seen much toil on the seas and fought many a battle with the elements. Although both were fond of Heather Ale, which was well known across the island, their liking for marijuana was known only to the cognoscenti. As a member of that order, as well as being their superior officer, Torquil turned a blind eye. As long as they were discreet and did not allow it to interfere with their duties, he thought it not unreasonable to take a liberal view about it.

'Well, we'd better be going,' Torquil said, pulling on his waterproof jacket. 'Wish us luck, Morag.'

Five minutes later the *Seaspray* coasted out of Kyleshiffin's crescent-shaped harbour, which was replete with small fishing vessels, yachts and cruisers, as it usually was in the summer months. When they hit open water, Wallace opened her up and they scudded across the waves as they headed north to do a circuit around the island.

It was a hazy day with patches of mist. As they cut a swathe through the water, parallel to the stacks and skerries of the coast, they attracted a following of gulls. Eventually, when they sensed that there would be no food forthcoming, they dispersed and rejoined the swarms of birds that seemed to eternally circle the great basalt columns. It took about twenty minutes to round the northern tip of the island, during which time Torquil had been scanning the shores with binoculars for any signs of a body. As they coasted down the west coast towards the curious star-shaped peninsula of the Wee Kingdom, the songs of the fulmar and gannets rose above the winds as adult birds zigzagged back and forth to countless nests in the cracks and hollows of the steep sea cliffs.

Torquil scanned the rocks and sea caves on the shoreline. 'It would be on these rocks that a body would most likely be swept up,' he said aloud to the twins.

'And thank God he hasn't been,' replied Wallace. 'It would be awful to find his body churned and hacked up like that.'

They skirted the three great basalt stacks, each a virtual islet, atop the last of which was the ruins of the old West Uist lighthouse and the derelict shell of the keeper's cottage. Then they rounded the south-west shore with the machair stretching to the lush undulating hills and gullies, beyond which was the small central Loch Linne. On the hills above the McKinley croft they saw the black-coated Soay sheep that old Alistair McKinley was so proud of.

As they headed south, passing the oyster beds and the little jetty alongside which the crofters' boats were moored, Douglas pointed towards the Wind's Eye croft where a large container lorry was parked beside the old thatched cottage. A tall metal tower had been newly erected and a couple of figures could be seen working on scaffolding around it.

'Well bloody hell! There's the first of those monstrosities on old Gordon MacDonald's croft. They haven't wasted much time.'

Wallace whistled. 'Just two men, as well. I must say though that I thought those windmills would be taller than that. It only looks to be about thirty or forty feet high.'

'It may just be an experimental one,' said Torquil. 'I guess they will have to put up all sorts of wind-measuring anemometers and things before they put up permanent structures.'

'Well I don't like it,' Douglas said gloomily. 'And nor would Ewan. When we last had a pint together, he was having a real go about them.'

And at mention of the big PC, they brought their minds back to the task in hand. Torquil shaded his eyes and peered seawards, towards the distant Cruadalach isles, an archipelago of about a dozen machair and gorse-covered islets.

'We'll go and check out the Cruadalachs now,' he said. 'It was beyond there that you found the *Seaspray* drifting wasn't it?'

'It was,' replied Douglas. 'But we checked them out already.'

'And the helicopters went over them, too,' agreed Wallace.

'I know, I read the reports. But I want to see for myself. And when we've done that we'll come back and do a full sweep round the east of the island.'

Wallace swung the catamaran around and they headed off

towards the mist-swathed Cruadalach isles.

Approaching the little islets, Torquil raised his binoculars as Wallace cut their speed. Then he picked up the microphone and clicked on the loudhailer. 'This is the West Uist Police,' his voice boomed out through the mist. 'Is there anyone on the island?'

There was silence except for the motor of the *Seaspray* and the wind.

'Are you expecting anyone to be here, Piper?' Wallace asked.

Torquil shook his head. 'No. But there's something odd about the atmosphere of the place, don't you think? I think there's something wrong.'

The twins looked at him blankly. 'Like what?'

'There is the smell of death in the air,' Torquil replied softly.

Wallace sighed. 'If you are after trying to freak us out, you're succeeding.'

Torquil smiled at his friends. 'I'm sorry, lads, but does it not just strike you as odd that there is no sign of life here?' He raised his eyes to the sky. 'No gulls. No seals.'

'Bloody hell, Wallace!' Douglas exclaimed. 'He's right. And there should be, there is rich fishing round here, as we well know.'

'Come on then,' said Torquil pointing towards the nearest isle. 'Let's take a look at them one by one.'

It took them the better part of an hour to land and have a look at all of the Cruadalach isles. And it was not until they landed on the last one, a long undulating beach and machair islet with tall, coarse marram grass and yellow-blossomed gorse bushes, that they heaved a sigh of relief.

'Ewan's body isn't here, thank God,' said Wallace.

'But someone has been here,' Torquil announced, after a few moments study of the beach. He pointed to a piece of driftwood that lay some feet away. 'Look at the pattern of sand on it. It looks as if it was used as a kind of rake, maybe to eradicate footsteps.'

And, as the twins watched him, he crouched down and started examining the machair. 'Bird watchers, do you think?' Wallace suggested. Torquil seemed to be on some sort of a trail, slowly working up the beach onto the machair. Finally, he disappeared behind a large clump of tall marram grass.

'Or maybe not just wanting to watch birds.' Torquil said, rising to his feet and coming out of the grass holding his cupped hand out. 'Maybe whoever it was had killing them in mind. Look at this. An empty cartridge.'

The twins joined him and examined the cartridge. 'That's a .308. That's more firepower than you need to pot a few gulls. That'd be enough to kill —' His face suddenly drained of colour and he looked aghast at his inspector. 'You don't think —?'

But Torquil didn't say anything for a moment. He was busy studying the cartridge. 'I don't know what to think yet,' he said at last. 'Except that maybe we had better check all the firearm licence holders on the island. Kenneth McKinley had a live .308 lying beside his body.' He took out a small plastic bag from a pocket and dropped the cartridge case carefully inside.

'Come on then, we need to get back.' Neither of the twins thought that a bad idea.

The Padre had played four holes before propping his bag in the porch of St Ninian's Church, which bounded the green of the hole called *Creideamh*, meaning 'Faith'. On the other side of the green was the cemetery, where his brother and sister-in-law, Torquil's parents, were buried. It had been his intention to go into the church to pray, but a thought struck him and he turned and strode over the green, filling his pipe on the way. He struck a light to the bowl and let himself through the wrought-iron gate into the graveyard.

'Well, brother,' he said, a few moments later as he stood over his brother's grave. 'A lot has been happening here lately.' He took his pipe from his mouth and stared at the bowl. 'But I suppose you know all that already. I just wish you could give us a hand and find Ewan's body. Torquil is fairly chewing himself up over it.' He leaned forward and ran a hand over the smooth marble face. 'You would have been proud of him, you know. He's made a fine officer — Inspector McKinnon, the youngest inspector in the west of Scotland.' He grinned to himself. 'But his friends all call him Piper —because he's the champion piper of the isles now. In fact —'

He was interrupted in his reverie when he heard a noise from the road on the far side of the cemetery and looked round.

Jessie McPhee was dismounting from an ancient bicycle. 'I am glad to catch you, Padre,' she said, letting herself in by the little iron gate, a bunch of pink carnations in her hand. 'I'm just coming to tidy Balloch's grave and lay a few flowers. I hoped that he'd — you know, look out for Ewan.'

Lachlan put his arm about her shoulders. 'I was going into the Kirk, Jessie. Would you care to come with me? We can say a prayer together if you like.'

Jessie nodded with a sad smile. 'That would be good, right enough. But another part of the reason I hoped that I'd see you was so that you could give Torquil this.' And she held up a small black book. 'Ewan was no great writer, but lately he'd taken to jotting things down at night. I think he was in love. I've not read it myself, I didn't think it was right. But maybe Torquil as his friend and Inspector could. I only thought about it after he had gone yesterday.'

The Kyleshiffin market was in full swing as the *Seaspray* cruised into its mooring. Holidaymakers and locals were milling around the market stalls that were clustered along the harbour wall, or bobbing in and out of the half moon of multi-coloured shops that gave Kyleshiffin a strange sort of kasbah atmosphere. Calum Steele was sitting on the harbour wall, eating a mutton pie, obviously waiting for them.

'*Latha math*! Good morning,' he called in both Gaelic and English as Torquil hopped off the catamaran while the Drummonds tied her up. He wiped a trickle of grease from the first of his two chins and raised his eyebrows hopefully. 'Any news, Piper?'

'Nothing, Calum,' Torquil replied with practised guardedness. Everyone on the island knew that Calum took his role as a newspaperman very seriously. He saw himself as a man of letters, an investigative journalist with a duty to keep the good folk of West Uist up to date with the news. He virtually produced the daily *West Uist Chronicle* by himself, which was how he liked it because it meant that he had no one to please except himself. And although most of the time the paper consisted mainly of local gossip, advertising, and exchange and barter columns, yet it managed enough of a circulation to keep a roof over Calum's head and enough in his expense account for Heather Ale and petrol for his Lambretta scooter. The truth was that the islanders liked local gossip as much as anyone else, and Calum was an avid peddler of it. Consequently, everyone was wary of him, especially if they might end up in the *Chronicle* the next day.

'Is that the truth, Piper, or is it the official response?'

Torquil raised his eyebrows and touched his own chin. Calum reflexively wiped another errant trickle of pie grease from his face and then rolled the paper bag that he had been using to collect pastry crumbs between his palms.

'I'm hoping that you're not thinking of littering, Calum Steele,' Wallace Drummond jibed as he jumped down onto the harbour.

'It's an offence, you know,' agreed Douglas, joining him. 'You don't want to be committing an offence in front of officers of the law.'

Calum spluttered. 'Officers of the law! You two are a couple of fishing teuchters. I've a good mind to write something up in the *Chronicle* about harassment of the press.'

'Is it a threat of defamation now, then?' asked Wallace.

'That's an offence too,' Douglas said. 'And you've got crumbs on your anorak now. You want to watch all those calories, you know.'

Calum flushed. 'You pair of malnourished, long-limbed Neanderthals, I'll give you calories — where they hurt!'

The twins looked at each other and nodded their heads. 'Oh, he's good with words, isn't he? No wonder he's the editor of the local rag.'

'A rag! You two should learn to read and then you'd know if it was a rag or not!' But then, as they both burst into laughter, and even Torquil grinned, he shook his head resignedly. 'One day I'll sort the pair of you out.' And then he said to Torquil, 'I saw Ralph McLelland. He told me about Kenneth McKinley. That's a sad accident, so it is.'

'Aye, I don't know what old Alistair will do without him,' Torquil returned.

'I'm going to go over and see him. Do a proper obituary.' He pulled out a small camera from his anorak. 'I thought I'd take a few pictures of the Wee Kingdom while I'm up there. Give it a bit of colour and link it up with the piece I'm doing about the wind farm.'

'Aye, there's some sort of wind tower being put up on Gordon MacDonald's croft now,' Torquil informed him. 'We saw it from the sea.'

'This new laird could change the whole nature of the island if he gets his way,' Calum said. 'I'm going to see if I can get an interview with him. It would be a good thing to introduce the folk of the island to the new laird with a photo-feature. What do you think, boys?'

'I'm wondering if you've got a licence for that digital camera, Calum?' Douglas Drummond said with a twinkle in his eye.

Jock McArdle was at that moment standing on the shore of Loch Hynish, tossing sticks as far as he could in the direction of the crannog with its ancient ruined tower. His two Rottweilers, Dallas and Tulsa, launched themselves in and swam powerfully to retrieve them, depositing them on the pebble shore with much barking as they pleaded for more.

McArdle was a dog lover. He especially loved big powerful animals like these. He appreciated their strong muscles, their loyalty and the verve with which they attacked life. They were both bitches; mother and daughter. Dallas was the youngest and seemed capable of swimming forever. Tulsa had been just the same when she was young, and, even now, amazed McArdle by being able to keep up with her daughter. Especially on this late afternoon, after she had seemed so off colour in the morning and had vomited up her morning meal. He had thought she was coming down with a bug.

'Fetch, girls! Fetch!' he yelled, lobbing a large stick as far as he could.

The dogs charged in together and after a couple of lolloping splashes were soon out of their depth and were swimming in pursuit of the stick. The laird of Dunshiffin watched the progress of the big black and tan heads, yelling encouragement to them both. He delighted in the fact that they were both revelling in the competition. They reached the stick together and turned, each with an end in their mouth as they started to swim for shore.

Then the younger Dallas growled and managed to wrench the stick from her mother.

'G'wan, Tulsa, don't let her get away with that!' McArdle shouted.

Dallas edged away and Tulsa seemed to put on a spurt as well. Then she gave a strange yelping bark and stopped. Dallas swam on, growling and working the stick into her mouth, her powerful teeth biting into the wood.

Tulsa's head momentarily disappeared beneath the surface of the loch.

'Tulsa!' McArdle cried, as Dallas reached the shallows and bounded out of the water with the stick.

Tulsa's head resurfaced again and McArdle began to heave a sigh of relief. Then her head started to sink again, but she spluttered and started to swim on weakly. Dallas, confused, stood in the water and barked continuously.

'Come on, you stupid bitch!' the laird screeched. 'Come on!'

Once again, her head started to sink and McArdle finally realized that his beloved dog was in real danger of drowning. He peeled off his jacket and tugged off his shoes, then went racing into the water, launching himself into a dive. As a youngster in Govan, he had learned to swim competently. Now with a powerful crawl, he swam as he had never done before, intent on saving one of the few living creatures that he actually felt anything for.

Ahead of him, he saw the dog's head spluttering as she attempted to swim on. And then he was on her. He grabbed her thick studded collar and immediately turned onto his back and began hauling her back towards the shore. A part of his mind reflected upon those life-saving classes that he had taken as a youngster, but never expected to use. And certainly not on saving a dog.

Tulsa was a dead weight by the time he reached the shore, and he himself was in a state of near panic.

'Shut the hell up!' he cried at Dallas, who was barking and running around in the shallow water in a frenzy.

He manhandled Tulsa through the shallows, immediately conscious of her weight increasing dramatically as they arrived on solid ground. He pulled her onto the pebble beach and stared, unsure of what to do next.

Then Tulsa began to convulse.

CHAPTER EIGHT

Katrina Tulloch bit her lip and rose from the dead body. She removed the earpieces of her stethoscope from her ears and coiled the instrument in her hand. 'I'm sorry, Mr McArdle, but she's gone.'

McArdle stared at her through tears. He swallowed back a lump in his throat. 'How the hell? She was only eight, for God's sake?' Katrina looked down at the Rottweiler's corpse lying in its own excrement, aware of the howling of Dallas in the back of the nearby 4x4. She had been in the vicinity when the laird's call had come through via her automatic redirect to her mobile.

'She was a powerful animal,' she said. 'Looked healthy enough and no obvious signs of death. Had she shown any symptoms in the last day or two?'

'She'd been off her food a bit. She puked up food this morning.'

'Anything else. Cough, weeing more? Any diarrhoea?'

McArdle shivered slightly as he stood in his sodden clothing. 'Aye, as a matter of fact she's had a bit of diarrhoea lately and seemed thirstier than usual. Oh, and Jesmond, the butler, was complaining about her slobbering on his precious hall floor.'

Katrina bent down and pulled open the dog's lower jaw. She sniffed, then rose looking puzzled.

'What's wrong?' McArdle snapped.

'I thought I smelled garlic. Dogs don't usually like that.'

'Tulsa would eat anything,' McArdle replied dismissively. 'But what killed her?'

'I won't be able to tell anything else without doing a post-mortem.'

The laird shook his head. 'No! You are not cutting up my Tulsa.'

Katrina shook her head sympathetically. 'I can understand that, but what about some blood tests? I can run a screen and might be able to come up with an answer.' She pointed to his wet clothes as involuntarily he shivered again. 'And I think you'd better get home and get into some dry clothes, Mr McArdle. You don't want to go down with something yourself.'

'I'll be OK. I've phoned for my boys to come and bring me some clothes. Can you take the blood here and now?'

Katrina hesitated. 'I suppose so; it's just that it might be easier if I took her body back to my surgery. If you want I could arrange for her to be cremated.'

McArdle shuddered rather than shivered this time. 'I'm taking her back to the castle. She didn't know it for long, but she seemed to like it well enough. Besides, I know that Dallas there will be feeling it, so burying her in the grounds seems right.'

Katrina went back to her van and got out her venepuncture kit and a few specimen bottles. She bent down by Tulsa's body. 'Did she have any different food in the last few days?'

'She always has the best, and whatever extra scraps the boys give her. Why, what are you thinking?'

'Just wondering if she could have taken something bad into her system.'

He glared at her. 'Do you mean poison?'

'I meant food poisoning, actually. But I suppose we'd need to consider if she could have eaten anything else. You don't have rat poison down at the castle, do you?'

He turned away as she sank the needle into a vessel and

329

pulled back on the syringe, dark purple blood oozing back into the plastic cylinder.

'Are you a wee bit squeamish, Mr McArdle?' she asked matter-of-factly.

His reply was curt. 'I'm squeamish about nothing! And I'm scared of nothing.'

'I didn't mean anything,' she replied apologetically. 'You've had a shock, what with having to pull her out and everything.'

'Never mind that,' he replied. 'What you were just saying though? About poison. Could someone have poisoned my dog?'

'I can't say without the results.'

'But it is possible?'

'Yes. If she was convulsing, like you said.'

The noise of a fast car coming along the road was followed by a screech of brakes and a skidding of wheels on gravel as a black Porsche Boxster ground to a halt. Liam Sartori and Danny Reid jumped out.

'You OK, boss?' cried Liam, as they jogged down to the loch side.

'God! Is that Tulsa?' Danny asked. 'Crikes, I'm sorry to see that, boss.'

'And is this the vet?' asked Liam, eyeing Katrina admiringly. 'Do you need a hand, dear?'

'I'd rather you didn't call me "dear",' Katrina returned, frostily. 'And yes, I am the vet — and no, I don't need any help.'

Sartori held his hands up in mock defence. 'No offence meant.'

'What are we going to do with Tulsa, boss?' Danny Reid asked. 'Dallas sounds upset.'

'We'll take her back to the castle,' McArdle replied sourly.

'Or rather you boys will in the 4x4. I've got an appointment in the town. Did you bring me fresh togs?'

Liam was returning from the Boxter with a holdall of fresh clothes when the characteristic whine of a scooter was followed by the appearance round the bend of Calum Steele. The *Chronicle* editor-in-chief parked behind the Boxter and came jauntily down the slope to join them.

'Hello, Katrina, what have you there? A drowned dog, is it?'

With the dexterity of a seasoned conjuror, his camera had appeared in his hand and he had taken a couple of shots before he even reached a standstill beside the group. He nodded at Jock McArdle. 'It's not the usual attire for swimming, so I deduce that you went in and brought the beast out?' He grinned and held out his hand. 'You must be Mr McArdle, the new owner of Dunshiffin castle? I was meaning to make an appointment with you and see how you're settling in. Get your comments on the wind farm and all.'

'I don't give interviews to the newspapers,' McArdle replied emphatically, ignoring Calum's outstretched hand.

Calum continued to grin good-humouredly. 'Ah, but maybe you don't know about the *Chronicle*. My paper is the epitome of responsible journalism. You ask anyone on West Uist. You see, it's the best PR you could have on the island.' He raised his camera and took a photograph of the new laird and his two employees. 'How about a more smiling one this time? Then we could maybe go and have a chat and a drink —'

'I don't do photographs either.'

'Och, as the new laird you are news, whether you like it or not,' Calum persisted bullishly. 'The public have a right and a desire to know all about you.'

Katrina had put her blood specimen containers away in her bag and now stood up. She felt uneasy at the hard expression that had come over McArdle's face. 'I'll — er — be away now then, Mr McArdle. I should have the blood results in a couple of hours and I'll be in touch if I find anything odd.'

Calum's head swivelled quickly on his stocky neck. 'Odd? Is there something odd about this dead dog?'

'This dead dog, as you so politely put it, was my dearly beloved pet. If there is anything odd about her death then it is nobody's business except mine and the vet's here.'

Calum was not renowned for his sensitivity. He pointed the camera at the dead animal and snapped another picture. 'You're not thinking that it was poisoned, are you?'

'Why did you ask that?' McArdle snapped. 'Why use the word poison?'

For the first time Calum discerned the hostility that Katrina had found almost palpable. 'Well, I suppose I meant polluted rather than poisoned. Blue-green algae in Loch Hynish, that sort of thing. But I'm sure it wasn't. Everything is pure and fresh on West Uist.' He smiled placatingly. 'I am sure there is no reason to be concerned.'

'But I am concerned about infringement on my privacy,' McArdle returned drily. 'Especially when I'm so recently bereaved.' He nodded at his employees and immediately Calum found his right arm pinioned in a vice-like grip by Liam, while Danny prised the camera from his hand.

Calum watched dumbfounded as the Glaswegian hurled the camera as far as he could into the waters of Loch Hynish.

'What the hell did you do that for?' he demanded. 'That's criminal! That was an expensive camera. I'll have the law on you.'

'I told you no interviews and no photographs,' McArdle said coldly, through gritted teeth.

Katrina saw Calum's face turn puce, just as she noted the

belligerent and insolent grins on the faces of Reid and Sartori. And she was all too aware that the young Rottweiler was howling anew and throwing herself against the closed door of the 4x4.

She caught Calum by the arm and pulled him away. 'Come on, Calum. Leave it for now.'

Dr Ralph McLelland had gone out on his rounds after his morning surgery and, as luck would have it, was just leaving the house of one of his elderly patients on the easternmost point of the island when Agnes Calanish, the wife of the local postmaster, went into labour. It was her fifth child and she wasted no time about it. The baby was delivered, her episiotomy was stitched up and the baby attached to the breast by the time Helen McNab, the midwife, arrived.

'A fine busy man you have been here, Dr McLelland,' cooed Helen, as she took over. 'And such a shame about Kenneth McKinley.'

'However will old Alistair manage the croft without him,' agreed Agnes, as her newborn babe suckled away contentedly. 'And what with all these windmills that they say are going up.'

'Windmills?' Ralph queried.

Guthrie Calanish came in with a tray of tea to celebrate his latest offspring. 'Aye, the first of them is up now and they are busy setting up a second. I was over at the Wee Kingdom this morning. There are two men and they seem to be setting them up like dandelion clocks.' He looked regretfully at the local GP. 'Are you sure you'll not stay for a cup, Doctor?'

'No. I'll be back in tomorrow. But I'm afraid I have work to complete after Kenneth McKinley's death.'

'Paperwork, eh,' sighed Guthrie. 'The bane of a doctor's existence, I'm thinking.'

Ralph smiled and left. He had work to do all right, but it was not nearly as pleasant as filling out a few papers.

Kenneth McKinley's body was waiting for him in the refrigerator of the Kyleshiffin Cottage Hospital mortuary. He had promised to do the post-mortem before lunch, and then let Inspector McKinnon have a report first thing afterwards.

While Ralph was carrying out the post-mortem on Kenneth, Katrina was back in her laboratory working with reagents on the blood tests she had taken from Tulsa. When she was at veterinary school, she had taken an intercalated BSc degree in toxicology and was well able to do the lab work herself.

The garlic smell had worried her, and her preliminary test had shown that she was right to be worried. She packaged up the specimens for later despatch and full analysis at the department of veterinary toxicology at the University of Glasgow, and put them in the fridge. Yet in her own mind, she had enough information. She phoned the mobile number that Jock McArdle had given her.

She hadn't felt at all comfortable about the way McArdle and his heavies had treated Calum Steele. The man was a bully, that was clear. Yet she felt sorry for anyone who lost their pet under such circumstances.

Arsenic was a particularly nasty poison.

Calum Steele was leaning against the front desk recounting his experience on the shore of Loch Hynish to Morag when Torquil came in. So deep into his diatribe was the journalist that he did not hear the Inspector come in.

'Thugs! They're just bloody thugs!' Calum exclaimed, hammering his fist on the counter.

'Who are thugs?' Torquil asked, clapping Calum on the shoulder.

'That new laird and his henchmen.' He recounted his meeting with them all over again, much to Morag's chagrin. 'One of them threw my camera into the loch. It was brand new. *Chronicle* property! I want to charge them with criminal damage.'

'Are you sure about that? He's a powerful man, I hear.'

Calum's face went beetroot red. 'The press will not be intimidated by a bunch of Glasgow bullyboys. I'm going to do an exposé on him.'

'An exposé?' Morag asked. 'And what are you going to expose about him?'

'His thuggery! His insensitivity. His intention to suppress the mouthpiece of the people.'

'Do you have a witness to all this?' Torquil asked, trying hard to suppress a grin. The newspaperman was well known for losing his rag.

'Katrina Tulloch. She saw it all. And she whisked me away just in time, or — or — I'd have shown them.'

'In that case I'm glad that she did. It's best to avoid physicality, as you well know.'

'Huh. I'm not afraid of anyone. I'm from West Uist, born and bred, just like you. I'll not be intimidated by Glasgow bullies.' Torquil put an arm about Calum's shoulders and gently moved him towards the door. 'Calum, I'll look into this, I promise. I'll have a word with this new laird and get his side of the story.'

'Aye, well, have a word with Katrina Tulloch, too. She'll tell you exactly what happened.'

'I'll do that, don't worry. I'm needing to have a word with her in any case.'

Calum nodded. 'Well I'm off to write a piece on thuggery right now. Just tell that laird to start buying the *Chronicle* from now on. If he wants to take on the might of the fourth estate, he's got a fight on his hands.'

Once he had gone Morag shook her head and frowned. 'Let's just hope Calum doesn't go over the top. You know what he can be like when he gets a bee in his bonnet.'

'Aye, he gets a sore head,' replied Torquil with a grin. 'And then we get a pain in the neck. He was like that when we were in school. But his heart is in the right place.'

Ralph McLelland was not happy. He had walked up to the police station with the manila folder containing his report on the post-mortem, and accepted Morag's offer of tea and biscuits in Torquil's office.

'There's something wrong, Torquil,' he said at last, as he dunked a shortbread in the tea.

'About Kenneth McKinley's cause of death?' Torquil asked.

'No, it's clear enough that he died as a result of the injuries he sustained in the fall. He had multiple contusions and fractures of his skull, spine, pelvis and all four limbs. His rib cage was smashed to pieces and he had a ruptured liver and spleen and a torn right kidney. No, he died instantaneously, there is no doubt.'

'Is it those marks on his face?' Torquil asked. 'Those scratches?'

'Aye, partly that. There were three ugly gashes on his face.'

Morag swallowed a mouthful of tea. 'Do you think someone scratched him?'

'Something, I think. They were vicious raking wounds, like a claw of some sort.'

'Or a talon,' Torquil suggested. He told them of his conversation with Annie McConville when she found his body.

'Aye, well, that would fit right enough. But eagles don't

attack people, do they?'

Morag interjected. 'There have been reports about the Corlin eagles attacking animals. Megan Munro telephoned in a complaint about them. She said they've been killing hedgehogs in her sanctuary.'

Torquil eyed her with amusement. 'And what does she want us to do about it? Arrest them?'

'Och, you know what some of the folk say about eagles attacking small animals. It's possible, I suppose.' said Megan.

'But not a man,' returned Ralph, pushing his mug across the table and smiling benignly, in the expectation that it would be refilled.

Torquil blew out a puff of air between pursed lips. 'What about if an eagle thought it was being attacked? If he'd been out there with a rifle, for example.'

Ralph and Morag considered the suggestion for a moment. 'That would be possible, I think,' said Ralph. 'But I'm no expert on birds. Maybe you need to ask someone who knows.'

'Nial Urquart might know,' Morag suggested, pulling out her notebook and jotting a reminder to herself.

'But he had no gun with him, did he?' went on Torquil. 'And I went back later and didn't find anything either at the foot of the cliffs, or up on the ledge that he looks to have fallen from. There were a few scuffs, but no sign of anyone else being there.' He shook his head and reached into his pocket. 'But strangely, this morning when the twins and I were out checking the Cruadalach isles, I found this.' He held out his hand to reveal the plastic bag with the empty cartridge. He laid it on the desk and opened his drawer, from which he took out another plastic bag containing a live bullet. 'This was the .308 that we found beside his body. The question is, if they were from a rifle owned by Kenneth McKinley, what was he doing out

337

there on the Cruadalach isles?'

'Maybe we'd better be asking Alistair McKinley a few questions,' Morag said. 'But we'll have to be easy with him. He'll be in a pretty fragile shape.'

'He said he felt guilty about letting Kenneth go off on his own,' Torquil said. 'And he told me that he had taken a rifle with him. The thing is — where is it now?'

Ralph clicked his tongue and drew the file towards him. He turned a page and tapped it with his middle finger. 'I said there were a couple of things. One was the presence of those wounds. The other was the contents of his stomach. It was full of a strange goo, half-digested of course. I had a look with the microscope and I'm pretty sure his last meal consisted of worms, slugs and a few snails. All raw!' He waited as Morag curled up her nose and covered her mouth to indicate her revulsion at the idea. Then said, 'Washed down with a few drams of whisky, judging by his blood alcohol level.'

'All in all, not normal behaviour,' said Torquil. He nodded at Morag. 'You're right, we need to ask Alistair a few questions. I'll go over and see him first thing tomorrow morning.'

After Ralph left, Torquil spent the following half-hour writing up his report for Superintendent Lumsden. He duly faxed it through and was just preparing to head off to the Corlins for another look around near the eagle nest and the point where Kenneth McKinley had met his death, when the telephone rang and Morag informed him that the superintendent was on the line.

'Good afternoon, Superintendent Lumsden, did you get my —'

'What the hell is it with you, McKinnon? Do you have to be antagonistic?'

'Antagonistic to whom, Superintendent?'

'To your superiors!'

Torquil's hackles rose immediately. 'Are you suggesting that I have been antagonistic to a superior officer, Superintendent Lumsden?'

'Christ, McKinnon, you're at it again right now! But no, that wasn't what I was meaning. I meant being antagonistic to your social superiors. This is the second laird who has come up against you and —'

'Hold on a minute, Superintendent Lumsden. For one thing I have no idea what you are talking about. I have had no dealings at all with the present laird of Dunshiffin. And as for him being a social superior, that is balderdash! I have not even met the man, but I do know that he has simply bought an estate on West Uist. That gives him no rights over anyone. He is a landowner, pure and simple.'

'Well, I've just had him on the phone for ten minutes ranting about the attitude of the people of some place called the Wee Kingdom, and the antagonism of the people in general and the uselessness of the local constabulary!'

'I repeat,' said Torquil as civilly as he could, 'I have had no dealings with him at all.'

'He says one of his dogs has been poisoned and he wants action. I want you to give it to him, McKinnon. We have to maintain a good rapport with important people like him.'

Torquil took a deep breath and forced himself not to lose his cool any more than he was doing. 'We will investigate his claims, sir.'

'Good. And what about that report I wanted faxing through?'

'It should be with you already, Superintendent.'

'Well it hasn't arrived. Send it again!'

There was a click, as of the receiver being slammed down on a telephone in Bara, and Torquil once again found himself staring at his dead receiver.

After sharing his frustration with Morag, Torquil telephoned Dunshiffin Castle and spoke to Jesmond.

'The laird is not available, Inspector McKinnon. He has left instructions not to be disturbed. He is upset about the death of one of his dogs.'

Torquil thought he detected a slight tone of irreverence as the butler mentioned the death of the dog. 'Well, tell the laird when he is available, that if he wishes to make a report about his dog's death he can jolly well come into the station and file one — personally. Goodbye, Jesmond.'

'I shall tell him exactly that, Inspector. Goodbye.'

Torquil thought he detected a note of glee in the crusty old butler's voice.

When Torquil arrived home that evening, he opened the front door of the manse and was immediately assailed by the aroma of devilled rabbit, one of Lachlan's specialities, and by the sight of his uncle on his hands and knees in the hall, leaning over the carburettor of the classic Excelsior Talisman that the two of them had been gradually restoring over the past umpteen years. Bits and pieces of the bike lay on oil-soaked newspapers along the side of the long hall.

'Have you a problem, Uncle?' Torquil asked, knowing all too well that when the Padre had something he needed to work out, he either went and hit golf balls or started tinkering with the Excelsior Talisman.

The Padre raised his eyes heavenwards and exhaled forcefully. Then he gave a wan smile, wiped his hands on an old rag and stood up. 'You might say that, laddie. But I'll solve it one day.' And giving the carburettor a mock kick, he pointed to the sitting-room with his chin. 'You look as if you've had a tough day. Why don't you pour a couple of drams while I check on the supper?'

And five minutes later, with a whisky in their hands, they sat on each side of the old fireplace and exchanged news of the day. Lachlan listened with a deepening frown as he heard about the superintendent's attitude over the telephone.

'That man is nothing but a boor, Torquil! An obsequious boor at that. I think he kow-tows to the gentry.'

Torquil sipped his whisky. 'I haven't met this McArdle yet, but I don't like the way he's taking on the mantle of "the laird" as if it gives him rights over the island.'

'But he has land ownership rights. The Dunshiffin estate is pretty big, and, of course, he has substantial rights apparently over the Wee Kingdom.'

'Well, I'm thinking that I'll be locking horns with him before too long.'

The Padre nodded sympathetically, then, 'I saw Jessie McPhee this afternoon. She was visiting her husband's grave.' He omitted to tell his nephew that at the time he had been paying his own respects at Torquil's parents' graveside. 'She's making peace with herself over Ewan, the poor woman.' He pulled out his pipe and was reaching into his pocket for his tobacco pouch when his hand touched the little black notebook that Jessie had given him. 'Oh, you'd better have a look at this. It's Ewan's. Jessie said that he'd taken to making lots of wee notes. She particularly wanted you as his friend and senior officer to have a look.'

Torquil laid down his whisky glass and reached out for the notebook. He skimmed it, immediately recognizing the big constable's untidy handwriting. It seemed to be quite

341

shambolic, having no set order; quite typical of Ewan, Torquil thought. There were bits and pieces of observations, things he'd highlighted to do, to say to various people, including Torquil. But interspersed among it there were personal thoughts.

The Padre noticed his nephew's change of posture, his expression of studied concentration. Slowly Torquil's head came up, his eyes sharp. 'He had a lot on his mind. It looks like he was feeling pretty desperate.'

CHAPTER NINE

Morag was looking bleary-eyed next morning after spending half the night looking after her youngest daughter Ailsa, who was subject to the croup. Sitting on the other side of Torquil's desk she read his summary of Ewan's notebook, which he had divided into three brief sections, respectively dealing with his feelings about Katrina Tulloch, his suspicions about something he suspected Kenneth McKinley of being up to, but which he hadn't been altogether clear about, and things that he was planning to discuss with Torquil and others.

'He seemed to have lost his heart to Katrina,' Morag said with a sigh. 'She's a bonnie girl, but —' She shook her head and stopped in mid sentence.

'But what?' Torquil queried.

Morag yawned as she thought. 'I don't suppose it is fair of me to say it, but she's a bonnie girl and she knows it. There's something ... sensual about her. I think she would not be a one-man woman.'

'But I understand that she's been upset since he disappeared. Lachlan told me about Gordon MacDonald's wake.'

'Oh yes. Just as we all have been upset. And she's been spotted wandering around the coast roads and the skerries. The Drummonds have seen her van parked overlooking St Ninian's Bay and Calum Steele says she burst into tears when he saw her in the Bonnie Prince Charlie the other lunchtime.'

Torquil nodded and pushed the latest edition of the *West Uist Chronicle* across the desk for her to see. 'Speaking of our esteemed journalist, I think he's well and truly peeved.'

Morag read the headline:

THE LAIRD, THE CAMERA AND THE LOCH

There followed a piece of Calum's most purple prose describing his encounter with the Laird of Dunshiffin, the dead dog, the Glaswegian bodyguards and the hurling of his digital camera into Loch Hynish. Morag smiled as she read it.

'So he's considering a claim for damages,' she mused, as she read that Calum had been forced to buy a very expensive substitute so that the *Chronicle* photographer would still be able to illustrate the articles in the paper.

'He's not planning to make friends with the new laird, then?'

Torquil frowned. 'And he's in danger of losing credibility as well. Look at the next page. He's written a piece about Kenneth McKinley.'

Morag turned the page to find a photograph of a golden eagle in flight, with an insert photograph of Kenneth McKinley above a headline reading:

DID A GOLDEN EAGLE MARK CROFTER OUT AS PREY?

Morag stared at the article with wide eyed disbelief, and then slowly read it out loud:

While out walking her dog at the foot of the Corlins yesterday, Miss Annie McConville, the well-known proprietor of the Kyleshiffin Dog Sanctuary, discovered the body of Mr Kenneth McKinley of Sea's Edge Croft. It seems that Kenneth had been climbing and tragically lost his footing.

But upon his face were the unmistakable marks of a bird's talons.

'No doubt at all, he was struck down by one of the eagle's,' Miss McConville told our chief reporter.

Miss McConville told us that she had discovered the body minutes before the arrival of our local Inspector Torquil McKinnon. Miss McConville reports that she pointed out the talon marks to the inspector, who seemed perplexed. A post-mortem examination is awaited at the time of writing.

Kenneth McKinley was the only son of ...

Morag slapped the pages together. 'That's typical of the wee ferret. He's wheedled gossip out of Annie McConville and speculated like crazy.'

'Aye, just like he usually does. But I think he's done it half on purpose. He knows that the golden eagles have caused mixed feelings on the island. There are the superstitious brigade and the bird lovers.'

'And the bird lovers are all up in arms about the proposed windmills,' agreed Morag. 'Calum will be loving all this.'

Torquil sipped his tea. 'Well, let's get back to Ewan's notebook. What do you make of the next section? What do you think he suspected Kenneth of? It is not clear from his notes.'

Morag looked at the notes then picked up Ewan's actual notebook. 'May I?'

Torquil nodded and watched her expression as she skimmed through it.

Suddenly, tears welled up in her eyes and she bit her lip. 'Oh my God! This bit makes me feel so guilty.' She read: *'Morag has her hands full, ask Torquil.* He must mean that I was so preoccupied about Ailsa and her schoolwork. She's missed so much school lately with this croup that she keeps getting. And Ewan didn't feel he could burden me with his worries!' And, despite herself, she sobbed anew.

In a trice, Torquil was around the desk and slipping a comforting arm about her shoulder. 'Now that is the last thing that you should be thinking, Morag. We don't know whether any of this is of the slightest relevance. Ewan was a good police officer. If he thought it was something you ought to know about then he would have asked. We mustn't get ahead of ourselves here.'

And pulling a tissue from the box on his desk she quickly controlled herself and resumed her customary visage of solid professionalism. She returned to the diary and flicked through the pages with barely a sniff or two.

Eventually she said, 'I think he's got two trains of thought going. On the one had it seems a bit personal, like he thinks Kenneth was watching him and Katrina. There's a hint there that he doesn't like the way that he caught him looking at Katrina and him when they were out having dinner at Fauld's Hotel one evening. And the other thing seems to be a suspicion that Kenneth was up to something. Look, there are times and dates when he's noted down when he saw him. And there are a few words in capital letters that he's boxed round — GUNS and BOND and FAIR FANCIES HIMSELF. I don't think he liked young Kenneth McKinley much. Maybe he saw him as a rival?'

Torquil clicked his tongue pensively. 'Aye, possibly. He was always a tad insecure, for all his great size. But with the word GUNS we come back to the missing rifle again, don't we.' He drummed his fingers on the desk. 'And what did he mean by BOND?'

'Beats me.'

'OK then, what do you think about those things he wanted to ask me about?'

The first was simply the name KATRINA, followed by a question mark.

'That's easy,' said Morag with a smile. 'You know he's always looked up to you as a friend, an older brother even, as well as his senior officer. He wanted to know your opinion about what he should do.' She shook her head and added wistfully, 'And the big darling thought I was too busy.'

Torquil frowned. 'Me, with my track record?' He shook his head, dismissively. 'What about FAMILY?'

'I don't know about that one.'

'We can come back to it. That leaves the last word, WIND?'

'I think everyone on the island has that word on their mind at the moment,' said Morag. 'What with windmills and wind farms.'

'Aye, and the more I think about it, the more I think it's an ill wind that's been blowing lately,' Torquil mused.

Sister Lizzie Lamb was busy, which was not at all unusual for her. No matter how many patients she had under her care, she was always busy. She could have six extremely ill patients in the cottage hospital and cope admirably, or just the one and be run off her feet. But patient care never suffered, or was in any way compromised. She just liked people to know that a nursing life was a busy life.

With Rhona McIvor as the only patient, her business extended to getting all of her administrative chores done, as well as overseeing a good spring-clean of the sluice, the supplies room and then an inventory of the mortuary equipment.

When the new laird presented himself at the reception desk, Maggie Crouch, the hospital clerk, scuttled off and found Sister Lamb in the supplies room. After a few words of exasperation, Lizzie left Giselle Anderson, her irreplaceable nursing assistant, to carry on with the spring-clean while she went to attend on the visitor.

'Rhona McIvor has had a heart attack and still must not be over-tired,' she said, leading the way into the side room where they had moved Rhona. 'Doctor McLelland was quite precise in his instructions.'

'Don't you worry, Sister,' returned Jock McArdle. 'I just want to pay my respects — I'll only be a couple of minutes.'

Sister Lamb was plump, forty-five, with an old-fashioned neatly starched uniform and an over-developed sense of the romantic.

'You sent her all those beautiful flowers, didn't you, Mr McArdle?' She smiled knowingly. 'She's a lucky lady.'

McArdle grinned affably, as he divined the real question that lay behind her remark. 'Ah no, Sister! You think that we —' He made a to-and-fro gesture with his hand. 'Nah. Nothing like that.'

Sister Lamb turned the corner and stood outside Rhona's room, her face betraying a slight disappointment that the romance she had speculated about was no such thing. She gave a little professional cough. 'I wasn't thinking anything, Mr McArdle. I was just looking out for my patient. Mind what I said now, she's not to be over-tired or over-excited.'

'I'll be two minutes with my friend. Sister. That's all.'

Torquil had to wait at the end of the causeway over to the Wee Kingdom, as the large container lorry edged across. It had emblazoned on its sides a picture of a row of windmills linked by lightning bolts and the words NATURE'S OWN ENERGY underneath it. The driver, a large man with a pony-tail and heavily tattooed arms, gave him a thumbs-up sign as he inched past. His companion, a younger man in a red baseball cap, was smoking a cigarette. Almost languidly, he flicked the dog-end out of the cab window so that it bounced off the front wheel of the Bullet. Immediately Torquil's hackles rose and he held up a hand for the driver to stop.

'Dropping litter is just as illegal on West Uist as it is on the mainland,' he said, turning off the Bullet's engine and hauling it up on its central stand. He ground the cigarette end under the heel of his heavy buckled Ashman boot then bent down and picked it up. 'I am Inspector McKinnon of the Hebridean Constabulary, and I am willing to overlook this — just this once!' He held up his hand to the open window. 'Take your litter home please and dispose of it appropriately.'

The youth glowered at him, but, after a dig in the ribs from the driver, he took the dog-end from Torquil and deposited it in the ashtray in the cab.

'Sorry about the boy here, Inspector,' said the driver, leaning towards the window. 'He's from the city and he doesn't know how tae handle himself at times.'

'I ken fine how to handle myself,' the youth returned sourly.

Torquil eyed him dispassionately. 'That's OK then. But just don't overstep the letter of the law while you're visiting this island, or you'll find that we enforce it pretty strictly here.' And then ignoring the youth he pointed to the two wind towers that had been erected on either side of the Wind's Eye croft cottage. Both of them were surrounded by scaffolding with ladders leading up to wooden platforms near the top. One had a slowly revolving three-bladed propeller and the other had a series of spinning anemometers at various heights above the platform.

'You didn't waste a lot of time putting them up. But they're a bit smaller than I imagined they would be. What are they, about forty or fifty feet tall?'

'That's right, Inspector. They're our standard fifty-foot towers. They are just basic ones to gather information. We measure wind speeds and directions with the anemometer one and the propeller has no turbine, it is just to record likely operating patterns. They're all recording data which the boffins back at the head office will work out later. We've done our work for now and are just off to bring the next lot over.'

'How many are you putting up?' Torquil asked.

'Ten more on this piece of land.' He said, indicating the Wee Kingdom. 'Then assuming everybody's happy with the estimates they get, who knows. It may be that we'll be putting up the real McCoys, the big turbines.' He grinned. 'Then it'll be proper wind farm here we come. And for that we'll have a whole gang of workers, not just gangers like me and the lad here.'

He turned and looked at the youth beside him, as if he had received a kick. The youth held up his watch and the driver pursed his lips. 'Would you excuse us then, Inspector? We need to catch the ferry.'

Torquil nodded and waved them on. 'Just watch your speed on these narrow roads,' he instructed.

'We'll go easy, Inspector,' returned the driver. He grinned as he nudged his companion. 'And maybe your wee ticking off will do the lad a bit of good, eh? I keep telling him to give up these coffin nails of his.'

When they had gone Torquil started up the Bullet and made his way over the causeway towards the McKinley croft. As he rode past Wind's Eye with its incongruous wind towers, he found himself mentally recoiling from them. These flimsy looking windmills were bad enough, but a wind farm with giant turbines would change the whole face of the island.

Rhona blinked myopically at Jock McArdle with ill-concealed disdain. 'What, no flowers for me today?' she asked coldly.

'No flowers,' he replied casually. 'Just a message.' His lips twisted into a smile that was curiously devoid of warmth. 'See, I'm here as a sort of postman.' He made a theatrical adjustment to the knot of his paisley pattern tie then reached into the inside breast pocket of his Harris Tweed jacket, and drew out a long envelope. 'Maybe I'm a wee bit over-dressed for the part, but I thought I'd deliver it myself. You'll be interested to know that it is all entirely legitimate.'

'Do you think I am remotely interested in anything you have to tell me, Mr McArdle?'

His mouth again curved into his mirthless smile and he smirked. 'And do you really think that I don't know who you are, or what you used to do for a living — Rhona McIvor? I've got the memory of an elephant, so I have. But you don't, it seems.' He tossed his head back and laughed, a cold sinister laugh. 'Have I changed all that much?'

A look approaching fear flashed across her face and she reached for her spectacles. When she put them on, McArdle quickly recognized that he had rattled her. And that she had recognized him. He grinned maliciously as he laid the envelope between a vase of flowers and a pile of cards on her bedside cabinet.

'Enjoy your reading,' he said, before turning and letting himself out. For a moment Rhona stared at the closed door with a look of horror, then she turned her attention to the waiting envelope. Her heart seemed to have speeded up.

Torquil found Alistair McKinley in one of his outhouses, vigorously working his handloom. Working out his grief and frustration, Torquil guessed.

'I've brought you a copy of the post-mortem report, Alistair,' Torquil said, as he pulled off his gauntlets. 'It's just a preliminary report, mind you, that we'll be submitting to the Procurator Fiscal for the Fatal Accident Enquiry.'

The old crofter sighed and laid down his shuttle. He heaved himself out of his high chair and held out his hand for the letter, which he immediately stuffed in the front pocket of his dungarees. 'I'll read it later, although I'm thinking that I already know what it will be saying.'

Torquil nodded grimly. 'Death from catastrophic head injury, multiple internal contusions and ruptures, and multiple fractures.'

'Aye! And I know well what it won't say. It won't say a thing about the culprits.'

'Meaning what?'

'Meaning the man who caused him to go off like he did. And the devil bird that made him fall.'

'You've read the *Chronicle* then?'

The crofter nodded. 'But I knew it anyway. I saw his bonnie face myself, remember? You were there when I identified his body. I recognized those scars as talon marks when I saw them.' He swallowed hard and tears formed in the corners of his eyes. 'But there will be justice coming.'

Before Torquil could follow up on the remark, Alistair straightened up and gestured towards the door. 'It's time for a cup of tea. Will you join me, Inspector?'

A few minutes later, as they waited for the kettle to boil, Torquil looked around the kitchen. It was surprisingly clean and functional. A row of basic cookery books were ranged along one half of the solitary shelf, the other half being home to a row of pots containing various herbs and condiments. Pans hung on the wall, crockery was stacked neatly in a dresser, and the old stove was in pristine condition.

'You have the eye of a policeman, Torquil McKinnon,' said

Alistair. 'You are wondering how two men managed to keep their kitchen so tidy. Well, it is respect for my late wife, God rest her soul.'

Torquil nodded politely and made no comment about his own home, the manse, which he shared with his uncle. Many of the nooks and crannies of the manse were filled with golf clubs, sets of bagpipes or bits and pieces of classic motorbike engines. Their home was not as neat as the McKinleys'.

With the teapot filled and the tray loaded, Alistair led the way through to the sitting-room. In ways, it mirrored the kitchen in its Spartan tidiness. The walls were painted a pale green and the brown carpet, although clean, had three or four frayed patches. There was little in the way of luxury in the room. No modern hi-fi system or computer, just an oldish television set, a box radio, two armchairs, a dining-table with three plain chairs around it, a few pictures and photographs on the mantelpiece. A bottle of whisky with two empty glasses beside it stood on one of those tall thin tables that looked as though it had once supported an aspidistra. Torquil noted the photograph of Kenneth McKinley propped against the bottle and imagined that the old crofter had been drinking a toast or two to his departed son the night before.

As Alistair poured tea, Torquil asked, 'You told me that Kenneth had gone out with a rifle. Are you absolutely sure about that?'

A thin smile floated across the crofter's lips. 'I wondered when you would get round to asking that. As you know from your records, we have licenses for all our guns.' And picking up his cup he crossed the room to the bottom of the wooden staircase. 'Come up and I'll show you our gun cupboard. It's all as it should be. We always keep the guns up here under lock and key.'

The gun cupboard was made of heavy oak and stood on an upstairs landing outside the bathroom. It was heavily padlocked and had been bolted to both the wall and the floor. 'There you are,' said Alistair, as he unlocked the padlock and opened the cupboard door. Inside, in wooden partitions, there were three guns: two shotguns — one 12-gauge and one 20-gauge — and a .22 Hornet rifle. The end partition was empty. At the top of the cupboard, above the partitions, was a locked metal cabinet that was also bolted to the back of the cupboard. 'The guns are just as you have them recorded on our firearm certificates, which I assume you have checked out.'

Torquil nodded, and pulling out his notebook opened it at his last entry. 'So it is the Steyr-Mannlicher Scout that Kenneth took with him?'

'It was. When can I have it back?'

'That's just it. We haven't found the gun!'

The crofter looked aghast. 'You haven't found it? That's not possible.'

'No sign of it at all. And that is serious. Were there any distinguishing features about the rifle?'

Alistair McKinley swallowed a mouthful of tea. 'I can let you have a photograph of it.' He went along the landing and opened a bedroom door. 'This was Kenneth's room,' he said, almost forlornly, standing aside for Torquil to enter.

The posters on the wall attracted Torquil's attention. They were recruitment posters for the marines: men in combat clothes charging through jungles, or wearing heavy camouflage gear stalking through woodland, guns at the ready. Then he noted the bookcase, neatly stacked with books about guns and weaponry, the SAS, and various manuals on hunting. On the bed was a scattered pile of clothing: dungarees, various camouflage jackets, rolls of thick socks. Beside the bed was a series of photographs of Alistair, Kenneth himself and his dead mother. Alistair leaned past him and picked up the framed photograph at the back.

'He liked this one. He got me to take it one day when we were up in the Corlins.'

Torquil took it. It was a carefully posed photograph of Kenneth with a rifle aimed at some distant target. 'It looks as though he's modified his rifle a bit,' he commented.

'Aye, he made his own sound modifier.'

Torquil looked him straight in the eye. 'Why did he need a silencer?'

Alistair shrugged the question away. 'If you are trying to take out half-a-dozen rabbits before they make it to their burrows then muffling the sound makes a good deal of sense.'

'What might also help,' Torquil said, as they made their way back along the landing, 'is a sample of the bullets he used.'

Alistair eyed him curiously then shrugged and unlocked the metal cabinet at the top of the gun cupboard. He opened a box and drew out a bullet. 'There you are. Just standard .308 cartridges. And the other box has .22s.'

He reached into the cupboard and unlocked the partition with the 12-bore shotgun. 'I might as well get this ready for tomorrow.'

'For the hedgehog cull?' Torquil asked.

Alistair McKinley nodded curtly. 'Aye, and I tell you one thing, Inspector McKinnon, I'm in a killing mood.'

CHAPTER TEN

Vincent had been working himself up into a rare temper as he fed Geordie Morrison's chickens and collected their eggs. He felt that he alone of the Wee Kingdom community actually saw through Geordie's façade as the jolly carefree eccentric, the natural father and perfect husband. Oh, he was affable enough, charismatic even, but he had them all eating out of his hand. No one carped when he just took off with his family, generally leaving Vincent or the late Gordon MacDonald to tidy up after him and cover for his chores. Rhona had always been smitten by him, of course, and the McKinleys never really bothered. They had always tended to be pretty self-sufficient.

Only now, in amidst the irritation, was Vincent starting to worry. This time the family had been away longer than expected. It was usually just a day or two on some joy-ride or whim of Geordie's. He wouldn't have thought too much about it, except that they seemed to have suddenly run into death and tragedy everywhere. Gordon had suddenly died of a stroke or heart attack. Young Kenneth had killed himself on some foolish climbing accident in the Corlins. Ewan McPhee was missing, presumed dead. And then Rhona had almost died from a heart attack. There were too many things going on.

Why didn't Geordie Morrison have a mobile like everyone else? But oh no, him and his bloody 'green' lifestyle!

The germ of anxiety had become heated on the flames of the irritation that he was feeling about having to do all these extra chores. He began to wonder whether Geordie really had taken his family and gone off in their boat. The boat had gone, right enough, but were they all OK? Could they be stranded somewhere — or even worse! He tried to shove the thought from his head, but he couldn't help thinking that Sallie would usually send one of the kids around with a note.

Except when Geordie pre-empted her and just took them off, of course. He had done it before, the big galoot, and only given Sallie time to write a note, which Rhona had found on the mantelpiece.

That'll be it! Vincent thought. For goodness sake, I'll have it out with the dim-witted pair of them if I find a note just waiting there. Putting us through all this!

With the basket of eggs in one hand he let himself into the unlocked back door of their cottage. The whole place smacked of family life. The smell of children, their toys, paintings, crudely written messages to their parents were everywhere — on the floor, the walls, attached to the fridge.

Entering the equally children-dominated sitting-room filled him with sudden dread. What if they had had an accident and no one had known about it?

Bugger! Ewan McPhee had died out there somewhere and his body hadn't been found yet. He cursed himself for a fool and ran up the bare wooden stairs to see if he could find some clue: a map, a book, anything that might point to where they had gone.

But there was nothing. Their beds had all been made, the bathroom was neat and tidy, the towels neatly folded and hanging from the rails. No toothbrushes! That meant that they had gone off somewhere, but that was all.

He was on the point of taking the liberty of checking drawers to see if he could elicit some information, although for the life of him he didn't know what sort of thing to look for, when he heard footsteps downstairs.

'Geordie? Sallie?' he cried, turning and descending the stairs two steps at a time.

Megan Munro was standing in the middle of the room, wringing her hands in agitation.

She was dressed in a baggy pink sweater with matching pink bobble hat, with her jeans tucked into pink patterned Wellingtons. He could see that she was trembling so much that her large hoop earrings were actually shaking slightly. When she recognized Vincent her lower lip started to tremble and she began to move towards him.

'Megan, what's wrong?'

He was silenced as she threw herself into his arms and buried her face against his chest. He felt her rhythmic sobbing.

'Is it ... Nial?'

She moved her head in answer back and forth and mumbled between sobs, 'We — we had a row! About ... birds ... and hedgehogs. And her!'

'Her?'

'Katrina Tulloch. He says he's worried about her.' She made a choking noise. 'I said he was more worried about her than he is about me! And he went off.'

Vincent stood patting her back, just letting her get rid of her emotions.

She looked up at him. 'I went for a walk, just to straighten my head out and I saw movement in the upstairs window here. I thought the Morrisons must be back. I thought I'd be able to chat to Sallie. I thought she'd understand.'

Ignoring an unexpected pang of disappointment and resentment, Vincent continued to make supportive, soothing movements on her back. 'There, there,' he said softly.

The sudden bang on the doorframe made him snap his head up to see Liam Sartori standing in the doorway, an insolent grin on his face.

'Well, well! What a cosy scene,' he said, holding up a hand with a number of envelopes. 'Listen, don't let me interrupt anything here. I've just come to deliver some letters. You two are crofters, aren't you? I met the lady at the — er — party, the other day.'

'You mean at the wake!' Vincent returned sharply. 'You know that you were not welcome.'

Liam smirked. 'Ah well, that's me. Thick-skinned I am. Anyway, here's a wee letter for each of you,' he said, looking at the names on the envelopes and reading them out. 'Miss Megan Munro of Linne Croft, and Mr Vincent Fitzpatrick of Prince's Croft. And there's one for Mr and Mrs George Morrison of Tweed Croft, wherever they are.' He eyed the two of them, still standing with their arms about each other. 'Convenient that they're not here though, eh? It means that folk like you can have a wee tryst here when —'

Vincent freed himself from Megan's embrace and took two swift steps towards Liam, who immediately adopted a belligerent fighting pose. He grinned and Vincent noticed the strong smell of whisky on his breath.

'You fancy your chances with me, do you, old man?' he jibed, his words slightly slurred. 'Come on then. I'll show you, too.'

Vincent stood with his fists balled and his elbows bent. 'What do you mean, you'll show me too?'

But Liam merely shrugged. 'Nothing, pal. Just say I had a run in with one of your locals recently. Only he turned my offer of satisfaction down!' His face twisted into a sneer. 'But, of course, if you'd like to make something of it!'

Megan put a restraining hand on Vincent's arm. 'Leave it, Vincent. He's just a minion of the new laird. A bully boy. Just take the letters.' And then to Liam, 'Now just leave this property.'

'Oh, I will, missy. I've just one more letter to deliver to the old boy who lost his son then I'll be away.'

And with an insolent wink he turned and left them to open their letters.

Nial Urquart was flushed, bedraggled and slightly out of breath when he came across Katrina's van. It was parked by the side of the high coastal road. It was empty.

He spied her on the shingle beach below, wandering along the base of the cliffs where at low tide the sea-caves that typified the West Uist coastline became visible. He descended quickly and weaved his way between the rock pools, and the seaweed and limpet-covered rocks towards her.

'Katrina! What are you doing down here?'

She had turned at the sound of his voice, her face distraught. 'I'm looking for, for —'

He encircled her in his arms. 'You're looking for Ewan?' He put a gentle hand under her chin. 'It's no use, Katrina. You have to accept it. Ewan has gone.'

She shook her head emphatically. 'But I can't stop. I care —'

'And I care about you, Katrina.' He took a deep breath. 'I want you to let me care for you.'

She stared at him in disbelief. 'But you can't. There's Megan! You —' Then her eyes rolled upwards abruptly and he had to catch her as her body went limp and she fainted in his arms.

Sister Lamb called for Nurse Giselle Anderson as soon as she found Rhona McIvor collapsed on the floor beside her bed. After a cursory examination revealed that Rhona was not breathing and that she was pulseless, Sister Lamb began cardiopulmonary resuscitation while Nurse Anderson ran to get the portable defibrillator. By the time she had returned to Rhona's side, Maggie Crouch had sent out an emergency call for Dr McLelland.

Sister Lamb had already tried two defibrillation shocks to Rhona's chest when Ralph arrived. With three of them at work they wired her up to an ECG monitor, put up an intravenous line and injected some adrenaline, sodium bicarbonate and lidocaine into her, before applying two more shocks. But, despite their best efforts, it was in vain. After ten more minutes, Ralph declared her dead.

As Sister Lamb and Nurse Anderson started to lay out her body on the bed, they noticed that there was a letter screwed up in her left hand. Ralph prised open her already stiffening fingers and removed the letter. He smoothed it out on the bedside locker.

'Looks like she was trying to write something on the bottom of this letter,' he mused, bending and picking up a pen that had rolled under the bed, presumably when she had collapsed. 'Her heart was obviously pretty fragile. I wonder if this letter had anything to do with it?'

'I bet that the new laird brought her that,' Sister Lamb said over her shoulder. 'He was just in here before we found her.'

'Was he now?' Ralph murmured as he scanned the letter. His eyes widened. 'I'm only guessing, but I'd think this letter would have pushed her blood pressure through the roof. And I'd say that she collapsed before she could finish her note.'

'What does it say, Doctor?' Sister Lamb asked, as she and Nurse Anderson pulled the sheet up to Rhona's chin.

'Just two words in capital letters — CARD IN — then there is a squiggle, which I assume is when she arrested.'

'A card? Shall I check out her locker, Sister?' Nurse Anderson asked.

Sister Lamb smoothed the bedcover and stroked a stray wisp of hair from Rhona's face. 'That's a good idea. We'll need to get everything ready for her next of kin.' Having said that she put a hand over her mouth. 'Oh mercy me, she has no next of kin! She was all alone.'

There was a tap at the door and then it was pushed ajar to reveal a sad-faced Lachlan McKinnon. 'Is it OK to come in?' he asked. 'Maggie Crouch said that Rhona just passed away.'

Ralph opened the door fully and ushered Lachlan in. 'Come away in, Padre. I'm afraid that Rhona had just one strain too many.' He showed him the letter and explained about the visit from Jock McArdle. 'I'm thinking that she had a shock, then she arrested — and although we did our best, we lost her.'

Lachlan looked down sadly at the body of his old friend. 'I'll say a wee prayer for her then, if you don't mind. Who are you planning to tell?'

'We were just talking about that, Padre,' replied Ralph. 'She was on her own, wasn't she? I suppose it must be the other crofters on the Wee Kingdom.'

'Aye, they'll all take it badly. I was heading over there after I'd seen Rhona anyway. Would you like me to do the needful?'

'It would be a great help if you would,' replied Sister Lamb. 'And if you tell them we've got her things here. The letter and cards and all.'

Morag had logged all the messages and enquiries that had come in throughout the morning and duly gave Torquil an update upon his return from the Wee Kingdom.

'Calum Steele called in for his usual snoop around. He said to tell you that he'll be going up to photograph the windmills.'

'There are two towers up already. I had a wee run-in with the chaps that were putting them up. They're not as big as I

362

imagined, but they are just experimental ones to gather information about the wind. The foreman said that they are planning to put up about ten. If all goes according to plan, then they may start building the big ones and that means a real wind farm.'

Morag grimaced. 'That new laird seems set to put the Wee Kingdom crofters' backs up, that's for sure.' She tapped the book with her pencil. 'And talking about him — the Laird of Dunshiffin as he likes to call himself — he phoned up too. He wanted to see you straight away, but I told him you were out on official business. He put the phone down on me, the ignoramus!'

'Well, he can go and boil his head!' exclaimed Torquil with exasperation.

Morag laughed. 'May I tell him that myself if he rings again?'

'Actually, Morag, I rather think I'll enjoy doing it myself. I'm not over-keen on his diplomacy skills, especially when he's a newcomer to the island.'

Morag ran through the rest of the messages then went through to the kitchen to make tea while Torquil began work on his report.

When Morag came back through with the tea-tray, she found him comparing the empty cartridge he had found on the Cruadalach isles with the two live cartridges — one that had been found beside Kenneth's body and the other that he had obtained from the McKinley house.

'These certainly look to me as if they're from the same batch,' he explained. 'And from my chat with Alistair it is clear that Kenneth had a thing about guns. He had a bookcase full of books about weapons, the SAS and hunting.'

He shoved the photograph that Alistair had given him across the desk. Morag swivelled it round and frowned.

'I see what you mean. And it makes you think about Ewan's entry about GUNS in his diary.'

'Aye, and his gun is nowhere to be found.'

'Is it a dangerous gun?'

'They all are potentially deadly, Morag. And this one is a .308. It could easily take down a stag.' He shook his head. 'Superintendent Lumsden is going to love this. And I have to say that I have a bad feeling about it all.'

Torquil was just about to go off to meet the Drummond twins at the harbour when his mobile phone rang. It was Lachlan.

'I think you had better come out to the Wee Kingdom. I have just found a body.' His voice hesitated for a moment. 'It looks nasty, Torquil. Somehow I don't think this was a natural death.'

CHAPTER ELEVEN

Morag had phoned through to the cottage hospital and managed to get hold of Ralph McLelland, who collected her from the station in the West Uist ambulance. Torquil had gone on ahead on his Bullet and parked alongside the Padre's Red Hunter on the island side of the Wee Kingdom causeway. Ralph parked behind them and he and Morag got out and looked over the edge of the causeway.

There was a fifteen-foot drop to a small shingle shelf covered in swards of slimy kelp with a couple of rock pools before the shelf disappeared into the sea. Torquil and the Padre were kneeling beside one of the pools looking at the body of Liam Sartori.

'He's dead all right, Ralph,' said Torquil, looking up when he heard their arrival on the causeway.

'He was lying face down in this rock pool when I found him,' said Lachlan. 'I was on my way to tell the crofters about Rhona's death and I saw him from the top of the rise. I pulled him out and turned him over to see if I could do anything for him. I assumed that he'd drowned. I tried CPR for a few minutes, but —' He shook his head despondently. 'Then I realized that things weren't what they seemed.'

Morag and Ralph scrambled down to them.

'What do you mean, Lachlan?' Morag asked. 'He must have fallen off the edge of the causeway, and knocked himself out when he fell in the pool. Isn't that what happened?'

Torquil shook his head. 'I agree with Lachlan. There's something that doesn't fit here. You can see where he must have landed. The shingle is all disturbed over there. I can't see how he would have ended with his face down in that pool. It is too far away.'

'Maybe he stunned himself, then got up and staggered about a bit before collapsing in the pool,' Morag suggested.

'It's possible,' said Ralph, kneeling beside the body, 'but look at those gashes on his face. They're like talon marks. Like the ones on Kenneth McKinley's face.' There were three ugly slashes running across the bridge of Liam's nose. His face and hair were damp and blood oozed from the wounds.

'That's what worried me,' said Lachlan. 'I am not sure that I —'

There was the click and flash of a camera and they all looked up to see Calum Steele standing on the causeway, a new camera in his hand.

'Looks like the eagles have been busy again,' he said. 'He's the one who threw my last camera in Loch Hynish, by the way, Torquil.'

Calum Steele had already been up to Wind's Eye croft to photograph the wind towers and he insisted on accompanying Lachlan, despite the minister's protestations, as he went to break the news about Rhona's death to the crofters of the Wee Kingdom. As expected, they were all devastated, and all rushed in to the Kyleshiffin cottage hospital to pay their respects.

Calum rode back on his Lambretta along the Dunshiffin road with the aim of getting a surreptitious photograph of the new laird and his other minion to illustrate his article on the windmills, and to link up with the piece he was planning to write about Liam Sartori's death and the ongoing 'Birds of prey' series that he was developing in his mind. The thought of a 'killer eagle' had raised visions of him making it into the national news, where in his heart he felt that he belonged. And maybe, he thought as he rode along, he might drop in at the castle if the laird was out and pump Jesmond for a titbit of news about that dead dog.

Turning a corner he had to swerve suddenly as a Porsche hurtled towards him in the middle of the road. As a result, he skewed off the road into a patch of bracken and fell sideways. By the time he got to his feet, with the intention of haranguing the driver, whom he assumed would stop and come to his assistance, he was dismayed, then outright furious, to find that the car was out of sight. And he had recognized the car, the driver and the passenger.

'That bloody laird! I'll have him!' he cursed.

He rode straight back to Kyleshiffin, along Harbour Street then up Kirk Wynd to the police station. He saw red when his eye fell on the Porsche parked directly outside the station.

He dismounted and made for the door, fully intent upon giving them a good ticking off, West Uist style, but he stopped on the threshold as he heard raised Glaswegian voices followed by Sergeant Morag Driscoll's calm remonstrance.

'Look, police-girlie, I had a call to say that one of my boys has been taken by the police. Now I want to see him and I want to see your head honcho, right now!'

Morag stared at Jock McArdle with steely eyes and tight lips, then, still maintaining her calm, said, 'Firstly, Mr McArdle, don't you ever call me a police-girlie again, or I'll be on your case so tightly that you won't even dare to drop dandruff in public. And secondly, I am not obliged to discuss whether anyone has been taken into custody with a member of the public.'

'Damn it — *woman* — has my boy been arrested?'

'You can call me Sergeant Driscoll, not woman,' Morag returned firmly, indicating the three stripes on her Arran jumper. 'And the answer is no, we do not have anyone in custody at this moment.'

McArdle frowned. 'Then why did someone call me and say he'd been taken away?'

Morag drew her ledger closer and picked up a pencil. 'Who called you, Mr McArdle?'

McArdle looked at Danny Reid. 'Did Jesmond say who called?'

Danny shook his head. 'Just a message to say he'd been taken away.'

'That message did not come from here,' said Morag, looking puzzled. She tapped the pencil on the ledger. 'What I can tell you is that there has been an incident involving a young man and we are trying to determine if he has any next of kin.'

Jock McArdle stared at her in shock, then he thumped his fist on the desk, 'Incident? Next of kin? What gives here?'

Calum Steele had come in silently. He coughed and advanced towards the duty desk, drawing his portly body up to his full five foot six. 'Do you need any help, Morag?' he queried.

Danny put a hand on his chest and prodded him back. 'Just get out, chubby,' he snarled.

Morag laid her pencil down. 'No, there's no problem, thank you, Calum.' Then sternly to Danny, 'And you — don't touch the him again. If you do, then maybe there will be someone under arrest today!'

Danny glared at her then shrugged and took a step backwards.

'There was an incident earlier today,' Morag went on. 'A fatal accident, I am afraid. That is why we are trying to locate next of kin.'

'For Christ's sake! Why didn't you tell me this straight away?' Jock McArdle demanded, his face purpling with rage. 'Liam's dead, is that what you're saying? How? Who did it?'

'I think you should calm down a bit,' said Calum.

'And I told you to get away from me,' said Danny. 'If my friend's been killed somebody's going to pay.' His eyes had murder in them. 'Don't you tempt me, pal.'

The door opened and Torquil came in. He quickly took in the situation. 'Mr McArdle, I am Inspector McKinnon.'

'At last, the organ-grinder!' said McArdle. 'There are a few things I want to ask you, but for now just tell me, where is my boy?'

'Are you related to Liam Sartori?' Torquil asked. 'We have found the body of a young man and we have a name from his driving licence.'

'Naw, I am not related. But Danny here and me are as close as any family to him. Apart from us, he is alone in the world. All three of us are alone.'

'In that case perhaps you'd care to come with me and identify the body. It looks as if he had a tragic accident.'

Alistair McKinley, Vincent Gilfillan and Megan Munro stood disconsolately about the bed and looked down at Rhona, their neighbour and friend. They all had tears in their eyes.

'Goodbye Rhona,' said Vincent and he bent down and kissed her on the forehead.

'It is a black day. I didn't think it could get any worse than it was when my boy died, but it just has.'

'It's like a plague,' sobbed Megan. 'Like the Black Death. One person after another. Gordon, Kenneth and now Rhona.'

'And Ewan McPhee,' Alistair McKinley added, as he made the sign of the cross and kissed Rhona's forehead.

Sister Lamb and Nurse Anderson had been standing respectfully by the door.

'I don't think she would have had much pain,' said Sister Lamb. 'She must have just collapsed. We found her on the floor there and tried to resuscitate her, but it was too late.'

Nurse Anderson pointed to the carry-all beside the bed. 'We packed all her things for you to take away. The letter she was reading is on the top.'

'Let's see that letter?' Megan said, drying her eyes and crossing the room to pick up the letter.

'It was a bit crumpled up in her hand and we smoothed it out,' Sister Lamb explained. 'We think she was trying to write something on it when she collapsed.'

'The swine!' cursed Vincent. 'It is the same letter that we all had. From the new laird about erecting those windmills on the Wee Kingdom.'

'What's that she was writing, Vincent?' Alistair McKinley asked. He looked over Megan's shoulder. 'It's shaky writing. Looks like CARD IN.'

'We thought she must have been trying to write something else when her heart stopped and she collapsed,' said Sister Lamb. 'See the squiggle.'

'Maybe there is something in one of her Get Well cards? They are all in the bag.' Nurse Anderson suggested.

'Or maybe it's a card at the cottage,' suggested Megan.

'Who knows?' said Vincent. 'One thing about it all is clear though, that laird killed her as good as if he put a gun to her head.'

'Aye, and he was responsible for my boy getting himself killed.'

Megan suddenly stiffened and pointed out of the window. 'Speak of the devil. There he is with one of his bully-boys. Where are they going with Inspector McKinnon?'

Alistair made to leave the room. 'I'm going to give him a

piece of my mind.'

But Vincent restrained him. 'No, Alistair, not now. Not while we're here seeing Rhona.' He bit his lip. 'We're all too shocked to start something now.'

Sister Lamb leaned over to see the three men entering the back door of the hospital. 'Hadn't you heard? About the young man, one of his employees? I thought you would all know, what with it happening at the Wee Kingdom.'

'What happened, Sister?' Vincent asked.

'There was an accident. He fell off the causeway and he's dead.'

Megan took a sharp intake of breath and threw herself into Vincent's arms.

'Inspector McKinnon will be taking him to see the body.'

There was a heavy footfall from the corridor then Nial Urquart came in. 'I came as soon as I heard,' he said, looking first at Rhona's body and then at Megan in Vincent's arms. 'I'm here now, Megan,' he said, giving Vincent a frosty stare as he held out his arms.

'And just where have you been?' Megan demanded. She sniffed disdainfully. 'You've been drinking!'

'Just the one at the Bonnie Prince Charlie,' he returned. 'I found Katrina. She fainted and I thought she needed a brandy.'

'I needed you, too, Nial!' exclaimed Megan, brushing past him and breaking into a run down the corridor.

Nial looked at the others then hung his head. 'I'd better go after her,' he said sheepishly.

Katrina was feeling confused. Everything was collapsing around her and she was finding it hard to maintain any clinical focus. It was fortunate that her surgery had been particularly quiet and the visits had been few. That had given her a chance to search.

But again she heard Nial's words, and although she knew that he was probably right, still she felt that she couldn't give up. Not until his body was found. She shivered at the thought of that, and of how her life had changed since she had come back to West Uist. In debt up to her chin, she had been finding it hard to cope with the small island practice. And then Ewan had changed everything — forever.

She looked in the mirror above the sink in her consulting-room. Although her eyes were bleary from crying, and she felt a bit heady from the double brandy that Nial had made her drink, the face that looked back at her was still pretty. She grimaced at herself.

Damn that face! Her looks had gotten her in trouble again and again. Men! Ewan with his insatiable jealousy, Kenneth with his puppy-dog drooling over her, despite her being quite firm in trying to shrug off his attentions. And now Nial.

Damn them all!

She rinsed her face and dabbed it dry with a paper towel.

Come on, Katrina, she chided herself. *Get a grip. You've work to do. Got to get those specimens off to the lab in Glasgow. And that means make the ferry within half an hour.*

And the courier would be waiting for the special package.

She donned her lab coat and pulled on protective gloves. Then she went to the fridge and pulled out all of the blood and urine specimens and the tissue samples that were awaiting despatch and wrote out the necessary lab request forms for each one. She knew that McArdle would soon be pressing her for the full results on his dog.

Then she packaged up the special tissue sample and laid it in the collection bag. It looked just like all the rest.

When she had finished she stripped off the gloves, rinsed her hands again and stared in the mirror. Despite herself, her thoughts returned again to Nial and she felt a tremble of excitement.

Then she chided herself again.

'What a mess, Katrina, you bloody fool! How do you get yourself into such messes?'

Once Jock McArdle and Danny Reid had left the cottage hospital, Torquil sat and drank a cup of tea with Ralph and the Padre in Ralph's out-patient consulting-room.

'That McArdle is an unpleasant fellow,' said Ralph. 'I know he was upset, but he's not going to win any prizes for politeness.'

'Calum Steele said something like that, too,' agreed Torquil. 'And Calum isn't himself renowned for that attribute.'

'I thought that you handled him rather well though, laddie,' said Lachlan.

Torquil gave a wan smile and sipped his tea. 'For now. But he's wanting to come back and talk to me about his dog. Apparently Katrina Tulloch says it may have been poisoned.'

'The world doesn't seem to be with Mr Jock McArdle at the moment,' mused the Padre. 'What do you think he meant when he said he'd deal with things?'

Torquil shook his head. 'I think he believes that Sartori was murdered. He saw the scratches on the face, but he didn't buy them being done by an eagle.'

Ralph McLelland stood up. 'Well, it's only speculation at the moment. The post-mortem may tell us more. Can I go ahead?'

Torquil took a final swig of tea and stood up. 'Absolutely. He's been formally identified. Let's see what you find.'

Jesmond was looking nervous when Jock McArdle stormed

into the hall with Danny Reid at his heel.

'I have bad news sir,' Jesmond said. 'I tried your mobile but there was no answer. It's Dallas, sir. I called the vet, and she's on her way. But I think it's too late.'

'What's happened?' McArdle snapped.

'I heard her howling, sir. I found her lying in the billiard-room, shaking and frothing at the mouth. Then she just — died! I think she may have been poisoned too, sir.'

Ralph called Torquil at home that evening, as he and the Padre sat sipping pre-dinner drams of whisky.

The Padre watched his nephew speaking to the GP-cum-police surgeon over the phone, then replace the receiver, looking grim-faced.

'It looks as though you were right, Lachlan. There's no doubt in Ralph's mind. He's pretty sure that it was murder. And he thinks he has strong evidence to prove it.'

CHAPTER TWELVE

The mouth-watering aroma of fried kippers greeted Torquil as he came down to breakfast the following morning. The Padre was standing by the Aga reading the latest edition of the *Chronicle*. He sighed and handed the paper to his nephew.

'Calum has been busy,' he announced. 'He sails close to the wind a lot of the time, but he may find himself in a spot of trouble with this.'

Torquil sat down and spread the newspaper on the table beside his place setting. There was a large photograph of the two wind towers on the Wee Kingdom and the headline: WIND OF DISCONTENT.

The article that followed it was one of Calum's rants:

The threat of wind farms in the Hebrides is now a reality. The self-styled 'laird of Dunshiffin', Mr Jock McArdle, has steam-rolled the local crofting community on the Wee Kingdom. These ugly wind towers are each about fifty feet tall and have been erected on the common grazing ground adjoining the late Gordon MacDonald's Wind's Eye croft. The new owner of the Dunshiffin estate, of which the Wee Kingdom is a part, has gone against the local wishes and put his ill-conceived plan into action.

The West Uist Chronicle *states that the plan is ill-conceived as the legality of erecting these wind towers on common grazing ground is in doubt.*

Torquil lifted the paper as his uncle handed him a plate and put the skillet of kippers on a cooling board in the centre of the table.

'It's not too bad as an article,' Torquil said. 'I guess he's just echoing local opinion.'

'Ah, but he then goes on to get a bit personal about McArdle and he calls his employees "henchmen". Not content with that he accuses them of intimidation tactics, and mentions again about them throwing his camera into Loch Hynish.'

Torquil picked up his knife and fork and began to eat as he continued to read.

'It's the article on the next page that I meant though,' Lachlan added, as he poured tea.

Torquil turned to the inside page and saw the photograph of the body of Liam Sartori lying below the causeway. The face had been digitally blurred, but beneath the photograph was the headline: HAVE THE KILLER EAGLES STRUCK AGAIN?

There was a blown up insert at the bottom left of the photograph, featuring a golden eagle swooping on some prey.

'Good grief, he's gone mad!' Torquil exclaimed. And he read:

The body of a man, believed to be in the employ of Mr Jock McArdle, the new owner of Dunshiffin estate, was found face down in a rock pool yesterday below the causeway to the Wee Kingdom. Our reporter saw the body and informed us that there was unmistakable talon marks across the dead man's face. He was able to confirm that these were identical to those found on the body of Mr Kenneth McKinley, who died in a climbing accident in the Corlins last week.

Two deaths! Both with talon marks! Isn't it time that someone did something?

'The bloody fool!' Torquil exclaimed. 'What's he playing at? It's bad enough that he's published a photograph of the poor chap's body but to write that drivel. It is as if he is inciting some idiot to go hunting for eagles.' He shook his head in exasperation. 'Blast Calum and his inflated ego. Why does he feel he has to sensationalize everything?'

'And there are a lot of hotheads around,' agreed Lachlan. 'But he'll get flak from people like Nial Urquart and the bird lovers.'

'Damn!' Torquil cursed, as he pushed his plate aside. 'That's all I need with a murder investigation on my hands.'

No sooner had he said it, than his mobile went off. Morag's name flashed on the view screen.

'Torquil have you seen —?'

'Aye, Morag. I've got the *Chronicle* in front of me. Calum is a prize idiot.'

'He is that,' Morag agreed. 'But I didn't mean that, I've just been watching the tail end of the early morning Scottish TV news before I take the kids to the minders. Kirstie Macroon has just done a piece on the *"Killer Eagles of West Uist"* and she had a tele-interview with Calum. We may be in for an influx of reporters and sensation seekers.'

Torquil groaned.

'I've got everything teed up for first thing though,' Morag went on. 'The Drummonds and Ralph McLelland are coming in. I thought we'd have the briefing in the recreation-room at the station. I'll have it all ready for when you get in.'

Superintendent Lumsden had left a message with Morag for Torquil to telephone him as soon as he set foot in the building.

'I think his gout must still be playing him up,' Morag said with a grimace that told Torquil exactly the sort of reception he could expect when his superior officer answered the telephone. And indeed there were no pleasantries or preliminary banter: the superintendent just went straight for the jugular.

'Why the hell is it always the same with you, McKinnon? Do

you set out to embarrass me with the chief constable? Why do I always seem to hear about what's happening on West Uist when I look at the TV news? Killer eagles for goodness sake! Have you no control over that numskull reporter Calum Steele?'

'The freedom of the press, Superintendent Lumsden,' Torquil returned.

'Bollocks! Why didn't you let me know about this?'

'I was going to contact you this morning, sir. I knew nothing about this story until I read the newspaper just now. In fact, it may be more complex than the report on the TV.'

There was a moment's silence on the other end of the telephone, and then slowly, Superintendent Lumsden growled, 'Go on, McKinnon, surprise me.'

Torquil took a deep breath. 'I was going to contact you this morning, sir, after my meeting with the police surgeon. Doctor McLelland did a post-mortem last night.'

'And?'

'We haven't had the meeting yet, sir. But there is a strong possibility that the man's death was more suspicious than we thought.' There was an interruption on the other end of the line and Torquil heard someone else talking in the background, and then Lumsden replying to them.

'Right, McKinnon, spit it out, I'm going to have to go. I'm about to take a call from the Laird of Dunshiffin.'

'It may have been murder, sir.'

Torquil winced as the superintendent howled down the other end of the line.

'Right! What a bloody fiasco! Have your meetings Inspector, then report back to me straight away. Meanwhile I'll see what your laird wants.'

'He isn't my laird, Superintendent —' But the line had gone

dead.

When she heard the phone being replaced, Morag popped her head round Torquil's office door. She sympathetically smiled at him. 'Everyone is here. Are you ready to start? I've got the tea and biscuits ready.'

The atmosphere was subdued in the recreation-room, because everyone was conscious that Ewan was no longer with them.

Torquil began by informing them all about the Scottish TV early news programme and about Calum Steele's piece in the *Chronicle*.

'Aye, but what I can't understand is that anyone would listen to the wee windbag's theories,' said Douglas Drummond.

'Och, it's because he is a man of letters and not an ignorant fisherman like you,' replied his brother. 'Or like me, for that matter — even though we both beat him in the Gaelic spelling contests when we were all at school. You remember them, don't you, Piper?'

Torquil grunted assent and brought the twins to order by clapping his hands and standing up. 'What Calum has done is done!' he said. 'But although he has made the national news with his talk about killer eagles, it actually looks as if there is a more sinister killer abroad than an eagle. It looks as if there is a murderer on West Uist.'

He gestured to the local doctor. 'Ralph, would you give us a summary of your post-mortem findings on the body of Liam Sartori?'

While Torquil had been speaking, Ralph had been plugging his laptop into the station projector.

'I've done this as a Power-Point presentation,' he explained. 'That way I can show you each stage of my examination, from the initial finding of the body by the causeway, through my preliminary external examination of the corpse, the post-mortem dissection, and the pathological and microscopic specimens that resulted from it.' He looked at Morag. 'Can we pull the blinds?'

And a few moments later with the room in partial darkness, he pressed the home button on his laptop and a photograph of Liam Sartori lying on the rocks by the causeway flashed onto the wall.

'As Torquil has just told us, the media have drawn attention to the so-called talon marks on the face of the dead man.' He pointed a laser pen at the wall and indicated the livid lines on the face with the little luminous red arrow. 'Quite clearly, if these are talon slashes then they lead us to think that they are the same marks that we so recently saw on the face of Kenneth McKinley.'

'And are they, Ralph?' Torquil asked.

'I'm not sure,' the doctor returned, changing the slide with the touch of a finger, to reveal the body of Kenneth McKinley and the deep gashes on his face. 'What do you think?'

The others all craned forward to look.

'I am not sure,' said Wallace.

'Isn't there some test that will tell?' Morag answered.

'I honestly don't know — yet,' replied Ralph. 'I've never come across a death as the result of an attack by a bird of prey. But the point is, it could have been. And we also have to ask several questions. First, could he have fallen off the causeway after being attacked by a bird, and then risen stunned from a knock on the head? Could he have then staggered forward to fall face first into a rock pool and drown?'

'What makes you doubt that?' Torquil asked, already aware of Ralph's findings.

Ralph moved to the next slide.

'This!' he said emphatically.

And they found themselves looking at the naked back of Liam Sartori, as he lay on the metal post-mortem table in the cottage hospital mortuary. Ralph directed the luminous arrow of his laser pen to a discoloured area that started between the dead man's shoulder blades and ran up to his neck.

'In my opinion this mark was caused by a foot.' Ralph said. 'You can see petechiae, tiny pinpoint haemorrhages dotted around and the spreading purple discolouration. This would be consistent with a foot having been stomped down hard on him — and maintaining pressure for some time. Possibly holding him underneath the water surface of that rock pool.'

'You mean after he had staggered there?' Wallace asked.

'Except that we think he was dragged there, rather than staggered there,' said Torquil. And he described the position of the dead man's collar, the disturbed shingle where he had fallen.

'Here's a photograph of how we found him,' said Ralph. 'Bearing in mind that the Padre had pulled him out of the pool, yet the position of his collar would be hard to explain.'

He then ran through a number of slides detailing the morbid anatomical dissection. Despite herself Morag felt decidedly queasy and had to look away. The Drummonds, well used to gutting fish and removing vast amounts of entrails, nodded with interest and sipped tea.

'As you can see there, I am squeezing water from the lungs. But the question is, did that water get there before or after he died?'

'What does that mean?' asked Douglas.

'Well, the presence of water in the lungs doesn't by itself tell us a lot. It could have got into his lungs after he was dead.'

Wallace slapped his hand on the table. 'Gosh, I see what you mean. It could have been made to look like he was drowned.' Then he eyed the police surgeon doubtfully. 'But how else could he have died?'

'From this,' said Ralph moving the slide to a photograph of a human brain resting in a large stainless-steel dish. Once again he manoeuvred the luminous red arrow of his laser pen to highlight a large clot of blood that had formed over the left temporal area. 'That could have killed him, although I think it may have just been enough to stun or knock him out. He could have sustained it in a fall, but equally, he could have been hit and then fallen.'

'Did you do a diatom test, Ralph?' Torquil asked.

'I did, and here it is.' And with a press of the button the wall was illuminated with a microscopic section of what looked like bubbles in a mush of red pulp. All over the field were small dots of a greenish hue. 'Those bubble-like structures are alveoli, the air pockets in the lungs, and those little dots are tiny unicellular organisms called diatoms. The water in the rock pool sample I took is full of them. This slide shows that they are present both inside and outside the alveoli. That implies that his heart was beating for some period of time after he was in the water. The diatoms have been inhaled and have entered the bloodstream. I have other samples that I have yet to analyse, but if I find them in other organs it is pretty conclusive that he drowned.'

'And with that strange bruise on his back it looks as if he may have been held under,' suggested Torquil. 'But he was a big bloke. Would it have needed a lot of strength to keep him under?'

'Not necessarily,' returned Ralph. 'His blood alcohol level was high enough to have anaesthetized half of the fishermen in West Uist.'

Torquil crossed to the whiteboard that was usually used to keep darts or table tennis scores and picked up the marker pen.

'All right, we have a suspected murder victim,' he said, writing the name Liam Sartori on the board and enclosing it in a box. 'What do we know about him?'

'He worked for the new laird,' Wallace suggested.

Torquil nodded, wrote the name Jock McArdle nearby and enclosed it in a circle. He joined the box and the circle with a line. 'What else?

'He was from Glasgow. Not much taste in clothes,' said Douglas.

'He had a run in with Calum Steele,' said Morag.

Torquil added Calum's name and circled it.

'And he had a run in with Ewan,' Morag added.

Torquil turned and stared at her in surprise. 'Did he now? When? I didn't know about that?'

Morag coloured. 'Sorry, Torquil. I thought I had told you. I've just — I mean I had — things on my mind. I'll get the report book.'

She got up and went through to the main office, returning after a few moments with the large loose-leaf ledger. She put the book down on the table in front of Torquil and thumbed back the pages.

'Here it is. Early last week, a couple of days before he ... was last seen. Ewan cautioned him and his companion, a Danny Reid, about messing about with a motorboat in the harbour. When he approached them, they didn't realize that he was a police officer and started giving him lip. You know what a gentle giant he is —' She bit her lip, and went on. 'Anyway, he showed them his warrant card and they just kept on being abusive and derogatory about West Uist, and about being the new laird's right-hand men. Then one of them tossed a cigarette end into the gutter and Ewan gave him the option of picking it up and taking it home or being run in there and then.'

Morag grinned as she recalled the scene of him telling her about it. 'When he began rolling up his sleeves — to use Ewan's words — "he fair scuttled down and picked it up." But Ewan thinks they went off muttering about getting him back.'

Torquil tapped the marker pensively on the table then turned and added Ewan's name. He hesitated a moment, then enclosed it in a box. 'We will use a box to indicate that Ewan is ... also dead.' He sighed and drew a line between the names. Then he added the name Danny Reid, circled it and drew interconnecting lines with Liam Sartori, Ewan McPhee and Jock McArdle.

After a moment he wrote the word 'dog' near Jock McArdle's name and enclosed it in a box, and underneath it wrote the words 'suspected poison', followed by a question mark.

'Right, now let's focus on the Wee Kingdom for a minute,' he said. 'Liam Sartori had been there, delivering letters, as I understand it; Lachlan told me about it. And the letters were all legal documents on behalf of McArdle, informing the crofters that he was going to have wind towers erected on the common grazing land adjoining their crofts.'

Ralph had been quiet since his presentation. Now he interjected, 'I am guessing that it is the same letter that the laird himself delivered to Rhona at the hospital!' His normally calm visage turned stern. 'I have every reason to believe that was the trigger for her heart attack.'

Torquil nodded, then turned and under the heading of Wee Kingdom added Rhona McIvor's name, which he duly boxed. He turned to Morag. 'We'll need a copy of that letter.'

Morag had been making notes. 'And I expect we'll need to interview all of the crofters.'

Douglas snorted. 'Aye, the ones that are still alive.'

And Torquil wrote the names as prompted by Morag: Alistair McKinley, Megan Munro, Vincent Gilfillan, all of whom he enclosed in circles. And then Gordon MacDonald and Kenneth McKinley, who received boxes.

'What about the Morrisons?' Morag asked.

'Good question,' replied Torquil adding their names alongside the other members of the Wee Kingdom community. Instead of a box or a circle he drew a large question mark beside their names.

As Torquil began making notes about the respective post-mortem findings on Liam Sartori and Kenneth McKinley, and then linking their names with the word EAGLE followed by a question mark, Wallace verbalized the growing anxiety that they had all been feeling ever since his brother's earlier comment. 'There seem to be an awful lot of folk's names in boxes on that board!'

Torquil moved to another part of the board and made similar notes about the contents of Ewan's notebook. He wrote the words: GUNS, BOND, FAIR FANCIES HIMSELF, then on another column KATRINA, FAMILY and WIND.

'SAS, camouflage clothes and guns,' mused Torquil as he tapped various entries on the board with the marker pen. 'And all that slug goo that was found in Kenneth McKinley's stomach — it all adds up to a rich fantasy life, I think. So BOND may have been James Bond! He saw himself as some sort of secret agent, it seems.'

Morag snapped her fingers. 'Maybe that's another link with Katrina Tulloch? Maybe he fantasized about her?'

Torquil circled Katrina's name, adding lines to Ewan, Kenneth McKinley and the poisoned dog.

'That's a spider's web you have there, Piper,' said Wallace.

'You're right,' Torquil mused. 'But where's the spider?'

CHAPTER THIRTEEN

Guilt had been a constant companion to Katrina for several days, but never more so than now, as she lay half-naked next to Nial in the long grass of the machair.

'I love you; you know that, don't you, Katrina?' Nial murmured, his lips playing over her throat.

'Nial, I — I —' Abruptly she sat up and began reaching for her discarded jeans and knickers. 'I think this was a mistake. It shouldn't have happened.'

He caught her wrist and pulled her back down. 'It was inevitable!'

'It's just that I feel so bad, so guilty about —'

'About Megan? She's my problem.'

Katrina bit her lip. 'I meant about Ewan.'

'Ah yes, of course. But even so, I think this was bound to happen. There's chemistry between us.'

And despite herself she had to agree. She had felt it for some time as well, but had done her best to suppress the feelings.

'How did you manage to find me?' she asked, as his roaming hands began to work their way under her clothes again.

'I suppose I knew that you'd be checking out the coast again.'

'You were lucky then. I had been busy and had to get specimens off on the ferry.'

He chuckled softly as she straddled him. 'Right now I feel I'm the luckiest man alive.'

Alistair McKinley whistled for Shep, his collie, and patted the rear seat of his old jeep. Beside him was his large leather hunting bag full of shotgun cartridges and his old 12-bore shotgun. He started the engine and set off.

As he turned out of his drive he saw Megan Munro waiting for him, arms akimbo. He stopped alongside her, immediately aware of two things. Firstly, she had been crying, and secondly, she was in a belligerent mood.

'Alistair McKinley, where are you off to with that shotgun?'

'Megan, lassie, I know that you've had a bad time of it, what with Rhona and ... your man, yesterday, but —' he sighed with a hint of exasperation — 'I'm not feeling that great myself. And where I go with my shotgun, for which I have a licence, is entirely my own business.'

'It's my business as well, if you are planning to kill hedgehogs. I'll stop you.'

Alistair grunted. 'Don't even think of messing with me, lassie. I've lost my boy and today I'm in a killing mood. I'm going to do what I need to do to ease my own pain.' He gunned the engine and engaged first gear. 'Now get out of my way.'

Megan stood staring after him, her temper seething.

'So much pain, so much hurt,' she mused. 'I've got pain of my own, you stupid old man. And I know how I'm going to deal with it.'

'Shop! Anyone home?' Calum Steele slapped his hand on the counter of the Kyleshiffin police station.

Wallace Drummond came through, a mug of tea in his hand. At sight of the tubby editor in his yellow anorak, he shook his head as if in disbelief. 'Dear me, you have a nerve, Calum Steele! Behaving like a hooligan after all that you've been doing.'

The smile that had been on Calum's face was quickly

replaced by a look of injured pride, and then by one of puzzlement, and finally by one of pure irritation. 'What are you babbling about, you teuchter? I hope you are not referring to my article —' the smile momentarily resurfaced — 'or my television appearance?'

'I thought it was an interview over the telephone that you gave, not an appearance,' said Wallace. 'But I should be warning you, Inspector McKinnon is not pleased.'

'So it's *Inspector* McKinnon today, is it?' Calum returned sarcastically. 'Well, is Inspector McKinnon in to have a word with me?'

'I'm here, Calum,' said Torquil, coming out of the recreation-room at the sound of the *Chronicle* editor's voice. 'And I'm glad to see you.'

Calum beamed and looked disdainfully at Wallace.

'Because I was meaning to give you a right royal telling off!' exclaimed Torquil. 'Just what on earth did you think you were doing with that piece of drivel about killer eagles? And printing that photograph was just downright irresponsible.'

'Ir-irresponsible?' Calum repeated. 'Me? I'm the most responsible reporter on the island.'

'Calum, you are the only reporter on West Uist,' replied Torquil.

'Aye, reporter, editor, photographer and printer. I am the media on West Uist.'

'You're a windbag!' Wallace interjected.

Calum looked thunderstruck and raised his hands beseechingly to Torquil. 'Did you hear that? I am —'

'You are a nuisance at the moment,' said Torquil. 'And why did you go and spread this gossip to Scottish TV?'

'I am a newsman. The public have a right to know about what's happening on the island. Even the folk in Dundee and

389

Glasgow have a right to know what's happening in the real world.'

'Well you may have shot the gun this time, Calum. We are treating the death of that young man as highly suspicious.'

The telephone rang three times and then stopped as someone answered it in the recreation-room.

Calum's face registered instantaneous excitement. 'Suspicious, did you say? Are you talking about suspicion of death caused by an eagle attack — or something else? Come on, Piper. Give me a piece of —'

'Calum, it's a good piece of my mind that you are getting now. You need —'

Morag popped her head round the corner. 'Sorry, boss, it's Superintendent Lumsden on the line. He says he wants to talk to you straight away.' She grimaced helplessly. 'Like right now!'

Torquil gave a sigh of irritation. 'OK Morag. Could you take over with Calum here?'

Morag nodded and moved aside to let Torquil pass. Then advancing to the desk, she asked, 'Right then, Calum, where were you with Torquil?'

'The inspector was ticking him off. Sergeant Driscoll,' Wallace volunteered.

'Away with you,' returned Calum. He leaned conspiratorially on the counter. 'Actually, he was just telling me that you lot suspect murder. Tell me more, Sergeant Driscoll.'

Torquil took the call in his office. As soon as he lifted the receiver, Superintendent Lumsden snapped; 'I've just come off the phone with your new laird.'

'You mean the new landowner, Superintendent,' Torquil interrupted.

'Don't mince words with me, McKinnon! The thing is, he's

upset. Not only has one of his employees been involved in a fatal accident, but his dog has been poisoned.'

'I was aware that he suspects his dog was poisoned, sir.'

'This is his second dog. He's feeling angry and thinks there may be a conspiracy against him.'

'There certainly seems to be bad feeling against him on West Uist. He has hardly endeared himself to the residents of the Wee Kingdom. He has started erecting wind towers before the situation has been clarified.'

'He's also fuming about the newspaper and the piece on the news.'

'I was just having a word with Calum Steele when you telephoned, sir. I understood that you wanted me to telephone you after the meeting.'

'Well, what was the result?'

'I think it was almost certainly murder, Superintendent Lumsden. I will fax the report through to you shortly. I think, under the circumstances, we will have to seal the island off.'

'Of course. Any suspects.'

'Too early to say, Superintendent.'

'Any leads?'

'A few. They'll all be in my report.'

There was a sharp intake of breath from the other end of the line, and a wince of pain. Torquil imagined the big policeman in his crisp uniform, with his foot bandaged. He felt little sympathy for his superior officer.

'OK, get on with it. Let me have that report as soon as possible. Meanwhile, I'll call the laird and tell him that there is now a murder inquiry going on.'

'Of course, Superintendent. Shall —' But before he could finish, there was a click and he once more found himself staring at the dead receiver.

Morag tapped on the door. 'I gave Calum the official line. We have no information to divulge and we are making inquiries. And I told him to behave.'

Torquil gave a half smile. 'And we can be sure that he won't! Ah well, let's get on with this thing. First of all, we have to seal the island off.'

'I took the liberty of getting on with that. No more ferries until further notice.'

Torquil smiled. 'What would I do without you, Morag?'

She returned his smile. 'The same as I'd do without you, boss. Just don't think of going! I hate to think what would happen if it was me who had to speak to Superintendent Lumsden.'

After Katrina had left, Nial continued his round of the coast, stopping every now and then to get out of his car and check out the nesting birds on the machair dunes and the cliffs. He mechanically jotted his recordings in a small notebook which he would later transcribe onto his laptop. The truth was that his mind was not fully on the job. Even spotting one of the eagles wing its way towards its high eyrie in the Corlins did not fill him with his usual enthusiasm. Instead, he was preoccupied by the women in his life.

Until a few days ago he had thought that he was madly in love with Megan. Then she had almost gone potty over those dead hedgehogs, and done a Lady Macbeth thing. It had spooked him, he had to admit, and it was then that he had become aware of the emotional door standing ajar. And shining through that opening was Katrina and his feelings for her. He grinned and felt a deep inner warmth as he thought of how rapidly those feelings had heated up until they had reached boiling point, for both of them, culminating in the passionate love-making that they had just enjoyed in the long grass of the machair.

Except that Katrina had emotional baggage. That policeman, Ewan McPhee. She felt guilty about him and he would have to work on that.

He was feeling torn between the two women. Megan or Katrina? He felt bad about his betrayal of Megan, but seeing her freaking out had altered his image of her. That was a weakness on his part, he felt. Yet he couldn't help it and part of his mind rationalized it by thinking that she had pushed him towards Katrina.

He grinned as he put his binoculars to his eyes and scanned the distant stacks and skerries.

'West Uist is a beautiful island, all right. And she's a beautiful woman.'

He had made up his mind.

Danny Reid was perspiring profusely. He was stripped to the waist and a coating of moisture covered his torso as he started heaping soil onto the grave. He hated digging. He hated all manual work if the truth be known, but burying bodies was one thing he hated above all else. And it had been a heavy body.

He had patted the turned earth into a smooth mound and was just replacing the turf that he had cut on top of it when he heard Jock McArdle's footsteps crunch on the gravel path behind him. He was carrying a decanter of whisky and two glasses.

'That's a good job you've done, Danny. And it is a good spot for them both. They hadn't been here long, but Dallas and Tulsa both loved tearing about this old patch of lawn.' He sighed and Danny noted the tears in his boss's eyes. 'We'll be able to see them from the snooker-room upstairs.'

Danny laid his shovel down and pulled on his T-shirt. 'Liam was right upset about Tulsa.' He nodded at the whisky glasses in his employer's hand. 'Are we going to have a toast to the girls, boss?'

McArdle held out the crystal whisky glasses for Danny to hold while he poured two liberal measures of malt. 'Aye, but we're also going to toast Liam. That was Superintendent Lumsden on the phone again. He tells me that Liam was definitely murdered. They're starting an inquiry.'

Danny stared at McArdle, his hand clenching the glass so that his knuckles went white. 'The bastards! Who do you think did it, boss?'

McArdle ignored the question for a moment. He raised his glass. 'To the girls! And to Liam! May we always look after our family.'

They both swilled their drinks back in one.

'It has to be one of those bastards on the Wee Kingdom,' McArdle replied. 'And I'm guessing there is no chance on earth that the local flatfeet will be able to find the buggers. We're going to have to do it ourselves, Danny.'

'How's that, boss?'

McArdle smiled, 'I've got an idea to flush them out.' He hefted the cut crystal glass in his hand and nodded towards the ornamental fountain in the centre of the lawn. In unison, they threw their glasses at the fountain.

Jesmond had been watching from an upstairs landing window. He winced as he saw the hundred-year-old crystal smashing on the fountain.

'Peasants!' he exclaimed. He reached for his mobile phone.

The Corlins were shrouded in swirling mist by the time that Alistair left his jeep at the foot of the cliffs, just at the spot where a few days ago, they had found the broken body of his son. He pulled off his shoes and socks and wiggled his feet, flexing the well-developed toes that typified many of the outer islanders — especially those who were descended from the old cliff-scaling families of St Kilda's. Alistair was proud of his heritage and had tried to instil that pride into his son. He had taught him to hunt, to survive in the wild when the weather was at its worst, how to forage for food under rocks and in pools, and he had taught him how to climb.

And that was what had been eating away at him for days. How could Kenneth have fallen? He was as sure-footed as any of the old St Kildans who used to scale the sheer cliffs of Hirta, the larger of the isles, in order to snare the Culvers and take their eggs as they nested. Alistair felt sure that it had been an outside agent that had caused his fall and he intended to investigate for himself. His soul burned to find satisfaction.

'If your spirit is here, Kenneth — come with me.'

He swung his hunting bag over his shoulder and then swung the shoulder sling of his shotgun bag over his neck and right shoulder so that the bag hung across his back and would not impede him as he climbed.

And he began to scale the almost sheer face, his fingers and toes finding holds and clinging long enough to hoist and pull himself up. Despite his age, he climbed with the effortless ease of a monkey.

'You were a good lad, Kenneth. You didn't deserve to die so young,' he whispered to himself, as he swiftly ascended towards the shelf of rock from which it was reported that his son had fallen. 'I know why you were coming here.'

He pulled himself up over the ledge and lay for a few

moments waiting for his breathing to settle to normal. And as he lay there, his shrewd eyes pierced the swirling mists until he caught a glimpse of the eyrie some distance away.

'You devil birds!' he cursed under his breath, as he pulled off his shotgun bag and drew out his 12-bore. He reached into his hunting bag and drew out two cartridges. Breaking open the gun, he slid them into place and snapped it shut.

'Now we wait until you go hunting,' he mused. 'Take your time. I'm in no hurry. I'm a hunter, too. Just like my boy.'

There was the sound of a toe scuffing rock and Alistair spun round, his eyes wide with surprise.

'You! What are you doing here?' he challenged.

CHAPTER FOURTEEN

Vincent Gilfillan had been busy all morning. He had dealt with his own chores before going on to feed Rhona's goats and then do some work on her weaving quota. He knew that he and the others would have to get together and work out what they were going to do about her croft. But of course, the complication was the new laird. The possibility that he would repossess her croft and rescind the right of transfer seemed highly likely.

'Damn the man,' he muttered to himself. 'We should have been in contact with the Crofters Commission to find out exactly what rights we have.' He shook his head sadly as he tidied up and left Rhona's weaving shed. It was exactly the sort of thing that Rhona would have seen to. And she would have done if she hadn't died so suddenly.

At the thought of her death, he pictured the new laird and he felt his anger seethe to boiling point. In his mind he saw him going into the cottage hospital with Inspector McKinnon and he thought back to what he had wished he had done. Part of him wished that he had not stopped from going out to challenge him. But then he thought of Rhona lying there, her face alabaster white.

He pushed open the door of her cottage, went through to the main room, lined with bookcases, antiques and numerous handmade mats covering the polished wood floor. He slumped down on the settee beside the holdall containing the things he had brought back from the hospital. The smell of her perfume and the odour of her cigarettes was all around him and he felt slightly heady. He gave a deep sigh of despair and leaned forward, sinking his head in his hands as he began to sob.

He was still sobbing when Torquil found him there ten minutes later when he pushed open the door.

'I thought I heard someone in here,' Torquil said, coming in and pulling off his large leather gauntlets. 'And I am glad to find that it is you. We need to talk. But first, I have to tell you that we are investigating a murder.'

Vincent looked up and wiped the tears from his eyes with the back of his hand. 'Whose murder, Inspector?'

'One of Jock McArdle's employees. The tall flashily-dressed one with attitude. It was his body that we found by the Wee Kingdom causeway.'

'He had a bad attitude, right enough. I met him yesterday. In Geordie Morrison's croft. I was there with Megan Munro and he came in and gave us a letter each from the new laird.' He wrinkled his nose distastefully. 'I thought that he smelled of whisky.'

'What were the letters about?'

'I think you know already, Inspector,' Vincent returned. 'The same as the letter that McArdle devil gave Rhona.' His face twisted in distaste. 'You know — the one that killed her! The one about having wind towers put up on the common grazing ground by our crofts.'

'Have you got your letter?'

'Not here. I think I may have just screwed it up.' He chewed his lip reflectively. 'But Rhona's letter should be here in this holdall. I haven't had a chance, or the inclination, to unpack her stuff.' He unzipped the bag, opened the sides and pulled out the letter.

Torquil read it and nodded. 'Enough to give anyone a shock, let alone someone who had just had a heart attack.' He held out the letter for Vincent to see. 'I understand from Dr

398

McLelland that it looked as if she was trying to write a message when she collapsed. Any idea what she meant by this CARD IN?'

Vincent shook his head. 'No idea. It may mean one of those Get Well cards that she had. They are all in there as well. As I said, I haven't had time to check her things.'

Torquil put the letter back into the holdall. 'I think that I had better take the bag back to the station. There may be something of relevance. I'll give you a receipt for it all.'

Vincent looked at him with puzzled brows. 'I thought you were investigating the murder of that young thug. Why do you need Rhona's things?'

'There have been several deaths. Too many for comfort. We're keeping an open mind about them all.'

'That's just what I was thinking yesterday, Inspector. That's why I was in Geordie's cottage. I was looking to see if I could find some clue as to where he'd taken his family.'

'And what was Megan Munro doing there?'

'I think she had the same idea. But she was upset.'

'Tell me more.'

Vincent stood up and stretched the muscles of his back. 'I'm not sure that I should be saying anything about Megan's problems.'

Torquil eyed him sternly. 'I repeat, I'm investigating a murder. Why was she upset?'

Vincent sighed. 'I think she is having trouble with Nial Urquart. She was upset, I comforted her, that's all.' He held his hands palms up in a gesture of helplessness. 'She threw herself into my arms and I was giving her a friendly hug. There was nothing more.'

'And what did Sartori say?'

'Nothing much. Just a smart comment, then he gave us the

letters and said he was going on to see Alistair McKinley.'

'And that was the last you saw of him?'

'Yes. I had chores to do and Megan was desperate to find Nial. I had already taken care of Geordie's chickens and collected the eggs. And to tell you the truth I was bit peeved with him. He's always going off and taking his family with him, and he's never too good at telling us where he's gone.'

'Who does he usually tell?'

Vincent hesitated for a moment, his expression grim. 'Rhona.'

'And presumably she hadn't told you where they went?'

'No, but she wouldn't, would she?' he replied brusquely.

'Do I detect a touch of pique there, Vincent?' Torquil asked.

Vincent ran his hands across his face. 'Aye, maybe. Look, the truth is that Rhona liked younger men. She always had. Never anything deep. She liked to be in charge of her life.' He gestured round the room at the bookcases packed with books, the upright piano by the wall, the old manual typewriter and the reams of neatly stacked paper on an old roll-top desk, then, 'Geordie was the latest.'

'And does everyone on the Wee Kingdom know that?'

The crofter shook his head. 'I knew it, and I suspect that Alistair knew it too. But I'm pretty sure that Sallie, Geordie's wife doesn't.'

'Or perhaps she found out and that's why they've gone off somewhere.'

'Maybe,' Vincent returned doubtfully. 'Geordie is an unpredictable man. I am just not sure what to think.'

'And were you one of Rhona's lovers?' Torquil asked matter-of-factly.

Vincent gave a soft whistle, and then smiled winsomely. 'You don't pull punches, do you, Inspector?' He glanced at a photograph of all of the Wee Kingdom crofters on the mantel-piece. A smiling Rhona was in the middle. 'The answer is yes, years ago, for a few months. When I first came to the Wee Kingdom to take over my croft when my mother's cousin died. But not since then. I loved her then.'

Torquil nodded. 'The Padre tells me that you've been here about twenty years now.'

Vincent nodded. 'That's right.' He seemed to look into the distance, into the past. 'Twenty years, how time flies. Rhona was sort of playing at crofting back then. She was still commuting back and forth to the mainland, and working as a writer in Glasgow or Edinburgh.'

'She was a journalist, I believe,' said Torquil. And crossing to the roll-top desk he looked at the piles of neatly stacked papers and the documents in the pigeon holes of the desk. 'It looks as if she was still busy with writing.'

'Aye, she hadn't written anything for years, but she started again — just articles — a few months ago. Mainly about lifestyles and crofting.'

'She seems to have been very methodical.'

'Rhona was the administrator of all of the Wee Kingdom business outlets. She did all the paperwork for us.' He shook his head. 'God knows how we'll cope now. I'm helpless at that sort of thing.'

'And what about the wind towers that McArdle is having put up?'

Vincent snorted with derision. 'He's got a lot to answer for.'

'It looks as if one of his men has already paid for him, with his life.'

'Aye, maybe so.'

Calum Steele had been busy on the internet. In his own mind he was an investigative journalist par excellence. He felt born to the job, being by nature both curious about his fellow citizens, and having an almost pathological urge to gossip.

'Calum Steele! You would spear the inside out of a calm with your questions!' Miss Melville used to say upon being barraged with his questioning in school. 'You need to go and be a journalist.'

And indeed that was precisely what he had done, the only thing being that he had done it locally. Being somewhat thick-skinned, it had never occurred to him that it had been Miss Melville's hope that he would leave the island to seek his fortune.

Calum had grasped the new technology with both hands. Although he liked to cultivate the image of always having a spiral-bound notebook with him, he always carried a state-of-the-art Dictaphone in his anorak as well as his latest love, his digital camera. He was still rankling at the criminal loss of his last one, which had forced him to shell out £500 on the new one at his elbow.

To his credit, he single-handedly produced enough copy to fill the eight pages that made up the local paper six days a week. Admittedly, four pages were taken up with advertising, but anything on the island that was remotely newsworthy, whether that was the purchase of a new tractor, the number of overdue library books, or the belief that eagles were attacking people, Calum would investigate and write it up. And a murder investigation to him was like manna from heaven.

Not being of a naturally sentimental nature, Calum had found himself in a strange place lately. The loss of PC Ewan McPhee had affected him more than he had thought it would. He had become maudlin and he found himself valuing his friends more than usual. Torquil McKinnon and the Drummond twins, who had all been at school at the same time, and Morag Driscoll, whom he had secretly adored for years, they all seemed vitally important in his life. He had become patriotic, territorial, and he had taken a great dislike to the brazenness of the new laird and his bully-boy tactics. He had decided to take up a crusade against the wind towers that were being erected on the Wee Kingdom.

'So, Mr McArdle, it's not just the king of ice cream that you are, is it?' he grinned to himself as he printed out his findings. 'Let's see what Kirstie Macroon at Scottish TV makes of this.'

And he reached for his mobile telephone.

Alistair McKinley lowered his shotgun.

'Lachlan McKinnon, what in the blazes are you doing up here?' He flicked his eyes at his shotgun. 'You shouldn't sneak up on a man with a shotgun. Accidents have been known to happen.'

The Padre waved a finger. 'Alistair, I was not sneaking up on anyone. If you must know, I came up here for inspiration. I am having trouble writing sermons and eulogies lately and I was preparing one for Kenneth. I thought that if I came up here, where he had his accident, I might get a sense of how he died. I imagine that is pretty much the same reason that you are up here yourself.' Then he pointed to the shotgun. 'Or were you here in some misguided sense of revenge?' He looked up at the misty Corlins. 'Were you hoping to pot a golden eagle? That would be foolish, you know.'

'Ach, maybe it would strike you as foolish, Padre, but you haven't lost your son. And it is better than me taking my gun and doing away with the real villain of the piece. The man who caused Kenneth's death and now Rhona's — that bastard

McArdle!'

Lachlan put an arm about the old crofter's shoulder. 'You are an old fool. Look at you, up here in these conditions in your bare feet! Is that the action of a sober man? Come on now; let's get you back safe and sound to your croft. I'll come with you and we'll have a dram.'

Despite himself Alistair gave a short laugh. 'You are not the usual type of minister at all, are you? Always encouraging me to have a dram. But I'll come with you. Will you need a lift?'

'I have my Red Hunter down below,' replied the Padre. He looked at the cliff edge. 'And if you will take my advice you will take the path down with me, and not make any more foolish attempts to climb in your bare feet.'

He waited while Alistair unloaded his shotgun and slid it into his shotgun bag.

As they made their way down the path, Lachlan fancied that he heard the heavy flap of eagle wings overhead. He smiled to himself, for he had no doubt that he had at least saved one life that day.

Morag sent the Drummonds off and went back into Torquil's office where she had left Megan Munro with a cup of tea.

'I've sent my special constables onto the job,' she said, sitting in Torquil's chair opposite Megan.

'He's not safe, Sergeant. He says he's off to start that hedgehog cull, but I don't believe him. He said he was in a killing mood, and with that poor man falling and getting killed the other day, I thought that I should report him to the police.'

'Well, the Drummond twins will investigate and see if they can locate him. Just to be on the safe side.' She produced her silver pen and her notebook and laid them on the desk in front of her. She had only met Megan Munro once or twice before, but she knew all about her and her hedgehog-rescue operation. A pretty girl, she thought. Pity that she has to cover up her hair in those beanie hats and wear those mannish dungarees.

'I am afraid that I have to tell you, that death you just referred to — well, we are treating it as suspicious.'

Megan's eyes opened wide. 'Suicide, you mean?'

Morag shook her head. 'Possibly murder.'

Megan let out a gasp and covered her mouth with both hands. 'But it couldn't be. I saw him myself yesterday afternoon. He was delivering those awful letters from the new laird, about the wind towers. I didn't like him. He smelled of whisky and I had to stop Vincent from getting beaten up by him. I'm sure if I hadn't been there he would have been violent.' As she recounted the meeting in Geordie Morrison's cottage, Morag made notes.

'Where is Geordie Morrison and his family?' Morag asked.

'We don't know. I think with all the other tragedies that have been going on lately, we're all a bit worried that something might have happened to them.'

'What does Nial think of it all?'

At the question Megan suddenly burst into tears. Morag patted her hand and pushed a box of tissues across the desk to her. 'I am sorry, Megan. Is there something upsetting you?'

'It — it's Nial. We had a row yesterday. Two actually, one in the morning and one when he got home last night. And he's barely talked to me this morning. He was up and out before I woke.'

Morag made a note in her book. 'Are you worried about him?'

Megan nodded. 'Oh, I don't think anything bad has happened to him. In fact, I think I know where he is. And who he's with!' Morag said nothing; experience having long since told her that people will often volunteer their information. 'He will be with that Katrina Tulloch. He drools over her. I know that now. He's gone from my bed to hers.'

'That isn't something that I can do anything about, I'm afraid.'

'No, but perhaps you ought to know about him. He's not exactly the harmless bird officer that everyone thinks. He's opinionated and he gets a bee in his bonnet about things. When he does that he can be ... tenacious.'

'I don't follow?'

'We first met at an animal rights meeting.'

'Go on,' Morag urged.

'He used to be an activist. He —'

'Has he a record, Megan? Is that what you are saying?'

Megan bit her lip as if she was having an internal argument as to what she should divulge. Then, finally, 'He told me that he once fire-bombed the warehouse of a factory that was involved in supplying a laboratory with animals for animal experimentation.'

Lachlan stood looking out of the window of Alistair's cottage, a glass of whisky in his hand. 'It is a magnificent view that you have here. I hadn't realized that you had such a good sight of the old lighthouse.'

'Aye, and from the other side of the house we'll soon be able to see all these wind towers that fool of a laird is planning.'

'Are you sure that it is all legal, though, Alistair? Have you had it checked out? I am no expert, but I would have thought he would have at least needed planning permission rather than just hoiking them up.'

Alistair sipped his whisky. 'Rhona usually saw to all the business and legal side of the Wee Kingdom. I suppose one of us will have to see to it now.'

There was a knock on the open door and Wallace Drummond popped his head round the frame. 'Ah Padre, we weren't expecting to see you here.'

His brother appeared beside him. 'It is Alistair that we are needing to see.'

'Come away in lads,' the old crofter urged. 'We were having a dram. Will you have one too? In memory of my lad.'

Wallace shook his head with a pained expression. 'I am sorry. We would have loved to join you, but we are here on duty. Our sergeant sent us on an errand. It's a bit tricky.'

'Out with it then,' said Alistair.

Douglas pointed to the shotgun bag leaning against the wall. 'We have been told that we are to confiscate your guns. Until further notice, the West Uist Police have put a ban on any hedgehog cull on the island.'

Jock McArdle and Danny Reid were watching the evening Scottish TV news in the large sitting-room at Dunshiffin Castle while they waited for Jesmond to call them to dinner.

'See that Kirstie Macroon, boss,' Danny said with a slightly lascivious tone as he handed his employer a whisky and lemonade. 'Liam fair fancied her.'

The redheaded newsreader went through the headlines while they sat and drank. Then the backdrop behind her changed to a picture of Dunshiffin Castle.

'Here that's us!' exclaimed Danny. 'We're on the news!'

Jock waved his hand irritably and sat upright. 'Let's listen then.'

And now to West Uist and the revelation by the editor of the West Uist Chronicle that the death yesterday of Liam Sartori, one of the employees of the new owner of the Dunshiffin Castle estate was not due to

407

an eagle attack, as we previously reported, but was in fact murder. The local editor, Calum Steele, is on the phone now.

Jock swallowed the rest of his whisky and lemonade and held the glass out to Danny for a refill.

Then Calum's voice came over the television:

The new owner of Dunshiffin Castle is himself causing quite a stir on the island. He has embarked on a programme of windmill erection, which is of questionable legality.

Jock McArdle cursed. 'Careful you wee bastard!' he said to the screen, which showed Kirstie Macroon nodding her head as she listened to Calum.

And our investigations have revealed that Mr McArdle has a cavalier approach to business. Today it can be revealed that whereas he is publicly proclaimed to be an ice cream and confectionary mogul, in fact he has many investments, most notably in a string of companies involved in animal research. He has previously been the target —

Jock McArdle shot to his feet. 'Get the Porsche. It's time that wee busybody learned not to meddle in my business.'

Nial Urquart had just walked into the sitting-room of Katrina's flat with a cup of coffee in his hand. He switched on the television and caught Calum Steele's piece on the news.

'Bastard!' he exclaimed.

'Who's a bastard?' Katrina called through from the kitchen.

Nial flicked the channel control to the BBC. 'Oh, no one. Sorry for my language. It's just my team. They lost in the league.'

Then he switched the television off.

The Bonnie Prince Charlie was busy, as usual. Mollie McFadden and her staff were occupied with pulling pints of Heather Ale and dispensing whiskies. At the centre of the bar,

Calum Steele was holding court, clearly enjoying his new-found celebrity status on Scottish TV.

He was just telling an eager group of listeners for the third time how he had winkled out the information from the internet, when he felt a tap on his shoulder and then felt himself being whirled round.

'I don't allow anyone to broadcast my business affairs,' Jock McArdle snapped.

'And I've warned you once before, chubby,' said Danny Reid, running a finger up and down the zip of Calum's anorak. He looked aside at his employer who nodded his head.

Calum swallowed hard and held his chin up. 'The press have a perfect right to keep the public informed.'

'Is that so?' Jock said, as Danny grasped the zip fastener of Calum's greasy yellow anorak. 'Well, let me give you a friendly warning, Mr Calum Steele. In future you will keep your nose out of my affairs and you will be ... respectful of my position.' He leaned forward and took the fastener out of Danny's hand. 'In other words — zip it!'

And he yanked the fastener all the way up and caught a tiny fold of Calum's double chin in the zip.

Calum howled in pain.

'Just a warning!' McArdle said. 'Good night everyone.'

As he and Danny Reid reached the door, Mollie's voice rang out. 'Aye, that's the door, Mr McArdle. Laird or no laird, you and your bodyguard are herewith banned! You are not welcome here again!'

McArdle turned and sneered. 'See, darling, that's OK. Why would anyone want to drink in this hovel anyway? Good night and God bless.'

It was ten o'clock by the old grandmother clock in her sitting-room and Megan Munro had cried all evening. She had sent three texts to Nial and tried to phone him half-a-dozen times, but without success. So desperate had she felt that she had even contemplated trying to drink a glass of wine, but the thought alone revolted her. But music usually helped her, loud music to try to lift her mood. Yet not even Queen nor the Red Hot Chili Peppers could help. She turned off the CD player and went to switch off the lights. It was then that she thought she heard the sound of crackling, and smelled smoke.

She looked out of the window and saw the glow from Gordon MacDonald's croft. The cottage was in flames and next to it, like a couple of beacons, the two wind towers were engulfed in flames.

CHAPTER FIFTEEN

The West Uist Volunteer Fire Brigade was scrambled upon receiving Megan's emergency call. They arrived within ten minutes in their 1995 Convoy van, which had been specially converted into a Light Fire Appliance. With its four-man team, lightweight pump and four fire extinguishers, it was doubtful that they would be able to deal with the inferno that was Gordon MacDonald's croft.

Torquil had been alerted as a matter of course and arrived moments after them on his Royal Enfield Bullet.

Alistair McKinley and Vincent Gilfillan had heard the crackling flames and had joined Megan Munro by the croft and all three had attempted to douse the flames with buckets of water from the nearby duck pond. It had been clear, however, that their efforts were in vain.

'Just thank the lord that there was nobody inside,' said Alistair.

'That we cannot be sure about, Alistair,' Torquil said, as they stood back to let Leading Fireman Fraser Mackintosh and his volunteers do the best that they could.

Vincent put a hand on Torquil's arm. 'You can't think that anyone is in there!'

Torquil bit his lip, his brow furrowed with anxiety. 'I doubt it, but one thing is clear — this is a case of arson. There is no way that the fire could have spread to the wind towers.'

Megan clapped a hand to her mouth. 'My God! Nial! Where is he?' She began to scream. And then she was running towards the cottage.

Vincent and Torquil both stopped her and drew her back.

Fraser Mackintosh came over. 'It is no use, Torquil. All we can do is contain it. It will have to burn itself out.' He pointed at the wind towers. 'At least those towers are metal and won't burn. The wood platforms we can probably put out, but it looks as if any equipment on them will have been destroyed.'

Vincent took Megan back to her cottage and the others watched and waited until the fire burned itself down and the roof collapsed. Fortunately, rain began to fall and helped to dowse the fire.

But even so, it was not until the first light of morning that they were able to enter the smouldering building. And it was then that they found the badly charred body of a man.

Doctor Ralph McLelland was doing an early morning call on Agnes Calanish's latest arrival, after her husband, Guthrie, had called him at five o'clock.

'We're right sorry, Dr McLelland,' said Guthrie, 'it is just that he seemed too young to be having the croup. We were worried that he might need to be admitted to the hospital.'

Ralph wound up his stethoscope and replaced it in his black Gladstone bag. 'No, there's no need,' he said, with a well-practised smile of reassurance. 'He's still getting rid of some of the secretions. His chest is as clear as a whistle. He'll be just fine where he is.'

The local doctor was well used to night visits, although the islanders by and large did their utmost to deal with problems until a respectable hour. For Guthrie Calanish who had to be up at four every morning to get down to the harbour for the early morning ferry, five o'clock seemed perfectly respectable.

'There might not be any post for some time, Dr McLelland,' said Guthrie. 'The ferries have been cancelled until further notice by order of the police. I was down at the harbour this morning just on the off chance, but nothing is doing.'

'It is all these deaths, isn't it, Doctor?' Agnes suggested, as she redressed the latest addition to the household on a changing mat.

'I am afraid so, Agnes. But the police will be making good headway.'

'Do you think so?' Guthrie asked. 'I heard from Wattie Dowel, the chandler, that they're pretty much in the dark. Could you —'

Ralph's mobile phone went off just then, which under normal circumstances would have caused him some alarm, since there was a good chance that it indicated another call and a receding opportunity to take breakfast before morning surgery. But he was well used to Guthrie Calanish's attempts to get gossip out of him, so he raised his hand for quiet as he answered the call.

He was not expecting it to be a call for him in his capacity as the police surgeon. His eyes widened as Torquil told him that they had found another body on the Wee Kingdom. He replied curtly, 'I'll be there in five minutes.'

'Something urgent?' Guthrie enquired, a tad too curiously for Ralph's liking.

He forced a smile. 'Just another call. A doctor's life is rarely dull, you know.'

Agnes smiled up at him. 'Oh, no one could ever accuse you of being dull, Dr McLelland.'

Guthrie gave her a withering look and showed Ralph to the door. He watched the doctor hurry up the path with shoulders hunched to protect his neck from the rain, then he nodded thoughtfully and reached for the telephone.

The rain stopped at about five o'clock. Morag and the Drummond twins had arrived before Ralph. Once Fraser Mackintosh had satisfied himself that the site was safe from further fire, and he and Torquil had checked to make sure that there was no possibility that the charred body showed any signs of life, they had withdrawn to preserve the crime site. For that was what Torquil had deemed it to be, especially after Fraser had informed him that he believed there to be strong evidence of arson caused by some incendiary device.

'The place was petrol bombed, Piper,' he had said. 'The cottage and the wind towers.' And he had pointed out the shattered fragments of milk bottles and the empty blackened petrol can that lay in a corner of the burned-out sitting-room.

Both Torquil and Morag Driscoll were CID and forensic scene-of-crime qualified, having both been seconded for training a few years previously. It was the chief constable's view that the Hebridean Constabulary should be totally self-sufficient and able to deal with all situations, without recourse to the mainland force. Accordingly, together with their ever-willing special constables, they had cordoned off the crime site with posts and tape barriers and then donned protective white coverall suits, as dictated by the Serious Crimes Procedure, while they awaited the arrival of Ralph.

'My God, I can guess what you've got for me. I caught the characteristic smell half a mile off,' said the doctor as he closed the door of his car and came over to them with his bag in one hand and his forensic case in the other.

'It is nasty, Ralph,' said Torquil. 'There is a badly burned — unrecognizable — body, in the ruins of the cottage.'

He waited while Ralph opened his forensic case and from it drew out a white coverall suit. 'An accident?' Ralph asked suspiciously, as he climbed into his suit and zipped up.

Torquil shook his head. 'No, it is suspicious all right.'

'It's a sight that you would be better seeing without having had breakfast,' Wallace said.

'I nearly lost mine,' Douglas confessed.

Ralph nodded sanguinely and picked up his case. Then he followed Torquil and Morag along the designated access path into the ruins to view the body.

It was a grisly sight. The blackened, shrivelled body lay sprawled on the floor near the hearth in what had once been the sitting-room of Gordon's croft. Ralph sucked air between his lips with a pained expression and stood looking about him for somewhere to lay his bag down. Finding a spot he put the forensic case down and placed his bag on top. He knelt down, opened the bag and drew out his stethoscope and an ophthalmoscope. Torquil and Morag watched him admiringly as he painstakingly examined the body as best he could without disturbing its position. An absolute stickler for routine and precision in all matters medical and forensic, he checked to ensure that the body was truly dead, and that there was no activity in the heart or nervous system.

'Dead as a piece of coal,' he announced, coiling his stethoscope and replacing it and his ophthalmoscope in his Gladstone bag, his bag for the living. Then he reached for his forensic case, which contained the instruments he used for examining the dead.

'Can you tell us how long, Doctor?' Torquil asked, his tone moving to the official.

The inspector was rewarded with a look of scorn. 'You're kidding me, Inspector!' Ralph replied, with a touch of sarcasm. 'A body found badly burned in a burned-out ruin of a house! The normal post-mortem changes mean nothing.'

'Not even the body's position?' Torquil persisted.

Ralph allowed a grim smile. 'Ah, you noticed,' he said. 'The fact that he was not curled up is suggestive that the individual was dead before the fire started.'

Morag grimaced. 'Another murder?'

Torquil looked at her with a troubled frown on his forehead. 'It looks like it. But we have a more immediate question to ask.'

'Aye', said Wallace. 'Who the hell is he?'

Ralph looked up at the special constable and shook his head. 'That is going to be difficult, considering the fact that his features have been burned beyond recognition — except perhaps to someone very close to him. We may have to get hold of dental records.'

Torquil pointed to the blackened body piercings on the lips, ears and above the eyes. Then to the mouth, which seemed to have fixed into a charred look of agony. 'What do you make of that?'

And, as Ralph looked, so he noticed for the first time the gold chain about the body's neck, disappearing into the mouth.

'It looks like a chain, possibly with a medallion,' Ralph returned. 'I will know better once I have done a full examination back at the mortuary. But first do you want to get the scene properly photographed and documented?'

And for the better part of an hour Morag, the Drummonds and Torquil set about recording the scene in notes, photographs and diagrams. While they did so, Ralph drove back to Kyleshiffin and swapped his car for the Cottage Hospital Ambulance. On his way back he passed the familiar sight of Calum Steele on his Lambretta scooter. Despite Calum's wave to stop, Ralph merely acknowledged him with a nod of his head and drove on. He knew all too well that the *Chronicle* editor had somehow scented out a story, and that he would be trying his damnedest to winkle out whatever information he could. But, with a suspected murder on the cards, Ralph knew it was best to leave that to the official force.

Torquil was busy in the ruins, but heard the tell-tale Lambretta engine approaching.

'Shall I intercept the wee man himself?' Douglas asked.

Torquil sighed. 'No, but thank you for the offer. It would be as well to make this official and I need to make sure that he doesn't do his usual thing and expound his own theories to the public rather than the official line.'

'Good luck, boss,' Morag murmured, as she continued making a detailed diagram of the charred cottage ruin.

'Good morning, Inspector McKinnon,' Calum greeted from the other side of the tape barrier. 'Arson attack, is it? Is somebody dead?'

'What makes you ask those questions, Calum?'

The newspaperman gestured to the burned-out ruins and the blackened wind towers. 'A cottage can catch fire, but I can't see how fire would jump all that distance to catch those towers. And this is Gordon MacDonald's cottage, there was no one in here, was there? Those windmill riggers were using it I know, but they left the island on —'

'So why do you ask about a death?'

Calum tapped the side of his nose. 'Let's just say that as a journalist I have my sources. And I passed Dr McLelland on my way here, which rather implies that he was coming here on professional business. All that and the fact that he wouldn't stop when he passed me, meant that he had information that he didn't want to divulge.' He grinned. 'And you are all wearing those official white dungaree suits. So what's up, Piper? Tell your old schoolmate Calum.'

Torquil shook his head good humouredly. 'All right, Calum.

This is the official statement, but don't go passing it on with any of your journalistic embellishments.'

'No, no, you can depend on me. I am a responsible journalist and there will be no poetic licence excuse from me. Just the facts.'

'And the facts are that the West Uist division of the Hebridean Constabulary are investigating a house fire on the Wee Kingdom, and the discovery of a badly burned body in the burned-out ruins of the cottage.'

Calum had clicked on the Dictaphone in his top pocket and for effect also jotted notes in his spiral-bound notebook. His eyebrows rose and he asked quizzically, 'Murder?'

'The fire and the death are being treated as suspicious,' Torquil replied.

Calum nodded sagely and wrote 'suspicious' in capital letters and underlined it emphatically. In his mind's eye he already saw the headline he would use for the piece. And more immediately, how he was going to deliver it by phone to Kirstie Macroon, the pretty red-headed newsreader with pert breasts that he frequently fantasized about, and whose voice melted his insides. Then, realizing that his mind was straying, he cleared his throat.

'The cause of death?'

'We are awaiting the post-mortem report. And that will be some time, since we have yet to remove the remains from the major incident scene.'

Calum leaned over and craned his neck to try to get a better view. Screwing up his eyes he could see the Drummond twins and Morag Driscoll inside, but that was all. 'And who is it?'

'We have not identified the body yet.'

'Any chance of a picture?' Calum asked, hopefully.

'Now you are pushing your luck, Calum. After that last stunt

418

of yours down by the causeway?'

Calum was about to protest, but the noise of the West Uist ambulance crunching up the drive halted the words before he had formed them. 'Ah the doctor, maybe I'll —'

'Maybe you will leave Dr McLelland to get on with his police surgeon duties, Calum. And that isn't a request, by the way.'

Ralph got out of the ambulance and came towards them with a pile of plastic bags and a folded-up body bag. 'Morning, Calum,' he said as he passed. 'I'm sorry that I couldn't stop earlier, but I had urgent work to be doing. Excuse me.' And he passed back along the designated access path. Once inside the burned ruin, he carefully put plastic bags on the head, hands and feet of the body to ensure that no important pieces of evidence were lost, before he and a very green-looking Wallace lifted the body and placed it in a plastic body bag before gingerly moving it into the ambulance.

Torquil jotted down in his notebook, 'Unidentified body of man, badly burned, removed from the crime scene at 06.25 hours. Doctor McLelland, police surgeon, will perform post-mortem as soon as possible.' Douglas was looking over his superior officer's shoulder as he wrote. He prodded Torquil in the back. 'Is that official jargon, meaning, after the doctor has had his breakfast?'

His brother joined them as Ralph drove off in the converted ambulance. He was still looking green about the gills. 'Which is more than I can say for me. I don't think I'll ever be able to eat anything again.'

Calum grinned at them. 'What's that? Two strapping big hulks like you feeling a bit squeamish. What is the island coming to?'

And before they could retort, as they usually did, Calum had left them with a wave as he ran over to his Lambretta.

'Is that what they mean about journalists following ambulances?' Wallace asked.

Jesmond tapped on Jock McArdle's door at seven o'clock and received a firm and colourful rebuke for disturbing his employer's repose. Nevertheless, he persisted with a further knock, adding the words, 'An emergency call from the local constabulary, sir.'

There was a rustling noise from the other side of the door, the tread of bare feet then the bedroom door was hauled open.

Jesmond held out the cordless phone. 'Inspector McKinnon would like to talk to you, sir. He says it is urgent.'

Jock McArdle frowned and grabbed the phone. He snapped his name into the mouthpiece, then stood listening, his expression growing grimmer by the second. 'I'm on my way!'

'A problem, sir?' Jesmond queried, as dexterously he caught the phone again.

'You could say that! This could be the start of the next bloody war!'

And, as Jesmond caught the murderous look in his employer's eyes before the door was slammed shut, he knew that if there was a war involving Jock McArdle, no prisoners would be taken!

The Padre had been roused from a fitful sleep by the telephone at his bedside. Groggily, he reached for the receiver and mechanically answered, 'St Ninian's Manse.'

He heard harsh breathing on the other end of the line.

'Hello, St Ninian's Manse,' he repeated. 'This is Lachlan McKinnon here. Can I help you?'

No one said anything. All he could hear was the harsh breathing. Then there was a rasping laugh and the line went dead.

'Now who on earth could that be?' he asked himself, reaching for his horn-rimmed spectacles in the dark so that he could see the luminous hands on the clock.

It was just after seven. He sighed, then threw back the blankets and got up. As he pulled on his dressing-gown and prepared to go over to his little praying stool he couldn't but help feeling that the phone call held some significance.

Torquil led McArdle through to the mortuary suite and tapped on the outer door. Through the frosted glass panels they saw the dim green-gowned shape of Dr Ralph McLelland approach and unlock the door.

'This way please, gentlemen,' said Ralph, leading the way through a swing door to the white tiled mortuary where a plastic sheet covered a body.

'We have reason to believe that this could be the body of a Daniel Reid, lately from Bearsden in Glasgow and currently residing at Dunshiffin Castle.' Torquil stated. 'I am afraid that the body has been very badly burned, almost incinerated. Do you feel that you would be able to identify the body?'

McArdle's face was pale and there was a noticeable patina of perspiration on his brow, but he nodded. 'If it is Danny, I'll know him.' Torquil nodded to Ralph who slowly pulled back the sheet to reveal the head and neck of the corpse.

McArdle looked shocked, colour draining even more than before. He swallowed hard, his expression pained. 'Yes. I am pretty sure that is my boy.' Then he spotted the chain around the neck and the ends disappearing into the clenched mouth. 'That's his medallion, right enough! Where was he? How did it happen?'

While Ralph pulled the sheet back Torquil gestured for

McArdle to follow him. 'I think we should go up to the station and have a talk, Mr McArdle. There are a number of questions that you will want to ask and also a whole lot that I need to ask you.'

'You're bloody well right there! And I'm going to have someone's head for this!' Torquil eyed the new laird dispassionately. 'As I said, we'll have a talk. But just so long as you know, Mr McArdle, this is police business now. We will deal with this and there will be no head-taking of any sort on my island.'

McArdle pulled out his car keys and stomped down the corridor. 'We'll see, Inspector. I'll meet you at your station.'

Ralph came out of the mortuary suite, bundling up his green gown. He deposited it in the wicker basket outside and reached for his jacket which was hanging on the peg above. 'I'm just away for a spot of breakfast, Torquil, and then I'll get on with the post-mortem. Is that OK?'

Torquil nodded assent. 'You must have a cast-iron stomach, Ralph.'

'Aye,' was the police surgeon's only reply.

'What do you mean, girlie?' Jock McArdle demanded of Morag. 'There are no ferries?'

Torquil heard the question as he came in the Kyleshiffin police station front door, in time to see Jock McArdle slam a fist down on the counter.

'I have just told you, Mr McArdle,' Morag returned, looking completely unflustered. 'All ferries to and from the island have been cancelled until further notice. The island has been sealed off pending investigations.'

'But I need to get some of my boys up here from Glasgow.'

Torquil intervened. 'As my sergeant just told you, Mr

McArdle, there will be no comings and goings until our investigations have been completed. And remember what I said at the hospital: this is a police matter, not a personal one.'

'Whoever killed my boys made it personal.'

'And we will find whoever did it,' Torquil said, and lifting the counter flap he held it open. 'We'll continue this in my office, I think.'

Ralph McLelland had gone straight to Fingal's Cave, the cafe on Harbour Street that boasted the fastest, biggest and cheapest breakfast in town. He was in a hurry and felt in need of a good fry-up before he began his forensic work. He was sitting down enjoying a mug of sweet tea when the tinkly bell at the back of the cafe door heralded another customer.

'Ah, Dr McLelland,' said Calum Steele, picking up a menu. 'Mind if I join you?'

'Ah, Calum,' Ralph returned with a long suffering smile. 'Of course not. Grab a seat.'

Morag glanced at her watch and rubbed her eyes. She could hardly believe that it was still only eight o'clock. So much had happened since she received the call from Torquil and there had been so much to do. Before Torquil had put a call through to Dunshiffin Castle, they had taken a few minutes in the Incident Room to add a new box with the name Danny Reid, followed by a question mark. The other information that Morag had obtained from her questioning of Megan Munro had been added and they had agreed that they needed to follow up about Nial Urquart's involvement in the animal rights movement, and about Jock McArdle's interests in a company that supplied animals to laboratories involved in research. Now that Torquil was busy interviewing McArdle, she switched on her computer and logged onto the internet.

After half an hour, she had printed out several sheets of paper. Then rising she went through to make tea. A few minutes later, as she sat down to read the printed sheets, her eyes opened wider as she read through them.

'Torquil will certainly be interested in these,' she mused.

CHAPTER SIXTEEN

Torquil eyed the laird of Dunshiffin with interest. The man was rattled, he could see that. He seemed genuinely shocked and upset, but anger lurked close to the surface.

'How long will this post-mortem be?' McArdle demanded.

Torquil shrugged his shoulders. 'An hour maybe and then there will be all the other tests. I would be hoping for a preliminary result some time this morning.'

'What is it with this place, McKinnon? My two dogs and my two boys. All dead. All murdered. What are you doing about it?'

'I am interviewing you for a start, Mr McArdle,' Torquil replied evenly. 'For one thing, we are not sure if Danny Reid was murdered. His death is just suspicious.'

'Suspicious!' McArdle snapped, showing his temper for the first time in the interview. 'You saw the frazzled state he was in. Of course he was murdered.'

'What was he doing at the Wee Kingdom last night?' Torquil persisted.

'How should I know?'

'He is your employee — I mean he was your employee. I would have thought you might have known, especially after your other employee's death.'

McArdle sucked air noisily through his lips. 'My boys are not in my employ twenty-four hours a day. I don't know what he was doing last night. I expect he'd been for a few drinks. My boys liked a drink. And they were very close. I expect he went up there because he wanted to investigate Liam's death.' He leaned forward and clasped his hands together on the desk in front of him. 'You lot don't seem to have got very far. And that's why I take grave exception to this cock-eyed ban on the ferries. I want some of my boys to come over here.'

'The ban is necessary, Mr McArdle. We are investigating a murder, possibly two. There will be no movement on or off the island, neither by sea nor air. And there will be no exceptions.'

'I don't like your tone, lad! I've had whipper-snappers like you for breakfast.'

Torquil stared him hard in the eye. 'You would find me most indigestible, Mr McArdle. Now tell me, what were you doing last night?'

McArdle's cheek muscles twitched. 'I was at home, in my castle, working on papers. Ask my butler Jesmond.'

'I will be doing so, of course. But do you think it is possible that Danny Reid could have been trying to start a fire in the croft cottage and been overcome by the flames and the smoke?' He paused and rested his chin on his fist. 'Perhaps he had been drinking as you suggested, and maybe drank too much?'

'Naw!' McArdle replied emphatically. 'My boys could both handle their drink. And there is no way that Danny would have played with fire.'

'But that isn't so, is it, Mr McArdle?' said Torquil, reaching into a wire basket beside his left elbow. 'We ran a check on your employees.' He smoothed the paper in front of him. 'They both had records. Liam Sartori for burglary and possession of drugs and Danny Reid for arson!'

Jock McArdle leaned back and shrugged. 'So what?'

'So it is suggestive, isn't it? A man with a criminal record for arson is found dead in a burning building.'

'Don't be an idiot, McKinnon. Danny wouldn't have torched

my property.'

'That's *Inspector* McKinnon, by the way,' he corrected calmly. 'In that case, do you have any idea why anyone would want to set fire to your property? Especially with one of your employees in it?'

The new owner of Dunshiffin Castle clenched his teeth. 'I am a businessman. A bloody successful businessman. I have had enemies in the past and I seem to have enemies now.'

'Why is that, Mr McArdle? Could it be because of the way that you do business?'

'Now you are beginning to get my goat. I am a successful businessman. Say anything else and I'll have your guts for garters — I'll sue you and your tuppence ha'penny police outfit for defamation.'

Torquil stared back with his best poker face. 'There is no defamation in my questioning, Mr McArdle. But since you are so sensitive, let me rephrase the question. You have a robust way of conducting your affairs. People on West Uist have called it bullying. Take those wind towers of yours, for example.'

'All perfectly legal.'

'I understand that the legality is under question,' replied Torquil. 'And then there were those letters you sent to the Wee Kingdom crofters. And the one that you delivered yourself to Rhona McIvor — who collapsed and died immediately afterwards.'

McArdle frowned. 'I regret her death, of course, but I hope you are not suggesting a connection between my letter and the McIvor woman's death?'

'It has been suggested that there may be a connection.' Torquil returned, casually.

'Who suggested it?' McArdle snapped.

427

'Doctor McLelland, our local GP and police surgeon.'

Jock McArdle shrugged dismissively. 'A country quack!'

'Dr Ralph McLelland is a highly respected doctor.'

The new laird of Dunshiffin merely smirked.

Torquil eyed him coldly for a moment then glanced at the notes on the desk in front of him. 'Yes, I'll be in touch when I have more news, or if I have more questions for you.'

McArdle nodded curtly, stood up and crossed to the door.

'Oh yes,' Torquil said, as the laird put his hand on the door handle. 'You always referred to your employees as your *boys*. Were you actually related to either of them?'

McArdle shook his head. 'Neither of them had any family. It's just an expression. Glasgow talk. I've always looked out for my boys.'

'Is that so?' Torquil asked, innocently.

McArdle's eyes smouldered. 'I should have looked after them better, maybe. But I'll be looking after their memory, you mark my words — *Inspector* McKinnon.' He tugged the door handle and stomped out, almost knocking Lachlan over as he did so. 'Excuse me, Padre,' He snapped, then left.

Lachlan came in and stood in front of Torquil's desk. 'Our new laird seems in a hurry to leave,' he remarked.

'I wish people wouldn't call him the new laird,' Torquil replied, with a hint of irritation. Then, noticing his uncle's look of surprise, 'Sorry, Uncle. It was just a difficult interview. He was not in a good mood, understandably, after he had to identify his employee's body.'

Lachlan winced. 'I heard from Morag that it wasn't a pretty sight. Was he —'

Torquil's telephone interrupted him and Torquil picked it up straight away. 'Yes, Ralph,' he said, into the receiver. He nodded as he listened. Then said eventually, 'Aye, it would help if you could confirm it with the other tests. Half an hour, that would be great.' He replaced the receiver just as Morag tapped on the door and came in.

'I'm sorry. Uncle, what was your question?'

The Padre had plucked his pipe from his breast pocket and was in the process of charging it with tobacco. 'I was wondering if he was murdered?'

Torquil sighed. 'I'm afraid so. Ralph says it is definite.' He looked up at Morag and explained: 'That was Ralph just now with the preliminary findings. He thought that there were a couple of things that I ought to be aware of. Firstly, that there was enough alcohol in his system to sink a battleship.'

'And secondly?' Morag queried.

'His trachea was crushed and his neck was broken at the fifth cervical vertebra. It was murder all right. Someone throttled him and then snapped his neck like a chicken's.'

In the Incident Room half an hour later, Torquil stood by the white board with the Padre beside him, while Morag, the Drummond twins and Ralph McLelland sat around the table-tennis table that had been converted into the operations desk.

'I know it is irregular, but has anyone any objection to Lachlan sitting in with us? We're depleted in numbers and I think he could prove useful in our investigations.'

There was a chorus of approval, and Lachlan sat down, immediately laying his unlit pipe down on the table in front of him.

'We'll start with Ralph's preliminary report,' Torquil said.

As the police surgeon gave a brief synopsis of his post-mortem examination, Torquil added the name Danny Reid to the whiteboard. He drew a square around the name and added relevant notes underneath:

ALCOHOL. THREE TIMES LEGAL LIMIT
BODY BADLY BURNED
MEDALLION IN MOUTH
MULTIPLE BODY PIERCINGS
BROKEN NECK — FIFTH CERVICAL VERTEBRA

'Thanks, Ralph,' Torquil said, as the local doctor finished his report and sat down. 'So we have two definite murders here.' He tapped the boxed names on the whiteboard and went on, 'And a missing police officer — presumed dead, an entire family missing, an accidental death in a rock-climbing accident and a sudden death from a heart attack.'

'A tangled skein, right enough,' mused Wallace Drummond. 'And don't forget the two dead dogs, Piper.'

The Padre picked up his pipe and tapped the mouthpiece against his teeth. 'And it all seems to revolve around Jock McArdle.'

'Who can hardly be a suspect though, can he?' said Douglas Drummond. 'He wouldn't be killing his own boys, would he?'

Torquil nodded. 'Ah yes, his *boys*. Well, while I was interviewing him earlier this morning, Morag was busy doing some research and liaising with her contacts on the Glasgow force. She has made some interesting discoveries about the "laird of Dunshiffin". He isn't quite who he seems.' He nodded to his sergeant, and then sat down.

'He certainly isn't,' went on Morag. 'Mr Jock McArdle died ten years ago.'

There was a chorus of surprised murmurings.

'Do you mean identity theft?' Lachlan asked.

'Not exactly. There was a Jock McArdle in Glasgow, but he had nothing to do with our supposed laird. No, he quite legitimately changed his name by dead-poll ten years ago from Giuseppe Cardini.'

'The plot thickens,' said Wallace.

'But why did he change his name?' Douglas asked.

Morag stared back at him with raised eyebrows. 'Presumably it was because he had just come out of prison after five years — for culpable homicide.'

The first thing that Jock McArdle did when he arrived back at Dunshiffin Castle was to pour himself a large malt whisky, which he gulped down in one. Then he poured another and carried it through to the library which he used as an office. He sat down behind the leather-topped desk, cluttered with papers and gadgets, and unlocked the desk drawer. He stared inside for a moment then smiled and reached for the telephone.

Superintendent Lumsden answered almost immediately and the two men talked animatedly for a few minutes.

'McKinnon is a bit of a maverick, I know,' Superintendent Lumsden said eventually. 'But I'll make sure that he plays ball.'

'I appreciate it, Kenneth. We Glasgow boys have to stick together, especially in a situation like this.' And after a few pleasantries he replaced his phone on the hook.

He took another sip of whisky and smiled to himself. He was still grinning when there was a tap on the door and he looked up.

'May I offer you my most sincere condolences, Mr McArdle,' said his butler.

Jock leaned back and gestured for him to come in. He smiled wistfully. 'Thank you, Jesmond. Take a seat. Let's not be so formal. That's not my way, you see.'

'Thank you, sir. I realize that you like informality, sir,' he said, gingerly taking a seat on the other side of the desk from his employer.

'So from now on, I'm going to call you Norman. That's OK,

isn't it?'

Norman Jesmond smiled uncertainly. 'That's good of you, sir. It is a privilege, sir.'

Jock smiled. 'Well, Norman, there's something that I've been wanting to talk to you about. Something I found in the pantry.'

The butler swallowed hard, conscious that little beads of perspiration had begun to form on his brow. 'In ... in the pantry, sir?'

'Aye, in the pantry, sir!' Jock McArdle repeated abruptly; then leaning forward his hand dipped into the open drawer and came out again with a tin that he placed on the desk. 'And I wanted to talk about my dogs — and this tin of — arsenic, I think!'

'I — er — don't understand, sir.'

The butler's eyes widened as Jock McArdle's hand again dipped into the drawer and came out again, but this time with a short-barrelled revolver. He laid it carefully on the desk beside the tin.

'Aye, let's talk about my dogs and how they may have had some of this ... arsenic,' he said in an unnervingly quiet and calm voice.

Torquil groaned when Morag told him that Superintendent Lumsden was on the telephone again.

'Your laird is mightily displeased with your attitude, McKinnon, and I have to admit that I think he's got a point. He is thinking of lodging an official complaint. He feels that you were heavy-handed with him this morning when he identified his employee.'

Torquil had felt his temper rise as his superior officer used the word 'laird' again.

'We have information about McArdle, sir. He isn't what —'

432

'Inspector McKinnon,' Superintendent Lumsden interrupted, 'you seem to have a problem with Jock McArdle, I realize that. But just let me tell you, he is an influential man.'

'You mean he has a lot of money, Superintendent?'

The voice on the other end of the line sounded as if it now came through gritted teeth. 'I mean that he has powerful friends. You would do well to realize that, Inspector. Two of his employees have been killed and he wants police protection.'

'Protection?'

'That's right. And I said you would see to it. So see to it and keep me informed about the case.'

There was a click and Torquil found himself staring at a dead line again.

Moments later he relayed the superintendent's message to the Incident Room.

'The man is a fool,' said the Padre, voicing his disbelief.

'Didn't you tell him about Morag's information, Torquil?' Ralph asked.

Torquil shook his head. 'I didn't really have time. The superintendent rarely listens. Besides, I'm not sure that he needs to know just yet.'

'Be careful, laddie. Remember that the superintendent had it in for you in the past,' said his uncle.

Torquil nodded. 'I'll be careful.'

He looked at Morag. 'Go on now, Morag. Tell us about McArdle, or Cardini.'

'Well, my contacts at Glasgow told me that Giuseppe Cardini served five years in Barlinnie Prison in Glasgow for culpable homicide. But apparently it was touch and go as to whether he went down for the murder of Peter Mulholland, one of the twins who jointly ran one of the biggest gangs in the Glasgow area. They were into drugs, prostitution and extortion in the

433

city. Giuseppe Cardini was thought to have murdered Peter Mulholland, although he claimed it was self-defence.'

Morag looked up at the assembled men in the room. 'And now comes the interesting bit. The police had been put onto him by an investigative journalist who had infiltrated the gang that Cardini worked for. Her name was Rhona McIvor.'

Ralph gasped. 'Well, I'm damned! I knew that she was a writer of sorts, but I didn't know she was into that sort of writing.'

'I thought I might be able to get a copy of her article off the internet, but I couldn't access it,' went on Morag. 'But I did manage to get a copy faxed from the records department. I have a cousin who works there. It was her first job of the day.' She opened a file and pushed a copy of the article across the desk for Torquil to see. 'I've highlighted a few interesting bits,' she pointed out. 'Matthew Mulholland, the other twin, had also claimed to have been attacked by someone, and a bullet-riddled car was pulled out of the River Clyde.

'So Cardini went to prison and while he was inside Luigi Dragonetti, the head of the gang, died of a heart attack. When Cardini was finally released, he just disappeared for a few months. It was then that he changed his name to Jock McArdle. And somehow he seemed to have been able to finance himself in the confectionary business, although the Glasgow police believe, and still believe but have been unable to prove, that he made his money through vice and extortion.'

'But what about the other gang?' Torquil asked, as he scanned Rhona's article.

'Matthew Mulholland died of a stroke on his way home from a Celtic match a week after Cardini reinvented himself as McArdle. Apparently he ran his Mercedes into a wall. Somehow the gang just disappeared — or rather a lot of the

434

gang "went straight" and ended up on the new Jock McArdle's payroll. He just went from strength to strength, invested in several companies and became a millionaire.'

'And what about this animal rights thing?' the Padre asked.

'Ah yes, that was one of his companies. They bred mice, rats and guinea pigs and supplied them to several university and government laboratories. Highly lucrative, until they attracted the attention of animal rights activists. Unluckily for them!'

'What do you mean?' asked Torquil, raising his head from the article.

'There is nothing concrete to go on here, but apparently there was an active cell of animal rights activists operating in the south of Scotland. There were a couple of attacks on the homes of some of the McArdle company workers, and even a fire-bomb attack on Jock McArdle's house. A few weeks later, a couple of bodies turned up in the river. They were identified as being members of the animal rights cell.'

The Padre whistled softly. 'Not a nice chap, it seems. And now he says he wants police protection.' He shook his head in disbelief. 'Well, I should let him wait a while if I were you. What about Sartori and Reid? Where do they fit in?'

Torquil tapped the article in front of him. 'I'm thinking that they were what Rhona called enforcers or punishers. That is how she described Cardini when he was a young man. That would certainly fit with their bully-boy antics on West Uist.'

Wallace raised a hand. 'Excuse me, but what was the significance of the bullet-riddled car?'

Morag shrugged. 'I am not sure. Rhona made the point that the Mulhollands had probably killed whoever was in that car.'

'But was there no body?' Douglas asked.

'No body, so no charge against Matthew Mulholland. He denied any connection. It was only supposition that it was connected. False number plates and everything. But inside the glove pocket they found a gun, a Mauser, and a library book about guinea pigs.'

'Guinea pigs?' repeated Wallace.

'Could that be the animal rights folk again?' his brother asked.

'The police checked and the book had been taken out by someone called Enrico Mercanti, who was on the Dragonetti gang payroll. The police think that he was a fellow punisher with Cardini-McArdle.'

Torquil stood up and went over to the whiteboard, and added a few more notes under Jock McArdle's name.

CARDINI PUNISHER PRISON — 5 YEARS

ANIMAL RIGHTS CELL — BODIES FOUND

He drew a line between McArdle's name and Rhona and added a balloon with the word ARTICLE inside.

'Cardini to McArdle. Sounds similar, as if he wanted to retain the sound of his name. So does the Italian connection have more significance than we thought?' He suddenly snapped his fingers and added in capital letters the word FAMILY to the notes under McArdle's name. Then he drew a line from there to the notes relating to Ewan McPhee's diary, where the same word stood out prominently.

'Could Ewan have been meaning this family is McArdle's *family*?'

'Are you thinking about the mafia?' Ralph asked.

Everyone started speaking at once, as the possibility hit home. But Torquil had been scrutinizing the ever-more complex spider web diagram that had been gradually developing. 'There is something here,' he mused, tracing out lines in his mind.

'Look there!' he cried, tapping the board under Rhona's

name. 'CARD IN! We've assumed she had written a message about a card. I reckon she was writing Cardini! But why? What else was she trying to write?'

The phone rang and Morag answered it. 'That was Calum,' she said a few moments later. 'He was wanting to tell us to turn on the television. Scottish TV have a bulletin scheduled for the next few minutes.' And as Wallace switched on the station television and found the channel, they found themselves confronted by Kirstie Macroon sitting at a desk behind which was a picture of the Kyleshiffin harbour. In a small square at the top of the picture was a smiling photograph of Calum Steele, to whom Kirstie was talking over a phone link.

'And have we any idea who the dead man was, Calum?'

'We have indeed, Kirstie. It was a man called Danny Reid, and he was in the employ of Jock McArdle, the Glaswegian millionaire who bought himself Dunshiffin Castle.'

'And you say that the wind towers around the house were burning, as well as the cottage?'

'It was awful. They were burning like beacons all night. It must have been a brighter sight from the sea than the old lighthouse itself. An inferno! And arson, without a shadow of doubt.'

'And are the police treating the death of Danny Reid as suspicious?'

'They have launched a murder investigation and Inspector Torquil McKinnon is leading the inquiry.'

'Thank you, Calum. I am sure we will be in touch again.'

'My pleasure, Kirstie.'

'Thank you again.'

Calum Steele's voice was heard again, but immediately cut off as Kirstie Macroon deftly continued with her bulletin.

'That was Calum Steele, the editor of the West Uist Chronicle who has been keeping us up to date on the current story about the windmills of West Uist. So now—' She stopped in mid-sentence and touched her earpiece. *'I am just informed that we have been able to contact Mr McArdle, the new laird of Dunshiffin, and the man at the heart of the wind farm scheme.'*

A picture of Jock McArdle on the day that he took possession of Dunshiffin Castle appeared, replacing that of Calum Steele.

'Mr McArdle, we understand that tragedy has afflicted you twice lately and we offer our condolences. Regarding the wind towers —'

She never finished her sentence. Jock McArdle's thick Glaswegian accent broke out and continued in a staccato barrage of anger.

'My wind towers have been criminally burned down and two of my employees have been murdered. This island should be called the Wild West, not West Uist! I am under attack here, and I have a pretty damned good idea who is behind it all — and why! I have been on the telephone this morning to the highest police officer I could contact and I demand police protection straight away. Meanwhile I am locking myself away in Dunshiffin Castle, and then I'm going to put the police straight. I'll get justice for
my boys.'

The phone went dead and Kirstie Macroon picked up again, as a photograph of Dunshiffin Castle now took up the backdrop behind her.

'As you have just heard, Mr McArdle feels that the situation in West Uist is becoming highly dangerous and he has asked for police protection. This is Kirstie Macroon for Scottish TV. We hope to have more information on the lunchtime news.'

Wallace turned the sound down.

'The wee fool,' cursed Douglas. 'What does Calum Steele think he's playing at, giving out information like that on national news?'

'Och, he's a journalist, Douglas. You know well enough what

438

he's like.'

'Well, I think he's a pain in the backside,' persisted Wallace.

'He's worse than that, I'm afraid,' said Torquil. 'He might not realize it, but he may have just signed someone's death warrant. Jock McArdle sounded as though he was preparing to pull up his drawbridge against a siege.'

Nial Urquart's hair was dripping wet from his shower as he came into Katrina's small sitting-room, a towel wrapped around his waist. Katrina was sitting in a silk dressing-gown with a mug of coffee in her hand as she watched the news flash on Scottish TV.

CHAPTER SEVENTEEN

'I thought you were going to make a great big fry-up after all our exertions of the night?' he asked with a grin, as he slumped down beside her and wrapped an arm about her shoulders. 'And right afterwards I'm going to sort things out with Megan.'

'Just a minute, Nial,' she said, raising a finger, her eyes wide with alarm, 'This is important. There was a fire on the Wee Kingdom last night — and a death.'

'A death? What? Who?'

Together they watched and listened to Kirstie Macroon's conversation with Calum.

'Thank God it was none of the Wee Kingdom folk,' whispered Katrina. She turned and looked at Nial. 'This isn't good. You ought to be there for Megan.'

But he was still watching the news as Kirstie Macroon talked to Jock McArdle, before signing off. 'The bastard!'

'Who?' Katrina asked, bemusedly. She noted the sudden gleam of anger in his eyes.

'McArdle! Him and his kind who profit out of suffering. It's all his fault. And now he's wanting police protection. Bastard!'

'It must have happened very late last night. I think you had better get in touch with Megan. She'll be frantic — as well as furious with us.' She bit her lip. 'It must have been awful. What did Calum Steele say, it was like a beacon, like the —' She suddenly stood up and switched off the television. 'Come on, we've got to get going. I've got a couple of visits to make then I have an operating session scheduled for this afternoon, and you need to go and talk to Megan.'

She disappeared into her room returning a few moments

later after having thrown on a jumper and pulled on jeans and trainers. Nial watched her gather her case, a water bottle and then open a cupboard under the stairs and pull out a rifle bag.

'Crikey, have you got to put some poor beast down?' he asked with a humourless grin.

She nodded. 'Always a possibility. Look Nial, could I borrow your boat?'

'Sure, the keys are on the bedside table. It's in the harbour, well-fuelled and ready.'

Katrina ducked back into the bedroom returning swiftly. She leaned over and kissed him on the lips. 'I need to rush. You talk to Megan. No, better still, you go and see her.'

He watched her through the window as she drove off in her van. He started humming as he flicked on the electric kettle and loaded a couple of slices of bread into the toaster.

'But first things first,' he mused to himself, as he reached for his phone.

Torquil finished his call then pocketed his mobile phone. 'That's Calum sorted,' he said with a scowl.

'How was he?' Morag asked.

'Peeved. He feels that he has pulled off a major coup and performed a public service, and he was surprised to hear me say that I may be pressing charges on him as a police nuisance.'

'And will you?' asked Lachlan.

'Of course not, but I just wanted to rattle him a bit, and get him off our case.'

Ralph had stood up and was packing his bag. 'I feel a bit guilty there actually, Torquil. He collared me at breakfast and pumped me for information. I didn't think he'd be straight on national news with it.' He shook his head guiltily. 'And I'm afraid I've got to be off. I have a surgery soon.'

Once he had gone, Torquil addressed the others. 'Right, we've got a number of leads to follow up. First —'

He was interrupted by the phone ringing on the station counter. Morag went through to answer it. They waited until she answered it and came back.

'That was Nial Urquart,' she volunteered. 'He says that he's worried about Katrina Tulloch. She's just left her flat in a hurry — he'd stayed the night, he told me — and she's taken some sort of a rifle. He says she looked preoccupied and went off as soon as she heard that news bulletin this morning.'

'Calum again!' said Torquil. And then after a moment's thought, 'But what could there be in that news bulletin to worry her?'

'There's more,' said Morag. 'She's taken the keys of his boat.'

'We'd better get after her and see what's going on,' said Torquil.

'We'll go,' said Wallace standing up. 'Shall we take the *Seaspray*?'

Morag stood in his way. 'No, with respect, I think I should go. I know her better than you. She's a woman and I've talked to her already. I know she's a bit confused at the moment.'

Torquil nodded. 'I agree; Morag should go.'

'And I'll keep her company, shall I?' suggested Lachlan. 'Better two people in the catamaran.' Then as she was about to remonstrate, he added, 'Remember that Ewan went missing after going off on his own.'

'Lachlan is right, Morag. Away you go. We'll sort out the rest of the tasks.'

Vincent was feeling exhausted and guilty after a sleepless night. After taking Megan back to her croft, he had listened to her rant about Nial's betrayal. He had wiped her tears away, and together they had speculated about the cause of the fire. At about five in the morning, they had drunk a couple of whiskies and each become aware of the chemistry that had been threatening to bubble to the surface for several months.

She kissed him and he recoiled.

'Megan, I'm old enough to be your —' She silenced him with another kiss. And then another. 'But what about you and Nial?'

'There is no me and Nial now.'

And then they moved to the bedroom where they stayed, cocooned from the world by their love-making, until the cockerel and the geese roused them back to reality, and the ever-increasing problems that surrounded them. But now the sex was like a drug and the hours seemed to drift by until Vincent finally heaved himself out of bed and started to pull on his clothes.

'I don't want you to go, Vincent,' Megan pleaded, and she insisted that he stay for breakfast. As she prepared food and boiled the kettle, Vincent settled down on the settee and turned on the television. As they ate, they watched the morning farming programme, which was interrupted by the news bulletin from Kirstie Macroon. They sat and watched in horrified silence.

'Oh my God,' gasped Megan. 'What is happening to this place? It is all falling apart.' She leaned forward and put her hand on his. 'But at least I have you now.'

Vincent shook his head. 'I don't know, Megan. It doesn't feel right.'

'It feels very right to me.'

'What should we do?'

She wiped her mouth with a napkin. 'We need time to talk and see where we're going here. But I have a job to do first. Wait a minute.'

And she disappeared into her bedroom, coming back after a few minutes with a large holdall and a rucksack. 'These are Nial's,' she said. 'Will you help me load them in the car?'

'I had better come too.'

'No, I have to do this myself.'

He helped her pack up the car and watched her drive off into the swirling mist. Then he purposefully strode back to his croft. He had an important job of his own to do.

Alistair McKinley had watched the firemen battle to contain the fire, then withdrew and watched the police go about their business after they discovered the body. After they had taken it away, Alistair went back to his croft and catnapped in his armchair before washing and breakfasting. Then, as usual, he went out and tended to his livestock and did some work on the loom. Half expecting a news report on the fire, he went in for a cup of tea and turned on the old television in time to see Kirstie Macroon's report. As he watched, he became more and more irate.

'So much death!' he whispered to himself. 'And all down to him!'

Methodically clearing up his breakfast things he set about doing the other chores that he felt could not wait, before going back to the outhouse that housed his loom. Pushing several boxes of wool aside, he prised up the flagstone in the corner, reached into the hollow beneath and drew out the rifle wrapped in polythene. He unwrapped it, gave it the once over, then reached into the hollow again and drew out his father's old hunting bag, which contained his spare ammunition.

'Just one more job to finish,' he mused. 'And this is in your memory, Kenneth my lad.'

Five minutes later his jeep disappeared into the mist, its red tail lights swiftly disappearing in the swirling yellow vapours.

Then a lone figure came round the side of the croft, heading swiftly across the ground towards the Morrison family croft. He sniffed the air as he went past it, heading up the rise towards Wind's Eye croft. He stood by the burned-out shell surrounded as it was by the plastic police tapes.

'Just one bloody great mess!' Geordie Morrison muttered to himself. 'Someone's going to pay for this. And I am going to see to that!'

Morag and Lachlan had arrived at the catamaran berth just in time to see Nial Urquart's motorboat disappear out of the harbour, heading northwards.

'It's a nippy little thing that she's got there,' said Morag, 'but we'll soon catch her.'

She donned a waterproof and life-jacket and started the *Seaspray* up while Lachlan untied the mooring ropes and then boarded beside her.

'Aye, as long as she doesn't disappear into the mists,' he said, as he donned waterproofs and life-jacket, while Morag went through preparations to leave harbour. 'Have you any idea where she may be headed?'

'None at all. But what worries me most is why she feels she might need a gun at sea.' As she expertly manoeuvred out of the harbour before accelerating northwards it looked as if Lachlan's fears might be correct. Already the boat had disappeared into the misty waters.

Morag switched on the radar and moments later she had a blipping image on the screen in front of her. 'We can't see her, but she's there right enough. And it looks as if she's heading around the coast.'

'Towards the Wee Kingdom, do you think?' Lachlan asked.

'Maybe,' Morag replied. 'Or possibly to Dunshiffin Castle.'

'Wallace, I want you to go to the Wee Kingdom and make sure that Vincent Gilfillan, Alistair McKinley and Megan Munro don't leave their crofts. We'll want to take statements from them later. Douglas, I want you to find Nial Urquart and bring him back here.'

'Are you going to question him, Piper?' Douglas asked.

'I am. But I'm going to go over things here first and get my thoughts in order. And I'd better give the superintendent a ring and put him in the picture.'

Once he was alone, Torquil went through to the kitchen and put the kettle on for a cup of tea.

Then, with his cup in his hand, he went through to the Incident Room and stared at the whiteboard.

Jock McArdle! And now he wanted police protection! He grinned. There was only him available to give that protection now. But protection against whom?

The answer came when the station telephone rang.

'Emergency!' The rasping whispered voice had an unmistakable Glaswegian twang. 'This is Jock McArdle at Dunshiffin Castle. I need help now! There's a nutter here — with a gun!'

There was the deafening noise of a gun being discharged, then a strangled cry, then silence.

'Bugger!' cursed Torquil. He dashed out, stopping only to pick up his helmet and his gauntlets. Moments later he was hurtling along the mist-filled Harbour Street on the Bullet.

Like many native West Uist people, Katrina had been used to handling boats since she was a youngster. She knew exactly where she was going and what she was doing. Her heart was racing and she felt more anxious than she thought possible.

She was unaware that she was being pursued.

It seemed to take an interminable time as she raced through the mist as fast as she dared go. And she was always conscious of getting too close to the coastline, with its innumerable stacks, skerries and hidden rocks. But at last she saw the Wee Kingdom loom out of the mists, and she steered a course parallel with it until she rounded the western tip, where three successive basalt stacks jutted out of the sea. On the top of the most westerly one, was the ruins of the old West Uist lighthouse and the derelict shell of the keeper's cottage. She headed straight for it, slowed the boat and manoeuvred to a stop by the aged jetty. Quickly tying up, she unsheathed her rifle from its bag and gathered her medical bag and water bottle. As she turned to look at the bleak ruins of the lighthouse, she felt a shiver of fear run up and down her spine.

She mounted the steps to the ruin, which was nowadays no more than the bare husk of a tower. The door had long since gone and the inside was full of collapsed masonry and years of guano from the gulls that even now were circling it, protesting noisily at a human presence. Then she turned her attention to the derelict lighthouse-keeper's cottage. She went along its frontage, trying to see through the wooden shutters that had been nailed in place years before. And then she was at the door, staring at the new looking padlock.

Another shiver ran up her spine as she tested her weight against the unyielding door. She listened with her ear at the door, but heard nothing.

Except the noise of an engine approaching through the mist.

Who the hell was this?

She had no time or inclination to find out. She dropped her bag and water bottle and taking careful aim with the Steyr-

Mannlicher rifle, she fired point blank at the lock.

Morag and Lachlan heard a popping noise as they approached.

'What was that?' Lachlan asked.

'It sounded like a muffled gunshot,' said Morag.

'You mean a shot from a gun with a silencer?' Lachlan queried. 'We'd best be careful here, Morag.'

And minutes later, having tied up beside the motorboat on the jetty, they made their way warily to the open door of the old lighthouse-keeper's cottage. Just inside the door a rifle was propped up against the wall, while inside they saw Katrina Tulloch sobbing her heart out and leaning over a body lying face down on the floor.

The turrets and battlements of Dunshiffin Castle, the thirteenth-century stronghold of the MacLeod family, were lost in the mist as Torquil approached. He stopped a hundred yards away and parked his machine by the side of the road and then advanced on foot. He had no intention of announcing his arrival, so he took to the grass verge and jogged along towards the bridge that crossed the moat. Unfortunately, there was no way of entering the castle by any other route, so he kept close to the walls of the gateway tower and thanked the mist for giving him some cover. Once in the gravel courtyard, he stepped carefully so as to avoid announcing his presence.

On the way there, he had stopped to call for back-up, but cursed when his phone failed to connect with any of his staff. He had thought of taking a detour to the phone box on the Arderlour road, but the sound of the gunshot when McArdle had called him had indicated the urgency of the matter. He knew that he would just have to use his wits and trust to the message he left in the voice box and his ingenuity.

There were no lights on, but one side of the large double front door was standing ajar. Torquil made his way towards it by following the courtyard wall and then climbing up the side of the steps to come at it from the side. He wrapped his goggles around the end of his baton and edged it into the doorway, using it like an angle mirror. Seeing nothing suspicious he crept through the door to stand in the hall as swirls of mist wisped through the door.

On the oak-panelled walls hung numerous stag heads, antlers, shields, with criss-crossed claymores and pikestaffs. On either side of the stairway leading up from the great hall stood empty suits of armour. Having been in the castle on numerous occasions over the years, as both guest and as a piper for formal occasions, he knew his way about the place. But the thing that led him at the moment in the chilly atmosphere was the unmistakable smell of a gun having been discharged. As he stealthily crept up the staircase, passed the larger than life size portrait of the Jacobite laird, Donal MacLeod, the odour became stronger. He reached the top of the stairs where twin galleries ran east and west with doors dotted along them and corridors at either end leading off into the interior of the castle. There the smell was very strong. Grasping his baton he headed for the west wing.

All of the curtains were closed and the long corridor was almost in pitch blackness, except for a line of light coming from a door at the end of the corridor. Torquil knew that this used to be the billiard-room in the previous laird's day. He stopped for a moment to take off his boots and then crept softly along the corridor in his stockinged feet. As he did so, he heard a click then a muffled thud, like the sound of a billiard cue striking a ball followed by it thumping into a pocket of a billiard table. It was then, as his eyes accustomed to the extra

449

darkness of the long corridor that he was aware of a figure ahead of him, creeping along the wall towards the door.

He stopped to watch as the figure reached the door, seemed to peer through the crack, then gingerly push the door open. As they did, the smell of a gunshot mixed with cigar smoke seemed to grow even stronger.

Then a voice cried out from the room, 'Don't move a muscle, Cardini!'

Torquil moved swiftly on his tiptoes towards the door. Inside, he saw the back of a man dressed in a smoking jacket bent over the billiard-table, as if frozen in time having just played a shot. Just behind him, a man was standing with his feet wide apart, arms outstretched, both hands holding an automatic weapon, pointed directly at the back of the other's head.

There was no time for thought. Torquil was in the room in a couple of strides. With a swift upward strike of his baton, he knocked the man's gun upwards, where it discharged with a deafening explosion, shattering a window. Then, moving swiftly before the man gained control of the gun, he brought the baton down sharply on the back of his head.

As the assailant fell face down, Torquil kicked the gun under the table, and then leaned down to turn him over.

He was surprised to see himself looking down at the unconscious figure of Vincent Gilfillan.

'Thank God for the West Uist police!' came Jock McArdle's voice. 'You know, McKinnon, I think you've saved me a job.'

CHAPTER EIGHTEEN

Katrina looked round as a floorboard creaked as Morag and Lachlan entered the ruined lighthouse-keeper's cottage. Tears were streaming down her eyes, but her voice was instantly authoritative as she moved into clinical mode.

'He's alive! But only just. Phone for Dr McLelland and get him to drive his ambulance down to the Wee Kingdom jetty.'

'Who is it, Katrina?' asked Morag, screwing her eyes up as she entered the dimly lit ruin.

'My God, Morag, it's Ewan!' gasped the Padre. His look of amazement turned instantly to anger as he saw the stout ropes about his ankles and his wrists. 'Who could have done this?'

But Katrina was not listening. She had her bag open and was making a quick examination of the almost comatose police constable. He was in a state of collapse and utter squalor, having clearly soiled himself several times over the last few days.

Morag went outside for a moment and called Ralph. She returned with her emotions in a state of complete turmoil.

She was so relieved, yet like the Padre, so angry that anyone could have done such a thing to her friend.

A low groan escaped from Ewan's lips as Katrina went over his chest with her stethoscope.

'Oh Ewan, I am so sorry, so very sorry,' she sobbed, as she slung her stethoscope round her neck and reached into her bag for an intravenous giving set and a bag of saline.

'He's dehydrated and looks as if he's lost a couple of stone,' she volunteered. 'He needs intravenous fluids, cleaning up and a good work-up in hospital.' She wrapped a tourniquet about his arm, found a vein and adroitly threaded a needle and cannula into it. With her teeth she pulled off the seal on the saline bag and linked it up to the cannula. 'Hold that high would you, Sergeant?' she said, handing Morag the bag, while she taped the cannula in place then applied a bandage around the site.

'I'm so pleased to see him alive,' Morag said at last, tears streaming down her cheeks. She pointed to the large polythene water flagon on an old table with a tube that hung down near Ewan's head. The flagon was empty but for about a few millilitres of brackish water. 'Whoever tied him up here obviously left water, but nothing else.'

'And I guess they didn't intend to leave him here as long as this. The monster!' exclaimed the Padre. Then he turned to Katrina. 'But how did you know he was here? You have probably saved his life; you know that, don't you?'

Katrina bent down and kissed Ewan on the forehead. When she looked up her face was racked with guilt. 'I didn't save him, Padre. In fact it's my fault that he's here in the first place!'

Torquil looked up at the unmoving figure bent over the billiard table. He saw that although the figure was wearing a smoking jacket it was clearly not the stocky Jock McArdle. As he slowly straightened he saw that it was Jesmond, the butler.

A very dead Jesmond.

His cheek was actually lying on the table surface, his sightless eyes staring straight ahead. From his mouth a frothy trail of vomit had trickled over the green baize. Clearly he had not died a natural death, but his body had been arranged thus.

'I can see why you look a wee bit shocked, Inspector McKinnon,' came Jock McArdle's voice from behind him. 'He's not a pretty sight, is he?'

Torquil turned round and found himself looking down the barrel of a short-barrelled revolver. McArdle was standing behind the door with the gun in his outstretched right hand and a cigar clamped between his teeth. 'I never liked the little pip-squeak,' he went on conversationally. 'He didn't really hide the fact that he resented me and my boys.'

'And so you killed him?'

Jock McArdle shook his head. 'Oh no, I didn't! It wasn't me; he did it himself. He was showing me how he poisoned my dogs.'

'And he did this while he was playing billiards with you?' Torquil asked, sarcastically.

McArdle laughed. 'You're having a wee joke with me, is that right, Inspector? No, you are right. He croaked in my office and I carried him here to bait my wee trap. And it was working fine, until you came charging in like the seventh cavalry.'

'It looked as if you were about to be shot in the head,' Torquil said, equally conversationally. 'As a police officer I couldn't allow that.'

McArdle nodded. 'Oh yes, I should be grateful, shouldn't I? And if you had just hit him a wee bit harder you would have saved me a job.'

Vincent groaned and put a hand to his head.

'But you see what I mean,' McArdle went on with a deep sigh. 'I'll have to finish him myself.'

Torquil stood straight. 'I can't let you do that.'

McArdle sneered. 'You are hardly in a position to do anything about it, Inspector. In fact, I didn't expect any of you flatfeet to arrive so quickly. It would have been convenient if you had come along afterwards, but as it is, I'll have to dispose of you as well.'

Vincent was trying to roll over.

'Just stay where you are Mercanti!' he barked.

At the mention of the name, Vincent went rigid, as if a button had been pressed. He slowly turned to face the laird. 'Cardini! You murdering bastard. I almost had you!'

McArdle waved the revolver in the direction of the snooker table and the propped-up body of Jesmond, 'Actually, I'm afraid not, pal. You fell into my trap, hook, line and sinker.'

Torquil had edged slightly away from the table, but McArdle snapped at him, 'Stay exactly where you are — both of you. This is a Smith & Wesson 360. It has a light trigger —which you might remember, Enrico. A quick move from either of you and I'll cut you in half.'

Vincent looked up at Torquil. 'He means it, Inspector. Don't do anything stupid.'

McArdle guffawed. 'Aye, Inspector. You see Enrico here — not Vincent as you know him —knows his guns. We were partners, you see. Comrades and punishers together.' Then his semi-affable grin suddenly disappeared. 'Until the little bastard betrayed me!'

Torquil nodded. 'I know who you are, *Giuseppe Cardini*. I know all about you and the Dragonetti gang.'

Giuseppe Cardini stared at Torquil in amazement for a moment, then he laughed heartily again. 'So you lot are not as stupid as I thought.'

'And I know all about your prison stretch, your petty little gang war and your change of name.'

Cardini pointed the gun at Vincent. 'And how much do you know about Enrico here? He was supposed to be dead, you know?'

'I know about the car in the river,' Torquil replied. 'And I know that it was a piece of investigative journalism by Rhona McIvor that sent you to prison.'

'The bitch!' McArdle almost screamed. 'I've wanted to get even with her for years, but she disappeared. It was only a few months ago when she started writing articles for the magazines that I realized where she was. I wanted her to suffer. And I have the means to do these things legitimately these days. I wanted an estate in the islands and this place came up. A snip for me. It was as if it was all meant to be.'

'And this wind farm plan, that was all part of your way to get even with her?'

'Of course. The stupid old bitch didn't recognize me after all those years.' He touched his cheek. 'Not surprising maybe, since I've had a spot of cosmetic surgery, but she was going blind as a bat. That made it easier.' He laughed. 'A wind farm! I ask you, why would I be interested in anything like that? It's pathetic. Give me the National Grid any day.'

Vincent had eased himself into a sitting position on the floor. 'You killed Rhona?'

'Not me, pal. She killed herself all those years ago when she took you in. Tell us about it.'

'*You* killed her!'

There was a thunderous noise as Cardini took aim and shot Vincent in the foot. Blood immediately gushed out of a hole in his boot and he gasped as he writhed in agony. Torquil made a move to help him but the sound of Cardini tut-tutting halted him.

'I said — *tell* us!'

Vincent's face was covered in perspiration, but he gritted his teeth and tried to talk.

'You were always a sadistic bastard, Giuseppe. That was one of the reasons I needed to get away. Rhona gave me the means of escape.'

Cardini snorted disdainfully. 'Aye, she was a good-looking

woman and we never suspected she was a journalist, a spy.' He turned to Torquil. 'She got herself a job as a cashier in one of Luigi Dragonetti's betting shops, then gradually worked her way up to be a manager. That allowed her to get properly in the know of things. And that's when she started shagging Enrico there.' He spat on the floor by Vincent's feet. 'And that's when he betrayed his family!'

'Does family mean mafia?' Torquil asked.

Cardini guffawed. 'Naw! You've been watching too many Godfather films. Luigi Dragonetti was just a god. He was like a father to us — him and me. Before him we were just slum tinkers. He gave us respect and gave us lives.' He shook his head and took the cigar out of his mouth. 'Like I tried to be like a father to Liam and Danny.'

'That's rubbish!' Vincent snorted. 'Luigi Dragonetti was a sadistic bastard who modelled himself on Al Capone. He used folk like us to punish people. He didn't give a stuff whose lives we pissed on as long as he got what he wanted. Rhona taught me that.'

'Then that was another reason for her to die! I hated that bitch for the five years I lost in prison.'

'So was that your real reason for coming to West Uist?' Torquil asked. 'To arrange for her death.'

Cardini shrugged noncommittally. 'That was the ultimate aim. But first I planned to destroy her. And it was happening too — until this bastard started killing my boys.'

'Did you?' Torquil asked.

Vincent's face was fast draining of colour as blood oozed from the hole in his foot to form a gory puddle on the floor.

'No — and yes,' he replied in a rasping voice. 'I killed the first little sod, but I didn't mean to. I just got so angry over that letter and how he talked to Megan. Especially when we were getting close. When I left Megan, I waited for him to come back by the causeway. When I confronted him, man to man, he spat in my face.' He glared at Cardini. 'That was one of the things you used to do before you hurt people. Anyway, he tried to throw a punch but he was drunk and slow. I knocked him off the causeway, then I jumped down and dragged him to the pool.'

Cardini let out a howl of rage. 'My boy! You drowned my boy!'

Torquil realized that Cardini's temper was brewing up to volcanic proportions. He needed to keep things flowing for the present. 'So what about the other man, Danny Reid? Did you kill him too?'

'I did. But it was because Rhona warned me about Cardini.'

'That's what she meant by CARD IN?'

Vincent nodded. 'I knew that Cardini would have some sort of revenge planned for Sartori's death. I saw the bugger sneaking into Gordon MacDonald's cottage, planning to set it on fire. A warning to us. I recognized he was trying to provoke whoever killed the first piece of shit. So I stopped him and snapped his neck. And that's why I left that message for him.'

'Is that what the medallion in the mouth was all about?' Torquil asked.

'It was a sort of signature that we used in the old days,' Cardini volunteered. 'But that was when I realized that bloody Enrico Mercanti was alive and well on this piss-pot of an island!' He laughed. 'And that's when I laid my wee trap for you. It actually worked out a bit earlier than I planned, but that TV woman forced my hand by giving me the opportunity to send out a message to you.'

He raised the gun and Torquil slowly raised his own hand. 'OK, McArdle or Cardini, whichever you want to be known by, it is time to give me that gun. I am arresting you both.'

Giuseppe Cardini looked back at Torquil in mock amazement. 'You are arresting me?' He guffawed. 'I don't think you quite understand. I am defending my property here. That bastard killed my boys, then he came here and killed my butler and tried to kill me too. I struggled with him and you, our heroic local flatfoot, rushed to help me, only to get tragically killed in the line of duty.' He shook his head with mock sympathy. 'There have been too many police officers killed while doing their duty and I will arrange with Superintendent Lumsden, my good friend, for some sort of local monument to be erected.'

Torquil was aware of a patina of perspiration on his brow, but he managed to keep his voice calm. 'I said I will take that gun now. I have to get medical attention for Vincent here. And, by the way, thank you for your confession.'

Cardini scowled and pointed to the gun in his hand. 'I am the one in the driving seat, McKinnon. Now how about just saying your prayers?'

'I don't think there is a need for that,' Torquil said, deliberately looking past Cardini at the open door. 'You have got all that, haven't you, Constable Steele?'

Cardini sneered contemptuously. 'Nice try, flatfoot. Now say your prayers. Both of you!'

Calum Steele's voice came from the open doorway. 'I have it all on tape here, Inspector McKinnon.'

In a trice, Cardini spun round into a broad-based crouch, both arms outstretched and steadying the gun.

There was a sudden flash from waist height, followed by a burst of fire from Cardini's gun.

But his moment of surprise had given Torquil the time he needed. He flew across the room, kicked the gun upwards and,

458

as he did so, grabbed Cardini's right wrist. They wrestled with the gun, and it scanned the room, spewing out two shots. Then Torquil managed to twist and bend Cardini's wrist back on itself. There was the snapping noise of bones crunching as the gangster's hand opened automatically and he screamed in pain as the gun fell to the floor.

But Cardini had been a street brawler and he immediately threw a left at Torquil's head. It was a shade too slow and he ducked and threw a straight left to Cardini's abdomen; then, as Cardini doubled over, he hammered an uppercut into his jaw. It lifted the laird off his feet and deposited him unconscious on the floor.

'And that's how we do things in West Uist.' Torquil said, blowing on his skinned knuckles. He turned to the door where Calum was climbing to his feet from the prone position he had adopted in order to hold up the digital camera and first dazzle then draw Cardini's fire.

'Well done, Calum. I've never been so happy to see anyone in my life. I thought that either you hadn't picked up my voice message or your Lambretta had finally packed in.'

'Never a bit of it, Piper. Mind you, that's the first time the West Uist investigative journalist has ever come under real live fire. And about that title "Constable Steele" — it has a certain ring —'

There was the sound of a click from the floor and they both turned to see Vincent propped against the leg of the snooker table, the crumpled body of Jesmond having tumbled into the bloody pool beside him. A rapidly spreading patch of blood was forming over Vincent's abdomen where one of the stray bullets had struck home.

'Just hold it where you are,' he rasped, his bloodied hands clenching a gun. 'Things are not — quite — finished!'

CHAPTER NINETEEN

Ralph McLelland broke just about every speed restriction on the island and arrived at the Wee Kingdom jetty within ten minutes of the Padre's call. Together with Katrina and Morag, he stretchered Ewan into the ambulance and drove straight to the cottage hospital. There, Sister Lamb and Nurse Anderson set about cleaning him up while Ralph took blood samples in order to determine his clinical state and electrolyte balance.

'He is dangerously dehydrated and still non-responsive,' Ralph told Katrina. 'I'll monitor him for a few hours to get him stable, but I have every faith that he will be on his feet in a week or so. Ewan McPhee is one of the strongest men I have ever known, but surviving this long on just sips of water has taken it out of his system.' He shook his head as he looked down at the haggard redheaded constable. 'I don't think many folk could have survived his ordeal.'

Katrina heaved an enormous sigh of relief then turned to Morag. 'And I think that you will want to have my account of all this?'

Morag's spirits had gone from rock bottom to sky high upon discovering that one of her best friends was still alive. Now, as an officer of the law, she snapped into professional mode. 'My thoughts exactly, Miss Tulloch. And I think it would be best if you accompanied me to the station to make your statement.'

Wallace Drummond had been on his way to the Wee Kingdom when he saw Alistair McKinley's jeep pulled off the road by the rough track that led up to the Corlins. He had a good idea of where he would find the crofter, so he coaxed the police

Ford Escort along the track and duly found him preparing to climb the cliff face.

'Alistair,' Wallace said, as he let the window down. 'I have already told you that you are not permitted to have a gun at the moment. You will give it to me now.'

The crofter shook his head, his face determined. 'Leave me alone, Wallace Drummond. I have something that needs to be done. I am going to shoot those bloody golden eagles.'

But Wallace was out of the car and, with a couple of quick strides, he caught hold of the bag carrying the gun that Alistair had about his shoulders. He slipped it off and held it behind him. 'And I am telling you that you will do nothing of the sort. There has been enough killing as it is. I am taking this gun and you back to the station with me. Inspector McKinnon says he wants to talk to you.'

'Put the gun down, Vincent,' Torquil said. 'You need medical treatment for that wound and you need it now.'

Blood was oozing from the wound in Vincent's abdomen and had soaked his trousers.

'I'm not worried about myself, Inspector,' he said, his voice losing power all the time. 'I am more concerned about that piece of excrement there.' He hesitated to gulp some air. 'He has a history of atrocities that you wouldn't believe. He liked to hurt people and watch them squirm. And he's murdered folk without batting an eyelid. I plan to be his judge, jury and executioner.'

'You can't do that, Vincent. That would make you a murderer, too.'

'I don't matter anymore,' he breathed. He gestured with the gun in his hand at Calum. 'Put those on the floor and switch them off.'

Torquil nodded to Calum, who acquiesced and laid down his camera and his Dictaphone.

'That's good, because I don't want any more of this being recorded,' Vincent said wheezily.

He stabbed the gun in the direction of the still unconscious Giuseppe Cardini. 'It is about him coming back into our lives. I thought that I had broken free from the Dragonetti gang and their ugly world of death and violence. Rhona helped to stage my disappearance and set me up with a croft here twenty years ago.' His eyes seemed to mist over. 'Clever woman, Rhona. She persuaded the old lady who owned it — she was ill and dying — to pass it on to me as if I was a relative. She sorted out my new identity, national insurance number, absolutely everything.'

Cardini began to stir as he made a slow return to consciousness.

Vincent rallied at the sight and aimed the gun at him. 'He deserves to die!' he exclaimed.

'The law will deal with him, Vincent. Don't do anything stupid.'

Cardini heaved himself up on his elbows, his eyes suddenly widening with alarm when he saw the gun in the hand of the blood-soaked Vincent. He gasped in horror as he realized he was staring death in the face.

The gun-hand began to waver and Vincent's eyes started to roll upwards. 'At ... at least ... I can now —'

Suddenly, as if every last ounce of energy had been used up, he slumped sideways and the gun fell from his hand.

Torquil swiftly produced handcuffs and cuffed Cardini. Then he and Calum turned their attention to Vincent. A quick examination failed to find a pulse and the enlarging pool of blood suggested that things were hopeless. Nevertheless, while

Calum called for medical assistance, Torquil attempted resuscitation.

By the time that Ralph had arrived, it was all too clear that the man they knew as Gilfillan was truly dead.

Giuseppe Cardini had been watching all that time, cursing them and making scathing comments. Now, he tossed his head back and began to roar with laughter. 'That serves —'

He suddenly went silent as Calum seemed accidentally to trip, and kicked him in the groin.

Neither Torquil nor Ralph McLelland saw it happen.

Katrina sipped the hot tea that Morag had brewed back at the station.

'I really liked him.' she explained. 'Ewan, I mean. But Kenneth McKinley just wouldn't leave me alone, and Ewan started to get jealous and suspicious. It is all my fault.'

'Why do you say that?' Morag asked, as she jotted things down with her silver pen.

Katrina put the mug down, her expression a mix of pain and guilt. 'Because Kenneth was working for me, and it all got out of hand. He was working ... clandestinely.'

Morag raised her eyebrows quizzically. 'Go on.'

'You have no idea how hard it is to make a living as a vet in the Hebrides. I was in debt up to my ears. I had a colossal student loan to pay back, and even working abroad in the East for a couple of years didn't make much inroad into it. When I took over my uncle's practice, I didn't realize that I'd be taking over his debt as well. He'd mismanaged things in a most appalling manner — as well as having a personal debt of several thousand with his gambling.' She looked beseechingly at Morag for some sign of sympathy. 'I was desperate and I had to make money as fast and as quickly as I could. There was no legal way I could do that.'

Morag made a conscious effort not to let her face register any sense of judgement. She had to let Katrina willingly offer the information. 'So what did you do?'

Katrina bent her head in embarrassment. 'I had contacts from my time in the East. Dodgy contacts with people working in the animal trafficking black market.'

Morag made notes and said nothing, merely encouraging the vet to continue with a nod of her head.

'In Thailand and China seal penises and genitalia are used to make virility medicines. In the Hebrides we have an almost limitless supply of them.'

Morag was unable to keep the revulsion out of her voice. 'But you are a vet! How could you contemplate such a thing?'

'I am a vet, but I eat meat. It is easy to judge me, but the seals were a rich source of revenue that I could tap into. I had a regular courier all lined up to take the stuff over on the ferry to the mainland along with my bona fide samples. From the mainland, he would arrange to ship them abroad. His exact route, I don't know.'

'We'll find out, don't worry,' Morag replied curtly. 'And what about Kenneth McKinley, how did he fit in?'

'He went out in his boat and shot them — procured their organs — then disposed of the bodies. He liked it, because he was a bit of a Walter Mitty. He liked to call himself the "assassin".' She leaned forward and pummelled her temples with her fists. 'I was such a manipulative cow. I fuelled his fantasy.'

'We know about his fixation with guns,' Morag said. 'And we are aware that Ewan McPhee suspected something about him.'

Katrina burst into tears. 'I know and I hate myself for it. That was how Ewan went missing. Kenneth told me that he had taken out — that was how he described it, as if he was a hit-man or something — a family group of seals. Ewan must have followed him and Kenneth jumped him or something. He said he had him holed up somewhere, and that he was teaching him — and me — a lesson. I think he had some idea that I would sleep with him to get Ewan free. He wore disguises when he was out shooting and I think he meant to frighten Ewan.' She bit her lip. 'Then it all went badly wrong. I met him up on the ledge in the Corlins and I tried to get him to tell me where Ewan was, but he was obsessed with shooting the golden eagles. Anyway, I didn't see it clearly in the mist, but I think one of them flew at him and seemed to hit him. He staggered over the edge and — fell to his death.'

She began sobbing again and Morag waited until she settled. Under other circumstances she would have made comforting noises, but she was feeling too angry and too revolted by the woman in front of her to do so.

'I went down to him,' Katrina went on at last, between sobs. 'He was dead, of course. Then I — I scratched his face, to make it look as if an eagle had struck him with its talons. I didn't know what else to do. I had to find Ewan, but I didn't know where he could be.'

'What about the rifle?'

'I took that and hid it. You've got it now.'

'And what made you go to the lighthouse-keeper's cottage?'

'I had scoured the whole island without luck over the last few days.' She looked up at Morag who was staring at her with her best poker face. 'I guess you probably know that I have just started an affair with Nial Urquart.'

Morag shrugged noncommittally. 'Go on.'

'Well it was this morning on the news. Calum Steele mentioned about those wind towers and the cottage burning like beacons — brighter than the old lighthouse. Then I thought that had to be it. Kenneth could have easily got to and from there from the Wee Kingdom. It is just below their croft. And, as you know, that's where he was. The poor man could have been dead, all because of me.'

'He could,' Morag replied coldly. 'And you can just thank your lucky stars that he isn't. Ewan McPhee is one of my best friends.'

Douglas Drummond pulled up outside the Morrisons' cottage just in time to see the family transporting bags from a huge wheelbarrow into the house.

'Ah, the police!' said Geordie, a well-built fellow with long hair and a full unkempt beard. 'I have a complaint to make. Someone has been into my house and made an almighty mess. Someone is going to have to pay!'

Douglas could hardly believe his ears, but rather than cause a scene with the youngsters about, he smiled and got out of the car. 'I was actually trying to find Nial Urquart, but there doesn't seem to be anyone left on the Wee Kingdom except yourselves. Maybe it would be as well if I took you down to the station to have a chat with Inspector McKinnon.'

'A good idea,' replied Geordie. 'I am not in a mood for shilly-shallying.'

'No, I can see that,' said Douglas. 'Neither is he.'

Megan Munro stood at the door of Katrina Tulloch's flat with the holdall and rucksack containing Nial Urquart's clothes. She had rehearsed the speech she was going to make, but when Nial answered the door with contrition written across his face, she merely dropped them on the mat.

'Megan, I'm an idiot!'

'You are.'

'I have made an awful mistake.'

'Me too.'

'Do you think we could —?'

In answer she flung her arms about his neck and he hugged her as if he would never let her go again.

'Of course we can!'

A week later, after an emotional rollercoaster trip, things started to settle down. The whole story about Jock McArdle came out and was duly written up by Calum Steele in the *Chronicle* and in interviews on Scottish TV with Kirstie Macroon. Giuseppe Cardini was transferred to a holding prison pending his trial, the windmills were taken down and the island saw a spate of funerals.

Vincent Gilfillan was buried in the St Ninian's cemetery next to Rhona McIvor, near to the grave of Kenneth McKinley.

Ewan McPhee slowly pulled through and was discharged from hospital into the doting care of his mother, Jessie. The entire division of the West Uist branch of the Hebridean Constabulary as well as the full staff of the *West Uist Chronicle* and the Padre descended on them and stayed far longer than they had intended, all eventually being ejected by Dr McLelland who gave them a lecture about over-tiring the patient.

Outside, Morag asked Torquil, 'So now that the big one is back safe and sound, have you given any more thought about leaving the Force?'

Torquil grinned. 'Of course I have. I am staying right where I am needed. With my friends.'

Calum was still nibbling one of Jessie's scones. 'About that roving commission we talked about, Piper? You know, me being a special sort of police assistant. I have been thinking and there could be mutual benefits —'

Torquil groaned and put an arm about the local editor's shoulder. 'Let's finish this at the Bonnie Prince Charlie, Calum. I'll even let you buy me a pint of Heather Ale.'

The Padre followed suit and put an arm about Morag's shoulders. 'Does Heather Ale sound good to you?' he asked.

'It does actually, Padre. And I think that we should drink to Superintendent Lumsden's fortune.'

'Why's that?' asked Wallace.

'Didn't you know?' Morag replied. 'He's been suspended, pending investigation of his association with McArdle.'

'Well, it couldn't happen to a nicer man, could it?' said Douglas.

'My sentiments exactly,' said Torquil with a laugh. Then, turning to Calum with a mock scowl, 'But don't quote me!'

BOOK THREE: MURDER SOLSTICE

PROLOGUE

Winter Solstice

The single beam from the Lambretta scooter's headlight cut a meagre swathe through the afternoon mist and drizzle. To make matters worse the light was failing fast as the sun descended rapidly towards the horizon to start the longest, darkest night of the year. Already a watery full moon was making its progress across the sky.

'Bloody mad, I must be,' mumbled Calum Steele, the editor of the *West Uist Chronicle*, to himself. He raised a hand to wipe his visor and cursed again. 'Cold, wet and miserable I am, and just before Christmas too. The folk of West Uist don't know what we journalists have to go through to bring them the news of the outside world.'

He tried to snuggle his thick neck into his sodden yellow anorak as he negotiated the snaking Dunshiffin road. 'I certainly didn't expect to be coming up here again today,' he grumbled.

Winter solstices had come and gone all of his life without him paying them the slightest bit of attention. Then The Daisy Institute, or as the locals called them, 'the flower people' had come and suddenly the solstices were big news. 'What do they think this is — a new Stonehenge?' he shouted to the elements, with a smug grin at his own joke.

Through the watery mist he could just make out the outline of Dunshiffin Castle, the recently acquired headquarters of The Daisy Institute. Several oblongs of light shone through the mist and he thought he could hear singing or chanting coming from within as he sped past.

'They have certainly had an impact on the island,' he said to himself. 'Them and their funny ways. I think I will have to write a series of —'

His attention was suddenly brought back to the task of controlling his scooter as he turned a bend and ran straight into a thick belt of opaque mist. He slowed down immediately, and then stared in horror as two headlights loomed out of the mist.

'Get over!' he cried in vain, as the vehicle hurtled towards him in the centre of the road. He swerved over to the side and almost lost his balance as he slewed precariously for a few seconds while a Jeep careered by at high speed with windscreen wipers working frantically. Calum stopped and looked round.

'And just what the hell are you playing at, Rab Noble?' he cried, as the tail-lights of the familiar Jeep rapidly disappeared into the mist. 'Are you drunk or what?'

But he knew that it was probably too early even for Rab to be drunk, by a couple of hours at least. It was milking time, he guessed, which could account for his haste. He was obviously rushing from the farm to the milking parlour on the far side of the farm.

As Calum's initial ire cooled, he realized all too soberly that if he had not had his wits about him, the island could have just lost the star investigative reporter and editor-in-chief of the *West Uist Chronicle*. At that he permitted himself a smile of self-satisfaction before continuing his journey.

Rab Noble was at least fifteen years older than Calum, which he realized may have been part of the reason that Esther, Rab's wife, had rung him half an hour earlier with her stark message.

'Get here right away, Calum Steele, and I will give you the biggest story you have ever had. The sadistic bastard! I will blow the lid on him and his band of sickos.'

There had been no explanation, just the exhortation to be quick if he wanted his reward. And so, natural-born busybody and professional newsman that he was, he had responded immediately and turned out in the inhospitable squall. Calum had never been able to resist a story. More than that, he had never been able to stop lusting over Esther Noble, or Esther Harrison as he always thought of her. She had been in his class at school, along with his friend Torquil McKinnon, now the local police inspector. Even then Calum had lusted over her, one of the best-looking girls on the island. As young adolescents they had groped each other on more than one occasion behind the bike sheds or in the bracken on the way home from school. She was bright too, which made it all the more surprising when she had left school at sixteen and married Rab Noble to become a farmer's wife, and a virtual recluse who rarely came into Kyleshiffin. Calum had barely seen her over the years, such was the way she had cut herself off from her roots, but as the man with his ear to every bit of gossip that was uttered on the island, he had heard that the marriage was stormy, presumably because as yet there had been no issue from the marriage. That and the fact that Rab Noble was a renowned drinker. And then there were the even darker rumours.

Calum turned off the road and headed up the track towards Hoolish Farm, catching a glimpse through the mist of the Hoolish Stones, the treble ring of megalithic stones a hundred yards or so out on the moor. They looked totally different from their appearance at sunrise when he had been up to watch the flower folk celebrate the solstice sunrise. He had written the article and was starting to put the *Chronicle* to bed when Esther had rung.

He heard the dogs howling before he turned the final bend and saw the lit-up windows of the dilapidated, sprawling farmhouse. He drew his scooter to a halt in the mud and dung-covered courtyard and switched off the engine.

There were three collies, all jumping and hurling themselves frenziedly about the wire-meshed kennel.

'Calm down, you doggies. Haud yer wheesht!' he cooed at them, to little avail. He thought that they looked fiercer than he remembered seeing them whenever he had come across Rab working with them on the farm near the castle. He tapped at the back door of the farmhouse, which was standing ajar.

'Esther? It's me — Calum.'

There was no answer, just the sound of a radio playing from inside the farmhouse. He pushed the door open and called again. Then he crossed the kitchen, avoiding bowls of dog food and entered the hall.

Esther Noble was hanging from the banister, her tongue purple and protruding from her mouth. A dog chain was cutting deeply into her neck and her face was livid, her eyes sightless and dead.

Half an hour later, Inspector Torquil McKinnon was patting the pasty-faced *Chronicle* editor's back while Dr Ralph McLelland, the local GP-cum-police surgeon, and another former school-mate, examined the body, assisted by Sergeant Morag Driscoll.

'And you say that Rab Noble almost ran you over?' he asked.

'Aye, Torquil. Like I told you, Esther phoned me to come up here straight away. She called him a sadistic bastard.'

'Well, we will see what he has to say soon enough. I sent Ewan McPhee to go and bring him back here. He will be milking the herd now, I am thinking.'

Calum was shivering slightly. He looked up at his friend. 'Suicide, do you think?'

Torquil shrugged his shoulders. 'Too early to say, Calum. And you know that, so be careful about what you write in the paper.'

'But I —'

Torquil's phone went off at that moment and he raised a hand for quiet while he answered it. Calum watched him talking and could tell by his facial expression that all was not well.

'That was Ewan,' Torquil explained a moment later. The others stopped what they were doing to listen to him. 'He has just been sick, poor lad.' He took a deep breath himself, then, 'He found the cattle howling and moaning as he arrived. Rab Noble was there all right, but it was more like an abattoir than a milking parlour. He had shot three cows, and then blown his brains out with a shotgun.'

CHAPTER ONE

The Kyleshiffin market was always busy on a weekday summer morning, but during the heatwave of the previous fortnight the number of market stalls had seemed to double. Bric-a-brac, second-hand books, arts and craft stalls occupied the roadside positions, while local produce sellers naturally held to their traditional pitches along the crescent-shaped harbour wall. With the town packed with holidaymakers, as witnessed by a veritable flotilla of yachts and cruisers bobbing up and down in the harbour itself, and an influx of what the local people called 'New Age flower people', the market workers and the proprietors of the multi-coloured shops that formed Harbour Street itself were enjoying a thriving trade.

Perspiring slightly and looking forward to a refreshing cup of tea at the station, Sergeant Morag Driscoll weaved her way through the throng only to find her way blocked by an unbelievably good-looking, blond, blue-eyed young man in his early twenties wearing a summery white hoodie. His smile seemed natural, as if he was genuinely pleased to see her. He was standing in front of a stall bedecked with pictures of stone circles, well-known religious sites from around the world and posters of an older, but similarly smiling man dressed in a yellow hoodie. Morag thought that the hoodies were designed to give them a modern, slightly monkish appearance. On the table were stacks of books all bearing the same photograph of the older man on the front cover.

'Can I interest you in the experience of a lifetime, lovely lady?' he asked.

Morag Driscoll was a thirty-something single mother of three. She was attractive by any standards, although she herself believed that she had a weight problem. It worried her and she worked hard to keep as trim as possible, since her husband had died from a heart attack when she was twenty-six and she vowed that she would always be there for her children.

Over the years she had heard just about every chat-up line, but this one took her by surprise, coming as it did from one who was at least a decade younger than she and who had a monkish look about him.

'I am a police sergeant, young man,' she replied, pointing to the three small stripes on the arm of her short-sleeved, navy-blue shirt. Wearing jeans and trainers as she was, the shirt was the only indication that she was a police officer, the local force being well known for its liberal attitude towards uniforms. She took the leaflet he had thrust in her direction. 'Do you still want to give me a wonderful experience?'

Unruffled, the youth stood smiling at her. And, as he did so, she realized that his question was probably more to do with the spiritual than the carnal. She felt a slight tinge of guilt and put it down to the natural cynicism that went with the job of policing.

'My name is Peter, Sergeant. I am one of the acolytes with The Daisy Institute,' he explained, pointing to the simple logo of a daisy flower on the front of his hoodie. 'It will be the summer solstice in a few days. We will be holding an all-night vigil at the Hoolish Stones to celebrate the solstice sunrise. Why don't you come along? It might change your life.'

Morag dabbed her brow with the back of her hand. This young man could have turned her head had she been ten or fifteen years younger. 'I know about your celebration, Peter,' she replied, allowing herself the ghost of a smile. 'In fact, I might even be there, officially. To make sure there is no trouble.'

'I will look forward to seeing you there then, Sergeant,' he replied. He reached over and tugged the sleeve of another white hoodie wearer. 'Henry, this lovely lady is a local police sergeant. I was telling her about the solstice celebration. We'll make her welcome if she comes, won't we?'

The hoodie wearer turned round and Morag found herself looking at another stunningly attractive young person with an enviable mass of auburn locks, a freckle- dappled face and glorious hazel eyes.

'Henry?' queried Morag, raising her eyebrows quizzically, for the face that had immediately fallen into a natural smile was most definitely female.

The girl laughed. 'Henrietta at birth, but Peter always calls me Henry.' She wrinkled her nose in mock disdain. 'He has a puerile sense of humour. But, of course, you will be welcome, Sergeant. Or you could come to one of our evening meetings. Scottish TV is doing a series on Logan Burns and The Daisy Institute every evening up at the Hoolish Stones. You might even find yourself on television.'

Morag glanced at the leaflet in her hand. It bore a photograph of Logan Burns, above a short text introducing The Daisy Institute, and explaining that it really stood for the DSY or The Divinity and Spirituality Institute. The reason for the daisy logo was thereby obvious. Morag suppressed the urge to tell them that she was sceptical of New Age religious leaders, gurus and cults, which was what Logan Burns and The Daisy Institute seemed to smack of. Instead, she smiled at them and shook her head.

'The trouble there is that like most police officers, I am a wee bit camera shy. But who knows.'

Ten minutes later as Morag pushed open the door of the Kyleshiffin Police Station, a converted pebble-dashed bungalow on Kirk Wynd, which ran parallel to Harbour Street, an evil odour assailed her sense of smell and she wrinkled her nose in disgust.

'Good Grief!' she exclaimed to PC Ewan McPhee, the large, freckled, red-haired wrestling and hammer-throwing champion of the Western Isles, and the junior officer of the West Uist division of the Hebridean Constabulary. 'What on earth is that awful stink? It's a thousand times worse than the fish market on a hot day like today. Is someone boiling a sheep's head?'

Ewan grinned as she covered her nose and puffed out her cheeks as if she was about to throw up. 'Och, you will get used to it in a few minutes, Morag. It is the boss. He is seasoning his bag and cleaning his pipes.'

'His bagpipes! Does he have to do that here? Goodness me, what a stench.'

The door behind the counter opened and Inspector Torquil McKinnon, often known to his friends on the island as 'Piper', came out of his office, working a large sheepskin leather bag between his hands. Five large bungs protruded from points around it, stopping up the stocks of the three drones, blowpipe and chanter. The bag made a curious squelching noise as he pummelled it between his hands.

'Is that my favourite sergeant that I hear complaining about me seasoning my bag?' he asked with a grin.

Torquil McKinnon was a tall, twenty-nine-year-old man with coal-black hair, high cheekbones and a slightly hawk-like nose. To many of the West Uist womenfolk he was a desirable and eligible male, but to Morag he was more like an impish younger brother, even though he was her superior officer. And she often treated him as such. She stood facing him across the counter, her arms akimbo.

'Torquil McKinnon, I respect your professional ability as a police officer. I applauded when you became the youngest inspector in the islands and the West Highlands. I admire your musical ability on the pipes. I was there, remember, when you won the Silver Quaich. But,' she said, slowly shaking her head, 'you have a lot to learn about public relations.'

Torquil frowned, stopped pummelling his bag and replied hesitantly, 'I am not with you, Morag. *Public relations?*'

'We are supposed to be creating a warm, friendly atmosphere for the public. We want them to feel at home whenever they come through that door. Instead of which you have made the place smell like a charnel house. It stinks in here, Torquil! It smells so bad that no one will want to spend more than ten seconds in this office. Just what odious mixture are you using in that bag?'

Torquil had initially thought that she was just teasing him, but now he realized that her scowl and her slow advance towards the counter flap meant that she was deadly serious.

Ewan was feeling uncomfortable with the way things were headed so he began edging sideways towards the kitchen, the door of which was lockable.

'It is a special formula prepared by Glen Carscal's of Inverness,' Torquil replied tremulously. 'It doesn't smell too bad, does it? It is mainly beeswax, treacle and lanoline.'

'So no wonder it smells like you are boiling a sheep! Torquil McKinnon, you may be the inspector here, but I am the station sergeant and I do not appreciate you turning my station into a —'

Torquil had stepped back a pace at her continued advance. He was about to remonstrate when the entrance bell rang out and the door opened. A moment later five dogs on leads appeared, closely followed by an old lady dressed in an ill-fitting Panama hat and a cheesecloth frock. A prodigiously big shoulder bag swung hither and thither as she strove to control three chirpy collies and a zestful West Highland terrier, while a restrained and slightly disdainful German shepherd stood dutifully at her side.

'Ah, Sergeant Driscoll, Inspector McKinnon and Constable McPhee,' beamed Annie McConville, a lady of seventy-odd years who was known throughout the Western Isles both for her vague eccentricity and for the dog sanctuary that she ran single-handedly. 'I was wondering —' She stopped abruptly and sniffed several times, her nostrils pinching with obvious distaste. 'Why, whatever is that disgusting smell?'

The three collies began barking in unison., followed a moment later by the Westie and the German shepherd.

'Wheesht, the lot of you,' cried Annie. 'Sheila and Zimba, you two ought to know better! I know it is an awful smell, but —'

'That is just what I was saying, Annie,' said Morag, darting a reproachful look at Torquil, who took it as his cue to beat a hasty retreat into his office.

'And what can I be doing for you?' Morag went on, tearing her gaze from the door that Torquil had left ajar.

'I was just going to ask PC McPhee if anyone had come in wanting to take any of these three beauties off my hands.'

Ewan had already made it to the kitchen door, behind which he vigorously shook his head and pressed his hands together as he looked beseechingly at his sergeant. Annie was well known for her loquaciousness and could, and often did, buttonhole Ewan for ages. Although he had been in the force for five years he had yet to develop the art of deflecting folk. Morag scowled at him, and then turned to Annie with a look of sadness, as if she was the reluctant messenger of bad tidings. 'Not a single offer I am afraid, Annie. You know you could —'

Annie McConville stopped her short as if divining what Morag was about to suggest. 'I could do nothing other than I am already doing! No dog under my care will ever be put down unnecessarily. No, Sheila, Zimba and I will just keep looking after the poor doggies — especially after all they have been through, what with the murder and suicide of their mistress and master.'

'I know that they have been through it, Annie,' said Morag, 'but we can't say that there was any murder involved. At the Fatal Accident Inquiry the sheriff said that culpable homicide of either Esther or Rab was not proven. He felt that it could have been a bizarre suicide pact.'

Annie McConville snorted derisively. 'Well, as good old Sir Walter Scott would have said, if that was the sheriff's decision, it was a "bastard verdict". I think it was otherwise and so does our local newsman, Calum Steele. Rab Noble killed his wife and then committed suicide.'

Morag was about to remonstrate further when the doorbell rang again and the dogs started up a cacophony of barking and howling. Then the door opened and another sprightly seventy-something woman entered the fray. Miss Bella Melville, the retired head teacher of the Kyleshiffin School had taught half of the adult population of the island and was therefore treated with deference by most of the islanders. She was an elegant lady with platinum-coloured hair, dressed in tweeds and a rust-coloured shawl. With her hands sheathed in prim black leather gloves she exuded a no-nonsense persona.

'Morag Driscoll,' she said, above the noise of the barking dogs. 'What exactly is that noxious effluvium? Did you not learn anything about aesthetics in my class?'

Morag had groaned silently upon seeing the apparition of her former teacher advancing towards the counter. She smiled nervously. 'It is the inspector, Miss Melville. He is seasoning his bagpipes on police property!'

She had deliberately raised her voice so that Torquil could hear her. Out of the corner of her eye she saw his office door silently close and she allowed herself a subtle smile. She intended to have further words with him later — after she had got rid of the esteemed head teacher and the equally celebrated dog saviour.

Miss Melville went on severely, 'Will you just tell the inspector that I am not pleased with him? Dereliction of duty might not be too strong a —'

'Excuse me!' snapped Annie McConville, turning squarely to face Bella Melville. 'But I was talking to the sergeant when you butted in.'

Morag took a sharp intake of breath. No one was used to seeing anyone stand up to Miss Bella Melville, but then again, Annie McConville was a law unto herself.

'I am sorry, Annie, I did not realize that —'

'You did not realize what, Bella Melville? That I was standing here talking to the sergeant with my dogs barking louder than the Hound of the Baskervilles?' She shook her head and eyed Miss Melville with an accusatory glare. 'You were just like this — overbearing — when we were in the same class at school.'

Despite herself, Morag let out a half snigger which did not go unnoticed by Bella Melville.

'I was never overbearing, Annie McConville. Why, you were just —'

The doorbell rang again, causing the dogs to raise their barking to another level. The door opened and a striking woman dressed in a pin-striped trouser suit entered. PC Ewan McPhee had just ventured out of the kitchen with a tray of mugs. He spied the new arrival immediately and asked above the protesting dogs, the arguing septuagenarians and his own, by now, fraught sergeant, 'What can I do for you, my bonnie lassie?' Then realizing that he had uttered his thoughts rather than the professional question he had intended, he blushed to the roots of his red hair. 'I mean, what can I do for you, miss?'

She was about twenty-seven, pretty with a tidy nose, hazel eyes and copper Titian locks that tumbled about her shoulders. She smiled at him without any obvious warmth. 'My name is actually Sergeant Golspie,' she said. 'And you must be Constable McPhee.'

Before Ewan could reply she had wrinkled her nose, delightfully wrinkled it, Ewan thought. She glanced at the dogs, and at the arguing women then held up her briefcase and leaned towards Ewan. 'Actually, if you could just let me through to the back office then I would be grateful.' She tapped the briefcase. 'I have something here that I have to give Inspector Torquil McKinnon.'

As Ewan raised the counter flap for her she whispered up to him, 'What is that awful smell, Constable? It isn't a dog smell, but it is quite disgusting.'

'That is just something the inspector is doing, Sergeant,' Ewan explained cryptically. 'You had better come through to the kitchen for a while. I'll take you through to the boss when World War Three out there has finished.'

Five minutes later in Torquil's office, when Morag had managed to persuade Annie McConville, her dogs and Bella Melville to leave, Torquil had a word with Morag. 'What was Bella wanting? I couldn't hear above the noise of those yapping dogs.'

'Your blood, I think,' Morag returned. 'She thinks that you should be doing more to prevent "undesirables" from coming to West Uist.'

'Undesirables? Who does she mean?'

'The flower folk among others. I don't think she appreciates people coming to celebrate at the Hoolish Stones.' She smiled, then told him about the two gorgeous representatives of The Daisy Institute who had accosted her on Harbour Street just a few minutes before. 'They were both good adverts for whatever it is they are studying. I don't think you could call either of them undesirable. I think Miss Melville is just getting even more strait-laced and territorial the older she gets.'

Torquil gave a short laugh. 'Goodness, what does she think we are? Passport controllers?'

Ewan tapped on the door and popped his head round. 'Torquil, I have a Sergeant
Golspie here to see you. She says she has something to give you.'

Torquil laid his bagpipe bag down on his desk and indicated for Ewan to show her in.

'And what can I do for you, Sergeant Golspie?' Torquil asked, rising from his chair as she came in. By his body language Morag could see that Torquil was impressed by the sight of his visitor.

'My name is Lorna Golspie, Inspector,' she said, producing her warrant card with the dexterity of a conjurer. 'I have been seconded to you from Superintendent Lumsden's office.'

Torquil nodded dumbly as Morag introduced herself and invited Lorna to sit down. Ewan had the tea tray at the ready and handed out mugs of his freshly brewed tea.

'I warn you that Ewan likes his tea strong,' said Morag with a grin at the big constable. 'Stewed, even.'

'So, what does the good superintendent want me to see?' Torquil asked cautiously. Indeed, at the mention of the name Lumsden all three members of the West Uist division of the Hebridean Constabulary had felt a tinge of apprehension. It had only been few months earlier that Superintendent Lumsden had been suspended from duty pending an investigation that arose from a case that Torquil had been handling. And some months before that Superintendent Lumsden had himself suspended Torquil during a murder investigation. To say that there was little love lost between them would have been an understatement of the situation. Since the superintendent's reinstatement the week previously, they had been awaiting a first contact.

Lorna Golspie opened her briefcase and drew out a manila envelope. She looked distastefully and suspiciously at the bulging bagpipe bag lying on Torquil's desk like the corpse of some grotesquely skinned animal. 'Do you mean he hasn't discussed this with you in person? I rather assumed that he would have talked it over already.' She shrugged and handed the envelope over. 'His orders are in there.'

It was Torquil's turn to look suspicious. He cast a glance at his two friends then slit the envelope open with his thumb. They watched him read, his eyes slowly widening. He handed the document to Morag, then leaned forward and casually picked up the sheepskin bag which he began kneading between his hands.

'So, you have been seconded to work with us,' he said. 'And I am to show you around the island and give you an area of responsibility, while you conduct an internal audit.'

'I am not sure that I am understanding about an internal audit?' queried Morag, knitting her brow as she reread the superintendent's orders.

The outer doorbell rang out and a moment later the door was pushed open to the sound of two male voices singing merrily away. Then there was a hammering of fists and a slapping of palms on the front counter, followed by the sound of the counter flap being raised and then dropped down as two lots of heavy feet came through.

'Gosh, Ewan McPhee, what are you doing in here drinking tea? We could have been a couple of real desperadoes,' said an extremely large man dressed in yellow waterproofs and heavy seaman's boots, as he unceremoniously barged into the office. A step behind him was a similarly dressed man of equal height and build. Both of them were wearing bobble hats.

'You ought to be having a word with the PC, Torquil,' said the second. 'Discipline, that's what he needs.' He winked at Morag, then seeing Lorna Golspie his face burst into a welcoming grin. 'But I am sorry. We did not realize that you were entertaining.'

Torquil continued to work his bag. 'Sergeant Lorna Golspie,' he introduced, 'Meet Wallace and Douglas Drummond. Our two special constables.'

'We fish for our living,' Wallace, the second of the twins explained.

Lorna gave them a wan smile. 'I think I might have guessed that.'

'The sergeant will be joining us,' Torquil said unenthusiastically. 'Superintendent Lumsden seems to be concerned with the way we run the station here.'

Lorna Golspie coloured slightly as she looked around the office. 'The superintendent has expressed reservations about discipline, procedures and efficiency levels,' she said. 'My orders are to observe and report back to him.'

Douglas Drummond slipped an arm about Morag's shoulders. 'No worries then, eh, folks? We are just one big happy family here.'

Sergeant Lorna Golspie did not seem to be smiling.

At Torquil's behest, Morag took Lorna off for a walkabout tour of Kyleshiffin while he got on with what he claimed to be pressing official business. When they returned at one o'clock they both sniffed upon entering the station, for the odour of Torquil's bagpipe seasoning still hung heavily upon the air. The bag itself was hanging like the corpse of some nondescript animal from a coat-hook inside the rest room, with a spread-out newspaper on the floor beneath to catch any drips of the seasoning fluid.

'The boss is out, Morag,' Ewan called through from the kitchen where he was busily cooking kippers and significantly adding to the aroma.

Throughout the tour Lorna had made intermittent notes in a small notebook, and she added a few more upon entering the rest room.

'The inspector is the piping champion of the Western Isles,' Morag hastily explained, jabbing a finger in the direction of the bag. 'He doesn't usually bring it in here to smell out my station. I expect his uncle has told him not to do it at home.'

Lorna Golspie flicked pages in her notebook. 'That will be his uncle, Lachlan McKinnon. He's a church minister, isn't he?'

Morag nodded. 'He's known as the Padre around here.' She pointed her chin at the book in Lorna's hand. 'How come you have notes about him? Has Superintendent Lumsden given you a rundown on everyone?'

Lorna smiled and snapped the notebook closed. 'Just some useful background.'

Morag eyed her suspiciously for a moment, then, 'Have you made arrangements about staying in Kyleshiffin?'

Lorna nodded. 'Yes, I'm booked into the Commercial Hotel.'

'You won't want to be there too long then,' Morag said. 'They know how to charge at the Commercial.'

'Oh the Force is paying,' Lorna volunteered.

Morag raised her eyebrows. 'Really? Then I guess the superintendent won't plan on this being a long secondment.'

Lorna shrugged noncommittally. 'Actually Morag, there is no time limit on it. I think that is why he wanted Inspector McKinnon to give me an area of responsibility. He sees me being here quite a while.'

'Oh,' Morag returned. 'So tell me, what exactly does —'

The front door had opened and Torquil's voice called through. 'Ewan! Good grief, man, what are you cooking? Morag will go spare when —'

He popped his head round the door and grinned sheepishly when he saw the two sergeants.

'Ah! Ewan just reminded me that it is lunchtime. I hoped you'd be back,' he said. 'I thought I would take our new member of the Force for lunch.' He nodded his head in the direction of the kitchen, where Ewan was tunelessly whistling away as his kippers sizzled in a pan. He crooked his finger at Lorna. 'Come on, Sergeant Golspie; let me take you away from this unwholesome smell.' Then, as he held the door open wide for Lorna Golspie to pass, he added in a hushed tone to Morag, 'See that Ewan opens the windows afterwards, would you, Morag? We can't have the station smelling like a fishmonger's.'

The Bonnie Prince Charlie Tavern on Harbour Street was busy as usual. The aroma of freshly cooked seafood assailed them as soon as Torquil pushed open the door. Mollie McFadden, the doughty landlady and her staff were busy pulling pints of Heather Ale and serving the lunchtime clientele. Mollie blinked myopically at them as they entered and, recognizing Torquil, waved at him.

'Mollie, this is Sergeant Lorna Golspie,' Torquil introduced. 'She is joining us for a while.'

Mollie, a woman in her early sixties, beamed and took Lorna's hand in a firm grip, for her forearm muscles were well built from having pumped a veritable sea of beer over the years. 'Pleased to meet you, Lorna. But aren't you going to get a bit crowded with two sergeants?' Then a suspicious look flashed across her face. 'Don't tell me that Morag Driscoll is leaving us?'

Torquil grinned. 'Nothing like that. Lorna here is — sort of an observer.'

Lorna pursed her lips and smiled at Mollie. 'Well, until I have seen the ropes.' Then she gave Torquil a mock scowl. 'You will be giving me some responsibility, won't you, Inspector?' she added. 'Just like Superintendent Lumsden ordered.'

Torquil held her eyes for a moment then gave a noncommittal smile.

'Maybe the sergeant would like a wee job now then,' Mollie said. And she pointed to the far corner of the bar where a group of men were standing, their voices getting louder and louder. There were about ten of them, a motley group of various ages and builds. Some were dressed in tweeds, others in outdoor working clothes.

'It's the Farmers' Collective Day at the Duncan Institute,' Mollie explained to Lorna. 'The local farmers have a meeting every fortnight and then they lunch either here or at The Bell at the other end of the street. They are usually a noisy crowd but they don't normally cause trouble.'

A heated argument was going on between two men in the middle of the crowd. One was a middle-aged man with a bushy, iron-grey moustache. He was dressed in a tweed suit with a canary-yellow waistcoat and a cravat. The other was a small, portly, bespectacled man in a yellow anorak. The bigger man was prodding him in none-too-friendly a manner.

'Calum has been in for his lunchtime drink as usual,' Mollie went on with a sigh, 'but you know how argumentative he can be. Well, he has seemed to inflame them all against him. Especially, that Tavish McQueen chap.' She leaned closer. 'I think it's something to do with one of his pieces in the *Chronicle*.'

Torquil gave Mollie a long-suffering smile that spoke volumes. He and Calum had been friends all their lives and Torquil had pulled his friend from enough scrapes no longer to be surprised to find him in yet another. If Calum Steele had a talent it was his gift for putting people's backs up. Torquil nodded to Mollie and began moving through the crowded bar.

'You little bugger!' came the voice of the man called McQueen, as he grabbed hold of Calum's anorak. 'You just keep out of my affairs.'

Calum pulled himself up to his full five foot six inches and flicked the man's hands off his anorak.

'I am a journalist and I will not be intimidated. You can just —'

A third man, who looked a younger version of McQueen, except that he was dressed in jeans and a nondescript rugby shirt, cursed and drew back his hand. But before he could bring it forward to strike the *Chronicle* editor, Torquil had grabbed his wrist in a vice-like grip.

'Police!' he snapped. 'Make one move and I'll be booking you folk for causing an affray in public.' He tightened his grip on the man's wrist and turned him round. He looked from him to the older man. 'You're the McQueens, who bought the Hoolish Farm, aren't you? I don't think you've had dealings with the police before,' he said, 'but that could all change.'

'Take your hands off me!' the other growled. He was in his late twenties and clearly had a hot-headed temperament. 'Or do you want me to make you?'

Before he could finish, Lorna had taken his other arm and deftly pinned it behind his
back, exerting enough pressure on his wrist to subdue him. 'Shall I cuff him, Inspector?' The crowd of farmers began shuffling back.

'You take your hands off my son right away, or I'll be having words with my solicitor,' said the older McQueen.

Torquil eyed the man sternly, then a thin smile passed over his lips. 'You may need to if I book you.' Then, to the son, 'Brawling in public is not tolerated on West Uist. Do I make myself clear?'

The other gave a grudging nod.

'Do you want to press charges on these men, Calum?'

Calum grunted and shook his head. 'Don't waste your time, Torquil. Just throw them out. The press will not be intimidated and it does not need the help of the police.'

491

Torquil nodded to Lorna and released his own grip. 'You heard the man. Now off with the pair of you. Take this as a warning.'

The older McQueen's face had turned puce and he took a pace forward, only to be stopped by a touch on his arm from another man with short cropped hair and a slightly cauliflower ear. 'I think you ought to leave it, Tavish. Why don't we all go along to The Bell?'

There were murmurings of agreement from the rest of the group.

'I'll remember you,' Tavish McQueen said angrily to Torquil. 'You had no call to interfere with us. We were just warning this little pipsqueak. I may take this further.'

But his companions started to move him through the crowded bar, which opened up before them.

'Thanks for that, Torquil,' Calum said, his voice seeming for the first time slightly slurred. He stared quizzically at Lorna.

'Calum, meet Sergeant Lorna Golspie. She's joining us as an observer for a while.'

'An observer?' Calum repeated incredulously. 'If what she did to that gorilla was observation I'd hate to see what she does when she gets started.'

He raised his hand to attract Mollie McFadden's attention. 'But for now let me buy you both a drink. What will it be, Heather Ale as usual for you, Torquil? And what about the sergeant?'

Torquil caught Lorna's questioning look and shook his head emphatically. 'We're on duty, Calum my man. We're just here for a spot of lunch.' He smiled at Lorna. 'I suggest you try the local mussels and wash it down with some of Mollie's homemade lemonade. It is the best in the islands.'

Calum winked at Mollie. 'You heard the inspector, Mollie. Make that two lemonades for the police people, a pint of Heather Ale for me — and a whisky chaser.'

'Are you going to tell me what that was all about?' Torquil queried, after he had given their orders for food.

The *Chronicle* editor shook his head and tapped the side of his nose. 'Just newspaper business. Nothing for you to worry about.'

Torquil nodded, having half expected some such response. He was all too aware that his old friend liked to play his cards close to his chest.

A few moments later with their drinks in their hands, they chinked glasses.

'Cheers,' said Lorna.

'*Slainte mhath*,' said Torquil, 'Good health.'

He winked at Calum Steele. He had a feeling that he would have to watch Lorna Golspie pretty closely.

CHAPTER TWO

The Reverend Lachlan McKinnon, known throughout West Uist as the Padre, crunched his way down the gravel path from the manse with his golf clubs slung over his shoulder. He had spent a couple of hours writing a sermon and planned to pop into the church to have his morning conversation with the Lord before meeting Finlay MacNeil, the Black House Museum curator, for their usual nine holes.

The Padre was a good-humoured man of sixty-four years with the ruddy cheeks of the outer islander, a pair of thick horn-rimmed spectacles perched on his hawk-like nose and a veritable mane of silver hair that perpetually defied brush or comb. As usual, he was wearing his clerical dog collar and a West Uist tweed jacket, his usual wear for both pastoral care and the golf course. He pushed open the iron gate and stopped a moment to light his briar pipe before striding along the metalled road to St Ninian's Church, a walk of a couple of minutes. There he propped his bag up in the porch, tapped his pipe out on his heel then let himself into the church.

A solitary figure in a white hoodie was sitting in the first pew, head bent as if in prayer. The Padre walked silently up the aisle and nodded at a pretty blonde-haired young woman who looked up sharply as he stopped to genuflect before the altar.

'I ... I am sorry, sir. I did not mean to trespass on your church,' she said tremulously, in a voice so devoid of an accent that the Padre suspected she was from one of the Scandinavian countries.

He put up a restraining hand as she shot to her feet. 'Everyone is welcome in the Lord's house. Please, carry on with your prayers or your meditation.' He smiled as he pointed to the flower logo on her hoodie. 'You're from The Daisy Institute, I perceive.'

She returned his smile. 'I am one of the acolytes. I am Johanna Waltari, from Helsinki in Finland.' She pointed to the altar with its wooden cross and the large stained-glass window behind it depicting St Ninian. 'I love your church, Father. It is simpler than the ones we have at home. It is good for sitting and talking to God.'

'That is just what I think, Johanna,' he returned, extending his hand. 'My name is Lachlan McKinnon, but folk round here call me the Padre. I like to think that the Lord enjoys coming to simple places like this.' He grinned then added with a merry twinkle in his eye, 'I am sure he needs a rest from cathedrals sometimes.'

Johanna giggled at his joke, immediately warming to him. She pointed to the ancient stone with its peculiar ancient markings that stood behind the baptismal font. 'It seems old, this church of yours. But I think that stone is older.'

'Aye, you would be right there, Johanna. The church was built in the eighth century, but the stone was here long before that. They just built the church around it. It was a common enough practice to build churches on top of old pagan sites. We call this one *Eilthireach*, the Pilgrim Stone.'

Johanna rose and crossed to the large obelisk-like stone which stood ten feet tall. It was covered in ancient carvings; a mix of curls, wavy lines, straight lines and with one or two carvings suggestive of human forms.

'The markings look like runes,' she said, running a finger over the surface. 'We have many of them in Scandinavia. Our founder and president, Dr Logan Burns, is an expert on all sorts of ancient religious writings. He tells us that many of the standing stones in the Hebrides are covered in a type of script that is older than runic or Ogham.'

'I have heard that he is some sort of an expert,' Lachlan returned. He pursed his lips thoughtfully. 'But as to exactly what language they are written in, I don't know if we will ever find out. Many a scholar has studied them and failed to come to a conclusion.'

Johanna seemed about to say something then thought otherwise. She pushed her hoodie back and shook her head to let her blonde hair escape. She ran a hand through her hair and smiled. 'Well, I had better get back. I have duties to perform and I am behind schedule. I have to take a class with some of our newest inceptors.'

Lachlan's eyes narrowed and it seemed as if he was about to say something before thinking otherwise. And indeed, it troubled him that The Daisy Institute had recruited several islanders over the last few months, much to the distress of several of his parishioners, for they had not seen their families since.

'I think I know what you were thinking, Padre,' Johanna said. 'You're concerned about the institute's policy of seclusion for three months.'

Lachlan gave a short laugh. 'Do they teach you to be mind-readers at the institute? Actually, you are quite right, Johanna, I was. It seems ... over-strict to me.'

She smiled. 'It is time for contemplation, that is all. Three months of intense meditation and contemplation on the wonders of the universe. It makes you find joy. Real joy.' She laughed, a spontaneous ripple of pleasure that seemed to bubble up from within. 'That is why we are all so happy. Logan Burns is a genius, Padre. A genius.' She shook hands and left quietly.

The Padre bit his lip. 'It seems a bit more like brainwashing to me,' he said worriedly. And he was not so sure that she really did feel as joyful as she suggested. He had the distinct impression that she had been crying when he came in.

Two hours later the Padre was on the ten-acre plot of undulating dunes and machair that he and several other local worthies had years before transformed into the St Ninian's Golf Course. Using the natural lie of the land they had constructed six holes with billiard smooth greens surrounded by barbed wire squares to keep the sheep off, in contrast to the coarse grass fairways where they were allowed to graze freely. Each hole had three separate tee positions, each one giving its route to the hole a special name in both English and Gaelic, thereby allowing players the choice of playing a conventional eighteen holes or any combination. The Padre was proud of telling people that while it was not exactly St Andrews, it was a good test of golf.

'Good shot!' he cried, as he watched Finlay MacNeil's tee-shot on the long eighth hole. The ball started left, heading towards the gorse bushes that abutted the fairway then gradually faded back into the fairway to roll on to about 250 yards. 'And that is despite the atrocious noise that new-fangled travesty of a club makes. It sounds as if you are hitting the ball with a tin can.'

Finlay MacNeil, the Black House Museum curator and an old golfing buddy of the Padre's, shook his head. He was a stocky little fellow with pebble-thick spectacles and a small goatee beard, minus the moustache. His cheeks had a network of dilated blood vessels that betokened a bucolic nature. 'Ach, Lachlan, old-fashioned you are. You must be about the only single-figure handicapper in the islands who still plays with woods. One day we shall drag you into the twenty-first century.'

'I will be kicking when you do,' returned Lachlan, bending to push a tee peg into the turf and balance his ball on top. He straightened up. Then, mentally selecting a spot on the fairway to aim his shot, he took a couple of practice swings before setting up over the ball. He swung freely and effortlessly. There was a satisfying click of wood on the ball and he held his follow-through as he watched the ball start right then draw back to bounce a yard ahead of Finlay's ball and then bob and roll along the fairway for another thirty yards.

'And another fine shot to you, Lachlan,' said Finlay. 'You should be on the green in two with a chance of an eagle. A birdie at the least.'

'Which I will be needing the way you are playing,' replied Lachlan, as he stowed his trusty old two-wood into his bag and pulled out his pipe. He struck a match to it and puffed it into action.

He waited while Finlay put the finishing touches to a roll-up cigarette and snapped a Zippo lighter into flame to light it. Then they walked on together, waving to another two-ball on the adjoining fairway.

'So tell me how are things going with your book?' Lachlan asked.

Finlay exhaled a stream of smoke then stopped with a scowl and reached into his pocket and drew out a hip flask. It was the fourth time that it had appeared during the round and he proffered it to Lachlan, who refused, since he restricted himself to a single dram during the course of a round, and that preferably well into the second nine. Finlay shrugged his shoulders and took a hefty swig.

'It was going well enough for a few weeks, but I have hit a block.'

'Writer's block?'

'You could say that. But really, it is more to do with this bloody Logan Burns and his Daisy people.'

Before Lachlan could say anything the museum curator had stomped off to his ball, grabbed a five-wood from his bag, then without a practice swing thrashed at the ball. The result was almost inevitable. He scuffed the ball off the heel of the club and it shot off diagonally to the left, sliding a mere twenty yards through the grass to come to rest at the foot of a standing stone that rose out of the rough and gave the hole its name of *Carragh*, the Pillar.

'*Luinnseach mhor,*' Finlay cursed. 'Clumsy lump that I am!' He shoved the five-wood back in the bag and strode on to check his lie. 'And now I will have to hit it sideways, back into play.' He pulled out a pitching wedge and chipped the ball back into the fairway.

Lachlan waited until he played his next shot on to the edge of the green, before taking a mid-iron himself and popping a shot into the heart of the green.

'Do you see what I mean, Lachlan?' Finlay said, as they walked up to the green and climbed over the barbed wire to reach the putting surface. 'That is my block. I get so cross at the garbage that man is peddling, it even unsettles my golf swing!'

'Peddling garbage about religion, do you mean?' Lachlan ventured. He thought about the young woman, Johanna Waltari that he had met that morning.

Finlay had pulled out his putter and was lining up his long put while Lachlan walked to the hole and attended the pin.

'No. It is the rubbish he talks about the Hoolish Stones and the inscriptions. It is all New Age nonsense in disguise and is no help to serious researchers like myself. And as for all this media attention that he has brought to the island!'

He putted and the ball rolled up to a couple of feet.

Lachlan bent and picked up the ball and tossed it back. 'Give you that putt,' he announced magnanimously. 'But he has certainly not had an easy press from Calum Steele in the *West Uist Chronicle*.'

'That was a wee bit generous with that putt, but it is only a six at that.' Finlay reached for his hip flask and took a swift nip. 'No, you are right there. For once Calum Steele has got it right. But it wasn't the local press I was talking about; it was this Scottish TV coverage that he is getting each night.'

'Ah!' Lachlan said in understanding. He lined up his own putt and smoothly stroked the ball to the hole, where it fell in with a welcome tinkle. He walked over to retrieve it and replaced the flag in the hole. 'But Calum is not giving the television programme much praise either.'

Finlay shrugged. 'I saw him the other day and from what I can gather that's personal. He doesn't care for the broadcast journalist. Anyway, he's a local man and he doesn't like people capitalizing on our Hoolish Stones, whatever the inscriptions are about.'

They walked on to the next tee. As they did so, Lachlan looked into the distance where he could just see the tops of the megalithic Hoolish Stones. Strange, he thought, how much of an enigma they had proved over the years. And equally puzzling was the fact that those strange carvings seemed to stir strong passions within people.

Calum Steele had left the Bonnie Prince Charlie a little after three o'clock; after he had partaken of another couple of pints of Heather Ale with Glen Corlin chasers to calm his temper down.

'Those bloody *teuchters*! I will show them,' he muttered to himself, as he walked to the *Chronicle* offices. 'The cheek that they have, accusing me of interfering with them. Well no one interferes with the *Chronicle*. Wait till I get to the newspaper offices.'

In fact, 'newspaper offices' was a somewhat grandiloquent title, for although there was a large printed sign attached to the wall beside the door, the newspaper offices consisted of two floors, both of which were exclusively used by Calum. The actual news office itself where Calum interviewed people and took orders for photographs which appeared in the paper, occupied the first room on the ground floor, with the archives of back issues in the room at the back. Upstairs was where the actual work took place. At the front was the room with a cluttered old oak desk where he wrote his articles and columns on a vintage Mackintosh computer or on his spanking new laptop. Sitting between the two computers was a dusty old Remington typewriter, which served no real purpose other than to help him feel the part of a writer. The rest of the room was occupied with his digital printing press, paper and stationary supplies, and in the corner was the space where he stacked the next issue of the newspaper ready for distribution. Across the landing was a larger room which had been divided up to form kitchenette, a shower, a toilet, and a room containing a battered old settee and a camp bed, which Calum used when he was either working late, or when he felt too inebriated to return home. As the editor, printer and sole reporter of the paper he worked flexible hours, his only rule being that however he managed it he would produce a paper every Tuesday and Friday. Sometimes he even produced extra editions, which he called 'specials' when there was something of significant newsworthiness that he felt the good folk of West Uist needed to know about. With the interest generated in the summer solstice and the population of the island suddenly swelled with holidaymakers and solstice-followers he had effectively been producing a daily *Chronicle* for the past fortnight.

Such was the popularity of the paper, albeit that at times it was merely a gossip press and a local advertiser, that not only did it generate enough money to fund itself, but it paid him a weekly wage, and sometimes also paid for an assistant. More than that, over the years his pieces had often been taken up by the mainland newspapers, and on occasion he had been commissioned to report on news items for Scottish TV.

And that had been a bone of contention with him lately, especially since it involved a matter of the heart. The fact was that Calum had been infatuated with Kirstie Macroon, the pretty, large-breasted Scottish TV newsreader and anchorperson. His occasional contacts with her by telephone, when she had interviewed him for some of the more sensational stories that he had covered, had led him to believe that he might have stood a chance of asking her out. And one day he had actually telephoned to ask her, only to learn as he stood, with the telephone in hand, that she was engaged. Worse, she was engaged to an irritatingly handsome and affable television reporter called Finbar Donleavy, with whom Calum had a run in before he had known about the engagement.

Finbar and a cameraman had been sent to West Uist to do a regular feature on The Daisy Institute in the week running up to the summer solstice, to be slotted into the daily Scottish TV six o'clock news bulletin. Grudgingly, Calum had to admit that Finbar, a dark-haired Irish demi-god from Dublin, who had clearly kissed the Blarney Stone, was a good reporter. He had seen him before and marvelled at his knack for smilingly lulling interviewees into a feeling of false security before screwing them down with what seemed to be a barrage of innocent questions, but which were indeed extremely penetrating. On more than one occasion he had thus exposed a shady character.

'Bugger him!' Calum often found himself saying whenever he came to mind. And that was a more regular occurrence than he would have liked, since he always saw him on the six o'clock news, as well as when he bumped into him and his pint-sized peroxide-blond cameraman, who all too clearly hailed from the London area. Somewhat maliciously, Calum had nicknamed them as *Ebony and Ivory, the piano-men* in one of his review articles on the Scottish TV programmes.

Calum mounted the stairs two at a time and went straight to the toilet to relieve his bladder from the diuretic effect of the Heather Ale and Glen Corlin chasers. Then he brushed his teeth, tossed off his anorak, tumbled into the camp bed and closed his eyes.

'Time for a think, Calum, lad,' he said, as he swiftly sank into one of his bleary moments before sleep arrived. He firmly believed this state was when he composed his best pieces, when his unconscious mind assembled the information in readiness for his conscious self to dredge it back in a vague semblance of order upon waking.

He had dropped into a doze and was enjoying the hinterland between sleep and wakefulness when he became dimly aware of a strange warbling note from somewhere close by.

'Bloody phone!' he groaned, mechanically reaching for the receiver and pulling it up to his ear. *'West Uist Chronicle.* Steele here. What can I do —?'

'You bloody little guttersnipe! Mind your own business or — you — will — be —' Calum's eyes blinked and he shot up, immediately aware that he was not dreaming. He was listening to an obviously disguised voice that was slowly and emphatically enunciating a threat.

'— a — dead — man. Butt out!'

There was a click as the phone was put down. Calum unconsciously ran the back of his hand across his brow, all too conscious of the film of perspiration that had suddenly appeared.

He cursed himself for not having a recorder attached to the phone. 'Who on earth was that? Surely not those *teuchters* in the pub. They wouldn't be so stupid, would they?' And, as he thought about the threat as his mind began to climb further into wakefulness, a slow smile spread across his face, despite the cold sweat that had moments before engulfed him.

'So it's death threats I am getting, is it?' he mused to himself. 'Well, whoever you are you can just bugger off. I am a newspaperman,' he said proudly. He opened a cupboard and took out a can of lager. He tugged the ring-pull in a defiant mood and took a hefty swig. 'The editor of the *West Uist Chronicle* will not be intimidated. Whoever you are.'

Logan Burns could never have been accused of being camera-shy. Conscious of his good looks ever since the first stirrings of adolescence, he had capitalized on his ability to charm and captivate members of both sexes. As a young divinity student in Glasgow, then years later as a researcher for an evangelical preacher in the USA, he had realized that people were fascinated by spirituality. After flirtations with Zen Buddhism in Japan, time in an ashram in Southern India and a gruelling four years writing up his Ph.D. at one of the minor American universities, he set off on what he believed was his life's work by setting up the DSY Institute.

He had always been careful to adopt the right image for the time. Part of him relished the role he had adopted as a cultural chameleon. Still a handsome man in his mid-forties, with a full head of distinguished-looking salt and pepper hair, a clean-shaven lantern jaw and a trim waist, he exuded the air of a man who had studied the world's mysteries and now felt at peace with himself. The silver, wire-framed spectacles that he wore perched halfway down his nose when reading lent him the intellectual air which was exactly the image he felt was needed as the director of the quasi-academic institute. In his yellow hoodie he looked like a slightly eccentric yet laid-back professor.

'Could we just do a sound check, Logan?' Finbar Donleavy asked, nodding to Danny Wade, his diminutive cameraman.

Logan winked at the two white hoodie-clad young acolytes, Peter Severn and Henrietta Appleyard, who were standing on either side of the central chambered cairn at the centre of the towering Hoolish Stones. 'Anything you want, Finbar. The three of us will just chat away about the nature of life.'

And although he sounded as if he was teasing, The Daisy Institute director began giving a mini-lecture on the tenets of Jainism.

'That's spot on, Finbar,' said Danny Wade, as he checked his sound meter. 'The wind is no problem at the moment and we can start shooting whenever you are ready.'

Logan pulled up the hood of his yellow hoodie. 'Good. But, Finbar, before we start I suggest that you take a shot of us with our heads dipped, as if in contemplation. Peter and Henrietta can do a Gregorian chant and then you can count me in. I will slowly lift my head and pull back my hood while you hone in on me.' He smiled. 'Then I will do my preliminary spiel.'

Finbar suppressed a grin. Logan Burns was as polished a performer as any of the actors, politicians and celebrities he had worked with over the years, yet he thought that there was something of the snake-oil salesman about him. They had filmed every evening for the past four days in the run-up to the summer solstice, each occupying a mere four minutes. So far they had gone out completely unedited, and most of them had been stage-managed by Logan Burns himself. Other reporters might have been resentful of that, but Finbar believed it was always best to give someone a lot of rope. If they wanted to hang themselves that was their affair.

And so, having agreed upon the introduction, they began filming.

Danny Wade was equally used to working with all sorts and had formed a similar opinion of The Daisy Institute director. He focused on the job in hand, sure in the knowledge that if he was a con-merchant, Finbar would find the weakness and hang him out to dry live on Scottish Television.

Torquil arrived home at the manse earlier than usual to find his uncle wiping his hands on an apron, having just replaced a simmering casserole in the oven of the Aga.

'Rabbit stew and dumplings followed by apple pie,' the Padre volunteered in answer to Torquil's unspoken question. Then, 'Time for a dram?'

They passed through the hall where carburettors and various motorcycle parts lay on spread-out newspapers along the wall, testimony to their mutual interest in renovating classic motorcycles. The two men had lived in the manse ever since Torquil's parents, Lachlan's brother and his wife, had died in a boating accident when Torquil was a youngster. Torquil had grown up under Lachlan McKinnon's guardianship, inevitably absorbing and sharing interests, such as the bagpipes, golf, classic motorcycles and politics. Over the years there had been two or three housekeepers, but none had stayed for long, either because they could not put up with the staunch masculinity of the manse, or because they just could not impose order amid the eccentric clutter of books, motorcycle parts or stray golf clubs and bagpipe chanters that somehow seemed to explode into every room.

The Padre poured a couple of drams and added water to two glasses while Torquil switched on the television before slumping into one of the armchairs.

'Tough day, laddie?'

Torquil grimaced, and then told his uncle about the coming of Sergeant Lorna Golspie. He smiled wryly. 'You could never accuse Superintendent Lumsden of subtlety.'

Lachlan nodded sagely. 'You're thinking that he blames you for his suspension. And if that is so then it is possible that this Lorna Golspie has been sent to spy on you. What is she like?'

Torquil pursed his lips in thought. 'I have to admit she is dynamic enough.' And he described the speed with which she had restrained one of Calum's interlocutors at the Bonnie Prince Charlie.

'Is she pretty?'

Torquil frowned. 'As a matter of fact she is, but that is hardly relevant, is it? I mean, she is just a colleague.'

Lachlan grinned. 'Just teasing, laddie. And that is the right answer, of course. It shows that you are not going to be taken in by a bonnie lassie.' The musical jingle of Scottish TV's *Six*

O'Clock News diverted their attention towards the television. Kirstie Macroon's familiar silky voice read out the headlines in neat staccato sound bites:

'ANOTHER SCOTTISH MINISTER ADMITS THAT HE SMOKED CANNABIS.'

'MORE TROUBLE OVER SUNDAY FERRIES TO THE HEBRIDES.'

The inter-slot jingle sounded, then:

'But first we go to West Uist for our usual look at the run-up to the summer solstice. We have an interview with Logan Burns of The Daisy Institute at the famous Hoolish Stones. Over to Finbar Donleavy —'

The link went like clockwork. The sound of seagulls and a light breeze merged into a melodic chant as the picture changed to give a distant shot of the Hoolish Stones. The shot then panned into the circle of megalithic standing stones arranged in three perfectly concentric rings and what seemed to be an aisle up the middle. Three hooded figures, two white ones flanking a taller one in yellow, were standing behind a central chambered cairn and before a towering column which was covered in weird carvings. All three had their heads bowed and two were chanting.

Then Finbar Donleavy's pleasant Irish brogue broke in as a voice-over.

'The Hoolish Stones. Possibly older than Stonehenge itself are the scene for tonight's coverage of The Daisy Institute. This evening we have come to the ancient stone circle where, in a few days, we shall see how Bronze Age folk used these stones, just as they did other rings like Stonehenge, to celebrate the summer solstice.'

The crescendo of chanting stopped abruptly as the view homed in on the central yellow-hooded figure. Very

508

deliberately, Logan Burns raised a hand and pulled back his hood to reveal his distinguished mane of hair.

The shot panned out slightly and Finbar stepped forward with a microphone in his hand. 'And this evening,' Finbar continued, 'we have the director of The Daisy Institute himself, Dr Logan Burns. Good evening, Dr Burns.'

Logan Burns's lips moved in the subtlest of smiles and he nodded, much as one might have expected from a medieval abbot. Then he spoke. 'I prefer to be called simply, Logan.'

'OK, Logan it is,' Finbar said, returning the smile. He turned to the camera and continued, 'We are at the very centre of the Hoolish Stones with its chambered cairn here before us and the famous Runic Stone behind us.' He inclined the microphone slightly towards Logan Burns. 'These strange carvings have been here for centuries, haven't they, Logan? Can you tell us something about them?'

Logan Burns nodded, like a professor acknowledging his introduction. He looked directly into the camera, as if aware that he was peering into innumerable television sets across the islands and the mainland. 'Yes indeed, Finbar. These are ancient carvings, similar to scores of other ones that I have studied around the world. I should say in beginning that I have a doctorate in epigraphy and am considered one of the world's foremost experts on ancient inscriptions.' He turned and ran a finger over a carved whorl. 'Beautiful, are they not?' he said, as if overcome by the beauty of the markings. 'Some academics, misguidedly and naively, believe these to be runic in origin.'

Finbar nodded. 'I believe it is called the Runic Stone. As I understand it, that implies a Viking origin?'

Logan smiled enigmatically. 'Others would have us believe that they are Ogham scripts.'

'Could you explain that, Logan?'

'Ogham is basically tree language. Some call it Celtic Tree language. It is another ancient script, but whereas runes represent a definite language of symbols, Ogham is made up of notches, coming off an edge or off an axis. It was originally used on wood, on trees, so you can see one simple flaw in that hypothesis straight away.'

'And what is that?' Finbar asked, with a quizzically raised eyebrow.

'West Uist has practically no trees.'

'So what does this all mean?'

Logan Burns again peered directly at the camera, directing himself to the viewers rather than the reporter beside him. 'I believe that these carvings are far older than either Runic or Ogham script. Indeed, I think there is good evidence that the Runic and Ogham are derived from these, rather than the other way around.'

'I am afraid I do not follow.'

Logan Burns smiled, like a benevolent schoolmaster explaining to a bright pupil.

'The usual thinking is that Runic and Ogham scripts were brought west by invaders from Scandinavia. I think the reverse may have happened. People from here travelled east, taking with them this proto-Runic or proto-Ogham writing.'

'But surely that can't be right!' Finbar exclaimed. 'Are you seriously suggesting that people from West Uist invaded Scandinavia?'

Again Logan Burns smiled. 'I didn't say invaders. No, that would hardly be the case, for a small island like this would not have been the home of a great warrior people. The population would never have been large. But travellers, possibly priests and scholars could have left here carrying knowledge. Ancient knowledge.'

Finbar knotted his brows. 'Ancient knowledge, you mean as in knowledge from an ancient civilization?'

'Exactly. And I refer to the lost continent of Atlantis. My researches have revealed that these stones form a direct link to Atlantis.' Before Finbar could interject, Logan Burns had returned to the Runic Stone and pointed out several carvings. 'These markings are remarkably similar to some of the ancient carvings that come from the Mayans of South America. They also look similar to the pre-cuneiform script of the Sumerians and some of the very earliest Egyptian hieroglyphics.'

'But you said Atlantis. Surely that is just a myth?'

Logan Burns looked at his two companions who both smiled knowingly for the camera, as if all three were aware of a great secret.

'Atlantis is no myth,' Logan replied at last. 'It is well established that before the great natural disaster that destroyed it, priests were sent out to all corners of the earth to establish sun and moon temples.'

Finbar nodded his head, yet did not look convinced. 'And do these barely discernible markings make any sense?'

Logan Burns smiled knowingly. 'Oh, I have a very good idea what they mean. As I said, I have studied inscriptions from all over the world and I have gone further than any previous scholar in understanding the origins of writing. Here we have a direct link to Atlantis, just as the ancient civilizations of Mu and Lemuria are linked to the civilizations that they spawned in China and India. Many of the major religions and philosophies in the world can be traced back to them, which partly explains The Daisy Institute's purpose. And these great peoples were all highly skilled in astronomy and astrology, which is why the solstices are so important.'

'And?' Finbar asked, hopefully. Although looking unconvinced, he certainly was at least intrigued.

'And it is too early to reveal all,' Logan Burns replied, pulling up his hood. 'But as we approach the great summer solstice, it will become clear.' He nodded to Peter and Henrietta, his white hoodie-clad companions and all three turned and walked past the Runic Stone up the aisle of stones.

'All very exciting,' said Finbar Donleavy to the camera. 'Perhaps we will indeed learn more as we approach the summer solstice. This is Finbar Donleavy bidding you goodnight from the Hoolish Stones in West Uist.'

The picture shifted to Kirstie Macroon in the Scottish TV studio as she did a link with the story about the Sunday ferries debate.

'All bonnie-looking folk,' the Padre remarked, as he drained his whisky and rose to his feet.

'Aye, I suspect that young blond-haired fellow is the one that Morag was going on about this morning,' Torquil said. 'Fair smitten with the young man she was.' He grinned as he finished his own whisky. 'Which is more than she was with Sergeant Lorna Golspie. There could be friction there, I'm thinking.'

Lachlan McKinnon clicked his tongue.

'Just as I am thinking there will be between Finlay MacNeil and that Logan Burns. Finlay is not at all happy with all the publicity that The Daisy Institute people are getting. He is feeling pretty territorial over the Hoolish Stones.'

Torquil followed him through to the kitchen. The aroma of rabbit stew was starting to stir up his gastric juices. 'It is to be hoped that he wasn't watching the news, just now.'

Finlay MacNeil had indeed been watching the news. After leaving the golf course he had gone back to the Black House Museum which stood on one side of a narrow metalled road about quarter of a mile off the coastal road from Kyleshiffin, with a fine view overlooking Loch Hynish. Beyond it was moorland leading to the clifftops. It was typical of the traditional dwelling of the islands and was at least 400 years old. Chimneyless, with a peat fire smouldering continuously through a central hole in the roof, it had in days gone by been home to generations of families and their livestock. Finlay had lovingly cared for it for twenty years as the island's museum curator. In the holiday season it had a fair amount of trade, and in the less clement months he was frequently visited by scholars, students and researchers. He had put the finishing touches to a small exhibition he was working on, then retired to his own home, a modern log cabin on the other side of the lane. While he waited for a pan of potato broth to heat up he had sat nursing his umpteenth whisky of the day as he stood watching his ancient black and white television.

'Bloody charlatan! You have no idea what the stones say — you and your New Age nonsense about Atlantis and Lemuria.'

Then his hand fell on his diary that he had left on the arm of the chair and he felt the usual old surges of guilt. Then his temper boiled furiously, just as his broth bubbled over the hob to make a sizzling noise that he barely noticed. 'I'll teach you, you — bugger!'

Ever since The Daisy Institute had taken over Dunshiffin Castle only one television set was allowed for the inceptors and acolytes. It was a pitifully small second-hand set that looked ridiculous in the great hall in which it had been installed atop a cheap set of stepladders.

And that was precisely how it was intended, for it was only switched on for the news bulletins, and only then because of the exposure that the institute was receiving. For many of the new inceptors it was the only sight they were permitted of the outside world during their period of three months' contemplation.

There were about thirty people in the room, all wearing the same style of hoodies. Two wore yellow ones, ten wore white and the rest pale-pink. The pink ones, supposedly representing the pale-pink tips of the petals of a daisy, represented the inceptors, the students of the institute. Everyone watched The Daisy Institute slot at the Hoolish Stones with evident interest.

There was much muttering around the hall. Mainly the mutters were of approval and awe. Veneration even.

Yet one person seethed with internal, well-disguised rage. The unspoken thoughts were anything but full of approval.

You lying, sanctimonious bastard! I would start counting my time, if I were you.

CHAPTER THREE

Finlay MacNeil woke at half past four in the morning, his habitual time to return to consciousness as the paradoxical action of his whisky-drinking kicked in. Dehydrated, with his tongue stuck to the roof of his mouth, yet with a full bladder that felt as if it could burst, he cursed his dependence on the *uisge beatha*, the so-called water of life. His head began to pound as he flung back his quilt and he began his habitual mantra 'never ever, never again', as he sat for a moment on the edge of the bed mentally reviewing his actions of the day before to ensure that he had done nothing too embarrassing. He spied his diary on his bedside table and flicked through it to his habitual last entry of the day. As usual, the handwriting showed the cumulative effects of his daily intake of alcohol. He ran a finger down the page, using his notes as a memory prompt to recall what had happened. He sighed with relief when he got to the end, and then absently let the pages flick backwards, his sore dry eyes threatening to produce tears.

And then with a tide of self-loathing he lay the diary down and sighed deeply.

'You bloody old fool!' he said, cudgelling the sides of his head with his knuckles. 'Guilty you are feeling, and guilty you should be for having no gumption.'

Padding barefoot to the bathroom, he relieved himself then sluiced cold water from the sink into his face. He poured water into his toothbrush glass and went through to the spartan sitting-room with his desk in the writing recess. He sipped the water then immediately gagged, as the taste of old toothpaste in the bottom burned the back of his throat. He dropped into the chair and eyed the ashtray on top of the desk with several stubbed out roll-ups and his tobacco pouch lying beside it. Inside it was half an ounce of Golden Virginia and a small packet containing the same amount of cannabis. He winced at his own weakness for the weed, and deliberately shifted his attention to the quarter-full bottle of malt whisky and the empty glass beside it.

'Ach, what the hell!' he said, grabbing the bottle and pulling out the cork to pour a finger in the whisky glass. 'A hair of the dog never hurt anyone. Better than the weed at this time of the morning.'

He swallowed it in one, relishing the liquid as it went down with an altogether more pleasant fiery sensation than the old toothpaste. He pressed the empty glass to his forehead and within seconds the pounding stopped. And as it stopped so did the self-loathing for his own weakness. Yet he was still angry.

The sun had already risen and rays were streaming through the gap in his curtains.

'It will be the solstice in a few days,' he mused. His glance fell on the piles of papers on his desk, on the half-open books and the screeds of handwritten notes he had made as he prepared the next chapter of his next book, entitled *The Hoolish Stones — the most westerly stone circle*. His computer stood on a neighbouring table, a fine patina of dust covering it, for he only used it once he had drafted the entire manuscript of whatever book he was working on. He had written thirty-two books so far, mainly small monographs for a quasi-academic publisher who specialized in archaeology, history and rural crafts. His work barely kept him in whisky, yet it helped to satisfy his literary aspirations and his belief in himself as a local scholar.

He was proud of the introductory chapter on *The Archaeo-astronomy of the Hoolish Stones*, and of the chapter he was

516

currently working on, *The Ancient Stone Carvers of West Uist*. He believed the book to be a valid and well-researched piece of work that made a genuine contribution to the enigma of the Hoolish Stones and the scattered monoliths that dotted the island. Just thinking about it made his ire rise again as he thought back to the previous evening's news programme with The Daisy Institute slot.

'I wonder what garbage that charlatan will be peddling to folk today.' And with a sudden snort of disdain he snapped the glass on the desk, tightened the cord on his dressing gown and went through to shave and dress. 'He pretends to be an expert. Well, maybe I'll just put him to the test.'

Pug Cruikshank was also an early morning riser. As a farmer he had little choice. He never needed an alarm, being used to waking at about five o'clock. Breakfast was usually limited to a couple of roll-ups and a jug of thick black coffee while he listened to *The Farming Programme*. Then it was out to the milking parlour by six, by which time his brother Wilfred would have herded the cattle into the collecting yard and started milking their small dairy herd of thirty Ayrshires, which had been swelled to fifty since they had bought Rab Noble's herd after the tragedy.

No one on the island, except for his brother, knew exactly why he was called Pug, although most folk assumed that it had something to do with being pugnacious. Indeed, pugnacious summed him up. He was a big unattractive man with a cauliflower ear and the physique of a light-heavyweight boxer, which in fact was what he had been in his youth before he opened a small debt-collecting business in Glasgow, prior to moving with his brother to West Uist to look after the farm when his uncle died two years previously. It had been a return to the life he had been brought up to in his native Galloway, where his father had been a tenant on a 200-acre dairy farm.

He crossed the yard into the parlour and glowered at Wilfred, his younger brother by five years. In many ways Wilfred was just a slightly smaller version of Pug, except that he had two missing front teeth, a legacy of arguing with Pug when they had been teenagers. From that day onwards, Wilfred, lacking in guile and cowed by his elder brother, had done virtually everything Pug had asked of him. He had enjoyed the physical aspects of the particular method of debt collecting that they had used in Glasgow.

'You still angry at that newsman, Pug?' Wilfred asked, as he attached the cluster, the four-cup unit, to the teats of one of the six Ayrshires that stood in the six-bay-abreast milking parlour.

'Aye, the jumped up little toe-rag. McQueen had every right to be pissed off at him. But if it had been me —' He pointed his thumb at his Adam's apple and made a choking noise in the back of his throat.

'I know. We'd have had him. You handled the situation well though, Pug. You got McQueen out of there pretty quick.'

Pug nodded. 'Tavish McQueen is a shrewd businessman, but he and his boy are hot-headed fools.'

'What did you think of that copper, what's his name — McKinnon and his tart?' Wilfred leered. 'She's a pretty piece, though. I wouldn't mind —'

'I don't want to hear what is on your dirty wee mind, you bugger!' Pug snarled. 'You know I don't like people talking like that. When I think of what happened at Hoolish Farm, it makes me feel sick.'

Wilfred bit his lip and straightened up, then moved over to start the milking machine.

Pug sighed and patted his brother's shoulder. 'Sorry, Wilf, I'm just a bit frazzled, that's all. I have a lot on my mind, what with all these complications. Let's just get these cows milked then go and see how Tyler is getting on with the pigs and the training.'

Wilfred grinned. 'That's OK. I don't know how you manage to keep all of these fancy business schemes in your head, really I don't.' He grinned even more broadly. 'I am always here to help though, you know that, don't you, Pug?'

Pug smiled absently and they lapsed into silence as they got on with the process of milking the herd. Doing six animals at a time, each milking taking five minutes, by the time they had disinfected each animal's udders, cleared them out and installed the next lot it took the better part of an hour and a half.

Once they had finished they returned to the farmhouse kitchen where they ate a bowl of porridge each before heading out in their old Land-Rover to the fields at the far end of the Goat's Head where they kept their saddleback pigs. Half-a-dozen corrugated arcs with fresh straw strewn outside each dotted the churned-up fields.

'Tyler has done his work already,' said Wilf, eyeing the contented pigs and piglets noisily mooching about. 'I reckon he's already working in the barn.'

Pug nodded as he slammed the door shut and started along the track towards the remote building perched not far from the cliff tops. It was a large, aesthetically unpleasing brick building that had deliberately been erected far away from prying eyes, and better still as far as they were concerned, from curious ears.

'I am looking forward to having this proper meet at the solstice eve,' Wilfred said with a grin, as he rubbed his hands together.

Pug grabbed the handle of the barn door and slid it open. Immediately a cacophony of howling and barking filled the air. 'Shut up!' Pug snarled, kicking the door with his boot. Almost instantly, the noise abated.

Pug Cruikshank grinned at Tyler Brady, a tall man in his early thirties with close-cropped hair, who was standing beside a cage inside which a large mongrel with the look of a retriever and the broad shoulders of a boxer was running inside a metal treadmill.

'You scared me there, Pug. I was miles away.'

Pug looked down at the electric prod in Tyler Brady's hand and at the wild look in the mongrel's eye as it dashed on the treadmill, its ears pulled back and saliva dripping from its muzzled jaws. 'Has it been giving you trouble?'

In answer, Tyler Brady, the brothers' pig-man and long-standing business partner, shoved the long cattle prod into the cage and applied a shock to the dog's buttock. It yelped, then increased its speed.

All three men laughed.

Pug slapped Brady on the back. 'OK, good job, Tyler.' He looked round at the line of fifteen other cages where a motley assortment of fighting dogs, some pacing, others just sitting, stared out at them. Although several of them made half-hearted attempts at wagging their stubby tails, all of them had a look of ferocity that made it clear that they had not been bred as pets. Indeed, each and every one of them had been bred as a biting machine.

'I take it that the pregnant ones haven't produced yet?' Pug asked, pointing to the end two cages.

'Naw. Another day I reckon, then the boxer should drop hers and the Stafford maybe next week. Do you think we'll be able to sell them all?'

'Reckon so,' Pug replied. 'I've got orders from the other islands and the usual ones up and down the west coast.' He grinned. 'Each of these little buggers is worth a tidy sum, to the right type of folk. I've even got orders down in Yorkshire and the Midlands.'

'Regular entrepreneurs, aren't we?' Tyler said. 'What with this and Wilf's little cannabis crop.'

'Aye, it's doing well for us, as long as the law doesn't come sniffing around. That means we had best be careful.'

'Of course we're careful, Pug!' Tyler Brady exclaimed sarcastically. 'We're a careful lot up on Goat's Head Farm. Ask anyone who dares come up here.'

Wilfred guffawed and was rewarded by a censorious glower from his elder brother.

'Get the food out of the Land-Rover, Wilf,' Pug ordered. He pointed to the circular wall that enclosed the pit that had been sunk in the middle of the barn. 'We'll give a couple of the younger ones a roll with their muzzles on. See if they can build up an appetite.'

'How about the Rotty and the mastiff?' Brady suggested, pointing to two of the cages.

'Suits me,' Pug returned.

Wilf returned with a large basin full of roughly chopped raw meat and bones. He walked down the line of cages depositing hunks of meat and a bone in each one, except for the cages with the young Rottweiler and what looked like a bull mastiff. The two animals inside stared at him and began barking at their omission from the food chain. And then they looked at each other and, as if knowing what was about to happen, they began growling menacingly at each other.

'Maybe a little wager?' Tyler suggested with a grin, as Wilfred returned with choke chains. He reached into the front pocket of his dungarees. 'And how about a smoke?'

'Of course,' Pug returned, and once again the three men dissolved into unpleasant mirth. 'A smoke is always good when the bets get high. And then we can talk about how we're going to settle some outstanding debts.'

Dunshiffin Castle had been the stronghold of the Macleod family, the hereditary lairds of West Uist since the thirteenth century up until the preceding two years when it had fallen into private ownership. The liquidation of the last owner's assets had once again put it on the market, only for it to be snapped up by The Daisy Institute and transformed into a residential centre for spiritual education.

At eleven o'clock, Logan Burns was sitting in the lotus position on a large nineteenth-century Persian rug in the centre of the castle library, which he now used as his private office. Opposite him, also in the lotus position, was a young woman dressed in a pink hoodie. A mere six inches separated their knees, as also was the gap between their outstretched palms. The girl's eyes were shut, a smile hovering over her lips as she breathed deeply in and out at his command. Logan watched the rise and fall of her pert breasts as he talked.

'Feel the energy flowing between us, Eileen. It flows from my hands, to your hands, and from my knees to your knees.'

Eileen Lamont's smile deepened and her attractive little snub nose wrinkled with pleasure. 'It ... it almost tickles, Dr Burns.'

'My name is Logan, Eileen. We have no sense or need of hierarchy here. Just concentrate on the energies. Become aware of your aura and of how it meets with mine. And yes, it will tickle. It will feel pleasant. You are starting to become aware of your higher self.'

He smiled as she sighed, her breasts rising as she did so.

'Now, just let yourself relax, feel yourself become aware of the heaviness of your physical body as I count backwards from five.' He paused, and then closed his eyes as he counted aloud. 'Five ... four ... three ... two ... one! Now just let your eyes open and feel yourself returning to the here and now.'

Almost reluctantly Eileen slowly opened her eyes, just as the director timed the opening of his own.

'Did you enjoy that?' he asked.

She nodded eagerly. 'That was fantastic, Doctor ... I mean, Logan. I have been so looking forward to my first session with you. The first couple of weeks had begun to drag.'

'The contemplation and meditation times are important, Eileen. You have to feel that you want to belong to our institute.'

'I almost asked to leave last week. Then Henrietta, Johanna and Peter, the senior inceptors, advised me to stay. They have all been a great help.'

Logan Burns nodded. 'Yes, they are all going to be great assets to the institute in time.' He clapped her hands in his and squeezed. 'As will you, I am sure. We need young people like you. You are the future.' He rose effortlessly to his feet and helped her up. 'Time to go and study now.'

He watched her leave then locked the door and crossed to the window which he slid wide open.

'Yes, she will do very well,' he mused to himself as he slumped into the leather chair behind the desk and pulled open a drawer.

With practised hands he rolled a spliff and lit it. He inhaled deeply. 'Very well indeed.'

Saki Yasuda, known to all of the inceptors at the institute as Miss Yasuda, was in the middle of her Kiko bodywork class when Eileen Lamont pushed open the squeaky door of the great hall and sidled into the back of the class.

'Sorry ... sorry, Miss Yasuda,' Eileen stammered, her face flushed. 'I was with Dr Burns ... I mean, I was with Logan. He was —'

Miss Yasuda was thirty-two years of age, but looked ten years younger. A mere five feet tall with the lithe supple body of a gymnast, she stopped, momentarily balanced perfectly on one foot and acknowledged Eileen with a smile of ruby-red lips and a slight inclination of her head.

'Please join the class, Eileen. I know that you were having your induction with Logan. Please, watch with the others and join in.'

She lowered her foot to the floor to stand with her feet together and with her hands raised perpendicularly above her head, fingers together.

'So now you ground yourself,' she said, as her dark eyes darted round the class of twenty inceptors and acolytes in their respective pink and white hoodies, and she suppressed a smile as she watched the less adept struggle to maintain their balance. Eileen Lamont certainly was not in that category. The thought that Logan Burns had kept her longer perhaps than was necessary, briefly intruded upon Miss Yasuda's mind before she instantly swept it away.

'And as you breathe in, please become aware of the energy within you. Draw that energy, your *ki*, down into your tummy.' She lowered her hands slowly and rested them on her own flat abdomen. 'This is your *hara*.' She moved her hands in a circular movement around her abdomen. 'Feel the energy, feel your *hara*.'

One or two giggles went round the room as people became aware of the strange butterfly sensation that Kiko bodywork often induced. The *hara* was so real, Saki Yasuda knew, a reassuring self-proof that there was more to life than just the chemistry of cells that modern science taught. And in that moment she felt the usual immense sadness when the image of her father crept into her mind. Doctor Toshiko Yasuda, one of the finest scientists of his generation, had been brought low by his own depression, that awful negativity that forced him to take his life by hara-kiri, the traditional ritual suicide of the samurai. *Hara-kiri*, which literally meant cutting the hara, the life force. She expelled the thought from her mind and swiftly finished the class.

She bowed to the assembly and they bowed back, then she left swiftly.

And then in the safety of her locked bedroom in the west wing of the castle she kicked off her trainers, peeled off her hoodie and joggers and flung them on to a chair. She stood naked before the mirror wincing at the scars on her arms, the old scratches where she cut herself when the need arose. Just as it was arising now, like a head of steam that needed venting.

Logan Burns! The thought of him would drive the bad thoughts from her mind. She closed her eyes and conjured up the picture of him as she liked to see him in her mind's eye — naked. She shivered, smiled and felt guilty. But then she saw Eileen Lamont's face and the spell was immediately broken.

Why did the thought of the director do this to her? Why did he send her into a spin? And why did she always feel so jealous? With a sigh she opened her bedside cabinet and took out the bag containing the scarifiers. And the bottle of vodka which helped her to reduce the tremor that even now was starting as she unzipped the bag and drew out the blade.

Drew Kelso was also sitting in his locked office, the former laird's billiard room. The table itself had been removed to one of the cellars and replaced by a large desk that was covered with books, ledgers, student files and a large laptop. The walls were covered with prints and posters of other Daisy Institute locations around the world. Immediately behind the desk was a clip frame containing the photographs of all of the inceptors and acolytes.

Drew was a well-built, dark, curly-haired man with an olive skin and pleasant, if not handsome features. He had high cheek-bones and hazel eyes, above which slightly drooping eyebrows gave him a faintly melancholic, puppy-dog appeal. He was drumming his fingers on the table as he pored over a sheaf of figures, his expression decidedly one of anxiety.

'Damn Logan!' he exclaimed to himself. 'The man has no idea about business. He could screw everything up —'

Something seemed to click in his mind and he thumped the desk, knocking over a glass of water in the process. He ignored it and, standing up, proceeded to pace the room.

'There has to be a way. He'll have to be — chained back, somehow.'

Torquil arrived at the station in the middle of the morning after a couple of meetings with various local worthies. He was met with stone-faced silence from PC Ewan McPhee and with a curt nod of the head from Sergeant Morag Driscoll.

'A word in your office please, Inspector McKinnon,' Morag said, through tight lips.

Torquil held open the door for her and followed her in. She turned and sniffed the air with a scowl. 'I am not happy, Torquil.'

'I know, I know, Morag. The bag seasoning is a bit strong, but I'll get some air-freshener and it will soon —'

'I am not talking about your bagpipes, Torquil. It's her!' she said, nodding her head sharply in the direction of the office wall.

'Her?'

'This Sergeant Golspie of yours. She's a nightmare.'

Torquil opened his mouth to reply, but she went on, 'It is like having a time and motion woman on my back. She's ticked off Ewan for the number of cups of tea he makes. She complained about the way he makes it.' She saw the start of a smile cross Torquil's lips and shrugged. 'OK, so the poor lamb always stews it, but that's the way Ewan makes tea, we all know that. She has gone over the times the Drummond twins have signed in for and queried them. She has gone through all of the files, grumbled about the way that I organize them, about how I draw up the duty roster, how I pin things to the board and even how I answer the telephone.' All of this had tumbled out in an exasperated manner in gradually increasing volume. She stopped, hands moving emphatically to her hips. 'You'll have to get her off our backs, Torquil, or I will —'

There was a tap on the door and Lorna Golspie pushed the door open, a file under her arm. She looked from one to the other.

'Excuse me, Inspector McKinnon. I thought I heard you come in and I just wanted to catch you to have —'

Out of the corner of his eye Torquil caught Morag's lips firming up.

'— a word?' he interjected. 'Of course. In fact, I'll do better than that, Sergeant. I'll take you for a wee outing.'

And, taking the file from under her arm, he handed it to Morag and deftly shepherded the sergeant out of his office.

Finbar Donleavy and Danny Wade had been waiting for half an hour up at the Hoolish Stones. One of the typical Hebridean sea squalls had passed over and they had sheltered inside the chambered cairn under one of the large umbrellas emblazoned with the Scottish TV logo until the worst of it had passed over.

Danny was the first to emerge into the fine drizzle. 'I think it will be OK, Finbar,' he said. 'I was worried that the lens would just get wet-speckle. What is the main theme of the slot going to be tonight?'

'Just a bit more about the geometry of the place, I think. Logan Burns wants to explain about the positions of the stones and the way the light will fall at the solstice.'

Danny had lit up a cigarette and was smoking it cupped inside his hand against the drizzle. 'What do you really make of him, Fin?'

Finbar looked about him then leaned forward with a grin. 'Now what sort of a question is that, with the man himself about to appear?'

'Come on, you've been as nice as ninepence with him all the way along. That's not like you.'

Finbar aimed a playful cuff at the cameraman's ear. 'Watch it, you wee tyke. I am being a responsible broadcast journalist, nothing more.'

'That's not what that little pot-bellied newsman called you in the pub the other night.'

Finbar guffawed. 'Calum Steele is jealous.'

'Of you going out with Kirstie?' Danny grinned. 'But so are half the men in Scotland. Come on, Fin. There's more to it than that, isn't there. He's not happy about you for some reason.'

'Well he's just going to have to lump it, isn't he? Anyway, here come Logan and his two side-kicks.' He held his hand out and gave a short laugh. 'And wouldn't you know it, the rain has gone for him. Maybe he is a bit of a shaman.'

Logan Burns greeted them effusively and, as before, outlined how he would like the slot to be filmed.

The sea had been choppy all afternoon and Lorna Golspie was looking decidedly green about the gills as Torquil put the West Uist Police *Seaspray* catamaran through its paces. After leaving the station that morning he had taken Lorna on his Royal Enfield Bullet classic motorcycle for a trip around the island, showing her the main features, the larger villages, hamlets and crofting communities. Then he had bought her lunch at the Bonnie Prince Charlie before heading off for a trip around the island and out towards the Cruadalach Isles.

'Don't be surprised if I go a bit peaky, Inspector,' she had jokingly protested as they left the crescent-shaped Kyleshiffin harbour.

He had thought that she was joking until they started back from the largest of the isles and she had suddenly dived for the side of the vessel, losing her lunch over the side.

'You'll be fine, Sergeant,' he said encouragingly, 'just keep your eye on West Uist and you'll be —'

'You ... did that on purpose, didn't you?' she blurted out, her eyes red and her face as white as a sheet. 'Sergeant Driscoll told you to give me a hard time.'

Torquil looked at her in horror. 'I did nothing of the sort! I just thought —'

She bent over the side and retched again. Torquil slowed down and patted the back of her life jacket. 'Can I do anything?'

'Get me back to dry land, please,' she returned, pleadingly.

'Aye, lass, I will that,' he said soothingly. He glanced at his watch, surprised to see how late it was. 'But like I said, you might feel better if you stare at the horizon. Look, you can see the Hoolish Stones from here. I am guessing that they will be filming again now.'

'I don't care! I think ... I am going ... to die!' groaned Lorna.

The Padre was watching the evening news, a whisky in his hand, his long legs stretched out in front of him.

'And so here we are again at the Hoolish Stones on West Uist. A rainy day on West Uist as it happens,' said Finbar Delaney to the camera. 'I am once again joining Dr Logan Burns and two of his young colleagues at the ancient Hoolish Stones on West Uist.'

Logan Burns walked into the picture flanked by Henrietta and Peter.

'Thank you, Finbar,' Logan said. 'This evening I want to give the viewers a brief description of these fabulous stones which were clearly constructed four thousand years ago as a temple to —'

'Liar! Charlatan!' a voice off-camera screamed.

Danny Wade spun round and picked up the lone figure of Finlay MacNeil staggering across the heather towards the stones.

'You are a lying charlatan, Burns,' Finlay cried, his voice slurred and his eyes threatening to go slightly crossed.

The Padre sat forward with his glass halfway to his lips. 'Oh, Finlay, my man, what are you playing at? You are fair sozzled.'

Finbar interposed himself between The Daisy Institute director and the advancing museum curator. He spoke into his microphone. 'It — er — seems that we have a heckler.'

'Ask him what his credentials are!' Finlay demanded. 'He is no scholar. He has no genuine academic background.'

A nervous, fixed smile had come to Logan Burns's lips. 'I assure you sir, I have impeccable qualifications.'

'Shall I help the gentleman away, sir?' Peter asked.

'Don't even think about touching me, laddie,' Finlay snapped belligerently.

Finbar tried to defuse the situation. 'Yes, well, if you would just be a bit calmer. It is Mr MacNeil, isn't it?'

'You know that well enough, Mr News,' Finlay replied sarcastically. Then turning directly to face the camera, which Danny Wade kept trained on him, he said, 'All this Daisy Institute and solstice nonsense has gone too far. It is dangerous nonsense this man is peddling. I know exactly what is going on here. I know all about you and your Daisy Institute, I tell you.' He stopped and glared at the bemused Logan Burns. 'I have studied these stones for years. I know all about them and I know all about the solstice. And I know all about the winter solstice as well.'

The television picture was suddenly cut and Kirstie Macroon appeared in the Scottish Television studio.

'Well, unfortunately we seem to be having technical problems in our item from West Uist. So now we shall go to Alistair Macintosh who is outside the Scottish Parliament with more news about another cannabis smoking MP.'

The Padre sighed and stood up. He cast a sour glance at his untasted whisky and put it aside. He had suddenly lost the desire for it.

Finlay MacNeil woke with a start to find himself sprawled across his settee, an empty glass on his chest and whisky fumes rising from his sodden clothes. It was dark.

531

'Oh man! What time is it?' he mumbled to himself, as he strove to sit up. 'What have I done now?'

He had the vague recollection of having gone to the Hoolish Stones to confront Logan Burns, of the television camera and the rain.

'It is late!' came a voice from the darkness. 'Perhaps a little too late.'

Finlay gasped and shot upright.

'Who's there?'

He fancied he heard a short laugh.

Then, before he knew it, something dropped in a loop about his neck and suddenly he was gasping for air.

CHAPTER FOUR

Ewan McPhee had been up since five in the morning in order to practise his hammer-throwing technique. Having virtually demolished his mother's outside shed roof he had taken to going for an early morning run up to the moor above Kyleshiffin where he could hurl his highland hammer with abandon. He had won the Western Isles heavy hammer championship for five years in a row, breaking his own record on each occasion and had even contemplated converting discipline to throw the Olympic hammer. Yet to do that filled him with a degree of anxiety, since it would necessitate trips to the mainland and beyond, a journey that he had only made twice before in his twenty-five years.

'Ewan my man, you are a poor specimen. A real timorous beastie!' he chided himself, as he stood just in front of the twelve-foot-tall ancient standing stone, knee deep in the heather, in track suit bottoms and vest, with the twenty-two pound steel ball on the end of a four-foot wooden cane at arm's length on the ground. 'You are lacking in gumption and no mistake.' He hefted the cane, tensing his muscles, then swung the ball up and around his shoulders three times, picking up momentum all the time, before hurling it over his shoulder on the fourth revolution.

He turned to look after it as it sailed away. Then he saw a flash of movement as the runner appeared from behind one of the undulating mounds.

'Look out!' he screamed.

The female runner stopped abruptly, looked round as the great hammer came hurtling towards her and with a cry of alarm threw herself on to the ground. The hammer sailed over her head and embedded itself in the heather ten feet away.

'Are you all right?' cried Ewan, jumping through the heather for all he was worth to get to her.

'You bloody maniac!' the woman cried, staring in horror at the cane sticking up at a forty-five degree angle from the heather. 'You could have —'

She turned as Ewan came bounding towards her, then: 'You! You great, red-headed baboon!'

Ewan stopped and stared down at Sergeant Lorna Golspie. 'G-Good morning Sergeant. N-Nice morning, don't you think?'

'What is it with you lot on West Uist?' she asked, declining his outstretched hand and pushing herself to her feet. 'Are you determined to kill me?' Then, after dusting down her track suit she set off on her jog again and called over her shoulder, 'I will see you at the station later this morning ... *Constable*.'

Annie McConville was up with the larks as usual and out walking her beloved German shepherd, Zimba, Sheila, her West Highland terrier and the three collies that she had taken into her care. She chose a different walk every day, sometimes going entirely on foot and sometimes, as on this morning, heading further afield in her ancient Hillman Imp. She had driven up to the Goat's Head, a peninsula at the north of the island that jutted into the sea and had started walking them up past the pig farm with its corrugated iron arcs, towards the cliff tops. Several dozen saddleback pigs were foraging about in their enclosures.

The collies began barking first, followed by Zimba when they saw the old green Ford van cross the rough ground from an ugly brick barn perched near the top of the headland.

'Wheesht, the lot of you,' Annie called, tugging on the collies' leads as the van passed them then described a complete U-turn and stopped beside her.

Annie smiled as the window was rolled down. '*Latha math*,' she said, 'Good morning to you. It is a good —'

'This is private property, woman! Did you not see the sign?' snapped Tyler Brady. Immediately, the large head of a Rottweiler appeared in the window behind him, its teeth bared.

'We are only walking,' Annie replied, undaunted. 'We will not be harming any of your animals. These dogs used to belong to Rab Noble at Hoolish Farm and I have them under control. I am Annie McConville and I am —'

'I don't care about the dogs and I don't care who you are. This farm is private! Now get off the land before I get the police on to you.'

The dogs under her care seemed to sense the animosity and renewed their barking, matched by a clamour from the Rottweiler.

'Oh, I will be going, don't you worry,' Annie replied, not in the least intimidated. 'But I will be remembering you, you impudent lump. You and your impertinent animal there.'

Tyler Brady's upper lip lifted in an ugly sneer and he gunned the engine. 'You and me both, sweetheart. Now, bugger off.'

The van wheels spun., spraying Annie and the dogs with mud and he sped off.

Torquil had slept poorly. The image of Lorna Golspie retching over the side of the *Seaspray* had haunted his dreams and he had spent half the night struggling with a feeling of mounting guilt. She had looked so ill when he took her back to her room at the Commercial Hotel, and her grudging thanks belied the impression that she had given him previously; that he had

535

deliberately set out to give her a rough time, literally by making her seasick.

He welcomed the coming of dawn, rose and dressed quickly. As usual his Uncle Lachlan was up and was himself preparing for a busy morning of pastoral visiting. As they ate a swift breakfast of porridge, soda-bread toast and half a pint of tea each, the Padre brought up the subject of the fiasco over The Daisy Institute slot on the news the previous evening.

'I fear that Finlay MacNeil is his own worst enemy,' said Torquil, as he pushed away his porridge bowl and began spreading marmalade over his toast.

The Padre shook his head. 'A great shame it is, since he has a great mind. The whisky is his weakness. I shall pop in to see him at the end of my visits. He may have sobered up by then and may be feeling a touch repentant.'

Ten minutes later, Torquil emerged from the manse in his leather jacket, with his tartan scarf tied about his neck, his Cromwell helmet dangling from his wrist and his bagpipe carry case in his other hand. Stowing the bagpipes in the pannier of his Royal Enfield Bullet, he donned his helmet, snapped on his goggles and gauntlets, then kicked the Bullet into action. Moments later he was on his way to St Ninian's Cave, the great basalt-columned sea cave that he used, as generations of pipers before him had done, to practise his piping.

Normally, a good blow on his pipes raised his spirits and helped him to clear his mind, so he approached his practice in the huge cave with enthusiasm. Yet when he got there and stood playing a decidedly poor *piobaireachd*, a pibroch, he gave it up as a bad job and headed off to the station at Kyleshiffin.

The pleasing aroma of freshly baked butter rolls and newly brewed tea greeted him as soon as he pushed open the door. Ewan and Morag were standing leaning against the counter, each with a roll in one hand and a mug of tea in the other. Knowing them both so well, a single look at the expressions upon their faces told him that they had been in the middle of some sort of counselling session.

'Trouble?' he asked.

Ewan drew himself up to his full six foot four inches and winced, his cheeks flushing with embarrassment. He put down his mug and self-consciously ran his fingers through his mane of red hair, then he cleared his throat. 'I am thinking that Sergeant Golspie will want to have a chat with you, Torquil. She and I had a — er — run-in this morning. That is ... we were ... both out on runs. Well, I was out practising the hammer up on the moor by the old standing stone and I — er — almost hit her.'

'Och, I am sure you did nothing of the sort, Ewan!' Morag interceded. 'She just wouldn't have been looking where she was going. How were you supposed to know she was skulking about up there?'

The big constable hung his head. 'I ignored the first rule of the hammer, Morag. I hadn't made sure it was safe to throw. I just kind of assumed that I had the whole moor to myself.' Almost absently he took a bite of his roll and chewed mechanically.

Torquil laid his bagpipe case on the filing cabinet and deposited his helmet and gauntlets beside it. Spying the third mug placed in readiness for him on the tray he poured himself a cup of Ewan's strong tea.

'Actually,' he said, as he added milk and picked up a roll, 'I think that Sergeant Golspie's ire may be directed more in my direction, Ewan, my man.' And he told them of their trip in the *Seaspray*.

Morag barely suppressed a smile of glee while Ewan gave a forlorn sigh.

Torquil shrugged. 'Well, we shall see,' he said, picking up his bagpipe case and heading towards his office.

'Oh, have you seen this morning's *West Uist Chronicle* yet?' Morag asked, wiping a fleck of bread from her lower lip. 'I've put it on your desk. Calum has written a hoot this time.'

Torquil took a slurp of tea then pushed open his door with a toe of his Ashman boot. Dumping his bagpipe case in the corner he sat down with his tea and smoothed the newspaper as he read the headlines:

STONED AT THE HOOLISH STONES

He grinned at the fuzzy picture of Finlay MacNeil berating Logan Burns at the stone circle. Clearly Calum Steele had taken the picture off his television set. Yet although it was hazy and distorted, still it gave the impression that Finlay MacNeil was in a distinct state of inebriation.

He read the article:

Our ancient stone circle, the Hoolish Stones, have probably gathered more media attention in the last six months than they have done in all their four-thousand-year history. The religious cult organization that calls itself The Daisy Institute, headed by a charismatic New Age mystic by the name of Logan Burns, has managed to grab national media attention as they gather to celebrate the coming summer solstice.

There is nothing wrong with that. The thing that does seem to rub people up the wrong way is their pseudo-scientific nonsense about the Hoolish Stones being an ancient temple of some sort, built by refugees from the mythical lost continent of Atlantis.

This in itself so incensed our local scholar, Finlay MacNeil, that he took it upon himself to interrupt a national television programme last night. Unfortunately, Finlay, who is known to like his cups as well as

538

many, came up against a stone wall in the form of Finbar Donleavy, the heavy-handed interviewer from ...

Torquil read the rest of the article with a grin. He was aware of Calum's admiration for Kirstie Macroon, the Scottish TV anchorwoman and his antipathy towards her Irish broadcaster boyfriend. A hoot, Morag had described it, but Torquil suspected that if Finbar Donleavy read it, then Calum could expect repercussions of some sort.

Sipping his tea and nibbling his roll he turned the page and read the headlines under a photograph of a lorry with the logo *Mcqueen's Regal Eggs — Straight From Mcqueen's Chicken Farm.*

WEST UIST TAKES A BATTERING — DUBIOUS PRACTICES BROUGHT IN BY INCOMERS

There was an insert photograph showing Tavish McQueen, one of the men with whom Calum had the run-in a couple of days before at the Bonnie Prince Charlie.

He read the *West Uist Chronicle* editor's diatribe about the new battery farm at the old Hoolish Farm. It was a blunt piece denouncing battery farming in general and the McQueen Regal Eggs business in particular. He recalled the anger in the bar the other day and shook his head.

'Oh Calum, my man. You have a rare talent for putting people's backs up, so you have.'

The great dining-room of Dunshiffin Castle, which had been converted into a refectory when the institute took it over, was humming with whispered conversations about the previous evening's newscast. Outside on the balcony the three directors were eating breakfast.

'I tell you, Logan, you're going to have to be careful,' Drew Kelso said.

Logan Burns finished pouring himself coffee and smiled at the financial director. 'I think I have everything in hand, thank you, Drew.'

Drew looked at Saki for support. 'Tell him, Saki. The Daisy Institute can't afford to lose credibility. That programme last night was a fiasco.'

'The man was drunk, that's all,' replied Saki. 'I think Logan is right. Everything is going well. The inceptors and acolytes are all happy.'

'Are they?' Drew returned, nodding his head at the glass door to the refectory full of inceptors and acolytes. 'What do you think they are all so animatedly talking about right now?' He shook his head. 'I don't think everyone is happy. Especially not with the contemplation period we impose on them.'

'It is the way it has to be,' said Logan firmly. 'It is the time they need to purge their minds of all the rubbish of consumerism.'

'There have been complaints from relatives,' Drew persisted. 'I field most of them. Maybe I field too many.'

'Complaints about what?' Saki asked, over the rim of her coffee cup.

'The usual thing. About not being able to see their darling young things. Accusations of being a cult.'

Logan Burns tossed his head back and roared with laughter. 'A cult! That is nonsense and you know it.'

Drew wiped his lips with his napkin. 'Of course I know that, Logan. But that's where you have to be careful about your Atlantis theories.'

'They are more than theories, Drew. They are firm conclusions based on solid research. I am the academic here, remember that if you will.'

'Yes but —'

'No buts, Drew. I am the founder of this institute and I shall steer the course that I see fit.' He swallowed the rest of his coffee then pushed his chair back. 'Now, if you will excuse me, I have work to attend to.'

Once he had gone Drew sat back in exasperation. 'That felt as if I was being told off by the headmaster.'

Saki gave him a wry smile. 'I think you deserved it a little. Logan is a genius.'

'You can see no wrong in him, can you? Well, all I can say is that we don't want another episode like Geneva. Have you seen how he is with that new girl, Eileen Lamont?'

Saki winced as if she had suddenly received a shock. 'Don't talk about Geneva like that, Drew. We still don't know what happened there. The police investigations cleared us entirely.'

Drew Kelso leaned forward. 'Let's just be clear on this, Saki. We can't afford to have another dead student. It would finish us.'

He turned at the sound of tyres crunching on the gravel of the castle courtyard. An old Land-Rover drew to a halt by the castle steps. He watched and frowned slightly as Pug Cruikshank got out and headed for the steps leading up to the front door.

'Speaking of the devil, this could be trouble,' Drew said, rising from the table. 'Just think about what I said, Saki. Logan may need to be saved from himself.'

He made his way through the refectory and was descending the main staircase as Pug Cruikshank came through the front door. 'Can I help you?' he said, descending quickly. Pug Cruikshank stared at him for a moment, then he shook his head emphatically. 'I've come to see the organ-grinder, not the monkey.'

'I think not!' Drew returned, reaching the bottom of the stairs and stepping towards the farmer. 'I deal with —'

He was stopped by Logan Burns's voice from an adjacent corridor. 'It is OK, Drew, we have an appointment.'

The director was standing talking to Eileen Lamont, who blushed when she saw Pug Cruikshank. 'If you don't mind, we'll talk later, Eileen,' Logan Burns said.

'Morning, Cousin,' Pug said, as he stood aside to let her pass. 'So this is what you meant when you said you were moving up in the world? To a castle. I am impressed.' Eileen gave him a wan smile and sidled passed him and Drew Kelso.

Drew stood staring as Pug Cruikshank then walked past him with a sneer and shook hands with the institute's founder before they disappeared back along the corridor.

'Damn!' he cursed under his breath, as he turned on his heel and returned upstairs, forcing a smile he did not feel as he passed three white-hoodied acolytes and let himself into his office.

'Number Two is looking pretty peeved,' said Peter, opening the door to let Johanna and Henrietta pass him into the hall.

'I think there is trouble brewing among the directors,' said Henrietta. 'Did you see them at breakfast?'

'I did,' said Johanna. 'I passed Miss Saki as she left the refectory. I think they have been arguing.'

Peter laughed. 'I reckon it is all to do with sex. A love triangle, what do you reckon?'

Henrietta grinned. 'What's that, an offer?' She put a hand on Johanna's shoulder. 'What do you think, Jo?'

Johanna jabbed her in the ribs. 'You have sex on the brain!'

Henrietta giggled and swayed her hips coquettishly. 'You never know.'

But as they all three burst into hysterics, Johanna had other things on her mind than rolling in bed with her two fellow acolytes.

Calum Steele rode up Harbour Street on his Lambretta, its two-stroke engine screeching and its exhaust belching fumes. He coasted in to the kerb by Tam MacAlias, the butcher's, to buy a couple of freshly baked mutton pies for his breakfast. He had just overseen the deliveries of the morning's *West Uist Chronicle* and he was hungry. He was still looking over his shoulder swapping a few words of good-humoured banter with the worthy butcher as he came out of the shop and almost tripped over a dog lead that was stretched across the doorway.

'Oh Calum Steele, you poor man!' exclaimed Annie McConville as Calum regained his balance, only to find his legs encircled by the collie on the other end of the lead. Before he knew it he was surrounded by three collies, a West Highland terrier and a large Alsatian, all of which began barking and salivating at the smell of fresh food. Calum hastily lifted the paper bag with one of the pies above his head and removed the other from his mouth, releasing a stream of juice that flowed down his two chins on to his yellow anorak.

'What the —?' he spluttered. Then, recognizing Annie and the prim Bella Melville, his old teacher, standing beside her, he swallowed hard and grinned obsequiously. 'Ah, Annie. And Miss Melville. Both out enjoying the air,' he said limply.

'We are not!' Miss Melville replied severely. 'Annie here just had a run in with an obnoxious idiot up at the Goat's Head Farm.'

'Incomers!' Calum pronounced.

'Exactly!' Annie agreed with alacrity, all the while expertly shepherding the collies from about Calum.

Calum eyed them suspiciously, holding his precious pie higher. 'These are the Noble dogs, aren't they?'

'They are that,' replied Annie. 'The poor souls miss their owners, I can tell.'

'Tragic business,' Calum agreed, a shiver running up his spine at the recollection of finding Esther Noble hanging from her banister. He had covered the story quite extensively and it still made him feel uneasy.

'And I don't even have Eileen to help me walk them any more,' Annie continued.

'Eileen?' Calum asked innocently, in his best journalistic manner, although he knew full well whom she meant.

'Eileen Lamont, as you know well enough,' Miss Melville interjected. 'You were always a nosy boy at school and I do not believe that you are any less so today.' She pulled her leather gloves up her wrists and Calum wilted before her withering glare, just as he used to when she was standing in front of the class.

'She is one of the four local folk who have gone and got themselves involved with the flower people up at Dunshiffin Castle,' Bella Melville went on, proceeding to tick them off on her fingers. 'Agnes Doyle, Nancy MacRurie, Alan Brodie and Eileen Lamont.'

'Aye, The Daisy Institute!' Calum exclaimed with a scowl. 'All incomers.'

'We are not happy about it at all,' Miss Melville said huffily. 'Eileen's parents have been going near frantic because they cannot get in touch with her. It is some sort of ludicrous rule they have. Stuff and nonsense!' She shook her head decisively. 'Well, we are going to report it all to the police.'

'About The Daisy Institute?'

'About our concerns over our local folk. We have no idea what they are up to at the castle. And all this business about the solstice; it smacks of cultism to me.'

Calum stroked grease from his chin with the back of his hand and absent-mindedly licked it. 'A cult, eh?' he mused, a twinkle coming into his eye. 'I think you could be right, Miss Melville. Reporting it would be your civic duty.'

'And I am going to have a word about that rude farmer,' said Annie McConville. 'I didn't like the look of him or his dog.'

Calum nodded sympathetically. 'There are far too many of these incomers to the island. They all seem to be interfering with the West Uist way of life.'

Bella Melville put a hand on his arm. 'You have a point there, Calum. I read your piece in the paper this morning about the egg man, McQueen. I do not think it is right having one of those battery farms on West Uist.'

'It is disrespectful to the Nobles, if you ask me,' added Annie.

Calum nodded, now eager to end the conversation. He was aware that his stomach was gurgling and that his pie was getting cooler by the minute. He knew that he would have to make the first move, so he stowed his barely touched pie into the paper bag with the other and took a step backwards towards his parked Lambretta.

'Well, if you will excuse me I had better be getting off. The press await —'

He felt himself bump someone then heard a curse as something heavy fell to the pavement.

'You bloody moron!' a voice cried. Then, 'You!'

Calum spun round to find himself facing Finbar Donleavy. Bending down beside him to retrieve a large black bag was Danny Wade.

'Bugger!' Danny Wade cursed, as he gingerly opened the camera case. 'I think you have broken it, you dozy fool! That camera is worth thousands of pounds.'

The glimmer of a smile passed over Calum's lips. 'You should watch where you're going,' he said with a shrug.

Finbar Donleavy's eyes narrowed and he jabbed Calum's shoulder. 'You need to watch it, Steele. Especially the garbage you write in that rag of yours.'

'You've read my latest review of your programme then?' Calum asked with a smile of satisfaction.

Danny Wade wailed, 'It is broken, Finbar. He did it on purpose, I reckon.'

Calum looked round, expecting some support from Annie McConville and Bella Melville, but they had already departed, the five dogs now padding obediently along with them in the direction of Kirk Wynd.

Unruffled, he turned back to the irate duo.

'So why don't you sue me?' he said with a smile, as he stowed his pies in the carry-basket on the back of his scooter.

'Don't worry, tubby, we might just do that,' returned Finbar. 'And maybe Kirstie will say something about you trying to sabotage us on the next news.'

Calum winced inwardly at mention of the woman he so admired, but outwardly he maintained an air of unconcern. 'If you'll excuse me, I have urgent work to do.'

'We might let you go now,' snarled Danny Wade, 'but the police might be calling to see you after we report you for this.'

Calum started up the Lambretta and studiously ignored the twosome. Then, just before he was out of earshot, he shouted, 'Bloody incomers!'

Morag was dealing with Finbar Donleavy and Danny Wade while Ewan was doing his best to placate an irate Bella Melville and an equally angry and voluble Annie McConville and her pack of animals when Lorna Golspie came in. Gone was the trouser suit, to be replaced by one of the West Uist Division's blue pullovers, yet still with smartly creased trousers rather than jeans like Morag's. She let herself through the counter flap and went straight to the back office where she removed a sheaf of neatly typed papers from her briefcase. She added a few notes to the last page in biro then stacked them in the fax machine. She dialled a number and pressed the send button before making herself a cup of weak tea. Then she sat down in one of the battered old easy chairs beside the table tennis table and sipped her brew. As she expected, her mobile phone went off within five minutes.

'Good morning, Superintendent Lumsden,' she said into the mobile phone. 'Yes, sir, you were right. It is a total shambles. And so far, in my experience, not the safest of places to be.'

Above the cacophony of barking dogs and raised voices from the outer office Torquil heard the telephone ring. Moments later his own extension rang.

'Superintendent Lumsden for you Torquil,' Morag announced. 'He sounds ... brusque.' Torquil thanked her for the warning, for he had been expecting a call sooner or later.

'Good morning, Superintendent Lumsden, what can —?'

The familiar voice snapped from the other end. 'What's been going on over there? I hear that you took Sergeant Golspie out in choppy conditions and that your constable, McFunny, or whatever his name is, tried to decapitate her with a hammer.'

Torquil took a deep breath. 'It is true I took Sergeant Golspie on a tour of the waters round West Uist, sir. No better way to get an idea of the island's geography than by seeing it from the sea. Apart from that if she is going to be with us for long, then —'

'She will be with you until she has completed her secondment,' the superintendent interrupted.

'I was going to say that she needs to be familiar with all of the surrounding islets. I had not realized that she was subject to sea-sickness. That could be a handicap working out here.'

'What about that constable, McFunny? He's dangerous.'

'Ewan *McPhee* is a very able constable, sir. And he is the Western Isles champion wrestler and hammer-thrower. I believe that Sergeant Golspie was out running and she ran into his throwing area. He is not dangerous.'

'She tells me that you fill the place up with strange smells, and that you boil your bagpipes on police property in police time.'

'I think I would need clarification on that, Superintendent.'

'Well, I have her initial report in front of me. It is all down here and it does not make good reading, McKinnon. Too many tea breaks, piles of things all over the place and a distinct lack of organization in the station. That sergeant of yours might need a bit of overseeing.'

'I think not, Superintendent.'

There was a thumping noise from the other end of the phone, as if a meaty fist had pounded on a desk. 'What did you say?' Superintendent Lumsden shouted down the phone.

'I said that Sergeant Driscoll needs no supervision, sir. I am happy with the way she runs this office.'

There was an indistinct noise from the other end, then, 'Have you given Sergeant Golspie an area of responsibility yet?'

'Not yet, sir,' Torquil replied. 'I am considering what would be the most appropriate area for her to look after.'

'Well, get on with it.'

The line went dead without any additional pleasantries. Torquil replaced the receiver with a smile then went over to the door and pulled it open. Lorna Golspie was standing there, her hand raised as if about to knock on the door.

'I wondered if I could have a word, Inspector?' she asked.

Torquil stood aside and gestured for her to enter. 'Of course, Sergeant.' Over her shoulder he saw Morag look at Ewan and raise her eyes towards the ceiling. 'I was just thinking it's about time we had a little chat about the way that we work as a team here on West Uist.'

The Padre had spent the morning doing pastoral visits. In the main they were visits to elderly folk and those with various chronic illnesses that precluded them getting to church. Not surprisingly, he often arrived at a visit only to meet Dr Ralph McLelland, the local GP, making a house call on one of his patients.

'Did you see the news last night, Padre?' he asked, as they came down the path from Agnes Mulholland's cottage, where they had both taken a cup of tea laced with a teaspoon of Glen Corlin malt whisky with her. 'A right state Finlay MacNeil was in. It doesn't reflect well on the island.'

Lachlan scratched his chin. 'I was talking about it over breakfast with Torquil. I'm guessing he will be feeling pretty sheepish by now.'

'I doubt if he will have a hangover, Padre. He has a rare tolerance to the whisky.' He opened the door of his old and much loved Bentley, which had done faithful service since the days his father had run the practice, and swung his battered Gladstone bag into the passenger seat. 'Still, we are fine ones to talk, eh? Tea and whisky before noon.' He grinned. 'We'd better both keep out of Torquil's sight.'

'Aye, Ralph,' the Padre replied with a wink. 'And I think I will pay a visit on Finlay before lunch.'

Lachlan watched the GP head off before straddling his classic 1954 Ariel Red Hunter and spurring it into action. Then he zoomed off himself. It was a pleasant fifteen-minute ride along the coastal road, past Loch Hynish with its crannog and ancient ruined tower, to the Black House Museum and Finlay's log cabin. He dismounted and tapped at the door before letting himself in the ever-unlocked front door of the cabin. He called out the museum curator's name with a jocular mention about getting up and having some nice fatty bacon and eggs. He knew that if Finlay was truly hungover, then he would have little stomach for a fat-laden brunch.

But there was no answer. The curtains were still drawn, an empty bottle of whisky stood next to an empty glass on his desk, and his bedroom was empty, the bed unslept in. He retraced his steps and crossed the road to try the door of the Black House, but it was locked.

'Where are you, Finlay, my man?' he mused, as he pulled his battered old briar pipe from his breast pocket and charged it with tobacco. He struck a light and puffed it into life, then went to explore the garage.

Right enough, Finlay's car was there.

Then he saw scuff marks on the gravel path. He imagined Finlay going for a walk, staggering about after too much whisky. 'Where were you heading? Surely not to the stones?'

He looked in the direction of the Hoolish stones, just making out the tops of them out above the undulating terrain. But the marks seemed to be going the other way. More towards the cliff tops. Then he started to feel a little anxious, for if he had gone out during the night, why wasn't he back yet? He tapped his pipe out against his heel and started walking across the heather in the direction of the cliff tops, some 300 yards distant.

'Oh, Finlay, my man, I am hoping that you've just fallen asleep in the heather.'

But as he approached the cliff tops he saw the Drummond brothers' fishing boat approaching the island. He began waving, but as he took a step nearer the edge he looked down and almost immediately felt his heart miss a beat.

There was a body lying on the rocks just above the fringe of seaweed-strewn beach that had been exposed as the waves began to recede.

CHAPTER FIVE

'Do you seriously mean you think that he was trying to kill you?' Torquil asked, incredulously.

'You weren't there. He missed me by inches,' Lorna returned, her eyes opened wide in alarm.

'And you think I tried to make you ill?'

'I never said that,' she replied, folding her arms defensively.

'Lumsden did.'

'Oh!'

Torquil tapped the end of his pencil on the pad in front of him as he faced Lorna across his desk. 'Morag would be upset if she knew that you criticized the way she runs the station.'

Lorna shrugged helplessly. 'It all needs tightening up in my opinion. There is not enough discipline. Take the special constables, for instance. They come and go as they please and Ewan is forever running around making tea for everyone.'

'We may lack formality, but we work well together.'

Lorna had been sitting upright on her chair, but now with a pout she slumped back. 'You think I was too harsh in my preliminary report, don't you, Inspector?'

'I do. And you were,' Torquil replied laconically.

Suddenly, Lorna clapped her hands to her face and gave a long pained sigh. 'Damn! Which means that I have blown it with you all, haven't I?' She removed her hands to reveal a deep frown. 'I could kick myself sometimes. I often get too ... officious. Does this mean that you won't give me an area of responsibility, something to get my teeth into?'

Torquil shrugged and sucked air between his teeth. 'That depends on your answer to my next question.'

Lorna sat forward again and waited expectantly, as if her future on West Uist depended on her superior officer's next utterance.

'Did you really tell the superintendent that I fill the place up with disgusting smells and that I boil my bagpipes?'

Lorna opened her mouth to retort, then she saw Torquil's mask begin to drop as a grin suddenly gave him a boyish look. Then he laughed infectiously and before she knew it they were both laughing their heads off. It was enough to bring a tap of enquiry to the office door and Morag popped her head round. Torquil waved her in.

'Come in, Morag. And bring Ewan. I think it's time we cleared the air, the lot of us.'

'Tea would be good,' Lorna suggested, hopefully.

Morag grinned, realizing that somehow Superintendent Lumsden's phone call had strangely resulted in a dove of peace flying in with an olive branch. 'Two ticks and we'll have a fresh brew. Will you take a biscuit, Sergeant Golspie?'

'Please, call me Lorna,' the sergeant corrected. 'I would love one.'

Five minutes later when Ewan came in with a tray laden with teapot, mugs and the biscuit barrel, Torquil and Lorna were still laughing away, as if they had been best of pals for years.

'I really am sorry, Sergeant Golspie,' Ewan said, his cheeks flushed. 'Do you think you can forgive me?'

Lorna waved her hand in dismissal. 'I think we should forget about the whole thing. I have just been so wound up. I think it was because of the picture Superintendent Lumsden painted of the set-up here. And please, Ewan, call me Lorna.'

The big constable grinned sheepishly. 'OK Serg — I mean, Lorna.'

And moments later, with mugs of tea and biscuits at hand they were sharing anecdotes and building bridges. Then Torquil's mobile went off barely seconds before the office telephone. With an apology, Torquil answered his mobile while Morag went through to pick up the office phone.

'My God! That's unexpected,' Torquil informed Ewan and Lorna a few moments later. 'That was the Padre. He's just been out to see Finlay MacNeil and he thinks he's fallen off the cliffs.'

'Is he hurt?' Ewan gasped.

'He thinks so. He says that the Drummonds are on the scene.'

Morag came in, an obviously pained expression on her face. 'He's dead, I am afraid, Torquil. That was Wallace on the phone. Douglas just checked him. He's fallen on to the rocks and must have smashed himself to pieces. It is not a pretty sight, apparently.'

Torquil sighed and heaved himself to his feet. 'Well we'd better get out there and take a look. Can you get hold of Ralph, Morag?' He turned to Lorna and gave her a wan smile. 'How are you with motorbikes, Lorna? Have you ever ridden pillion?'

Lorna was already on her feet. 'My brother used to have a Yamaha. I think I can say I won't get travel sick.'

'Don't speak too soon,' Torquil replied, tossing her his spare helmet as he gathered his own Cromwell helmet and goggles. 'We're going on a real motorbike.'

Torquil left Kyleshiffin and then opened up the throttle on the chicane-like coastal road. As he put the machine through its paces, cornering at speed, he was aware of the ease with which Lorna rode pillion. He was also conscious of her arms about his waist and her body close to his. It had been a long time since he had allowed anyone to ride with him and he was vaguely pleased that it did not upset him, as he had expected it might.

They passed Loch Hynish and then took the road up past the Black House Museum and Finlay MacNeil's log cabin, outside which the Padre's Ariel Red Hunter was parked on its stand.

'Hold on, we're going cross country for a bit,' Torquil said, turning his head and grinning as his tartan scarf blew over Lorna's face. She tapped his waist in confirmation and he turned off the road on to a sheep track leading across the heather and the cliff tops in the distance, where his uncle's unmistakable figure could be seen, pipe in mouth and white mane of hair blowing in the wind.

'Ah Torquil,' he cried upon hearing the Bullet's familiar approach. 'Glad I am to be seeing you. And who —?'

Torquil cut the engine and waited for Lorna to dismount before doing so himself. 'Uncle Lachlan, meet Sergeant Lorna Golspie.' Then, turning to her as he pulled off his gauntlets, 'Lorna, this is my uncle, Lachlan McKinnon, known to virtually everyone as the Padre.'

They shook hands fleetingly, then the Padre turned again to the cliff edge.

'The Drummonds are down there. I saw them coming in from their fishing just before I spotted Finlay. They landed and checked to see if he was still alive.' He shook his head sadly. 'Poor devil, he had no chance after falling that far. But you'll still need a medical opinion, I'm thinking.'

'Aye, Morag sent out a call for Ralph,' Torquil returned. 'Although how he can get down there will be another matter.'

'Well, we'll see soon enough,' said the Padre, pointing the stem of his pipe in the direction of the Black House Museum and Finlay MacNeil's cabin. 'Here he comes.'

And as they all looked round, the ringing bell of the Kyleshiffin Cottage Hospital ambulance sounded out above the wind and they saw the old vehicle leave the road and come buffeting along the coarse track through the heather towards them. It was not a purpose built ambulance, but a fairly old camper van that been donated by a former laird and adapted at public cost. The door opened and the GP-cum-police surgeon jogged across the heather with his Gladstone bag swinging from his hand.

Ralph was one of Torquil's oldest friends. He was the third generation of his family to minister to the local people of West Uist. He had trained at Glasgow University then embarked upon a career in forensic medicine, having gained a diploma in medical jurisprudence as well as the first part of his membership of the Royal College of Pathologists. His father's terminal illness had drawn him back to the island to take over the practice, which he had then run single-handedly for seven years.

Torquil introduced him to Lorna, then said, 'Lachlan and the twins found him almost simultaneously. He's dead, they say, but you'll need to certify him. Do you need us to get you down there? I'm thinking it will be a case of taking you out in the *Seaspray*.'

Ralph scratched his chin as they looked over the edge to where the Drummond twins were standing beside the body of Finlay MacNeil. Their fishing boat *The Unicorn* was anchored and their small rowing boat was moored in the shallows. Wallace was gesticulating up at them and trying to shout above the wind. Ralph shook his head. 'I cannot see that it would be necessary to see him there. It looks clear enough. He's had a fall, possibly when —' he looked at the Padre and shook his head — 'when he had taken a few drinks too many. We were talking about that earlier weren't we, Padre?'

The Padre nodded with a frown. 'The whisky! I think everyone thought it would be the death of him one day.'

Torquil's phone went off and he answered it. 'Aye, Wallace, we were just talking about what to do. Dr McLelland is here and he agrees. If you could take him back to Kyleshiffin harbour we'll meet you with the ambulance and take him to the Cottage Hospital.'

'Is there much of a drink and drug problem on the island?' Lorna Golspie asked, once he had put his mobile phone away.

Torquil opened his mouth to reply, but Ralph beat him to it. 'People drink here, just the same as other places, Sergeant. Sometimes they might drink too much, but I wouldn't have said there was a big problem.'

The Padre struck a light to his pipe. 'It is big enough though. Especially if it causes a man's death.'

Calum Steele had ridden out past Dunshiffin Castle and taken the narrow track up to the Hoolish Stones. Cutting the engine of the Lambretta he parked behind one of the great gateway stones and then flattening himself on the ground he edged into a position in the bracken to get a view of the Hoolish Farm. From his vantage point he could see the large sign boasting *MCQUEEN'S REGAL EGGS — STRAIGHT FROM MCQUEEN'S CHICKEN FARM.*

He glanced at his watch and waited expectantly. Five minutes ticked by, then he saw movement and a battered minivan came down the drive. As it passed him he saw that it was full of about six men, including young Gregory Todd, the insider who had given him the rundown on the conditions that he and his fellows worked under, and the state that the hens were kept in at the battery farm.

'That's the staff off for a good liquid lunch,' he grinned to himself.

He waited until it was out of view then he pushed himself to his feet, zipped up his yellow anorak and patted his pockets to check that he had the three precious accoutrements of a twenty-first-century journalist — a digital camera, mobile phone and spiral-bound notebook. Then buoyed with the mutton pies and the half bottle of cola he had consumed, he felt in the mood for some honest to goodness investigative journalism.

'OK, Mr High And Mighty McQueen, so you think that you can give me orders, do you? Well let's see how you like it when I expose you to the world.'

By the 'world' he of course meant the good folk of West Uist, although on several occasions in the past some of his news stories had been picked up by Scottish TV and broadcast nationally.

'Bugger Finbar Donleavy and that half-witted, white-headed camera-jockey! Ebony and blooming Ivory, they are all right,' he mused, as he ducked down and began creeping towards McQueen's battery farm. 'I don't know what Kirstie Macroon could be thinking of. The man is a boor. She could have had me if she had played her cards right!'

And the thought of Finbar Donleavy canoodling with the full-breasted television anchor-woman had a galvanizing effect on him. Seeing himself as a journalistic commando he quickly covered the ground to the end of the dyke that ran up the length of the drive. He stopped and looked around, squinting slightly, not because it helped him to see any better, but because it suited the mental image he had of himself as a commando spying on enemy territory.

The old farmhouse had been tidied up and renovations were clearly underway. Similarly, the old dog kennels had been demolished and two large functional barns had been erected. Taking up half of one was another huge sign proclaiming that this was MCQUEEN'S CHICKEN FARM. Beside that was a huge rustic picture of Tavish McQueen, grinning as if he had himself laid the proverbial golden egg.

'I bet the bugger has never seen a proper farm,' Calum sneered to himself. He pulled out his digital camera, looked to right and left then crept along the wall and over the yard to the sliding doors of the first barn. He noted with glee that there was no lock.

'A doddle this will be. Quickly in, snap a few shots, and then I am out of here.'

And that was exactly what he did. He slid the door open, popped his head round to see if there was anyone there, then crept in.

'Bloody hell!' he exclaimed to himself, as he slid the door behind him and turned to inspect the interior. The stench was indescribable and he was forced to cover his nose with his cupped hand as he gagged despite himself. Almost as bad was the plaintiff clucking of innumerable hens.

And yet the sight that greeted him was even worse than he had imagined it would be. The barn was suffused with bright glaring overhead strip-lights. From floor to roof were rows of stacked battery cages, each containing four or five hens in cramped wire-mesh-bottomed cages, with tiny feeding areas in front of them and plastic chutes running along the rows to collect the eggs. Calum estimated that there had to be something over 5,000 hens cramped in this barn alone. Straw was strewn over the dirt floor and trenches under the rows of cages reeked with accumulated chicken manure.

Calum felt anger rise like a palpable force within him. It was accompanied by revulsion and a strange sense of impotence. Part of him wanted to run along the barn unlocking the cages to release the birds, to orchestrate a great avian escape. Yet he realized how futile that would be. It was one thing for animal rights campaigners to behave like that, to take the law into their own hands, but not for him, the responsible face of journalism. No, the best help he could give these beleaguered creatures was to expose the practice.

He began taking pictures of the cages; shots of the wire-mesh bottoms that deprived the birds the comfort of sitting on a solid base, the faecal-covered feathers, and the sores on their bottoms. Even the four or five carcasses that had not been noticed and which other poor birds were forced to live with.

He had moved along and was bending over photographing the pallets full of egg trays, testimony to the vast output of the farm. He did not hear the footsteps behind him, so had no warning of anything amiss until he felt something snake round his neck and suddenly squeeze, causing him to drop his camera and claw at his throat as he fought for air.

It was a sombre group that collected at the harbour in the heat of the afternoon, with holidaymakers thronging the harbour markets, all completely oblivious to the transfer from *The Unicorn* to the Kyleshiffin Cottage ambulance of the bundle wrapped in an old tarpaulin cover.

'He'll smell a bit of herrings, I am sorry to be telling you, Dr McLelland,' said Douglas.

'Don't worry, Douglas,' Ralph returned, as he snapped the door closed. 'The smell of fish has never worried me yet. I have to deal with other odours more noxious than that in my work.'

Lorna Golspie visibly shivered. 'Will you be able to tell us the cause of his death, Doctor?'

Wallace Drummond stared at her in amazement. 'I think even dumb fishing folk like my brother and I can tell what killed the poor man.'

Torquil put a hand on Wallace's shoulder. 'We cannot assume anything, Wallace. Finlay MacNeil might have fallen to his death, but we have to go through the motions.'

The Padre knitted his brows and shook his head emphatically. 'I do not think that suicide is at all likely. Not Finlay.'

'You will be wanting a post-mortem as soon as possible, I imagine?' Ralph asked.

'I would be grateful, Ralph.'

Lorna leaned towards Torquil. 'Would you like me to liaise with the doctor, Inspector? Remember, you said you would give me a job.'

Torquil clicked his teeth pensively. 'Ah yes, Lorna. A job. I am still thinking about that.'

Calum's hand came in contact with a bare muscular forearm that held him in a vice-like neck-lock. He patted it frantically as the pressure on his trachea increased and the only noise he could make was a plaintive gurgling.

'Bloody snooper!' a voice at his ear rasped. 'You need a lesson. A final lesson!'

Panic bells began to ring in Calum's mind. A final lesson! He nipped the skin of the forearm, only to feel the grip about his throat strengthen. He felt a wave of dizziness and nausea sweep over him.

Then vaguely he had a picture of a series of articles on self-defence he had published a couple of years before in the *Chronicle*. Line drawings that he had copied from a series of bubble gum cards he used to collect as a boy. He saw them now, each with the title Bazooka Bob's School of Judo. Each card had three drawings of a judo throw.

Dizziness increased as he almost fell into a trance-like state, and he became the character in the line drawings.

He stiffened, tensed his neck muscles, before suddenly letting all his muscles go floppy as if falling. At the same time he grabbed the arm and jack-knifed forward, tugging as he did so.

To his amazement, never having actually done anything like it before, except in the rich fantasy world in which he saw himself as the hero of a thousand situations, he felt a large body hurtle over his head to land on his back on top of a large pallet of eggs. There was an almighty cracking of several dozen eggs and a deep grunt of pain.

Calum looked down at the sprawling figure of Angus McQueen, the battery farm-owner's son. Tempted though he was to bring his foot down on his attacker's face as he wiped egg yolk from his eyes, he desisted, choosing instead to scoop dirt and chicken dung from the barn floor and throwing a handful into the man's face.

It seemed the right thing to do, for it made him cough and splutter and gurgle with rage. More importantly, it gave Calum the time he needed to gulp air into his lungs and act. He picked up his camera, took a picture of his aggressor before beating a hasty retreat.

'Mission accomplished, Calum, my man,' he grinned to himself as he sprinted down the drive.

It was not until he reached his hidden Lambretta that he realized the enormity of what had just happened. Then a surge of nausea doubled him up.

Regretfully, he lost his breakfast of mutton pies.

After a late lunch for which no one had much of an appetite, Torquil called his staff into his office. 'OK, Morag, let's see what jobs we've got and let's divvy them up.' He smiled at Lorna. 'Sergeant Golspie is keen to get her teeth into something.'

'Let's be hoping it is not one of us then,' said Wallace with a grin. 'Or then again —' he added, with a roguish wink at the new sergeant.

He was immediately rewarded with a jab in the ribs from his brother, who addressed Lorna with an even deeper grin. 'Ignore my boorish brother, Sergeant. He got the bad genes.' Torquil eyed the twins with mock severity. 'That's enough lads. OK, Morag, what have we got?'

Morag shook her head and began hesitantly. 'Calum tops the list, I am afraid. This morning we had a complaint from that TV reporter Finbar Donleavy and the cameraman —' she referred to the duty log book to refresh her memory — 'Danny Wade, about him deliberately breaking their camera. Apparently, it might mean they will not be able to broadcast on the news tonight.'

'Doesn't sound like Calum,' Torquil said defensively.

'I am not so sure, Torquil,' said Douglas Drummond. 'Our Calum is a clumsy wee man.'

'And he doesn't think much of Finbar,' agreed his brother. 'He thinks more about Finbar's girlfriend though.'

Torquil said nothing. Calum's feelings for Kirstie Macroon were well known by them all.

'Also a complaint against him for trespass, criminal damage and assault.'

Torquil slapped his hand on the desk. 'That's rubbish. They're going too far.'

'It is a different complaint, Torquil,' Morag interjected. 'It just came in while you were at lunch. It is from the McQueens. They say he's broken into their *farm*, taken unauthorized pictures and beaten up the son.'

The Drummonds and Ewan looked at one another for a moment, then all three burst out laughing. 'Calum Steele beating up that big McQueen fellow! That's ridiculous, Inspector,' said Ewan. 'He couldn't knock his way out of a paper bag.'

Lorna snapped her fingers and looked at Torquil. 'Wasn't that fracas in the Bonnie Prince Charlie to do with the McQueens?'

'It was. Maybe they have a vendetta against him. Calum sees himself as an investigative journalist, you see.'

'There is more,' Morag went on. 'And it is to do with Calum again. Logan Burns, the man from The Daisy Institute phoned while you were out. He was complaining about Calum's piece in the paper. He said that he wanted him charging with defamation of character and that he would be taking legal action.'

'That is nothing to do with the police,' said Torquil with a trace of irritation. 'He needs to see his solicitor, not be bothering us.' He gave a long-suffering sigh. 'Calum really knows how to stir people up against him, doesn't he? What else, Morag?'

'Curiously, there is a complaint about Logan Burns himself and The Daisy Institute. Annie McConville and Bella Melville were in. It is like a menagerie when Annie brings her dogs.

Anyway, they say that they represent some of the families.' Once again she consulted the log book and read out the names. 'Agnes Doyle, Nancy MacRurie, Alan Brodie and Eileen Lamont.'

'They are all over eighteen, though, aren't they?' Torquil interjected.

'They are, but Miss Melville says that their families are concerned that they cannot get access to them. They say that the institute is just a cult and they demand that we investigate it.'

Torquil looked ceilingwards and groaned. 'Investigate what, exactly?'

'They are claiming that they may be keeping people there against their will.'

'That is an unpleasant thought,' said Wallace.

'A serious accusation,' Douglas agreed.

'So we had best check it out,' Torquil acquiesced. 'Anything else, Morag?'

Morag sighed. 'Annie McConville was also complaining about the Goat's Head Farm people. She was out walking her dogs this morning and she was stopped from going up to the actual headland by some boorish chap in a big green Ford van. He had a Rottweiler or some big dog with him. She says he was needlessly rude to her.'

'Hardly a police matter though, is it?' Torquil queried.

Morag eyed him askance. 'It is Annie McConville though, boss. You know what she's like. If we don't do something she'll be living on the doorstep with her pack of dogs.'

Torquil put his hands over his face in exasperation. Then, turning to Lorna, he said, 'Do you see the sort of things we have to put up with here? This is our bread and butter. Sorting out bickering between folk. If you want crime you've come to the wrong place!' He tapped his fingers on the desk. 'OK, so let's get cracking. I'll go and see Calum. Morag, how about you and Lorna going over to Dunshiffin Castle and doing a bit of digging around. We could do with knowing a bit more about The Daisy Institute and I think the female touch is required.'

He looked up and grinned at Ewan. 'How's about a trip out to the Goat's Head and having a wee word with these folk about being nice to one of our celebrity senior citizens?'

'Sure thing, Torquil,' the big constable said enthusiastically.

'Then you can liaise with Annie McConville.'

Ewan's face dropped. 'If you insist, Torquil.'

Wallace Drummond put an arm around his brother's shoulder. 'Looks like there are no jobs for the handsome specials? I guess we could go —'

'I didn't say that, Wallace,' Torquil cut in. 'It would help if you two followed up on that last task.'

'What was that, Torquil?' Douglas asked warily.

'The post-mortem on Finlay MacNeil. It would be good to know what Ralph McLelland thinks. Why don't you two pop along and see him?'

Wallace shrugged. 'No bother, Inspector McKinnon. But would it be OK if we just popped along to the Bonnie Prince Charlie for a snifter to give us a bit of Dutch courage?'

Ewan McPhee answered on behalf of his superior. 'Drinking on duty! Away with the pair of you before I get my hammer to you!'

'What's the matter, Padre? You look as if you have seen a ghost.'

'Worse than that, Mollie. A tragedy, so it is. I found Finlay MacNeil at the bottom of the cliffs beyond his cabin.' He shook his head sadly. 'He is dead.'

Mollie gasped. 'Do you think he was —' She hesitated, then went on in a half-whisper, 'Drunk? I saw him on the TV last night.'

Lachlan shrugged. 'It is not for me to say, Mollie. I believe Dr McLelland will be doing a post-mortem examination.' He pointed at one of the optics. 'A single Glen Corlin, if you please. And will you join me, Mollie?'

'A real shock for you,' Mollie said, reaching for a couple of glasses. 'These are on the house, Padre.' And reaching above her head she tapped the bell then raised her voice to announce to the rest of the clientele, 'We have a tragedy here. Finlay MacNeil has died in an accident. If anyone would care to join us we are having a drink on the house in his memory.'

Amid gasps of astonishment and much murmuring of sorrow the bar came to life. The words of sympathy came thick and fast, and before long the subdued mood was gradually replaced by a lightening of spirits as people fell into anecdotage.

'Do you remember the time Finlay caught a fish in his trousers?'

'He was the most erudite of writers.'

The Padre raised his second glass to Mollie and winked at her as she bustled about with her bar staff raising glasses to optics and pulling a veritable spate of Heather Ale into fresh glasses. Her offer of drinks on the house was a sure-fire way of generating extra custom, as she well knew. A show of generosity by the landlady was inevitably reciprocated by two or three rounds of magnanimity from her loyal customers.

Lachlan was just filling his pipe preparatory to taking his leave when he felt a hand on his shoulder. Turning he found himself confronted by Finbar Donleavy and Danny Wade, each with a pint of Heather Ale in their hands.

'A sad business this is,' said Finbar with a sympathetic shake of his head. 'To think that we were — er — talking to the man just last night.'

The Padre frowned. 'Not exactly talking to him though, were you? More like filming his outburst.'

'He was pretty vitriolic about Logan Burns. We felt we had to halt the interview.'

'I know. I saw the news,' the Padre nodded affably. 'And I read Calum Steele's piece in the papers.'

Finbar's face darkened. 'That newshound is chancing his arm. He made some defamatory remarks about me in that local rag.'

'That local rag is highly respected in West Uist,' the Padre countered.

'He broke our camera you know,' Danny Wade said. 'We reported him to the police.'

The Padre bit his lip. 'That doesn't sound like Calum.'

Danny Wade snorted. 'It was an expensive piece of Scottish TV property. We expect action from the police for criminal damage. We're just waiting for the next ferry to bring in a replacement camera so we can film for the news tonight.'

'You will be continuing the pieces about the institute then?'

'The solstice won't stop for Finlay MacNeil's death,' Finbar replied unemotionally. 'It is just two days away. I will say a few words about the tragedy, of course.' He sipped his beer, and then asked casually, 'What do you as a man of the church think about The Daisy Institute? They seem to be getting a lot of attention. Have you seen the number of people that are coming into the island?'

The Padre had been half-expecting the question. 'Aye, the island is pretty busy right now, but it is the height of the summer and it is a beautiful island. But I am afraid that I have no comments to make about The Daisy Institute. I am eagerly awaiting whatever revelation Logan Burns is promising us.' He clenched his pipe between his teeth, nodded, then left.

The two newsmen stared after him.

'Nothing there then, eh, Finbar?' Danny Wade commented.

Finbar shrugged his shoulders noncommittally. 'Who knows? If the Padre does know anything he isn't saying. That was just a brush-off.' He took a hefty swig of beer. 'Looks like we will still have to do some spade-work ourselves.'

Danny Wade laughed. 'And get it all on camera.'

They both grinned and clinked glasses, neither having noticed the hoodie-clad figure sipping a cola a few feet along the bar from them.

CHAPTER SIX

Calum had recovered by the time he got back to the *West Uist Chronicle* offices. At least, he had recovered from the shock of the fracas with the younger McQueen, but not from the emotional trauma of being up at the Hoolish Farm again. It had only really hit him when he reached his scooter and hurled up his late breakfast. From that moment, as he rode his Lambretta back along the coastal road, he could not free his mind of the image of Esther Noble hanging from the banister in the hall of the farmhouse.

Resisting the urge to pull out the bottle of Glen Corlin that he kept in the R-S drawer of his filing cabinet — 'R' being for 'restorative' — he went through to the kitchenette, filled the kettle and brewed himself a strong pot of tea. He was just stirring the pot when the bell went and the outer door opened and closed.

'If that is tea I hear being made, I'll have a cup,' Torquil's voice called up the stairwell.

Calum grinned as he heard his friend mounting the stairs two at a time.

'Aye, you have come for a decent cup of tea then, instead of that ditch water that Ewan McPhee dishes up,' Calum replied with a grin. 'What brings you to the fourth estate, Piper?'

Torquil gave a mock scowl. 'Semi-official business, I am afraid, Calum. Complaints about you.'

The newspaper editor produced an extra mug from the cupboard and poured tea.

'About me? Havers, man. I am a model of respectability. Who is complaining?'

'Just about everyone, Calum,' Torquil replied, dropping on to the battered settee and accepting the mug. He poured milk into it from the half-empty bottle and stirred it to an agreeable cream colour. He winked to indicate that he was teasing.

'Three complaints actually. In order, criminal damage, trespass and bodily harm, and defamation of character. The complainants respectively being, Finbar Donleavy and his cameraman Danny Wade, Tavish McQueen and Logan Burns.'

Calum took a sip of tea and wiped his lips with the back of his hand. 'You are joking me, are you not?'

Torquil shook his head. 'I'm investigating, Calum. I'm here for your version on each count.'

Calum sighed and sat down on the edge of his camp bed. 'Criminal damage, so they are talking about their camera, right? Well, that is simple, it was an accident. They weren't looking where they were going and barged into me. Clumsy buggers. They were peeved because of my review of their news slot.' He sneered. 'What sort of a journalist is he? The simple fact is that he can't take criticism and he's tried to get back at me with this trumpery.'

'Sounds reasonable. Your word against theirs then.'

'Aye, and what's this nonsense from McQueen?'

'They say you broke into their egg farm and assaulted Angus McQueen, the owner's son.'

Calum thumped his knee with his fist. 'He says I assaulted him?'

Torquil could barely keep the grin from his face, as he recalled the all too recent banter between Ewan and the Drummond twins about Calum's fighting ability. 'Aye, he says that you broke into the farm, beat up Angus McQueen and took a lot of unauthorized photographs.'

'Ha! I took photographs all right. That is what we investigative journalists do. But I didn't break in, the door was open and I popped in to — er — make an appointment. When I was there I was shocked at the state of the poor birds there and I did take a few pictures. I will be writing up the article later and it will appear with the photographs in the next edition of the *Chronicle*. It is a scandal, so it is. The place is a health hazard and I am thinking of reporting them for cruelty.'

'Do you want to make that formal, Calum?'

The newsman pursed his lips for a moment then shook his head decisively. 'No. The power of the press will bring other powers to bear. A bit of good old-fashioned exposure should set the wheels in motion.'

'And what about this assault claim?'

'Pah! The bugger attacked me.' Calum sat upright, his chest expanding with ruffled pride. 'He should have thought better than to tangle with a martial artist.' And with a sudden guffaw, he told Torquil about the attack from behind, and of his recollection of the Bazooka Bob bubble-gum cards and the drawings of the judo throw. He chuckled as he put down his mug, stood up and demonstrated the throw with a cushion.

'And here is the picture I took of him after I threw him,' Calum went on, showing his friend the picture on his digital camera. 'That will be going into the paper as well.'

Torquil grinned. 'Spiky wee gink, aren't you?'

'You said it, Piper. Now what about this defamation rubbish?'

Torquil shrugged and swallowed the remains of his tea. 'I think you said it. Sounds like rubbish to me. Logan Burns claims that you have defamed him and his institute. It is nothing to do with us, of course. I just thought I'd warn you in case he decides to take legal action.'

'The *Chronicle* will not be suppressed. Let him do his worst.' He finished his own tea and stood staring at the mug for a moment. 'But going back to the Hoolish Farm, I have to say that it brought back bad memories.' He bit his lip and swallowed hard. 'I keep seeing Esther's body hanging there. I don't sleep well these days because of it.'

Torquil nodded in agreement. 'An unpleasant business, but you have to put it out of your head, Calum. There was nothing you or anyone could do. Remember what the Fatal Accident Inquiry said.'

'But maybe if I had got there sooner. He passed me on the road, remember. Almost knocked me down.'

Torquil put his hand on his friend's shoulder and squeezed.

'Anyway, I'd better be off,' he said. 'I have to write up my reports on these three "cases". Thanks for your co-operation, Calum.'

Calum grinned sheepishly. 'Always a pleasure, Piper.' He sighed and cracked his knuckles. 'And now I had better get the wheels of the press rolling. I have articles to write.'

Torquil grinned and descended the stairs. But, by the time he reached the door, the grin had disappeared. He had to admit to himself that he had never felt easy himself about the tragedy at Hoolish Farm back in the winter. There was something about it that didn't seem right, but he just couldn't put his finger on it.

Morag drew the station's tired old Ford Escort into the Dunshiffin Castle courtyard and pulled to a halt beside a parked Rolls Royce, a Porsche Boxter and one of the latest XK Jaguars. Lorna got out and looked up admiringly at the great Scottish baronial castle, with its original structure dating back to the fourteenth century when the first of the McLeod lairds had built it. An impressive flight of stone steps led up to the huge main doors, beside which was a seemingly incongruous sign with the logo of a daisy on it. Underneath it, large italicized yellow letters proclaimed it to be 'The *West Uist HQ of the DSY Institute*' with small letters underneath explaining that it was: 'Centre for the Study of Divinity and Spirituality.'

'Looks as if there is money to be made in daisies,' she joked, as Morag came round the car to join her.

'The cars are all owned by The Daisy Institute, not by individuals,' came a voice from the top of the steps.

The two sergeants looked up and saw Drew Kelso standing at the open doors, his hands folded inside the voluminous sleeves of his yellow hoodie, like a modern day monk.

'Very nice,' said Lorna, feeling rather caught on the hop.

Drew smiled down at them, his smile reminding Morag of the fixed smile on a ventriloquist's dummy. 'I am Drew Kelso, the Financial Director of The Daisy Institute. Won't you come in? You are police, are you not? We were expecting you.'

'You were expecting us?' Morag repeated, as she mounted the steps, where they introduced themselves and both produced warrant cards.

'Yes, Logan Burns is waiting in his office with Saki Yasuda. We want to co-operate as much as possible.'

The two sergeants looked at each other as they passed him into the great hall, which Lorna noticed was bedecked with deer heads, antlers and innumerable crossed claymores, shields, and pikestaffs. A large portrait of a kilted laird looked down at them from the top of a magnificent oak staircase.

'Hideous, aren't they?' Drew Kelso said, as he caught her look of wonder. 'Hardly the right message for an institute like ours, but Logan insisted that the castle should still retain its identity. He has very clear views about maintaining character. This way, please.'

A door opened and a stream of young people teemed out, the majority dressed in pink hoodies, but with several dressed in similarly cut white garments.

'Why exactly were you expecting us, Mr —?' Lorna asked.

'Drew, just call me Drew.' His smile faded and he looked bemused. 'It is about the tragedy, is it not? About MacNeil's death?'

Morag stopped. 'How did you hear about Mr MacNeil's death?'

Drew shrugged. 'Someone heard about it when they were in Kyleshiffin. Everyone at the institute knows. So sad, so very sad.'

'Actually, we were here to have a chat about some complaints,' said Morag.

'Complaints? From whom?'

'Perhaps we could explain in the office as you suggested,' Morag went on.

'Of course,' Drew replied. He turned to lead the way again.

Another door opened and more young people came into the corridor. Morag caught sight of two young women and waved to them.

'Actually, do you mind if Sergeant Golspie has a chat with you all? I've just seen a couple of my neighbours. I'll just have a word with them.'

And before either Lorna or Drew could say anything Morag had linked arms with Agnes Doyle and Eileen Lamont and loudly and assertively proposed that they take her for a cup of tea.

Pug Cruikshank was in good spirits, almost literally, as he showed his latest customers around the cages of the barn, while Tyler and Wilf put a couple of the dogs through their paces on the treadmills. There were four customers, two from Ireland, one from Birmingham and the last from Norway. As was usual, Clem O'Hanlan and his uncle had brought hip flasks of poteen with them, and Lars Sorensen had produced a bottle of vodka. Between them, apart from the teetotal Brummie, known always as Mr Borawski, they had drunk half of each, as well as half a bottle of Glen Corlin before leaving the farmhouse.

'Hey, Mr Borawski, why won't you drink with us? You worried we'll poison you, eh?' Clem OHanlan queried cheerily.

Mr Borawski was a stocky little fellow, widely known throughout the international dog-fighting fraternity as not being someone to trifle with. He had many brothers and uncles and there were rumours of many business interests that would have made the Kray brothers interested at the very least. He said nothing as he lit up a Marlborough and eyed Pug meaningfully.

'Mr Borawski is a religious man,' Pug said quickly. 'The booze is against his religion.'

Clem's Uncle Sean guffawed. 'Sure, I understand that all right. You have to follow your religion and do what your priests tell you. My auld dad, he was a priest and he taught by example. Drinking is everything to a good Catholic.' With which he produced a hip flask of poteen and took a hefty swig.

Lars Sorensen scowled, screwing his beetle brows so that they became a corrugated series of lines across his forehead. 'Catholic priests don't have children!'

'Not in Norway, maybe,' interjected Clem. 'But in our country, well, let's say things are a lot more liberal.'

Wilf turned and beamed. He began a lewd anecdote, but was quickly halted by Pug who had no wish to allow alcohol to get in the way of business.

'All right, lads!' he said firmly. 'Let's get down to brass tacks. You've seen our stock and you can see that we've got more on the way soon. Who wants to make me an offer?'

Mr Borawski blew a cloud of smoke from between thin lips. 'I am slightly impressed, Pug. Maybe if —'

'Slightly impressed!' Tyler Brady exclaimed stiffly. 'Why you don't —'

Suddenly, a red light on a wall began flashing and a buzzer started to emit a pulsed warning.

Pug darted to a window and pulled back a shutter slightly. He picked up a pair of binoculars that were perched on the sill and focused them through the gap on the long sweeping track that led from the cattle grid 400 yards away, just beyond which they had strung the pressure wire that alerted them to anyone approaching.

'Shit! This could be trouble.' He let the shutter slip back and turned to the others. 'Looks like the police. Everyone stay here. Wilf, you keep the dogs quiet. Tyler, you and me will go walkies with these two.' He snapped his fingers irritably. 'Quickly, for fuck's sake!'

PC Ewan McPhee felt that he had drawn the short straw, both in terms of the investigation that had been allocated to him by Torquil, and by the mode of transport that he had been forced to take. Ordinarily he would have chosen to use his mountain bike, but twisted front forks had forced him to plead with his mother to borrow Nippy, as everyone in Kyleshiffin lovingly referred to her forty-year-old *Norman Nippy* moped. It wasn't that he minded using it, for it had belonged to his late fisherman father, but rather the fact that a six foot four red-headed police constable looked ridiculous riding it. When it was new, its 50 cc engine had a maximum speed of thirty-five miles an hour, but time had considerably slowed Nippy down. Ewan's eighteen-stone frame reduced that figure to an almost pedestrian speed.

Having first of all checked that there was no one at home in the Goat's Head farmhouse he had set off towards the Goat's Head itself, where Annie McConville had said that she had been turned away by one of the farm staff.

He steered Nippy along the track past the pig fields towards the large distant barn. As he approached, he saw a door open and two men emerged, each with a large dog on a lead. Despite himself, Ewan cringed.

He was not overly fond of dogs.

Morag sat back in one of the refectory chairs and smiled at the four pink hoodie-clad Daisy Institute inceptors sitting around the table. Within minutes of sitting down with Eileen Lamont and Agnes Doyle, they had been joined by the two other locals who had recently enrolled. Morag knew them all, at least by sight, but she suspected that their period of seclusion from the other islanders may have somehow stimulated a feeling of homesickness and heightened a need to talk to one of their own. She had no doubt that news of the arrival of two woman police sergeants would have spread instantly round the castle.

'So, how are you all enjoying yourselves?' she asked, picking up her tea and sipping.

'It's fantastic!' enthused Agnes Doyle, a tall, twenty-year-old with long braided hair and prominent, uneven teeth.

'The best thing I've ever done in my life,' agreed Alan Brodie.

Morag nodded, partly because Alan, a nineteen-year-old, had a local reputation as a misfit.

Nancy MacRurie, an attractive brunette like Eileen, sat forward with her arms crossed on the table in front of her. 'We're just fine, Sergeant Driscoll. Why do you ask? What is it to the police?'

Morag shrugged the question aside with a wave of her hand. 'Actually, my colleague is here seeing your director. She has just joined us so I was showing her around. And seeing Eileen and Agnes here, I just grabbed the opportunity to buy you a cup of tea.'

Eileen Lamont sniggered girlishly, almost a little hysterically, Morag thought. 'It is brilliant, Sergeant Driscoll, really it is. Even though I didn't think so in the first couple of weeks. I almost left, you know.'

'Why was that?' Morag asked casually.

'I was lonely. I missed my folk. I missed Mrs McConville and her dogs.'

'Of course, you used to help her with the dog sanctuary, didn't you?'

'I did. In between my work at the vet's, but I suppose I just felt I needed a change from all the animals for a while, and that was why I joined the institute. And I am glad I did. Logan Burns is a ... a ... genius.'

'What stopped you leaving?'

Eileen smiled and pointed to a group of three white-hoodied individuals who had just come in and sat down at a nearby table. 'Those three acolytes stopped me. Especially Johanna Waltari. She is fabulous.'

Morag pretended not to notice the meaningful looks that the other three inceptors about the table exchanged between themselves. Her suspicions seemed to be confirmed by the wave from Eileen that was reciprocated with a little smile by the one called Johanna.

'Well, well,' called out Peter, upon spotting Morag and the inceptors. 'Look, Henry, it's the lovely sergeant we met the other day.' And as Henrietta beamed and waved he gave Morag a wink.

Morag acknowledged them with a wave. 'That is Peter, isn't it?' she whispered softly to the others. 'I met him in Kyleshiffin the other day. He seemed —'

'Totally up himself,' Alan volunteered.

'He and Henrietta are practically an item,' said Nancy. 'More's the pity. I think he's hot!' And before long the floodgates opened and they were filling Morag in on all the gossip, far more freely and eloquently than they would if she had been formally interviewing them. And that was just what Morag wanted. She made mental notes that she would transcribe on to paper later on.

If there was one thing Lorna prided herself on it was her ability to think on her feet and to assess situations quickly. That had been part of the attraction of the Force in the first place, being presented with a situation and having to come up with an action plan in one's mind immediately. As she sat down in the chair proffered to her by Drew Kelso her eyes took in the decor of the office with its large thick Persian rug, the plush leather armchairs, the murals hanging on two of the walls and the old bookcases full of a mixture of original leather-bound books and numerous brightly coloured works that she assumed were more recent additions to the old castle library.

'We have added substantially to the old library,' Logan Burns said from the other side of the old oak desk, as if divining her thoughts. 'And you are Sergeant —?'

'Golspie. Sergeant Lorna Golspie.'

'May we call you Lorna?' Drew asked, as he took a seat on the settee beside Saki Yasuda, the impression of a twinkle in his eye. 'And would you like tea, coffee?'

Ordinarily Lorna would have preferred to maintain a strictly professional manner, especially as she felt somewhat outnumbered by the three directors of the institute, but instead she smiled and shrugged her shoulders. 'Lorna is my name,' she said, with as much casualness as she could muster. 'Nothing to drink, thank you.'

'People do not show enough of themselves,' Saki Yasuda said with an encouraging nod of her head. 'There is a tendency to hide behind titles and job descriptions.'

'Do you think so?' Lorna returned. She noted the way that Saki Yasuda sat, gracefully like a cat. Her voice almost purred.

'I do. That is what we go to such great lengths to instil into our inceptors. They have to let go of the strict uniforms that society makes us wear.'

Lorna raised an eyebrow and added jokingly, 'Really? Aren't we all still wearing uniforms? I've got on my police pullover and you are all wearing these hoodies. Aren't they uniforms?'

Saki Yasuda's brows wrinkled slightly and for a moment Lorna thought she was going to lose her feline-like composure. Logan Burns came to her rescue.

'Well said, Lorna. It is true, no one can truly escape the confines of their position in society. But these hoodies of ours are designed to be loose, casual.'

'But they show a hierarchy, do they not?' Lorna asked. 'You three are all in yellow, some of your staff are in white and the newer members are in pink.'

Logan clapped his hands. 'You have us there. But it is a hierarchy of attainment, not of supremacy.'

'Isn't it? It looks a bit like teachers, prefects and pupils to me. In fact, that is one of the reasons I and my colleague Sergeant Driscoll have come to see you. There have been complaints.'

Logan Burns leaned on his desk, his hands interlocked. 'Against the institute? Tell me more, Lorna.'

'The families of four of your — what do you call them — inceptors, have complained that they have been denied access to their relatives. They claim that the institute is too regimented and that it is, well, that it is a cult.'

The three directors looked at each other in amazement then burst into synchronized, disbelieving laughter.

'That is utterly ridiculous,' Logan Burns said at last. 'The Daisy Institute is a serious study organization. Our purpose is to waken people up to the divinity and spirituality that is all around us, in every religion and philosophical system that there is. Our inceptors and acolytes — and we have centres in five countries — all come to us of their own free will for instruction on how to get in contact with their own inner selves and inner spirituality. We don't stop anyone from communicating with their families. If they don't communicate it is their choice not to, and not because they have been prevented in any way.'

'We teach them how to communicate with themselves,' Saki volunteered.

Lorna frowned. 'I don't quite understand.'

'We teach them to meditate, to get in touch with their energy systems and through that with their higher selves.'

Drew sat forward. 'It is through one's higher self that one can communicate with the divine.'

Lorna felt that the conversation was getting too metaphysical. She decided to bring it back to her purpose. 'So the inceptors can call out and they can receive phone calls here?'

'Not exactly,' Logan Burns replied, with a shake of his head. 'We do not allow mobile telephones in the institute. They can, if they wish, use one of the directors' lines.'

'How do you explain the complaints about not being able to speak to their relatives?'

Drew Kelso shook his head. 'It can't have happened often. Perhaps the inceptors have been in different parts of the castle, meditating, or doing personal study. Or doing one or other of the vigils that we ask them to do. For example, we use the old dungeon as a room of contemplation for focusing on fear and eradicating it. And one night an inceptor keeps a vigil over the Hoolish Stones from the top of the north tower.'

Logan Burns unlocked his hands. 'We really can assure you that if anyone would like to speak to their relatives they may do so.' He laughed. 'And as you can see, we have no locks on the doors, no chains. Everything that you have mentioned can be put down to free will.'

'So they can visit them whenever they wish?'

'Preferably not in the first three months. We do like that time to acclimatize them to meditational practices. After that, they may come and go as they please. Just ask any of our senior inceptors, or any of the acolytes.'

Lorna nodded. 'That is good to get that cleared up. Which brings me to the other matter. I believe it is a complaint that you made, Dr Burns, against the editor of the *West Uist Chronicle*.'

'Call me Logan, please,' he returned with a smile. 'And let us just say that I would like to withdraw my complaint. I was a little piqued by something the good editor wrote in his paper. I have calmed down now and really have no wish to pursue it.'

Lorna smiled. 'Nice to make short work of that then. I won't keep you any longer.'

They all stood and Drew opened the door for her.

'Oh yes, there was just one thing,' Lorna said at the threshold, as she stood looking Drew straight in the eye. 'Why did you think we would be coming to ask you about Finlay MacNeil? You did say that you all wanted to co-operate with us. Why was that?'

Drew looked at the others before replying. 'We heard about his sudden, tragic death. After his drunken rampage at the Hoolish Stones last night we thought that you might —'

'Might what?' Lorna prompted, as he hesitated.

'That people might think that we had put a spell on him,' said Saki Yasuda, with the
suggestion of a sarcastic smile on her lips. 'That's what people think cults do isn't it, Sergeant?'

Logan Burns guffawed. 'But we are no cult, are we, Saki?' He held out his hand to Lorna. 'Feel free to call anytime you like, Lorna.'

Drew Kelso shook her hand. 'Absolutely anytime,' he added, holding her regard for a moment and making her feel conscious of that odd twinkle she had noticed before. Somehow it gave her a tingle down the spine. It was at variance from the feeling of antipathy that she had picked up from Saki Yasuda.

She gave a professional smile. 'Thank you all for your cooperation,' she said, as she heard Morag's voice outside in the corridor. 'Meeting you all has been very ... enlightening.'

Ewan rode up the track towards the two men, each with a muscular dog on a chain.

'You are on private property!' Tyler Brady said, waving his hand as if to indicate that Ewan should stop and go back. Ewan thought he saw the other man grunt something and the gesticulating one dropped his hand to his side.

He rode up to them and drew Nippy to a halt.

'*Latha math*, good morning,' Ewan greeted, as he sat on the moped saddle planting his long legs firmly on the ground. 'I am PC Ewan McPhee of the local police force. I have come to see you about —'

Immediately the two dogs started to strain at their leashes and growl menacingly.

'— I have come to see you about a complaint,' Ewan went on, his mouth suddenly going very dry.

Pug Cruikshank's face registered astonishment. 'A complaint, Officer? About what?'

'Your attitude for one thing. One of our respected citizens was told in no uncertain manner that this was private property and that she should not walk here.'

'That will be that mad old dog woman I told you about, Pug,' said Tyler Brady. 'I saw her off this morning because she and her dogs were disturbing the pigs.'

'Mrs McConville would not have allowed her dogs to disturb your pigs, I am sure,' Ewan returned. 'She is an expert in dog-handling.'

One of the dogs growled and bared its teeth.

'I hope you keep those dogs under good control,' he added. 'What breed are they?'

'This is an American Staff and Tyler there has got a boxer-terrier mix,' Pug explained quickly. 'Both perfectly legal. And both expertly trained and controlled.'

'And this is still private land,' Tyler Brady said belligerently.

Ewan did not like the man's tone. Sitting astride the moped he felt slightly disadvantaged, since both were tall men. He dismounted and kicked the moped's stand down and drew himself up to his full height, which was a couple of inches taller than either of them.

'As you should know,' he said. 'Mrs McConville was free to walk over your land as long as she did no harm to your crops.'

'Or livestock,' Pug interjected. Then, with a smile, 'But look Officer, we have no objection to anyone walking over our farm, just as long as they stay away from the pigs. The saddleback sows are highly strung animals and soon get upset. If they get upset, their milk dries up and the poor wee piglets are at real risk.' He patted Tyler Brady on the shoulder. 'Tyler here is mad about our pigs and can be a wee bit territorial, that's all.'

Tyler Brady eyed Ewan fiercely. 'Aye, territorial, that's me. And I don't take any crap from anyone. Not even the police.'

'Tyler, calm down,' Pug soothed. He turned to Ewan. 'We lost three piglets recently. He's chewed up, so he is. Will that be all then, Officer?'

Ewan stood a moment pensively chewing his lip. 'I think so. Just as long as there are no more complaints about rudeness, or about your dogs.'

'There will be no complaints about our dogs, don't you worry,' Pug returned, bending down to pat his brown-headed American Staff firmly, which began furiously wagging its stumpy tail. 'And tell your Mrs McConville she is welcome to walk our farm as long as she keeps well clear of the pigs.'

Ewan nodded to them, remounted Nippy and set off, vigorously pedalling until the Norton motor kicked in.

Once he was well out of earshot Tyler Brady spat then sneered, 'We could have kicked that big oafs arse!'

He was rewarded by Pug Cruikshank grabbing a handful of his shirt and yanking him almost off his feet. 'You bloody idiot! You could have had him on to us. If you ever make a bollocks like that with the police again, I'll knock your bloody head off! Understand?'

Tyler Brady, stared in horror at the unbridled anger written across Pug's face. He
swallowed hard and nodded eagerly. He was all too well aware of the damage that temper of Pug's could inflict.

Wallace and Douglas Drummond had taken Ewan's advice and gone straight to the Kyleshiffin Cottage Hospital rather than make a detour to the Bonnie Prince Charlie. Ralph McLelland was pulling into the car park just as they were entering the main door. He jumped out of his old Bentley, hauling his Gladstone bag along with him.

'Are you here to watch me, lads?' he asked. 'I had to dash out on a house call to the south of the island first so I haven't had time to start.'

He saw their simultaneous looks of disappointment. 'Why don't you pop along to the Bonnie Prince Charlie for a half-pint while I get changed and get the body ready?'

Wallace shook his head and made a sad clacking noise with his tongue. 'We are not allowed. Duty, you see.'

'Ewan McPhee said he'd get his hammer to us, the big lummox,' Douglas added with mock fear.

Ralph stroked his chin. 'But post-mortems are not for the faint-hearted. You need a good stomach.'

The twins gave each other a swift appraisal. 'I think we can safely say that neither of us is faint-hearted,' said Wallace.

'And gutting fish the amount of time we have to probably means that we have good enough stomachs, thank you, Dr McLelland.'

'That's a pity,' Ralph said, eyeing the two of them good-humouredly. 'I was going to offer you both a dram from my special medicinal bottle before we begin.'

Their eyes lit up.

'Well, if it is for medicinal purposes, Dr McLelland, then who are we to refuse?'

'Aye, you wouldn't want us getting light-headed while you are working, would you?'

'No,' Ralph replied. 'To the mortuary it is then.'

CHAPTER SEVEN

The skirl of the bagpipes greeted Morag and Lorna when they arrived back at the police station just as Ewan chugged up Kirk Wynd on Nippy.

'Don't mind me asking, will you, Morag,' Lorna said as she got out of the station Ford Escort, her expression a study in concealed disdain, 'but is Torquil good?'

Morag looked bemused for a moment, then beamed. 'Good? He's the best, Lorna. Torquil is a Silver Quaich champion. We are proud of him on the island. That's why so many folk just call him Piper.'

'That's what I thought,' Lorna replied, as she followed Morag in. 'He sounds — great.' She suppressed a smile at the unconscious phonetic connection. In truth, she had never been a fan of the great Highland bagpipes.

Ewan fell into step behind them. 'Great, isn't he?' he said with a grin.

'Just what I was thinking,' Lorna replied, with a blush.

'Ah! Just in time,' Torquil said, dropping the blowpipe from his lips and instantly silencing the pipes with a swift chop to the bag. 'I have the kettle on and was just having a quick practice before you all came back.'

He grinned at Lorna. 'You will not have heard the pipes properly, I'm betting. You will need to hear them outside. I'll give you a recital when we get some time.' And at her smile, he winked. 'Maybe even let you have a go.'

'You are honoured,' Morag said, with a look of surprise as Torquil disappeared into his office. 'He doesn't usually let anyone within fifty yards of his pipes. Maybe he is —?'

But the blush that appeared on Lorna's cheeks stopped her from speculating further. Instead, she turned to Ewan and patted him on the shoulder. 'How about you making the tea, eh, my precious? You know how the boss makes it too weak.'

Five minutes later they were all gathered in Torquil's office ready to report on their individual investigations.

Morag was the first to report on her interview with the four local inceptors of The Daisy Institute. 'They really couldn't have been more content. Every one of them seems on a high and they seem to regard the three directors as sort of demigods. They are all looking forward to the solstice.'

'And why is that?' Torquil asked. 'Just what is so special about this summer solstice? They have been coming and going for thousands of years, so why all the big interest now?'

'Logan Burns is going to reveal something mind-shattering,' Morag replied blankly. 'They say it has something to do with revealing ancient knowledge and bringing enlightenment, but that seems to be as much any of them knows.'

'So there is no problem as far as they are concerned with access to their families?' Ewan asked over the top of his tea.

'None at all,' Morag replied. Then turning to Lorna, she asked, 'Did Logan Burns say anything interesting?'

Lorna consulted her small black notebook. 'He just refuted any problem. I didn't really explore about the solstice, but all three of the directors, that is Logan Burns, Drew Kelso and Saki Yasuda, all seemed pretty spiritual. A bit hippy-ish, actually. Logan Burns is clearly in charge, but I get the impression that there is something between them.'

'Woman's intuition?' Torquil asked with a mischievous grin.

'Don't knock it, Inspector,' Lorna returned with a raised eyebrow. 'But yes, I would say there is some sort of relationship going on there. At least between Drew Kelso and Saki Yasuda.'

'And why do you think that?' Torquil queried.

'Because he was giving me the eye and she saw it and didn't like it. She became icy towards me as if she was trying to show that he belonged to her.'

'Interesting,' Morag remarked, tapping her lips with her silver pen. 'Because Eileen Lamont told me that all the students think she has the hots for Logan Burns.' She looked at her notebook and absently drew a circle round one of her entries. 'And then again, they all think that Logan Burns has an eye for anyone female.'

Torquil dunked a ginger biscuit in his tea and then held it up and watched as it went floppy before popping it in his mouth. Then he nodded. 'So we can really put that complaint to bed, can't we? There is no restriction. The young folk are not being held against their will and it isn't a cult.'

Lorna shook her head. 'I would just say it was a slightly off the wall New Age organization. Harmless.'

'And what about the complaint against Calum Steele?' Torquil asked.

'Logan Burns says he wants to drop it,' Lorna replied.

Torquil nodded with relief. 'That's good. It seemed a waste of time anyway.' He nodded at Ewan, who was also in the middle of watching a dunked ginger biscuit bend. 'What happened up at the Goat's Head Farm?'

Distracted momentarily, Ewan flinched as the biscuit dropped into his tea, splashing his jumper. He laid the mug down, wiped his jumper and blushed to the roots of his red hair.

'Nothing really, boss. I met two of the chaps. The owner, Pug Cruikshank and a bloke called Tyler Brady. I think he is the pig man.' He shivered. 'And two great hulking dogs. Ugly buggers, I thought.'

Morag gave him a mock scowl. 'Ewan, you don't talk about members of the public like that.'

'No, not ... not them,' he stammered, before realizing that his sergeant was teasing him. 'At least, although I didn't mean it, they were fairly big lads. Handy in a fight, I expect. In fact, the Tyler guy was a bit pushy. I think he was trying to intimidate me. But anyway, I meant the dogs, not the men.'

'You do know that Cruikshank was a boxer? A former contender for the British light-heavyweight title,' Torquil informed him.

Ewan accepted the information without enthusiasm. As the wrestling champion of the Outer Isles for three years in a row he had always believed that if it came to a scrap, a wrestler would have the edge over a boxer. 'Actually, Torquil, that's funny, because I asked him what breed the dogs were and he said one was an American Staff and the other was a boxer-something cross.'

'And what did they say about intimidating Annie McConville?'

'That was the Tyler chap. He was a bit belligerent and was going on about it being private land, so I told him about the law. I think he would have argued it out with me, but his boss shushed him up. He said that in future Annie can walk her dogs as long as they don't go up there near the pigs.'

Torquil nodded. 'Which sounds pretty reasonable, I suppose. Thanks, Ewan.' He grinned. 'How was Nippy, by the way? He got you there and back.'

Ewan coloured again. 'As a matter of fact, Torquil I was going to ask you about that. Now that there are so — er —

many of us, what with Sergeant Golspie and all, do you think we could do something about police transport?'

Lorna sat forward. 'Actually, Inspector, I have taken action on that. I have hired a car from the local garage and should have it in action tomorrow.'

Ewan persisted. 'I was thinking about something for me, actually. My mum doesn't mind me using Nippy, but I wondered if the division funds would stretch to buying me a bicycle. I know where I can get a good one.'

'Tell us then,' Torquil said, humouring the big constable.

'Dairsie, the ironmonger, has a mountain bike for sale in his window. I popped in and asked him on my way back from the Goat's Head. It used to belong to Rab Noble.'

Morag shivered despite herself. 'Och, are you sure you would want to be riding that, after the tragedy and everything? Was it not up at the milking parlour when he ... died?'

'It wouldn't bother me. I could just do with some wheels. And it would be good for my exercise regime.'

Torquil grinned. 'Have a look at the finances will you, Morag? Now, about Calum.' And he told them about his own interview with the *West Uist Chronicle* editor.

Ewan shook his head. 'I still cannot believe that he pulled off that judo stunt.'

Torquil grinned back. 'I assure you, he must have. I saw the photograph that he took. And I must say that I don't really like the idea of this battery farm. It doesn't reflect well on West Uist.'

'Should we investigate it, Torquil?' Morag asked.

'I don't see how we can,' Torquil replied pensively. 'It is not illegal, is it?' He scratched his chin. 'Although I think that I had better interview the McQueens and get the whole picture. It would probably be as well to establish a baseline before Calum writes his next piece in the paper, and really stirs things up.'

'Aye, he's a wee firecracker when he gets going,' Ewan agreed.

The bell in the outer office rang out, followed by the sound of heavy boots and the raising of the counter flap.

'It is only us,' called out Wallace Drummond.

'Two drip-white characters from the local mortuary, in need of a resuscitating cup of Ewan McPhee's tea,' Douglas called.

And a moment later they entered, looking anything but drip-white.

'What news, lads?' Torquil asked. 'Did Ralph finish the post-mortem?'

Wallace held up a large manila envelope. 'We have the report, Piper. He says that he has a lot of other tests to finish it off, but in a nutshell he was full of whisky and every bone in his body was broken.'

'Entirely consistent with a fall from the top of the cliffs while under the influence of alcohol,' added Douglas. 'Doctor McLelland said that his inner organs just about exploded on impact.'

Torquil noticed that Ewan's face had suddenly drained of colour. 'Are you OK, Ewan?' he asked concernedly.

In answer, the big constable clapped a hand to his mouth and rushed from the office. They heard him race through to the toilet and a moment or two later came the sound of violent retching.

'Always a bit queasy is our Ewan,' Wallace explained to Lorna.

'How about a tune on the pipes, Piper?' Douglas asked, pointing to Torquil's pipes on the top of the filing cabinet and then nodding in the direction of the toilet and Ewan's retching. 'We could do with drowning out the lad's tummy frolics.'

The Padre had felt pretty miserable after finding Finlay MacNeil's body and had gone back to the church to say a prayer for him before having a few holes on the golf course to calm his nerves. He was kneeling before the altar when he heard the door open and footsteps as if someone had entered and was letting their eyes adjust to the dimly lit church interior.

He turned in time to see a white hoodie-clad figure retreat through the door and pull it after them. He felt sure that it was the girl Johanna, whom he had met the other day. He smiled and returned to his prayers, content to think that she found his church worthy of a second visit.

And yet as he finished and thanked the Lord for listening to him, his eye fell on *Eilthireach*, the Pilgrim Stone, and as he surveyed the ancient carvings upon it, his mind turned again to Finlay.

'You knew as much about these strange markings as anyone, didn't you, old friend?' he mused, feeling strangely close to his old golfing partner as he did so. 'I wonder if you ever actually translated their meaning.' He sighed as he broke free from the spell of the stone and turned to leave. 'Perhaps you never did. And maybe that is why Logan Burns at The Daisy Institute bothered you so much. Perhaps he actually has.'

Collecting his waiting clubs from the porch he headed off to the course and played the ninth, then the short fifth before cutting across to play the eighth, his intention being to finish off with the ninth then pop back to the manse. He was one over par as he stood on the tee, debating whether to go for his usual two-wood or go for the big one with a driver. With a click of the tongue he decided on the driver and teed the ball appropriately high. After a couple of practice swings he set up and drove, trying for extra length. But, as so often happened when he tried to force a few extra yards, he pulled the shot. It started travelling to the right of the fairway then curved back to roll some 270 yards from the tee in the light rough. Unfortunately, it was almost directly behind the ancient standing stone that they called *Carragh*, the Pillar.

'Oh man, that is just where Finlay was when we last played,' he mumbled morosely to himself as he struck a light to his pipe and ambled up the fairway.

By the time he reached it he had quite lost the taste for his pipe and tapped it out on the side of the stone as he absently inspected the lie of his ball. There was no way that he could clear the Pillar so he pulled out his seven iron with the intention of chipping out sideways. His eye fell again on the wavy lines and whorls of the ancient carving on the stone and he felt his spirits sink.

'I am going to miss you, Finlay my friend. You and your ever-ready hip flask.' And he felt the desire for a dram come over him, coupled with the desire for some company, for, as often happened, he was the only player on the course. He sighed and lay his seven-iron against the ancient monolith while he reached into his jacket pocket for his mobile phone. He rang Torquil's number as he traced the pattern on the stone.

'Is that you, laddie?' he said into the instrument. 'I don't know about you, but I am feeling the need of company this evening. I am making finnan haddie tonight and there's a problem.' He smiled as he waited for Torquil to respond. 'No, not a big problem. Just a question of quantity. Aye, there is too much for the two of us. I thought it was probably about time we invited that new sergeant of yours.' He grinned to himself

596

as he heard his nephew speaking at the other end. 'She'll come! Excellent! We'll have a dram while we watch the news then we can show her some West Uist hospitality.'

He deposited the phone in his pocket then reached for his seven-iron. He felt confident that he could still make the green in three and with luck sneak a birdie to get back to par.

Eileen Lamont and Nancy MacRurie were sitting studying in their shared room in the west wing of the castle when they saw Johanna cycle into the courtyard. Nancy smiled to herself as she saw Eileen's eyes light up.

'I wonder where she's been?' Nancy asked. 'Must be nice to be able to ride off to Kyleshiffin, or wherever you want, without having to get permission from the Gestapo.' Eileen shook her head as she shut her study folder and stood up. 'Och, it isn't that bad, as we told the sergeant. Anyway, I need to catch Johanna. It's the last chance I will have today, what with it being my turn to do the Hoolish Stones vigil tonight.'

'You like her, don't you?'

Eileen blushed and nodded.

'And she likes you?' Nancy probed, ever one to enjoy confidences. She giggled as Eileen nodded again.

'OK, so how about if I do your vigil tonight, then you can — do what you want.' Eileen let out a little gasp of delight, threw her arms about her friend's neck and planted a kiss on her cheek. Then she knocked on the window to catch Johanna's attention. As Johanna looked up a smile of recognition lit up face. Eileen gesticulated to say that she was coming down.

'Good luck!' Nancy said to Eileen's fast retreating back.

Saki Yasuda peered out of Logan Burns's office window and watched the two young women talking animatedly together in

597

the courtyard below.

'Eileen and Johanna are getting very friendly,' she announced.

Drew Kelso looked over her shoulder and frowned. 'Yes, but we can hardly discourage it, can we? I mean, people often pair up.'

Logan Burns took two quick steps across the room, his brow furrowed. 'Well, I think we ought to discourage these liaisons. This is a serious study enterprise, not some kind of dating agency.'

Eileen and Johanna crossed the courtyard hand in hand and were met by Peter and Henrietta coming down the great steps. They seemed to enjoy a few words of banter then they all retreated back up the steps into the castle.

'See what I mean?' Logan said warmly. 'These sexual tensions are bad for them. They muddy the waters.'

Drew and Saki looked at each other in concern.

'It is just youthful attraction, Logan,' Saki ventured, placatingly.

'It isn't actually causing any harm, is it?' Drew asked.

Logan spun round. 'I don't like it. It is too near the solstice. It is all too important to be screwed up by — by —' His phone rang and he crossed the room and snatched up the receiver. 'Burns!' His expression altered almost immediately. 'All fixed and ready? Excellent. I will be there.'

Replacing the phone he ran a hand through his hair, his ire all dissipated. 'That was Finbar Donleavy. They have managed to get a replacement camera so they are going to run a piece as planned.' He frowned. 'I suppose I had better make appropriate noises about our late unlamented friend, Finlay MacNeil.'

Peter and Henrietta had made the most of the afternoon and gone to bed with a bottle of Niersteiner. When they finally rolled apart after their passionate love-making, each bathed in perspiration, they lay in post-coital bliss staring breathlessly at the ceiling.

'You are a horny devil, aren't you?' Henrietta said at last. 'I know what set you off. It was seeing Johanna and Eileen getting it together.'

Peter turned on to his side and leaned on his elbow. He grinned. 'I just like to think about sex. It turns me on.'

'Thinking about other people having sex makes you horny? So am I just here to gratify your needs?' she said, tongue very much in cheek.

He gently stroked her breast. 'You are a pleasure in your own right, dearest Henry — as you well know. But what is wrong if thinking about your friends having it off stimulates one?'

'As long as it is only thinking about them.'

'Hey, come on. You were the one making lewd jokes to Johanna about having a threesome.'

'She is an attractive girl.'

Peter laughed. 'Ha! So you fancy her as well!' He pouted. 'But at least now you know that she is into other girls.'

'I suspected it already. She never mentioned it, but I have seen her look at a photograph in her room. It is of another girl. A good-looking girl. I suspect she was in love.'

'It all makes sense now then,' Peter said, the feel of Henrietta's breast under his hand arousing him again. 'And talking of thinking about other people having sex,' he said, lasciviously, 'what do you think of Miss Saki?'

She playfully elbowed him in the ribs, and then turned to him with a coquettish smile. 'Come here,' she purred. 'Let me show you what I think.'

The mouth-watering aroma of slowly poached finnan haddie greeted Lorna as Torquil opened the front door of the manse and ushered her in.

'Ignore the motorcycle bits and pieces,' he said, indicating the line of carburettors, chains and shards of gears and brakes that lay on oil-soaked newspapers along the length of the hall. 'My uncle is not the neatest of men.'

'I heard that!' boomed out Lachlan McKinnon, emerging from the kitchen, wiping his hands on an apron. 'At least twenty-five per cent of this debris belongs to my scatterbrained nephew here, another twenty-five per cent is mine, and the rest are spares for the Excelsior Talisman that we have both been rebuilding over the past decade.'

Torquil stood wrinkling his nose apologetically. 'It is slow work.'

Lorna gave him the slightest of winks. 'Like seasoning bagpipes?'

Lachlan tossed his head back and laughed. 'Don't get started on that, lassie. I am forever moving chanters and drone reeds. But come on through, we'll have a dram before dinner.'

Lorna followed him through and began by refusing a drink on the grounds that she would somehow have to get back to her hotel in Kyleshiffin. 'I'll probably get a taxi,' she said with a questioning look at Torquil. 'That way you can have a drink without worrying about taking your bike out.'

'No need to go back,' Lachlan stated. 'Stay the night, Lorna. We have rooms galore, a well-stocked bathroom with all conveniences, spare toothbrush and all.'

'Yes but —'

'And where could you be safer than with a minister and a police inspector?'

'But —?'

'But nothing, my dear.' The Padre's face creased into one of those smiles that few could resist. 'Just say that it is about time you got to know the locals and this old local could do with a bit of company tonight.' He poured three Glen Corlin malt whiskies and handed her a glass. 'Now sit you down, it's time for the news.'

Torquil switched on the television and then dropped on to the settee beside Lorna. The credits were rolling at the end of one of the imported Australian soaps and then the theme music for the Scottish TV *Six O'Clock News* rang out. And then Kirstie Macroon was reading out the headlines:

'SCOTTISH MINISTER RESIGNS AMID CANNABIS CLAIMS: TRAGEDY OF THE WEST UIST ARCHAEOLOGIST.'

The familiar inter-slot jingle sounded then:

'First we go across to West Uist where Finbar Donleavy is joined at the Hoolish Stones by Logan Burns, the Director of The Daisy Institute. Good evening, Finbar.'

The scene moved to the periphery of the Hoolish Stones where Finbar Donleavy was standing with a microphone beside Logan Burns.

'Thank you, Kirstie. I am here with Dr Logan Burns at the famous stone circle where last night we were joined by local historian and archaeologist Finlay MacNeil. It is with great sadness that I have to report that early this morning Mr MacNeil's body was found at the foot of nearby cliffs.'

He slanted the microphone in Logan Burns's direction and The Daisy Institute Director began talking.

'Thank you, Finbar. Yes, it is a great tragedy. Finlay MacNeil was one of the great local historians and he will be sorely missed on the island.'

'You didn't always see eye to eye with him, though, did you?'

'No, we had different opinions about the stones' carvings on the island, and the purpose of these great stones. I am afraid that often happens. A local amateur feels that he has a monopoly on knowledge, even greater than that of an acknowledged scholar.'

'And you are a scholar, Dr Burns, are you not?'

Logan Burns made a self-deprecating gesture.

'I don't really want to expand on that now. Not in the light of this tragedy. This evening I would just like to symbolically pay my respects and the respects of my institute to the late Finlay MacNeil.' He held up his hands and produced a long daisy chain. 'I made this today and would like to just drape it across this stone in memory of a great local historian.'

He skilfully tossed it upwards, like a lasso, to drop over the top of the great stone. He then bowed.

'In memory of Finlay MacNeil. We will be thinking of you in two days when we celebrate the summer solstice.'

The shot moved to Finbar Donleavy who also bobbed his head and gave a wan smile.

'And on that sombre note, it is good night from us at the Hoolish Stones.'

Kirstie Macroon took over and moved smoothly into the other stories.

The Padre raised his glass. 'To Finlay! Although I am not sure what he would have made of that daisy-chain stunt.'

'Was it a stunt, Padre?' Lorna asked. 'He seemed genuine to me. An ageing, but genuine, hippy.'

'Lorna interviewed Logan Burns today,' Torquil explained.

'He is a smooth operator,' Lorna volunteered. 'And so were the other two.'

'Except Saki Yasuda didn't care for you, did she?' Torquil pointed out.

Lorna smiled at him. 'There is no accounting for who we like and dislike, is there?'

The two pinpoints of colour that instantly developed on Torquil's cheeks did not go unnoticed by the Padre.

By nine o'clock, Calum Steele had finished production of the morrow's edition of the *West Uist Chronicle* and was debating whether to settle for a fish supper and a pint or shove a ready meal into the microwave and wash it down with a can or two of lager. He had just opted for a trip out to The Frying Scotsman for a supper before dropping in for a nightcap at the Bonnie Prince Charlie, and was zipping up his anorak when the window exploded and a brick caught him on the side of the head. He slumped unconscious on to the floor, a pool of blood trickling down his face to form a pool about his head.

Nancy MacRurie looked over the battlemented wall of the north tower at the silhouette of the Hoolish Stones in the moonlight. Although she had lived on the island all her life yet she had never until recently taken the slightest notice of the Stones. Now she thought they were both beautiful and incredibly meaningful.

'Thank you, Logan, and The Daisy Institute,' she mused to herself, as she leaned against the wall, enjoying her vigil. 'You have put some purpose into my life.' And reaching into her pocket she pulled out her tobacco pouch and rolled a spliff.

'No harm in a little comfort, is there, girl?' she said, lighting up and taking a deep inhalation to hold the smoke in her lungs for a few seconds. And within moments everything seemed to become more relevant, even the purpose of the Stones and her own presence in the institute. 'I wish I could fly,' she mused to herself.

She did not hear the muffled footsteps behind her. She felt something drop over her head and tighten about her throat. She clutched at it but rapidly felt her grip on consciousness start to slip away. Then a hand landed on her shoulder and spun her round. Momentarily she felt her senses return and she saw the face suddenly looming towards her.

'What the —?' she gasped in horror, then, 'You!'

She opened her mouth to scream, but the ligature tightened again and a blow to the side of her head made her reel so that she was only dimly aware of arms sweeping behind her knees, lifting her upwards to somersault over the parapet.

Then she was airborne. Thrashing wildly with arms and legs in some vain attempt to fly or catch something solid. The spliff fell from her fingers and landed on the ground a fraction of a second after her. Blood trickled from her mouth on to the ground and her sightless eyes stared out at the distant Hoolish Stones, as if in death she was maintaining her vigil until the morning.

CHAPTER EIGHT

Torquil was woken at six in the morning by Morag's call. He shot up in his bed as he received the news that Calum had been admitted to the Cottage Hospital at four in the morning.

'He woke up in a pool of his own blood,' she explained over the phone. 'Someone had thrown a brick through the *Chronicle* office window and unluckily he must have been standing in the wrong place. Anyway, he managed to call Ralph McLelland on his mobile and Ralph dashed round and admitted him.'

'Is he badly injured?' Torquil asked concernedly.

'He is concussed and needed half-a-dozen stitches, but there is no fracture.'

'Thank the Lord for that. Any idea who did it?'

'You know Calum, he has a way of putting folk's backs up. His main concern apparently was about getting the morning edition of the *Chronicle* out in time. He hasn't been interviewed yet; I just thought I'd let you know as soon as possible. Do you want one of us to pop round and see him?'

'No, that's all right. Lorna and I will go and see him after we have had breakfast.' There was a moment's pause on the other end of the phone.

'Did Lorna stay the night then?'

Torquil felt a strange feeling deep inside him at the question. Somewhat nonplussed, he replied simply, 'Aye.'

'Oh!'

'See you later then,' he said, replacing the receiver with a grin.

After a frugal breakfast, despite Lachlan's offer to send them off with a decent fry-up, Torquil and Lorna sped off to Kyleshiffin. As they hurtled along the chicane-like bends of the coastal road Torquil fancied that Lorna's arms were holding on to him just a tad tighter than before. He grinned to himself, for he had to admit that they had enjoyed a pleasant evening, and had talked about all sorts of things, apart from work, after the Padre had retired and left them to their own devices.

Calum was in one of the side rooms of the Cottage Hospital, lying with a cold compress on his forehead and the room in shadows.

'Torquil, do me a favour and talk sense into Ralph. He will not discharge me and I have a newspaper to run.'

'I saw him on the way in, Calum,' Torquil replied. 'He wants to observe you for a while. He says you were lucky and that it's a good thing you have such a thick skull.'

'I'll give him a thick skull! And I'll give the bugger who did this to me a —'

'A piece of your mind?' Lorna interjected with a smile. 'You don't want to get in trouble with the police yourself, do you?'

Calum shoved himself up on his pillows and sighed. 'Aye, you are right. I meant I was going to give them a proper telling off. An erudite piece of purple prose in the *Chronicle*. Remember the pen is mightier than the sword.' He rubbed his hands together. 'Torquil, pull up the blinds, will you? Lying here like an invalid is getting on my nerves.'

Torquil complied and the early morning sun made Calum blink. Torquil grinned. 'You are concussed, Calum. You are bound to have a sore head for a while.'

Calum removed the compress to reveal a waterproof dressing over the stitches on his temple. 'Ach! It's a bit sore, but no worse than a half-decent hangover.'

'Any idea who did it, Calum?' Lorna asked.

'No. We crusading journalists make the odd enemy along the way. It could have been any of half-a-dozen folk.' He nodded his head with satisfaction. 'At least that many.'

He recounted all that he could remember of the previous couple of days, right up until the moment the brick came through the window and knocked him out.

'When I came round the bloody thing was lying next to me. Whoever threw it had the cheek to wrap it in a copy of the *Chronicle*.'

'Which issue?' Torquil asked.

'Don't know. I didn't look. I felt so wretched all I could do was phone Ralph, and then I must have passed out again. The next thing I knew I was waking up in this bed while they got me ready to X-ray my head.'

Torquil pulled out his phone. 'I'll get Morag to send Ewan round to get the brick. And let's see what you were writing about on the day of the paper your assailant used to wrap the brick.'

'You think he'd taken issue with something I wrote?' Calum asked with a grin.

'Glad I am to see that you haven't lost your sense of humour,' Torquil replied as he called Morag.

Calum laughed. 'It's the only way, Piper. When someone tries to kill you I say laugh as you spit in their face.'

Alan Brodie had risen at 6.30, breakfasted on toast and black coffee, smoked half a spliff then made his way to the north tower to relieve Eileen from her vigil at seven. His own vigil was the shortest of the day, only lasting until ten o'clock when it was time for a group meditation. When he found the top of the tower deserted he assumed that she had sloped off early, so he went to check the room that she shared with Nancy. Finding their room unoccupied and their beds obviously unslept in, he began to panic.

Saki Yasuda was the director on duty and after she and Alan did a swift check throughout the main communal rooms of the castle she rapidly put the wheels in motion. By 7.30 a more formal search was underway and all of the inceptors and acolytes were roused from their beds.

Johanna and Eileen emerged from Johanna's room, both bleary-eyed from lack of sleep. They were immediately surrounded by friends and fellows all uttering sighs of relief.

'But where is Nancy?' she asked Saki Yasuda, after she had heard that everyone had been looking for her. 'Nancy kindly did my vigil for me.'

'Why did she do this?' Saki returned sharply. 'It was your vigil and your duty.'

'She off-offered to do it while I-I —'

'While you what?' Saki demanded, her arms folded in front of her.

Johanna answered for her. 'While Eileen stayed with me. We had long conversations in the night.'

Saki Yasuda's lips tightened and she was about to remonstrate, when from somewhere at the other side of the castle, someone shouted. Then there was a clamour of people calling to one another and before many moments the castle was bubbling with activity and noise as people moved quickly out into the corridor to congregate at the steps leading up to the north tower.

'Outside!' someone called. 'She's outside. She looks —!'

Logan Burns and Drew Kelso came bounding down the steps from the main hall and sprinted through the main gate.

'We'll take if from here, Saki,' Logan called over his shoulder. 'Keep everyone inside the castle.'

'And better call an ambulance,' Drew said, as he went past. 'We need a doctor.'

Nancy was lying in the shadows at the foot of the tower, barely visible from the top. She was lying on her front, with limbs splayed outwards and her right cheek resting on the ground in a pool of blood.

It was clear to both men as they knelt down beside her that she was long past the care of any doctor.

Morag had sent Ewan straight round to the *West Uist Chronicle* offices. Ralph had left the door open when he and Alex Lamb, the cottage hospital nursing sister's husband and cottage hospital multi-purpose porter-cum-handyman, had taken Calum off to hospital. There was glass all over the main upstairs office and a pool of blood had soaked into the already multistained carpet. Ewan photographed the room from several positions, as Morag had instructed him, then he took further pictures of the broken window and the newspaper-covered brick that still lay on the floor. Then he gingerly put it in a polythene bag ready to take back for Torquil to examine.

He was bending over to tie it when he fancied he heard a floorboard creak behind him. He was just in the process of looking round when he heard a definite noise as of a heavy step, then something thudded into the back of his head and he started to dive into a deep pool of unconsciousness. As he drifted down he had two fleeting impressions, one auditory and one olfactory.

He heard the familiar ring of the West Uist Cottage Hospital ambulance dashing off somewhere.

And he seemed to register a faint agricultural smell.

Doctor Ralph McLelland had arrived at Dunshiffin Castle minutes before Torquil roared up the road on his Royal Enfield Bullet. Torquil found him kneeling beside the body of a young woman, with the two male directors of The Daisy Institute looking on a few feet away.

'What happened?' Torquil asked, as he approached, pulling off his goggles and stripping off his gauntlets. 'Morag told me that there had been an accident. I came straight away.'

Logan Burns held out his hand and introduced himself and Drew Kelso. 'We had already called for the doctor here, but when we found her and saw that she was dead we thought we had better alert the police.'

'A tragedy,' Drew Kelso said, shaking his head and almost seeming to shiver with emotion.

Ralph removed his stethoscope from his ears and stood up. 'Poor girl! She's been dead a number of hours, I would say. She's had a tumble from the tower.'

Torquil grimaced at the sight of her lying there, her body obviously smashed. 'It is young Nancy MacRurie, is it not?'

'It is,' Logan Burns confirmed. 'She is — or rather — was one of our inceptors.'

Torquil was looking about and spotted the spliff. He picked it up and sniffed it, then knelt down and gingerly sniffed the dead girl's mouth. 'Cannabis,' he said. He reached inside his jacket and drew out a small polythene bag into which he dropped the spliff. 'Will you be able to detect it at the post-mortem, Ralph.'

'If it is in her system, then yes. Will you be informing the next of kin?'

Torquil sighed. 'Aye, we will get straight on to it. She will have to be formally identified. Can you take her back to the hospital, Ralph? Make her look ... respectable?'

And as the local GP-cum-police surgeon went over to the ambulance, Torquil pulled out his notebook and pen and started to make notes. 'What would she have been doing up there in the night?'

'It was a vigil,' Logan Burns returned. 'All of the inceptors have to do an overnight vigil on the Stones.'

Torquil was about to ask more when a scream rang out from the top of the tower. Looking up they saw two females leaning over the top of the battlement. Screwing up his eyes Torquil recognized one as Eileen Lamont. The other was a blonde-haired young woman that he did not know. Like Nancy, Eileen was wearing a pink hoodie, while the blonde girl was wearing a white one. The blonde girl had her arm about Eileen and seemed to be comforting her.

'No! Not Nancy!' Eileen Lamont cried. 'It shouldn't be you. It should've been me!'

Torquil stared at the faces of the two directors. He was not sure what emotions they were going through, except they both looked extremely worried.

Wallace and Douglas Drummond had been called in by Morag when Ewan failed to return from the *West Uist Chronicle* offices and failed to answer his mobile phone. She explained about the attack on Calum Steele and the accident at the castle.

'What do you want us to do, Morag?' Wallace asked.

'Go and check that he's all right,' she replied worriedly. 'It isn't like Ewan to dawdle.'

'We're on our way,' said Douglas, heading for the door, only for it to be pushed open as he reached for it.

'Ewan!' Morag exclaimed, at the sight of the big red-haired constable as he staggered in clutching a blood-soaked handkerchief to the back of his head. 'Whatever happened, my wee darling?'

The twins grabbed an arm each and helped him through the counter and sat him down while Morag prised his improvised dressing away from his head and inspected the wound.

'I've got it,' he said, with a wan smile, holding up the polythene bag containing the brick. 'But some devil was hiding and biffed me from behind.' He reached into a pocket and drew out a smashed camera. 'And while I was out he smashed this up.' He held it out apologetically. 'I'm sorry, Morag. I know it is police property.'

'Never mind about all that,' Morag said, replacing the handkerchief while she went to get a damp flannel and the first-aid kit. 'It is you that I am more worried about. Who could have done such a thing?'

'The same bugger who threw the brick, I am guessing,' said Douglas, through gritted teeth.

'We'll get the swine, whoever it is,' Wallace announced, meaningfully smashing a fist into the palm of his other hand. 'And when we do we'll show that you don't push West Uist men around like this.'

'You'll do nothing hasty at all,' Morag said firmly as she cleaned dried blood from Ewan's hair to get a good sight of the wound. She winced as the big constable yowled with pain. 'Och, I think we are going to need to get Ralph to put stitches in.'

'Shall we go and have a look at the *Chronicle* offices, Sergeant?' Douglas asked.

'No,' Morag returned. 'It is an even more serious crime scene now. Before it could just have been hooliganism, but now it is the scene of the serious assault on a police officer.' She dabbed antiseptic around the edges of the wound. 'It could even be attempted murder.'

'Aye, you will be wanting a proper police person then,' said Wallace. 'What about the lovely Sergeant Golspie. Could she not go?'

Morag was silent for a moment. 'I am not sure where she is at the moment. She went for tea last night with the boss and this morning when I called him about Calum he said they'd go straight round to see him. She hasn't answered her mobile.'

The twins and Ewan all looked round at her at once.

'She stayed the night at the manse then?' Douglas asked.

'Then she'll be with him now,' Wallace mused. 'At the castle.'

'I expect so,' Morag replied.

'Oh,' said Ewan.

Lorna Golspie was at that moment concluding a deal.

Torquil had dropped her off on Harbour Street as he made his way to Dunshiffin Castle. She had gone straight to Drysdale's Garage and managed to haggle the price down on a second-hand Golf GTI. It was only as Padraig Drysdale went to the office for the paperwork that she switched on her telephone to receive three messages. The first two were from Morag, both asking her to call her immediately. The third was from Superintendent Lumsden abruptly demanding she phone him, in his terms, 'yesterday!'

She phoned the superintendent first, before rapidly signing her hard-earned money away on the Golf GTI. She was feeling anxious and her mouth was dry even before she phoned Morag. She had not realized how much Superintendent Lumsden clearly hated Inspector Torquil McKinnon.

As soon as Torquil received Morag's phone message about Ewan, he excused himself with the assurance that they would be back in touch very soon. He left Ralph to organize the removal of Nancy's body to the Cottage Hospital mortuary, then he almost flew back on the Bullet to Kyleshiffin. He felt desperately sorry for young Nancy and her family who had yet to be informed, and he always felt responsible for his staff, regarding Ewan more as a younger brother and friend than a junior officer. And then there was Calum. Just thinking about his two friends, both victims of violence, made him feel even angrier and he opened the Bullet's throttle right up.

Lorna was waiting behind the counter for him as soon as he entered the station. 'Inspector McKinnon, I need to tell you something —'

'Just give me a minute, Lorna. I need to see Ewan. Is he through the back?'

She nodded with a pained expression on her face. 'He's with Morag and the Drummond twins. I think they're debating about taking him to see the doctor.'

'The doctor will be a while. He's busy taking Nancy MacRurie's body back to the mortuary.' And he told her of the discovery of her body.

Lorna sighed. 'That is an awful shame. A young girl like that.'

'It was a horrible sight, Lorna. It was all the worse since she was one of us.' He bit his lip. 'But as I said, I need to see Ewan.'

Lorna nodded, all too aware that he did. Another native of West Uist, or 'one of us', as he had just said. Not for the first time she felt an outsider.

They were all in the rest room, drinking tea. Ewan made to stand up as soon as Torquil came through the door, but he was immediately pushed back into the settee by the strong hands of the two Drummond brothers. Torquil listened to a joint summary on the events from Morag and Ewan.

'We'll get whoever did this to you, Ewan,' Torquil promised, his face grim.

'I should have been more on guard,' Ewan replied. 'I just wasn't expecting anyone to be there.'

'Did you notice if whoever it was did anything, moved anything while you were unconscious?'

Ewan shifted uncomfortably on the settee. 'I ... I didn't notice, Torquil. Sorry.'

Torquil waved his hand. 'No problem. We'll get it checked out soon enough. The most pressing matter though is to inform the MacRurie family and have one of the family identify poor Nancy's body.'

Morag nodded. 'I know them pretty well, boss. Shall I do that?'

'You're a star, Morag,' he replied giving her a wink. Then he turned back to Ewan. 'As for you, a trip to the hospital to see Ralph, then home and off to bed.' He looked at the twins. 'Will one of you take him over to the hospital?'

'I'll take him, Inspector,' came Lorna's voice from behind him. 'I have wheels now.'

'That would be a big help, thank you,' he said, turning and seeing her grimace uncomfortably.

'I am afraid that I have something else to tell you,' she said, apologetically. 'I had a call from Superintendent Lumsden. He wants to talk to you — like straight away.' She shrugged her shoulders apologetically. 'I'm sorry, but he didn't seem in a very happy mood.'

Torquil smiled at her. 'It would be a first if he was.'

To say that Superintendent Lumsden was not in a happy mood was something of an understatement, as Torquil found out a few moments later when he called his superior officer on Bara.

'About time, McKinnon,' the gruff, lowland voice snapped over the telephone. 'Just when were you planning to let me know your progress on the MacNeil case?'

'The MacNeil case, sir? Are you talking about Finlay MacNeil?'

There was the noise of a sharp intake of breath from the telephone on Bara. 'Of course I mean Finlay MacNeil. He's the local historian whose body was smashed on the rocks yesterday, in case you had forgotten.'

'But there is no MacNeil case, Superintendent Lumsden.'

'What! You mean to say that the outburst he had on national television the day before didn't ring some kind of an alarm with you? He insults that hippy man and his odd-ball outfit and then he is found at the bottom of cliffs. You don't think that is suspicious?'

Torquil himself took a deep breath and forced himself to speak slowly, politely. 'There was a post-mortem, of course. And there will be a Fatal Accident Inquiry. All the documentation is already on its way.'

'Except for your report that should have been faxed through to me straight away! I want you to investigate this and report to me pretty damned quick. And why has Sergeant Golspie not been given an area of responsibility yet?'

'That isn't how we work on West Uist, Superintendent.'

'That is how I want you to work, Inspector McKinnon. I gave you an order and it hasn't been carried out.'

'With respect, Superintendent, we have been rather busy. And Sergeant Golspie has been investigating things together with Sergeant Driscoll. And then of course with the events of today everything has got —'

'What do you mean events of today?'

Torquil made a face at the phone. 'The attack on the *West Uist Chronicle* offices last night and the assault on Calum Steele, the editor. He is in hospital with a head injury. And then the death of the young girl, Nancy MacRurie, at Dunshiffin Castle. And the attack on my constable, Ewan McPhee.'

'You are kidding me?'

Torquil replied icily. 'There is nothing there to joke about, Superintendent, I assure you.'

'Why didn't Sergeant Golspie tell me about any of this?'

'I presume because she did not know about it, sir.' Then he added with a touch of mischief, 'Perhaps you didn't give her a chance to talk, Superintendent.'

'Don't be impertinent, Inspector.'

'No impertinence intended, Superintendent. It is just that you don't seem to listen very often.'

There was a spluttering noise from the other end. 'You have me worried, McKinnon. You seem to be infecting a potentially good sergeant with your own brand of lethargy and indolence.'

'Thank you, sir,' Torquil replied glibly.

'It wasn't a compliment, McKinnon. Now get on with it. And let me have a faxed report by the end of the day. It would be nice, just once, to get a report from you before I see and hear about some disaster on national television news.'

'Of course, Superintendent. Shall I —?' He heard the click of the line being disconnected and he looked down with a hint of amusement at the dead receiver.

Together with the Drummonds, Torquil cursorily examined the *West Uist Chronicle* offices, making sure not to handle anything before Morag returned later to dust the place for fingerprints.

As he expected, there was some damage. Calum's computer had been trashed, and five bundles of the latest edition of the *Chronicle* had been tossed out of the back window, where they had scattered all over the back lane. Already there were a few people who had picked up copies and started reading them as they went about their business.

'Looks like whoever did this didn't want Calum's latest edition to be read,' said Wallace.

'Aye,' his brother agreed, 'but the damned fool doesn't know some of the good folk of West Uist. There are free papers here just for the taking. Everyone will have heard about this and will want one. They'll soon do the rounds.'

'I doubt that The Frying Scotsman will be getting a consignment of the residue of this edition to wrap fish suppers up in.'

Torquil gave a short laugh and slapped them both on the shoulder. 'Come on then, boys. Let's get a copy or two and see just what our local investigative reporter had been up to. There should be a clue or two to get us started.'

But although he didn't say it, he wondered whether instead of clues and fish suppers there might just be a red herring or two in the latest edition.

After playing four holes of golf, the Padre had set off on his Ariel Red Hunter to do a few outlying pastoral visits before heading into Kyleshiffin to chair a meeting of the St Ninian's Benevolent Fund for Fishermen and Lighthousekeepers. It was his plan after that to call in to the Cottage Hospital to see

Calum and two of his other parishioners.

He was not sure exactly why he took the turn up towards Loch Hynish, except that he felt somehow compelled. It was one of the island's beauty spots, with its *crannog* and ruined tower in the middle of its still waters.

He drew to a stop as the road reached a slight crest above the loch. Down below was a small jetty and moored to it was a small rowing boat, known locally as the 'wee free ferry,' for it was there for anyone who cared to row out to the *crannog*, the artificial Iron Age islet, to explore the old ruin that rose from a swathe of bracken and dwarf rowan tees. It was a place of bittersweet memories, for he had often rowed his nephew there when he was a boy, left in his care when Lachlan's brother and his wife, Torquil's parents, had drowned in a boating accident. Happy were those days. Yet unhappy was the memory of the tragedy that had befallen a friend of Torquil's a little more than a year before. He sighed, as memories of happier times came flooding back. And then he realized just why he had taken this road today. He wanted to see the Black House Museum, and probably pop along to the cliff top from whence he had spotted Finlay's body lying on the rocks below. He tapped the Bible in his pocket and nodded.

'A prayer over the spot is the least I can do for you, old friend,' he mused as he set off again.

He rode on and passed the sign for the Black House Museum, which had the CLOSED UNTIL FURTHER NOTICE board hanging below it. He smiled, for although Finlay rarely closed the museum, whenever he did he would do so without forewarning and without information as to when it would reopen. It was his way of broadcasting his freedom to pursue other work and interests, like his writing or his golf.

The road snaked round and the Black House Museum and the nearby log cabin came into view. Parked outside it was a maroon four by four. The Padre slowed down as he approached the Black House Museum and saw that the door was standing open. He stopped and switched off his engine, kicked down the stand and dismounted.

'Hello there,' he called out, as he went over to the open door. He looked in fully expecting to find the driver of the four by four, but the old house was empty. He came out and pulled the door after him, feeling a momentary surge of irritation that whoever had come to look at the place had wandered off and left the door open. He shook his head in despair, thinking of how that would have angered Finlay.

Mechanically, he had pulled his briar pipe from his top pocket and was contemplating filling it when he heard voices from nearby.

To his surprise they seemed to be coming from Finlay MacNeil's log cabin. That really fanned the smouldering embers of his ire and he crunched across the road and tried the door handle, which opened at his touch.

'And just what on earth do you think you are doing here?' he demanded upon seeing Finbar Donleavy standing by Finlay's desk, moving papers about while he talked into a microphone in his free hand. A few feet away from him Danny Wade, the blond-haired cameraman was busily filming.

Finbar Donleavy stopped talking and signalled Danny Wade to stop filming.

'You are trespassing on a dead man's property!' the Padre said accusingly. 'I think you had better explain yourselves.'

'No harm, Vicar,' said Danny Wade. 'We're just doing a —'

'I am a minister, not a vicar,' Lachlan said curtly. 'And I think that you may be doing a good deal of harm.'

Finbar Donleavy came forward, a placatory smile on his lips. 'We were just doing a piece on Finlay MacNeil for this evening's news, Padre. We didn't think we'd be doing any harm.'

'I don't think that going through his personal papers is justified,' Lachlan returned. 'Finlay MacNeil was my friend and I do not think that intruding like this is either a seeming way for the media to behave, nor a respectful act to someone who has just passed away so tragically.'

'The piece we were doing was quite respectful,' Finbar returned. 'I was just demonstrating that he seemed to be in the middle of some research.'

'He was writing a book,' Lachlan conceded.

'About the Hoolish Stones?'

'That is correct.'

'And you saw the way he interrupted the live broadcast the other night?'

Lachlan had seen out of the corner of his eye that Danny Wade had started filming again, just as he was aware that the broadcast journalist was attempting to extract information from him, presumably to be included in the broadcast. He had no intention of being drawn into saying anything contentious.

'Yes, I saw the programme. I told you that yesterday, as I am sure you remember. Finlay MacNeil was upset, right enough.'

Finbar's mouth almost registered a smile as he pressed on. 'He did not approve of Dr Logan Burns and The Daisy Institute, did he? Would you think it was fair to say that he vehemently disagreed with Dr Burns's theories about the Hoolish Stones?'

Lachlan reached into his side pocket and drew out a box of matches. He casually shook it and drew out a match. Then he struck it and reached past Finbar to light a small candle that stood in a Toby jug candleholder. Straightening up he smiled benignly. 'It would not be right for me to speculate on that.' And before Finbar could formulate another question, he produced his Bible. 'Now since you are here, would you care to join me in saying a few prayers in Finlay MacNeil's memory?'

Then turning directly to the camera he began, 'Finlay MacNeil was a local historian, a respected member of the West Uist —'

'Actually Padre, before you get started,' Finbar said hurriedly, 'I think we will be going.'

'Yes, we have other places to visit,' agreed Danny Wade, dropping his camera from his shoulder.

'Of course,' Lachlan replied affably. 'But about this little piece of footage, I would suggest that you do not show it on the television. You don't want to alienate the West Uist viewers, do you? I am sure that they would regard this invasion of Finlay MacNeil's home in a poor light, what with him not even buried.'

The two men took their leave.

'And pull the door closed after you, will you?' Lachlan called after them. 'We don't want anyone coming in here uninvited, do we now?'

A few moments later the four by four was started up and shot off. Only then did Lachlan permit himself a smile. 'Almost a case of bell, book and candle, eh, Finlay?' he said to the ether. 'Exorcising unwanted spirits.'

His eye fell on the whisky bottle and the tobacco pouch lying on top of the desk, and the piles of papers that the journalist had been rifling through. He straightened the piles and cast an eye over some of the notes his friend had been making. Then he noticed the old diary in one of the recesses of the desk. Finlay had always been a keen diarist, he knew.

He held up his Bible and said a prayer before blowing out the candle and preparing to leave himself. Then he clicked his tongue thoughtfully and turned back to the desk to pull out the diary. 'It wouldn't do to leave your personal thoughts here, would it, Finlay?' He popped his Bible in one pocket and the diary in the other. 'I will look after them for you.'

CHAPTER NINE

Annie McConville was just returning from the outhouses where she had fed all of the dogs under the care of the Kyleshiffin Dog Sanctuary. Zimba, her own German shepherd, and Sheila, her small West Highland, padded along beside her, like a sergeant major and corporal in her personal canine army. The amazing thing was that Annie did indeed seem to have a magic connection with most animals, but dogs in particular. She was passionate to the nth degree and was rewarded by the affection of all those waifs and strays under her care. Now well into her seventies, she was still remarkably fit for her years. Although she missed the help that Eileen Lamont used to give her in walking the dogs, yet she was still able to fit in a walk for all thirteen of them throughout the day. Everyone on the island knew her well, so raising money to keep her charges in food and medicine was never a problem. On the other hand, finding new homes for them was always difficult.

She was humming and swinging the large basket back and forth against her wellingtons as she made her way back up to the house. First Zimba stopped, his hackles rising as he emitted a low-pitched growl. Then Sheila started jumping up and down making an altogether less restrained barking noise. Immediately, the kennels erupted in an assortment of sympathetic barking and yowling.

'Wheesht! Wheesht, the lot of you,' Annie cried, putting a whistle to her lips and receiving instantaneous quiet in response.

And looking up the path she saw two men waiting for her. Father and son, almost certainly. Tavish McQueen was standing feet apart and hands clenched by his sides, while his son Angus leaned against the wall of her house, arms folded in front of him.

'Ah, it is Annie, isn't it?' the elder McQueen said, coming down the path towards her, his leather-soled brogues clacking assertively on the concrete. 'I am Tavish. That is Tavish McQueen of McQueen's Regal Eggs.'

Annie shook his hand. 'I know who you are, Mr McQueen. I have seen your face on the billboard by your farm and on your egg vans.'

'The face will soon be on TV, too, Mrs McConville. We are a growing business. It will be good for West Uist.'

'That I am not so sure of,' Annie replied dispassionately. 'You are still a newcomer, you know.'

Tavish McQueen's brow tightened somewhat, but he did not allow his smile to fade. 'Well anyway, let me get down to business. You may have heard that we were broken into?'

'I heard rumours, but I saw an article in the *Chronicle* today.'

'Oh, I heard there was no *Chronicle* today,' McQueen returned.

'There was indeed, no thanks to whoever attacked poor Calum Steele and tried to sabotage his paper. The folk of West Uist are not so easily hoodwinked. The galoot who attacked him threw the papers away, but Calum's distribution lads salvaged some and got them out to those who are loyal to the *Chronicle*.' She tilted her head and eyed both McQueens askance.

'That just about means all of the islanders,' she added meaningfully.

'Aye, and that is good. Folk should stick together. But what I meant to say, Annie, was that —'

'*Mrs McConville*,' Annie interrupted.

'Pardon me?' McQueen asked, taken aback.

'My name is Mrs McConville. I have been a widow for twenty-three years and you have not been invited to use my Christian name.'

'Aye — right — sorry. Mrs McConville, I would like to buy a couple of your dogs. A couple of the collies that used to live on our farm.'

'No. I am sorry, you cannot buy two of them.'

Angus McQueen pushed himself off the wall with his elbows. 'What about if we bought all three, Mrs McConville? We could do with them as guard dogs at the farm.'

'You cannot buy any of them,' Annie replied firmly.

'But — but this is a dog sanctuary isn't it?' Tavish McQueen spluttered. 'I am offering to take the dogs off your hands.'

'They are no trouble,' Annie replied. 'Which is more than I can say about a battery farm on West Uist. I saw the article in the *Chronicle*. And I saw the pictures of the good hiding this young hooligan got from Calum Steele when he attacked him from behind.'

'Now just a minute, woman!' Angus McQueen began, taking a pace forward.

Immediately Zimba's hackles went up and he bared his teeth menacingly. Sheila did a respectable imitation of the same and the younger McQueen retreated a pace.

'I love my doggies,' Annie went on. 'And I have respect for all of God's creatures. You battery farm people clearly do not. You don't look after your chickens and so I will not let you look after these poor doggies.'

Tavish McQueen had been chewing the ends of his moustache as his face grew redder and redder.

'Come on, Angus. We'll see if we can have a word with Pug Cruikshank. He'll maybe sell us a real dog.'

'And I won't be buying any eggs from you!' Annie called after them, as they stomped away.

The great hall of Dunshiffin Castle was full of hoodie-clad inceptors and acolytes. They sat cross-legged on the floor watching the three directors walk to the front to stand before them. There had been much muttering and chatter, but it was silenced as Logan Burns raised his hands.

He pushed his wire-frame spectacles back on his nose and stood surveying them with a sad expression.

'My friends, you all know the tragedy that has befallen us today. We are one less in number after Nancy's terrible accident.'

Eileen Lamont was sitting in the second row and immediately she began to sob. By her side, Johanna Waltari put a comforting arm about her shoulder and drew her close. Other people in the hall began to weep freely.

'That is it, my friends, let the emotion out. Show the universe that we are sad to have lost one of our number. Do not be afraid of your emotions.'

'Let them free,' Saki Yasuda echoed.

'Show her spirit it is not forgotten,' Drew Kelso added.

'That is right,' Logan Burns went on. 'Our emotions give us a chance to connect with the divine, with the spirit. And so in a curious way Nancy has taught us something. By her passing — and note that she passed from this world when she was doing her vigil over the Hoolish Stones — she has given us a link with our greater purpose. The summer solstice is almost upon us and we must not allow anything to lessen the experience of it for us. It is going to show us the link. The real link between the ancients and ourselves. Nancy has shown herself to be a messenger. She is the first to light up the way, to show us that Atlantis is with us here.'

His voice had been gradually gaining in fervour, just as his eyes had almost seemed to glow in intensity.

'Nancy hasn't gone!' someone cried.

'Her light lives!' yelled someone else.

'She sacrificed herself to show us.'

Logan Burns raised his hands again. 'The solstice is symbolic of the link. We must celebrate it, just as many people are coming to the island to celebrate it with us. The television coverage has brought them here, to the last great temple, the last great link with Atlantis. And this evening, on Scottish television, I shall reveal the secret of the Hoolish Stones. For it was here that great messengers carried their wisdom to the top of the world.' He raised his hands higher, looking ceilingwards, yet through the ceiling almost as if he could see to the stars and through time to the infinite beyond.

The mood of the hall rose with him. Instead of the tears and the sobbing, people started to laugh, to chant, to lift their arms in imitation of Logan Burns.

'There will be no more accidents,' Logan Burns went on. 'I myself shall do the vigil tonight and tomorrow we shall all go and gather round the Hoolish Stones through the whole night to watch the sunrise. To communicate with the divine. And we shall be full of love. We shall all love one another — just like they did in ancient Atlantis.'

The whole hall erupted into rapture and people embraced one another.

Drew Kelso caught Saki Yasuda's eye and gestured out of the window, where Finbar Donleavy and Danny Wade could be seen getting out of their four by four. They smiled at one another and began clapping Logan Burns. Amazingly, their founder appeared to have averted the disaster that had seemed inevitable after the death of Nancy MacRurie.

They both felt there would be need for celebration.

Torquil sat back in his chair and listened as Morag briefed Lorna, the two Drummond brothers and himself about her meeting with Nancy's family.

'Her mother is distraught, of course, but Hamish, her father, is worryingly calm. Even when I took him to identify her body at the Cottage Hospital, he seemed like a man in control of his emotions. It was afterwards that he had me most worried.' She sighed. 'I can't say that I blame him, but he said that it was all the fault of The Daisy Institute. He said that he would not rest until he finds out just what happened.'

'Understandable,' Torquil remarked.

'I would probably want to tear Dunshiffin Castle apart, stone by stone,' said Wallace Drummond.

'But he said it without raising his voice or anything,' Morag went on. 'That is what worried me.'

'We had better keep an eye on him, don't you think, Inspector?' Lorna asked.

Torquil sniffed and sat forward. 'Absolutely. We don't want him doing anything rash. Now this afternoon, we have some things that we need to follow up on. I need to have a word with the McQueens.' He tapped the newspaper that had been wrapped around the brick and smoothed out on his desk. 'The main article is no surprise. Calum went to town on the article about the battery farm. He might have just shot himself in the foot this time though. He admits that he entered the farm without permission.'

'But he was attacked,' Douglas Drummond said, pointing at the picture of Angus McQueen sprawled on a pallet of smashed eggs. 'The wee man did well!'

'That is why I need to interview this Angus McQueen,' Torquil went on. 'It looks as if he could have had a score to settle with Calum.

'Morag and Lorna, will you go back to the castle? Interview Logan Burns and Eileen Lamont.'

'Why Eileen?' Morag queried.

'She cried out that it should have been her, not Nancy,' Torquil replied. And he recounted the events when he had arrived.

'What about us, boss?' Wallace asked.

Torquil clicked his tongue. 'Despite everything we still have this event tomorrow that we have to police. Go up to the Hoolish stones with the ropes and cordon off the main site, then start sorting out car-parking.'

The Drummonds scowled at one another. 'A pair of traffic wardens, that's what we are, Brother,' said Wallace.

'Aye, but it might be fun giving out tickets.'

'Tickets! You've got to be joking!' Tyler Brady exclaimed, slapping the table in front of him so hard that several of the pints on it wobbled precariously and beer slopped on to the tabletop.

The public bar of The Bell was busier than usual, and several people looked round at the group drinking in the corner.

'Keep it down, Tyler,' Pug Cruikshank said through gritted teeth. 'Of course we'll have tickets. We don't want any busy-bodies straying into the meeting tomorrow night. They won't exactly be tickets; nothing to say what they are for, but they'll be identifiable to us all right.'

'I'll be collecting them at the cattle grid when they come in,' explained Wilf in a hushed voice, producing a small green piece of paper with the print of a stone circle on it and showing it to Tyler. 'No one would have any idea what this was about.'

'How many have you got rid of so far?' Tyler asked.

'Fifty odd,' replied Pug. 'I've mailed out thirty-five, and Wilf has distributed the rest to the usual punters.'

Clem O'Hanlan grinned and lifted his half empty pint to his mouth. 'And we have ours. It will be a good do, so it will. I am looking forward to taking some money off you all.' He winked at his uncle Sean, and then addressed his neighbour.

'Do you not fancy putting your new purchase up to the test Mr Borawski?'

Mr Borawski shook his head and contemplated his glass of lemonade. 'I will have a few bets, but I am taking my dog back home in one piece. We will try him out there, once he is used to his new home.'

Lars Sorensen nodded in agreement. 'I am with you there. I am not going to cripple my own investment before I have personally done some training.'

'Ach, you boys should live a bit more dangerously,' said Sean O'Hanlan, cheerfully. 'Me and the young fellow there have bought a good piece of action and we plan to clean up.' He downed the rest of his pint and tapped the glass on the table.

'Another one, boys?' Pug asked, standing and picking up the Irishman's empty glass. 'Just one thing though. We've taken all precautions for the meeting. Make sure you hold on to your tickets and don't gab to anyone you don't know. I for one don't plan to live in the least bit dangerously.'

'We'll get these,' came a voice from behind him. Pug turned to see Tavish McQueen and his son Angus.

'Get a round in, Angus,' McQueen ordered, as he took a seat beside Pug. 'Did you hear about that Steele idiot?'

Wilf Cruikshank guffawed. 'Someone cracked him one and he's in the hospital. Couldn't have happened to a nicer chap.'

'Just what my Angus thinks,' Tavish McQueen replied. Then, leaning forward and lowering his voice, 'Tomorrow night is still on, I take it?'

'Of course,' said Pug.

'Good. But I need to do a bit of personal business, Pug. Since that bloody little reporter broke into our place I feel we need a couple of guard dogs. I went to that old mad woman's dog sanctuary this morning and tried to buy the Noble collies, but she sent me away with a flea in my ear.'

Tyler Brady snorted. 'She's another one who could do with a crack! She had the police up at the farm after I told her to keep off our land.'

Pug eyed him coldly. 'There will be no more of that talk, Tyler. Remember what I told you.' He turned back to Tavish McQueen. 'So what business do you want to do, Tavish?'

'I want to buy a couple of dogs.'

Pug pressed his lips together. 'They're not exactly guard dogs. They are all *special*.'

Angus McQueen came back from the bar with a tray of fresh pints. He distributed them then drew up a seat beside his father.

'Did you hear —?' he began enthusiastically.

'They know all about Steele,' Tavish McQueen cut in without looking round. 'I know that, Pug. I need special animals to deter nosy parkers from prying into my affairs.'

Pug considered for a moment. 'In that case I think we can accommodate you, Tavish.' He grinned. 'For the right price.'

Tavish McQueen picked up his pint and took a hefty swig. Then, putting the glass down, he wiped froth from his moustache. 'You know me, Pug; I always pay my debts.'

Calum Steele was getting bored, as a result of which he was starting to lead the cottage hospital staff a merry dance. Having read all of the magazines that visitors had brought him and counted all the cracks on the wall of his room, he had developed a passion for his buzzer. Three times he had Sister Lizzie Lamb come to check his stitches, reassure him that the headache would go and that he would be seeing Dr McLelland when he did his round later on. Twice he had called Maggie Crouch, the ward clerk, and got her to bring him a notepad and pen, then pop out to bring him back a mutton pie and a bottle of Irn-Bru. Four times Nurse Giselle Anderson had answered his buzz, each time for increasingly frivolous tasks.

'Calum Steele, if you press that buzzer one more time,' Giselle snapped, eying him
threateningly, 'then it will not be your head that will be hurting.' And she brought her hands from behind her back and let a long plastic tube dangle from her fingertips. 'Sister Lamb thinks that all this attention may be due to constipation. Maybe it is a soapy water enema that you need.'

Calum pulled his sheets up slightly and slipped down on the pillows. 'I ... er ... think maybe I'll take a nap,' he said, his face draining of colour.

Giselle hung the tubing over the bottom rail of the bed and left with a malicious smile on her face.

Ten minutes or so later Calum was wakened from a doze by a firm hand on his shoulder. His mind immediately flashed a picture of the enema tube advancing before him and he shot up in bed with a start.

'Easy, Calum, easy does it,' said the Padre. 'You must have been dreaming, I am thinking. I have brought you some grapes — and a copy of the *Chronicle*.' He pointed to the bedside cabinet where he had deposited the grapes and the slightly soiled newspaper. 'I am sure that you heard about how they got delivered. Whoever did this to you dumped them out of the window, but they have been gathered up and have just about sold out. It is a good edition.'

'Thanks, Padre. It is the first one that really has cost me blood.'

'Have you any idea who did it?'

'As I told Torquil, there could be a queue of folk.'

Lachlan shook his head. 'You know that is not true. But this is not what we expect on the island. Violent crime should have no home here.' Then he raised an eyebrow and added, 'Mind you, that picture of the younger McQueen lying on his back covered in eggs has made many folk giggle. That was you throwing your weight around,' he said jokingly. 'You'll need to stop that.'

Calum eyed the enema tube and shuddered. 'Nurse Anderson said something similar just a wee while ago.' He pumped up his pillows and sat back against them. 'But I need to be out there, not lying in bed like this, Padre. I have news to cover.'

'Aye, it is sad about Nancy MacRurie. A terrible accident.'

Calum's eyes widened. 'What's that?'

The Padre raised his eyebrows questioningly. 'You didn't know? Ah well, I only heard about it myself. I thought you might have heard, what with her parents having to identify her body in the mortuary.' And he told Calum as much as he knew.

'I didn't know anything about it, Padre. I guess they deliberately kept it from me on Ralph McLelland's orders. I am to be kept in bed apparently.' He folded his arms petulantly. 'It is hard though. I am a newsman and I should be reporting. I expect that Irish TV bletherer has been on to it.'

'Finbar Donleavy? Actually, I don't know if he has. At any rate he seemed very interested in Finlay MacNeil's house.' And he described his earlier encounter with the broadcast journalist and his cameraman.

'Ebony and Ivory strike again! That is scandalous!' exclaimed Calum. 'Highly unprofessional!' Although he knew that was exactly what he would have done himself if he had been following a story.

After the Padre left, Calum was still rankled about being cooped up in hospital. It bothered him that he was missing all the news, his very *raison d'etre*.

'So Finbar Donleavy has been breaking and entering, has he?' he mused to himself. 'I wonder what Kirstie Macroon would think of that?'

And with that thought he risked Nurse Anderson's threat of the enema tube and pressed the buzzer. He needed to make a phone call.

Finbar Donleavy pulled his four by four into the side of the drive leading up to Dunshiffin Castle to allow the Golf GTI to pass. Lorna raised her hand in thanks and drove into the courtyard, braking hard as she did so to skid slightly on the gravel surface. Once she switched off the engine, Morag let herself out and nodded approvingly.

'It is certainly smoother than the station's old Ford Escort. Ewan will be envious when he sees it. I think he's getting fair embarrassed about having to use his mother's old moped.'

They mounted the stairs to the hall and were met at the door by Peter and Henrietta. To both sergeants' surprise, they seemed quite upbeat. A stream of pink-hoodie-clad inceptors passed them, giggling among themselves.

'You'll have come about the accident,' Peter asked with a smile.

'We are all so upset,' Henrietta agreed, with an equally unruffled manner. 'I expect you will want to talk with Logan. He's expecting you.'

Morag nodded as the duo started to lead the way to Logan Burns's office. 'Well actually, Sergeant Golspie is going to see him, while I have a chat with Eileen Lamont and her friend.'

Peter pointed to the great staircase, at the top of which hung the portrait of a tartan-clad eighteenth-century laird. 'They are both up in Johanna's room. Eileen has moved in there after the accident. I'll take you up, shall I?'

Morag followed him while Lorna went off with Henrietta. He led the way upstairs then along the long east wing and knocked on a door. Floorboards creaked and a moment later it was pulled open by Johanna Waltari. Inside, sitting on the edge of one of the two beds Eileen was sobbing with her head in her hands.

'I am Sergeant Driscoll,' Morag introduced herself. 'May I come in and talk with Eileen?'

'Of course,' Johanna replied. 'I will go with Peter and let you have some peace.'

'No need for that,' Morag said, raising a restraining hand. 'In fact, it would be as well if I could have a word with both of you.' She turned her head and smiled at Peter. 'Perhaps I can have a chat with you afterwards, Peter.' Peter beamed at her, then gave her a wink that disconcerted her and worried her that he might have misconstrued her meaning. 'Later it is, Sergeant,' he said and left.

When the door closed Eileen looked up. Her eyes were red-rimmed and swollen. 'Sergeant Driscoll,' she said, trying to force a smile. 'You've come about Nancy, I suppose.'

'Awful news.'

'It should have been me, Sergeant!'

Johanna had sat back beside her and put an arm about her shoulders. Morag sat on the other side and did the same.

'That is nonsense, Eileen,' she said.

'But she took over my vigil so that ... so that —'

'So that what?'

Johanna took over. 'So that she could come and see me. We had a long talk into the night. Almost all night.'

Morag noticed the framed photograph beside the other bed. It was of a young woman of Eileen's age. Scandinavian, by the appearance.

'And what were you talking about?'

'The Daisy Institute and the reason we are all here. About the solstice and everything.'

'You said before that you had thought of leaving?'

'I had but Johanna, Peter and Henrietta persuaded me to stay.'

'And what did Nancy feel? Did she ever have any doubts?'

'No, she was brilliant. She loved it here. She liked the way everyone gets on. And she liked — well, she liked having sex. I think that was one of the things she liked about the place.'

Morag was used to receiving all sorts of information in interviews. She maintained an interested, but unshocked visage. 'Do a lot of people have sex here then?'

Johanna answered for her. 'Everyone here is an adult. Free love is not exactly encouraged, but ...' Her voice trailed away meaningfully.

'What do you think happened to Nancy?' Morag asked.

Eileen took a deep breath and leaned closer to Johanna. 'I think she smoked too much weed, got high and leaned too far over the edge of the tower.'

'Did she smoke a lot?' Morag asked, knowing full well that she did.

'Yes. All the time. Both she and Alan were always sharing spliffs. I tried to tell her it was no good for her.' Tears welled up in her eyes and she began to weep again. 'How ... how right I was,' she said between sobs.

Lorna thought that Logan Burns seemed to be in a strange mood. He was more relaxed than he had been at their previous interview, and yet he was also more animated. In part, she thought that it was due to the fact that he had clearly taken some sort of stimulant very recently. She had seen enough of drug taking in her time in the Force to recognize the signs. She suspected that it was simply cannabis.

'Forgive me for mentioning it, but no one seems desperately upset by the death of Nancy MacRurie,' she stated in her opening gambit.

The corners of his mouth cured up slightly. 'It is a terrible accident, of course, and awful that she was so young, yet we all know that she has gone to a better place. To a higher realm.'

'And that is what? Heaven?'

Logan leaned back in his chair behind his desk and shrugged. 'The name is immaterial. It is a higher state beyond the physical. That is what all religions teach, and they are all correct. How can one be sad about someone going further on their spiritual journey?'

'But she is dead.'

'She has left the ties of her physical body.'

Lorna decided not to get tied down in a spiritual discussion. 'That is as may be, but we, the police, have to investigate all fatal accidents. There will, you realize be a Fatal Accident Inquiry.'

Logan Burns nodded. 'Ask whatever you like, Lorna.'

'OK. Why was Nancy up the tower in the middle of the night on her own?'

'She was doing the night-time vigil. We expect the inceptors to do that, to look out over the Hoolish Stones as the solstice approaches. It gives them a sense of the importance of the place. We do the same thing in our other centres across the world. They are always based near to an ancient religious structure.'

'Why?'

'To communicate with the divine and tap into the spirituality of the place. These sites allow us to link up with the ancients and their great knowledge.'

'And I understand that you believe that the Hoolish Stones have some connection with Atlantis?' Lorna knew enough to keep the disbelief from her question.

'I do. There is absolutely no doubt in my mind. In fact, you'll get a good idea about it on this evening's news. The news team left just before you arrived.'

At the mention of the news team Lorna felt a shiver run up her spine. Superintendent Lumsden had castigated her because he had heard about Finlay MacNeil's death from the news instead of directly from them.

Peter was leaning against a wall when Morag emerged from Johanna's room. He smiled as he ambled towards her.

Morag returned the smile, aware now that he was a young man who was very sure of his charms. She recalled how her

639

first impression of him had been so favourable when she saw him at his stall at the harbour market in Kyleshiffin. Clearly he was close to Henrietta. Indeed, she remembered Nancy herself saying that they were practically an item, and that she herself thought he was 'hot.' Seeing him move towards her made her suspect that fidelity was not high on his list of virtues.

'So, lovely Sergeant Driscoll, what do you want to talk to me about? Would you like to go somewhere more comfortable?'

Morag felt herself bristle. Outrageous, she thought. The young pup actually thinks he could bed me, a mother of three young ones! And this morning one of his fellows died when she fell from a tower. Whereas she had previously thought him an attractive young man, now he made her flesh crawl. Yet she could not allow that to show.

'Here will be fine, Peter. I just wanted to ask you why everyone — Eileen and Johanna apart — seem singularly unaffected by what happened today?'

Peter stared at her intensely for a moment and then he smiled. 'Everyone has to die some time, Sergeant. Nancy was here to learn about the divine, about spirituality. Now she knows.'

Morag could scarcely believe her ears. 'Thank you, Peter. That was all.' She walked past him. She badly needed to get to fresh air.

The great hall was packed as usual for the Scottish TV Six O'Clock News. Kirstie Macroon ran through the headlines with her usual aplomb.

'PARLIAMENT ROCKS OVER ALLEGATIONS OF CORRUPTION IN THE CIVIL SERVICE. TRAGEDY ON WEST UIST.'

There was much shuffling about as the assembly waited to hear about Nancy MacRurie's sudden death.

And sure enough, the screen showed a picture of Dunshiffin Castle and honed in to reveal the north tower. Then a picture of Nancy appeared in the bottom left quarter of the screen.

'Tragedy occurred on West Uist early this morning at The Daisy Institute, which as viewers may be aware, is now based at historic Dunshiffin Castle. The body of Nancy MacRurie was found at the foot of the tower. It is speculated that she fell from the tower during an overnight vigil that she was keeping, overlooking the famous Hoolish Stones.'

Eileen Lamont was sitting with Johanna, Agnes Doyle and Alan Brodie. She immediately burst into tears and had to be comforted by her friends.

Kirstie Macroon gave some background to the accident.

'Earlier today Finbar Donleavy met with Dr Logan Burns, the Director of The Daisy Institute as part of our regular series about the Hoolish Stones in the run-up to the summer solstice tomorrow night. Dr Burns told us about how well Nancy MacRurie was doing at the institute and of the plans that she had been making.'

Eileen continued to sob, but all around her people were chatting and murmuring happily as they heard Logan Burns talk about Nancy.

'Finbar also spoke to Dr Burns about the solstice, and he finally revealed his theories about the Hoolish Stones.'

At the back of the hall Drew Kelso and Saki Yasuda exchanged worried glances.

Calum watched the news from his bed in the cottage hospital. He had his spiral notebook on his lap and had been making copious notes as was his custom.

Logan Burns and Finbar Donleavy were standing beside a screen in a room of the castle that Calum recognized as the old gun room, where successive lairds had kept their shotguns, pistols and fishing tackle. With practised ease he had been giving a Powerpoint demonstration to Finbar.

'So you see, these carvings are undoubtedly Atlantean in origin. The significance of this is that the knowledge of the Atlanteans directly spawned the Ogham script and runes of the Scandinavian countries. I have studied early language and epigraphy for years and this discovery effectively turns history on its head.'

Finbar nodded his head noncommittally. 'But does this really matter, Dr Burns?'

'It is of vital importance, Finbar. Because the writings reveal much more about the knowledge of the Atlanteans. And tomorrow, at the solstice, all will become clearer.' He tapped a button on his laptop and an aerial view of the Hoolish Stones appeared on the screen. 'As you can see, the Hoolish Stones are formed by three perfect concentric circles, with the great chambered cairn in the centre and the aisle leading all the way through.'

He waited expectantly, as if this revelation alone would produce a reaction in the journalist.

'The significance of this is that this is a direct ground-plan of the city of Atlantis. It is exactly as Plato described it. The writings on the stones, which I have deciphered, confirm not only this fact, but that this ground-plan was used for all of the temples of Atlantis that were built after the great cataclysm that destroyed the continent.'

Calum had been watching with ever increasing amusement as he jotted down notes. 'So that is your great revelation, is it?

The Hoolish Stones are what is left of a temple built by survivors of Atlantis. Good one, Logan!'

The usual Scottish TV jingle sounded out and the shot returned to the studio. Kirstie Macroon was studying a sheaf of documents. She looked up and smiled.

'We are extremely sorry to hear of more news from West Uist today. Apparently our old friend and sometime special correspondent, Calum Steele, was attacked last night and sustained a head injury. He is now recovering in the Kyleshiffin Cottage Hospital. We all wish him well for a speedy recovery. Get well, Calum.'

The *Chronicle* editor had watched entranced. Although he had talked to her by telephone that afternoon, basically to protest about the way that Finbar Donleavy had breached one of the first rules of responsible journalism by breaking into Finlay MacNeil's cabin, he had not expected a personal message from her on TV. He felt that the smile had been deliberately aimed at him and he felt his heart miss a beat. And then she was talking again.

'The solstice is due tomorrow and our series of meetings with The Daisy Institute is just about over. Yet our reporter, Finbar Donleavy, feels that there are some important questions to be posed. We go back to Finbar.'

Finbar Donleavy appeared in front of Dunshiffin Castle, in front of the large sign with the daisy logo.

'The Daisy Institute has been based on the island of West Uist for eight months now. Their purported aim is to further the study of divinity and spirituality, and as you can see their logo is that of the humble daisy. This is reflected in the uniforms that they wear. The directors, of which there are three, including Dr Logan Burns, the founder, wear yellow hoodies. As you will note from our past features these bear more than a passing resemblance to monks' gowns. The acolytes, that is those members who have reached a certain state of awareness and understanding, wear white hoodies, while the newest members, the ones they call inceptors, wear pink ones.' He pointed to the logo of the pink-tipped daisy. 'Truly this looks like a harmless throwback to the days of flower power and the hippy movement.'

Calum watched, his jaw dropping as he did so. He was beginning to see Finbar Donleavy in a new light. This was brilliant! True investigative journalism.

'Yet there may be a darker side to The Daisy Institute. Enough to be alarming. The first question we ask is, why choose a castle as your base? Is it to keep people out? Or to keep people in? There have been allegations that inceptors have been prevented from talking with their families for three months. After that time they show no desire to make contact. The question is, could there be a form of brainwashing going on? And then we have the sudden death of Finlay MacNeil, a critic of Dr Burns, as shown on Scottish TV News just the other night. And now this tragic death of one of the inceptors. A lot of questions are cropping up, the main one being, are we witnessing the emergence of a powerful cult right here on West Uist?'

The jingle sounded again and Kirstie Macroon did a link to the next news item.

'Well what do you know!' Calum exclaimed to himself. 'That's a story, Donleavy. A damned good story. And while you are working on that, I reckon I had better get started on a bit of investigation of my own.' He pressed his buzzer and threw back his covers. When Sister Lamb came in he was pulling his clothes out of his bedside cabinet. He cut her remonstrations short. 'Have you got one of your dockets, Sister. No offence, but I need to discharge myself.'

After clearing his desk at the station, Torquil had typed out his report of the day and faxed it through to Superintendent Lumsden. He phoned his uncle to say that he would not be returning for dinner that evening, because he had other plans. It had been more of an impulse than a plan if the truth be told.

He asked Lorna to have dinner with him and she, to his surprise and pleasure, accepted. A quick call to Jenny McVicar at the Peat Inn resulted in a candlelit dinner for two upstairs in the special annexe to the inn's restaurant, where they shared a meal of roast grouse and a half carafe of claret. Over the meal they chatted superficially about work, the Force in general and Superintendent Lumsden in particular, both agreeing that as a line manager he was as supportive as a sponge yet as prickly and poisonous as a sea urchin. Then they talked about their interests; Torquil's piping, his passion for motorbikes; and about Lorna's love of cars, horses and racing. It was not so much that they had interests in common, as that they were aware of a chemistry that had been working between them. By the end of the meal their hands inadvertently touched as he poured her wine, and the touch lingered.

By moonlight they rode out on the Bullet to St Ninian's Cave and crunched down the shingle beach to watch the crabs frolicking in the shallow waters. There seemed an inevitability about their first kiss. And about all that followed.

The Padre had taken a relaxing bath before heading to his study in his dressing-gown with a whisky nightcap and Finlay's diary. He flicked on the green-shaded desk lamp and charged his pipe before settling down in the old armchair to read. The grandfather clock ticked sonorously away as he strained to read Finlay's handwriting. It was not an easy task, for the handwriting varied, depending upon the museum curator's state of sobriety. The best written pieces were neat, scholarly entries, compared to the spidery segments that were scrawled in marked states of inebriation. And the frequency of the latter had been increasing as he went through the diary.

The whisky by his side stayed mostly untouched and his pipe grew cold as the import of the writings became clearer — apart from the entry about 'the dogs'. Finally, he reached for his phone and left a message on Torquil's mobile. 'Oh Finlay, Finlay!' he said, shaking his head as he thought of his old friend. 'If only you had said something I think you might still have been with us.'

CHAPTER TEN

Saki Yasuda enjoyed making love in the moonlight. Particularly, she enjoyed sex with a modicum of pain on both sides. The rubber clothes, chokers and flails set the mood as their perspiration-covered bodies gleamed in the moonlight that flooded through the slats of her window shutters and enhanced the build-up of passion. Then with a gradual disrobing and tearing away of remaining clothes, so that there was only naked flesh, she scratched, bit and slapped, and enjoyed having the same given back. The release was simultaneous and they lay gasping side by side for some moments.

Drew began to laugh.

'Not quite the reaction I expected,' she said coyly.

He rolled his head to face her. 'I'm sorry Saki, that was as fantastic as usual. It is just that I was thinking about Logan.'

'Because you know I do the same with him?'

'No. That doesn't bother me. Why should it? Jealousy is a waste of time. I was just thinking of him up there in the tower on his vigil, while we — pleasured and destressed each other.'

'And do you feel less stressed, Drew? That Finbar Donleavy has been treacherous. He called us a cult.'

'Well, we are, aren't we? Let's be fair, Saki, that is just what we are.'

Her brows beetled. 'No, we are not. We are a serious scholarly institute. We study spirituality and we teach love.'

'Love like this?' He gave another deep throaty giggle.

'That is not funny, Drew. Logan Burns is a genius. He has made earth-shattering discoveries. And he is feeling stressed right now, just like you and I. Just think what he must be feeling up in the tower on his own right now.'

'Then I suppose you would rather that he had been here for you to thrash and make love with instead of me,' he returned sarcastically.

She jumped up and stared down at him, her chest heaving. 'I would like you to go, Drew. Now!'

He rolled off the bed and gathered his things into a pile. 'It is all falling apart Saki, you know that, don't you? We can't survive another Geneva. That's what could happen when they have the Fatal Accident Inquiry over Nancy. We should all be worried. Especially Logan.'

She shook her head. 'I think you are worried about something else, aren't you? You are worried that Logan will find out about the finances?'

His eyes narrowed. 'What do you mean?'

She stared back at him, arms akimbo. 'I have seen the books, Drew. You should be worried.'

He squeezed the riding crop in his hand. Then he smiled and swished it gently too and fro before dropping it on his pile of things. 'You be careful too, Saki,' he said, as he pulled on his hoodie.

Logan Burns had many times proudly, yet modestly, announced that he could meditate anytime, anywhere. Indeed, in some of his lectures he showed photographs of him taken in trance perched on top of a flagpole during a world congress on transcendental meditation held some years previously in Simla. It had been a technique that he had developed to a fine art and which had been his personal salvation over the years, during bad patches when he had faced adversity about his beliefs and his teachings.

When things were really bad, he found that a spliff of cannabis helped to get him in a susceptible mood. He had smoked two since taking up his vigil, overlooking the Hoolish Stones and, as he flicked the butt of the last one over the battlement wall, he made a mental note to commend Pug Cruikshank on the quality of the latest batch that his brother had grown.

He was sitting in the lotus position atop the north tower of Dunshiffin Castle, his hands resting palm-upwards on his knees, to open his palmar chakras and allow him to free his mind from the shackles of consciousness. He had emptied his mind of all extraneous thoughts and sensations, thinking of nothing except the Hoolish Stones and the key that they gave to the wisdom of the Atlanteans. He was unaware of the breeze that played over him, brushing wisps of his abundant hair about his face. He was unaware of the gradually dropping temperature. And he was unaware of the figure in black with a black balaclava that had emerged from the stairs leading on to the top of the tower where he sat.

He didn't see the metal flask being produced, or hear the movement of metal on metal as the top was screwed off and the sulphurous smell arose from the liquid inside.

Johanna crept slowly nearer, raising the flask in both hands, ready to pour the contents of the flask over his head.

He was also unaware of Eileen Lamont moving swiftly behind Johanna and putting a hand across her mouth and grabbing her wrist with the other.

Johanna twisted her head round and saw Eileen vigorously shaking her head. And then, as if a spell had been broken, she felt her resolve suddenly disappear and she allowed Eileen to draw her back towards the stairs.

Logan Burns was unaware of the footsteps retreating back down the stairs. And he was unaware of how close he had been to having a flask of concentrated sulphuric acid poured over his head.

Torquil left the Commercial Hotel rather sheepishly at six in the morning and rode back to the manse in high spirits. It was only when he dismounted outside and pulled off his goggles and gauntlets that he switched on his mobile and received his uncle's message of the night before. He did not imagine that it would be a matter of real urgency so he tiptoed along the hall to the foot of the stairs, planning to have a quick shower then a spot of breakfast before leaving for a quick practice at St Ninian's Cave on his way in to the station. He thought that if he was careful his uncle might just imagine that he had come back late in the night.

'Morning, laddie,' came the Padre's voice from the kitchen. He appeared a moment later, already dressed with his dog collar on and his dressing-gown on top of his clothes, a saucer in one hand and a steaming cup of tea in the other. 'Busted, is the term they use nowadays, I am thinking. I popped my head round your door and saw that your bed had not been slept in.'

'Ah,' Torquil said, turning to face him with a guilty grin.

'And you have either been running, or the colour in your cheeks indicates some secret that you have been keeping.'

Torquil averted his eyes for a moment, then nodded and looked his uncle straight in the eye. 'Uncle Lachlan, would you think I was mad if I told you I think I am in love?'

'With Lorna?'

'Aye. We seem to have a certain ... er —'

'Chemistry? I had noticed. And you look like a man in love.' He deposited his tea on the side table and advanced towards his nephew with his hand outstretched. The Padre pumped Torquil's hand, then said, 'You have needed some luck, Torquil. Especially after all that you have been through. And she seems a nice, bonnie lassie. I am pleased for you. But —'

Torquil's eyes widened slightly. 'But what?'

The Padre sighed. 'But, I have something important to show you. Something that I think you need to see. About Finlay MacNeil. Come through to my study.' He led the way and pointed to the diary laid open on the desk. Beside it was a sheet of paper with notes written in Lachlan McKinnon's neat handwriting.

Torquil sat down and read the notes. Then he scowled before picking up the diary and flicking through the entries.

'I see what you mean, Uncle. It is all quite worrying.'

'I was planning to say a few words at the clifftop where he fell,' the Padre explained. 'But on the way I saw this four by four outside the Black House Museum. It was empty, so I tried Finlay's cabin and found that broadcaster Finbar Donleavy and his cameraman filming inside. He tried to bamboozle me and do a bit of sneaky filming while I was there, but I rather saw them off.'

Torquil looked up with a thin smile. He was all too aware of his uncle's abilities and almost felt sorry for Donleavy.

'I didn't like the fact that they had just sneaked into his place without permission, so I locked it up.' He nodded at the diary. 'And I took that away with me. It was only when I saw Donleavy's piece on the news last night that I thought I had better have a look at it.' Then, when Torquil made no comment, 'You did see the news, didn't you?'

When Torquil shook his head Lachlan told him about Finbar Donleavy's little diatribe and his questions about The Daisy Institute being a cult.

Torquil blew air through his lips. 'I think I had better have a shower and we should have breakfast, Uncle. Then I had better go in and go over everything with the team.' He pulled out his mobile phone. 'I'll get Morag to tee everything up for nine o'clock.'

A few minutes later after speaking to his sergeant he sat back and looked hopefully at his uncle. 'Would you mind coming and sitting in on the meeting? Finlay's handwriting is not easy and you may be able to help us.'

'For Finlay, anything,' the Padre replied, picking up his empty cup and saucer. 'You go and shower while I knock something up to eat, then I'll race you to Kyleshiffin.'

Torquil grinned at his uncle's retreating back. Then he phoned Lorna's mobile. His face creased into a smile when she answered. 'Hi, it's me,' he said. 'I need you in early, Lorna.'

He felt a tingle run up his spine when she replied softly, 'And I need you too, Torquil.'

The Macbeth ferry, *Laird o' the Isles*, from Lochboisdale in South Uist slowly manoeuvred into the crescent-shaped harbour of Kyleshiffin. Eventually, the great landing doors slowly and noisily descended to allow the walking passengers to disembark before the inevitable cascade of traffic. Sitting as unobtrusively as he could on the harbour wall, finishing off a mutton pie, Calum Steele picked up his old polaroid camera and took photo after photo of various passengers and an assortment of cars.

It seemed a very mixed population. The usual bands of holidaymakers; young families come to visit the island's famous harbour town, groups of nature-watchers with cameras, binoculars and folded up tripods, and many with the same bright-eyed enthusiasm that he had noted on the faces of The

652

Daisy Institute people. Yet with his eagle eye Calum was also aware of another sub-section of people, mainly men, without any particular outstanding features that would differentiate then from the average traveller, except that they had the look of gambling folk. No one seemed to notice him, yet some journalistic sixth sense suddenly made him aware of goose-pimpling at the nape of his neck. Gathering up his pile of photos from the spot on the wall where he had been depositing them, he slid off the wall and merged into the crowds that were milling around the ever-busy market stalls. He ducked down and circled a couple of stalls, finally hovering at Alice Farquarson's second-hand book stall.

He raised a finger to his lips and tapped the side of his nose when she began to hail him. Alice grinned, all too aware that Calum was in the middle of his 'newspaper snooping', as all the locals who knew him referred to the activities that he preferred to think of as investigative journalism.

Picking up a coffee-table book he peered over the top and watched the spot he had just vacated. He recognized Wilf Cruikshank and Tyler Brady from the Goat's Head Farm. They were talking to one of the recent disembarkees from the *Laird o' the Isles* ferry. He could not hear what they were saying, but he immediately spotted Wilf Cruikshank's hand disappear into his Barbour jacket and come out a moment later to hand over a green card surreptitiously in exchange for a number of banknotes, equally surreptitiously passed over.

Calum raised his camera above the book and snapped the transaction. He took another six photos of other similar dealings before shoving the camera inside his anorak.

'Thanks, Alice. See you later,' he said at last, winking at the stall-holder, as he made to lay down the book.

'I think that the least you can do is buy that book, Calum Steele,' said Alice with a stern look as he made to leave. 'We all have to make a living, after all. I am not just a bit of camouflage for your snooping.'

'Oh — aye,' Calum returned, checking the price then delving into his pocket for a couple of pounds. He grinned as he looked at the title for the first time. '*The Complete Book of Dog Training and Grooming*,' he read out. 'Couldn't be more apt, Alice. Couldn't be more apt.'

Morag had arranged the station rest-room as Torquil had instructed and had phoned the Drummond twins. Fortunately, they had not set off in their boat and they told her they would be there at the back of nine. Ewan had felt fully recovered after a good night's sleep and had already opened the office when she herself had arrived. But Dr Ralph McLelland was out on an emergency home visit and was not answering his mobile phone, so she was unable to invite him to Torquil's emergency meeting. Accordingly, she had sent Ewan off to the Cottage Hospital to see if they could find anything out about where he had gone.

'Good morning, Sergeant Golspie,' Morag greeted Lorna with a knowing smile when she came in. 'Did you have a good evening with the boss?'

Lorna blushed then smiled demurely. 'Only one word, Morag. Fabulous.'

'Do I detect a sea change in the emotions around here?'

Lorna nodded. 'Torquil and I are — getting on really well.'

Morag pointed to the rest-room. 'Tell you what, why don't you get the white board all set for Torquil? He said he wants to make notes on it, and I'll put the kettle on. They should all be along soon enough.'

And indeed, the twins came through the door instants before the noise of a couple of motor bikes heralded the arrival of Torquil and his uncle.

'I have asked Lachlan to join us,' Torquil explained shortly afterwards as they sat round the ping-pong table in the rest-room. Morag had laid out paper and pencils in front of each place setting. Torquil picked up the diary in front of him. 'This is Finlay MacNeil's diary, which Lachlan recovered from Finlay's log cabin yesterday.'

He glanced at his uncle and asked him to describe the encounter with the broadcast team while the others took notes.

'I watched the news last night,' the Padre went on, 'and when Finbar Donleavy made that jibe about The Daisy Institute being a cult I thought I would have a peek through Finlay's diary.'

'Thanks, Uncle,' said Torquil. 'Essentially, like all diarists Finlay was pretty obsessional about making a daily entry. They vary in the content and the way they are written. Sometimes they are just single line entries, other times they are observations about life, or recaps about the day's events or about how his work was going. Sometimes he gets angry and his writing reflects that. And again, at times he seems the worse for drink and his handwriting becomes pretty scrappy, and at times it is just a scrawl.'

He looked round the room with raised eyebrows. 'But some of the entries, especially the ones over the last seven or eight months, are quite venomous and vindictive. And they raise some uncomfortable questions.'

'Basically, ever since The Daisy Institute took over Dunshiffin Castle and they started studying the Hoolish Stones,' the Padre added.

'Is this not just Finlay getting territorial?' Morag asked.

Wallace nodded sagely. 'I am thinking that could be right. He almost thought of the Stones as his own.'

Torquil shook his head. 'I doubt it. Listen to this first reference: *10 October — Met Dr Logan Burns of The Daisy Institute today, up at the Hoolish Stones. He was photographing the inscriptions. Bloody fool! Tried to tell me that he was an expert on epigraphy and that he would decipher them within a week!*'

Lorna tapped the end of her pencil on her note pad. 'Not a good start to a relationship.'

'It didn't get any better,' Torquil went on. 'Listen to this: *17 October — Saw Burns at the Pillar Stone on the golf course. The idiot had the audacity to tell me he has deciphered the inscriptions and that he was studying the markings on the Pillar Stone. He thinks it confirms his decipherment and confirms his theory. And his theory is — ATLANTIS! Good grief, what an idiot! The bugger put me off my round.*'

The Padre gave a soft chuckle. 'I remember that. And I also remember that just playing his ball near the Pillar would almost send him apoplectic.'

'His entries go on like that. Then we come to this alarming one. It is hard to read, almost a scribble that looks as if he was the worse for wear when he wrote it, as if he had a couple of stiff drinks before he sat down: *21 December — I watched the flower fools up at the stones at the winter solstice. They know nothing about the significance of the solstices. And that Burns idiot and his henchfolk — Kelso, a shifty bugger, and the little woman, Japanese, I think — they are telling the benighted folk that come to study with them all sorts of nonsense.*

'*It was pissing it down up at the stones when I went to take some moon positions late afternoon. Got caught in the thunderstorm. I trudged back by Hoolish Farm and saw the shapes through the curtains. I heard the voices, going hammer and tongs. The dogs were going mad outside. Then I*

saw him dash out and get in the Jeep. I thought it didn't look like Rab.
Shit that I am, I sat down and sheltered against one of the outer stones
and had a dram. Then I fell asleep in the rain and woke when I heard
Calum Steele on his scooter. Then all hell broke loose.'

Morag gave a soft whistle. 'It didn't look like Rab? Did he
say anything else?'

Torquil shook his head. 'No more entries for a week. Maybe
it was just because it was Christmas.' He shrugged then
continued, 'I couldn't read the next one, so if you wouldn't
mind, Lachlan.'

The Padre reached across for the diary and turned it towards
him. He pushed his spectacles back on his nose and read:

'30 December — I feel bloody awful. Poor Esther and Rab. It wasn't
Rab. But how can I say anything? I've left it too late and they would all
think I was just drunk again. Or stoned. Damn these addictions of mine.
I'll have to give up the drink and the weed.'

The Padre shook his head. 'Then he writes another whisky-
sozzled bit the following night: *31 December — Cruikshank wants*
his money. Bloody weed.'

Lorna frowned. 'Does he mean Cruikshank is a weed, or is
he on about smoking cannabis?'

'The latter, I think,' Lachlan replied.

Torquil looked sternly at the Drummond twins. 'Do you
know anything about this Cruikshank? Is he a supplier of
cannabis?'

Wallace and Douglas shook their heads in unison.

'No idea, boss,' Wallace replied.

Torquil frowned. 'Well, anyway, the entries about Logan
Burns and the institute get more and more irate, as I said.' He
consulted the sheet of notes that his uncle had supplied him
with. 'Then he wrote this piece just the other night, after he

had been up at the Hoolish Stones and interrupted the television broadcast. Would you read it, Uncle?'

The Padre cleared his throat and squinted to read the diary entry:

'*I confronted the bugger on the TV news last night. Rattled him I think. And I made it clear that I know about them. That I know about what really happened at the winter solstice. Maybe I could make some money here. Enough to retire and finish my books in peace. Anyway, just one more drinkie I think, then we'll see.*'

The Padre held up the diary and pointed to a discolouration of the paper. 'It looks as if he even spilt his whisky on the diary at that point.'

Lorna chewed the end of her pencil. 'Am I missing something here? Did something happen at the winter solstice?'

'We had a tragedy,' Douglas replied.

'A local farmer hanged his wife and — well, not to put too fine a point on it, blew his brains out,' Wallace explained.

'We don't know any such thing, Wallace,' said Morag. 'Remember that an open verdict was declared at the Fatal Accident Inquiry.'

Wallace and Douglas looked at each other doubtfully. Wallace shrugged and Douglas sat back and folded his arms.

Torquil gave Lorna a brief summary of the events surrounding the deaths. Lorna sat through it all making notes.

'Is this the Hoolish Farm? The one that is now a battery farm?' she asked.

'The very same,' replied Torquil.

'And Calum Steele found the wife, Esther Noble's body?'

'He did and he hasn't been himself since then. You see, he had a thing about Esther Noble going back to our schooldays. I think that is partly why he has had a thing about incomers to the island since then.'

Lorna gave a wan smile. 'Which as one of the most recent incomers must make me *persona non grata* with him.'

Torquil hummed noncommittally. He stood up and crossed to the white board. 'OK, so Finlay's diary has raised a serious question. Let's see what we have so far. We have the winter solstice tragedy.'

He picked up a marker and wrote the words *MURDER SOLSTICE* at the top left corner, then underneath it in a box the name *ESTHER NOBLE* and under it *Found hanged in hall — murdered?* Then under that in another box the name *RAB NOBLE* and beneath that *Fatal head wound — shotgun — suicide?*

'And then we have Finlay MacNeil.' And at the top of the board he wrote *FINLAY MACNEIL* and surrounded it with another box. Under it he wrote *Diary.* He looked round the others. 'What else? Let's brainstorm.'

Morag raised a hand. 'The Fatal Accident Inquiry declared the Nobles an open verdict.' Torquil nodded and wrote *FAI open verdict* next to the Noble boxes, then he drew a circle round it and added lines to connect the circle with their boxed names.

Wallace bit his lip pensively, then said, 'I'm thinking that the Hoolish Farm is awfully close to the Hoolish Stones. Finlay says he was out there the night the Nobles died.' Torquil nodded and wrote *HOOLISH STONES* in the middle of the board and surrounded it with a circle. Then he added a line to Finlay MacNeil's box, before writing *HOOLISH FARM* in another circle under the Noble boxes. He then added dotted lines linking the farm to the stones.

'So I suppose we need to add the new owners of the Hoolish Farm below that,' suggested Lorna. 'And how about the battery farm?'

'I suppose so,' replied Torquil, adding the words *BATTERY FARM* and the name *MCQUEENS* beneath it.

The Padre cleared his throat. 'I'm thinking that Calum Steele could do with a little circle; he has had a bad time of it, what with discovering the Nobles and then being attacked and having his office trashed.'

'I agree,' said Torquil, adding a circle for the *West Uist Chronicle* editor. 'And the question about who attacked him is fairly open.'

'What about these television interviews?' Lorna asked. 'Finlay MacNeil died after the drunken episode on the news.'

'Absolutely,' Torquil agreed, writing TV and circling it, then adding the names *FINBAR DONLEAVY* and *DANNY WADE*. He added lines connecting this circle to *FINLAY MACNEIL,* and the *HOOLISH STONES,* then another to *CALUM STEELE.* Beside the latter he added a question mark. 'And since we have added this we have to put *THE DAISY INSTITUTE* into the picture, don't we!' And so saying he drew another circle with *DAISY INSTITUTE* inside and the names *LOGAN BURNS, DREW KELSO* and *SAKI YASUDA* underneath. 'And it links up to *TV* and *FINLAY MACNEIL.*'

Morag sighed. 'And now we have Nancy MacRurie. I think her accidental death has to go up there, since she was one of the inceptors.'

Torquil added her boxed name and added a line to join it to *THE DAISY INSTITUTE* circle.

'And don't forget that Eileen Lamont said it should have been her, not Nancy,' Morag added.

Torquil frowned as he added another circle with Eileen's name. 'And we have the question about cannabis to add. Remember that Finlay said in his diary entry that he would have to give up weed. And Nancy seemed to have been smoking a joint when she died.' He added *CANNABIS,* circled it and drew lines to *FINLAY MACNEIL* and *NANCY MACRURIE.* 'And he also said something about Cruikshank wanting his money and "bloody weed!"' He added another circle with *GOAT'S HEAD FARM* inside it and underneath it the name *CRUIKSHANK.*

'And what about dogs?' Lorna asked. 'That old lady, Annie McConville, had complained about one of the farm people's attitude and didn't like the look of his dog. And then Ewan had a run in with them.'

There was a few moments' silence while Torquil wrote on the board. Then the Padre spoke the disquieting thought that was becoming all too apparent to them all. 'The boxes show the people who are now no longer with us, right? I am thinking that there are too many dead people on that board.'

There followed another tense silence, which was broken by the office telephone.

'We could do with that being Ralph,' said Torquil, as Morag went through to answer it.

She put her head round the door a moment later, a look of pained chagrin upon her face. 'It's Superintendent Lumsden for you, Torquil.' She shrugged her shoulders sympathetically. 'It sounds as if he's on the warpath.'

Ewan was on his way back from the Cottage Hospital when he was side-tracked as he passed Dairsie's, the ironmonger's shop. In the window he spied Rab Noble's mountain bike with its price ticket showing a reduction of twenty-five per cent. Ewan decided to buy it straight away before someone else snapped it up.

'You are lucky, Constable McPhee,' said Dan Dairsie as he rang up the old-fashioned till that had been installed by his grandfather before the Great War and which had occupied the same spot on Dairsie's counter ever since. 'I've had no end of enquiries since I reduced the price.'

And, as Ewan happily wheeled it towards the door, he added with a wink, 'Mind you, I am happy to be having it taken away. I am not so sure that I like the thought that it was up at the milking parlour when Rab Noble — you know what.'

'In that case, Dan Dairsie, if you are so pleased to get rid of it, maybe you should be throwing in a little extra.'

The ironmonger shoved his hands deep into the pockets of his brown shop coat and smiled apologetically. 'Business, Constable McPhee. It was never my grandfather's practice to offer free gifts, and it is not the policy of the current proprietor. The reduction has squeezed my profit margin as it is.'

Ewan shook his head with a good-natured smile, for he had expected such an answer. He left the shop and wheeled the machine across the pavement to the road. He was in the act of mounting it when he heard a shrill voice that made him squirm.

'Constable McPhee, just the person I was looking for,' came Annie McConville's voice.

Ewan turned to see the old lady advancing upon him with her dogs on leads, one in each hand. Both dogs recognized Ewan and approached with wagging tails.

'Ah, Mrs McConville,' he said warily, forcing a smile to his lips. 'What can I do for you?'

Annie looked back and forth to ensure that no one on the crowded street was eavesdropping, before leaning towards him. 'It is more what I can do for you, Ewan McPhee. Information, that is what I am offering you.'

Ewan looked at her hesitantly. 'I am afraid I am not at liberty to offer any money, Mrs McConville.'

Annie looked scandalized. 'Money! Civic pride is all that motivates me. No, I wanted you to know about that awful egg man, McQueen. He tried to buy two of the Nobles' doggies from me.'

'But there is nothing illegal in that,' Ewan pointed out.

'Of course not. I wouldn't sell him one anyway, so guess where he is going to buy one?'

Ewan stared back at her in puzzlement. 'Where?'

'The Goat's Head Farm. From those rude men that you went to see.'

'Ah well, remember that I told you that you can walk your dogs there whenever you want, just as long as you don't upset the pigs.'

Annie snorted derisively. 'I know that. But it is the type of dog he wants to buy. He wants a guard dog. I had a word with Netty Lamont, you know, Eileen Lamont's mother.' Then as Ewan continued to stare at her vacantly, 'Eileen used to help me walk my doggies. You know her well enough; she was one of the veterinary nurses before the flower people got to her. She was a great friend of poor Nancy.'

'Ye-es,' Ewan replied slowly. 'A tragic accident. Tragic.'

'Tragic indeed. The two of them were such friends. Well, I was talking about Eileen. She used to help out at the Cruikshanks' farm when old Watty Cruikshank was still alive. He was her uncle. Then, when the new folk came — they are her cousins you see — she stopped going. Netty says she didn't like what they were doing to the farm. And she didn't like the type of dogs they were breeding.'

Understanding came to Ewan. 'But they are not breeders, are they?'

Annie's eyes sparkled. 'Ewan McPhee, not everything that happens in this world is done by the board. Netty says that was partly why she stopped going. That and the fact that she didn't take to her cousins.'

Ewan ran a hand through his mane of red hair. He recollected the two dogs that he had seen the other day.

'And have you been looking about you?' Annie went on. 'Have you not noticed some of the folk that have been coming to the island today?'

'You mean the folk coming for the solstice, Mrs McConville?'

'You just start looking, Constable McPhee. If you ask me, it is not just the solstice that's attracting people to West Uist at the moment. You just think about what I have said. Tell the Inspector about McQueen and the Noble dogs.'

'I will tell him, Mrs McConville,' Ewan replied.

'And you might also tell him that I told Calum Steele the very same thing. He seemed more interested than you,' she added cryptically, as she headed off into the throng of the market.

Torquil was still in his office talking to Superintendent Lumsden when Ewan came in. Morag filled him in on the meeting so far while he poured himself a mug of tea.

'What about Dr McLelland? Did you track him down?' Morag asked.

'No, he's not expected back until his late morning surgery at eleven.'

The door opened and Torquil returned. 'I take it that is Rab Noble's old mountain bike parked behind the counter?'

'Oh, aye,' Ewan replied quickly. 'Is it OK parking it indoors, Torquil?'

'Fine,' Torquil replied diffidently. 'Morag will reimburse you later.'

'What did the superintendent want, Inspector?' Lorna asked somewhat anxiously.

Torquil pursed his lips. 'Basically, my teeth. He said he is furious about learning about what is happening in part of his jurisdiction from watching the news instead of from my reports. He has given me a warning. He said that if he has one more problem with me then I will be suspended.'

'That is outrageous!' exclaimed the Padre, thumping his fist upon the ping-pong table.

Ewan shook his head. 'That man has it in for you, Torquil.' He pointed at the network of names, boxes and circles on the whiteboard. 'But, before I forget, I'd better tell you about my meeting with Annie McConville.'

The group listened, then Torquil added some notes beneath the circled *GOAT'S HEAD FARM*. He stood tapping the end of the marker on the board. 'There certainly seems to be a lot that needs investigating here. Let's divvy the tasks up.'

Lorna coughed. 'Did you tell him about these lines of enquiry, Inspector?'

Torquil shook his head. 'It didn't seem a good time to mention it.'

Ewan frowned. He was trying to puzzle out what Annie McConville had meant about Calum Steele being so interested in the fact that Tavish McQueen wanted to buy a dog from the Goat's Head Farm folk.

CHAPTER ELEVEN

Tavish McQueen handed over a wad of twenty pound notes to Pug Cruikshank and stood nodding his head admiringly as his son Angus took possession of the boxer.

'You will find he is a good guard dog, Tavish,' Pug said, with the reassuring tone of one who has just sold a commodity for a good price.

'Aye, a good guard dog is what I need. To stop any more shenanigans from that Calum Steele and his like.'

Angus McQueen snorted derisively at the mention of Calum Steele's name. 'He'll maybe be minding his own business now, eh, Dad?'

Tavish McQueen ran a finger across his moustache. 'A good thing too. But I don't want anybody else looking into my affairs. Like that television crew that have been giving the flower folk a bad time.'

'My cousin is one of the flower folk,' Pug said meaningfully, in case Tavish McQueen had it in mind to be too derogatory about them.

Tavish McQueen took the hint. He pointed with his chin at the large fighting arena. 'Is this one vicious?'

Pug shook his head. 'He is no fighting dog. Not like these ones,' he said, pointing to the cages of sleeping animals. 'Oh, he'll make plenty of noise to frighten off any intruders and given half a chance he'll nip the arse off anyone who tries to get into your place, but that's it.'

Tavish gestured to his son to take the dog out to their waiting car.

'About tonight then,' he began, once they were alone. 'Have you had a thought about letting me in on some of the action?'

Pug gave a short laugh and slapped the other on the shoulder. 'There will be plenty of rich pickings, Tavish. And what are friends for, that's what I say. You scratch my back and I'll scratch yours.'

Logan Burns looked exhausted. His eyes were red-rimmed and his normally cleanly shaven cheeks were showing a fine dark stubble. Yet there was an unmistakable sparkle in his eyes as he addressed the assembled institute in the great hall at Dunshiffin Castle.

'We are on the verge of the great revelation, my friends. This evening we shall be starting the final vigil — all of us — at the Hoolish Stones. We shall stay through the night and watch the sunrise on the day of the solstice. And you will see how the stones are so perfectly aligned with the sunrise, just as the ancients set them up.'

There was a murmur of wonder and nodding of heads in the audience. Saki Yasuda and Drew Kelso, standing a little back from and on either side of Logan Burns looked at each other and nodded approvingly.

'And on Scottish TV we shall show our critics how wrong they are.'

Alan Brodie and Agnes Doyle were sitting cross-legged on the floor in the front row. Agnes prodded Alan in the ribs. He looked at her then with a nod of assent, raised his hand.

'Excuse me, Logan, but are you sure the television will be coming? What with that outburst by Finbar Donleavy.'

'And after Nancy's death,' Agnes Doyle added.

Logan Burns's lips tightened. 'I have no reason to think otherwise. They want the story just as much as we want the world to receive the message.' He held out his hands, almost beseechingly. 'Are you all still with me on this?'

Peter and Henrietta both cried out assent in unison and turned with raised hands to orchestrate a cheer from the assembly. When the clamour calmed down after a few moments, Saki Yasuda took a pace forward and put a hand on the director's arm.

'And you should get some rest first, Logan.'

Logan Burns patted her hand affectionately. 'You are right, Saki. I will go. Could you do a group meditation now? It would be a good preparation for this evening.'

The sitting inceptors and acolytes began shuffling apart to leave an aisle for Logan Burns to leave by. He pressed his fingertips together in a gesture of thanks and made to leave.

'And while you are resting I shall contact the police,' said Drew Kelso, as he followed the founder. 'Just to make sure that they are on hand this evening in case there are any troublemakers.'

Logan Burns stopped and held his hands out to the assembly. 'Do you see how my fellow directors look after me? How fortunate I am.'

Dr Ralph McLelland replaced his ophthalmoscope in its case on his desk then reached across to pull up the window blind and allow the light in again.

Calum Steele blinked and muttered an indistinct curse, which was rewarded with a stern look from the GP.

'You have been a lucky bugger, Calum Steele,' he said, rebukingly, as he sat behind his desk and reached for his prescription pad. He thought for a moment then dashed off a prescription in the classical scrawl shared by all doctors. He tore it from the pad and held it out, but held on to it as Calum went to take it. 'But you were a damned fool to discharge yourself last night. I am not surprised that you have a headache. I wanted you to rest for another day.'

Calum gave him a lopsided grin. 'Och, Ralph, man — I needed to find out what was really happening in the big world. I couldn't wait there and find out from the news.' He pointed his thumb at his own chest. 'I am the news on West Uist and I have a newspaper to run. Besides, I am here, am I not, your first patient?'

Ralph released the prescription and watched as Calum folded it and stowed it in a pocket of his anorak.

'Poor Nancy MacRurie,' Calum remarked casually. 'I heard about her accident. You told the nursing staff to keep it from me, didn't you?'

'I didn't want you to get too agitated, Calum,' Ralph returned. 'I knew you would want to get up and start snooping around.'

Calum shrugged. 'Actually, I ran into Annie McConville and she told me that Nancy was a good friend of Eileen Lamont.'

'Possibly,' Ralph returned slowly.

'Eileen used to help out at Goat's Head Farm, as well as helping at the vet's and at the dog sanctuary.'

'Out with it, Calum,' said Ralph, glancing at his watch. 'I have other patients waiting.'

Calum gave one of his cheesiest smiles and rose to go. 'Oh, I heard that Eileen was gay. I just wondered if you had any idea whether Nancy —'

Ralph's brows almost seemed to join together and his manner turned frosty. 'Calum Steele, we have known each other all our lives, but you never seem to learn.'

Calum smiled nervously. 'Learn what, Ralph?'

'One, that doctors are bound by the Hippocratic Oath. And two —' He stood up and made to march round the desk, only halting when his telephone started ringing. His hand hovered over it and he wagged a finger of his other hand at the newspaper editor.

'Just you remember that I am considerably bigger than you and I used to play shinty for the Western Isles. Now off with you, Calum Steele!'

Calum retreated swiftly, massaging his ego with the sentiment that investigative journalists were sometimes forced to annoy even their best friends in the pursuit of the truth and a good story.

'Aye, thank you, Ralph,' Torquil said into the receiver. 'I understand. Oh, and did Calum say where he was going? I need to talk to him, but he is not answering his phone, which is unusual.'

He nodded as Ralph replied, then replaced the receiver and stood for a moment tapping the saddle of the mountain bike that Ewan had stashed behind the office counter. Something was niggling him, but he could not put his finger on it. With a scowl of frustration he returned to the rest-room where the others were waiting.

'Ralph doesn't feel able to commit himself. He cannot add anything about his examination of any of the bodies. The clinical findings were consistent with accidents in the case of Finlay MacNeil and Nancy, and the Noble case is closed.'

'But it could be reopened, couldn't it?' Lorna asked.

'It could if we had any reason to reopen it,' he mused, as he strode over to the whiteboard with its network of squares, circles and notes. He tapped it with his fingertips. 'There is something here that isn't right, folks. But I can't see it.' He rubbed his eyes, suddenly feeling very tired. He stifled a yawn and caught sight of Lorna doing likewise. Then he was stifling a grin that had threatened to erupt.

'I think we should break for an early lunch then reconvene this afternoon. Let's all mull things over.'

The others stood up and gathered notes together.

'Well I think I will be off, laddie,' said the Padre, pulling his pipe from his breast pocket in readiness for hitting the open air. 'Will you be home for tea this evening?'

Torquil shook his head, a trifle too readily, he realized. 'I think we'll need to keep an eye on the crowds up at the Hoolish Stones for a while, at any rate. I'll see you later, Uncle.'

The Padre understood only too well. He gave them all one of his practised pastoral smiles, revelling in the blush that ascended to Lorna's cheeks. Then he left.

Morag turned to the Drummonds. 'Why don't we head up to the stones now, and just check on the parking arrangements, so that we are prepared for later?'

'Ach, Sergeant, we have it all in hand. Everything is marked out and cordons are in place,' said Wallace.

'You can trust us,' Douglas affirmed.

'I'll buy lunch afterwards,' Morag persisted.

The twins bumped into each other as they both went to open the door for her.

'I'll get on with a bit of tidying, Torquil,' Ewan volunteered. 'Then I'll get some of my reports written up.'

'Excellent,' Torquil said, beaming at his constable. 'And meanwhile Sergeant Golspie and I shall ... go for a think.' He picked up his Cromwell helmet, goggles and gauntlets and pointed to the spare passenger helmet on the filing cabinet.

When they had left, the Drummonds and Morag grinned at each other. Wallace began whistling 'Love is in the air,' and Douglas and Morag joined in with him.

The Padre rode home, gathered his clubs then played six holes. He had intended playing a full nine, but gave up at the sixth having had, by his standards, a poor result. His concentration had not been good and his swing had felt out of sync. Accordingly, he left the course and strolled up to the church to say a few prayers before heading back to the manse to prepare a late lunch.

Unusually, the door was standing ajar and he fancied that he heard a mixture of sobbing and plaintiff voices from within. He laid his clubs against the wall in the porch and entered. Sitting in the front pew were two women, one with her arm about the other, clearly trying to offer comfort. They were both members of The Daisy Institute. The one who was sobbing was wearing a white hoodie and the other, offering consolation was wearing pink. As he approached along the aisle they looked round sharply and he recognized both of them.

'Why, Johanna, what is the matter?' he asked concernedly. Then said, with a nod at the girl in the pink hoodie, 'Hello, Eileen. It is a while since I have had the pleasure of your presence in my church.'

'*Latha math*, Padre,' Eileen said. 'I hope you don't mind us coming here like this, but Johanna has had a bit of a shock.'

'Not another accident at the castle?' the Padre queried.

Johanna looked up at him and wiped tears from her eyes with the back of her hand. 'No, not an accident, Padre. It is something that didn't happen. Something terrible that Eileen stopped me from doing.' She sighed and then her whole body started to tremble. 'I am so ashamed of what I was thinking of doing.' She pointed to the metal thermos flask on the stone floor in front of her. 'I have been mad, I think. I was going to maim someone.'

Eileen held her close and stroked her hair. 'She has been carrying a great secret burden around with her for too long, Padre.'

'What secret is this, Johanna?' the Padre asked, sitting down beside her.

'Guilt, Padre. I feel so guilty.' She turned and squeezed Eileen's hand. 'When Nancy died, I felt so worried about Eileen and I felt I had to bring my plan forward.'

The Padre picked up the thermos and was about to unscrew the lid.

'No! Be careful!' Johanna cried, snatching it away from him. 'It's acid and it's dangerous.'

Lachlan pushed his spectacles further back on his nose and whistled softly. 'Acid? This sounds serious, Johanna. Would you like to tell me what has been happening?'

Johanna looked at Eileen for guidance. Eileen nodded encouragingly.

'It is a bad story, Padre,' Johanna said. 'But I would like to tell you, because I am so scared.'

The Padre patted the back of her hand. 'Go ahead, lassie. You are in the right place. Nothing bad can happen to you here.'

Torquil and Lorna had bought sandwiches and a couple of bottles of water and then rode the Bullet along the coastal road for a couple of miles before taking sheep tracks across the moor to reach the sanctuary of the tall bracken. All thought of their picnic disappeared as they fell into each other's arms, before dropping to the ground to carry on where they had left off that morning. They made passionate love, unaware of the passage of time until a few flecks of rain on their bare flesh and a slight breeze brought them back to reality.

'My God, if Superintendent Lumsden could see us now,' Lorna giggled as she kissed his nose.

'He would have a blue fit!' Torquil replied with a laugh. 'As would anyone else. You just make me feel so happy, Lorna. I can hardly believe that this is happening. Here and now, and all so quickly.'

'Yes, we barely know one another. But it feels so perfect. As if it was meant to happen.'

Torquil's brow clouded. 'I didn't think I would ever meet anyone again,' he said. 'After what happened before. I need to tell you —'

She silenced him with another kiss. 'I know all about it,' she said softly. 'Morag told me.'

Rain started to fall and reluctantly they separated and gathered up their clothes and dressed quickly.

'I don't seem able to think when you are about,' Torquil said as he ran his fingers through his thick black hair. 'All of these problems, all these unanswered questions back at the station, they just don't seem to bother me.' He bit his lip. 'And that is bad, isn't it?'

Lorna threw her arm about his shoulder. 'Look, Torquil, we know where we are for now, don't we? I feel exactly the same way about you. We'll just have to pinch ourselves and get back to reality.'

'I agree, let's get back to problem-solving. I think I can now that my head has been cleared of all my lustful thoughts.'

'Not all of them, I hope.'

He looked up at the darkening sky then winked at her as the rain began to fall. 'Looks like we are in for one of our classic West Uist squalls. Let's get the Bullet back on the road.' Lorna tossed her head back and laughed. 'I love all these odd things about you. Your bagpipes, your insubordination to the superintendent, your old motorized bike.'

'Motorized bike! How dare you!' he exclaimed, making to grab her hair. Then his eyes opened wide in amazement. 'Good grief, Lorna. That's it. That's the thing that has been bothering me about the whole thing. The bike! Come on, we have to get back.'

'We were getting worried about you two,' Morag said as Torquil and Lorna came in, their clothes sodden. 'You got caught in the squall, I see. Well, the pair of you had better just get dried off and slip into the interviewee dressing-gowns before you catch a chill.'

'Morag, I am fine really —' Lorna began.

'I would just do as she says, Sergeant Golspie — I mean, Lorna,' said Ewan. He pointed at the puddles that were accumulating around their feet. 'Morag is a bit house-proud, you see.'

'Aye, comes from looking after her three bairns,' Wallace ventured.

Morag eyed him sternly. 'And the bairns that I have to look after here. And that includes you two, Wallace and Douglas.' Her withering eye caught Torquil. 'And as for the inspector —'

Torquil raised his hands. 'OK, we're going. How about hot tea and we'll be with you in the ops room in a minute. Morag, get out the file on the Hoolish Farm case; I think we have something to chew over.'

And indeed, when Torquil and Lorna reappeared a few minutes later in yellow dressing-gowns, still towelling their hair as if fresh from showers, the tea was ready. As were the other members of the division.

'Ewan's bike is the thing that has been bothering me,' Torquil said immediately. 'Or rather, Rab Noble's bike.'

'I don't understand, Torquil,' Morag replied.

'It was up at the milking parlour, wasn't it?' Morag flicked the pages over then nodded. 'It was. He often cycled there, apparently. What are you getting at, Torquil?'

'The puzzle. It is a puzzle, because all of the dogs were at the farm. Don't you see, the bike and the dogs were in the wrong places.'

Lorna pulled the file across the ping-pong table and started reading to familiarize herself with the main aspects of the case.

Ewan nodded. 'It was a terrible sight. But the bike was parked at the parlour. It was leaning against the outer wall. I remember that because I ran out after finding the carnage inside and I almost puked over it.'

'But what do you mean about the dogs?' Douglas asked in bemusement.

'Well, you would have expected him to take the dogs to bring the cattle up. Even if he cycled there, you would have expected that, wouldn't you? They would have run alongside of him.'

'But Calum Steele said that he was almost knocked off his scooter by him driving like a maniac.'

'*If* it was him!' Torquil announced. 'What if the reason the dogs were not with him was because he had cycled directly to the milking parlour from somewhere else? And what if the reason the dogs weren't with him was because he had been somewhere that they would have been a nuisance?'

Morag had raised her tea to her mouth, but quickly replaced it on the table untouched. 'I see what you are getting at. If the bike was there, it couldn't have been Rab Noble in the Jeep. And that means that —'

Torquil shook his head. 'It means that there is a possibility that whoever was in the Jeep went to the milking parlour and may have shot him with his own shotgun. Made it look like the suicide of someone who had lost the plot.'

Lorna looked up from the file, her eyes wide in horror. 'And that might mean that the Jeep driver had already murdered Esther Noble.'

Silence fell about the room as the import of it all fell upon them. The storm clouds had darkened the sky and a fork of lightning outside was followed by a peal of thunder.

'Bloody hell! That is spooky!' exclaimed Douglas Drummond.

'It is more than that, Douglas,' said Torquil pointing at the whiteboard. 'It looks as if we are about to open up a can of worms.'

He stood and went over to the whiteboard and picked up the marker. It squeaked on the board as he wrote beside the boxed names of Rab and Esther Noble the word: *MURDER?*

'It raises questions about where Rab Noble could have been on his bicycle? Who gained by their deaths? And, most importantly, who killed them?'

'There are a lot of links to the Hoolish Farm on that board,' Wallace pointed out.

'And to the Hoolish Stones,' Douglas added.

'And to The Daisy Institute,' offered Ewan.

Torquil made a fist and tapped his forehead. 'Damn! All of which makes it look as if the other deaths, of Finlay MacNeil and Nancy MacRurie should be regarded as suspicious.'

Lorna bit her lip and winced. 'Then maybe it would be an idea to have a word with Superintendent Lumsden, Inspector? Remember what he said.'

Torquil glanced at Lorna and gave her a fleeting smile. Then he turned to the whiteboard. 'There is not anything here that directly links the institute with the Noble deaths, is there? I am just a bit wary of talking to the superintendent until I have this fleshed out a bit more.'

'Is there anyone who would be a suspect in the case?' Lorna asked. 'What do we know about the wife, Esther Noble?'

'That is one of the reasons I wanted to talk to Calum Steele,' Torquil replied. 'If only he would answer his mobile.' He tapped his teeth with his fingernail. 'It makes me think that he's up to something.'

Morag sipped her lukewarm tea. 'But she was in your class at school, wasn't she, Torquil?' she asked, rhetorically. 'What you don't know, Miss Melville almost certainly will.'

'I know that Calum used to have the hots for her, but she left school at sixteen and got married. I totally lost touch with her. I supposed she had just dropped into the farmer's wife role. Rab Noble had always been a bit of a recluse.' He pointed at the file. 'What did Calum Steele say in his interview?'

Lorna shoved the file across the table to Morag. 'Perhaps you would like to check, Morag? It is your file, after all,' she said, diplomatically.

Morag graced her with a smile and flicked the pages over. 'Here we are. He said that she telephoned him and said that she told him — and I quote — "*Get here right away, Calum Steele, and I will give you the biggest story you have ever had. The sadistic bastard! I will blow the lid on him and his band of sickos*".'

Torquil's eyes opened wide. 'The *sick bastard*? Was that a reference to Rab Noble, as we originally thought, or was it someone else. Someone who then killed her? And if so, was she killed because she was going to talk to the press about something?'

'Dogs!' Ewan suddenly exclaimed.

'Yes, Ewan?' Torquil asked. 'What about dogs?'

'Sorry, boss, I just had an idea. Rab Noble might have left his dogs at home because he was going to visit somewhere that there were other dogs.' He pointed at the notes Torquil had made earlier, when he had told them about his meeting with Annie McConville. 'He could have cycled easily to the Goat's Head Farm. They have dogs, as we all know.'

'Good thinking, Ewan. We will have to check that out.' He tapped the box containing Finlay MacNeil's name. 'Now what about this? The links are clear between the Hoolish Stones and The Daisy Institute, especially Finlay's animosity to Logan Burns.'

'We have to interview him again, I think, don't we?' Morag said.

'And we have to look at that poor girl, Nancy.' The sky darkened and another fork of lightning flickered outside.

Torquil pointed to the word *TV* and the name *FINBAR DONLEAVY*. 'The Padre told me about the news last night and Finbar Donleavy's little piece.' He wrote the word *CULT* underneath the circled *DAISY INSTITUTE* and added a question mark. 'This word begins to make me feel very uneasy. It is the eve of the summer solstice tonight, the time that the institute has been harping on about for ages. That they have been getting TV coverage about. If the death of Finlay and Nancy have something to do with the institute, and if it is a cult, then maybe we have reason to be really worried.'

Morag bit her lip anxiously. 'I keep thinking about Eileen Lamont saying that it should have been her that had died, not

Nancy. Poor kid.' She shook her head, and then asked, 'You don't think that this solstice has something sinister about it, do you? That Eileen Lamont could still be at risk?'

'Worse than that, Morag,' Torquil said. 'The whole institute could be at risk. If it is a cult, remember some of the atrocities that have happened in other parts of the world. There was that mass suicide in Jonestown in Guyana back in the seventies.'

'And the Waco siege in Texas,' Lorna continued. 'How many people died in that?'

No one answered immediately, for a succession of lightning flashes made them all aware that the atmosphere was full of electricity. But they were all also aware that it was not the static that was making the hairs on the back of their necks seem to stand up.

Lachlan had let Johanna Waltari pour out her tale, interspersed here and there with comments from Eileen who kept her arm about her through it all.

'So let me get this straight,' he said at last. 'Your real name is not Johanna Waltari, but Jaana Hakinen. You joined the institute the year after your elder sister Aila died in Geneva.'

'That is right, I know I didn't explain it well. There was only me and her left when my parents died. But she joined this crazy group and I couldn't see her. Then she died in an accident. She fell from the top of a building and died instantly. There was an inquiry, but it was declared an accident.'

'But you did not believe this? Could it have been suicide?'

The girl Jaana shook her head vigorously. 'No, Aila was level-headed before she joined the institute and fell under the spell of Logan Burns. She was a graduate of Helsinki University and was going to be physiotherapist — until they turned her head.'

Eileen nodded emphatically. 'It is true, Padre. They are so persuasive about everything. You really believe that they have the answers to all that you could ever ask.'

Lachlan smiled thinly but made no comment. Instead, he asked, 'So you think that your sister was murdered?'

Jaana frowned. 'Perhaps not in so many words, but I think she was put in a bad state and may not have known what she was doing.'

'And put in this state by the process that they put you through?'

'That and the jealousy that she had for the other woman. She had kept a diary, although she was not supposed to. They do not allow such things. But one of her friends sent it to me after she died. It told me that she was having an affair. She just wrote "with the director". But this other woman, another inceptor, a British woman, she stole her lover.'

'And you planned to get even?' the Padre asked. 'But why with this acid?'

'He deserves it. He is a charlatan. He has fooled everyone and he wants the world to accept his crazy ideas. Tonight he means to reveal everything.' She turned to Eileen and kissed her cheek. 'I bless the day that I met Eileen. She has saved me from much stupidity.'

'Maybe from prison,' the Padre said. 'But tell me again why you were so worried about Eileen?'

Jaana sighed. 'When Nancy died I thought — I thought that she had been killed, like my sister.'

'It was supposed to have been my vigil, you see, Padre,' Eileen explained. 'Only Nancy did it for me so that I could go and see Johanna, I mean Jaana. When Jaana told me some of her story, we sort of thought that it could have been me, because Logan had taken a shine to me.'

681

'Are you serious though? Do you really think that Logan Burns is a murderer?'

'I think he is a monster.'

'And what about this evening? Are you planning to go and stay up to see this solstice?'

The two girls nodded in unison. 'We feel that we must be there. For Nancy's sake, and also because some of our friends are there.'

The Padre nodded and sucked air in through his teeth as a crack of thunder seemed to rock the rafters of the church. 'Well, let us hope that the weather brightens up a bit or you will all get soaked to the skin.' He stood up and nodded. 'And now I think I had better be off myself. I need to have a word with my nephew, Inspector McKinnon. Especially after this tale. Do you have any objections about me telling him all this? If you are really suspicious about what happened to your sister, then I think he should know.'

'You tell him, Padre. And if he wants to talk to me I will tell him everything.'

CHAPTER TWELVE

Calum Steele had gone to ground. That was the way he liked to describe his extra special thinking time when he was working on a case and did not wish to be interrupted by anyone, friend or foe. And, at the present time, he believed that he had plenty of the latter. Going to ground sometimes just meant unplugging his phone and retiring to his camp-bed in the *West Uist Chronicle* offices for a nap. On this occasion he did not wish to risk another attack like the last one, when his window and his head had been smashed with the brick. Accordingly, he had gone off to the old but 'n' ben cottage, the traditional two-roomed crofter's cottage, at the end of Loch Hynish that he had inherited from his grandfather and which he had used to develop his photographs before the days of digital cameras. While not exactly liveable, it still had a sound roof, a water supply and a gas stove so that he could knock up a meal and brew tea.

And so, tucked up in the old sleeping-bag that he left in the cupboard for such occasions, he had whiled the rainy afternoon away as he worked out his plan of campaign. Not that it was anything too subtle. He had stowed his Lambretta round the back of the but 'n' ben and planned to set off for the Goat's Head in the early evening.

'This is meant to be, Calum my man,' he cooed to himself. 'Some old-fashioned West Uist weather, a fine sea squall that brings plenty of rain and mist.' He glanced at his watch then unzipped his sleeping-bag. 'Time for some soup, a dram and a mutton pie.'

He struck a light and turned on the gas stove. Then, while the soup heated up, he assembled the equipment he needed. His old polaroid camera, his hand-held tape-recorder and the old two-foot long sawn-off axe-handle that he carried as a cudgel, just in case. Then he turned his attention again to the photographs spread out on the old trestle table and picked up the magnifying glass that lay beside them. He selected the photograph of the green card that he had taken of Wilf Cruikshank exchanging for a wad of notes down at the harbour.

'Eight o'clock,' he mused to himself with a grin. 'Soon be time for me to get into a good position then. Somewhere upwind so that I don't give any of those mutts the chance of sniffing me out.'

Outside the rain had stopped and the mist swirled against the window panes. Calum ate his soup unaware that at that very moment his but 'n' ben was being closely watched.

Superintendent Lumsden was in a foul mood when he called the West Uist station to talk to Torquil. He was in an even worse one when Morag answered and told him that Inspector McKinnon was not available.

'And just why is he not available. Sergeant Driscoll?'

'It is the weather, sir. He is out of the station on an investigation and his mobile isn't working. No mobiles work out here when we get one of these sudden sea storms. Even these telephones can ... be ... unpredictable and —' There was a sudden loud whistling noise, then the line cut out.

Morag looked round from the office counter at Ewan McPhee who stood with a whistle halfway to his lips. Behind him Torquil stood grinning.

'Well done, Morag. And good man, Ewan,' Torquil said.

Lorna was standing with her hands in her dressing-gown pockets, a worried look on her face. 'Are you sure that was a good idea, Torquil?'

The phone rang again and Morag signalled to Ewan to be ready with his whistle.

'A necessary subterfuge,' Torquil whispered, before Morag picked up the phone.

He tapped the watch on his wrist and picked at his own dressing-gown sleeve. 'Time to get changed,' he mouthed quietly.

Five minutes later they had congregated back in the restroom.

'That was him again,' Morag said. 'I think he believed me, because he started talking quickly before he was cut off.'

'And?' Torquil asked.

'I don't know. He got cut off by the storm.'

Wallace and Douglas laughed. 'She has a wicked streak in her, true enough,' said Douglas.

'Aye, just as Ewan McPhee always says,' added Wallace.

Ewan was quick on the defensive. 'I never said any such thing, Morag. They are just a pair of *teuchters*.'

'OK, let's get back to brass tacks,' said Torquil. 'We have serious work ahead. Firstly, Morag had better stay here and man the phones. If the superintendent calls, then the electrical interference will cut him off. If it is a genuine member of the public we deal with it as usual.'

Morag nodded. 'What are we going to do about the solstice? Are we going to cancel their meeting?'

'Impossible,' Torquil replied. 'We have no grounds. Nothing concrete except supposition. We police it as usual, but while we do so we will keep our eyes open and opportunistically interview the various people.'

The bell in the office rang to indicate that someone had entered the station. It was followed a moment later by the tread of heavy brogues on the linoleum floor and by Lachlan's dulcet tones.

'It is only me. Can I come through?'

Moments later he was standing in the rest-room explaining about his meeting with the two girls.

Torquil filled him in on their conclusions, directing his attention to the whiteboard and its web of associations.

'We were just talking about whether we could cancel the meeting,' he said.

The Padre shook his head. 'You should see the numbers of folk that are finding their way up there right now. I think you would have a riot on your hands.'

'That is what we were thinking, Uncle. We were planning to interview the directors up there.'

'If we can get them away from the television crew,' Lorna said.

'If you like, I think that I could create a diversion if needs be,' the Padre suggested. 'I have had dealings with Finbar Donleavy as you know. I think I could handle him if you need to talk to the others.'

'What about us?' Wallace asked. 'Do you want us to interview any of the flower folk?'

'No, I think you will both be needed to sort out parking and make sure there are no skirmishes or anything of that sort. We have not had a big meeting like this and we have no knowledge of whether these solstice watchers will be drinkers. You two take the station Escort.

'And me, Torquil?' Ewan asked.

'You need to check out the folk at the Goat's Head Farm.'

Ewan was fiddling with the whistle that hung on the lanyard from his neck. He nodded and grinned. 'I'll use the station mountain bike, if that is OK.'

'And your whistle, if you run into any bad folk,' jibed Wallace, much to his brother's amusement.

'So that is set then,' Torquil said. 'Lorna and I will grab the opportunities to interview the directors one at a time and the Padre here will keep the TV bods busy if needs be.'

'And we need to talk to Eileen and Jaana,' added Lorna. 'I suggest we go in my car.'

'Fine,' replied Torquil. 'That's about all we can do. The proper investigation will start tomorrow, if we find we have enough to go official.'

Morag sighed. 'Let's just hope I can keep the superintendent off our backs until then.'

'Amen,' said the Padre.

A sizeable crowd had already started to gather around the Hoolish Stones. The ground was wet and the sky was virtually obscured by banks of cloud. Mist swirled eerily around the ancient standing stones.

The Daisy Institute members had assembled in the positions that had been allotted to them earlier that afternoon at Dunshiffin Castle. The three directors were standing in the middle by the chambered cairn, the white hoodied acolytes were positioned each to one of the megaliths of the inner circles, and the pink-clad inceptors were similarly placed by stones around the outer ring.

'It is impressive, Logan,' said Saki Yasuda. 'From the air this will look like a real daisy.' Logan Burns seemed restless, a little irritable. But he nodded at her. 'Just as it would have looked in the days of Atlantis, Saki. And when this temple was built all those millennia ago, the stones would have been painted in these colours.'

Drew Kelso patted Logan on the back. 'It is all coming together for you now, Logan. Just a few hours and the sunrise on the solstice will light up the stones, just as you have predicted.'

'Yes, but where is that blasted television reporter?'

'He said he would be here for the news slot as usual,' Drew returned. 'I spoke to him just a couple of hours ago.'

Peter Severn and Henrietta Appleyard were standing a few feet away from them, each beside a great stone. 'Would you like me to go and look for Finbar?' asked Henrietta.

Logan Burns shook his head. 'There is still time. We should get ready to show the people. I will address them soon.'

'I could phone him,' Henrietta offered.

'I said there is time,' Logan Burns snapped. 'Besides, your phone won't work out here in this weather.'

'Let us hope the mists clear,' Saki said.

Logan Burns snorted irritably. It was clear to everyone around him that he seemed like a man about to fulfil his life's destiny. And he seemed scared.

He pulled up his hood and stood with his hands pressed together. 'Pass the signal. It is time to begin the chant.'

Calum Steele left his Lambretta in bracken some distance from the drive leading up to the Goat's Head Farm then took to the route he had planned out, circumnavigating the cow pastures and the pig pens to get to the far side of the farm. Keeping to the undergrowth and blessing the cover of the mist he had spotted the younger Cruikshank brother positioned at the bottom of the drive by the cattle grid. Several vehicles had already gone through and made their way towards a makeshift parking area in front of the old barn.

'Looks like the old girl's tip was right enough,' he mused to himself, as he lay on his stomach peering through binoculars at the activity unfurling before him. Every now and then the door of the barn opened, light from within spilled out and he could hear a tumultuous barking and a hum of raised voices.

Then a McQueen Egg van arrived and he saw the father and son emerge, to be greeted by the older Cruikshank and disappear inside the barn.

'Time for a closer look,' he whispered between his teeth. Then, stealthily, when he judged that the time was right and no more cars were coming up the old track, he made his way to the rear of the building.

As he suspected, there was a window, protected by bars, yet with enough room for him to see inside. The action had already begun. He saw the cages of dogs, the crowd of men, gamblers all, encircling an enclosure inside which two men were crouched at opposite corners, holding fast to the collars of a couple of snarling, wide-eyed fighting dogs. The men were crying out, braying almost. Then at a signal from Pug Cruikshank, the dogs were released. A blur of movement saw the two dogs crash into each other, jaws snapping, teeth bared and immediately blood and saliva starting to spurt.

Calum had his camera at the ready, and his tape recorder in his hand to catch the noise, yet even his seasoned sensitivities were shocked. He stood staring in horror.

Then a hand was clamped firmly over his mouth and he felt his arms pinned to his side. Something hard, like a gun barrel, was jabbed into his back and he froze in terror.

The narrow road up to the Hoolish Stones was packed on either side with cars. The Drummond twins were doing their best to maintain some order, but the crowds were considerable and they were already having some difficulty in controlling the flow.

'No one is going to be leaving in a hurry,' Lorna said, as she edged into a free spot created by Wallace.

The Padre was the first out. 'That certainly sounds eerie,' he remarked as the monotonous chanting from The Daisy Institute members assailed their ears.

Torquil, Lorna and the Padre made their way across the moor to the edge of the great crowd that had assembled around the ancient monument, despite the inclemency of the weather. It seemed a completely disparate group: New Age people, holidaymakers and locals stimulated to find out what all the fuss was about.

Among the first people that they met as they joined the outside of the crowd were Miss Melville and Jessie McPhee, Ewan's mother.

'Are the television people here yet?' the Padre asked them.

'Not a sign of them,' replied Bella Melville. 'They are just chanting away there. I am not sure that I fancy standing here in this weather listening to them caterwauling all night until the sunrise.'

'Is my laddie Ewan not here?' Jessie McPhee, a petite lady in a duffle coat asked.

'He is on a job, investigating elsewhere,' Torquil replied. 'Now, if you ladies will excuse us, we had better have a closer look at what is happening.'

He made to move off, then snapped his fingers and turned back to Bella. 'Just one question, Miss Melville. It is about the

Nobles at Hoolish Farm. Do you know if Esther Noble was happy?'

'Happy! You are joking, aren't you, Inspector McKinnon? Didn't I teach you anything? You need to keep your eyes open. No, Esther was never happy since the day she married Rab Noble. He drank and he gambled and he kept low company. It is no wonder that she was ... tempted by other men.'

'Other men? Here on West Uist?'

Miss Melville nodded curtly. 'She left him for a few months, you know. Went to Switzerland to sort her head out. But I think she met someone there. Anyway, it didn't last and she came back.' She shook her head again. 'No, she was not a happy woman, Torquil McKinnon.'

Torquil looked at Lorna, both aware of the possible link with The Daisy Institute that they now had to follow up on. 'Thank you, ladies,' he said. 'Don't get too cold.'

They left and gradually sidled through the crowd to the edge of the stones, where the chanting hoodie-clad figures formed an impressive yet incongruous sight.

As they did so, the figure of Logan Burns raised his hands and the chanting suddenly stopped. He stepped up on top of the chambered cairn.

'My friends!' he called out, his voice seeming to boom and echo around the great standing stones. 'Thank you all for coming here today, on this night to wait until the solstice sunrise. As you will all know from the televised slots on Scottish TV — although for some reason the television crew are not here tonight — the summer solstice is the longest day of the year, and on that day the sun will seem to stand still. I, my fellow directors and our acolytes and inceptors plan to stay here until the sunrise, at which point there will be a great revelation. You will all see that —'

'*Liar! You filthy liar!*' someone screamed.

Logan Burns blinked, looked slightly taken aback, then began again. 'You will see that my predictions —'

'*Liar! Bloody murderer!*' the voice screamed again. A man's voice, that quaked with rage.

Torquil and Lorna were craning their necks to spot the heckler, as were most people in the crowd.

'*You killed my girl! Now die there in your precious stones!*'

There was an explosive noise of two shots and Logan Burns spun round and seemed to be knocked backwards, to fall off the cairn, an arc of crimson trailing from his body.

The crowd began to panic as people realized that a gun had been discharged.

Torquil and Lorna immediately went into action in an attempt to quieten the crowd and pinpoint the gunman, but it was in vain. They were jostled to and fro as people attempted to escape lest there should be further firing.

Then, as the crowd started to move away, Torquil saw Hamish MacRurie advance towards the group of three inside the inner stones. All of the inceptors and acolytes had either taken cover behind their stones or had taken to their heels with the rest of the onlookers.

Logan Burns was lying on the ground, blood pumping from a wound in his chest. Saki Yasuda was kneeling beside him, attempting to cradle his head in her lap. Drew Kelso was backing away from the approaching gunman.

'Hamish MacRurie!' Torquil shouted. 'Police! Stand still!'

But the distraught father was moving as if in a trance, the gun in his outstretched trembling hand.

'Lorna, get hold of Ralph,' Torquil ordered, as he launched himself free of the crowd and charged after Hamish. He realized that the man was not going to listen to logic. So he dived at him, ensnaring his arms and dragging him with him to the ground. The gun went flying.

The Drummond twins were quickly on the scene and ran to help.

'Help me!' Saki Yasuda screamed. 'I need a doctor here. My God! I think Logan is dead!'

Calum's mind was racing and the pressure of the object in his back rooted him to the spot. 'Not a sound, Steele!' a familiar voice hissed in his ear. 'I am going to take my hands away in a moment, OK.'

Calum made to nod and the hand slowly withdrew from his mouth.

'Good! Now let's get some proper footage of these sick bastards,' Finbar Donleavy said. 'In you get, Danny, and start shooting.' Calum eased away to let the white-haired Danny Wade take his place with his camera.

'How did you find me?' Calum gasped.

'We followed you,' Finbar whispered back. 'We realized you were on to this lot as well.' He winced as he looked in the window at the carnage that was taking place in the ring. 'Make sure you get some pictures of the punters as well, Danny.'

'This is my story, Donleavy!' Calum said, between gritted teeth as he recovered himself.

'Don't worry, Kirstie made me promise that you'll get your credits. We will interview you properly once we get away from here, then later we'll do a stake out and confront some of these sick sods.'

'Kirstie said that? Well, get the McQueens over there,' Calum said, shooting out a hand to point at the two men through the window. But in doing so he jolted Danny Wade's hand and the camera lens struck the window.

Immediately, a man at the back of the crowd looked round and saw them. He cursed, then shouted out a warning. Before they knew it two-score or so of angry faces were turned in their direction. Worse, men were making for the door.

'Shit! Now it's hit the fan. Let's get going,' cried Finbar Donleavy.

And indeed the three of them needed no further prompting. They belted for it and were already a couple of dozen yards away when the barn door burst open and people started racing out. One of the first was Pug Cruikshank.

'Get those bastards or we're scuppered!' he cried. Then, 'Wilf, get your dogs on them!'

In the general melee of people running for their vehicles the three journalists ran for all they were worth. They were all too aware that in moments, as some of the fighting dogs were loosed, they could well be running for their very lives.

'He is just in shock,' the Padre said, as he knelt beside Saki Yasuda and Logan Burns. 'We are getting a doctor to him as soon as possible. I am no doctor myself, but I would say that he has been lucky. The bullet has passed through the top of his chest and missed his heart. We need to keep him conscious and comfortable, and just maintain pressure on that wound.'

Saki Yasuda heaved a sigh of relief. She looked up. 'Is Drew here?'

Wallace and Douglas had come running at the sound of gunfire and were in the process of helping Torquil put handcuffs on the wild-eyed but now subdued Hamish MacRurie.

'Is that the other guy in the yellow hoodie?' Wallace asked. 'He went off with Lorna.'

'She said she was going to get Ralph McLelland and that we should help you,' said Douglas.

Torquil stood and looked round, his eyes opening wide in alarm. 'Where is the gun?' The twins shook their heads.

'I don't like this,' Torquil said, turning and running towards the cars. People were running everywhere, cars were being started and horns beeped as everyone wanted to get away from the Hoolish Stones.

But no one could, for two cars were blocking the narrow lane, and both had their tyres slashed. Lorna's Golf GTI was gone.

'Wallace, see if you can get through to Morag,' Torquil snapped. 'And, Douglas, try and get hold of Ralph.'

'What are you going to do, boss?'

Torquil was running for the other side of the road where he had spied Nippy, Jessie McPhee's Norton moped.

'I am going after the bastard. He's got Lorna!' Torquil exclaimed. 'And he's a murderer.'

Calum's heart was pounding and felt as if it could easily burst as he ran as he had never done before. Cars were being revved up and driven off, slewing from side to side in the mud.

'Where is your car?' Calum called to the other two.

'Miles away,' Finbar gasped.

'Fuck! The dogs are coming,' cried Danny, chancing a look over his shoulder.

'Make for that Hillman Imp,' Calum said. And, as the words tumbled out, he realized that he recognized the car parked just inside the cattle grid.

The noise of panting dogs seemed ominously close and the three men tried to put on a spurt.

A stream of cars was flashing past the Hillman and, as they watched, they saw the driver's door open and an old lady got out.

'Annie! For God's sake,' screamed Calum. '*Get back in the car!*'

But the old lady just pulled the door as wide open as she could and casually reached inside and took something out. 'You get in the car, Calum Steele,' she called. 'And your friends.' And, as they approached, they saw that she had a parcel, which she tossed to the side. Then she pulled out a whistle and blew. But no noise came out.

Finbar arrived at the car first and dived in, followed shortly after by Danny Wade who tossed his camera in first. Calum brought up the rear and with what seemed the last of his strength, he dived in.

'C ... come on, Annie!' he gasped, turning as quickly as he could to help her.

But then they saw that the old lady was doing nothing of the sort. She was standing over the two black pit bull terriers as they sniffed and snuffled over the parcel of meat. Annie had a hypersonic whistle between her lips and was blowing it. And to the amazement of the three newsmen, looking from the safety of her old Hillman Imp, the dogs began to settle and moved towards her, tails between their legs looking thoroughly cowed.

'I thought you might need a wee bit help, Calum Steele,' she said, taking the whistle
from between her lips. 'And see that I found a good use for your newspaper,' she added with a twinkle in her eye, pointing to the parcel of raw meat that she had thrown to distract the dogs.

Lorna had been unable to do anything other than obey with the gun in her back. Then, once in the car, Kelso had produced an S&M choke chain from a pocket of his hoodie and dropped it over her head. She had gagged as he demonstrated how easily he could garrotte her.

'Just drive to that police boat of yours,' he had commanded.

Unable to do otherwise she had obeyed.

It had been difficult driving, with her as yet unsure of the roads, and trying to go quickly with repeated reminders not to do anything foolish. She had taken two wrong turns, for each of which she received a choking reprimand, yet she managed to drive to the police docking point on the harbour where the *Seaspray* police catamaran was waiting.

'Start it up and let's get off!' Kelso snapped at her. 'Set a course for the mainland. Be good to me and maybe you'll live through all this.'

Lorna acquiesced, despite her protests about being a poor sailor and getting sea-sick. 'Just go.'

'Why ... why are you doing this?' she ventured once *Seaspray* was clear of the harbour and heading out to sea.

'I am escaping,' he said simply. 'I would have been leaving soon anyway, but that fool precipitated my egress. I had no intention of you clods getting hold of me.'

'You mean because you killed —?'

'All of them!' he said with a laugh. 'That's right. That snivelling bitch who was going to shop me. Her cuckolded husband, that drunken idiot MacNeil.'

'And ... and Nancy?'

'Her too. Stupid bitch. What was she doing on that vigil anyway? I was going to have a quick interlude with that little Eileen girl, but then it was the wrong one. She had to have an accident.'

The *Seaspray* scudded over the waves and Lorna began to feel nauseated, though whether from the confession or from the buffeting of the boat, she was unsure.

'The fool Burns can take the rap. It is only a matter of time before they make the link with Geneva.'

'With Jaana's sister? We know about that already,' Lorna ventured.

Kelso tugged on the chain and Lorna gagged. He laughed, and stroked her neck with the barrel of the gun. 'You are quite attractive, you know that, Sergeant? We might have a slight stop before we get to Benbecula. You might grow to like this little chain, what do you think?'

Lorna tasted vomit and retched.

Kelso looked at her distastefully. 'Still, I don't need to kiss you. Your body will do.' Lorna felt her skin crawl as he moved the gun, letting it trace the contours of her left breast.

'You ... you like this S&M stuff, do you?'

'I like to be in control.'

'And ... where are you going to go?'

He laughed. A brutal laugh. 'That you will never know. Suffice it to say that I will be going to enjoy the money that I have siphoned off from this mad bastard's organization. I am going to enjoy a very long retirement, incognito.'

'You told me why you killed Nancy, but why Finlay MacNeil?'

'No reason why you shouldn't know. He saw me leave the Hoolish Farm after I killed the bitch. After all I did for her. I brought The Daisy Institute to this god-forsaken island after she left Geneva. She liked it at first, being able to continue our affair, until I developed ... other interests. Other women.'

'A crime of passion?'

tumbled into the fighting ring in an unconscious heap, Ewan blew on his fist. 'Always wanted to do that,' he said. 'But I can't say that I am too impressed with this boxing of yours. You wouldn't last half a minute in a proper wrestling match.'

The caged dogs had been watching and seemed to go wild, hurling themselves against their prisons and howling.

Ewan raised his finger to his lips. 'Wheesht, doggies. You'll wake these scunners up.'

He grabbed Tyler Brady's collar and dragged him across the floor then flung an arm over the side of the fighting pit. Then he stepped inside, slipped a handcuff on the unconscious Pug Cruikshank's wrist and coupled him with his henchman.

'Oh yes, I didn't answer the question, did I? I am arresting you for resisting arrest.'

CHAPTER THIRTEEN

The following day, after a hectic time of interviews, meetings and reports, Torquil, Lorna and Morag sat in the sitting-room of the manse while the Padre poured drinks prior to serving dinner.

'There we are, a dry sherry for Morag and Glen Corlins for the rest of us,' he said, approaching with the small tray that he loved to use when he and Torquil entertained. 'Here is to a more peaceful time,' he said, raising his glass. 'That will help your throat, Lorna. West Uist's own malt whisky.'

Lorna self-consciously touched her bruised throat and smiled. Then she raised her drink and they clinked glasses and sipped their drinks.

Torquil glanced at the clock on the mantelpiece, then rose and switched on the television. 'It's just about time for the news.'

The Scottish TV news jingle sounded out and then Kirstie Macroon's familiar voice read out the main headlines.

'SCOTTISH FIRST MINISTER DEMANDS THE RETURN OF THE JACOBITE HOARD. SERIAL KILLER ARRESTED ON WEST UIST AND LOGAN BURNS SHOT AT THE SUMMER SOLSTICE. DOG FIGHTING SYNDICATE EXPOSED. DISGRACE OF THE WEST UIST BATTERY FARM.'

The Padre raised his eyes heavenwards as the news anchorwoman read the report about the Jacobite hoard. 'I cannot say that I like this move to separate Scotland from England. There is too much petty nationalism these days.'

And then she was reporting on the things they had been waiting to hear.

'Last night the controversial director of The Daisy Institute, which we have been featuring in our regular news bulletins over the last week, was shot during the start of the proposed night-long vigil at the Hoolish Stones. It seems that he was shot while addressing a crowd of onlookers, by the distraught father of a young woman who died in an accident at Dunshiffin Castle, the West Uist headquarters of the Daisy Institute, earlier in the week.

'We have to report that evidence has come to light to show that her death was not an accident, as was previously thought. Similarly, the death of noted local historian Finlay MacNeil —'

'How did Superintendent Lumsden take it all?' the Padre asked.

Torquil gave a wry smile. 'A bit like a wild boar, Uncle. He went on for about quarter of an hour about breaking me to constable, having me keel-hauled, flogged, you name it.'

Lorna gave a short laugh. 'But he had to accept that we — or rather Ewan and Calum Steele — broke that dog-fighting crowd. They will all be prosecuted.'

'And since the McQueens were in on it they have been totally discredited,' Morag added.

Kirstie Macroon went on to report about Drew Kelso's connection with The Daisy Institute and the death of Jaana Hakinen's sister in Geneva, and the fact that Esther Noble had spent time in Switzerland.

'Police are following a trail of investigation which suggests that there may be a link with the suspicious deaths last winter of Esther and Rab Noble. It had been thought that the husband might have murdered his wife and then committed suicide. The evidence now points to a double murder by Kelso.'

Morag put her sherry down on the coffee table. 'So Kelso persuaded Logan Burns to move the institute to West Uist, knowing that he would jump at the opportunity to use the Hoolish Stones to further his crackpot Atlantis theories.'

'That's right,' said Torquil. 'Kelso didn't care, because he was just siphoning money away into a numbered account in Zurich. He and Esther started up their affair again. And seemingly he was a sadist and had a passion for S&M. He must have told her everything in some of his sessions and then when he started fancying someone else, presumably Eileen Lamont, she threatened to expose him. So he killed her.'

'I feel so sorry for Nancy. She died because she was in the wrong place at the wrong time. Eileen was right, it was meant to be her. Although he might just have meant to rape her, rather than kill her.'

'We are pleased to report that Logan Burns, the Director of The Daisy Institute, is recovering in the West Uist Cottage Hospital. We talked earlier to his fellow director, Miss Saki Yasuda, who informed us that The Daisy Institute is planning to leave West Uist as soon as Logan Burns has recovered.'

The Padre shook his head in sorrow. 'All those deaths. So unnecessary. So evil. Poor Finlay MacNeil. It was his televized outburst that made Kelso suspect that he knew about him and led to his death.'

'We turn now to the discovery of a dog-fighting syndicate, using specially, illegally bred and trained dogs on West Uist. A joint investigation by *West Uist Chronicle* Editor Calum Steele and Scottish TV's Finbar Donleavy, uncovered an illegal group. I warn you that the footage we are about to show may offend those of a sensitive nature —'

The footage was indeed alarming, but quite damning.

'That will be the end of the McQueens and the Goat's Head Farm lot,' said Morag. 'Ewan, Calum and Finbar Donleavy all come out of it well.'

'Aye, and Calum is pretty hopeful,' said Torquil. 'Apparently Finbar Donleavy has been offered a post with CNN. That would mean that his and Kirstie's relationship might be difficult, with them on opposite sides of the pond.'

'And during their investigations the police discovered that Tyler Brady had been responsible for the savage attack on Calum Steele and on PC Ewan McPhee.'

The Padre stood up. 'Well, Lorna, you have had a pretty baptism of fire on West Uist, haven't you? Are you sure that you want to stay?'

Lorna looked at Torquil and smiled as he reached out a hand to her.

'Yes, Padre, I think that I very much want to stay.'

Morag stood up. 'Let me help you serve the food up, Padre,' she said quickly. 'I — er — think we are in danger of feeling like a couple of gooseberries in here.'

The Padre grinned as Torquil and Lorna stared dreamily at each other. He winked at Morag. 'Aye, you could be right, lassie. Bring your glass and we'll have another dram while I strain the tatties.'

A NOTE TO THE READER

Dear Reader,

Thank you for taking the time to read this collection, I hope that you enjoyed reading about the dark things that can happen on my idyllic little Scottish island on the edge of the world.

It is true that characters in a novel often take on a life of their own. That happened several times with these novels, when the story did not follow the path that I had imagined it would take. The characters felt so at home on the island of West Uist that they felt empowered to pay the piper to play their macabre tune.

I have been a lifelong fan of crime fiction, but to my mind the use of the laboratory and the revelations that DNA testing can instantly give, somehow rob many modern crime novels of their sense of romance. That was why I set my stories on the remote Hebridean island of West Uist, so that it would be far removed from the modern forensic crime thriller. Also, because the island has the smallest police force in the country, it would not be another gritty, urban police procedural. Crimes would have to be solved in a very old-fashioned manner.

I studied medicine at the University of Dundee and did some of my training in the highlands. I loved the sense of community in villages and determined that if I ever wrote a crime novel it would feature a Scottish detective working in a remote place, aided by friends, family and the local newspaper. Years later when Inspector Torquil McKinnon walked into my imagination I set about learning to play the bagpipes, although unlike Torquil, the winner of the Silver Quaich I have never been anything other than dire. Nonetheless, playing around with my pipes helps me as I am working out my plots.

Since golf is also a hobby and I had played on the remotest Hebridean courses, those sheep-nibbled links complete with dive bombing gulls had to appear in the stories. When I venture onto my local golf course I imagine the Padre, a steady 8 handicapper, playing alongside me, advising me on how to hit the green, sink a putt – or solve the newest clue.

If you have enjoyed this collection enough to leave a review on **Amazon** and **Goodreads**, then I would be truly grateful. I love to hear from readers, so if you would like to contact me, please do through my **Facebook** page or send me a message through **Twitter.** You can also see my latest news on the **West Uist Chronicle Blog** and on my **Website.**

Keith Moray

https://keithmorayauthor.com

Sapere Books is an exciting new publisher of brilliant fiction and popular history.

To find out more about our latest releases and our monthly bargain books visit our website:
saperebooks.com

Printed in Great Britain
by Amazon

55287981R10421